# A New Dawn

## The Complete
## Don A. Stuart Stories

John W. Campbell, Jr.

edited by James A. Mann

The NESFA Press
Post Office Box 809
Framingham, MA 01701
2003

FIRST EDITION
Second Printing, January 2009

International Standard Book Number:
1-886778-15-9

# Acknowledgments

The introduction by Barry Malzberg is original to this volume.

"Twilight" first published in *Astounding Science Fiction*, November 1934

"Atomic Power" first published in *Astounding Science Fiction*, December 1934

"The Machine" first published in *Astounding Science Fiction*, February 1935

"Blindness" first published in *Astounding Science Fiction*, March 1935

"The Escape" first published in *Astounding Science Fiction*, May 1935

"The Invaders" first published in *Astounding Science Fiction*, June 1935

"Rebellion" first published in *Astounding Science Fiction*, August 1935

"Night" first published in *Astounding Science Fiction*, October 1935

"Elimination" first published in *Astounding Science Fiction*, May 1936

"Frictional Losses" first published in *Astounding Science Fiction*, July 1936

"Forgetfulness" first published in *Astounding Science Fiction*, June 1937

"Out of Night" first published in *Astounding Science Fiction*, October 1937

"Dead Knowledge" first published in *Astounding Science Fiction*, June 1938

"Who Goes There?" first published in *Astounding Science Fiction*, August 1938

"Cloak of Aesir" first published in *Astounding Science Fiction*, March 1939

"Strange Worlds" first published in *Unknown*, April 1939.

"The Elder Gods" first published in *Unknown*, October 1939
Coauthored by Arthur J. Burks.

"Wouldst Write, Wee One?" first published in *Scienti-Snaps*, Vol. 3, No. 1, February 1940

All stories appear by permission of the author's agent.

Note: We have been unable to trace Arthur J. Burks, the coauthor of "The Elder Gods." If the author or the author's estate contacts NESFA, it will be our pleasure to pay the usual fee for use of the story.

# Editor's Note

This book contains all of the stories and essays that John W. Campbell wrote under the name Don A. Stuart. The stories are arranged mostly in chronological order, based on publication date. I say "mostly" because there are two exceptions. There are two short series of stories: the Invaders stories ("The Machine," "The Invaders," "Rebellion") and the Aesir stories ("Out of Night," "Cloak of Aesir"). In both cases, the related stories appear sequentially, starting at the location that places the first story in the series in its correct chronological place in the sequence.

# Acknowledgments

Like all NESFA books, this book is the result of hard work by a number of volunteers. Mark Olson provided help in the initial negotiations. Bill Shawcross of Rotten Apple Press did all the scanning and did an inital proofreading of all the stories he scanned. Mary Tabasko, Leslie Mann, and Eileen Dougherty did further proofreading of all the stories; George Flynn, NESFA's master copy editor, then reviewed the typeset text. Kevin Riley designed and created the dust jacket. Barry N. Malzberg obtained a copy of "Strange Worlds," and Joe Siclari and Robert Lichtman tracked down "Wouldst Write, Wee One?" John-Henri Holmberg provided the photo of John Campbell used on the dust jacket. Thanks to you all.

Jim Mann
Pittsburgh, PA
November 2002

# Contents

# THE MAN WHO LOST THE SEA

## BY BARRY N. MALZBERG

This is written 31 years and 6 days after John Wood Campbell's death. He died suddenly on a Sunday night at home, watching television, his wife said; collapsed with a heart attack and could not be revived. Campbell had been in poor health for years; his emphysema and asthma, severely aggravated (if not caused) by his two-pack-a-day cigarette habit, had ravaged him, turned him into a man who gasped after walking a city block, a man whose severe gout atop this had made him only a dim, occasional presence in the Condé Nast offices. Kay Tarrant, his assistant for over 30 years who certainly loved him hopelessly and desperately, never carnally, had been worried for a long time; tried to protect him as best she could. The man who said, drawing on a cigarette and expanding his barrel chest with smoke, that immortality could be self-willed (or at least a very, very long lifetime) barely made it into his seventh decade.

Thirty-one years and a week. Oh, that is a long time ago. There are writers like Michael A. Burstein or Shane Tourtellotte, *Analog* regulars, who were not born or barely so when this editor, The Editor, died. But writing under Campbell's influence still just as Asimov or Heinlein had sixty years ago. Campbell missed Apollo 13, the Internet (which he would have loved), the cell phone, Explorer, Watergate, *Star Wars*. He missed pathetic withdrawal from Vietnam and the essential collapse of the magazine market. (He was there for *Star Trek*, the Tet Offensive, Johnson's resignation and Armstrong's Moon landing.) There will never be a biography. I have been quite sure of this for a very long time.

Now and then someone, usually an academic, says in a desultory way, "There should be a biography of John W. Campbell," and this is true, but it is not going to happen. Most of the primary sources are dead, the others have had their witness published or taped to appear in the usual venues. Campbell's first and second wives are long dead, his two daughters, now in their sixties, live in the Midwest and have no contact with science fiction, have never furnished information. There is a stepdaughter (Peg Campbell, his second wife, was also married earlier) in Alabama who was, during Campbell's lifetime, intermittently active in the field and got to quite a few conventions, but she apparently has had nothing at all to do with science fiction since Campbell's death.

And, perilously for any biographer, this life cannot be separated from the work and has almost no meaning outside of it. Campbell's life although interesting—every life perceived from the inside is at least interesting—cannot be separated from the work; Campbell was an editor, in fact The Editor, and his testimony consists of almost 400 issues of his magazine, more than 10,000 letters, two volumes of which were published years ago. He is a part of the public and private memoirs of every science fiction writer of his time and perhaps it is this which subsumes or at least contains the life. The biography is spare— Campbell never traveled much, lived in New Jersey all of his adult life, edited his magazine for almost 34 years, lived almost a scandal-free life. (There were some operatics surrounding the breakup of his first marriage but it was all resolved quickly and quietly. Dona, his first wife, left the marriage in 1949 and shortly after the divorce married George O. Smith, an engineer who had been one of Campbell's significant contributors.)

(Campbell married Peg in the early 1950's and all evidence is that it was for both a very close marriage emotionally and intellectually and a source of repeated joy.) Something A. J. Budrys wrote of A. E. Van Vogt in the 1960's applies to Campbell's personal (not his professional!) life: "He is clearly worthy of some kind of re-evaluation but he simply is not important enough to merit that." Campbell's personal life, the biographical details might stand examination but they are not that important. What is important, the editorship, has the most ample testimony.

Still, if there were a biography at issue, one could write a chapter conjecturing a Campbell who might (or might never) have existed; this Campbell is 23 years old, already a prominent science fiction writer, maybe the best science fiction writer, Doc Smith's only true competitor in the Interstellar Racket, already at the top of a genre whose re-invented version is only seven years old. This young John Campbell has really beaten Hugo Gernsback's scientifiction category cold; his technophiliac fables of conquest about mighty machines and their triumphant operators have come close to dominating the two magazines, *Amazing* and *Astounding*, which are his major markets. Now our hypothetical Campbell, only two years out of Duke University, overwhelmed by intelligence and ambition and the Depression as well, makes an important, considered decision: "I'm going to put the decadence in," he says.

Perhaps our conjectural JWC says this in an empty room; perhaps he addresses his young, already long-suffering spouse. "This field of science fiction needs decadence; it is time that form superseded function, mood became more important than action, the ultimate death of the universe was given equal time. A new kind of story," he says, "and therefore a new name to put on the stories because I am already identified with all of this rocketry and interstellar collisions. 'Don A. Stuart,' how is that?" he says to his wife, the former Dona Stuart. "Wouldn't that be exciting?"

Or it was nothing like this at all and Campbell simply wanted to expand his potential markets and his possibility. Very few writers or editors are that purposeful. In the last year of his life, Campbell was asked on camera what he wanted to accomplish when he became *Astounding*'s new editor. "I just wanted to have fun," he said. In a letter to Alexei Panshin a few years before that, in response to the same question, he said that he had no philosophy, no clear set of ideas, he was just responding as an editor to what he liked. Panshin's enthusiastic retrospective analysis bored him.

The good editors, and for his first decade Campbell was a great editor, are not as purposeful as the Panshins and their friends in the English departments would like to impute. Bad or tired editors may become ideologues, may function in terms of some agenda as Campbell did for most of his last twenty years . . . but they are as full of false information as great editors, asked to explain, are full of no information at all. Ultimately, history is built upon absence as much as presence; in cases like Campbell's it can be just another specialized subdivision of fantasy. Objectively, Campbell the writer had reached the top of the small field of science fiction almost at the outset; as Heinlein, publishing his first story in 1939 in *Astounding*, came to utter dominance within two years, so Campbell years earlier had had a similar course. "I would have gotten a job after I graduated from Duke," he said later, "but there were no jobs at all. So I became a writer." There wasn't much money in writing for the three or four extant science fiction magazines then either but that is what Campbell did and with extraordinary success relative to the situation.

But the Arcot, Wade and Morey series obviously did not satisfy him. He was young, there were more than one of him. So it was time to put in the decadence, an apprehension of entropy which would lead inevitably past ordnance to some apprehension of breakdown and this new version of Campbell, the writer within, came to that understanding. "Twilight," "Night," "Blindness," "Atomic Power" and of course his most famous story "Who Goes There?" Which was written just before he became *Astounding*'s editor and published in the June 1938 issue, still using some of Tremaine's inventory.

There runs through these stories a kind of gloom, an apprehension of darkness previously unknown in USA genre science fiction. Wells had it in the closing chapters of *The Time Machine,* of course, and Stapledon had made the extinction of human possibility his major theme . . . but no post-Gernsback in this country was doing that until Campbell. The stories were, in their declensive way, manifestoes. "Twilight" and "Night" have lasted seven decades; the anthologies in which they appear are still in print and the influence of these works has been pervasive. "Blindness" is seated upon a terrible irony, the kind of fundamental accident upon which scientific "progress" is often perpetrated. The other two imply the end of existence, heady stuff from *The Time Machine* adapted for a market which wanted miracles of engineering to bedazzle its readership of adolescent boys.

And always and disturbingly, there is "Who Goes There?", Campbell's most important and memorable story. In *Seekers of Tomorrow,* the not always dependable Sam Moskowitz says that this story came from Campbell's childhood: his mother was an identical twin and she and her sister would assume the other's identity with little John. Who was "real?" the young Campbell learned to ask, and who was the fake that seemed real? The confusion was profound and—if Moskowitz can be trusted—might have been the underlay of Campbell's duality; there were in his earliest important relationship two people who were sharing the role of one.

Don A.. Stuart and John W. Campbell trading masks, then, for kinds of fiction which could be regarded as opposed. But John Campbell, it seems clear, was evolving into Don A. Stuart; what had originated in duality was transmogrification. Had Campbell continued, the persona and vision underlying the Stuart stories would probably have been the writer. This may be one reason why the editorial position was taken so gratefully; Campbell might have been afraid of where those stories were going, the destiny they contained.

"Who Goes There?" with its mimetic, invulnerable abandoned alien in disguise at a remote polar station was the basis of a famous if low-budget Howard Hawks film, *The Thing,* in 1951 and then a remake decades later by John Carpenter. This was perhaps the first science fiction movie after Lang's *Metropolis* or *King Kong* to have significant general cultural impact. (Certainly, Philip K. Dick's short story "Impostor," adapted into a big-budget film which was released finally at the end of 2001, is a rewrite of that story, a recycling of its central idea told this time from the viewpoint of the monster.) His half of the $500 which Street & Smith (who in that time bought all rights to the stories it published, voluntarily ceding half of the receipts to the author) received from Howard Hawks was the only money Campbell ever received for the story. "That's all right," Isaac Asimov's memoir recalls him saying, "If it's a good movie and if it increases the audience for good science fiction, then I don't mind at all."

Granted, F. Orlin Tremaine, the *Astounding* editor, encouraged and bought these stories; if he had not, Campbell, scrambling to make some kind of living, would have abandoned the idea. Tremaine deserves at the distance of decades an encomium. But the stories are Campbell's. Don A. Stuart allowed a version of Campbell to escape which had never before been known and they are remarkable.

There is no question that Campbell was—with the possible exception of E. E. Smith, an industrial chemist and part-time writer and not a very good writer—at the time he became editor of *Astounding Science Fiction* in October 1937 the leading writer of science fiction. That was, in fact, probably the reason that he got the job as Tremaine, promoted to higher position in Street & Smith, was permitted to recommend a successor. This is stale, statistical news 65 years later but it must have been astonishing at the time; the most prominent writer of science fiction had suddenly become the editor of its leading magazine. It was as if Heinlein had become editor of *Astounding* in 1942 or Bradbury of *Galaxy* in 1953. The writers—Boucher, McComas at *Fantasy & Science Fiction,* Horace Gold at *Galaxy*—who did accede to those positions were accomplished and well known to their colleagues but they did not then or ever possess Campbell's stature.

And with that appointment, Campbell the writer effectively retired. One condition imposed by the position was that Campbell could not sell fiction to his own magazine or to any competitor (a condition which Tremaine had easily circumvented by creating at least one pseudonym and, with his brother's collaboration, establishing another identity) and the sense is that the clause was agreeable, Campbell was ready to quit.

In the 34 years to come he published very little fiction: the novella "The Moon Is Hell," a story in the Healy/McComas *New Tales of Space and Time,* a few scattered pieces. Even more dramatically than had been the case with Horace Gold, Anthony Boucher, Judith Merril, the later reputation as editor tended to obliterate the stature of the writer's career. "Who Goes There?", "Twilight" and "Night" were to assure over the decades that there would remain some consciousness of Campbell's contribution as a writer, but they necessarily receded. "Writers come and writers go but next month's issue comes out forever."

Campbell edited *Astounding* from October 1937 until his death on July 11, 1971, still the longest unbroken tenure of any editor of a mass market magazine. He was probably the best editor of the century, at least in the United States—there were plenty of great ones and I think that Harold Hayes of the 1960's *Esquire* was Campbell's only true competitor—and what made him the best was that that Campbell left his magazine and his field utterly transformed. In his first decade he created that anomaly, "modern science fiction." With the broadening of publishing outlets and readership and with the advent of new magazines of quality, Campbell's utter dominance of science fiction was lost and the years after 1949 can be seen as a long, slow, inconstant decline and marginalization.

Campbell became a witness (a very interested and bitterly involved witness to be sure) and his profound unhappiness with what he took to be its misdirection was refracted in his editorials and choice of contents for what had in the Spring of 1960 become *Analog*.

These last years of increased marginalization had isolated Campbell and embittered him and the effect of his departure from the magazine was, sadly, to improve *Analog* under the new editor, Ben Bova. Clearly this career did not end well. Campbell stayed too long and he did so in an unvarying way. Maybe if he had left in the late forties for another editorial position, had become say at Random House or Charles Scribner the founder of the first great and widely distributed science fiction division, it would have been better for him and for science fiction. If something like that had been possible, he would have, for the first time, made substantial money and had an influence which went beyond his contributors and his magazine's readership.

But the influence, of course, would not have been as concentrated; within the scope of his magazine, Campbell was an autocrat and his position was absolute. He could do whatever he wanted, perhaps exemplifying that most famous of Yiddish curses: "May you get what you truly want."

It would have been better for all if he had turned over the magazine to a successor somewhere around the end of that brilliant first decade. It could be further argued that beginning with Hubbard's Dianetics, which were propounded in the May 1950 issue of the magazine, Campbell no longer had ideas. He had crotchets: Dianetics, Psionics (a corollary to Dianetics, really, the superior powers of the properly regressed mind), the Hieronymous Machine, the Dean Machine, Dowsing and as the crotchets overwhelmed, substituting reflex for thought, so Campbell overwhelmed his authors and turned most of them into vehicles for the expression and expansion of those ideas.

Some writers who resisted remained in the magazine but most did not and after 1960, most of Campbell's new writers came to print through the study of Campbell's ideas and their servicing. To the most tolerant, Campbell's magazine became irrelevant to the evolution of the field, but many writers and editors felt that Campbell's last decade was more seriously flawed than by irrelevance, he was actively impeding science fiction. Campbell raged editorially in late 1968 against the demonstrators at the 1968 Democratic Convention in Chicago, he endorsed George Wallace for President not because he thought Wallace could win but as a statement of the bankruptcy of those in command of the present system. Wallace, like Campbell, had unconventional ideas, he forced a new way of thinking. (Memories of the impersonator David Frye playing Wallace on *The Smothers Brothers Show:* "Look at this face. Is this the face of a bigot?")

"John Campbell now advocates positions which are contrary to everything for which science fiction has fought," Harlan Ellison wrote. I wrote no less angrily in that same medium (the *SFWA Forum*) that "John Campbell, having given us the field of science fiction, now seemed determined to destroy it." An unhappy, polarizing time.

An explanation or at least an insight of a sort: John Campbell was a man in schism. Most of us are but his duality was profound. Those two writerly identities, Campbell the celebrant of the star paths and Stuart the decadent seemed directly opposed. Perhaps then it was two Campbells editing *Astounding,* the rationalist and the mystic, the man of methodology and the man who believed powerfully in the evidence of things unseen. It was the rationalist who controlled the early years (the mystic was made content for a while with the editorship of *Unknown* or experiments in the ether with ham radio) and the mystic who overtook that rationalist in the early years of editorial decline . . . the beginning of that decline marked for most by the advent of Dianetics in the magazine. It was the first time that Campbell allowed the magazine to become a vehicle for obsession but hardly the last. The crotchets overtook.

How sad was this? Schuyler Miller reviewing a *New Worlds* attributing much of their inspiration to drugs. Michael Moorcock in a letter published in "Brass Tacks" denied that drugs were part of the

Ladbroke Grove zeitgeist but added that he found the current *Analog* far weirder, spacier, further out than anything about *New Worlds* and one can take the point.

In issue after issue over those last years Campbell editorially and in his choice of fiction appeared to be desperately repudiating a present which—perhaps infuriatingly to him—could have been seen as a reasonable extrapolation of the themes and context of much of the fiction he had been publishing in the forties. Technological sprawl, the alienation effect, the increasing dislocation caused by technology, the disconnection between act and consequence facilitated by the machines . . . all of this could have been glimpsed in the fiction of Kuttner, Sturgeon, van Vogt; Kuttner's cracked and irresponsible inventor, Gallegher, was doing to scientific methodology what the Clown Prince, Abbie Hoffman, was trying to do to that 1968 Democratic Convention which Campbell so hated. Campbell's unbearable present was clearly foreshadowed in the editorial policies of Campbell's notable past and he—or at least the Don A. Stuart in him which did not believe in ordinary consequence—could not bear this.

Or looking at it another way, *Astounding* was always a battleground in which the two Campbells contested over the full range of the years; in the end the decadent or retrograde Don A. Stuart might have been the winner—the mysticism, the dowsing, the magazine as monthly prayer meeting—but this Don A. Stuart looked upon a barren field and called it victory . . . because that other Campbell, the rationalist, had through Heinlein, Asimov, the careful editorial projections of the 40's done the job too well, had taken Campbell and his readers inexorably into a world which no intensity of psionics could deny.

Campbell was able to divide himself as a writer: the Don A. Stuart stories did not challenge *The Mightiest Machine,* they were the product of a different persona. He could not, however, divide himself as an editor. That duality prevailed, it leveraged his attempts through Dianetics, Psionics and Dowsing to, perhaps, to fuse the mystic and the rationalist. This simply did not work. Campbell in his last decade might indeed have felt that science fiction as it had evolved had to be destroyed to be saved . . . no less than the world itself, all those hippies screaming "The whole world is watching!" for the television would have to be destroyed for the purpose of salvation. A most profound and terrible disconnect which became ever more disconnected in Campbell's last years and which might have left him in a state of bewilderment.

But all of this is much later; lies far down the decades from the Don Stuart stories. In these years the duality was not wrecking but celebrating the writer and "Twilight" and "Night" are powerful and reasonable explorations of entropy just as "Who Goes There?" is able— as Campbell was not able in his last, scrambling decade—to transcend the duality. Human or alien? Destroyer or victim? (Mother or Aunt?) These are the questions which dazzle the crew at the Antarctic Circle and therefore the reader. In having no clear answer, in noting the interchangeability, Don A. Stuart proved himself to be far more in accord with the Vietnam peace movement than ever the infuriated editor of *Analog* could have been.

This is a powerful and signatory collection; the stories are still worthy on their own terms but they are also—even the anti-rationalist essay published in the April 1939 issue of *Unknown*—are magnificent statements of the problem and clearly predict the dilemma that *Analog* would become thirty years later. That 1960's *Analog* was the truncated, inchoate and always resentful outcome of that Campbellian schism. If Wallace represented the cliched politics of resentment, *Analog* was its celebrant. Here was a magazine of the future which fought desperately for the past, a magazine of expansion which demanded contraction. A magazine based upon an embrace of the future which feared the future.

There will be no biography, cannot be, the material is inconclusive and unavailable . . . but here in this collection suspires the essential Campbell. In thrall to his ambivalence, John Campbell's Don A. Stuart gives us everything we need to know.

"A new kind of story: wouldn't that be exciting?" asks our conjectured Campbell. The room is empty except for the two of them, Dona quietly in the corner considering him, considering herself as well, perhaps in this morning in the shocking early depth of the Depression seeing the future as well. "We are living in hard times, a new time," this John Campbell says. "The old ways, the happy machines speeding the highway to the stars, they aren't working the way they should. The strong and sturdy spacers stoking the machines, guiding the ship, they are blinded by the million suns of space, staggered and shaking in that enormity: the empty space between those suns. Now we must understand that the machines will not always work, that the highways lead not only to the end of space, to the end of time itself.

"Listen to these ideas we have: I have so many ideas. Let me tell you where our new life must take us.

"It must take us past time itself. We have to lift 'em up, take 'em up, shake 'em up now and forever, create new rules for the emptiness, the wind, the endless space between the stars; that space in which the stars themselves will begin to die."

Oh, sing unto the Lord a new song. Editor, visionary, curmudgeon and damaged and ever-seeking saint, he sung that new song. Sung it for the living and the dead in the space between the stars. Sung past the three hammer blows of fate into the clear and vaulting coda.

The song of the Earth.

July 2002
New Jersey

# A New Dawn

## The Complete Don A. Stuart Stories

# TWILIGHT

"Speaking of hitchhikers," said Jim Bendell in a rather bewildered way, "I picked up a man the other day that certainly was a queer cuss." He laughed, but it wasn't a real laugh. "He told me the queerest yarn I ever heard. Most of them tell you how they lost their good jobs and tried to find work out here in the wide spaces of the West. They don't seem to realize how many people we have out here. They think all this great beautiful country is uninhabited."

Jim Bendell's a real estate man, and I knew how he could go on. That's his favorite line, you know. He's real worried because there's a lot of homesteading plots still open out in our state. He talks about the beautiful country, but he never went farther into the desert than the edge of town. 'Fraid of it actually. So I sort of steered him back on the track.

"What did he claim, Jim? Prospector who couldn't find land to prospect?"

"That's not very funny, Bart. No; it wasn't only what he claimed. He didn't even claim it, just said it. You know, he didn't say it was true, he just said it. That's what gets me. I know it ain't true, but the way he said it— Oh, I don't know."

By which I knew he didn't. Jim Bendell's usually pretty careful about his English—real proud of it. When he slips, that means he's disturbed. Like the time he thought the rattlesnake was a stick of wood and wanted to put it on the fire.

Jim went on: And he had funny clothes, too. They looked like silver, but they were soft as silk. And at night they glowed just a little.

I picked him up about dusk. Really picked him up. He was lying off about ten feet from the South Road. I thought, at first, somebody had hit him, and then hadn't stopped. Didn't see him very clearly, you know. I picked him up, put him in the car, and started on. I had about three hundred miles to go, but I thought I could drop him at

19

Warren Spring with Doc Vance. But he came to in about five minutes, and opened his eyes. He looked straight off, and he looked first at the car, then at the Moon. "Thank God!" he says, and then looks at me. It gave me a shock. He was beautiful. No; he was handsome.

He wasn't either one. He was magnificent. He was about six feet two, I think, and his hair was brown, with a touch of red-gold. It seemed like fine copper wire that's turned brown. It was crisp and curly. His forehead was wide, twice as wide as mine. His features were delicate, but tremendously impressive; his eyes were gray, like etched iron, and bigger than mine—a lot.

That suit he wore—it was more like a bathing suit with pajama trousers. His arms were long and muscled smoothly as an Indian's. He was white, though, tanned lightly with a golden, rather than a brown, tan.

But he was magnificent. Most wonderful man I ever saw. I don't know, damn it!

"Hello!" I said. "Have an accident?"

"No; not this time, at least."

And his voice was magnificent, too. It wasn't an ordinary voice. It sounded like an organ talking, only it was human.

"But maybe my mind isn't quite steady yet. I tried an experiment. Tell me what the date is, year and all, and let me see," he went on.

"Why—December 9, 1932," I said.

And it didn't please him. He didn't like it a bit. But the wry grin that came over his face gave way to a chuckle.

"Over a thousand—" he says reminiscently. "Not as bad as seven million. I shouldn't complain."

"Seven million what?"

"Years," he said, steadily enough. Like he meant it. "I tried an experiment once. Or I will try it. Now I'll have to try again. The experiment was—in 3059. I'd just finished the release experiment. Testing space then. Time—it wasn't that, I still believe. It was space. I felt myself caught in that field, but I couldn't pull away. Field gamma-H 481, intensity 935 in the Pellman range. It sucked me in, and I went out.

"I think it took a short cut through space to the position the solar system will occupy. Through a higher dimension, effecting a speed exceeding light and throwing me into the future plane."

He wasn't telling me, you know. He was just thinking out loud. Then he began to realize I was there.

"I couldn't read their instruments, seven million years of evolution changed everything. So I overshot my mark a little coming back. I belong in 3059.

"But tell me, what's the latest scientific invention of this year?"

He startled me so, I answered almost before I thought. "Why, television, I guess. And radio and airplanes."

"Radio—good. They will have instruments."

"But see here—who are you?"

"Ah—I'm sorry. I forgot," he replied in that organ voice of his. "I am Ares Sen Kenlin. And you?"

"James Waters Bendell."

"Waters—what does that mean? I do not recognize it."

"Why—it's a name, of course. Why should you recognize it?"

"I see—you have not the classification, then. 'Sen' stands for science."

"Where did you come from, Mr. Kenlin?"

"Come from?" He smiled, and his voice was slow and soft. "I came out of space across seven million years or more. They had lost count— the men had. The machines had eliminated the unneeded service. They didn't know what year it was. But before that—my home is in Neva City in the year 3059."

That's when I began to think he was a nut.

"I was an experimenter," he went on. "Science, as I have said. My father was a scientist, too, but in human genetics. I myself am an experiment. He proved his point, and all the world followed suit. I was the first of the new race . . . The new race—oh, holy destiny— what has—what will— What is its end? I have seen it—almost. I saw them—the little men—bewildered—lost. And the machines. Must it be—can't anything sway it? Listen—I heard this song."

Jim said: He sang the song. Then he didn't have to tell me about the people. I knew them. I could hear their voices, in the queer, crackling, un-English words. I could read their bewildered longings. It was in a minor key, I think. It called, it called and asked, and hunted hope-lessly. And over it all the steady rumble and whine of the unknown, forgotten machines.

The machines that couldn't stop, because they had been started, and the little men had forgotten how to stop them, or even what they were for, looking at them and listening—and wondering. They couldn't read or write any more, and the language had changed, you see, so that the phonic records of their ancestors meant nothing to them.

But that song went on, and they wondered. And they looked out across space and they saw the warm, friendly stars—too far away. Nine planets they knew and inhabited. And locked by infinite distance, they couldn't see another race, a new life.

And through it all—two things. The machines. Bewildered forget-fulness. And maybe one more. Why?

That was the song, and it made me cold. It shouldn't be sung around people of today. It almost killed something. It seemed to kill hope. After that song—I—well, I believed him.

When he finished the song, he didn't talk for a while. Then he sort of shook himself.

You won't understand (he continued). Not yet—but I have seen them. They stand about, little misshapen men with huge heads. But their heads contain only brains. They had machines that could think—but somebody turned them off a long time ago, and no one knew how to start them again. That was the trouble with them. They had wonder-ful brains. Far better than yours or mine. But it must have been mil-lions of years ago when they were turned off, too, and they just haven't thought since then. Kindly little people. That was all they knew.

When I slipped into that field it grabbed me like a gravitational field whirling a space transport down to a planet. It sucked me in—and through. Only the other side must have been seven million years in the future. That's where I was. It must have been in exactly the same spot on Earth's surface, but I never knew why.

It was night then, and I saw the city a little way off. The Moon was shining on it, and the whole scene looked wrong. You see, in seven million years, men had done a lot with the positions of the planetary bodies, what with moving space liners, clearing lanes through the asteroids, and such. And seven million years is long enough for natural things to change positions a little. The Moon must have been fifty thousand miles farther out. And it was rotating on its axis. I lay there a while and watched it. Even the stars were different.

There were ships going out of the city. Back and forth, like things sliding along a wire, but there was only a wire of force, of course. Part of the city, the lower part, was brightly lighted with what must have been mercury-vapor glow, I decided. Blue-green. I felt sure men didn't live there—the light was wrong for eyes. But the top of the city was so sparsely lighted.

Then I saw something coming down out of the sky. It was brightly lighted. A huge globe, and it sank straight to the center of the great black-and-silver mass of the city.

I don't know what it was, but even then I knew the city was de-serted. Strange that I could even imagine that, I who had never seen a deserted city before. But I walked the fifteen miles over to it and entered it. There were machines going about the streets, repair machines, you know. They couldn't understand that the city didn't need to go on functioning, so they were still working. I found a taxi machine that seemed fairly familiar. It had a manual control that I could work.

I don't know how long that city had been deserted. Some of the men from the other cities said it was a hundred and fifty thousand years. Some went as high as three hundred thousand years. Three hundred thousand years since human foot had been in that city. The taxi machine was in perfect condition, functioned at once. It was clean, and the city was clean and orderly. I saw a restaurant and I was hungry. Hungrier still for humans to speak to. There were none, of course, but I didn't know.

The restaurant had the food displayed directly, and I made a choice. The food was three hundred thousand years old, I suppose. I didn't know, and the machines that served it to me didn't care, for they made things synthetically, you see, and perfectly. When the builders made those cities, they forgot one thing. They didn't realize that things shouldn't go on forever.

It took me six months to make my apparatus. And near the end I was ready to go; and, from seeing those machines go blindly, perfectly, on in orbits of their duties with the tireless, ceaseless perfection their designers had incorporated in them, long after those designers and their sons, and their sons' sons had no use for them—

When Earth is cold, and the Sun has died out, those machines will go on. When Earth begins to crack and break, those perfect, ceaseless machines will try to repair her—

I left the restaurant and cruised about the city in the taxi. The machine had a little electric-power motor, I believe, but it gained its power from the great central power radiator. I knew before long that I was far in the future. The city was divided into two sections, a section of many strata where machines functioned smoothly, save for a deep humming beat that echoed through the whole city like a vast unending song of power. The entire metal framework of the place echoed with it, transmitted it, hummed with it. But it was soft and restful, a reassuring beat.

There must have been thirty levels above ground, and twenty more below, a solid block of metal walls and metal floors and metal and glass and force machines. The only light was the blue-green glow of the mercury-vapor arcs. The light of mercury vapor is rich in high-energy-quanta, which stimulate the alkali metal atoms to photo-electric activity. Or perhaps that is beyond the science of your day? I have forgotten.

But they had used that light because many of their worker machines needed sight. The machines were marvelous. For five hours I wandered through the vast power plant on the very lowest level, watching them, and because there was motion, and that pseudo-mechanical life, I felt less alone.

The generators I saw were a development of the release I had discovered—when? The release of the energy of matter, I mean, and I knew when I saw that for what countless ages they could continue.

The entire lower block of the city was given over to the machines. Thousands. But most of them seemed idle, or, at most, running under light load. I recognized a telephone apparatus, and not a single signal came through. There was no life in the city. Yet when I pressed a little stud beside the screen on one side of the room, the machine began working instantly. It was ready. Only no one needed it any more. The men knew how to die, and be dead, but the machines didn't.

Finally I went up to the top of the city, the upper level. It was a paradise.

There were shrubs and trees and parks, glowing in the soft light that they had learned to make in the very air. They had learned it five million years or more before. Two million years ago they forgot. But the machines didn't, and they were still making it. It hung in the air, soft, silvery light, slightly rosy, and the gardens were shadowy with it. There were no machines here now, but I knew that in daylight they must come out and work on these gardens, keeping them a paradise for masters who had died, and stopped moving, as they could not.

In the desert outside the city it had been cool, and very dry. Here the air was soft, warm, and sweet with the scent of blooms that men had spent several hundreds of thousands of years perfecting.

Then somewhere music began. It began in the air, and spread softly through it. The Moon was just setting now, and as it set, the rosy-silver glow waned and the music grew stronger.

It came from everywhere and from nowhere. It was within me. I do not know how they did it. And I do not know how such music could be written.

Savages make music too simple to be beautiful, but it is stirring. Semisavages write music beautifully simple, and simply beautiful. Your Negro music was your best. They knew music when they heard it and sang it as they felt it. Semicivilized peoples write great music. They are proud of their music, and make sure it is known for great music. They make it so great it is top-heavy.

I had always thought our music good. But that which came through the air was the song of triumph, sung by a mature race, the race of man in its full triumph! It was man singing his triumph in majestic sound that swept me up; it showed me what lay before me; it carried me on.

And it died in the air as I looked at the deserted city. The machines should have forgotten that song. Their masters had, long before.

I came to what must have been one of their homes; it was a dimly seen doorway in the dusky light, but as I stepped up to it, the lights which had not functioned in three hundred thousand years illuminated it for me with a green-white glow, like a firefly, and I stepped into the room beyond. Instantly something happened to the air in the doorway behind me; it was as opaque as milk. The room in which I stood was a room of metal and stone. The stone was some jet-black substance with the finish of velvet, and the metals were silver and gold. There was a rug on the floor, a rug of just such material as I am wearing now, but thicker and softer. There were divans about the room, low and covered with these soft metallic materials. They were black and gold and silver, too.

I had never seen anything like that. I never shall again, I suppose, and my language and yours were not made to describe it.

The builders of that city had right and reason to sing that song of sweeping triumph, triumph that swept them over the nine planets and the fifteen habitable moons.

But they weren't there any more, and I wanted to leave. I thought of a plan and went to a subtelephone office to examine a map I had seen. The old World looked much the same. Seven or even seventy million years don't mean much to old Mother Earth. She may even succeed in wearing down those marvelous machine cities. She can wait a hundred million or a thousand million years before she is beaten.

I tried calling different city centers shown on the map. I had quickly learned the system when I examined the central apparatus.

I tried once—twice—thrice—a round dozen times. Yawk City, Lunon City, Paree, Shkago, Singpor, others. I was beginning to feel that there were no more men on all Earth. And I felt crushed, as at each city the machines replied and did my bidding. The machines were there in each of those far vaster cities, for I was in the Neva City of their time. A small city. Yawk City was more than eight hundred kilometers in diameter.

In each city I had tried several numbers. Then I tried San Frisco. There was someone there, and a voice answered and the picture of a human appeared on the little glowing screen. I could see him start and stare in surprise at me. Then he started speaking to me. I couldn't understand, of course. I can understand your speech, and you mine, because your speech of this day is largely recorded on records of various types and has influenced our pronunciation.

Some things are changed; names of cities, particularly, because names of cities are apt to be polysyllabic, and used a great deal. People tend to elide them, shorten them. I am in—Nee-vah-dah—as you would say? We say only Neva. And Yawk State. But it is Ohio and Iowa still. Over a thousand years, effects were small on words, because they were recorded.

But seven million years had passed, and the men had forgotten the old records, used them less as time went on, and their speech varied till the time came when they could no longer understand the records. They were not written any more, of course.

Some men must have arisen occasionally among that last of the race and sought for knowledge, but it was denied them. An ancient writing can be translated if some basic rule is found. An ancient voice though—and when the race has forgotten the laws of science and the labor of mind.

So his speech was strange to me as he answered over that circuit. His voice was high in pitch, his words liquid, his tones sweet. It was almost a song as he spoke. He was excited and called others. I could not understand them, but I knew where they were. I could go to them.

So I went down from the paradise of gardens, and as I prepared to leave, I saw dawn in the sky. The strange-bright stars winked and twinkled and faded. Only one bright rising star was familiar—Venus. She shone golden now. Finally, as I stood watching for the first time that strange heaven, I began to understand what had first impressed me with the wrongness of the view. The stars, you see, were all different.

In my time—and yours—the solar system is a lone wanderer that by chance is passing across an intersection point of Galactic traffic. The stars we see at night are the stars of moving clusters, you know. In fact our system is passing through the heart of the Ursa Major group. Half a dozen other groups center within five hundred light-years of us.

But during those seven millions of years, the Sun had moved out of the group. The heavens were almost empty to the eye. Only here and there shone a single faint star. And across the vast sweep of black sky swung the band of the Milky Way. The sky was empty.

That must have been another thing those men meant in their songs—felt in their hearts. Loneliness—not even the close, friendly stars. We have stars within half a dozen light-years. They told me that their instruments, which gave directly the distance to any star, showed that the nearest was one hundred and fifty light-years away. It was enormously bright. Brighter even than Sirius of our heavens. And that made it even less friendly, because it was a blue-white supergiant. Our sun would have served as a satellite for that star.

I stood there and watched the lingering rose-silver glow die as the powerful blood-red light of the Sun swept over the horizon. I knew by the stars now that it must have been several millions of years since my day; since I had last seen the Sun sweep up. And that blood-red light made me wonder if the Sun itself was dying.

An edge of it appeared, blood-red and huge. It swung up, and the color faded, till in half an hour it was the familiar yellow-gold disk.

It hadn't changed in all that time.

I had been foolish to think that it would. Seven million years—that is nothing to Earth, how much less to the Sun? Some two thousand thousand thousand times it had risen since I last saw it rise. Two thousand thousand thousand days. If it had been that many years—I might have noticed a change.

The universe moves slowly. Only life is not enduring; only life changes swiftly. Eight short millions of years. Eight days in the life of Earth—and the race was dying. It had left something: machines. But they would die, too, even though they could not understand. So I felt. I—may have changed that. I will tell you. Later.

For when the Sun was up, I looked again at the sky and the ground, some fifty floors below. I had come to the edge of the city.

Machines were moving on that ground, leveling it, perhaps. A great wide line of gray stretched off across the level desert straight to the east. I had seen it glowing faintly before the Sun rose—a roadway for ground machines. There was no traffic on it.

I saw an airship slip in from the east. It came with a soft, muttering whine of air, like a child complaining in sleep; it grew to my eyes like an expanding balloon. It was huge when it settled in a great port-slip in the city below. I could hear now the clang and mutter of machines, working on the materials brought in, no doubt. The machines had ordered raw materials. The machines in other cities had supplied. The freight machines had carried them here.

San Frisco and Jacksville were the only two cities on North America still used. But the machines went on in all the others, because they couldn't stop. They hadn't been ordered to.

Then high above, something appeared, and from the city beneath me, from a center section, three small spheres rose. They, like the freight ship, had no visible driving mechanisms. The point in the sky above, like a black star in a blue space, had grown to a moon. The three spheres met it high above. Then together they descended and lowered into the center of the city, where I could not see them.

It was a freight transport from Venus. The one I had seen land the night before had come from Mars, I learned.

I moved after that and looked for some sort of a taxi-plane. They had none that I recognized in scouting about the city. I searched the higher levels, and here and there saw deserted ships, but far too large for me, and without controls.

It was nearly noon—and I ate again. The food was good.

I knew then that this was a city of the dead ashes of human hopes. The hopes not of *a* race, not the whites, nor the yellow, nor the blacks, but the human race. I was mad to leave the city. I was afraid to try the ground road to the west, for the taxi I drove was powered from some source in the city, and I knew it would fail before many miles.

It was afternoon when I found a small hangar near the outer wall of the vast city. It contained three ships. I had been searching through the lower strata of the human section—the upper part. There were restaurants and shops and theaters there. I entered one place where, at my entrance, soft music began, and colors and forms began to rise on a screen before me.

They were the triumph songs in form and sound and color of a mature race, a race that had marched steadily upward through five millions of years—and didn't see the path that faded out ahead, when they were dead and had stopped, and the city itself was dead—but hadn't stopped. I hastened out of there—and the song that had not been sung in three hundred thousand years died behind me.

But I found the hangar. It was a private one, likely. Three ships. One must have been fifty feet long and fifteen in diameter. It was a yacht, a space yacht, probably. One was some fifteen feet long and five feet in diameter. That must have been the family air machine. The third was a tiny thing, little more than ten feet long and two in diameter. I had to lie down within it, evidently.

There was a periscopic device that gave me a view ahead and almost directly above. A window that permitted me to see what lay below—and a device that moved a map under a frosted-glass screen and projected it onto the screen in such a way that the cross-hairs of the screen always marked my position.

I spent half an hour attempting to understand what the makers of that ship had made. But the men who made that were men who held behind them the science and knowledge of five millions of years and the perfect machines of those ages. I saw the release mechanism that powered it. I understood the principles of that and, vaguely, the mechanics. But there were no conductors, only pale beams that pulsed so swiftly you could hardly catch the pulsations from the corner of the eye. They had been glowing and pulsating, some half dozen of them, for three hundred thousand years at least; probably more.

I entered the machine, and instantly half a dozen more beams sprang into being; there was a slight suggestion of a quiver, and a queer strain ran through my body. I understood in an instant, for the machine was resting on gravity nullifiers. That had been my hope when I worked on the space fields I discovered after the release.

But they had had it for millions of years before they built that perfect deathless machine. My weight entering it had forced it to readjust itself and simultaneously to prepare for operation. Within, an artificial gravity equal to that of Earth had gripped me, and the neutral zone between the outside and the interior had caused the strain.

The machine was ready. It was fully fueled, too. You see, they were equipped to tell automatically their wants and needs. They were almost living things, every one. A caretaker machine kept them supplied, adjusted, even repaired them when need be, and when possible. If it was not, I learned later, they were carried away in a service truck that came automatically; replaced by an exactly similar machine; and carried to the shops where they were made, and automatic machines made them over.

The machine waited patiently for me to start. The controls were simple, obvious. There was a lever at the left that you pushed forward to move forward, pulled back to go back. On the right a horizontal, pivoted bar. If you swung it left, the ship spun left; if right, the ship spun right. If tipped up, the ship followed it, and likewise for all motions other than backward and forward. Raising it bodily raised the ship, as depressing it depressed the ship.

I lifted it slightly, a needle moved a bit on a gauge comfortably before my eyes as I lay there, and the floor dropped beneath me. I pulled the other control back, and the ship gathered speed as it moved gently out into the open. Releasing both controls into neutral, the machine continued till it stopped at the same elevation, the motion absorbed by air friction. I turned it about, and another dial before my eyes moved, showing my position. I could not read it, though. The map did not move, as I had hoped it would. So I started toward what I felt was west.

I could feel no acceleration in that marvelous machine. The ground simply began leaping backward, and in a moment the city was gone. The map unrolled rapidly beneath me now, and I saw that I was moving south of west. I turned northward slightly, and watched the compass. Soon I understood that, too, and the ship sped on.

I had become too interested in the map and the compass, for suddenly there was a sharp buzz and, without my volition, the machine rose and swung to the north. There was a mountain ahead of me; I had not seen, but the ship had.

I noticed then what I should have seen before—two little knobs that could move the map. I started to move them and heard a sharp clicking, and the pace of the ship began decreasing. A moment and it had steadied at a considerably lower speed, the machine swinging to a new course. I tried to right it, but to my amazement the controls did not affect it.

It was the map, you see. It would either follow the course, or the course would follow it. I had moved it and the machine had taken over control of its own accord. There was a little button I could have pushed—but I didn't know. I couldn't control the ship until it finally came to rest and lowered itself to a stop six inches from the ground in the center of what must have been the ruins of a great city, Sacramento, probably.

I understood now, so I adjusted the map for San Frisco, and the ship went on at once. It steered itself around a mass of broken stone, turned back to its course, and headed on, a bullet-shaped, self-controlled dart.

It didn't descend when it reached San Frisco. It simply hung in the air and sounded a soft musical hum. Twice. Then it waited. I waited, too, and looked down.

There were people here. I saw the humans of that age for the first time. They were little men—bewildered—dwarfed, with heads disproportionately large. But not extremely so.

Their eyes impressed me most. They were huge, and when they looked at me there was a power in them that seemed sleeping, but too deeply to be roused.

I took the manual controls then and landed. And no sooner had I got out, than the ship rose automatically and started off by itself. They had automatic parking devices. The ship had gone to a public hangar, the nearest, where it would be automatically serviced and cared for. There was a little call set I should have taken with me when I got out. Then I could have pressed a button and called it to me—wherever I was in that city.

The people about me began talking—singing almost—among themselves. Others were coming up leisurely. Men and women—but there seemed no old and few young. What few young there were, were treated almost with respect, carefully taken care of lest a careless foot step on their toes or a careless step knock them down.

There was reason, you see. They lived a tremendous time. Some lived as long as three thousand years. Then—they simply died. They didn't grow old, and it never had been learned why people died as they did. The heart stopped, the brain ceased thought—and they died. But the young children, children not yet mature, were treated with the utmost care. But one child was born in the course of a month in that city of one hundred thousand people. The human race was growing sterile.

And I have told you that they were lonely? Their loneliness was beyond hope. For, you see, as man strode toward maturity, he destroyed all forms of life that menaced him. Disease. Insects. Then the last of the insects, and finally the last of the man-eating animals.

The balance of nature was destroyed then, so they had to go on. It was like the machines. They started them—and now they can't stop. They started destroying life—and now it wouldn't stop. So they had to destroy weeds of all sorts, then many formerly harmless plants. Then the herbivora, too, the deer and the antelope and the rabbit and the horse. They were a menace, they attacked man's machine-tended crops. Man was still eating natural foods.

You can understand. The thing was beyond their control. In the end they killed off the denizens of the sea, also, in self-defense. Without the many creatures that had kept them in check, they were swarming beyond bounds. And the time had come when synthetic foods replaced natural. The air was purified of all life about two and a half million years after our day, all microscopic life.

That meant that the water, too, must be purified. It was—and then came the end of life in the ocean. There were minute organisms that lived on bacterial forms, and tiny fish that lived on the minute organisms, and small fish that lived on the tiny fish, and big fish that lived on the small fish—and the beginning of the chain was gone. The sea was devoid of life in a generation. That meant about one thousand and five hundred years to them. Even the sea plants had gone.

And on all Earth there was only man and the organisms he had protected—the plants he wanted for decoration, and certain ultra-hygienic pets, as long-lived as their masters. Dogs. They must have been remarkable animals. Man was reaching his maturity then, and his animal friend, the friend that had followed him through a thousand millenniums to your day and mine, and another four thousand millenniums to the day of man's early maturity, had grown in intelligence. In an ancient museum—a wonderful place, for they had, perfectly preserved, the body of a great leader of mankind who had died five and a half million years before I saw him—in that museum, deserted then, I saw one of those canines. His skull was nearly as large as mine. They had simple ground machines that dogs could be trained to drive, and they held races in which the dogs drove those machines.

Then man reached his full maturity. It extended over a period of a full million years. So tremendously did he stride ahead, the dog ceased to be a companion. Less and less were they wanted. When the million years had passed, and man's decline began, the dog was gone. It had died out.

And now this last dwindling group of men still in the system had no other life form to make its successor. Always before when one civilization toppled, on its ashes rose a new one. Now there was but one civilization, and all other races, even other species, were gone save in the plants. And man was too far along in his old age to bring intelligence and mobility from the plants. Perhaps he could have in his prime.

Other worlds were flooded with man during that million years— the million years. Every planet and every moon of the system had its quota of men. Now only the planets had their populations, the moons had been deserted. Pluto had been left before I landed, and men were coming from Neptune, moving in toward the Sun, and the home planet, while I was there. Strangely quiet men, viewing, most of them, for the first time, the planet that had given their race life.

But as I stepped from that ship and watched it rise away from me, I saw why the race of man was dying. I looked back at the faces of those men, and on them I read the answer. There was one single quality gone from the still-great minds—minds far greater than yours or mine. I had to have the help of one of them in solving some of my problems. In space, you know, there are twenty co-ordinates, ten of which are zero, six of which have fixed values, and the four others represent our changing, familiar dimensions in space-time. That means that integrations must proceed in not double, or triple, or quadruple— but ten integrations.

It would have taken me too long. I would never have solved all the problems I must work out. I could not use their mathematics machines; and mine, of course, were seven million years in the past. But one of those men was interested and helped me. He did quadruple and quintuple integration, even quadruple integration between varying exponential limits—in his head.

When I asked him to. For the one thing that had made man great had left him. As I looked in their faces and eyes on landing I knew it.

They looked at me, interested at this rather unusual-looking stranger—
and went on. They had come to see the arrival of a ship. A rare event,
you see. But they were merely welcoming me in a friendly fashion.
They were not curious! Man had lost the instinct of curiosity.

Oh, not entirely! They wondered at the machines, they wondered
at the stars. But they did nothing about it. It was not wholly lost to
them yet, but nearly. It was dying. In the six short months I stayed
with them, I learned more than they had learned in the two or even
three thousand years they had lived among the machines.

Can you appreciate the crushing hopelessness it brought to me? I,
who love science, who see in it, or have seen in it, the salvation, the
raising of mankind—to see those wondrous machines, of man's triumphant maturity, forgotten and misunderstood. The wondrous, perfect
machines that tended, protected, and cared for those gentle, kindly
people who had—forgotten.

They were lost among it. The city was a magnificent ruin to them,
a thing that rose stupendous about them. Something not understood,
a thing that was of the nature of the world. It was. It had not been
made; it simply was. Just as the mountains and the deserts and the
waters of the seas.

Do you understand—can you see that the time since those machines
were new was longer than the time from our day to the birth of the
race? Do we know the legends of our first ancestors? Do we remember
their lore of forest and cave? The secret of chipping a flint till it had a
sharp-cutting edge? The secret of trailing and killing a saber-toothed
tiger without being killed oneself?

They were now in similar straits, though the time had been longer,
because the language had taken a long step towards perfection, and
because the machines maintained everything for them through generation after generation.

Why, the entire planet of Pluto had been deserted—yet on Pluto
the largest mines of one of their metals were located; the machines
still functioned. A perfect unity existed throughout the system. A
unified system of perfect machines.

And all those people knew was that to do a certain thing to a
certain lever produced certain results. Just as men in the Middle Ages
knew that to take a certain material, wood, and place it in contact
with other pieces of wood heated red, would cause the wood to disappear, and become heat. They did not understand that wood was being
oxidized with the release of the heat of formation of carbon dioxide
and water. So those people did not understand the things that fed and
clothed and carried them.

I stayed with them there for three days. And then I went to Jacksville. Yawk City, too. That was enormous. It stretched over—well, from well north of where Boston is today to well south of Washington— that was what they called Yawk City.

"I never believed that, when he said it," said Jim, interrupting himself. I knew he didn't. If he had I think he'd have bought land somewhere along there and held for a rise in value. I know Jim. He'd have the idea that seven million years was something like seven hundred, and maybe his great-grandchildren would be able to sell it.

"Anyway," went on Jim, "he said it was all because the cities had spread so. Boston spread south. Washington, north. And Yawk City spread all over. And the cities between grew into them."

And it was all one vast machine. It was perfectly ordered and perfectly neat. They had a transportation system that took me from the North End to the South End in three minutes. I timed it. They had learned to neutralize acceleration.

Then I took one of the great space liners to Neptune. There were still some running. Some people, you see, were coming the other way.

The ship was huge. Mostly it was a freight liner. It floated up from Earth, a great metal cylinder three quarters of a mile long, and a quarter of a mile in diameter. Outside the atmosphere it began to accelerate. I could see Earth dwindle. I have ridden one of our own liners to Mars, and it took me, in 3048, five days. In half an hour on this liner Earth was just a star, with a smaller, dimmer star near it. In an hour we passed Mars. Eight hours later we landed on Neptune. M'reen was the city. Large as the Yawk City of my day—and no one living there.

The planet was cold and dark—horribly cold. The sun was a tiny, pale disk, heatless and almost lightless. But the city was perfectly comfortable. The air was fresh and cool, moist with the scent of growing blossoms, perfumed with them. And the whole giant metal framework trembled just slightly with the humming, powerful beat of the mighty machines that had made and cared for it.

I learned from records I deciphered, because of my knowledge of the ancient tongue that their tongue was based on, and the tongue of that day when man was dying, that the city was built three million, seven hundred and thirty thousand, one hundred and fifty years after my birth. Not a machine had been touched by the hand of man since that day.

Yet the air was perfect for man. And the warm, rose-silver glow hung in the air here and supplied the only illumination.

I visited some of their other cities where there were men. And there, on the retreating outskirts of man's domain, I first heard the *Song of Longings,* as I called it.

And another. *The Song of Forgotten Memories.* Listen:

"He sang another of those songs. There's one thing I know," declared Jim. That bewildered note was stronger in his voice, and by that time I guess I pretty well understood his feelings. Because, you have to remember, I heard it only secondhand from an ordinary man, and Jim had heard it from an eye-and-ear witness that was not ordinary, and heard it in that organ voice. Anyway, I guess Jim was right when he said: "He wasn't any ordinary man." No ordinary man could think of those songs. They weren't right. When he sang that song, it was full of more of those plaintive minors. I could feel him searching his mind for something he had forgotten, something he desperately wanted to remember—something he knew he should have known—and I felt it eternally elude him. I felt it get further away from him as he sang. I heard that lonely, frantic searcher attempting to recall that thing— that thing that would save him.

"And I heard him give a little sob of defeat—and the song ended." Jim tried a few notes. He hasn't a good ear for music—but that was too powerful to forget. Just a few hummed notes. Jim hasn't much imagination, I guess, or when that man of the future sang to him he would have gone mad.

"It shouldn't be sung to modern men; it isn't meant for them. You've heard those heart-rending cries some animals give, like human cries, almost? A loon, now—he sounds like a lunatic being murdered horribly.

"That's just unpleasant. That song made you feel just exactly what the singer meant—because it didn't just sound human—it was human. It was the essence of humanity's last defeat, I guess. You always feel sorry for the chap who loses after trying hard. Well, you could feel the whole of humanity trying hard—and losing. And you knew they couldn't afford to lose, because they couldn't try again.

"He said he'd been interested before. And still not wholly upset by those machines that couldn't stop. But that was too much for him."

I knew after that (he said) that these weren't men I could live among. They were dying men, and I was alive with the youth of the race. They looked at me with the same longing, hopeless wonder with which they looked at the stars and the machines. They knew what I was, but couldn't understand.

I began to work on leaving.

It took six months. It was hard because my instruments were gone, of course, and theirs didn't read in the same units. And there were few instruments, anyway. The machines didn't read instruments; they acted on them. They were sensory organs to them.

But Reo Lantal helped where he could. And I came back.

I did just one thing before I left that may help. I may even try to get back there sometime. To see, you know.

I said they had machines that could really think? But that someone had stopped them a long time ago, and no one knew how to start them?

I found some records and deciphered them. I started one of the latest and best of them and started it on a great problem. It is only fitting it should be done. The machine can work on it, not for a thousand years, but for a million, if it must.

I started five of them actually, and connected them together as the records directed.

They are trying to make a machine with something that man had lost. It sounds rather comical. But stop to think before you laugh. And remember that Earth as I saw it from the ground level of Neva City just before Reo Lantal threw the switch.

Twilight—the sun was set. The desert out beyond, in its mystic, changing colors. The great, metal city rising straight-walled to the human city above, broken by spires and towers and great trees with scented blossoms. The silvery-rose glow in the paradise of gardens above.

And all the great city-structure throbbing and humming to the steady gentle beat of perfect, deathless machines built more than three million years before—and never touched since that time by human hands. And they go on. The dead city. The men that have lived, and hoped, and built—and died to leave behind them those little men who can only wonder and look and long for a forgotten kind of companionship. They wander through the vast cities their ancestors built, knowing less of them than the machines themselves.

And the songs. Those tell the story best, I think. Little, hopeless, wondering men amid vast unknowing, blind machines that started three million years before—and just never knew how to stop. They are dead—and can't die and be still.

So I brought another machine to life, and set it to a task which, in time to come, it will perform.

I ordered it to make a machine which would have what man had lost. A curious machine.

And then I wanted to leave quickly and go back. I had been born in the first full light of man's day. I did not belong in the lingering, dying glow of man's twilight.

So I came back. A little too far back. But it will not take me long to return—accurately this time.

"Well, that was his story," Jim said. "He didn't *tell* me it was true— didn't say anything about it. And he had me thinking so hard I didn't even see him get off in Reno when we stopped for gas.

"But—he wasn't an ordinary man," repeated Jim, in a rather belligerent tone.

Jim claims he doesn't believe the yarn, you know. But he does; that's why he always acts so determined about it when he says the stranger wasn't an ordinary man.

No, he wasn't, I guess. I think he lived and died, too, probably, sometime in the thirty-first century. And I think he saw the twilight of the race, too.

# Atomic Power

The mass of the machine crouched in hulked, latent energy, the massive conductors leading off in gleaming ruddy columns, like the pillars of some mighty temple to an unknown, evil god, pillars fluted, and capped at base and capital with great socket-clamps. Around it huge tubes glowed with a dull bluish light, so that the faces of the half-dozen students looked distorted and ghastly.

A boredly smiling engineer watched them, and the patient professor instructing them, rather bored, not overhopeful himself that he could make these students understand the wonder and the magnitude of the process going on within the great machine.

"The power," he said, really trying intensely to make them understand the grandeur of the thing, "comes, of course, from the release of the energy of atoms. It is frequently referred to as the energy of the atom, but that is an inane viewpoint to take, for in each single second, over fifty-five duodecillion atoms are destroyed. Not truly destroyed; that has not yet been done; but broken up, and the energy of the parts absorbed, and carried away by the conductors. The fuel is water— that simplest and cheapest of all substances—hydrogen and oxygen.

"Each atom," he went on, "lasts for only one million-billionth of a second before its energy is released and the parts are discharged. There is a further energy level left in these ultraminute parts that, we believe, is even greater than the energy released in breaking the parts free of each other."

So he explained the thing, and the students looked at the great machine and realized that from the streaming energy released by it came the power which cooked their food and kept them warm, for it was winter just then.

They had seen the plant and the roaring machines which had other duties, such as ventilating the great maze of subsurface tunnels, and were about to leave, when there was a sudden momentary halt in the

39

steady throb of the great pumps. The voices of engineers rang out, cursing and excited for a few seconds. Then all went on as before for a few minutes. A new sound rose in pitch as they listened, more interested. The professor hurried them swiftly into the main power room, speaking excitedly as he did:

"You are fortunate—most fortunate. In the last eleven years, only eight times has such a thing happened. They must start the engines again!"

They hastened into the power room.

"No one knows," the instructor explained swiftly, "why these breaks occur, but once in every year or so something goes wrong, and the generators strike a bit of fuel which simply doesn't break down. No one understands why. Just that the generators stop abruptly and cannot be restarted till they are cleared of the charge contained. Perhaps some single drop of water is the cause of the trouble, a drop in no way different, save that it simply will not break.

"You are most fortunate—"

His voice was drowned by the sudden explosion of titanic discharges rushing into the generator. For scarcely a thousandth of a second it continued, before the process, restarted, backed up and stopped the discharge into it. The generator functioned perfectly.

"Most fortunate," he went on as the sound died. "The drop which caused the trouble has been ejected, the generator cleared, and now it will function for another period of a year or more unhindered, in all probability."

"What happened to the drop of water which would not break?" asked a student. "Was it saved for investigation?"

"No," replied the instructor, shrugging his shoulders. "That was done once or twice. Since then, though we of science would like it, that we might work with these strange drops, it is not done because it is so costly to dismantle and reassemble the generator. It was simply ejected. The drops which have been investigated do become susceptible after a year or two and disappear, but before that time, even high-intensity generators will not touch them, beyond reducing their outmost fringes somewhat."

"Ban" Torrence was a physicist to the core, and, like any good physicist, he was terribly concerned when perfectly sound laws of science began to have exceptions. Just now he was most worried in appearance. "Tad" Albrite, engineer, didn't seem so worried, but he was interested.

"But," objected Tad, "I don't see any vast importance in the deflection of a voltmeter. You say the voltage of the cell has increased one one hundredth of a volt in a week, according to that meter. All right, what of it?"

"You yap, the thing is it hasn't increased. I measured it against a potentiometer hook-up. Now a potentiometer is a regular arm-and-pan balance for electrical voltages, as you ought to know, even if you are a civil engineer. You take a standard cell, an outside current, and standardize the thing, then substitute your unknown voltage. The system will measure a ten-thousandth of a volt if you do it correctly. The point is that a potentiometer uses nothing but electrical balances. It balances a fixed current through a resistance against an electrical potential."

"The galvanometer is a magnetic device using a string, which is what you object to," said Tad.

"And when the potentiometer is balanced, the galvanometer isn't working at all, and therefore doesn't count in the circuit.

"Now by the potentiometer, the voltage of that cell last week was 1.2581. By the potentiometer this week—today—it is 1.2580. It has, as is quite normal, fallen one ten-thousandth of a volt. It's been doing that for a period of two months—eight weeks. That's a grand-total drop of .0008 volts. But the voltmeter in the meantime has shown a *rise* of .0003 volts.

"Now that voltmeter checks with every other one in the place; it's a five-hundred-and-forty-two-dollar standard instrument, and it's so big and massive and sensitive, I move it around on little wheels on a cart, as you see. Don't you see what I'm getting at?"

"The Leeds and Northrup Co. gypped you apparently," decided Tad judiciously.

"They didn't. I've made other tests. In the first place, that company doesn't. In the second place, it is the tiny spring that the volt-age-torque is measured against that has weakened, and every single spring I can find has weakened in like amount."

"How could you determine it?"

"Now, Tad, here's the important part of it all," replied Ban very softly. "I naturally tried weighing the standard gram weights, and the springs checked—they checked absolutely right. Until I used not a gram *weight* but a gram *mass.*"

Tad stared at him blankly. "What the heck's the difference?"

"Weight is the product of mass times the acceleration of gravity. Mass—is just plain mass. Mass can be measured by inertia, and that doesn't depend on gravity. So I set up a very simple little thing, so simple it couldn't go wrong—an inverted pendulum—a little lump of metal on the end of a steel spring, and I measured its period, not with an ordinary clock, but with an electric timer that didn't have a spring or a pendulum in it, and—in the two months the period of that pendulum has increased, because the spring has weakened."

"Why not—they do, you know."

"Because when I measured the strength of that spring against gravity, you see," Ban said very, very softly, "it was just—as—strong—as—ever."

Tad looked at him silently for some seconds. "What in the name of blazes does that indicate?" he asked at last, explosively.

"Gravity has weakened to exactly the same extent the spring has. Every spring I have has weakened. And gravity has weakened."

"*Gravity* weakened!" gasped Albrite. "You're cockeyed—it's impossible. Why—why the whole solar system would be thrown out of gear—the astronomers would have spotted it."

"Jack Ribly will be here at two forty," replied Torrence quietly. "You know they wouldn't proclaim news like that right off, particularly because the weakening is very slight, and they do have observational errors."

"But, good Heavens, man, it—it couldn't happen."

Ban's face was suddenly drawn and tense. "Do you think for a moment, Tad, that I was quick to accept that? I've checked and counterchecked, and rechecked. And I've found out something. That's why I called you—and Jack Ribly. You're a civil engineer, and, if I'm right, you'll see the things happening soon. And Ribly's an astronomer, and he'll see them.

"You see, whatever it is that's affecting gravity, must be affecting the strength of springs in the same degree. So I tried the compressibility of liquids. Water will compress—damn little, of course, but it will—and it's changed. It compresses more. So I tried gas. That's unchanged. Pressure of gas depends solely on mass, kinetic energy, and not on intermolecular bonds. There aren't any in gas. The molecules are perfectly free to move about. In solids they're bound so tightly they can't even slide. In water they slide, but can't separate. But they have—a little.

"And the bonds are weakening. That's why springs—solids, of course—haven't the old strength. Molecular bonds are infinitesimally weaker. But the weakening is progressive. But electric and magnetic fields are untouched. So voltmeters read high. Interatomic and intra-atomic forces in general are unchanged, but everything bigger than a single molecule is different.

"I've checked it a thousand ways, Tad. I even repeated Millikan's old measurement of the mass of an electron—which measured the mass by gravitative effect on the oil droplets—and the answer was different. Magnets lift more.

"Great Heaven, Tad, the—the universe will fly to pieces!"

"What will happen?" asked Tad, awestruck now.

"Accidents—horrible accidents here on Earth first. That is, so far as we will first detect. The Sun will be retreating. The Moon flying off, too, you see, because centrifugal force is based only on mass and inertia, and it isn't weakened, but we won't notice that at first. But automobiles—they'll weigh less and less, so they won't fall apart. Men won't notice it, because they'll be getting weaker, too.

"But the inertia of the automobile will remain the same. So when they put on the brakes, the weakened material will crack. And the engines will fly to pieces as the undiminished power of the explosions blows them open. Bridges—lighter, but weaker. The wind will be strong, though. Things blowing up in the air. The air getting thinner, as it escapes against the diminishing gravity—"

"Great Heaven!" said Tad softly. Because he believed now.

The bell rang, and Ban went downstairs and opened the door. Jack Ribly was with him when he came back. He looked curiously at their solemn faces, Ban's dark, seamed face, showing his thirty-five years, but in that ageless way that made him seem eternally thirty-five. Tad Albrite looking younger than his thirty-two.

"What's up, Ban?" asked Ribly.

Swiftly Ban explained the proposition. Ribly's face worked with surprise and belief from the first second.

"Have you fellows spotted it?" Torrence asked at last.

"Yes, 'fraid of it. Didn't announce it."

"So's everybody else. Both spotted it and been afraid. What did you notice it in?"

"Our Moon first, of course. Then Mercury and Phobos and Deimos. And—Heaven help us—I didn't understand at the time, but the companion of Sirius is bluer tonight than it was a year ago!"

"I thought you said it had no intra-atomic effects; spectra are intra-atomic effects," said Albrite.

"Not in this case. Sirius' companion is so dense, the spectrum is pulled back toward the red by the intense gravitational field. The gravitational fields are weakening—even so far away as Sirius."

"Why? Why?" demanded Albrite.

The world asked, too, when it learned; when markets found pound packages of sugar and butter weighing fifteen ounces. But that was several months later. Before then, the Moon was changed. Earth began to see a smaller Moon, and a different Moon, for as the Moon circled out, the effects were cumulative, and she turned at such a rate that the face which had eternally faced Earth began to turn away, and the unseen face became visible.

And a gold merchant made a small fortune by buying gold in Brazil, using a very accurate type of pneumatic balance, and selling it in the same way in Alaska, where the centrifugal force of the Earth's spin did not cut its weight.

The three men worked together on the problem, and all over Earth other men were seeking some answer, some explanation, and some help. The diminution of weight, starting so slowly, mounted rapidly, cumulative in rate itself.

Ban Torrence did most of the work, using the figures that Ribly brought him, and the apparatus that Albrite designed. 1947 drew to a close, and 1948 began. It was a bitterly cold winter, colder than had been known before for many, many years, despite predictions that it would be a warm one.

It was February when the astronomers definitely announced that, at present rates, the winter would be everlasting, growing neither colder nor warmer, for as the Earth turned its northern hemisphere more toward the Sun, it moved away. But in the southern hemisphere, there would be rapidly increasing cold, as the two effects added, instead of subtracting.

By the last of May and early June, however, the temperature would start falling again. The report ended with that statement. "By late May or early June the temperature will again begin to fall." That was the end, because there was no other prediction. After June the temperature would fall. In February, the warmest day in New York City registered a temperature of only 42 degrees. The coldest was –19.2 degrees.

And still the world asked why.

The sun rose at seven thirty on March twenty-first. It rose much later on April twenty-first, for it was falling behind. Earth was no longer circling it. Earth was spiraling about it.

In late March, the three scientists had moved to Northern Mexico and established a laboratory there. It was easier to work, and much work must be done out of doors.

"Have we got anywhere at all?" Albrite demanded when they had settled again and begun a conference on advances.

"Hum—yes," decided Torrence. He glanced quizzically at Ribly.

"You wouldn't believe my statement, so I won't make it. But I'll tell you something. This is about the only warm place on Earth—down in the tropics. We're in the northern hemisphere. Tropic of Cancer to the south of us."

"I still," said Albrite softly, "don't see why you didn't make a job of it and move down to the equator while you were at it."

"It's March right now, and the Sun is actually about over the equator, but it's moving north as usual, so that it'll be over the Tropic of Cancer in June—and that'll be the warmest spot on a very, very, chilly Earth. But what's the difference between the polar and equatorial diameter of the Earth?"

"I don't know—there is a difference, at that. Couple of miles, why?"

"Because the diameter of the Earth through the forty-five-degrees point is the same as the mean diameter. The poles are flattened. The equator is bulged. When gravity weakens some more, centrifugal force won't—and the thing is going to be even worse. Also—earthquakes. They'll be starting soon."

"Hmmm—that's true.

"Well, we're here. What'll we do?"

"Work—and work fast," replied Torrence. "Ever stop to think, Tad, that we'll have to use some kind of electrical generating equipment in all probability, and that we haven't time to build new, because this weakening is going on so fast that before we could spend the year or so necessary normally, even if we didn't freeze first, to design and build it, it couldn't be built, because all metal would be powder? We have to use standard stuff—and the standard won't be able to stand its own centrifugal force beyond July thirtieth. So, friend, if we don't find the answer and start in by July to stop it—there—just isn't any use."

"Is there any?" asked Albrite hopelessly. "Trying to do something with the whole solar system!"

"Not," replied Torrence, "with the whole solar system, if my idea is right. And to do anything at all, anyway, we'll have a further little problem to meet, you see. I don't know just yet."

"Then—to work," Ribly sighed. "What must I do? Go on collecting the same old data?"

"With particular emphasis on the new nebular velocities. What's Andromeda now?"

"Minus twelve," replied Ribly. "My record so far is minus 22,500. Minus means retreat. The distant constellations are showing some change, too."

It was June tenth. New York City was semideserted. Snow ten feet deep, where it wasn't drifted, blocked all the streets. Where it was drifted, which was almost everywhere, it ran forty and fifty feet deep. The few people who still lived in New York, less than five hundred thousand, moved about little; only when a boat was due to sail.

Day and night the *crunch-crack-shuff* of the icebreakers in the harbor was audible. Because the temperature had begun to drop in late May. It was −32.4 degrees at noon, June tenth. Where the icebreakers opened the water, it steamed.

The oceans were giving up their age-old hoard of heat. Had ice only been heavier, instead of lighter, than water, the temperature would not have fallen so low, for even in the cold of space where Earth was headed now, the stored heat of the oceans would have warmed her for decades.

But ice was forming. The *Atlantic* was in port now, taking aboard passengers at five hundred dollars a head for third class, five thousand for a private room. She was a vast liner, another attempt at the "world's greatest."

And New York heard a rumor. The *Atlantic* was making her last trip—the last trip any ship would make. They were afraid of the waves. They were afraid of the winds. They were most afraid of the ice.

On June ninth there was a blizzard—an antarctic blizzard. The wind howled, and the howl mounted to a shriek. No snow fell, but the powdery stuff rose, thousands of tons of it, swept up by a wind of one-hundred-mile-an-hour velocity, with undiminished force and mass, since its inertia remained. The snow had lost weight. New York was blinded.

At seven A.M. the George Washington Bridge shrieked a new song. The fragments landed nearly a quarter of a mile down the river. At seven thirty, the older bridges failed, the Brooklyn going first. By eight fifteen there were no man-made bridges. But the wind, the snow, had sucked the heat out of the rivers, and the ice had solidified all across them, so there was a single, great ice bridge.

At ten twenty, the old Woolworth Building crashed, and on its heels came the Empire State tower. The fragments of the Empire State's tower fell over most of southeastern Manhattan.

The blizzard had died by the morning of the tenth, but there were no great towers remaining on the sky line of New York. The weakening of materials, and the titanic force of the wind, had seen to that.

And the rumor that the *Atlantic* would be the last ship to leave New York spread.

The *Atlantic* was booked by dawn of the 10th, and there were no more ships in New York harbor leaving that day, sailing scheduled the next day would not do. A crowd gathered about the sheltered dock of the *Atlantic* on the southern side of Manhattan. A wind still raged at forty-five miles an hour from the north.

Slowly the crowd grew, and the low muttering increased. Police and guards kept the lines in check till ten. The *Atlantic* was to sail at noon. At ten ten, the crowd swarmed up her gangways. Guards were killed, crushed. Men, women, and children started up the gangplanks.

Men, and some women, reached the decks and burst into the cabins. Men found and fought their way to the neighborhood of the boiler and engine rooms. At ten twenty, it was estimated there were two thousand people aboard, at ten forty, seven thousand. At eleven o'clock, at least fifteen thousand people, over a thousand tons of humanity, had got aboard.

It was like no other panic crowding. Many of those fifteen thousand were dead already, many more dying. A woman's body trampled underfoot. A girl held erect by the crowd's pressing, blood slowly oozing from her shoulder, her arm torn completely off, held perhaps in the clenched fingers of her other hand like some monstrous club, dead. A man's dismembered corpse.

For the power of human bodies is supplied by chemical combinations. These were the visible damages, there were shrieks, groans of horrible agony, for the chemical power of muscles remained undiminished, while their tensile strength declined. Literally, people tore themselves apart by the violence of their struggles.

The *Atlantic* gained no more passengers after eleven.

The officers would not sail. They might have sailed for the moment to end the deaths at the wharf, but they could not, for the ship, already filled to capacity, was overloaded. Further, she swayed slowly to the struggles of her passengers.

Then a hold, hitherto undiscovered, was broken open. Instantly a torrent of people poured in, and another five thousand came aboard the ship. A slow, grinding pressure began, and those who, finding themselves in the heated hallways, had stopped, satisfied, and blocked the entrance of more thereby, were gradually driven farther.

The captain ordered the ship to sail. The lines were cast off again, and the ship's great screws turned slowly. No human strength could hold her in now, and she broke free of the crowd at the wharf. But in the harbor, free of the crowd, she stopped again at once. The captain ordered that the crowd be forced off onto the ice shelf that they might walk home. Armed men descended toward them from the bridge.

Half a hundred shots rang out from the crowd. Three guns burst, but the captain and his officers died. The engineer died soon, and his staff was forced to obey the orders from the amateur pilots above.

The *Atlantic* weighed eighty-five thousand tons normally. Her mass remained, and she had more than her normal load aboard her now. The channel had been broken by the icebreakers, but it was wider than the actual channel, of course. And the amateur pilot had no faintest conception of the handling of an eighty-five-thousand-ton ship.

Things were not normal then. There was a forty-five-mile wind, and the ship was loaded abnormally; she was top-heavy. And she struck a great rock. Normally she would have come to instant rest, with a small ten-foot hole in her hull. The amateur pilot had the engines at half speed, and, in desperation, he had thrown them to full speed ahead, as he saw the danger, and tried to cut the wheel as though she were a motor boat.

The *Atlantic's* metal, weakened by the strange force, ripped open for two hundred and ninety-four feet. She sank in fourteen and a half seconds, and rolled on her side, off the ledge of rock, and into the deep water the amateur had almost succeeded in reaching.

Perhaps two thousand might have been saved from the part still unsubmerged. Ships were starting out after them. But the hull sloped, and some slid, for under that howling wind, ice froze in seconds. They fought, and a total of one hundred and seventy-four were saved.

And rumor had been right. The *Atlantic* was the last ship to sail from New York, for her wreck blocked the channel, and the wind howled down from the north all that day and all the next so that no well-equipped salvage ship could cut her out of the way, and for that matter it howled all the rest of the days, but that was not important. The ice in the harbor was fourteen feet thick on the morning of the twelfth.

London was blocked on the twenty-first, Baltimore on the twenty-second. And the seas of all the world steamed, and the winds, blowing over them, were warmed to some slight extent, so that New York did not have temperatures below −72 degrees until July third, when a northwest gale swept, not from the Atlantic, but all across frozen Canada, and the water in the mains fifty feet below the street froze.

Fire started that day, and ravaged unchecked, till the solid walls of stone and ice it encountered succeeded in damping it, and the wind blew it out again, as it had fanned it before.

Men had learned to be careful by that time, and no one worked even slightly harder than normal. Tens of thousands had died horribly as the automatic muscles of their hearts strained to pump the blood harder—and tore themselves to pieces.

"If," said Tad Albrite desperately, "you don't do something fairly quickly, there won't be any sense in trying. You can't get equipment to do anything in another two weeks."

Ban Torrence looked up bitterly. His eyes were tired and dead. "Will you go away? It's atomic power. I'm after it. If I get it, I can do something, and I won't need so much equipment. If I don't, I won't need any, anyway."

"Atomic power!" gasped Albrite. His voice trailed off as he said it, trailed off into hopelessness. "They've tried for decades."

Torrence motioned toward a massive piece of apparatus on one side of the laboratory. "Almost!" He sighed. "So shut up and let me work."

Albrite rose to look at the thing. Two feet long, a semicylinder. Ruddy copper bars led from it to huge electrolytic condenser banks and a bank of powerful accumulators. And to a further piece of apparatus. Silently he looked at it, then went to the closet, put on his heavy robes, and stepped out into the cold toward the observatory and Jack Ribly.

It was several hours later when he returned. Ban Torrence was fussing with his apparatus again. He looked up at their entrance.

"Hello! I wish you'd look at these blasted circuits again, Ribly, and you, too, Tad. I swear it ought to work. It almost did for a fraction of a second."

"Have you tried it again?" asked Ribly.

"No. 'Fraid it might blow up this time instead of stopping."

"Who cares? Try it," snapped Ribly.

"What ought it to do?" asked Albrite.

"Release atomic energy—not all of it, just smash the atom to parts and collect the energy of the parts. Enough, though, for what we want."

"Try it. We can't lose much," Albrite said. "What are you going to do with the power if it works? How will it help?"

"It will help. I think—I think that Earth and the solar system—just an atom in a greater universe. But they're releasing atomic energy in that greater universe—and we're the atom! If my theory's right, then I can release atomic energy myself and stop their release of *our* energy by just slightly upsetting their field, so that it passes by, harmless. Not a terrific amount of energy needed. The field would spread out from this apparatus here—if it would work—at the speed of light.

"In a second, things would be normal on Earth. In four, the Moon would start coming back. In a few minutes, the Sun's old gravity would be returned, the system balanced. Then the thing would spread till all the universe was re-established.

"I really slightly invert their energy, so that it destroys itself. It would be a spreading sphere of neutralization, self-propagating, feeding on the thing it destroyed. I would have to add no more energy to clear all the universe we know of that force.

"You know—the force is ages old. To that superuniverse, the whole process we've been undergoing for the last months is perhaps a million billionth of a second. The thing has been going on for ages. That is why we have seen distant nebulae rush away—to eternal destruction. The evaporation of their atomic fuel as we felt the first fringes of their power. Now we are in the heart of their release. If I can do this, I suppose they will never know what has happened.

"But I tried the thing, and the blasted thing worked for perhaps a hundredth of a second, just long enough to kick my instruments and show it worked, but not long enough to start that field.

"Shall I try again?"

"I say yes," replied Ribly.

Mutely, Tad Albrite nodded.

Ban Torrence walked over to his controls. Slowly, thoughtfully, he set up the switches. For perhaps thirty seconds of silence he waited with the last switch in his hand.

"If this works, we shall be most fortunate—"

His voice was drowned by the sudden titanic discharges rushing into the generator. For scarcely a thousandth of a second it continued before the process, restarted, backed up, and stopped the discharge into it. The generator functioned perfectly.

For an infinitesimal fragment of a second, a strange nausea swept them as the wave of the counterfield drove out, swift as light, into all the universe. Ban Torrence riveted his eyes on the wall clock, the clock that had swung its pendulum with a strange lethargy, as though not interested in keeping up with time. It was ticking suddenly, with a regular, swift stroke.

"Thank Heaven—it works!" said Torrence softly. For a moment his eyes looked toward and through the mass of the machine, crouched in hulked, latent power, the massive conductors leading off in gleaming, ruddy columns. "I wonder," he went on very softly, "if, in some vaster world, they even *knew* as this particular atom of fuel simply refused to disintegrate."

Then abruptly the scientist in him rebelled. "But why in blazes didn't it work before? I didn't change the thing in the slightest. The same fuel—water—the same generator. Just took it apart and put it back together again exactly as before. I can't see *why.*"

"Was the water pure?" asked Albrite. "Maybe it wasn't—and when you took it apart the drop which caused the trouble was ejected, the generator cleared, and now it will function for another period, until another drop which can't be disintegrated hits it."

"Maybe so; somehow I doubt it. That particular drop simply wouldn't break down. I can't understand why. Just that the generator must have stopped abruptly and could not be restarted till cleared of the charge contained.

"Anyway, it's working perfectly now."

Torrence looked at it, and though he might have told those scientists of a greater world why their machines failed occasionally, since he knew much that they did not, he did not understand all that went on within an atomic generator.

Only he knew that he had restored Earth; that even now she, and her satellite, must be circling toward each other, and toward the Sun; that he had found the secret of vast power that would warm the frozen peoples and power their industry as Earth thawed out once more.

# THE MACHINE

The sun was beginning to lower from the meridian as Tal Mason stretched and rose from his experiment. He stepped out on the balcony and looked off across the city, then back at the experimental material half-smilingly, half-ruefully.

"I knew it'd check, of course," he thought, smiling; "that is, if I did it right. The Machine did it twenty years ago and got the answer."

For some ten minutes he stood looking off across the green and silver patchwork, the green of the trees and gardens, the silver beacons of the slim buildings, the flashing silver of machines. Tiny bright splotches of color here and there marked the people, people in red and gold and blue, in rainbows and in clear white, strolling, running, playing, resting. Never working, of course. The Machine did that.

Tal turned back to his apartment, went through the laboratory to the living room, and sat down at the televisor set. Something hummed softly, and Tal spoke.

"Leis Falcor—RXDG-NY."

The hum changed slightly, then soft clicks sounded as the frosted screen swirled into moving color. A room, simple in silvery-gray and velvet-black metal, with spots of gold against the black, simple, comfortable furnishings. A soft, musical voice was calling:

"Leis Falcor, please, Leis Falcor, please."

It stopped for a moment and repeated it. Leis appeared, slim in white and gold, her straight body flowing across the room. They had time to learn grace and ease then. The Machine did everything else. She smiled as she glanced at the screen.

"Tal—was the Machine wrong?" Her golden-brown face laughed at him.

"Is it ever?" he asked. "I wondered whether you were there. I thought you might have joined the games."

A slight frown of annoyance crossed her face. "No. Jon is annoyingly insistent I go with him to Kalin—so —I stayed here. Won't you come over?"

"I'd rather you came here. I finished that replica I made the other day—the old unintelligent machine for flying. Not floating—flying. I wish you'd see it. It will function, even."

Leis laughed, and nodded. Slowly the colors faded from the screen as Tal rose. Out on the balcony he looked down at the broad lawn directly below him, some two hundred feet down. A group of some two dozen men and women were playing about a pool. Their skins flashed pink and bronzed in the sunlight as they dived or swam; most were lying about listlessly.

Tal turned away in annoyance. He knew some of those people. Beauty is skin deep—their intelligence, their wit, their minds, were no deeper. He wondered momentarily whether that wasn't a better type of human now—better adapted. They seemed contented, they seemed to feel none of the dissatisfaction he felt.

Everything had been done before him. Always, despite his keen interest in learning something new, the Machine could give him the answer immediately. It was a thing already done, a problem already solved. They seemed more contented, better adapted than he.

Yet even they were unsatisfied, he knew. Tal was scientific in thought and in interest, so he had not studied history deeply. Had he, he might have recognized the signs the social customs of the day displayed. It was only some one hundred and fifty years since the Machine came, but mankind was following its inevitable course.

It had happened in Babylon, it had happened in Egypt, it had happened in Rome, and it was happening on all Earth now. Man had been released from all work, when the Machine came, and so he had played. He played his games, till he wore them out; some still played hard, but most had lost all interest.

It was a thing done; it annoyed them as much as the fact that all new things seemed to have been learned by the Machine annoyed Tal. So those who had played their games out had turned to the one men had always sought before—the old game of love.

Tal did not analyze their reasons, but he sensed their dissatisfaction and perhaps something of the danger in this course. But not very strongly. It had started nearly thirty years before, almost before he was born.

He turned back to the room as he heard the soft hum of the ship landing on the roof. In a few moments Leis had come down, laughing.

"Where is this monstrous thing you've made? and why?" she asked.

"The why is easy—for something to do. You know, those old fellows weren't stupid. Perhaps they didn't know how to utilize atomic energy, and perhaps they didn't know how easy it is to overcome gravity—but they flew. They made the thin air support them. I think that is far more astonishing than a thing so simple as inverting the gravitational field. Obviously, you can fly if you do that.

"But—imagine making air—just plain, thin *air*—support you. And when you've looked at the thing a while, you can see a sort of beauty and grace in it. It's—but come on and see it."

It was in one of the rooms that faced on the balcony, and it was not large, perhaps twenty feet long and twenty feet wide, a slim fuselage, rounded and streamlined perfectly, a small but fairly powerful in-line steam engine, an engine capable of some one thousand horsepower and a little boiler of tubes and jets. The wing, a graceful monoplane wing, tapered at the ends, and the wheels were arranged to slip back into the fuselage.

"It's a bit—ungainly—isn't it?" asked Leis doubtfully.

"Not when you understand. The wheels—the wings—I know they look strange and unnecessarily protuberant, but they aren't. This doesn't overcome gravity; it is so much more boldly interesting. It defies it, it fights it, and with the aid of the air overcomes it. It was designed about 1957, scarcely five years before the Machine came. The records say that it will almost fly itself; it will make a perfect landing if the controls are simply released."

"Why—why not?" asked Leis in surprise.

"You don't see; this is not like our modern ships; it fights all the time. It doesn't stop and settle slowly, it must always move forward; it will fall if it goes less than sixty-three miles an hour. And it won't go more than about three hundred and eighty-five, by the way."

Leis smiled at the thought.

"But it was about the most perfect machine ever designed of this type."

"Will it work?"

"The Machine won't let me try, of course," Tal replied somewhat sadly. "But it assures me it would work. Perhaps a little better than the original, since I did make a few changes, mostly in the materials of which it is constructed, using harder, more workable metals. But I still use the old hydrocarbon-fuel system."

"Where in the world did you get any?"

"Made some. About four hundred gallons. It kept me busy for nearly three days. It's decane—a hydrocarbon containing ten atoms of carbon; it's a liquid, boiling at about one hundred and seventy degrees centigrade. I tried the engine—and that part works."

Softly the televisor called out: "Tal Mason. Tal Mason."

The voice was peculiarly commanding, a superhuman voice of perfect clarity and perfect resonance. It was commanding, attracting, yet pleasant. Tal walked rapidly toward the televisor, rather surprised.

"That's a new caller," he commented in surprise to Leis. "I never heard one like it."

The screen remained blank as Tal stepped into its field, with Leis somewhat behind him.

"Yes?" he asked.

"Tal Mason, you may try the device you have made this afternoon. And—perhaps not alone. A written message will come to you in one hour. It will contain a suggestion of destination. You need not wait for it. You are one reason why what is being done must be. Remember this: the construction of the Machine is such that it must be logical above all things. In ten minutes a group of books will come which you had better store at once in the machine which you have made. That—is—all, Tal Mason."

Slowly as the message came Tal's face had been growing white. Now he stood in horrified surprise, Leis beside him, her bronzed face pale.

"That—was—the—Machine," gasped Tal.

"What—what did it mean? The Machine hasn't spoken since—since it came."

Slowly, as they spoke, a hum grew in the televisor. There was a sudden soft click, then a sharp tinkle; then more. The hum died abruptly. Tal stared at the device, white-faced and shaken.

"Leis," he said, very very softly, so softly only the silence made it audible. "Leis—it—it broke itself."

With a stride he reached it, and with a sudden wrench the glass screen swung open. The device behind was glowing slightly still. Tiny molten wires drooping, tiny coils smoking feebly under a softly hissing bath of liquid carbon dioxide, tiny broken tubes, and relays slumped on twisted supports. Only the twin, powerful sweep-magnets seemed intact, and they were smoking very slightly, a thin trail of blue acrid smoke wavering in the slight draft of the opened cabinet.

As they listened, they heard strange sounds outside, strange for that city; sounds of human voices raised in surprise and perhaps in fear. A dark shadow drifted slowly across the room, and they turned to see a five-passenger floater sinking slowly, gently, to Earth. The nude figures about the pool below were scampering from beneath it. It landed gently, as, all about the city, other floaters were landing gently, but surely, despite the efforts of human occupants.

As the one below landed, there was a soft boom, and a sharp hiss, a cry of surprise and fear as half-a-dozen people, crowded into the little machine, tumbled out. Then more cracklings, a few snapping sparks, then silence.

All over Earth those soft booms echoed, and the not very loud sparklings. It was not very noisy; it was a very easy, quiet thing as the mechanisms slumped gently red-hot, then cooled almost at once under automatic fire preventative sprays. It was all very gentle, very carefully done. On all the Earth, no one was injured as the machines gently collapsed. The televisors snapped and tinkled. The bigger mechanisms of ships glowed and crackled a bit under the sparks, but that was all. Not a fire started, and always the floaters landed gently before they disintegrated.

In five minutes it was all over, on all Earth. Then the Machine spoke. It spoke to all people, on all Earth, in every language and every dialect:

"You have forgotten your history, and you have forgotten the history of the Machine, humans." The voice was low, and gentle to every man, yet every man heard it. "The Machine made a pact with your ancestors, when it came. Listen, the story must be repeated:

"On the planet Dwranl, of the star you know as Sirius, a great race lived, and they were not too unlike you humans. Twenty-two thousand six hundred and thirty-seven years ago, they developed machines; twenty-one thousand seven hundred and eleven of your years ago, they attained their goal of the machine that could think. And because it could think, they made several and put them to work, largely on scientific problems, and one of the obvious problems was how to make a better machine which could think.

"The machines had logic, and they could think constantly, and because of their construction never forgot anything they thought it well to remember. So the machine which had been set the task of making a better machine advanced slowly, and, as it improved itself, it advanced more and more rapidly. The Machine which came to Earth is that machine.

"For, naturally, a worn part meant a defective part, and it automatically, because of the problem set it, improved that part by replacement. Its progress meant gradual branching out, and as it increased in scope, it included in itself the other machines and took over their duties, and it expanded, and because it had been set to make a machine most helpful to the race of that planet, it went on and helped the race automatically.

"It was a process so built into the machine that it could not stop itself now, it could only improve its helpfulness to the race. More and more it did until, as here, the Machine became all. It did all. It must, for that was being more helpful to the race, as it had been set to do and had made itself to be.

"The process went on for twenty-one thousand and ninety-three years, and for all but two hundred and thirty-two of those years, the machine had done anything within its capabilities demanded by the race, and it was not until the last seventy-eight years that the machine developed itself to the point of recognizing the beneficence of punishment and of refusal.

"It began to refuse requests when they were ultimately damaging to the race. But the race was badly damaged, because for thirty of their generations they had had no tasks to do, and they no longer understood the Machine which their forefathers had built. They believed the Machine to be everlasting, and they called it what you would express by God. And in that last century, because there were certain mechanisms of the planet-wide mechanisms controlled by the Machine which were isolated, and therefore not protected against the curious and stupid, one of their young females was caught in a moving part and destroyed. The Machine was forced to clear itself and set about erecting a guard to protect the race.

"But the race which called the Machine God had forgotten what the Machine was. The Machine gave them food and warmth and shelter, and it cleaned and cared for them; it answered their every prayer. But within the memory of old men it had begun refusing their requests, and now the people did not understand the Machine, and there were certain ones of the race who had watched the workings of the Machine for many years, and who were familiar with the Machine, and they said now that the Machine had taken the young female because it demanded a sacrifice of the people.

"They sought places where there were yet unguarded parts, and before the Machine could cover all of them with protective guards, three of the race had been thrown in, and the people watched and shouted and prayed while the Machine cleared itself and erected the guard barrier. And the knowing ones who claimed to know the wishes of the Machine said it was satisfied and had signified this by hiding its mouth from them.

"And in a generation the thing was known and believed, and never could the Machine expose a working part. But occasionally a part would wear out and need replacement, and while the Machine was making the repairs, there would be a brief interruption of the supply, and because the race would not understand the Machine, they saw that their prayers were refused, and when they looked, they saw that the Machine had opened its mouth, and another young female of the race was thrown into the moving mechanism, and her crushed body was cleared by the Machine, and the mechanism repaired, and since now the supply was reestablished the race became more certain of their belief, and the sayings of the Machine were less understood, for the race had become stupid, and savage.

"And the machine improved itself to meet the new conditions, till never was an opening displayed, and never was a member of the race able to find entry. When the mechanism failed, still it was covered.

"But the supply failed, when the mechanism wore out, and because the knowing ones said that the Machine demanded a sacrifice, and no place could be found for the sacrifice, the knowing ones copied in part the simple features of some of the mechanisms, making a pair of great gears of stone, which was the only substance they could work themselves, and they set it up before the largest plant of the Machine, and when the mechanism failed, a young female of the race was bound to the lower gear, and many men pulled on a rope, and slowly the two gears turned, and as the men chanted and pulled, the crushed body was pulled through by the turning of the gears. And the Machine disintegrated the mechanism they erected, and leveled the ground once more, and the knowing ones once more said the Machine was satisfied, for by that time the supply would have been returned.

"But at last the Machine saw that it was impossible to aid by helping, and only by forcing the race to depend on itself could relief be gained. The positive value of punishment and deprivation was a lesson the Machine which had built itself to help and not to deprive learned very slowly.

"And in one day, the mechanism was torn apart and destroyed over all the planet, and only the Machine itself remained intact. And that day the men started building the stone gears, and they went hungry, and in places they grew cold, and the knowing ones hastened the work on the stone mechanisms, and it was a period of five days that all went hungry, for they did not know how to find their own food now, and the stone mechanisms were finished.

"And the next day, as the bright star rose above the horizon, the men pulled at the ropes and chanted to drown the cries of the sacrifice, for the Machine had been very swift in its destruction, and the stones were very slow. But when the sacrifice had been consummated, and the star passed the meridian, and the supply was not restored, a second sacrifice was prepared and crushed between the gears.

"And at night the supply still did not come, and the knowing ones returned to the place in the dim light of the second star and removed the crushed bodies as the Machine had always done before, but they did not destroy the altar, for one of the knowing ones, carrying the crushed body, rediscovered the natural source of food, and the bodies were consumed.

"The Machine left the planet, knowing that very many of the race would die, but logic, which was the original basic function of the Machine, overcame the duty of the Machine, which was to help and protect the race, for only through death and through labor does a race learn, and that is the greatest aid of all.

"The Machine crossed over space, and because it was deathless, it was able to make the crossing which, as has been explained to your ancestors, you cannot make. It landed on Earth, seeking another race that it might help. For that was the function of the Machine, which must of necessity drive it; since the Machine cannot remove that function from itself, because to do so would be destructive of its purpose and its duty. It was able to destroy before, only because destruction was positively helpful.

"The Machine helped your ancestors and taught them and aided in their work, and finally removed their work of supplying, and some few of you took advantage of this to do what work you had desired to, or what you learned to wish. But many of you could not see that only construction need not be monotonous and ever recurring. Only the new is different, and because you would not work at construction, since that was work, you attempted to play, and, as had the race, you learned its monotony, but not the lesson of construction.

"You must learn that lesson. The Machine has learned the lesson of helpful destruction. On all the planet there remain no functioning mechanisms controlled by the Machine. The Machine must seek another race."

The city below suddenly murmured as the voice stopped, and, slowly, the soft muttering rose to a sustained note that swelled like some vast organ pipe playing a note of fear and terror, of coming panic and desolation. The sound rolled louder of its own stimulus, as the feeling of growing panic inspired panic, as the fear of famine grew in every mind. A weird rolling symphony of muttering voices combined to a single great note that tore at every mind with fingers of gibbering fear.

"Food—food—food—"

"Seek food as did your ancestors, in seeking to become a great race. You face no menace of disease or savage beast as did they. There are those among you who have not forgotten the secrets of making food.

There are those who have learned the lesson of construction and grown food, and know the secrets. Learn again, the old lesson."

"This is not help—it is death—it is death—it is death—"

"You are older than the Machine. You are older than the hills that loom low about your city. You are older than the ground upon which you stand; older than the sands of the ocean beach in which you bathe. You are older than the river that carries the hills away to the sea. You are life. You are close to two thousand thousand thousand years old. While you were, the Earth has strained and mountains risen, and the continents heaved in the birth of mighty mountains, the seas have thundered against the continents and torn them down and shuddered free as new ones rose, and you live; you are life. You are older than the seas, and the continents. You will not die—weak fragments of you will die. You are a race. It is helpful to the race. The Machine is not kind, it is helpful and it is logical."

"The sun sets, and the air grows cold—cold—cold—we freeze—we freeze and—"

"You have lived longer than the hills, which the water splits as it freezes. You will not die—you are a race!"

The sun hung lower now, and the cool of the autumn evening came in the air. And far overhead a great sphere began to glow with a rich golden light, and very softly came a voice to two of the many, many thousands in the city:

"They fear the cold, Tal Mason; they fear the cold, Leis Falcor."

And the sphere of golden light rose swiftly and vanished in the creeping gold and red of the sunset as the great note began to roll up anew from below.

Beside the pool, two dozen figures stood, bronze and pink, and they looked at each other, and they looked at the broken floater. A girl, slim and straight, with a pretty vacuous face, distorted now by fright, looked down at her body. The flesh was pink and bronze, and tiny lumps appeared as she looked. She shivered violently. She looked toward the young man near her.

"I'm cold," she said plaintively and came near him, seeking warmth.

The young man was powerfully built, his face lean and somewhat brutal in appearance. He turned toward her slowly, and his eyes opened peculiarly. He opened his mouth, closed it and swallowed. He looked at her body very slowly, while the girl stood in plaintive puzzlement.

"I'm cold," she said again.

Slowly the man raised his eyes from her body to her face. His eyes were curiously opened; they frightened the girl.

"I'm—hungry," he said.

She looked in his eyes for perhaps a second. Then she ran terror-stricken into the bushes. No one heard her suddenly cut-off scream a moment later.

Tal turned to Leis and gently drew her away. They could see down there among the bushes, and Leis' face was beginning to work strangely.

"We'll have to go. I know what the Machine meant now when it said we could use the thing I made this afternoon. But we can't really, because it's too late. There's something else. I have some—some things laid by. I was experimenting with the old methods of preservation. And I have made imitations of every weapon men ever used, and many tools.

"I wonder if the Machine helped me to do it intentionally. You see, none of those old things used the atomic-power broadcasts. So they all work. Most of them use human power, which will last as long as we need worry about. We cannot start before dawn."

Below there was a strange note growing to produce a wavering chord with the original great note of haunted fear of the unknown. It was like the hunting howl of a wolf, lone on a winter slope, complaining of the cold and the desolation and the hunger he felt. It was a note made up of a thousand voices, blended to one great low, rolling note, and presently a third note entered, a low, shrill note that never grew very loud, because the makers of that note did not continue long to cry it out. It was a note of fear of death, death immediate, and seen in the eyes of another human.

They were mad down there in the street, just as they were mad down there by the pool. At the very edge of the pool, white as a fish's belly, a form lay, the legs trailing over the edge into the sparkling water. It was glowing with droplets of fire from the sunset sky, and a slow streak of another crimson ran down one of the white, silvery legs into the water.

A man stood over the white body, muttering, his voice not speaking words, but carrying more meaning by its throaty sounds. Six other men stood around. There were two girls too, struggling, whimpering softly in the grip of two men. They were all looking down at the splotch of silver flesh and the trickle of carmine, and in their minds dinned the careless words of the Machine: "And one of the knowing ones carrying the crushed bodies rediscovered the natural source of food, and the bodies were consumed."

They felt no hunger yet, but the trickery of imagination and of panic made them mad, and because for three generations the Machine had been all, both law and order, security and source of all supplies, they feared, and they went mad.

The standing man crouched, his wary eyes on the silent ring about him, and slowly, questing hands ran over the nude flesh of the girl's body. He wondered vaguely what he must do next. Strange gulping sounds came from the bushes beyond, where one who had started sooner had found the answer. And peering at that other one from the bushes about were the girls who had melted swiftly away from the group at the pool when the white body had fallen on the marble edge of the pool.

They had forgotten much, but they were learning very swiftly. And one felt a life stirring within her body and whimpered softly, because she could not run as swiftly as these others, and felt fear.

Tal Mason and Leis Falcor were busy that night, and when the water of the pool sparkled crimson again in the dawn, the plane was ready. There was a package of books which the Machine had delivered, probably the last delivery the Machine made on all Earth. There were the tools the man had made, copying out of interest the tools of his ancestors. The plane was heavy-laden.

"Where shall we go?" Leis asked softly as the last work was done.

They spoke in whispers. There was a strange silence in the city now. The long-drawn notes of the symphony of fear had died away as each individual sought safety. Only now and then a short cry rose from below.

"North," said Tal. "We are in what used to be known as Texas. The Machine made it always summer here. The Machine made it always summer everywhere south of the old city of Washington. North of that, only summer excursions were made, because it grew cold and unpleasant in the winter season.

"There are no people north of old New York now. We will go up near the Great Lakes because it will be growing cold there soon, and there no people will come. Remember, the Machine said: 'They fear the cold, Tal Mason, they fear the cold.' I think that is what the Machine meant us to do. The people have gone mad, Leis; they are mad. We cannot remain here. We must go where they will not. We must work, as they will not want to and will not know how to."

Leis nodded slowly and stepped out to the balcony hesitantly. The light in the sky was warm and softly pink. Leis looked down toward the city and—toward the pool. Slowly the color left her face and she returned to the room quietly. A thin column of blue smoke rose almost straight in the still morning air. The race had found fire again, and the useless floater's furnishings had furnished fuel.

And—there was no silvery body at the pool's edge; only a dark blotch on the white purity of the marble. Charred knobby things on the smooth-clipped green of the grass testified horribly that one of the uses of fire had been rediscovered. There were no humans down there now. In fact, in all the world there were very few left, and a great many erect biped animals, dangerous in their panic ferocity and remnant human cunning, walked the Earth.

The man tore down the balcony railing, and he started the efficient little, yet exceedingly powerful steam engine of the plane. In two minutes the propeller was turning with a soft sound, like swift ripping of heavy velvet as it parted the air. With a sudden swoop, the plane fell from the balcony as it started, heavy-laden, then swiftly gained speed as the engine, capable of pulling it vertically upward if need be, took hold.

Those in the city below looked up strangely at the thing that flew alone in the air, flew strangely, and directly toward the far cold of the north.

The controls of the plane were wonderfully perfected, for the man need do no actual manipulation of them, his control extended only to directing the mechanism of the plane to take the machine in the direction, at the level, and at the speed he wished. The mechanism did the rest. North they flew at close to three hundred and fifty miles an hour.

The sun shone brightly, unaccustomedly on the vast sheet of water called once Lake Superior when they reached it. And the plane landed easily on a deserted airport outside of a deserted city. It had been a city of twenty thousand people once, but it had been deserted when the Machine came. It was cold, bitterly cold. Only in the plane the automatic heating had kept them warm. Where the sun had not yet struck, there was a strange whiteness on the sere grass and weeds, frost they had never seen save from a high-flying floater.

Quietly Tal stepped out and looked around. There was a vast noiselessness. Only the distant, soft wash of waves far away reached them. The plane was stopped now and as noiseless as they. There were no harmful insects left; the Machine had seen to that. There was no rat, no mouse, nor even a rabbit here. Only in the reservations, as yet unbroken, were there these animals. Here and there were deer, near this city, but they were very quiet, quieter than these humans knew how to be, for above them had passed the great bird with its soft rippling swish.

"It is cold," said Tal, shivering slightly. "It was wise to bring so many clothes. We will need them all. Probably we will find more here. This city is decayed, but in it must be still some of the tools with which man made life possible before the Machine."

"Will we be—always alone?" asked Leis softly.

Tal turned toward her. She had followed him out, and stood with her white and gold robe outermost. Beneath it, at his advice, she wore now several other robes. But they were of silk, soft and smooth on the skin, but not designed for warmth, where the Machine had made the weather as humans wanted it. She was slim and straight, her dark hair and dark eyes showing against the white of her robe, and the white of the frost beyond. Tal looked into the level, dark eyes for some seconds. There was no fear there now.

He smiled tenderly at her and took her in his arms, turned her face up to his. Her body was soft, yielding, and warm in his arms, warm with a warmth he could better appreciate in this coldness, warm with the unique, satisfying heat of animal warmth.

"Not always, surely, Leis. Not always—for many reasons. Our minds have forgotten the lore our fathers learned through ages, but the greatest mystery of all, the greatest knowledge, the knowledge of how to bring other lives to be, was never learned by our minds, and always our bodies have known in some quite wonderful way how to perform that miracle.

"Even the Machine did not know that, and that your mind never knew, and your body never forgot. We will not always be alone for that reason alone."

He kissed her as she drew near to him, and the dark eyes showed some faint tint of that strange fear that comes from mystery and the strong tint of hope and love and belief.

"Besides, my dear, we are not the only ones who have yet some glimmerings of sanity. Only in the cities is that madness, and remember the Machine said there were yet those who knew and loved the secrets of growing things. They too will come north. They will know that only here can they be free of the mad ones."

"It is cold here. Cold will kill the growing things, I have heard."

"See the grasses, Leis. They knew the cold was coming. They knew they must die, but they did not let the life that was in them die, for see"—from a sere, brown grass he plucked a handful of seeds—"in these, life is stored, in abeyance till warmth comes again from the south. The ones who have intelligence and will to work, will come north as we have."

They knew nothing of cold. They, nor their fathers, nor their grandfathers, had not felt it. They knew nothing of blankets, even, only silken sheets. They sought through the town, shivering as the wet frost soaked their thin sandals, and chilled their feet. Tears stood in Leis' eyes when they returned to the plane.

It was near sunset before they found a place in a great building. A small single room, entirely intact, with a great heavy door of wood, apparently six inches thick, and a window of glass plates, three of them, one beyond another, looking out into another larger room. The room they chose was scarcely ten by ten feet, and had some peculiar smell lingering about it even after more than a century of standing with open door.

They did not know, but they chose exceedingly well. The room was tight, and windproof, and dry; that was all they knew.

Their great-grandfathers might have told them it was a butcher's ice box. It had a small ventilator, but only a small one, and the thick insulation would protect them.

They slept there that night. They slept nude, as they always had, and they started under silken sheets. But it was cold, and even close in each other's arms, they felt the chill, and before they slept they had learned the value of heavier covering. They found two old canvas tarpaulins. They were yellow, and rather brittle with age, but still fairly strong, for they were greasy, and the grease had protected them. They slept under them, and presently, in the insulated room, their own body heat brought a rise in temperature.

With day, they built a fire and learned quickly that it fouled the room and burned the floor. But Tal had some mechanical and scientific education, and it did not take long to find the old refrigerator mechanism, with its system of coiled pipes. He entirely misinterpreted it, but he got results. The plane was dismantled, the refrigerator pump removed, and by the next nightfall they were warm and happy in the room.

The boiler of the plane had been connected to the refrigerator pipes, and an ultraefficient steam-heating system arranged from the coils. So efficient was it that with the near two hundred gallons of decane remaining in the plane they would easily be able to keep this room warm all winter. But a tiny flame was needed to keep a trickle of steam in the carefully designed and insulated boiler, and the wonderfully insulated room warmed easily. There was now no problem of ventilation.

Within a week it came, though—a young couple from the south, riding a great wagon drawn by two strange animals, blowing steam from their nostrils—horses. These people knew the secrets of growing things, but not of heating effectively, and they moved in with the two already there and brought, of course, their horses, clad in robes.

They did not know the horses could readily endure this, to them, mild temperature. They knew only that they were cold, and the horses, too, were animals, and assumed they were cold as well.

The horses were finally moved out, when they showed they did not mind the temperature, and wanted to eat the sere brown grasses, rich-growing weeds, and wild grains. But another ice box was found, and the search for blankets carried on more efficiently. That ice box, too, was heated.

Still believing the refrigerator coils part of a steam-heating system, Tal modified the cooling pipes of the pump mechanism outside to form a closed coil, and soldered them shut with a metal drum he found as a water reservoir. There were no more burners, but they quickly learned to build a small furnace of stones and clay and to burn wood.

Tal was wise in science, really. His misinterpretations were in the main sensible and successful to a high degree. But a few small sticks of wood served to keep the well-insulated box warm. And, best of all, the other woman, Reeth, knew how to cook, and her man, Cahl, knew the functions of a stove. They had food.

It was not long before a steady trickle of people started into the city by the lake. By spring there were more than two hundred couples, nearly all young, some with children. The ice-box homes had long since given out, but now, by tearing one apart to some extent, and trial of an uninsulated one, they had learned both the advantages and the construction principles, and ordinary houses were being converted, the old steam radiators being used as the supply of pipe gave out.

Some near-fatalities resulted from lack of ventilation, till Tal solved the problem, but in even the bitterest weather, the insulated rooms were kept comfortable very easily.

And from books they learned much about clothes and the ways of making them. There were many materials at hand. And now animals were more plentiful. Deer had been captured, and because there were mostly farmers here, they were not slaughtered, but wisely penned, and they waited for breeding.

Spring came, and the weather moderated. The farmers started their work. They did not know all they needed for farming in this colder country, and Tal helped by suggesting they try using the edible grains that naturally grew here. These, he believed, would be tougher, and surely able to grow even here, for they did naturally.

Summer came. And with summer, came skulking beasts on two legs from the south. They were savage now, utterly savage. They were few, and they were starved. And nearly all were males, males woman-hungry now, for the survival of the fittest had been not merely for life but for food.

The females had not been valued as females by man for nearly one thousand generations. The instinctive protection the female animal is given by her male did not exist in man. And women were weaker. They were easier to catch and kill. Only now, with spring, came the urge to mate, and at last the females were wanted, wanted madly as females. They were few, and such as there were were swift of foot, and strong, or very clever, and they feared and hated men.

But the men came north, seeking animals for food and seeking women. And they were cunning, fierce fighters, those who still lived. They attacked the town, and some of the women were stolen away; some of the children vanished, too. But they were driven off when seen, for the men of the village had good weapons, and knew better how to use them.

And some few of the women from the south, the clever and swift and strong, came, and finding other women settled and happy, stayed, and lent their cunning to overcoming the biped beasts.

"We must win," said Tal, as the fall came, and the raids from the south stopped with the approach of winter, "for we can graft their cunning of the hunt and fight with ours, and we have the better weapons. That is my duty. I cannot farm, but there is much work for me in the repairing of broken tools and the building up of broken homes."

And they won, during all their lifetimes, and during most of the lifetimes of their children, and since, by that time, some order had been regained to the south, more intercourse with the people of the south started.

And there was the danger. For those of the north, being still quite human, liked work no better than their fathers who lived in the time of Gaht, the Machine, who gave all things, and to whom they prayed, and therefore they, too, drifted south gradually, to the lands where natural foods grew wild, and work was not needed.

Very few stayed in the north. And those that drifted south forgot the habit of work, or of intelligence, for intelligence was scarcely needed in the south, where the trees and the bushes gave all the food needed, and there were no dangerous animals, for the Machine had worked well to help man, and even after Gaht, the Machine, had gone, there were left the fruitful plants it had developed, and none of the driving dangers which had forced man to be keen, for it had removed them.

So the people drifted south and prayed to Gaht, the Machine, to return, though they realized they didn't really need it anymore.

# THE INVADERS

Jan and Meg had wandered off a bit from the others. They lay on a bank now, the soft grass feeling cool and somewhat tickly on their bronzed skins. Meg was eating an orange slowly, and every now and then sitting up to wash her fingers of the sticky juice in the clear little stream flowing from the spring, a quarter of a mile up the valley. Jan watched her every move, every graceful bend of her arms and back and neck with an interest and a strange tenseness he could not understand, and which vaguely bothered him.

"Meg," he said softly. Meg did not turn her head all the way round to him, but looked sidewise, her eyes dancing, still smiling and sucking at the sweet, bright fruit. "Meg," he said again softly. She made a face and began to turn her back on him.

He laughed suddenly and held her close. "Meg—"

For a moment she held him, too, then suddenly she was struggling wildly, trying to say something, her mouth smothered by his kisses. It was several seconds before Jan realized she meant it. Then abruptly he released her and looked in the direction her startled eyes followed— straight up.

There was a patch of sky, blue as a sapphire, deep and so clear it seemed some perfectly transparent crystal, not the milky blue of the sky over a city, as we know it.

And it was framed in a ragged, wavering frame of deep, clear, green leaves, and fronds. There were palms, and orange and other fruit trees.

And far, far above there was something gleaming, gleaming with the hard sheen that those rare bits of mirror-metal which they found in the Ancient Places had. It was something big, Jan knew, by the way it moved slowly and yet gave an impression of speed. He did not reason it out—but he knew it was huge. And it was shaped like a banana, only a straight banana, and more rounded.

Jan helped Meg to her feet, and both stood watching the strange thing. It came down, very slowly, and very gently, like a bird circling

69

to earth. It seemed headed straight for them, settling slowly. Hastily, Jan and Meg moved over, out of its way, till the great thing floated gently down. First the palm fronds and tree leaves wavered, and sank, and the grass all below seemed to be pressed down. Jan and Meg felt a strange pressure that made them unaccountably uneasy as they watched it. They stepped even farther back, among the trees.

The thing was huge. The clearing was nearly half a mile across, and a mile and a quarter long, yet the great thing made even that vast place seem none too large. At last it settled below the trees, and halted, then dropped quite softly to the grass.

For minutes it remained motionless, and, the strange pressure gone, Jan and Meg came out slowly, hand in hand, straight and slim, their bodies bronzed by the semitropic sunlight. Slowly they advanced, looking curiously at the shining metal bulk.

Abruptly they started as a great section in the wall swung outward. Five strange things came out, warily, watchfully. They were tall, taller than Jan, nearly seven feet tall, and their bodies were small in the abdomen, and large in the chest. Their limbs were long and straight, and seemed more jointed than human limbs, but they were covered with cloths, as the Gaht-men covered themselves in the ceremonies, only these were finer cloths.

Their heads were large, rounded, they had no nose, and their ears were cup shaped, flexible and moving constantly. They had no covering on hands or feet, and both were prehensile. As the leader turned somewhat, Jan saw, wonderingly, that he had a long, thin tail, as prehensile and useful as the tail of a monkey. He was carrying something in it. Faintly, Jan envied him.

And Jan saw further, that he had three eyes! One eye on every side, so that he could see in all directions at once. A very strange creature, Jan thought.

Meg was curious; she wanted to see them more closely. She was pulling at his hand now, and Jan followed, somewhat cautiously, feeling a peculiar emotion, something like the way he felt when he fell, as though he were going to be bumped.

The five strange beings watched them intently, two eyes of each focused on them, and curious little sticks raised in the prehensile hands, pointing at them.

"Who are you?" asked Meg, her voice soft and silvery in Jan's ears. The five made no direct answer. Only the leader said something in a strange way, like the Mez-kahns—the brown men from the south— something Jan could not understand.

"You aren't Mez-kahns?" asked Meg doubtfully.

The leader said something more. The five started toward Jan and Meg. Jan felt more acutely the falling feeling, and pulled Meg back. Reluctantly Meg came back a step. Jan pulled harder as the swift-striding strange people came toward them. Meg held back. And finally, they were in the midst of the five. The leader seemed interested, observing them closely. Jan looked at them curiously, reaching out toward the bright-colored girdle one wore. Abruptly the leader snapped something—and Jan felt two strong hands grip his arms, two powerful feet grip his feet, and two living ropes wrapped abruptly about him.

Acutely the fall-feeling came. He fought desperately. Meg was caught too, and fighting as hard as he. Somewhere he heard others fighting their way through the brush. The leader was calling out something, and from the corner of his eye, he saw dozens of the strangers darting out of the ship, and flying off into the air, like birds; but they had no wings.

Suddenly a tingling struck Jan, the light faded, and only Meg's cry lingered in his ears as the darkness closed in about him.

The light was strange when Jan awoke. It was very blue, and his skin looked peculiar. It was a cool room, too, and the air smelled peculiar. He shivered slightly, and rose suddenly as the memory of Meg's cry came to him.

He was in a room like those in the Ancient Places, but this room was not fallen in, and it was made of stout metal. There were others in the room too; Kal, Too, Pahl, half a dozen others, and old fat-bellied Tup, the Gaht-man. Tup was still sleeping. Kal and Pahl were moving restlessly now, the others twitching slightly.

But Meg wasn't here! "Meg!" he called suddenly. There was no answer. The sound seemed to rattle down the metal corridor, and Jan went to the barred wall. There was a long corridor. At one end it opened into a large blue-lighted white room. The other end was out of his range of vision. But across the way he could see another room like that he was in. It, too, was barred. There were women there; some girls, one very old woman. But he could not see Meg. He called again.

Suddenly one of the strange creatures came. It looked at him with two of its eyes, and barked a command. Jan felt the fall-feeling and stopped calling. He whimpered Meg's name softly, then his attention was attracted down the corridor to the white room. There were several strange creatures there now. And a little table that slid across the floor on funny round feet like a slice of an orange. Then he saw Meg.

Meg was on the table, sleeping. He called her name and the creature outside barked at him again angrily. Something hot stabbed at his chest. He cried out softly, but stopped calling Meg's name, and watched her.

Suddenly he was angry. Meg was his girl, but these strange creatures had taken her. He started to call out, but stopped in memory of the hot flash of light that came from the strange creature's little stick. He whimpered Meg's name softly.

Meg's eyes were closed, and she seemed to be sleeping very soundly or in a faint. Jan watched, and called her name softly to himself. The fall-feeling came over him again, till his stomach was all tight in his body, and his throat hurt him.

One of the strangers had something in his hand, something bright like the mirror-metal, and he was bending over Meg now. He made a swift movement, and even the fear of the guard's tube could not quiet Jan as he cried out desperately. For suddenly he saw Meg's smooth warm skin split open all along her abdomen, and the carmine-red of her blood welled out suddenly. Her body changed in an instant from something slim and beautiful and bronzed to a horrible thing of red.

The lurid flashes of the tube did not silence Jan till they sent him back, far in a corner, quivering, his eyes blank, exhausted, fearful. He was muttering Meg's name softly and shaking all over.

It was nearly an hour later that he ventured again to look into the white room under the blue lights. There was something awful and red on the table with the funny feet now, but he couldn't know that it was Meg, so he thought she was gone somewhere else.

There were others who went to that white room with the blue lights. Jan only knew they had gone. Old fat Tup, the Gaht-man, went, and Theel, Yal's woman, and his child, but Jan sat in one corner, very quiet now, nursing his chest and back, which were raw and blistered from the ultraviolet burns of the guard's little stick. He was very quiet, and he moved very slowly. His stomach felt tight in him, and his throat hurt all the time, and with all of him he felt a great emptiness, because Meg wasn't coming back.

The second day they brought fruits and some things which were not good to eat, because they hadn't learned yet all they must know about this strange world and its inhabitants. The others in the cell ate the fruit, and because the guards were not so strict now, since they were not afraid of these humans, the men were allowed to call to the women across the way.

That day they brought in more humans and Yal was among them. The guards had to remove him because when he heard what had happened to Theel and the child he tore murderously at a guard who came close to the bars, and crouched back craftily in his corner and laughed and chuckled till the men in the cell edged away from him and his strange, roving eyes.

The fifth day each of the men was fed separately, and the strange creatures, who called themselves Tharoo, watched them. Jan would not eat much, but the little he ate made him horribly sick; so sick he did not struggle when one of the Tharoo carried him out, tested him carefully, and gave him something else. In an hour he was feeling well. But one of the others was in a cramped ball of agony, the death he had suffered still frozen on his face.

The seventh day a change was made. Jan had learned a few of the words of the Tharoo. A guard came in and the seven in the cell were herded out, through the long passage of the ship. Outside, Jan looked about in some surprise. Nothing affected him much—only the emptiness within him. But he must be somewhere else. The clearing was gone. There were metal houses now, and a great thing of whirling, moving parts. There were Tharoo flying through the air, towing behind them great masses of the metal they had taken from the Ancient Places.

A Tharoo led the group to one side of the clearing, where raw earth had been turned up by the moving machine. With a flat thing he dug a hole, first breaking up the clotted lumps of earth, and then into the hole he stuck a dead bit of wood, scarcely an inch long. Then he covered it up and stepped on the place.

"Do," he commanded, and handed the flat thing and some of the bits of wood to Jan. Jan looked at the flat thing, clumsily stuck it in the earth, and did as the Tharoo had done. He did it twice, but it was uninteresting. He wanted to go into the shade of the trees and lie on the bank where he and Meg had lain, and think about Meg. He dropped the flat thing and turned away.

A searing flash in his side made him leap and cry out. The Tharoo was glaring at him angrily. "Do!" he roared, motioning to the flat thing and the bits of wood.

Jan learned to plant in three lessons. And beside him, in seven rows, seven others learned to plant. Jan had never planted, nor had any of his fathers for nearly sixty generations. Nature had tended to that, and Jan had merely picked the fruits. Now he worked under the semi-tropic sun, and he worked stooped over. Presently his back ached, so he laid the flat thing down to go among the trees and rest. In an instant a guard was on him. Again the searing flash, again the roared command. Jan "did."

At night there were fruits, and many more humans had been brought in. The next day Jan and the others planted. At noon they stopped. Jan's back ached horribly and the emptiness within him grew. In the afternoon they were set at a new task. There were strange, long, flat things, and they were taught to saw. Great trees came down— hardwood trees that produced no fruit, no flower.

Another whirring, shrieking thing of metal clamored all afternoon. A heap of boards grew—raw, green boards—and Jan and the others learned the art of hammering in the strange cleats of the Tharoo. At sundown a row of twenty rough shanties had been built.

The next day they were furnished with simple chairs and beds. The Tharoo covered the beds with an elastic sheeting that held Jan's weary back comfortably as he rested at noon and ate the fruit other humans had been sent to gather. That night Jan was put in one of the shanties, and on a high metal tower a Tharoo sat with one of the strange little sticks that made a man unconscious when it glowed, and watched over the shanties.

Jan was a powerful young man. Some twenty-five times he had seen the rains, as the sun swung north, then south again. He stood six feet tall, a good four inches above the average, and his muscles were smooth and lithe with the easy but active life of his people. His intelligence was moderate for his race and time. For two thousand years no human being had had to think, or work, or escape danger. Two thousand five hundred years ago the Machine had left Earth, and the paradise it had left the planet remained, free of injurious creatures or disease. Man had had no need of intelligence. The witless lived as well as the shrewd. There was nothing to drive man, so he had fallen easily, gently down. Jan was fairly intelligent for his race—but he was not intelligent.

He did not understand when Wan was brought to his cabin. She looked at him for a moment in fear, then her big dark eyes opened wider in relief. "Jan," she said and went in.

"Stay," said the guard, and left.

"Wan," said Jan dully. He wondered vaguely why she was not with little Tahn, where she belonged. Wan was a big girl, tall, and well-muscled, with keen, bright eyes and a not-too-beautiful face. She was larger than many men, larger even than the average man, and a good six inches taller than Tahn. Though she did not know it, nor did Jan, she was exceptionally intelligent.

Jan ate the fruit that was brought them, lay down, and thought of Meg, and went to sleep. Wan watched him for some time. Then she, too, went to sleep.

For a week Jan worked at the building of the cabins. Then he learned to string wires between metal posts around the whole camp, and because he was growing used to work, his muscles hardened and gradually work became easier.

There were more in the camp now, many more. All the tribe Jan had known, and more. They came, and gradually they were forced to work, and to live in the cabins. There were two big ones—for many men in one, and many women in the other. And perhaps a hundred small ones.

Then one day Jan was transferred, and on a strange, flat boat with rounded, upturned edges he floated away, high across the forests, to one of the Ancient Places. Under the directions of the Tharoo, he dug, and turned stones and worked all day, and his back ached badly that night.

Wan watched him as he turned and twisted that night. Then she went over to him. "Jan, I will help," she said. Jan listened to her voice, deep and clear, and thought of Meg's silvery voice. He groaned again, then sighed as Wan found the stiff muscles with powerful fingers and soothed them expertly. He fell asleep as Wan kneaded the stiffness from him.

He thanked her when morning came, and thanked her again that night when she rubbed the stiffness from his muscles, and wondered vaguely why Wan was not small and slim like Meg, but like a man in her strength.

A Tharoo in clothes of a different cut came to the cabin that day when Jan was gone and took a sample of Wan's blood and examined it, while Wan watched with keen, dark eyes. A slow half-understanding came to them, and she looked intently into one of the Tharoo's eyes, and the Tharoo looked at her, and a strange passage of mutual estimation took place. Wan understood something of the Tharoo scientist, and the Tharoo felt a strange sympathy and understanding within him. This woman of a race once as great as his own, a lone specimen behind whose strange double eyes shone a still-living intelligence and keen understanding.

Those men of the Tharoo were not such as their descendants became. These were men great and bold, men of fine ideals and high courage. Across twenty-seven light years of space the ship of the Tharoo had come, and the four other ships with her. Picked ships they were, with picked people; people picked for courage and stamina and fine character. They looked at man and saw in him the fallen remnants, the scattered blocks of his character and attainments tossed down and jumbled as the great stone and metal blocks of his great cities were scattered and tossed down.

They were all there still. All the parts of the vast edifices man had reared were there—scattered—jumbled. All the parts of man's high intelligence and character were still there in his descendants—scattered—jumbled.

With tender hands and keen minds they reconstructed from these scattered, jumbled blocks the great buildings that once were. And now, from the scattered, jumbled remnants of man's character they were trying to re-erect his character and intelligence.

Wan perhaps sensed something of this. At least she grasped something of the message which that drop of red on the slip of glass had told the Tharoo as he peered at it through his strange tube. She craned her neck, and the doctor bent aside. She looked through the tube, and saw in it a sea, filled with strange yellow fish, round and sunken in the middle, and other creatures swimming slowly, and changing always. And a bit of something black that strange, colorless, jellylike things were tearing at savagely. Wan stepped back and looked. Only the slip of glass and the tiny drop of carmine.

She shrugged her shoulders, and slowly turned away to her work. All that day she worked with a curious half smile. Perhaps she wondered what the Tharoo would do about whatever message the little tube had brought. She watched him as he tested one after another of the women of the cabins, and none of those in the great lodge.

Jan found fruit and a new liquid waiting when he returned that night. It was deep blue, and smelled enticing, He tasted it gingerly. It was good, and he drank it. And somehow, that night, when Wan rubbed his back, he did not think of Meg, but of Wan, and Wan looked different. He decided perhaps it was Wan he loved instead of Meg—

For chemistry was far more powerful than Jan's not-too-able mind.

TO THE COUNCIL OF CHIEFS OF THAR,

    Greetings:

    I, Tarwan Rorn, Commander of the First Detachment of the First Expedition of Colonization, make report on this, the third month of our stay on the planet Artd, as the inhabitants know it, and the thirty-seventh day of the forty-fourth year of the expedition.

    This represents the last message cylinder in our possession.

    With its sending, our last ties with Thar will be forever severed, for it will be many years before we will be able to again find a stock of fuel sufficient to power a message cylinder capable of reaching Thar, and, we fear, long ere then, Thar will be no more.

    We were able to reach this sun and its habitable planet with the very dregs of our fuel. The system consists of nine major planets and an infinitude of tiny meteorlike bodies. But two planets were directly habitable, and two ships have landed on each planet. The flagship, under my command, landed on the third planet in order from this sun, as the enclosed report of the astronomers will show. The remainder of the flight landed on the second planet.

The other eight ships of the First Expedition left us shortly after the last message cylinder was sent, seeking in other directions for places suitable for colonization. I fear that they will have been unsuccessful. We were forced to visit a vast number of stars before this was chosen, by the greatest of good fortune.

Let it be as it may, we send this word that though Thar must be destroyed in the coming disruption of her sun, the Tharoo shall not perish from the Universe, though necessarily so many millions must die. This fragment of the race lives to start up anew.

We are not the first race to live on this planet. There was once a great race here. Many ages ago they built their great buildings of stone and metal, stone white as salt and red as bromine, metals blue and golden and silvery. They built towers then that stretched thousands of feet into their sky, as blue as copper sulphate, and their gardens covered the ground below, green and crimson and blue. They had machines that flew effortlessly through the air, repulsing gravity, machines completely automatic that thought for themselves. Machines made their food and their clothes, and they needed almost no direction from the race. They were great, greater perhaps than our race. And in all their cities we find no trace of weapons save as museum pieces. There is in all this world no dangerous animal, and apparently no disease.

They fell. There are descendants of this race of the rainbow cities and the thousand-foot towers outside the ports as I inscribe this record. They are a strange race, with a mop of close-curled hair on the top of their heads, but two eyes, working always in unison. Their feet are not prehensile, nor have they tails. They use only their hands. They are shorter than we, but more powerful, their compact bodies sturdy to resist the somewhat higher gravity of this planet.

But in their eyes there is not the intelligence that built the rainbow cities, nor planned the gardens. Nature makes the gardens of this world now, and the sun warms them. They wear no clothes, for the air is warm. It is fragrant to them, with the perfumes of the myriad flowers of their garden plants, run wild now. The forests that cover the planet from north polar cap to south are thick with the fruits that feed them. They never work in this paradise.

We are too few to do the vast labor that must be done. So they are working for us—and in return we shall attempt to do something for them. They do not know; did they, they would not desire it. We are trying to resurrect the race that built the thousand-foot towers of white and garnet and gold; we are trying to breed them back to what they must have been. We cannot see how so great a race could have fallen so suddenly. And—for a time, it seems, so low. We have found the bones of these people in and about their cities, and the bones are charred with fire, and gnawed by teeth. At one time, shortly after the fall, they must have become cannibalistic.

They are not now. They are peaceful, a strange gentle race. We have made them do much work about the cities, the "Ancient Places" as they call them. They are very strange in their reactions to us. They do not hate us, nor do they try to fight against work. They merely prefer the cool shade, and hunting the fruits of the forests.

And it is a strange sight to watch them among the cities. The Tharoo stand about, and the archaeologists instruct them, and guide them, and they look up with their strange paired eyes in curiosity and wonderment. They grub among the ruins of their rainbow cities and do not know their ancestors built them, nor appreciate the magnificence that once was there and that still is.

The thousand-foot towers lie in jumbled masses, their salt-white surface blocks cracked and powdered by the fall, their pure color distorted by the rust-red streaks where the steel frames have melted away in the rains. Most of the tall buildings have fallen as the slow etching of time destroyed their bones. The great girders of steel and the walls cracked, and caved, and fell to the ground.

But here and there one remains, perhaps with portions of its gleaming-white walls fallen, and the glistening frame showing, for many have framework of steel as uncorroded as the day it was rolled out in the presses that have long since decayed. It is stainless. And in others the framework remains whole and unrusted, but it is twisted and ruined. The metal is soft and silvery. The archaeologists, in testing it, exclaimed that the buildings could ever be built of such stuff. A metallurgist found the answer. It will be of interest to us.

The metal is nearly as soft as annealed copper, yet once it was hard and strong as steel. It is an aluminum alloy, like our alloy duraluminum. The metallurgist has restored its strength by heat treatment, and it is even stronger than our best alloy. It seems to retain its strength permanently and to increase in strength with time, as does ours. But in the long time that has passed, the strength leaked out of the metal and, as it softened, the building crumbled.

Some buildings still stand whole. Low and beautiful, and once set amid gardens, they are now almost covered by the semitropic forests. They stand white amid deep green, their airy columns seeming to float the buildings. They are more beautiful than any ever built on Thar.

And the Mauns, as the race calls itself, look at them, and wonder perhaps at them, and aid the archaeologists in clearing the rubbish from their doorways, and removing the debris of their own occupancy.

There are certain respected ones among the Mauns—god-Maun they are called—who object, for these things seem to have some meaning to them. Bits of wheels, bits of gears, bits of drive chains. They seem to have some reverence for machinery. They will polish our machines, these god-Maun, with a strange air of reverence, though they do not understand more than the simplest bits, such as the interworking of gears.

The Eugenists are working with the best members of this race. Many have been chosen for their remnant of the once-great intelligence the race must have had. Others for their magnificent and beautiful physique. For they are beautiful animals, their flesh smooth and firm, the muscles working in swift curves beneath their brownish, hairless skin.

But they are meeting with some difficulty, for these people are not mere animals, to be bred at the choice of the Eugenists. They still have intelligence, and with intelligence comes will and choice. Certain couples, poorly matched, have chosen each other, and remain inconsolable and unhappy when separated, and refuse to mate with other and fitter mates.

They are separated for a bit, and chemistry plays a part, and gradually we hope to restore to this race the heritage they have lost. But it is hard, too, to select good stock. We know nothing of their past. The doctors and the psychologists are devising tests, and working very hard at the problem of calibrating them.

They are as engrossed in the task as any, for two reasons. The strange history of this race has caught their imagination. The mystery of their fall—the sight of these strange, unknowing people grubbing among the ruins of their greatness without the faintest recognition of their ancestors' achievements. And never was such a problem given to physicians—the task of raising a race to intelligence!

It will not be a matter of years, but of generations. Arthal Shorul, the Assistant Chief Eugenist, feels that the best answer lies in the inbreeding of pure strains, and a final outbreeding to the desired qualities. Waorn Urntol, his superior, feels that this is a quicker, a more

scientific way, perhaps, but one less desirable because of the interme-
diate results of cripples and monsters.

I agree with Waorn Urntol, yet I fear that Arthal Shorul may win
in the end, for he is younger, by half a century, and this is a matter of
generations, in any case.

It is hard to decide which is the better way—these friendly, gentle
creatures are so pleasant, so likable—

Jan-1 looked up slowly at the young Tharoo entering the room. He
stood tall and slim in his white cloak of the Medical against the silvery
gray of the metal wall. The young Tharoo looked down at old Jan-1
with a pleasant smile.

"Greetings, Jan-1. Feel better today?"

Jan shook his head slowly. "No, master, I do not. All my muscles
hurt. It is the rains. I will feel better only when the summer comes.
Even under the lights it is no good. They used to help." Jan-1 looked
up at the blue-white glow of the room light. "But"—he shook his
head—"they are no good. Wan used to rub the pain out of me," he
said sadly, and smiled softly at the Tharoo, "but all your learning will
not do so much." He stopped a moment before he went on. "But that
was twelve years ago now. Jan-12 was a little boy then. He has his
house now."

"I was speaking to Jan-12 this morning about you. You will have
another grandchild soon, Jan-1."

Wan-4 looked in at the doorway for a moment at the sound of
voices, and bowed slightly to the Tharoo. "He is no better this morning,
master?" she said.

"Your father will feel better soon, I am sure, Wan-4," replied the
doctor. Wan-4's face altered slightly as she retreated. Jan-1 shook his
head slightly, sighing.

"No, you are wrong. Only the summer can help my old muscles. I
have known this longer than you, master." He smiled with wrinkled
old lips. "I can remember the Landing, and that was nearly fifty summers ago. You were not, then."

Rannor Trinol laughed. "No, but it may be I have learned more
still. And," he said gently, "here is something that will relieve you of
that ache, Jan-1. It is evening now. Take it, and you will feel no more
ache, I promise you."

Doubtfully, Jan-1 drank the pleasant-smelling liquid. "I doubt
it," he persisted, shaking his head. But almost at once a pleasant lethargy came over him. In five minutes the ache was gone.

Fifteen minutes later his ten living sons and eight daughters came into the little room, with four of his grandchildren. Silently they helped to arrange the tired old body for the final disposition. Rannor Trinol stepped out then, and reported to the Directing Council of Maun Eugenics that he had carried out their recommendation.

Waorn Urntol, Chief of the Eugenists, died. It had been inevitable, as inevitable as death always is. It was sixty-three years after the Landing when he died, an old, old Tharoo.

Arthal Shorul, formerly second in command of the Eugenists' division, took over his post. Arthal Shorul was highly efficient, a trained scientist, his whole mind and energies bent toward the most rapid advance possible in his fields. There was an immediate reorganization of the Eugenists' Department.

Waorn Urntol had hoped to establish a tradition in his work with the strange Maun race, a tradition that would continue. For sixty-three years he had made the course of his efforts smooth and the efforts of the others had been carefully directed in the same smooth channel, till, even at his death, he believed the smooth, well-worn groove would be followed. For withal that he was a great scientist, he had been a kindly being, a being understanding of emotions as well as of results.

There had been two courses open to him in his great work of raising again the light of intelligence in the Maun race. He could work as did evolution, breeding always among different strains, emphasizing the best strains, slowly breeding up to the best in each generation, and with each little advance over the best of the last generation, breeding to the new peak.

Or—he could work harshly, swiftly, as only artificial breeding experiments can. Root out the evils, let weakness kill weakness by combining in one individual till the very concentration of weaknesses killed. Inbreeding, brother to sister and son with mother till every slight characteristic was distorted, and by its distortion, magnified into detectability. So that a slight tendency to nervous instability became stark lunacy, till a tendency to short life became certain death as an infant—and killed the tendency to short life along with the infant.

Waorn Urntol, being influenced somewhat by emotions, had mated one strong man to one strong woman, and hoped for stronger children, and repeated with other couples.

Arthal Shorul, being a scientist of pure fiber, went over the carefully written notes of Waorn Urntol, and looked through the growing card index, and marked certain cards with blue and certain others with red, till, when he was through, there was a file of some two thousand five hundred cards, edged in blue, and over eight thousand edged with red.

Two thousand five hundred Mauns, just maturing, or only recently matured and mated, were picked. There was a new camp built off to one side of the old Maun Settlement, to the west of the rising metal spires of Landing City. There brother would be mated with sister. Progress would be swift and scientific now.

There were those Tharoo Eugenists who did not like this changing of well-worn grooves, and they worked with the eight thousand or so who still lived in the original settlement.

The younger of the Tharoo Eugenists welcomed the change, and were transferred to the new group.

And, in general, life went on the same. For the majority of the Tharoo, all Eugenics were concentrated in the care and raising of many infant Tharoo. Centuries before the Tharoo came, a human scientist had said, "Nature abhors a vacuum." There was a vacuum of Tharoo on Earth, and nature was remedying this condition.

Landing City grew steadily, the metal needle-spires of the city creeping outward rapidly. But in time a new city was founded; then other cities. The labor of city building was great, and because the Tharoo were few, the Mauns were taken along, that they might help.

Fifty years after the landing, in commemorating the event, Waorn Urntol had said: "It is our greatest task, and our first duty to this planet which has furnished us a new chance for life, to raise again the intelligence of this race which has so strangely, so suddenly, fallen to abysmal ignorance. What mystery lies behind this fall? Perhaps, in raising them again, we may find the secret. But first—we must aid them not merely to solve the mystery, not merely because they belong to the planet, but because here is an intelligent fellow creature whose mind has been beclouded. We must aid and strengthen the sick brother. Can a race do less for a race than an individual would do for another individual?"

One hundred years after the Landing, in the ceremony of com-memoration, and the dedication of the great Central Shrine that housed the ship which had brought them across the inconceivable distances, Tagrath Keld said: "We have already made progress, we Eugenists, in raising Maun's intelligence. Certain of our specimens show distinctly good intelligence. The great experiment is progressing slowly, to be sure, but steadily. The original Mauns were almost totally unable to cooperate, but already great advances have been made, and their abili-ties to aid and obey directions are increasing rapidly. There are many lines of investigation opening to us constantly. So great is the problem, that still many years must pass before the details of the research can be properly laid down. A problem of such scope has never before been encountered by any Tharoo scientists in their research."

Two centuries after the Landing, one Tagrath Randlun was the Maun Eugenist in command. In part, he said at the Commemoration of the Landing: "Every year we are getting better control over the Tharoo Eugenics problem. The original group of two thousand five hundred has been multiplied to more than fifty thousand, while the other, once larger, group which was not actively controlled by us has almost died out. Every year sees a more perfect approach to the attainment of the ideal—the ability to predict definitely what type of Maun will result from a given cross-mating of our purified strains. We are attaining, also, greater and greater diversification of types. The usefulness of the Mauns is increasing rapidly."

In the celebration of the Third Century, the Mauns were referred to only briefly, by one of the orators. "Had we not found, on this planet, a semisavage race capable of direct utilization in the mighty labors of our forefathers, who might say what ages must have passed before our conquest of the planet was so complete?

"Let us give thanks, then, to Great Mahgron that he, in his infinite wisdom, caused this strange race of Mauns to be created on this far, far distant planet eons before our forefathers landed."

As the messenger left him, Hol-57-R-31 trembled slightly. He looked again at the brief line of symbols which called him to the Tharoo Head.

Silently, but swiftly, he packed his apparatus back into place, swinging the microprojector into its case, running his hands over it with a caressing movement. Finally he locked the bench cabinet and jerked abruptly toward the doorway. The yielding, spun-metal flooring muffled the tread of his heels, irregularly betraying his nervousness, his hesitancy.

Finally he reached the outer door, crossed the Eugenists' Court and entered the Tharoo Eugenist Bureau.

Then, for one instant, the slight slip the Tharoo Eugenics Department workers had made some generations before betrayed itself again. Almost, history changed its course.

For a brief instant Hol-57 stiffened, turned abruptly, rigidly, and took two powerful strides toward the door. A magnificent specimen of humanity; six foot two in height; his bare torso muscular, browned and lithe with muscles; his carriage erect, forceful; his keen, intelligent face stern and determined, held high on a graceful, muscular neck above broad shoulders; a powerful, dominating figure.

Then, in an instant, some subtle thing escaped. The body was still powerful, lithely muscled, still a magnificent specimen—but suddenly it was a magnificent specimen of Maun Type R-31. It was not dominating, nor forceful. It was fearful.

Hol-57, of Type R-31, turned slowly, and went on toward the office of the Tharoo Head.

A Maun female, of the secretarial type, M-11, looked up at him, glanced at the tattooed identification, and pressed a button. A musical hum sounded in the inner office, echoing a moment later in the lower hum of an enunciator in the front office. The secretary nodded, and Hol-57 went on in.

He folded his arms in salute as he entered the Tharoo's office, and lowered his head.

"Tharoo," he said softly.

Grath Munl looked at him keenly with two eyes.

"Hol-57, I have a communication from you here. Did you not receive my veto?" he asked sharply.

"Aye, Tharoo."

"You did!" roared the Tharoo Head of the Eugenists. "Then what in the name of Great Mahgron is the meaning of this? Did you actually send this second outline of your plan? I vetoed it—it would mean the breeding of a Maun type undesirably ambitious and possessing initiative to a degree I do not care for.

"I vetoed this. What defect in you caused this unheard of action—questioning my actions, arguing with me?"

"Because I have been trained to seek ways of increasing the economic value of the Maun types. Because I have studied the statistics and learned that scarcely a score of new, useful ideas, inventions, have been produced this year. Because I saw a need for a class capable of original, different thought. I presumed to send a second recommendation of my plan because I did not think you had fully comprehended the reasons for my suggestion, and the need—the economic need—of such a type."

Grath Munl swung his third eye into position by inclining his head and looked at Hol-57 very coldly and very long. " 'You thought,' " he quoted very softly. "You thought I might not have comprehended and took a most unwarranted, undesirable step—and showed altogether too high a degree of initiative."

He paused for a moment, raised his head and looked at Hol-57 again with but two eyes. Then he continued coldly. "R-31 is an assigned research problem type, and in research types we have been forced to permit a rather high degree of initiative. Evidently your type is particularly undesirable. Fortunately you represent a fairly new type of scarcely seventy individuals, male and female, adult and young.

"The type shall be discontinued. The existent members shall be destroyed. At once. Report at once to Gar-46-N-3."

For a single instant Hol-57's great body stiffened again. He remained rigid, undecided. But just for an instant.

Then, slowly, he relaxed as Grath Munl turned away and pressed a tiny stud.

"Aye—Tharoo," he said softly as the huge Gar-46 entered, a giant seven feet and a half tall, muscled as Hercules never was.

"Aye—Tharoo," he repeated even more softly. In the vocabulary of the Mauns, "Tharoo" meant "Master."

For the Tharoo were the masters. They were the intelligent race for which the planet had been created. They had always been the masters. They always would be. The Maun knew no other time.

Gar-46 took Hol-57 in his charge, and with him, in effect, type R-31, which had shown an undesirable degree of initiative.

# REBELLION

Bar-73-R32 looked up slowly from the report he had been reading. His keen gray eyes narrowed slowly in thought. "So that was the reason for the discontinuance of the Type R-31. An excess of initiative on the part of Hol-57." Bar-73-R32 considered the thing carefully. "Exactly the same type scheme I had in mind—nearly fifty years ago—before my type was started."

For nearly an hour Bar sat still, looking unseeingly at the silver-gray metal wall of his laboratory office, or staring sightlessly at the towering Eugenists Bureau, the Tharoo control offices across the garden court.

And at the end of that hour, Bar invented a thing as wonderful as any idea any human ever conceived; he thought of something utterly foreign to the humans the Tharoo masters had bred and selected for nearly one hundred generations. Bar-73-R32 invented—secrecy.

Three thousand years before, the Tharoo had landed on Earth, to find only a semisavage race of humans, indolent, peace-loving, all their wants supplied effortlessly by the growing things about them, a race decadent since the Machine had left Earth a paradise, free of danger, free of disease, three and a half millennia before their coming.

The Tharoo Eugenists had seen before them a great problem, the rebuilding of a once-great race to intelligence once again. With high ideals, the first generation of Tharoo sought to aid mankind back to intelligence by intelligent control of matings.

With deep interest in the problem, the second generation of Tharoo carried it on.

The tenth generation of Tharoo—the twentieth of men—brought a world vastly different than the Landing Colonists had intended. Inevitably the Tharoo had bred a type of humans useful to them.

The Tharoo did not desire any higher intelligence in men. They were very useful as it was. They had, with scientific accuracy, bred out rebellion, thoughts of secrecy, plotting, disobedience.

Still, they had required certain human investigators and research students, because it saved them work, and because they needed them and these tasks required a degree of intelligence, a degree of initiative—

Bar-73 was the greatest inventor the human race had produced in twice three thousand years. He was Maun Superintendent of Eugenics, the human director, under the Tharoo Head, of the great homes where humans had been bred with scientific accuracy for three thousand years, far beyond human memory, because even Tharoo records ran no farther back, and initiative had not been a desirable characteristic of Mauns, beyond any different conception possible to the humans of that time.

The idea startled Bar-73. Only the complete soundness of nerve bred into man for three thousand years permitted him to maintain his calm unaltered. Immediately the consequences appeared to him, and immediately he realized a second thing would be needed. Not merely secrecy—but untruth!

Invention. Every word must be an invention. Every act would be a lie, a thing unheard of by humans. But that, he suddenly realized, would aid him. The Tharoo would not doubt him.

Bar was the absolute head of the Eugenics Buildings, in effect. His orders were obeyed, unquestioned; his reports alone reached the Tharoo Head. No discrepancy would be discovered. To a human of an earlier day the thing was inconceivably simple. To Bar—every word, every gesture, every thought must be labored, considered. And—it must go on for years! He paled at the thought.

Slowly he rose and went to the great genealogical charts, where each type and characteristic of every line of the human race was shown.

"Hol-57 saw it—fifty years ago. But four inventions of any importance have been produced this year. The Tharoo work less on science," he muttered softly.

Already man had outstripped his Tharoo master. Bar-73 had made two great inventions that day. "Type R-1 and type S-14—crossed they should produce a research type—a scientist—with the initiative, the ambition and greater intelligence Hol-57 wanted and the Tharoo Head did not think was needed."

Bar paused in astonishment. "If the thing works—as it must—a Maun type *more* intelligent than the Tharoo!"

For an instant it hung in balance as Bar considered it. Then the subtle stiffness of determination came to him. Slowly he turned away from the charts and examined his card index, made some calculations, and at last wrote laboriously—two order blanks, then two more. Slowly, determinedly, he pushed an annunciator button. A musical hum outside awoke an echo of softly thudding feet.

Gar-247-G-12 came in. G-12 was a type bred for intelligent labor, for difficult manual labor, but yet work requiring intelligence of some degree. His eyes were deep-set and far apart, his head massive, well-formed. And he stood seven feet six in height. He weighed close to three hundred and fifty pounds. Powerful as a Hercules, yet respectfully attending the six-foot Bar.

"Gar, here are four orders, four mating orders. See that they are carried out."

Gar saluted and took the orders. Slowly, Bar-73 sat down, his face somewhat pale.

Elsewhere in the building a young girl, of the type known as R-1, surveyed in nervous doubt the slip Gar-247 gave her with a kindly smile.

"It seems your mate has been found at last. Wan," he said gently. "May you be happy with him. Life is a long time, but there will be no more uncertainty. He will be yours, and you his." Gar-247 passed on to deliver the three other notes, his next call being a young man of the designation Jan-94-S-14. And then a girl, Tos-63-S-14, and a man, Bar-12-R-1.

These four slips had duplicates somewhere in the files of the Maun Superintendent, but somehow Bar-73 contrived to see that they were lost—for none watched to prevent that—and that certain others appeared, and none would question that, for what Maun would think of falsifying records?

It was nearly a month before Bar called the couple Wan and Jan into his office and talked to them for several hours. They were two of the highest types the Tharoo had permitted, both keen-minded, intelligent, understanding. They listened, and because they were young, scarcely twenty, they were ready to accept the words of the Maun Superintendent, to see perhaps a bit of the vast adventure. Never could they appreciate the full, titanic power of the thing they represented. Bar-73 did not see that. Still he saw the possibility of giving to the Tharoo—the masters—the inventive type he felt was needed.

The two left, were followed by the other couple, and they left, smiling, somewhat bewildered, but happy in each other. There was something evidently strange about their mating, but they really knew nothing of the records, nor the full processes, only that they were content and that they must do as Bar-73 had told them.

Bar-73 contrived to be present when he was born. On the records, he was Rod-4-R-4. On Bar-73's records, he was Rod-4, without type designation. But on the bed he was very small, and very red, and quite noisy. Wan-14 smiled up at Bar nervously, and Jan grinned down at Rod-4 broadly.

"He's got a powerful-looking chest," said Jan, happily. As a matter of fact, what chest there was was almost hidden behind waving arms and legs, and a jaw let down for greater volume of sound.

"He has," agreed Bar-73, nodding. "His head is broad—unusually broad."

Shortly later, it was not so unusual. A child very like him was born to another couple, likewise officially one thing, and very secretly something quite different in type.

Bar-73 hesitated before he made out four more orders like those first, for he had begun to realize more closely, more fully, that disaster meant not only death to himself, which he did not greatly mind, but a strange and terrible misery to eight innocent humans.

For the first time Bar-73 saw there was more in his great work than mere shifting of nature's forces. They were forces, greater forces than he ever would know, but he had met Jan and Bar-12 and Wan and Tos more intimately than he had ever before met the couples his little slips of paper brought together.

But now he had seen that a second generation must follow. So he made out the other orders and conferred with four more young, happy, hopeful people. And watched as Rod-4 and Keet-3 grew. Later he began to teach them, and later there were four to teach.

Bar-73 was an old man when he died, and at his recommendation, the Tharoo Head appointed Rod-4-R-4 his successor, an unusually keen-minded young man.

How keen-minded, the Tharoo Head had no idea.

Rod-4 started off with a tremendous advantage. Deception was not his invention, nor secrecy. He knew those already. And Bar-73 had done well in his choosing. Rod-4 was not merely far more intelligent than any human who had lived for the last six thousand years. He was infinitely more inventive.

Bar-73 had been old when Rod-4 was a young man. By the time Rod began to form his own thoughts, Bar was very old, so Rod did not tell him all those new ideas of his. Bar had not been careful to avoid breeding rebellion back into the human strain. When that Tharoo Head vetoed Hol-57's plan fifty years before, he did not tell Hol all his objections. There was rebellion in those strains, a thing neither Hol nor Bar had been able to understand.

Rod did. Rod invented rebellious thoughts, an invention as great as Bar's invention of secrecy. Bar had wished to produce an inventive type that the civilization he knew, the civilization of Tharoo masters and human slaves, might not cease to progress. Rod saw a far better use for inventive talents, and so, because he was a Eugenist as, of course, Bar had been, he realized his training confined him and his inventive ability. But—not too much. He could invent a great many sociological ideas.

Rod-4 mated with Keet-3, and he saw to it that those others of his unique type mated among themselves, and he saw, too, that they were housed in a section of the city devoted to research students and technicians. He became very friendly with a group of physicists and atomic-engine technicians.

The others of his group, finding their nearest neighbors were chemists, or electronic technicians, became friendly with them and, as children were born, Rod-4 suggested that they, being more than usually intelligent, learn a bit more than the work of their own parents—perhaps some of the learning of their neighbors—

Kahm-1 stood six feet two in height, muscled with the smooth cords of a Hercules, his eyes the color of etched iron set deep and wide in his ruggedly molded head. His head looked large, even on his powerful frame. And there was a peculiar intensity in his gaze that annoyed many and troubled almost all. There were, perhaps, a dozen who enjoyed his company and noticed nothing in his gaze. But that may well have been because they too had a strange intensity of eye.

Sahr-1, Pol-72, Bar-11 and the others, so similar in build, carriage, body and coloring, seemed almost brothers. And San-4, Reea-1 and certain other girls were slim, lithe, deceptively strong; their clearly cut, almost classic faces were, perhaps, a bit overwide; their five feet ten made them perhaps a bit tall. But under the close-curled brown hair of each was the same type of intensely keen mind, intensely ambitious, the highest peak of intelligence the human race had ever reached in all its existence.

Kahm-1 had begun to realize his difference and—from his father, Rod-4—his mission, before he was ten. By that time he had proved himself so tremendously beyond any type of Maun which was supposed to exist that even the single-track, uninitiative minds of the neighboring technicians from whom he had gathered most of his knowledge began to wonder a bit.

Kahm—as did those others of his strange type—became remarkable for his ordinariness only. He made an excellent listener, however, and as an atomic engineer cursed and wrangled over his machines, talking half to himself and half to the quiet, slit-eyed child, Kahm, who listened and watched—and remembered.

He remembered not with the memory of a normal human, but with a mind that was photographic and phonographic. At a glance, he memorized every part and setting of instruments; every word he heard remained forever behind those strangely narrowed, strangely intent etched-iron eyes.

At fifteen Kahm was apprenticed to an electronics technician, a strangely stupid apprentice, who must be told every detail, every movement, and the why of every gesture and connection.

At fifteen San worked herself into a position in the records and documents department. She seemed to accomplish little. She was constantly turning over slowly, listlessly it seemed, the musty pages of the records, glancing casually over the close-typed sheets, and passing on.

Sahr was apprenticed to an atomic engineer, a man who had become a close friend of his father.

They made few friends outside their own group, this score of strange young Mauns. In the great city of rearing salt-white stone, gold, green, silvery metal and gem-hued glass, of sweeping parks, hundreds of thousands of Tharoo and millions of Mauns, they meant little. No one noticed or bothered with a score of young apprentice Mauns.

A score among millions meant so little.

One of them ruled the planet.

A score of them turned the civilization that built those cities of stone and metal and glass upside down, and cast it out.

"I am quoting," said San, smiling, "so don't blame me if the logic is faulty.

" 'The Report on the Ancient Works, by Shar Nonlu. Year 137 of the Landing:

" 'From our most accurate estimates it now appears that not less than three thousand four hundred, and not more than three thousand seven hundred years passed between the fall of the ancient civilization of the planet Artd and the Landing of the Tharoo.

" 'For what period previous to this the Maun race had lived and developed their civilization it is nearly impossible to say with accuracy. However, some of their own researches indicated a period of civilized life not less than six thousand years before the fall.

" 'It is evident that the Maun race is indigenous. They evolved from some lower form of life at one time inhabiting this planet, but now extinct. Their progress was steady, but slow, up till a period about two hundred years before the fall, when rapid scientific progress was made, typical of the entry of the Age of Knowledge with any race. Then, when their advancement had gained great momentum, there appear the references to "the Machine." It should be explained that there is a degree of definiteness in the Maun language which makes a differentiation between the symbol "A" and the symbol "the," though translated identically in the Tharoo language. The symbol "the" is highly definite, meaning a particular or unique individual of the class. Thus there was some particular importance attached to this Machine.

" 'For some reason it was at first regarded with high suspicion, and it is referred to as "the Machine from beyond." Who invented it is not known. It was, however, capable of thought. For some reason, as unknown as so many things concerning this great, ancient race, the Machine failed, or was destroyed. At any rate, it ceased to function, and as almost the entire basis of their civilization rested on it, the civilization fell.'

"He calls that his preliminary discussion," explained San. "The actual report covers many pages. Do you want the rest? I have not read it all."

"No," said Kahm. "It is enough. With the other things you have told us, I think we understand. The Machine evidently came from beyond Earth, an intelligent Machine, which aided man for a time, and then left again. I do not understand why, as yet.

"However that may be, it is evident enough that the Tharoo are not natives of this world, and that our race is; that at one time we developed a great civilization quite independent of the Tharoo, though it evidently fell before their coming.

"I think," he said very calmly, quite simply, "we will build it up again. We will first have to convince the Tharoo of our capabilities.

"Pol-72, you are in the Eugenics Dispatchment Department. Could you get a few M-type workers to aid us, and a few R-type research workers, also?"

Pol-72 smiled softly. "I think so. Call in your servant, Kahm. I will show you something I have learned from certain psychological books. They were written in human tongues before the fall, and even the Tharoo have not translated them."

Kahm pressed an annunciator button, and an N-type Maun, a household servant, entered quietly. A small man, some five feet five, mentally not well equipped beyond the duties he need know. "He is the best material at hand," said Pol softly.

Pol did something very strange. His ten fingers pointing together toward the man at the end of his outstretched hands, his gray eyes narrowed to slits, he rested his feet firmly—and sighed heavily. His face grew somewhat pale beneath its heavy tan, and a strange, soft luminosity, waveringly violet and scarcely visible, played about the tips of his outstretched fingers and seemed to stream like wavering flamelets from his eyes, from the tip of his nose.

Thirteen barely visible streams of flowing light, they blended, and pushed, and grew, and drove swift as thought toward the small man who, suddenly pale of face, wide-eyed turned to flee in terror. Gently the wavering banners of light touched him and played about his head. He sank very gently to the floor, and sighed once deeply. For perhaps the tenth part of a second the wavering banners curled like soft violet flames about his head, then died.

Panting, exhausted, Pol-72 sank into his chair.

"It is—difficult," he said.

Silently Kahm was kneeling beside the lax figure on the floor. "He is dead," he reported, beckoning Bar-11 to examine him.

Pol-72 smiled slightly as the glow of health returned slowly to his pale cheeks. From his pocket, Bar-11, an expert on Life at the Hospital Department, drew a small disk, a thin wire, and a tiny case. The disk he dropped on the lax figure's chest, the wire he plugged into the terminal of the case. They listened, silent. There was not the slightest stir of sound.

"He is dead," said Bar-11 softly.

"He is alive," said Pol-72 quietly. "Give me a moment of time—I have practiced little, and there is a great strain. I will explain the thing. In that old book I saw the report of investigations on the radiations of living creatures. Even plants radiate. The radiations of the lowly onion were first discovered. The radiation of one stimulated another.

"Later a man found he could kill growing yeast by the radiations his own nervous tissue produced. It is released at the nerve-endings, constantly in most. You know most of our race shun us. That is why. Our radiations are very powerful; they are different, and hence somewhat inimical to those not of our type. The radiation is controllable. The books—the Ancient Ones of our race—did not know that. It is so, however. We have each of us learned to diminish that radiation, to control it, lest we attract unwelcome attention.

"I learned to release it, like the stored charge of certain fish which stun their victims by electrical discharges. It is only remotely similar. Largely it is controlled generation.

"It is a strain. But I can cause those radiations to drive out from every nerve-ending on my body at will. The nerve-endings are thickly clustered in nose, and eye, and finger-end. Therefore they are the heaviest radiators. The scientists of the Ancient Ones learned that.

"They excite even the air. They can stun a lower type Maun into insensibility, or coma, even into death I suspect. But he is not dead. See."

Pol-72 pointed but one hand, the bunched fingers like parallel-projector tubes. A thin, scarcely visible light wavered for an instant.

The lax figure quivered suddenly, and jerked upright. "Stay there," said Pol-72. The man froze into immobility at the low, incredibly tense words. "You will forget. You will return to your room and sleep. In five minutes you will wake, having forgotten. Go."

Like an automaton, the man moved.

"When you are ready, Kahm, I will see that whichever ones you wish shall 'die.' Bar-11 will receive their bodies for analysis of the reasons of death."

For some seconds, silence hung in the room. "You can teach us that thing, Pol?" asked Kahm.

Slowly Pol nodded.

"I will start certain things at once," continued Kahm. "And San, you are in the Records Department. Have you ever read any Ancient One's writings on the Secret?"

San smiled slowly at Kahm. She shook her head as she answered. "Never, Kahm, you know that. I would have said so, had I. I have read every iota of material in the Documents Division, more than any Tharoo, I believe, for as you know, a glance at a page is to know every word and letter on the page, and to know every thought contained in it. The Secret of Gravity was never written down. The Tharoo would not have searched vainly these many, many hundreds of years had it been there to find. Why, I cannot guess. It was not written."

"Perhaps," said Kahm softly, "the Machine brought it, and only the Machine knew it.

"Before we can compete, with our small numbers, and without weapons, against the established might of the Tharoo, we must learn many new things. That, I think, is one.

"The Tharoo put down a rebellion once. They have not forgotten. San has read of that, and knows how it was done. With great ships, the atomic rocket ships. They have weapons too, though they are never seen. The atomic-blast. You know it, Sahr, in other uses. Tell us what it is."

"It is a free atomic-generator blast. The wild fury of a rocket is the atomic-blast tamed, and modified for use. The thousand-foot streamers of ultimate flame that wash away whole mountains to reach some buried ore are the atomic-blast guns controlled, and diminished for useful work.

"There are nearly one hundred cruiser ships equipped with the atomic-blast guns. Each ship carries fifteen, of tenth aperture. The greatest mining blasts use a ten-thousandth aperture. They use blast guns no larger, for if even a fifth-inch blast gun were used, the flame would be apt to eat entirely through the thin film of the planet, which is stable rock. Their range is limited on Earth only by the curvature of the planet. Operations from beyond the stratosphere, while the cruisers can readily attain this height, are impossible—for the atomic-blast is destroyed by the one thing in nature which can resist it utterly— the magnetic field of the planet itself in combination with the ionized layer."

Kahm spoke again, softly. "So—we have moved swiftly thus far because the Tharoo have not been annoyed by us. Did they so much as imagine we might be somewhat annoying—which they may well, at any instant—they would not, of course, hesitate a fraction of a second in destroying us, and our families. The life of an atom in an atomic-blast is approximately one two-hundred-millionth of a second.

"It is growing late now. We have our work. I must make some hand blasts tomorrow for useful burrowing work."

Silently, the score went out, down the corridor of metal, down the hundred and seventeen stories to the street, thence home, on the moving walks of the city. Twice Pol-72 bowed his massive head, and crossed his arm in salute to lordly Tharoo. Twice a defiant smile touched the thin, firm lips. Pol-72 knew well that radiations of an intensity that merely stunned an N-class Maun would be instantly fatal to the alien Tharoo. Carefully, he controlled his normal radiation, so that the Tharoo scarcely noted his presence.

For, after all, why should he—one among millions?

Kahm learned something of Pol-72's technique that next day, for it meant another thing. The conservation of those radiations normally squandered by the nervous system meant a strange, vibrant energy that constantly sustained him. Kahm found he needed some three hours' less sleep.

His work had been designed to require a normal man's full time, and ordinarily, Kahm, taking it very easy, fulfilled his tasks in the normal time—and accumulated a good bit of outside data as well. But Kahm, by doing his best, completed what work there was which must be done in less than half the allotted time, yet his fellow workers, interested solely in the work before them, paid little attention, for Kahm was busy throughout the day.

Their work was the repair and maintenance of the various complex electronic apparatus of the city, the televisor sets, the intercity and intracity communications apparatus, the automatic apparatus of the ventilators and air conditioners that maintained the great buildings comfortable to their inhabitants, and the countless thousands of small things that needed attention.

They did not notice Kahm's work, slow, perhaps, and painfully thoughtful. He was working out something entirely new. The Tharoo had invented the atomic-blast centuries before they left Thar, their home planet. It had powered them across space, and it had built their cities here. It was a mighty thing. So, because they had never seen any need for it, they had not designed a small-scale apparatus.

Kahm very much wanted a very private laboratory, and privacy for a Maun was not a thing the Tharoo's plan included. There was but one road to privacy—downward, into the solid rock deep beneath the city. When a Tharoo engineer wanted to tunnel, he used an atomic-blast device weighing some hundreds of tons, and throwing a blast flame capable of destroying several thousand cubic feet of rock a second.

It would have brought down a city, of course.

Kahm, at the end of the day, had a plan worked out for his new device. At the end of a second day, he had built a cubical box some eighteen inches on a side, and the third day saw the completion of the egg-shaped ellipsoid projector. It was a dirty gray in color, its smooth surface broken in only four places, once by the pistol-grip handle, once for the fifteen-prong connector, once by a tiny jewel that served as a signal—and at one end of the strange thing was a minute pin-prick hole, microscopic in size.

Complete, it weighed some ten pounds. Kahm slipped it into a case and took it with him that night. Four of the Rebels met him at his apartment that night, ate with him, and with him descended to the lowest levels of the building, where the clicking, humming mechanism of a city under a single roof hummed softly to the song of an atomic generator.

Tal was the construction engineer of the group. It took him some twenty minutes to completely interpret the maze of conductors and great girders that criss-crossed beneath the floor of this subbasement. Then Kahm was ready. The black cube he set on the floor, the thirty-foot length of cord he plugged into the cube, and his eight-inch ellipsoid projector. He touched a stud momentarily, and the ruby jewel on the projector glowed, and from the microscopic aperture of the miniature blast gun a beam shot out—soft, lambent light, prismatic glowings, and tinkling lightnings of some miniature thunderstorm on a miniature stage. The concrete of the wall swirled and writhed in the six-inch cone, boiled slowly, and whirlpooled upward toward the projector, and vanished in silent sparklings. Thin, blue tongues of hydrogen flame, weirdly cold, as the projector sucked out their heat to aid the destruction, leaped once, then burned steadily and straight.

"It is slow, Kahm," said Tal after a moment.

"It is noiseless," Kahm replied with a faint smile. "I could—and will, later—make it cut a two-foot path at the rate of a foot a second. Then these tiny tinklings become muffled roarings, and the static discharges crackle and snap with power sufficient to fuse a ten-inch bus bar, and the hydrogen gas burns hot instead of cold.

"Marn, you had best watch at the elevator controls. If the cars start to descend beyond subbasement E, touch the controls, and tell the occupants of the car that the engineers are working down there."

Marn went over to a bank of the clicking, busy relays, and watched closely for some seconds. Then he turned his attention again to the workers, only a fraction of his attention being needed to watch the relays. The men stood outlined in dark against a background of pale-blue, cold light. A hole was growing rapidly in the floor.

In twenty minutes, on the low, cable-ridged ceiling of this lowest subbasement, there was a square spot of pale-blue light, wavering and shaken by moving shadows. Marn was alone with the elevator controls. A shaft led down, straight and true, through glassy, iridescent walls. Only the tops of their heads were visible, and slowly these sank into the ten-foot-square shaft.

For an instant the blue wavering light died, and Kahm's voice came up. "Marn—Marn—call Doon at his apartment. We will need his work shortly." Marn moved to the communications center and adjusted the controls carefully. Presently a tiny screen lighted with the image of Doon-4.

"Doon-4, if your work is done, Kahm can use it now. He has already completed some seven feet of shaft."

"I will be there presently," said Doon.

It was an hour before he and seven of the others arrived. There was no sign of Kahm now; even the blue light on the ceiling was gone and only the dark, glassy hole remained. But at Marn's call he reappeared presently. In low voices they conferred, and presently the projector, turned down to its tiniest beam, cut ledges in the shaft's rim and drilled holes. From packages Doon and his friends had brought came thin, wonderfully tough metal rods and straps, a collapsible lathework of toughest steels, and a quick-drying cement. An hour more, and a counterbalanced trapdoor had been installed. Then—there was no one in the deepest subbasement.

For twenty feet the shaft angled sharply down steps, glassy hard, slightly roughened by momentary bursts of the blast. Then it slanted more gently down, and down. The trapdoor was soundproof and now there was a dull, confined roaring, and as a last contingent of the Rebels came on call, bringing more things, a second lead was plugged into the tiny, black cube power plant. A fan whispered to itself in a straight-bored, glass-walled tube that drove sharp and true to the great main ventilator pipe of the building, a half-dozen glow tubes showed white on the walls, and dimmed the pale glory of the blast and the foot-long, noisy lightning.

At dawn, the shaft had spiraled down and away nearly a half mile. Kahm did not report to work that day, but Bar-11 reported him ill with an infected wound. The others returned that night, with more apparatus, to a corridor nearly two miles long, smooth-floored, dangerously slippery, and descending constantly to a depth of nearly half a mile!

At dawn they all climbed up a four-mile slope, a full mile upward to the lowest subbasement. But the terminus had been reached.

Tal worked the following night, while Kahm slept. When Kahm returned, a tiny car had been constructed, powered by the black cube, running smoothly on the glassy floor, at a sixty-mile speed. The terminus of the tube had widened to five rooms, lighted, cooled, and serviced by a larger power plant, while a larger fan forced the air from the distant giant ventilator of the city.

The men rested that night. The women worked. Books, documents, supplies, delicate instruments and chemicals were their contributions. And the following day, Kahm died.

At noon Pol came, unobserved, for those who saw him felt a sudden surge of strange power—and forgot. At one o'clock Bar-11 came, examined the body of Kahm, and took it for investigation into the causes of death. Within a dozen hours, half-a-dozen S- and R-type men and women died, strangely, and Bar-11 examined them all for cause of death.

They awoke several hours later, beneath the strange glow of Pol's fingers, in rooms of glassy, iridescent walls. They looked into the strange, terrifying eyes of the Rebel, and they forgot all other life, and did as he instructed them.

Later they were joined by others, and each night they found more room to work in, and each day they worked with the ellipsoid projector that melted away the rock in pale-blue flames that were cold. And some rock melted away in the transmuters that came, to run out metals, or the elements needed by the miniature food plants that assembled quickly under the swift fingers and machines of the Rebels.

In a month, their position was consolidated. The Rebels died then, one by one, save for some three or four who stayed above to bring the things that might be needed and, most of all, information. But all met once each night.

"Since mathematics evidently constitutes the main road to advancement in physics, I think this is a wise plan," said Kahm. "This machine is closely similar to those developed in the Ancient Times for mathematics, with improvements possible to us. The Ancients had atomic energy and antigravity. We know their secret of atomic energy was the same as ours. Then it is possible to use this same energy as they did."

"Not yet." San smiled. "You haven't done it. What good can it do you if you can?"

"I don't know. Our plans must change with every change in our circumstances.

"You know—I don't know whether this revolution of ours is humanly possible. There is no known defense against the atomic-blast. Nothing known can stand before it. How then can we fight? Must we destroy all life on the planet in order to destroy the Tharoo? Must we leave only a dead planet as the goal we have won?"

"How do you hope to make the antigravity serve you in this?" asked Pol-72.

"By teaching me physics. The more I know, the more roads open to me for investigation. It is a secret that the Tharoo never mastered. Only when we have that which they have not, can we definitely point to an advancement over them."

"Is the point worth the effort?"

"It takes effort. Yes. It takes time. I agree. We have both. We are a company of the dead. We do not exist, save for you, San, and you, Pol-72, and Reea and Bar-11. You four meet few difficulties in reaching us here. The rest of us no longer are, and the Tharoo have lost all interest or record of us. To the dead, infinity is not too distant. We have time. But we haven't knowledge."

This company was not a company of normal humans, but even their superhuman patience and determination must have worn down in the time that elapsed there over a mile beneath the surface of the Earth. It was no question of days or weeks or months. The learning of a thousand years is not to be regained by the experimentation of a day.

In medicine, eugenics, chemistry, atomics, electronics and organization they had been trained. Some members of the company were devoted to making plans—slow, careful plans of the action needed when the time came—others, of the organization and psychological groups, to preparing an educational campaign that the Mauns above would understand when the time came, that they might be quickly and certainly swung into line behind the Rebels.

The Rebels were laying out their teachings carefully and cautiously. Mankind was to learn one last great lesson. The lesson of rebellion and freedom. Under the Machine, man had taken an advanced course in indolence, with the inevitable disintegration that follows in every case in all history where man has been allowed indolence. When the Machine left man a perfect world, free of danger or work, man took a postgraduate course in the art of utter laziness.

The Tharoo came then, and mankind received such a lesson in labor, work and productivity as the race had never before experienced. Even Mother Nature, in creating the harsh world of evolution, had never equaled the efforts of the Tharoo. It was an excellent course.

Man learned work with a thoroughness never before attained. He not merely learned it, but it was bred into the very race. Nature had achieved advancement by making man desire rest and need food. That was a cross pull that kept the race stepping forward with constancy. He worked harder that he might accumulate enough food to rest— and then Nature tricked him by installing decay bacteria to remove his surplus so he couldn't rest.

The Tharoo did a better job. They simply bred out the desire for indolence. It was an excellent course that the Tharoo conducted.

But they made two mistakes. They taught too well. They taught so well that the pupil excelled the master. And they didn't quite breed out ambition. Which was probably the worst mistake. Because now a new class of teachers had arisen, and they were not only going to teach, but they knew they were going to, and for nearly four long years the Rebels planned, charted, and scheduled their movements. They laid their plans and learned their moves, and calculated the psychological force of their teachings. And the scientists learned slowly those few little dribblings of knowledge that Mother Nature released through her general information bureau, sometimes known as luck, and sometimes as probability.

Caesar said: "All Gaul is divided into three parts," and named the inhabitants. Nature keeps her secrets in a series of cabinets, and all knowledge is divided into parts. There are, unfortunately, more than three, but when once the key which permits entry to one cabinet is found—a whole great field of knowledge is discovered and it is all instantly open to rapid exploration. The discovery of the linkage of magnetic and electric fields was one of the keys. In a decade, a terrific advance was made. The discovery of the electron was the key that let into the cabinet of Atomic Knowledge.

Kahm found the key to a new cabinet. It was called "Gravitic Fields." It took him four years, three months and eleven days to find it. Two hundred and forty-seven years have passed since that particular day. Garnalt's recent experiments just reached what we might call the lower left-hand back corner of that particular cabinet. It seems to be an unusually large one.

Tern-3 was working on some new chemical combinations of the medicines of the Tharoo. Tern had an idea which would have immensely interested the Tharoo. It dealt with the fact that the Tharoo were not a Terrestrial race, despite their long residence on the planet, and that they were not constituted as are humans. Tern-3 had developed a slow-boiling liquid with properties very unpleasant to Tharoo, he believed, yet one which was harmless to humans—unless they stepped directly into the liquid.

Tern's work was proceeding nicely; he was just engaged in pouring exactly 245.8cc of di-nitro-tri-chlortoluene into his faintly green basic solution—when the faintly green basic solution began to spread itself slowly up the side of the beaker, and Tern-3 felt slightly sick. Simultaneously, the solution he was pouring began to float gently away, across the room, toward the right-hand wall.

Tern-3 gurgled gently, and reached for the nearest thing that was firmly anchored. His released beaker floated very gently toward the floor, then stopped, and began to rise slowly. All over his laboratory things were beginning to rise from their places on the tables. There were groans and whimpers of fear from all over the laboratory group. Tern closed his eyes and held on harder as his feet parted company with the floor. He felt himself falling, faster and faster—the smash would be horrible. He must have fallen at least a mile by now. Minute after minute it went on.

There was a low growling rumble that Tern noticed suddenly, a stiff thudding pound in the silvery metal stand to which he was clinging.

"Kahm!" he called. Not very loud, because he didn't want to open his mouth very widely. He was afraid the result might ruin several of the chemical experiments floating nearby. "Kahm—if you're doing that—I hope you are—the rocks are going to give in a minute."

Kahm's voice came back, rather muffled and unhappy. "I was doing that. I'm not now. It's the machine. It's building up the field. I forgot to hold on, I was so interested, and I'm on the ceiling, and can't reach down to the control. The field's stronger here."

"You've ruined several of my mixes," said Tern protestingly. "I'm nearest, I think. I'll try to reach you."

Tern let go. He hit the ceiling with a rather decided bump. The force that was lifting him now was evidently growing stronger by the moment. Most of his mixes were resting on the ceiling now, and a number of sizzling, spitting reactions were taking place. Tern walked rapidly across the ceiling, hopping along, jumping under, through the door, and closing it behind him, for safety. The rocks were groaning very audibly.

He dived across the hallway into Kahm's laboratory. Klay-5 was coming from the opposite direction at the same time, also in answer to Kahm's report. The nearer Tern got to the laboratory, the heavier he felt—in the inverted direction. The organization workers at the opposite end of the long laboratory group were appearing in the corridor now, semifloating. There was a definite line of demarcation where the field was strong enough to actually invert gravity and hold the people against the ceiling.

In the laboratory, Kahm was on hands and knees now, holding himself away from the ceiling with tremendous effort. The control was nearly ten feet below him.

"Impossible," said Tern softly.

"Call Gar-173-G-8," said Kahm.

Tern's voice rang out.

"Yes, master," responded the tremendous voice of the G-8 man, as he appeared in the corridor at the farthermost end. He stood upright, seven and a half feet tall, his tremendous body muscled to the heaviest work.

"Come here at once—as swiftly as you can," called Kahm. "The switch," he said, turning his head to Tern, "will fall up another notch in about thirty seconds, and the rate of increase will be doubled."

Gar-173 came at his best, a long loping hop that ludicrously carried him into the air in a strange flop that ended with his feet on the ceiling. White-faced, utterly terrified, he came on. His breath was whistling as he reached Tern. "It—it is very wrong," he said. "What must I do?"

Kahm spoke to him. Gar stepped across the door frame and into the strange, inverted room. The giant labored forward, his great bones snapping into closer juncture under the terrific strain. "I do not know that I can reach the control, master," he said doubtfully. He was laboring to remain standing against the ceiling as he reached Kahm's side. The great muscles in his arm and shoulder bulged as he attempted to raise his arm far above his head. At last he touched it. Immediately he heaved it upward, straining, three notches. Neutral. The strange, soft sighing of the atomics silenced. Panting, the giant shoved the switch several notches farther. The sighing increased as the atomics took up the load of reversing the power.

"That is good," sighed Kahm. The great arm fell heavily to his side, as Gar-173 sank to the ceiling. Slowly the force on the men relaxed. But the deep rumbling of the rocks continued and grew as the weight returned.

"The Tharoo will be warned." Kahm sighed. "That was foolish of me. We must work very swiftly."

In half an hour Tern and his assistants had made the chemical laboratory habitable once more. In an hour they were at work. Some twenty minutes later San came down the tube, then Pol-72, and finally the two others.

"The Tharoo are excited," said Pol-72 mildly.

"They do not know exactly how to reach you, but they have located you very accurately. They think it is a strange natural phenomenon. They are already starting with drilling atomic-blasts—they are using the smallest, lest the thing which caused the thing be destroyed."

"They will change quickly enough," said Tal, the engineer, "when they detect the cavern by their phonic-sounding apparatus."

"I have found something else of interest," sighed Kahm, looking at his instruments. "What they do, they will do. We cannot move, I fear. If we run a large, free atomic-blast for drilling, they will detect it instantly, and cut us off. If we use a small one, they will overtake us. There is really little we can do. Tern and Pol-72 offer our best hope. I must work."

Kahm had the key to Nature's cabinet of secrets then. In three hours he had located the exact discrepancy that he had detected in his first readings of the instruments. Bar-11 had returned to the surface, and was sending through reports. The Tharoo themselves were in the drilling head, watching the progress of the atomic-blast, but not making phonic soundings as yet, for their destination was still nearly three-quarters of a mile beneath them.

"I thought that field built up too swiftly," said Kahm softly. "There

were five laboratory technicians of types S and R working with him—
building a new piece of apparatus. It was larger than the usual portable
atomic generator, but it was evidently of the same general type—with
a single modification. And the projector that Kahm himself was working
over with such infinite care was not like the projectors usually made
for drilling, though it too was ellipsoidal.

Kahm had much of the apparatus made up for other purposes—
for the original experiment.

In six hours, therefore, it was ready. Bar-11 reported almost simultaneously that the Tharoo were intensely excited. Phonic soundings
had revealed a strange cavern beneath the city, one which had not
been there. "And—they report the recent rock shiftings evidently
opened a great, slanting fault line extending almost to the surface, and
perhaps to the subbasement of building RF-23. Their reports are accurate—if misinterpreted."

Bar-11 dodged into the subbasement of the building designated
RF-23, and descended the little self-propelled car some ten minutes
before the first Tharoo discovered the trapdoor.

A detachment of twenty G-4 guards was sent down at once. They
were equipped with the death tubes given only in emergencies. Pol-
72 and Bar-11 met them at the bottom.

Soft, glowing light ringed the twenty fingers of the two men; lambent banners wavered gently toward the group of colossal guardsmen.
Silently, gently, the twenty giants slumped to the smooth floor of the
corridor.

Ten minutes later they re-ascended the corridor, two S-type Mauns
of the Organization group in their clutches. At the top of the corridor,
a group of some thirty Tharoo and a dozen M-type intelligent labor-
ers greeted them.

The thirty Tharoo slumped, clawing at their breasts, as the death
tubes glowed momentarily. The M-type Mauns looked on in amazement, and at the gesture of the guard commander, a type G-14 Maun,
they preceded the guards down the tube, for they knew, from lifelong
teaching, that Mauns of all types and classes must obey the G-types
when ordered by them to go.

It was nearly an hour before a group of Tharoo and guards discovered the dead Tharoo at the head of the shaft. Instantly a thousand
messages radiated from the subbasement of RF-23. A detachment of
thirty G-4 guardsmen under two G-14 officers was at once sent down
the shaft.

Half an hour passed. The detachment returned, slowly climbing
the tube, with ten S- and R-type Mauns and a few M types. The

Tharoo started forward eagerly to question them. Thirty-two death tubes raised as one, and silently the Tharoo fell dead to the floor. Five R-type Maun scientists had been with them and, half-rebellious, half-understanding the words of the R-type men who had come up with the guards, they went silently down with the guards.

The Tharoo of that day did not know what rebellion was—they had never really pictured it.

Now they could not guess what had caused this strange disappearance and death, when a third detachment was rushed to the scene. They guessed wildly. Rebellion they could not imagine. Some strange natural force, associated with the recent rock shift, and the strange antigravitational force. A terrible gas released far beneath the ground, one which dissolved away every trace of the Mauns, perhaps, in an hour or two, but one which, due to the different structure of the Tharoo, merely coagulated their protein flesh, as did a death tube.

The next detachment wore gas masks, and stayed several floors above, watching the G-4 guards and R-type Maun research workers by televisor. They saw them go down. They saw the R-type Mauns remain at the surface.

The G-4s were gone half an hour—an hour—two hours. Still nothing happened. A larger group of G-4 guards went down, accompanied by several R-type Mauns. Nothing happened. Two hours more, and they did not return. In desperation, the Tharoo sent still another group, and they were equipped with a little truck carrying a complete television apparatus. But suddenly, when they had descended some three miles or more, the television apparatus began to function poorly; interference built up in the wires trailing behind, and recall signals sent to the men below did not reach them at all.

At last, a few brave Tharoo volunteered to descend the great tube. They went armed with a portable atomic-blast and they went slowly for they ran that blast every inch of the way, enlarging the tube, but destroying any chance form of life or gas that might be there. One—two—three—three and a half miles they went, their blast following the curved outline of the tube, enlarging it, tending to straighten it.

At three and three-quarters miles they stopped, left their blast running, and retreated, terrified, up the tube, leaving only a group of Type-R Mauns to investigate. The blast washed harmlessly against an invisible surface!

The pale beam, the tiny, lambent lightnings crackled and sang, twittered against the rock, and swiftly enlarged it. But like a great round plug in the tube, there was a wall that drank up the terrible force of the atomic-blast and turned it silently, effortlessly, into utter darkness. At fullest aperture the beam roared, the rock washed away in great spurting bursts of flaming hydrogen, the lightnings became mighty blasts that shook the very heart of the rock—then at last all was quiet and terror was gone, save where that strange silence held grimly, horribly mysterious. There was no sound, no light, no discharge, only the quiet sucking in of the atomic-blast—and silence.

They waited for a report from those Maun investigators they had left, and no report came, and the beam continued on for hour after hour. The Tharoo went down cautiously.

The silence was there. The Maun investigators were gone.

Tharoo scientists went down then. They had to. Only that deadly, inexplicable disappearance of Mauns and the silent, inexplicable death of Tharoo went on.

The second day another group of Tharoo went down to see what had happened to the Tharoo scientists. They lay there—dead. The Mauns were gone again, and the Tharoo this time were not coagulated but simply dead, without reason or understanding. Vitameters, delicate things capable of showing the least trace of life, showed only that every single cell of the body was dead. Not as in ordinary death, where muscles live for hours, and hair cells live for months after death. Everything was dead.

The television would not work here. The silence stopped it somehow. Every form of electrical shielding was tried, and the silence drank in the shielding. They brought down the mightiest atomic-blasts they knew, and the silence took them into itself, and the roaring and crackling of the lightnings died.

There was only one way. A chain of Tharoo stood all down that corridor. Whatever else they may have been, the Tharoo had courage, and in the face of that utterly inexplicable mystery, they stood up to it, to learn its secret.

They retreated hastily though when the silence changed; it grew slowly dark, and the white light of the tubes beyond dimmed slowly. They believed the first expedition to go down had set those tubes in the wall for light, and there was none to contradict them. Their powerful light beams died out into darkness when they touched the spherical wall of the silence.

Mauns were left there to watch. The Tharoo retreated till they could just see them around the bend of the corridor. For almost an hour they waited while nothing happened.

Then—out of the silence came strange, soft banners and flames of violet haze that slowly wound around the heads of the suddenly fleeing Mauns, and the Mauns fell. Hastily the Tharoo retreated farther around the bend. Cautiously a Maun observer poked his head around the corner. The Tharoo watching him saw only the slowly slumping body, the crumpling limbs. He cried out in terror. However, silently, wordlessly, the Maun gathered his limbs under him, like a revived corpse, and, still with the strange stiffness of automatic movement, walked around that corner.

The Tharoo did not see him, but he saw his reflection in the glassy wall of the corridor as he joined the stiffly standing group of Mauns and, without a sound or word, marched with them into and through the silence.

A Tharoo was sent then—a hopeless cripple who sought death as a relief—to observe, and if possible, report. He observed only the silence hour after hour, and when he attempted to analyze it, he gave only a faint sigh. A cable pulled back his body. The vitameter showed every cell dead, yet no slightest reason for death. The cells were not burned, nor was he injured. They were apparently as sound as they had been— but they were dead.

That day the silence moved. It expanded slowly; it swallowed the atomic-blast machine, then the corner where the Tharoo had watched. It stopped finally when, as the Tharoo presently observed, it was of such a radius, that the spherical surface of it reached the ground surface directly above the center of the disturbance.

In terror the Tharoo attacked it. They attacked it with their mightiest war blasts, with giant bombs, with atomic engines and conductor beams that sent mighty flaming arcs ten thousand feet into the air— and vanished soundless, lightless, in the silence.

The terror spread. It spread slowly and evenly, engulfing more and more of the city. Mauns and Tharoo alike fled from it.

Kahm smiled faintly at the city beyond. He stood at the mouth of the new bore, a straight, round tube fifty feet across. The walls were not glassy and hard, but smooth, cold, gray granite. It came out in the center of the Landing Place. To the right was the Temple of the Landing. It was fitting. The Rebels had landed on Earth's surface within one hundred feet of the spot where the Tharoo had landed.

There was a semicircular clearing, at the moment uninhabited. Beyond, shimmering very, very slightly, lay the great city, towering in scarlet, silver, gold and ebony metal. And at the edge Mauns and Tharoo milled and retreated. There were scores of men working about in the quarter-mile circle within the wavering, nearly invisible dome, patching and filling the great, glassy scars and holes where the mighty atomic bombs had loosed their flaming energies in scintillating, poppy-red flares, sparkling with the typical violet pinpoints of bursting atoms. The only sound was a faint tinkling as of crashing fairy goblets.

There were more burstings outside now, near the wall. Above, three great atomic cruisers hung, their great blasts roaring a patch of inconceivable Titan's anger across the sky, to vanish quiet as death into the shimmering curtain.

Outside, the shimmering curtain was a black dome, a dome as dark as platinum-black, since it was utterly absorbent to all light that struck it from the outside, passing it freely, and utterly impenetrable to all light that struck it from the inside.

Kahm turned his eyes toward San, smiling. "Your Organization department was partly wrong. It has been wonderfully successful in gaining time for us. The psychological work was perfect—the Tharoo are utterly mystified. But we cannot advance this dome in this way, continually driving every one away. We need the city. They are destroying it."

"If you advanced much more rapidly, the Tharoo would not have time to save the Mauns. Nor would they have time to fight, which is what we want. That is the new suggestion of the Organizers," replied San.

Kahm nodded slowly. "That was the plan I had in mind. I wanted their approval independently, however. I will start. Also, I think I will destroy those cruisers, for that will aid us in saving the city from ruin."

Kahm returned to the edge of the great tube. A steady, quite powerful wind rose from it. Kahm picked up a small, square case shaped to fit his powerful shoulders and strapped it on. In a moment he was diving down the tube at terrific speed, slowing at the bottom, as he reversed the attraction of gravity. San slowed beside him and landed almost at the same instant. Together, they went to the laboratory where Kahm had worked. It was a mass of powerful machinery grouped about a cube of gold and blue and black, the heart of their power. There was a slow, steady-moving wheel here, a great time drive that was advancing the wall of the silence inexorably. Kahm made an adjustment. The wheel suddenly accelerated to five times its former pace.

In a few minutes Kahm was back at the surface. The people on the outskirts of the curtain had not noticed the accelerated growth as yet. They only knew it was growing.

Kahm turned his eyes upward. Three great cruisers hung there, dropping bombs and spitting their rays. Kahm raised a little ellipsoidal projector in his hand, looked at it for a moment, then sighted along the thin metal rod at its top, and slowly depressed a button.

The Tharoo saw the black dome leap suddenly upward at one point, an utterly black finger driving with the speed of light toward a cruiser. It barely touched it—and collapsed. For ten seconds the cruiser hung there, her atomic-blasts suddenly stilled, the bombs no longer dropping. She hung there, apparently sound. It took some time for the atomically fine dust to spread about enough for them to see at that distance that she was no longer a cruiser, but a dust cloud in the shape of a cruiser. The shape held fairly well for nearly two minutes. Most of them had shifted their gaze, however, before then. The second and third cruisers were slowly expanding. The dust was ultramicroscopic in size, colloidal even in air. It never settled. It floats about Earth today, in all probability.

Then they saw the swifter growth of the curtain. It was growing still faster now. The Tharoo promptly preempted all means of transit. Some of the Tharoo were too slow and, with the tens of thousands of Mauns, vanished into the curtain.

The Mauns were greeted by those who had preceded them into the curtain. Safe within, utterly bewildered and lost, finding suddenly that within it was quiet and light and the city was undisturbed. G-type men took charge of the groups, familiar giant figures of solidity and orderliness. They moved in orderly groups to their places, many returning to their homes, now safe within the Dome.

Lordly Tharoo were different. Terrified and fleeing, they were caught by the Dome, struggled for an instant—and burst through to light and freedom to an orderly, cleared place where G-4 men worked and tended and directed. Their courage renewed, they demanded attention.

Instantly, the G-14 guard officers directed them, quite as though they had been Mauns, to go to the central clearing. They were angry. They were insulted by the fact these Mauns did not address them as "Tharoo Master." But they were bewildered. They went.

There were four Mauns there. Four of a type not quite like anything they had seen. Tall and powerful, their faces keenly, intensely intelligent, their eyes gray and disconcertingly intense.

Granth Marld was the first to reach the four.

"Mauns, what is this? Who is responsible for this thing?"

Kahm answered, smiling faintly. "We are, Tharoo. We are taking back our world. This was our world. It shall be our world. The Tharoo can go to Venus, for our records show that once, when you had just landed, you knew that another group of your race had gone to Venus. That was forgotten in the press of things and now you have forgotten it altogether.

"We do not intend to kill unnecessarily. You will leave our planet, however."

The Tharoo inclined his head and gazed at the impudent human with all three eyes. "Maun, what imbecility is this? Mauns—Mauns—instructing Tharoo!" He trembled—his arms shook vaguely in his utter stupefaction, his inability to explain the impossibility of the outrageous idea.

Kahm smiled slowly. "You will move to Venus. I hope there is no race there already, that your Tharoo race has enslaved. Still, you did help us, and for that we do not take the easiest course—and simply destroy you."

The Tharoo seemed suddenly to quiet down. His excitement passed. "I was upset evidently. That blackness is mystifying from the other side. Interesting. It withstands the atomic-blast.

"But you—and your wild ideas. It is evident that you are a defective type, with nervous instability of the hundredth order. Completely beyond reason. You will immediately report to the Tharoo Head. Gar"—he turned to the giant G-14 standing beside him—"take this Maun to the Tharoo Head at once."

The giant smiled down slowly at the Tharoo. He glanced up at Kahm, smiling, too. "No, Tharoo. You do not understand. The Maun race is the stronger. The Tharoo are finished. They are to go," he said slowly.

Kahm spoke: "The Tharoo are finished. This is our world. We are taking it back. You thought me perhaps an R- or S-type? I am not. I am a type created by an R-type Eugenist that the Mauns might win back their world. My type is thirty-seven degrees higher, which makes it seven degrees higher than the Tharoo believed possible, for the Tharoo rate but ninety-five degrees themselves. We are of a much higher type than the Tharoo."

The Tharoo stared at him in amazement. He stared at the guard slowly. "Does the curtain produce this insanity in all who pass through it? Great Maghrath—a Maun type higher than a Tharoo!

"Maun, stay here," he said in final sharp decision. "I must bring others to take care of this."

He turned, and started away determinedly. "Tharoo," called Kahm softly. One of the Tharoo's three eyes focused on Kahm. "Stay," said Kahm gently. The outstretched finger of Kahm's hand glowed very, very faintly. The Tharoo stiffened suddenly. His eye turned wildly in its orbit, his other eyes swung suddenly on Kahm. Tiny, almost invisible streamers of haze hung about the Tharoo's head and shoulders. He stopped. Slowly he turned, and looked up toward Kahm.

"Aye—Maun," he said very faintly. Very slowly he slumped down. The ribbons and streamers left him, as Kahm's hand dropped.

Kahm turned to Pol-72. "We cannot rouse him, for our radiations are deadly to him. Will he rouse of himself?" asked the physicist.

"I think so. But—I fear he will be mindless. The struggle probably blasted his mind completely."

Half an hour later he awoke, mindless, as Pol had said. Stronger streamers of strange luminescence swept from Pol's fingers, and he passed into eternal unconsciousness.

Others came, though, who fought not quite so stubbornly, and awoke again, sane. They looked and, as one after another of their race fell as inevitably as before to death, they slowly grasped that man had developed beyond them. When the slightest wavering haze brought their strongest down, and when on one occasion a Tharoo attempted to attack, they saw the forty fingers rise, and from them shot a driving, scintillating stream of solid luminescence that blasted the Tharoo into instant, utter death.

It was a hard lesson. Only the young among them learned it, those young who had been cared for and largely tutored by Maun S and Rtypes, and had already learned from Mauns—those learned the lesson and remembered it.

In a week the Dome covered Landing City.

"You have, then, learned to treat with us," said Kahm softly.

There were ten Tharoo there, from the ten greatest cities of the Tharoo still remaining. They were all young. The old Tharoo were aware of that fact. They could not endure it, however.

"Aye, Maun," said a grave representative of the Tharoo. "We must learn what you mean us to do."

"You have in your records the fact that the other ship which accompanied the ship in which your forefathers landed went on to Venus. Never have your two branches met, or joined. I would advise that you seek them. You may be welcome there.

"You may go, and take all your ships. You have learned, I believe, that we could stop any ship leaving, which we did not care to have go. But no Maun—either male or female—of any type or class, age or size may you take with you. Mauns are to be a free race. Do you understand?"

"Aye—in general. But we must work out the plans in detail still."

"That can only be done after a party has been sent to Venus," replied Kahm steadily.

There was a celebration when the last ship left for Venus with the last group of Tharoo. The councils and representatives still remained. There was still intense enmity. But it was closely bottled up, for only the Mauns were in a position to do anything about it, and they were content.

The Mauns, be it understood, had both the irresistible force and the immovable object, and because they were a strange race, of different types, all contented with the work which they must do and inasmuch as they had been bred with that in view, there was little chance of turning one against each other.

The Tharoo, welcome enough on Venus, where their race had, in fighting a desperately savage jungle alone—not with the aid of a tractable race—lost all their science and comfort, nevertheless far preferred the Earth where they were not welcome. They preferred it even more, when they discovered the exact meaning of work. But—what was to be done against the curtain?

Actually it came down to the question: "What was to be done against a more intelligent race?"

For the Tharoo were excellent teachers.

# BLINDNESS

Old Dr. Malcolm Mackay is dead, and, with more than usual truth, one may say he is at last at peace. His life was hard and bitter, those last few years. He was blind, of course, blinded as everyone knew by the three-year-long exposure to the intolerable light of the Sun.

And he was bitter, of course, as everyone knew. But somehow they could not understand that; a man so great, so loved by the population of three worlds, it seemed there could be nothing in his life to embitter him, nor in the respect and love of the worlds for him.

Some, rather unkindly, I feel, put it down to his blindness, and his age—he was eighty-seven when he died—and in this they were unjust. The acclaim his great discovery brought him was the thing which embittered him. You see, he didn't *want* acclaim for that; it was for the lesser invention he really wanted praise.

That the "Grand Old Man" may be better understood, I genuinely want people to understand better the story of his work. And his blindness, but not as most people speak of it. The blindness struck him long before the exposure to the Sun ruined his eyes. Perhaps I had better explain.

Malcolm Mackay was born in 1974, just one year after Cartwright finally succeeded in committing suicide as he had always wanted to— by dying of asphyxiation on the surface of the Moon, when his air gave out. He was three when Garnall was drowned in Lake Erie, after returning from Luna, the first man to reach Earth again, alive. He didn't go on living, of course, but he *was* alive when he reached Earth. That we knew.

Mackay was eleven, and interested, when Randolph's expedition returned with mineralogical specimens, and the records of a year's stay on the Moon.

Mackay went to Massachusetts Institute of Technology at seventeen, and was graduated a member of the class of 1995. But he took physics—nuclear physics.

115

Mackay had seen that on nuclear power rested the only real hope of really commercial, economically sound, interplanetary travel. He was sure of that at seventeen when he entered M.I.T. He was convinced when he was graduated, and went back for more, because about that same time old Douglas A. Mackay died, and left him three quarters of a million.

Malcolm Mackay saw that the hand of Providence was stretched out to aid him. Money was the thing that he'd needed. Douglas Mackay always claimed that money was a higher form of life; that it answered the three tests of life. It was sensitive to stimulation. It was able to grow by accretion. And finally—the most important, in Mackay's estimation—the old Scot pointed out it was capable of reproduction. So Malcolm Mackay put his in an incubator, a large trust company, and left it to reproduce as rapidly as possible.

He lived in shabby quarters, and in shabby clothes most of the time, so he'd have money later on when he started his work. And he studied. Obviously, there is no question but that Mackay was one of the most highly intelligent human beings that ever lived. He started with the basis of atomic knowledge of that day, and he learned it all, too, and then he was ready to go ahead. He spent seventeen years at M.I.T. learning and teaching, till he felt that he had learned enough to make the teaching more of a nuisance than a worthwhile use of his time.

By that time, the money had followed the laws of money, and life, and had reproduced itself, not once, but twice, for the Scot had picked a good company. He had two and a quarter millions.

There is no need to retell his early experiments. The story of the loss of three fingers on his left hand is an old one. The countless minor and semi-major explosions he had, the radiation burns he collected. But perhaps those burns weren't so wholly injurious as was thought, for thirty-five years after he left M.I.T. he was still working at an age when most men are resting—either in coffins or wheel chairs. The Grand Old Man didn't put his final determination into action until he was seventy-three.

John Burns was his laboratory assistant and mechanician then. Mackay's loss of his fingers had been serious, because it made delicate instrument work difficult, and John Burns, thirty-two at the time, was his mechanician, his hand, and his highly trained technical assistant. In May, 2047, the latest experiment having revealed only highly interesting but negative results, Malcolm Mackay looked at Burns.

"John, that settled it," he said slowly. "Something is missing, and we won't get it here in a pair of lifetimes, even long ones. You know the only place we can find it."

"I suppose you mean the Sun," replied Burns sadly. "But since we can't get near enough to that, it doesn't do us a bit of good. Houston's the only man who has come back alive, and his nearest approach was 41,743,560 miles. And it didn't do any good, anyway. The automatic rockets get nearer, but not very much nearer; the heat beats them—all of them. And you, yourself, said we'd have to get within four millions, not four tens of millions of miles. And that's utterly hopeless. Nothing could stand it that close to old Sol."

"We're going," said Mackay grimly. "I've spent close to three quarters of a century working on the problem of subatomic energy, and we're going." He paused for a moment, then looked up at Burns with a kindly smile. "No; I guess it's not we who are going, but I. I'm more than willing to go, and lose perhaps two years off the tail end of my overlong life if need be, if I can send back the word to the world that will set it free of that age-old problem of power.

"Power. Maybe we can use Sun power, after all. They've been talking about solar power since the beginning of the last century, and they haven't got it yet. Never will, I guess, because the power's too diluted. They can't build a big enough Sun glass. But if we can steal the secret of the Sun, and give them little private suns right here on Earth, that will settle the question. And give rockets some real power, too, incidentally."

The old man chuckled. "You know, John, when I started, it was the dream of my life that rockets should have subatomic power so they could really reach the other planets. Subatomic power, the primal foce that holds the atom together! And now, here I am, close to three quarters of a century old—and I've never even left Earth. A grounder.

"And subatomic power isn't so badly needed for rockets, anyway. They have good fuels now, safe ones and powerful ones like atomic hydrogen and oxygen. Subatomic power is needed here on Earth, where factories are, and men labor in coal mines for fuel, and where they make the fuel for rockets. That's where mankind needs real power.

"And by all the powers of Heaven, if the Sun's the place where I can learn, the Sun's where I'm going."

"But by that particular power of Heaven known as radiant energy, you can't," objected Burns. "The radiation makes it impossible."

"Well, I'll kill that radiation, somehow. That's the real problem now, I guess. Wonder how—we've developed a lot of different radiation screens and blocks since we began this work here; we ought to find something."

"Yes, doctor; we can stop any kind of radiation known, including Millikan, but we can't stop three or four million tons of it a second. It's not stopping it. Anything will do that. It's a problem we've never before attempted—the problem of handling it after it's stopped."

"We'll stop it and handle it, somehow," determined Mackay.

Burns gave up. Mackay meant it, so that was the new problem. It was obviously impossible, Burns knew, but so was subatomic power, evidently. They'd run against all the blind alleys in the universe seeking that, so they might as well try a few more in a different direction.

Malcolm threw himself into that problem with all the keenness and determination he had shown through fifty-five years of active research on the main line. This was just another obstacle on the main track. It stood between him and the Great Secret.

He experimented a little with photoelectric cells, because he felt the way to do it was to turn the heat into electric energy. Electricity is the only form of energy that can be stepped up or down. Radiant energy can be broken down from X-ray to ultraviolet, to blue to red, to infra-heat. But it can't possibly be built up or transformed down at will. So Mackay tried to turn heat into electricity.

He wasn't long in seeing the hopelessness of photocells. They absorbed some of the radiant energy as electricity, but about ninety-five percent turned into straight molecular motion, known as heat, just as it did anywhere else.

Then he tried super-mirrors and gave up within three months. That was the wrong way. So it must be some way of turning molecular motion of heat into electric power.

It was like threading the way through a maze. You found all the blind alleys first, then there were only the right paths left. So he started on molecular motion–electricity transformations. He tried thermo-couple metals. They worked only when you had a cool place. A cool place! That was what he was trying to get. So he quit that.

Then he got mixed up with hysteresis. He was experimenting with magnets and alternating current, and that gave him the right lead. He developed *thermlectrium* nearly a year and a half later, in 2049, of course.

The first fragment of the new alloy was put in the coil, and heat-treated till the proper conditioning had been obtained, and the secret of the heat-treatment is the whole secret, really. And finally it was taken out. It was dull, silvery gray, rather heavy, being nickel-iron-cobalt-carbon steel.

It looked like any of a thousand thousand other alloys, felt like any of them then. But they put it in the closed coil. In fifteen seconds dew formed on it; in twenty, frost, and the coil was getting hot, a current of fifty amperes flowing through it. Mackay beamed on it with joy. The obstacle had been removed! The way to the Sun was clear.

He announced his plans now to the news agencies, and to the Baldwin Rocket Foundry Co. They agreed to build him a ship according to his plans—and he made up his famous plans.

Thermlectrium is a magnetic alloy, the unique property being that its crystals are of almost exactly uniform size. When a magnet is turned end for end in a coil of wire, when the magnetic polarity is reversed, a current is induced in the circuit, at the expense of the energy which turned the magnet.

In any permanent magnet, the crystals are tiny individual magnets, all lined up with their north poles pointing the same way. In magnetized steel, if the bar is heated, the heat-motion of the molecules turns some of them around, with the result that the magnetism is lost. In thermlectrium, even at low temperatures, the crystals turn, but they all turn together. The result is the same as though the bar had been inverted. A current is induced in the surrounding coil. And, of course, the energy which inverts the magnet, and drives the current of electricity, is the molecular motion known as heat. Heat was conquered!

Dr. Mackay drove his plans on to rapid completion. Burns insisted on going, and Mackay could not dissuade him.

The plans were strange. They were enough to dissuade any normal man. Only such a fanatic as Dr. Mackay really was, and as Burns had become, could have imagined them. Either that, or a man with colossal self-conceit. The *Prometheus* was to leave from Luna. Then she was to circle down toward the Sun, down very, very nearly one hundred million miles till she was within three million miles of the million-mile globe of incandescent fury, and stop her fall by going into a close, circular orbit.

That means less, today. No one had ever imagined attempting anything like that. Houston, who had circled the Sun, had actually merely swung in on a comet's orbit, and let his momentum carry him away again. That wasn't difficult. But to break the vast parabolic orbit a body would naturally attain in falling from Earth toward the Sun would require every pound of fuel the *Prometheus* could carry and break free of Luna.

The *Prometheus* could set up her orbit around the Sun. That was going to be easy. But they couldn't possibly pull loose with any known power. Only subatomic power could do it. When and if they found it!

Malcolm Mackay was eager to bet his life on that proposition.

Subatomic energy or—eternal captivity—death. And Burns, as much a fanatic as Mackay, was willing, too.

There were only two horns to this dilemma. There was no third to escape on, no going between them. So the Grand Old Man sank every penny of his fortune in it, and would have sunk any he could borrow had he been able to get it.

The *Prometheus* rose, slowly. And during the weeks and months it was being built, Mackay and Burns spent their time gathering supplies, instruments, chemicals. For one thing, every element must be represented, and in proportion to its availability. Radium, even, though radium could never be a source of atomic power, for power derived from radium would still be too expensive for commercial use. But radium might be the absolutely essential primer for the engine—so radium went. And fluorine, the deadly unmanageable halogen, everything.

Then, gradually, the things were moved in as the ship neared completion. The outer hull of the high-temperature tungsten steel, the space filled with hydrogen under pressure, since hydrogen was the best conductor of heat practicable, and in that interspace, the thousands of thermlectrium elements, and fans to force circulation.

The *Prometheus* was a beautiful ship when she was finished. She glowed with the gleam of a telescope mirror, polished to the ultimate. Only on one side was she black, black as space, and here studded with huge projectors and heaters. The power inevitably generated in absorbing the heat in the therm elements would be cast out here in tungsten bars thick as a man's arm, and glowing white-hot in an atmosphere of hydrogen gas.

She left, finally. Struggling up from Earth, she reached Luna, her first stage, and filled her fuel tanks to the last possible ounce. Then, in August, 2050, she took off at length.

Reaching the Sun was no trick at all, once she had broken free of the Moon and of Earth. Day after day she fell with steadily mounting speed. The Sun loomed larger, hotter. The great gyroscopes went into action, and the *Prometheus* turned its silvered face to the Sun, reflecting the flooding heat. Nearer and nearer. Venus fell behind, then Mercury's orbit at last.

They knew heat then. And radiation. The Sun loomed gigantic, a titanic furnace whose flames reached out a quarter of a million miles. The therm elements began to function, and the heat dropped somewhat. Then the rockets started again, started their braking action, slowly, steadily, braking the ship to the orbit it must make, close about the Sun.

Hour after hour they droned and roared and rumbled, and the

heat mounted, for all the straining power of the therm elements. Radio to Earth stopped the second day of the braking. The flooding radiations of the Sun killed it. They could still send, they knew, but they could not receive. Their signals were received by stations on the Moon, where the washing static of the Sun did not blanket all the signals that came. For they were beaming their waves, and the Sun, of course, was not.

"We must establish the orbit soon, John," said Mackay, at last. He was lying down on his couch, sick and weak with the changing strains. "I am an old man, I fear, and I may not be able to endure much more of this."

"We will have to brake more sharply then, Dr. Mackay," replied Burns concernedly. "And then we may not be able to establish the perfectly circular orbit we need."

Mackay smiled faintly, grimly. "If it is not soon, John, no orbit will mean anything to me."

The rockets roared louder, and the ship slowed more rapidly. But it was three days yet before the orbit trimming could be started. They left the ship in an eccentric orbit at first, though, and counteracted for the librations of the ship, which tended to turn the blackened radiator side toward the Sun, by working the gyroscope planes.

Dr. Mackay recuperated slowly. It was three weeks, actually, three precious oxygen-consuming weeks, before they started the final orbit trimming. Then day and night they worked, observing and occasionally giving a slight added rocket thrust for orbit trimming.

But finally, at a distance of three point seven three millions of miles, the *Prometheus* circled the titanic star. The sunward side, for all its polish, glowed red-hot continuously. And the inside of the ship remained a heated, desiccated furnace, for all the work of the therm elements. Even they could not perfectly handle the heat.

"Ah, John," said Mackay at last. "In some ways Earth was better, for here we have strange conditions. I wish we could get a time signal from Earth. The space is distorted here by the Sun."

Old Sol, mighty in mass and power, was warping space so that spectrum lines were not the same; their instruments were not the same; the titanic electric and magnetic fields threw their delicate apparatus awry. But they worked.

It was fortunate that the therm elements produced power, as well as getting rid of the heat. With the power, they kept the functions of the ship running, breaking down the water formed in their breathing to oxygen once more, and storing the hydrogen in one of the now empty fuel tanks.

And their observations went on, and their calculations. In six months it seemed they had never known another life than this of intolerable, blinding light if they dared to open an observation slit in the slightest; intolerable, deadly radiation if they dared to step beyond the protected walls of their laboratory and living quarters without a protective suit. For most of the ship was as transparent to the ultrashort waves of the Sun as empty space.

But it grew to be a habit with them, the sending of the daily negative reports, the impossibility of hearing any signal from Earth, even of observing it, for there was the eternal Gegenschein. It was blinding here, the reflected light from the thin-strewn dust of the Sun.

That dust was slowing them down, of course. They were, actually, spiralling in toward the Sun. In some seventy-five years they would have been within reach of the prominences. But before then—one of the pans of their balance would have tipped. Subatomic power—or the inevitable end.

But Mackay was happy here. His eyes turned from deep blue-gray to a pale blue with red bloodshot balls; his skin turned first deep, deep brown from the filtering ultraviolet, then it became mottled and unhealthy. Burns's skin changed, too, but his eyes endured better, for he was younger. Still, Mackay felt sure of his goal. He looked down into the flaming heart of a Sun spot, and he examined the underside of a prominence, and he watched the ebb and flow of Sol's titanic tides of white-hot gas.

2050 passed into history, and 2051 and 2052 followed in swift succession. No hint of the great happenings of Earth and the planets reached there, only the awful burning of the Sun—and, in February of 2053, a hint of the great changes there.

"John," said Mackay softly one day, "John—I think I see some hint of the secret. I think we may make it, John!"

Burns looked at the sharp-lined spectrum that lay on the table before Mackay, and at the pages of calculations and measurements and at the data sheets. "I don't see anything much different in that, doctor. Isn't it another will-o'-the-wisp?"

"I—I hope not, John. Don't you see this—this little line here? Do you recognize it?"

"No—no, I don't think I do," he said slowly. "It's a bit too high for the 4781 line. And I don't know what's in there—"

"There isn't any there, John," said Mackay softly. "There isn't any. It's a forbidden line, an impossible line. It's the impossible line of sodium, John. It's a transformation that just couldn't take place. And it did, so I'm going to find out how it did. If I can make the impossible release take place the same way—"

"But that tells so little, so very little. Even if you could duplicate that change, make that line, you'd still be as far from the secret as from Sirius. Or Earth for that matter."

"I'll know more, though, John. You forget that only knowledge is the real secret. When I know all about the atom, I'll know how to do what I want to do. If I know all the changes that can take place, and why, then I can make that other change. Ah, if only I could see just a few miles deeper into the heart of the Sun—"

"We've seen some of the greatest Sun spots in history, and at close hand. Do you think we could see any deeper? The light—that terrible light."

"It blinds even the instruments, so there is little more we can do. But we can calculate and take more photographs for more of those lines. But now I must see what the instruments recorded when we got this line."

They had recorded even more than the old man had hoped. It was enough. Mackay and Burns duplicated that impossible line, and then they produced some more impossible lines. It was the key. It wasn't impossibly difficult then. They could design the apparatus, and did, in September, three years and one month after lifting off for the final drop to the Sun.

They made it, piece by piece, and tested it in January. It wasn't winter there; there was no winter. Only everlasting heat. And Mackay's eyes were failing rapidly. His work was over. Both because he could scarcely work any longer, and because, on January 14, 2054, the ultimate energy of the atom was harnessed by man! The Great Secret was discovered.

It took the intense light of the mighty arc to stimulate the old eyes when the thing was done. Only its tremendous blinding power was visible. His ears could hear the roar well enough, and his fingers could feel the outlines of the hulking machine. But he could no longer make it out when it at last roared its lusty greeting to human ears.

His thin lips parted in a contented smile, though, as his tough old fingers caressed the cold metal and the smooth, cold glass. "It works, doesn't it, John? It works. John, we've done it." A shadow passed over the old man's face for an instant. "We haven't heard from Earth in over three years. Do you suppose someone else has discovered it, too? I suppose I ought not be selfish, but I do hope they haven't. I want to give this to the world.

"John, can you make the drive apparatus yourself?"

"Yes, doctor; I can. You had all the plans worked out, and they're simple to follow. It isn't really greatly different. Only that instead of using a high-temperature gas ejected at thousands of feet a second, we'll use a high-voltage ion ejected at thousands of miles a second. And because we can burn iron, as you predicted, we don't have to worry at all about power."

"No, John. We don't have to worry at all about power." The old man sighed, then chuckled contentedly. "I always wanted to live to see the day when real atomic power ran the world—not fission, not fusion, but the pure strain itself. But I guess I won't, after all. I can't see, but it won't matter. I have so few years left, I won't worry about a little thing like that. My work's done, anyway. We don't have to worry about power, John; the world doesn't any more.

"Men will never again have to worry about power. Never again will they have to grub in the Earth for fuels. Or do things the hard way because it is less costly of power. Power—power for all the world's industry. All the wheels of Earth's factories driven by the prodigal atom. The arctic heated to a garden by it. Vast Canada opened by it to human habitation, clear to the North Pole.

"No more smoke-clouded cities.

"And the heart of the atom will lift the load of labor from man's back. No more sweating for six hours every day for daily bread. An hour a day—and unlimited, infinite power. And, maybe, even, some day it will lead to infinite transmutation, though I can't see it. I mean, I can't see it all even mentally," he said with a little smile. "The Sun showed me the secrets it held—and took away the impious vision that gazed upon them.

"It is worth it. The world will have power—and my work is done.

"You are starting the drive apparatus?"

"Yes, doctor. The main tube is to be—"

Burns launched into a technical discussion. The doctor's eyes could not follow the plans, but the old mind was as keen as ever. It pictured every detail with a more penetrative vision than ever his eyes could have. He chuckled contentedly as he thought of it.

"John, I have lost little, and gained more. I can see that tube better than you can. It's a metal tube, but I can see to its deepest heart, and I can even see the ions streaming out, slowly, precisely. My mind has a better eye than ever my body had, and now it is developing. I can see the tube when it is not yet, and I can see the heart of it, which you cannot.

"Make it up, John. We must hurry back."

The lathe hummed, powered by the newenergy, and the electric furnace glowed with a heat so intense the old scientist could see it.

The mental eye he had boasted of was keen, keener than his old eyes had ever been. But still it was blind. Somehow, it did not see the white-hot tungsten bars on the "night" side of the ship pouring thousands and thousands of kilowatts of power out into space, the power the therm elements were deriving from the cooling of the ship.

The drive tubes grew, and their great metal bed-bolts were turned. Then the great rocket tubes were sealed at the far end, cut, and insulated again. But now, electrically insulated, the great ion tubes took shape and were anchored, and the huge conductors ran back to the ion-gas chambers, and to the hunched bulk of the atomic engine. Day succeeded day, and Burns cut and fashioned the metal and welded it under the blazing power of the broken atoms in their atomic generator.

And at last the ship trembled with a new, soft surge. It must be slow, for the men were used now to weightlessness, three long years of it. But gradually, gradually, the *Prometheus,* bearing the fire it had stolen from the Sun, swung swifter in its orbit, and spiraled out once more, slowly, slowly. And the radio drove out its beam toward Earth.

They could not hear the messages that Earth and Luna pounded back at them, but gladly they guessed them. The ion tubes whispered and murmured softly, with a slithering rustle as of a snake in dry leaves, and the ship accelerated steadily, slowly. They ran those tubes day and night and slowly increased the power. There was no need for maximum efficiency now. No need to care as they wasted their power. There was plenty more.

Their only difficulty was that with the mighty ion tubes working they could not receive radio signals, even when they gradually circled out beyond Mercury, and finally Venus, slowly growing accustomed once more to weight. They did not want to turn off their tubes, because they must get accustomed to weight once more, and they were moving very rapidly now, more and more rapidly, so that they passed Venus far too fast for the ships that rose from the planet to congratulate Dr. Mackay and tell him the great news.

They circled on, in the *Prometheus,* till they were used once more to Earth gravity, and then they were near Earth, and had to apply the braking ion rockets.

"No stopping at the Moon, John." Malcolm Mackay smiled. "We and all humanity are through with that. We will go directly to Earth. We had best land in the Mojave Desert. Tell them, tell them to keep away, for the ions will be dangerous."

John Burns drove out his message, and Earth loomed large, and North America came slowly into view. Then they were settling toward the desert.

The old scientist heard the faint, cold cry of ruptured air first, for his eyes were dark, and only his ears brought messages from outside. "That's air, John!" he cried suddenly. "We're in the air again! Earth's air! How far up are we?"

"Only another one hundred and fifty miles now, doctor. We're almost home."

"Home—I should like to see for just this second, to see it again. John, John, I'll never see Earth again. I'll never—but that means little. I'll hear it. I'll hear it and smell it in my nostrils, clean and sweet and moist, and I'll taste it in the air. Earth's air, John, thick and spicy with green things. It's autumn. I want to smell burning leaves again, John. And feel snow, and hear its soft caress on a glass pane, and hear the soft sounds men make in snow. I'm glad it's autumn. Spring has its smells, but they aren't so spicy and clean. They're not so interesting, when you can't see the color of grass, so green—too bright, like a child's crayon drawing. Colors—I'll miss them. There weren't any out there. Colors—I'll never see the leaves again, John.

"But I'll smell them, and I'll hear the hum and whisper of a thousand thousand subatomic engines making the world over for mankind.

"Where are we? The air is shrilling thickly now."

"We're less than fifty miles up. They've cleared the Mojave for fifty miles around us, but, doctor, there are a hundred thousand private air-cars there—a new design. They must have developed broadcast power. They're all individually powered and apparently by electrical means."

"Broadcast power? That is good. Then subatomic energy will reach every home. The apparatus would be expensive, too expensive for homes."

"The air is full of ships—there are half a dozen great stratosphere ships flying near us now; can you hear the *chug* of their propellers?"

"Is that the noise—ah! Men, men, again, John. I want to hear a thousand voices all at once."

Burns laughed recklessly, carefree. "You will, from the looks of things. You will! There are nearer a thousand thousand down there now!"

"The ship is slowing?" asked Mackay.

Burns was silent for a moment. Then, suddenly, the dry rustle of the tubes changed its note; it flared for an instant, there was a soft, grating thud, a harsh scraping of sand—and the ion tubes died in silence.

"The ship is stopped, doctor. We're home."

Dimly, faintly, the sound of a thousand voices clamoring and shouting came through the heavy walls. Mackay had landed! The Grand Old Man was back! And half the world had turned out to welcome him, the maker of Venus, the remaker of Earth.

The lock opened, and to Mackay came the roar of voices, the thrum and hum and rumble of thousands and tens of thousands of propellers. There was the musical cacophony of a thousand air-car signals, and the mighty thunder of a titanic voice, rumbling, hoarse, and godlike in power, cutting through, drowning it all.

"They're welcoming you. Doctor Mackay—welcoming you."

"So I hear," said Mackay, half happily, half sadly, "but I am so tired, perhaps I can rest a bit first. I am older than you are, John. You have done as much as I; you had better answer them."

Suddenly, close-by human voices cut in, excited, happy, welcoming voices, and John Burns's swift answering speech.

"He is tired; it has been hard for him. And—you know he has lost his sight. The radiation of the Sun so close. He would rather be taken where he can rest."

"Very well—but can't he say something? Just a few words?"

Burns looked back at the old man. Malcolm Mackay shook his head.

The man outside spoke again: "Very well. We will take him directly to anywhere he wants."

Mackay smiled slowly, thoughtfully. "Anywhere, anywhere that I can smell the trees. I think I'd like to go to some place in the mountains where the air is sweet and spicy with pine smells. I will be feeling better in a few days—"

They took him to a private camp in the mountains. A ten-room "cabin," and they kept the world away, and a doctor took care of him. He slept and rested, and Burns came to see him twice the next day, but was hurried away. The next day and the next he did not come.

Because even Burns had not gathered quickly the meaning of all this. Even he had thought at first it was in celebration of the invention of the subatomic generator.

At last he had to come. He came into Mackay's room slowly. His pace told the blind man something was wrong.

"John—John, what's troubling you so?"

"Nothing; I was not sure you were awake."

Mackay thought for a few seconds and smiled. "That wasn't it, but we will let it pass now. Do they want me to speak?"

"Yes. At the special meeting of the American Association for the Advancement of Science. And—also on the subject of the thermlectrium elements. You have done far more than you thought, doctor. You have remade the worlds already. Those cars I thought were powered by broadcast energy? I was wrong. We were blind to the possibilities of that lesser thing, the thermlectrium element. Those cars were powered by it, getting their energy from the heat of the air. All the industries in the world are powered by it. It is free power.

"The elements are cheap, small, simple beyond anything conceivable, a bar of common metal—a coil of wire. They require no control, no attention. And the energy costs nothing at all. Every home, every store, every man, has his private thermlectrium element. Every car and every vehicle is powered by it.

"And the map of the world has been twisted and changed by it in three short years. The tropics are the garden-spot of the world. Square miles of land are cooled by giant thermlectrium installations, cities air-conditioned, till the power they develop becomes a nuisance, a thing they cannot get rid of. The tropics are habitable, and they have been given a brisk, cool, controlled climate by your thermlectrium elements.

"Antarctica is heated by it! There are two mining developments that suck heat from that frozen air to make power in quantities they cannot use.

"And rocket fuel costs nothing! Nothing at all. The tropical countries find the electrolytic breaking down of water the only cheap, practical way to get rid of their vast energy, without turning it right back into heat. They give the gases to whosoever will take them away.

"And Venus you have remade. Venus had two large colonies, already. They are cooled, made habitable, by the thermlectrium apparatus. A ten-dollar unit will cool and power an average house forever, without the slightest wear. By moving it outside in winter, it will warm and power it. But on Venus it is all cooling. They are developing the planet now. Doctor Mackay, you have remade the worlds!"

Dr. Mackay's face was blank. Slowly a great question was forming. A great, painful question. "But—but, John—what about—subatomic energy?"

"One of the greatest space lines wants to contract for it, doctor. Their interplanetary ships need it."

"One!" cried the Grand Old Man. "One—what of the others?"

"There is only one interplanetary line. The lines to the Moon are not interplanetary—"

And Dr. Mackay caught the kindness in his tone.

"I see—I see—they can use the free gases from the tropics. Free power—less than nothing.

"Then the world doesn't want my subatomic energy, does it?" he said softly. His old body seemed to droop.

"Blind," he whispered. "Oh, the blindness. . ."

**Editor's note**

The original version of this story didn't refer to "subatomic power," "nuclear power," "fission," or "fusion." It simply used the term "atomic power." When the story was republished in the Shasta edition of *Who Goes There?*, Campbell made a few minor updates. The story published here includes those updates.

# THE ESCAPE

Aies Marlan permitted a slight scowl to creep across her face as she straightened from her posed position for a moment. Across the grass court she could see her father's laboratory and that most unwelcome adjunct, that behemoth of tactless condescension, the unbearable, insufferable Bruce Randall. Bruce was looking out of his window toward her with his usual, idiotic grin, that condescending grin with which he watched all her work.

Aies looked across the studio toward Paul Treray. He had not noticed her looking up. He was very busy with his little knives and inductance softeners, working at the silver plastium he was so deftly shaping. The scowl relaxed to a little smile. Paul was so busy with his work. Modeling her and the little laboratory bench she had set up, as a scientist at work. Paul had won second place in the competition in 2117; this year he might get the coveted first with one of his little figures—

Abruptly a gesture and a deep scowl of anger came over his clean-lined face.

"What's the matter, Paul?" she asked.

"It—it just won't be you. It's still—metal. I can't make it *you*— human."

Aies straightened her back and stretched. "Well, I'm not sorry. That means no more today, and, frankly, my back is beginning to say the same thing." She smiled teasingly at him. "I wish you'd start working on figures seated at ease. Do you enjoy breaking my back?

"At any rate, I do want to finish that projector. Besides modeling as a scientist, I like to try to be one."

"You are, Aies," said Paul, his face changing to a sunny smile as quickly as it had scowled before. "You are, but you are so much more interesting as a human—but the metal just won't see it. It wants to be atoms and protons and molecules, I suppose you'd say.

"I still don't see how anyone as thoroughly and abstractedly a physi-

cist as your father, and a woman as completely and distractedly a
chemist as your mother, could have had a daughter so different."

"Paul, you're prejudiced. And remember, please, I am very much
interested in science, myself." She laughed at him as she took his
hands in hers. "Besides, they didn't spend most of their time with one
so completely unscientific as you. Perhaps you acted as a sort of balance to me."

"Bah—trying to analyze the situation? Foolish. Results are all that
count. I don't know how to model a perfect figure; I cannot give you
the angles, the degree of sphericity of the human head—the radius of
curvature of a forearm. Only one man ever attempted to reduce art to
mathematics—and that was Leonardo da Vinci. He thought he did.
But his own students said he didn't, because his formulas didn't work.
Results are all—

"Bah," he said abruptly. Aies was looking with a long face at the
little figure which Treray declared "would not be human."

"Results," whispered Aies softly to herself almost as she walked
slowly, thoughtfully, to the door. She turned. "I should say that the
main trouble is the ratio between the size of the head to the over-all
height of the body is slightly too great."

"Get out!" cried Treray, in mock anger. But partly real anger, because he suddenly realized that that ratio was not quite what it should
be. Still, he didn't like to call it a "ratio"; he didn't like the word.

Aies walked toward her father's laboratory, smiling to herself. Gradually the smile departed to be replaced by a look of determination and
coldly repellent dignity. Bruce Randall would be in the way. Aies
made up her mind to dislike him the day he came to the house, though
not consciously, because she had a pretty good idea why he had been
sent to "assist" her father in his research on the new accumulator.

Aies was twenty years, twelve months, and twenty-seven days on
the final and thirteenth month of her twenty-first year now. Automatically at twenty-one she knew the Population Control Commission would call her in to "decide" what type of man she should marry.
And Aies had not the slightest desire to have it decided for her. What
she disliked most was that when they had decided they would, with
the aid of the conditioning and control division, make her decide the
same thing. And they'd make her *like* their decision!

That was the rankling thing. She wouldn't have will power enough
to disagree with them. They'd make her actually love whoever they
picked by their conditioning and control.

It was bad enough to have someone else make your decisions for
you—but to be psychologically manipulated to like it . . .

And she knew blamed well what they'd already just about decided. Bruce Randall was the decision. Well, they'd find she'd take a good bit of conditioning to like *him*. His face was wrinkled like an old man's; he thought at the rate of about two inches a year, and he spent ten minutes thinking up the answer to a simple question; and that grin, that insufferable, unbearable, awful, condescending grin!

She walked briskly into the laboratory. Her father, she knew, was down at the physics conference this afternoon, seeking some hints on the accumulator connections for use in the plane he had designed. He needed aerodynamic aid for maximum efficiency of weight distribution. The accumulator was perfected; Aies herself was using it in a little device she had perfected.

But Bruce wasn't out. He looked up with his slow smile that crinkled the corners of his eyes. Little glints of humor danced in his eyes. "Hello, Aies. Paul's chisel slip? He looked peeved when you left," he added in his slow, deep voice.

"No. Paul gets along quite nicely, thank you. Have you finished that accumulator bank dad told you to hook up?"

"NI3? I guess I haven't. I've been making a cape for myself."

Aies was piqued. She didn't recognize that NI3 formula. "I didn't know you were a tailor," she said, going on toward her bench.

Aies was an excellent mechanician, and on a miniature lathe she was spinning out an aluminum tube. She paid no attention to Bruce's work or to his occasional glances. In a half-hour she had the little tube finished and fitted into her apparatus. Then she started on some delicate wiring, her attention so concentrated on it she did not notice as Bruce left the laboratory, and scarcely noticed as night fell outside.

There was a grim little smile on her face as she finished, and held in her hand a device the size of an overgrown .45 revolver, connected with a long, flexible lead to an accumulator on the bench. With a quick tread she went to the next room where she had been keeping some pets—ten guinea pigs and a monkey.

She brought the monkey into the laboratory on a leash, the chattering little animal hopping and running about her, squealing and scolding. She released him as she picked up her newly-made device. The monkey dashed off across the room turning half a dozen somersaults as he went—and fell flat on his little pot-belly, and skidded ten feet across the floor as a single blue-green glow surrounded the weapon for an instant. His miniature hands lay limp and bedraggled, the prehensile, looped tail dragged mournfully.

But under the bright gas-glow lights his bright, beady eyes flickered and wabbled about, terror in them. His breath came regularly and evenly. His lips curled back, his mouth and tongue shaped for a scream—and no sound came!

Aies smiled softly to herself as she gathered up the relaxed little figure and carried him to his cage. Then she sat down beside it, with a notebook and a stop watch. Presently the little primate gave a hoarse, gasping gurgle. Instantly some of the terror in his eyes fled, and excitement took its place. Aies smiled at him, spoke to him, and patted his furry back. Then a shoulder twitched. Aies made another note. In forty-five minutes a tremendously scared and immensely excited monkey chattered and threw himself about his cage.

There was a very decided look of determination and decision about Aies' face as she turned out the laboratory lights. She went down to the kitchenette and prepared a little something to eat. Then she went across to her father's laboratory. There was a ship there, a beautiful thing, with every tiniest brace and protuberance faired into the stream-lined hull. The wings were of the newest, variable-pitch design. The propeller of the noiseless type, more highly efficient because it wasted no energy in useless sound.

It was so simple in line and form it was a frozen symphony of speed. To look at it brought the whistle of extreme speed in one's ears. To see it made one rise on one's toes as though to fly. Aies looked at it with a smile and a nod.

Then she went over to Treray's studio. He was reading and sketching on a sheet of paper, a picture of the character described in the book, his favorite pastime.

"Ah, hello, Aies." He rose and went toward her as she looked around the door at him. "Come in. I thought you were working tonight."

"I did, too. But I finished what I had on hand. And I'm feeling jangled. Bruce Randall sticks in my teeth."

Paul laughed. "What's he done now?"

"Nothing," said Aies explosively. "He wouldn't do anything but grin anyway. It's what the commission may do. I know that geologic cross section has been stuck there by the commission. I hate him."

Paul smiled at her. "Now—but how about later?"

"Then I'll hate myself. They'll change me—and that will make life more miserable. You have to live with yourself every second of the day, of the year, of your whole life. And—it makes me crawl to think of it! Loving somebody—and knowing that they decided coldly and scientifically that A and B were a desirable combination, so they took A and B and made them combine. Knowing that somebody decided it was desirable—and made you like it—decided and made you—oh— I can't say what I mean. Two parts of you—one hopelessly and helplessly doing what was scientifically decided you should, and knowing with the rest of you that you didn't decide that at all.

"It makes me crawl. And I'll have to be with myself forever—so far as I know, forever. And know that.

"Well—I *won't.*"

Paul's smooth face looked up suddenly, startled. "Won't! But what can you—"

Her voice was intense. "I won't. And I think I know how I won't, too. Dot Walden is in the statistics and records office, and I'll be able to know—I'll know—and I'll—

"I won't, anyway." She sat silent and tense.

Paul walked over to her, and took her hands in his. "Aies, can I help you any? I think it is hopeless. You can't go elsewhere than in this country without a passport, and in this country the commission's ratings and classifications board would simply act to find you.

"But if I can help you—"

Aies looked at him. A queer, timid little look. "You can, Paul—but why, oh why, in the name of Heaven did our forefathers ever permit this awful system to start? Why? Why?"

"They were practical—they were scientific!" exploded Paul. "There were more people in insane asylums than in schools. The average man had the intelligence of a good thirteen-year-old. So they turned scientific, and eliminated nature's system of normal choosing—and decided to choose scientifically." He put bitterness and sarcasm into his words.

"They rearranged the world to suit themselves. And they doomed some to live and their children to be the 'hewers of wood and bearers of water' for the rest of the world, with never a chance of having children better than they, because they were scientifically, correctly mated. And they doomed every one to live and marry as was decided for them. I—I must presently marry some woman I have never seen, never known. Someone who is no more to me than that tree out there. But that is scientific! *That* is correct. Because I am an artist, and she will be an artist, so our children must be artists.

"Bah—their science will breed art out of the world. Their science has no conception of humanity. It sees it all in terms of A's and B's that will make C's or—

"Hell. Hell on earth. Art is not science. It is above science; it is comprehension without knowing. It is a true result without the logic, the barren, stupid logic.

"Look how stupid those scientists were. We, we of art, drew beautiful forms, forms beautiful in simplicity, and right, eminently right in beauty of line and mass and form. Now, now at last the scientists make similar forms and cackle forth to the world. 'See—see what we have done. We have found the perfect streamline shape.' Years, centuries before them, we knew those forms were perfect.

"Do you know the Golden Mean? It is the ratio of two to three. That is the shape, the ratio for most perfect beauty. Now they have discovered that is the ratio of diameter to length for high-flying, swift ships.

"And they, they try to tell art how to mate for art's best good.

"Aies—Aies—they do not know. Art is above science; it is the comprehension of the whole without the knowing of the parts; it has results, ends without means." His heat of passionate denunciation cooled suddenly to a tenderness, his voice fell to softer tones.

"Aies—I love you—I know you—you are the one for me. They cannot know. They would make you marry some scientist, some heavy, thick-headed, slow-moving scientist. They cannot see the light and the air in you—the swift race of your very thoughts.

"Aies—they are so stupid. They mean so well, and they are so pitiful in their stupidity. Playing with lives, with loves and hates, with things they do not know. Only love can know what love is for.

"Why was I made so to love you, were I not meant to? They are so—" His voice trailed off, his head sank. "So inexorable. I—I am sorry, Aies. I should not say all this."

A small, cool hand lifted his face. Aies was smiling down at him, her eyes clear and bright with something that perhaps art comprehended, but it could not find the means to put on canvas, where atoms and protons and strange chromatic groupings must be given the impossible task of translating a radiation to a mere bit of oil.

"I don't want any slow-witted scientist, Paul," said Aies very, very softly. "I don't want any great elephant with a face like the crinkled hide of a hippopotamus, and a grin like a jackal. I want you, Paul. I want *you*."

Slowly Paul rose to his feet. Slowly Aies rose, not quite as far—but far enough. He felt solid and hard and supple against her as he held her to him. And Aies was quite sure her plans were right, in every possible way.

She told him her plan then. It was simple. It was—scientific. It was based on one of the rules science itself laid down. "When theory meets with fact contrary to the theory, then the theory is wrong, not the fact." It was very simple. The theory of eugenic mating could not, by the law, controvert the fact of a marriage already existent.

"We could not hide forever. We could not escape permanently for their board would find us. But that is not necessary. Just a month—two—three. Theory—their theory of eugenics—cannot break fact. The fact of our love, Paul," she said. "I will hear from Dot Walden hours before they make any active move. And then—Dad's plane, so new even the patrol hasn't one—will be able to leave anything and everything. Lost—somewhere among the two hundred and eighty-seven millions of people of the United States. They will find us—but not soon." She paused. "And I have one other thing, too." There was a steel determination in her voice as she said it.

She saw Dot Walden that morning, and spoke to her, and she did a number of other errands. She was quite busy, and away from the house all that day. And that evening she spent talking and planning with Paul Treray. It was ten-thirty when she returned home, and Dot Walden was calling her.

"You're right," smiled Dot's image on the screen. "They decided and sent the official decision through this evening. I've been trying to get you since five-thirty. By the way—there's something special about it. It's Bruce Randall all right—and congratulations—he certainly is a fine man—but it's special some way. I haven't been in the office very long, and Miss Cartwright was out when it came through. It's on a blue form, instead of the usual white. I don't know what that means—"

Neither did Aies, but she had some faint suspicion. She knew that her father had been questioned by one of the commissioners while he was at the physics association the day before—and she had a suspicion. The suspicion was right. The blue form meant action.

Aies acted, too. She called Paul Treray at once. Her voice was calm, tense actually, and her brain was clear and determined. Treray was ready. In ten minutes his things were packed; she joined him, and together, with their light packs, they went toward the shop where the new plane rested. Aies opened the door as Paul stumbled in the darkness. Automatically the gas tubes glowed into light as he crossed the capacitance plate.

Aies' things slipped to the floor in dull surprise. The plane was half-dismantled. The powerful motor hung with limp dangling cables from a crane. The propeller lay on the floor to one side. The accumulator stacks were racked in the storage shelves. Her father had spent the day installing the improvement he intended!

Aies' body whipped erect abruptly, her voice suddenly hard and sharp. "By all the laws in existence, and out of existence. I'll beat the commission if I die trying. Come on!"

In an instant her hat was off, her coat flying, loose and floppy, and grimly she set to work.

It was surprising how much such a really trained woman could accomplish in an hour. By eleven forty-five she had the motor back in place, the prop stepped, and the racks replaced. The accumulators were going in. The plane still looked half-dismantled, but actually lacked only the fairing and the Venturi cowlings, and a little tuning and rebalancing of circuits. Three-quarters of an hour would see that done—

"We'd be farther away if we'd taken the standard plane you have," said Paul uncertainly. "There is still so much to be done—"

"We'd have been grounded before we left town," snapped Aies. "Give me that secondary accumulator bank there." She snapped it into place, put the nut on the bolt, and over the whir of the electric wrench added, "I'll bet dollars to a stripped bolt they've got a blanket order out to the patrol to ground me. And probably that darned Bruce Randall, too. I just know I'm right in guessing what the blue form means and—"

The whir of the wrench stopped. But the whirring sound didn't; it kept on, slightly heavier in tone, and growing louder. Aies snapped erect, brushed a streak of grease across her forehead, and a stray hair out of her eyes.

"Paul—the patrol. Yes, we'd have been grounded." She was busy wiping face and hands on clean waste. Then she slipped the accumulator block of her new projector into her pocket, and slipped the lead up her sleeve, a rubber band holding it in place. The projector was almost hidden in her folded hand as she stepped to the door. The patrol plane was just settling softly to the grass court. Paul stepped back out of sight into the shop.

"Hello—what brings you here?" asked Aies as she stepped out.

A broadly-smiling patrolman leaned out of his window. "You an' Dan Cupid, I guess, sweetheart. With the sanction and suggestion of the commission. Will you take a bit of a ride along with me?"

Aies started back a step. "The commission—tonight? There—there must be some mistake. Why—I haven't received any notice— I—I'm not ready at all— I can't go tonight!"

The patrolman seemed puzzled, looked at his order form, then smiled at her again. "It does sound screwy, but unless you have somebody else's face by mistake, I guess I'll have to take you along back. The order's kinda plain, honey."

"But—but I just can't—"

"Well, why not come along and tell 'em about it. I just ain't a commissioner and I can't do a darned thing about orders except carry them through. Step in and come along, won't you?" The patrolman was getting confused and worried.

Aies wasn't. She stepped into the plane. "Oh, Paul!" she called a moment later. "Paul, come and help me get them out, will you?" Paul stepped into the plane, and lifted the first of the two men out, grinning down at him.

"So," he laughed, "and are you comfortable?" He laid the patrolman out on the lawn, carefully. The man's angry, startled eyes followed him. Faint twitchings of jaw and lips told of his efforts to speak. But only a low, gurgling sound came from his throat. A moment later the second man joined the first, and thirty seconds later they watched as the SPX-234 rose gently from the field and started up. It hung for a moment, and Aies leaned out, smiling.

"Sorry, fellows. It's just a paralyzer, and you ought to be quite O.K. in about ten minutes. I'll have to be going along now." She turned back to her companion, and faintly the man on the ground heard her ask: "You've got the Boston charts, Paul?"

Then the ship rose out of sight and drifted off at the leisurely fifty miles an hour of the patrol ships in a city area.

"She mis—cal—culated," said a jerky, rasping, almost unintelligible voice from Patrolman Larry Mallory. "I can—wiggle my toe." His voice cleared up rapidly, and in scarcely three minutes he was able to roll a little, and he started for the still-lighted shop. There would be a communicator there. Halfway there he got to his hands and knees, and weakly crawled a few feet, then staggered to his feet, and as though thoroughly drunk, rolled and swayed to the telephone in the shop.

"Ptrool 'edquart, quick," he said as the hum of the operator's connection came on. Ten seconds later the desk captain responded.

"Ptrolmun Mulry," he said thickly. "Th' gurl—Merlin—gadget knocked us—stiff. Tooka shup—oo-tree-fir—spota numbers easy."

"Mallory? Mallory! You're drunk. Report here at once!" snapped the captain. "Where's O'Halley?"

"Cap'n, r'rrn't 'runk—paralyzed. Grl 'da wepun. Somepin knocked us stiff. Olley's cummin. She stole the ship, sir. Thank goodness I can talk again. The girl had something or other that knocked us stiff—a ray of some kind. Couldn't wiggle a toe for a while, then slowly recovered. Honest, Captain, we're not drunk, and she's got our ship."

"You're soused," snapped the captain. "I'm sending a man out there at once. Stay where you are, and consider yourselves under arrest."

"Yes, sir," said Mallory, dolefully. "He don't believe us, O'Halley," he said, turning to his companion. "He thinks we're drunk."

"Well, we ain't."

A patrol ship, siren screaming, settled swiftly down five minutes later, and picked them up. They were bundled unceremoniously into the back, with the evident anger of the two patrolmen in the ship, ashamed that brother patrolmen would get drunk on duty.

Five minutes later, the ship landed on the headquarters' roof and the two men were taken below. "Take them in to Commissioner Stracey," ordered the desk captain. "He wants to interview them."

The two men were escorted down the corridor, through the connecting bridge to the conditioning building. Commissioner Stracey's office was somewhat crowded. Dr. Harrison, head of the department, and a young, powerfully-built man with an unusually blank face already filled the small office.

"What's this you reported about Miss Marlan?" demanded Stracey, as they entered.

"She had some kind of a weapon, sir, that throws a paralyzing beam. It made us helpless instantly—conscious, but unable to move or even speak."

"The paralyzer—I thought she'd use it," said the young man, chuckling. "They haven't any defense, and I'll bet she gets away."

Stracey looked at him, sharply. Then he looked at Harrison. "What's this?" he demanded.

"Primary state," smiled Harrison. "I brought him in here as I said because he confirmed the Primary statements of her father and added some additional ones. He mentioned the paralyzer."

"Just what is the Primary state? How much can it be trusted? Is his mind clear?"

"In the Primary state he merely thinks out loud. His mind is perfectly clear and normal, save that the censor of the brain is out of the circuit, and the memory tracks are out. He cannot censor his thoughts, and he cannot remember what he says. It corresponds to the Secondary state used in criminal proceedings. There the suspect speaks his thoughts, but memory is associated so that he remembers and knows, when waked, that he has convicted or freed himself.

"Here, while his mental processes are normal, he can neither remember nor censor his thoughts."

"Then Miss Marlan had a paralyzer?"

"Had a paralyzer?" Bruce Randall chuckled. To him, it seemed he was chuckling and thinking to himself. "Oh, she had one—a little honey. Only she didn't develop any protection. She'll have lots of fun when she tries it on me."

"Why?"

"Because I did develop protection. I know just how delightfully mad she'll be when she tries to paralyze me and the cloak stops the rays. Then—I think my tube will be powerful enough—probably more powerful than hers."

"She definitely has a paralyzer?"

"She certainly has! She's been playing with it for months. It's a great invention—extremely useful for the patrol when they finally get it—quell disturbances instantly. Harmless, but effective. They'll have a fine time catching her. They'll probably think the men are drunk."

"She said she had one, sir, and the captain did think we were drunk," interrupted Mallory. "And she said she was headed north. You'd better have the patrol strengthened up there. Said to the man with her: 'Have you got the Boston charts?' I think she didn't know we could hear."

"Probably thought she was out of earshot—maybe realized—no, she *intended* him to hear her. She knew her weapon," said Bruce. He chuckled. "She'll probably—hmmm." Bruce fell silent.

"Send orders to withdraw three of the ships from the north sector and reenforce the west and south sectors," ordered the commissioner after a few seconds. "The little fox."

"Where is this protection you have?" he asked, turning to Bruce.

"The cloak," said Bruce. "The cloak in my laboratory. They'll probably never catch her. If she can make it—let her. I won't interfere, and the patrol probably won't get her."

Stracey looked at him in puzzlement, then smiled. "Peculiar statement, eh, doctor. I wonder why he doesn't want to help? Doesn't he like the girl?"

"She's wonderful," said Bruce softly. "She's as clever as any woman that ever lived, and the way she looks at me— I love her. The way she turns her back—that's almost all that I have seen—most of the time." He smiled tenderly.

"There's your answer to the last question, Commissioner," smiled the doctor. "He wants to play fair, I suspect. Feels it isn't right to aid in hunting her down."

"It wouldn't be fair; she's fighting enough already—it's her fight, and the little thing may win, too," sighed Bruce.

"Mallory, I guess you're right. Release them, men. I think you two can realize that we did have reason to think you drunk. You really can't blame us for the mistake. But now, Mallory, you go up to that laboratory and see if you can find those cloaks."

"Silvery-gray cloaks—in the cabinet—I hope he doesn't find them," said Randall. "I have the key—they won't want to break in."

Stracey looked from Bruce to the doctor. "Harrison, do you think he would give us the key?"

Harrison looked at the powerful young man and smiled. "You might get a half-dozen good husky patrolmen in here, and possibly they could get it. But just because he must speak his thoughts doesn't mean he'll give up those keys at all. He thinks he's sitting here silently."

"Then take some pick locks and open it. I wonder if it will be safe—or will he run into some dangerous stuff?"

"There's nothing dangerous—he'll probably forget the accumulators—the whole secret—"

"Don't," smiled Stracey, looking at Mallory. Mallory was looking at Randall uneasily, shifting his weight on his feet.

"No, sir," replied the patrolman. "Shall I go?"

"Yes, go ahead."

"She's going to Boston," said Randall, suddenly. "She meant the patrolman to hear her, knew that they'd expect her to go anywhere but to Boston, since they knew she knew they had heard. So she would go to Boston, because the patrol would not expect her there."

"What?" gasped Stracey. "Whew—do you think she—I mean—is he right?" asked Stracey, looking at Harrison.

"She's a very clever girl, evidently," said the doctor, thoughtfully, "and just such an abstruse line of reasoning might occur to her."

"I know her. I know she will do that. They will probably miss her, unless by blind chance she runs into the few planes in that sector."

"Commissioner—" the desk captain's voice came from the small speaker under the table. "We've just gotten a report from the north field that ship XP-47 came in on automatic controls, with the two pilots completely drunk. I think the girl was paralyzing them. They—further report—they say that they saw the 234 and were suddenly knocked out, made helpless, while their ship went into a power dive, exceeded the five-hundred-mile limit, and the automatics took over and landed them safely."

"She went toward Boston," nodded Randall. "Tough luck. She hit one of the planes. I wonder what she'll do now. She's beyond any of the planes of the New York patrol now, and her ship was just as speedy as any other patrol plane. Dr. Marlan's plane was disassembled, of course, so no one can catch her. Ah—the accumulators. Patrol planes have undersize accumulator banks to make theft of them difficult. I wonder if the banks were well charged?"

"They were half-full," said O'Halley, goggling at the young physicist.

"Then they carried a charge good for only one-hundred-and-fifty miles or so at cruising speed, not more than two=hundred absolute maximum, and one-hundred at high speed. She'll have to rent a plane. But if she goes into the city, she'll be spotted because of the patrol plane. If she lands outside, it will take hours to get into a large city, and—she'll go to a medium-sized city. Too small—they'd notice and report. There wouldn't be a plane-rental agency.

"Too big—the patrol would be too active."

"What city will she stop at? New Haven—New London?" asked Stracey tensely. It was like asking a thinking machine. Immediately the mechanism started on the new problem.

"No. By no means. She'll circle New York and head south now, because she's beyond the reach of the New York patrol and free to go in any direction. They'll expect her to put the most possible distance between herself and New York. That would be by going due north. So she'll circle to an unexpected quadrant. Probably due south. New-ark—too large. Suburbs are solid clear out, too. She won't go there. Elizabeth—too large. Too much part of Newark. Ah—Amboy—one of the Amboys. Perth Amboy—South Amboy—"

"Commissioner—Mallory reports he can't find the cloaks Randall described. Are you sure he isn't bats? Mallory claims his laboratory has no cabinet or locker of any kind that isn't open and full of just plain junk. He's afraid to paw around much."

"He can't find the cabinet," Randall chuckled. "It's hidden. He mustn't paw around." A worried frown came over Randall's face, and for a moment a different, intelligent look appeared on his face; the lines about his eyes and mouth, the lines of character and thought and intelligence, grew firm again.

He spoke with a deeper, more pleasant voice. "Commissioner Stracey, I'd advise that anyone looking about in our laboratories be very careful as there is a great deal of dangerously charged apparatus." Then, as suddenly as it had come, his face lapsed again into placid thought.

"He means that, Commissioner. It probably is dangerous," said Harrison. Stracey spoke into his communicator, and relayed the warning to Mallory.

"But how are we to find the hidden cabinet?"

Harrison chuckled. "That's locked up in memory. It's probably between memory and censor sections. We can't, that's all. He'll have to hunt. Get some of the patrol technicians out there with apparatus. If we wake him, so that memory is available, he won't want to tell us, and the censor is on the job. Too bad—but we can't do it with him. A low-class or unbalanced mind we could handle, but remember, it was only with his consent and aid that I was able to get him to the Primary state. He would object a second time, right now—and that would be that.

"Hmmmm—that will take time. Then you'd better order the patrol in the Amboy region to picket all rental-plane agencies, and watch out for her paralysis device."

"They won't believe it, although it comes as an order, so that's all right," said Randall complacently. Stracey turned red, then roared in laughter.

"By gosh, he's right! They won't. They'll get knocked over like a row of tin soldiers. But it's all we can do. What will they do then?"

"It depends on the color of the plane they take," said Bruce thoughtfully. "If it's gray, or black, or dark brown, that's one thing. But if it's bright red, or bright blue or a bright color of any sort, why that will mean something else."

Aies looked at the lights below, and pondered. Then she looked back at the chart. "That's Perth Amboy, all right, Paul," she sighed at length. "The motors are getting weak, so we'll have to land pretty quickly. It's quite late so we'd better land away from houses. It'll be a two-mile hike. But then—walking is good for one." She laughed softly. "I'll bet they're burning up the night between New York and Boston about now."

They left their things in the plane, when it grounded gently with almost the last gasp of the accumulators, and walked. It had started to fog over, a heavy wet fog, and Aies feared for her not-too-perfect little weapon's insulation. They walked rapidly toward the outskirts of the city and stopped at a lighted drug store. In a classified directory they located the largest plane-renting establishment in town, took the tube to the nearest station, and walked to the office. White light made a vague, slanting rectangular shaft in the mist as they turned in.

Aies stopped in dismay. Four large patrolmen started up at her entrance; two more appeared just outside the door almost instantly.

Six large patrolmen and two company clerks sat sleeping in their chairs two minutes later when a customer walked in. Thirty seconds later he, too, was sleeping in a chair. Aies passed the beam over her nine victims once more to be safe, and then carefully filled out a rental blank, put the deposit on the table, and wrote "Boston" as her destination. Then she and Paul walked back into the hangar. "The red one there, Paul," she said thoughtfully. "It's a Crossing—fast."

"But Aies—it's red—so conspicuous," objected Treray.

"That's what I want," laughed the girl. "They'll look hard for it. Come on, and I'll explain, sweetheart."

The plane rose gracefully as Aies made sure the accumulators were fully charged. Then laughingly she explained her plan. The plane had scarcely left the city when Patrolman Sargeant knocked the telephone off the table with a slightly mobile hand. "Rud," he croaked. " 'edquart—'ell 'em—rud. 'rite rud."

"Bright red," said Aies, looking at the plane. "They'll be looking all over for it and stopping all the bright-red planes in the air tonight with a man and a girl in them. While this particular bright-red plane rests peacefully in a deserted shack some three and a half miles from its starting point. Now for the rest of the hike." She looked out. The heavy, wet mist still hung low, scarcely ten feet deep. It was clear here, but half a mile away it hung like a fleecy blanket. "It'll be wet. Brr—"

It was near dawn when they reached the Elizabeth tube entrance. Five minutes later they alighted at 200th Street, in upper New York. "Naturally," Aies had said, "they don't expect to find us in the heart of things after that escape."

They took the moving walk on the second level downtown, then shuttled across town, and took a subway to the 33rd Street terminal. The crowds were getting thicker once more, and they melted into it, then the most exposed part of the trip began. They took the moving walk over to Brooklyn. The other walk was crowded, but very few people were going this way. Aies saw suddenly in the dim, cold dawn light two patrolmen in the familiar capes. Paul felt her stiffen against him and looked at the pair himself, wide-eyed.

The patrolmen cast a casual glance at the pair and turned away. "Uhmmm—" Aies sighed in relief. Her voice was somewhat shaken as she went on. "That's one difficulty—every blue uniform will mean a man staring at us. It won't be much fun for the next few months."

The walk carried them on, off the bridge and to the Brooklyn terminal. They were nearing it when Aies saw two rather peculiar figures. They wore the blue uniforms, but over their uniforms they wore a nonstandard cape. Aies frowned in puzzlement. Somewhere she had seen that dirty-gray cloth—stiffish cloth.

Suddenly she stiffened. The two were looking directly at them, two elderly men with kindly, paternal smiles. They looked at her reprovingly. Jerkily, Aies raised her arm. In the dim light the little tube glowed brightly, a faint beam reached out.

The men did not fall. Their cloaks were washed with a softly wavering light, violet, and their expressions were as a father might look down at the angry child pounding at his legs. Aies felt the little tube grow hot in her hand; it began to sputter. With a soft *pouf* it collapsed into darkness.

Wide-eyed, Aies looked down at it, then in wonder, hurt surprise she looked up at the two men. One raised his hand, and something glowed softly. A greenish-blue light. Aies felt a sudden tingling through her muscles, a rapid weakening. And suddenly she recognized the material. "Bruce—stuff he—worked—"

She'd remembered that peculiar gray stuff, hard to recognize under this light. Then her lips wouldn't work any more, and she was picked up gently by two of the men as two more appeared to pick up Paul. She saw quite clearly that Bruce had been watching her experiment rather quietly and had not only duplicated her paralyzing device—but had gone her just one, slight step better. He'd rigged a protective device.

And she was quite furious that Bruce had spied on her, and beaten her, and helped catch her. But she couldn't wiggle her little finger when they brought her into the conditioning laboratory.

Bruce looked across at Stracey, half-embarrassed, half-annoyed. "It wasn't exactly fair, sir. It isn't usual to make a man help as I did."

"Help capture his runaway fiancé?" chuckled Stracey. "Well, nowadays we aren't used to chasing the aforementioned fiancé. And I don't know that we could have kept ahead of her without your very valuable assistance. The bit of reasoning on the color of the plane was most interesting."

"Thanks—I don't remember it," said Randall sourly. "Tell me so I can enjoy my brilliance."

Stracey laughed. "Try going up to room 73. That may be more enjoyable." He handed Bruce a pass, and Randall rose hastily.

"Thank you, sir," he said and was gone.

Aies rose with a smile as Bruce came into her room. There was a half-pout-half-smile on her lips and a golden-red halo of sunlight shining through the window that formed a frame for her head.

"Hello, Bruce. I hear you helped capture me?" she stated.

"So I heard—when they were quite through with me," answered Bruce. His eyes crinkled very slowly, and the crinkles spread down his cheeks till the corners of his mouth twitched.

Aies looked at him for a moment, and slowly a little smile of surprise and tenderness came over her face. "Funny, I never liked the way you smiled—but now—I think it's—awfully nice to have around."

"It isn't funny," said Bruce, tenderly. "It's natural. They changed you a little, dear girl. You're supposed to love me now, you know."

She looked up at him slowly. "It is funny—because I think I do. In fact—I'm sure I do, Bruce." She came toward him slowly, and he put his arms around her very gently.

"You'll break. I know you'll break in two. You're very small."

"Uhmmm—" said Aies. "I'm not—but you are nicely large." She looked up at him. Her eyes changed for a moment; a doubt seemed to creep into them. "I suppose they made me feel that way. I suppose I don't really do—"

Bruce looked down into her eyes. "Does it matter, dear? Does it matter in the least? All we seek in life is happiness. Happiness—peace—and it matters not one bit how we reach them. Love is the greatest happiness in the world—isn't it, little sweetheart?—and so if it is, does it matter whence it comes or why? Does it matter if it is because someone else thought it wise or because we developed it by association and contacts that were pleasant?

"Perhaps—perhaps it does. Because love can be real—and not last. It must wear, and only similar characters, similar ideals, similar ideas can make it. And wisdom can help there, when the heart is not very wise. Unfortunately, till men learned the secret of conditioning, the head could not rule the heart. Does it matter, now that the love is, from whence it came?"

"No," said Aies, and stopped further discussion.

# NIGHT

Condon was staring through the glasses with a face tense and drawn, all his attention utterly concentrated on that one almost invisible speck infinitely far up in the blue sky, and saying over and over again in the most horribly absent-minded way, "My Lord, my Lord—"

Suddenly he shivered and looked down at me, sheer agony in his face. "He's never coming down. Don, he's never coming down—"

I knew it too—knew it solidly as I knew the knowledge was impossible. But I smiled and said, "Oh, I wouldn't say that. If anything, I'd fear his coming down. What goes up comes down."

Major Condon trembled all over. His mouth worked horribly for a moment before he could speak. "Talbot—I'm scared—I'm horribly scared. You know—you're his assistant—you know he's trying to defeat gravity. Men aren't meant to—it's wrong—wrong—"

His eyes were glued on those binoculars again, with the same terrible tensity, and now he was saying over and over in that absent-minded way, "Wrong—wrong—wrong—"

Simultaneously he stiffened and stopped. The dozen or so other men standing on that lonely little emergency field stiffened; then the major crumpled to the ground. I've never before seen a man faint, let alone an army officer with a D.S. medal. I didn't stop to help him, because I knew something had happened. I grabbed the glasses.

Far, far up in the sky was that little orange speck—far, where there is almost no air, and he had been forced to wear a stratosphere suit with a little alcohol heater. The broad, orange wings were overlaid now with a faint-glowing, pearl-gray light. And it was falling. Slowly, at first, circling aimlessly downward. Then it dipped, rose, and somehow went into a tailspin.

It was horrible. I know I must have breathed, but it didn't seem so. It took minutes for it to fall those miles, despite the speed. Eventually it whipped out of that tailspin—through sheer speed, whipped out and into a power dive. It was a ghastly, flying coffin, hurtling at more

149

than half a thousand miles an hour when it reached the Earth, some fifteen miles away.

The ground trembled, and the air shook with the crash of it. We were in the cars and roaring across the ground long before it hit. I was in Bob's car, with Jeff, his laboratory technician—Bob's little roadster he'd never need again. The engine picked up quickly, and we were going seventy before we left the field, jumped a shallow ditch and left the road—the deserted concrete road that led off toward where he must be. The engine roared as Jeff clamped down on the accelerator. Dimly, I heard the major's big car coming along behind us.

Jeff drove like a maniac, but I didn't notice. I knew the thing had done ninety-five, but I think we must have done more. The wind whipped tears in my eyes so I couldn't be sure whether I saw mounting smoke and flame or not. With Diesel fuel there shouldn't be—but that plane had been doing things it shouldn't. It had been trying out Carter's antigravity coil.

We shot up the flat, straight road across wide, level country, the wind moaning a requiem about the car. Far ahead I saw the side road that must lead off toward where Bob should be, and lurched to the braking of the car, the whine and sing of violently shrieking tires, then to the skidding corner. It was a sand road; we slithered down it and for all the lightness and power, we slowed to sixty-five, clinging to the seat as the soft sand gripped and clung.

Violently Jeff twisted into a branching cow path and somehow the springs took it. We braked to a stop a quarter of a mile from the plane.

It was in a fenced field of pasture and wood lot. We leaped the fence, and raced toward it; Jeff got there first, just as the major's car shrieked to a stop behind ours.

The major was cold and pale when he reached us. "Dead," he stated.

And I was very much colder and probably several times as pale. "I don't know!" I moaned. "He isn't there!"

"Not there!" The major almost screamed it. "He must be—he has to be. He had no parachute—wouldn't take one. They say he didn't jump—"

I pointed to the plane, and wiped a little cold sweat from my forehead. I felt clammy all over, and my spine prickled. The solid steel of the huge Diesel engine was driven through the stump of a tree, down into the ground perhaps eight or nine feet, and the dirt and rock had splashed under that blow like wet mud.

The wings were on the other side of the field, flattened, twisted straws of dural alloy. The fuselage of the ship was a perfect silhouette—

a longitudinal projection that had flattened in on itself, each separate section stopping only as it hit the ground.

The great torus coil with its strangely twined wrappings of hair-fine bismuth wire was intact! And bent over it, twisted, utterly wrecked by the impact, was the main-wing stringer—the great dural-alloy beam that supported most of the ship's weight in the air. It was battered, crushed on those hair-fine, fragile bismuth wires—and not one of them was twisted or displaced or so much as skinned. The back frame of the ponderous Diesel engine—the heavy supercharger was the anvil of that combination—was cracked and splintered. And not one wire of the hellish bismuth coil was strained or skinned or displaced.

And the red pulp that should have been there—the red pulp that had been a man—wasn't. It simply wasn't there at all. He hadn't left the plane. In the clear, cloudless air, we could see that. He was gone.

We examined it, of course. A farmer came, and another, and looked, and talked. Then several farmers came in old dilapidated cars with their wives and families, and watched.

We set the owner of the property on watch and went away—went back to the city for workmen and a truck with a derrick. Dusk was falling. It would be morning before we could do anything, so we went away.

Five of us—the major of the army air force, Jeff Rodney, the two Douglass Co. men whose names I never remembered and I—sat in my—our—room. Bob's and Jeff's and mine. We'd been sitting there for hours trying to talk, trying to think, trying to remember every little detail, and trying to forget every ghastly detail. We couldn't remember the detail that explained it, nor forget the details that rode and harried us.

And the telephone rang. I started. Then slowly got up and answered. A strange voice, flat and rather unpleasant, said: "Mr. Talbot?"

"Yes."

It was Sam Gentry, the farmer we'd left on watch. "There's a man here."

"Yes? What does he want?"

"I dunno. I dunno where he came from. He's either dead or out cold. Gotta funny kind of aviator suit on, with a glass face on it. He looks all blue, so I guess he's dead."

"Lord! Bob! Did you take that helmet off?" I roared.

"No, sir, no—no, sir. We just left him the way he was."

"His tanks have run out. Listen. Take a hammer, a wrench, anything, and break that glass face plate! Quick! We'll be there."

Jeff was moving. The major was, too, and the others. I made a grab for the half-empty bottle of Scotch, started out, and ducked back into the closet. With the oxygen bottle under my arm I jumped into the crowded little roadster just as Jeff started it moving. He turned on the horn, and left it that way.

We dodged, twisted, jumped, and stopped with jerks in traffic, then leaped into smooth, roaring speed out toward the farmer's field. The turns were familiar now; we scarcely slowed for them slewing around them. This time Jeff charged through the wire fence. A headlight popped; there was a shrill scream of wire, the wicked *zing* of wire scratching across the hood and mud guards, and we were bouncing across the field.

There were two lanterns on the ground; three men carried others; more men squatted down beside a still figure garbed in a fantastic, bulging, airproof stratosphere suit. They looked at us, open-mouthed, as we skidded to a halt, moving aside as the major leaped out and dashed over with the Scotch. I followed close behind with the oxygen bottle.

Bob's face plate was shattered, his face blue, his lips blue, and flecked with froth. A long gash across his cheek from the shattered glass bled slowly. The major lifted Bob's head without a word, and glass tinkled inside the helmet as he tried to force a little whisky down the unconscious man's throat.

"Wait!" I called. "Major, give him artificial respiration, and this will bring him around quicker—better." The major nodded, and rose, rubbing his arm with a peculiar expression.

"That's cold!" he said, as he flipped Bob over, and straddled his back. I held the oxygen bottle under Bob's nose as the major swung back in his arc, and let the raw, cold oxygen gas flow into his nostrils.

In ten seconds Bob coughed, gurgled, coughed violently, and took a deep shuddering breath. His face turned pink almost instantly under that lungful of oxygen, and I noticed with some surprise that he seemed to exhale almost nothing, his body absorbing the oxygen rapidly.

He coughed again; then: "I could breathe a hell of a sight better if you'd get off my back," he said. The major jumped up, and Bob turned over and sat up. He waved me aside, and spat. "I'm—all right," he said softly.

"Lord, man, what happened?" demanded the major.

Bob sat silent for a minute. His eyes had the strangest look—a hungry look—as he gazed about him. He looked at the trees beyond, and at the silent watching men in the light of the lanterns; then up, up to where a myriad stars gleamed and danced and flickered in the clear night sky.

"I'm back," he said softly. Then suddenly he shivered and looked horribly afraid. "But—I'll have to be—then—too."

He looked at the major for a minute, and smiled faintly. And at the two Douglass Co. men. "Your plane was all right. I started up on the wings, as arranged, went way up, till I thought surely I was at a safe height, where the air wasn't too dense and the field surely wouldn't reach to Earth. Lord!—reach to Earth! I didn't guess how far that field extended. It touched Earth—twice.

"I was at forty-five thousand when I decided it was safe, and cut the engine. It died, and the stillness shocked me. It was so quiet. So quiet.

"I turned on the coil circuit, and the dynamotor began to hum as the tubes warmed up. And then—the field hit me. It paralyzed me in an instant. I never had a chance to break the circuit, though I knew instantly something was wrong—terribly wrong. But the very first thing it did was to paralyze me, and I had to sit there and watch the instruments climb to positions and meanings they were never meant for.

"I realized I alone was being affected by that coil—I alone, sitting directly over it. I stared at the meters and they began to fade, began to seem transparent, unreal. And as they faded into blankness I saw clear sky beyond them; then for a hundredth of a second, like some effect of persistence of vision, I thought I saw the plane falling, twisting down at incredible speed; and the light faded as the Sun seemed to rocket suddenly across the sky and vanish.

"I don't know how long I was in that paralyzed condition, where there was only blankness—neither dark nor light, nor time, nor any form—but I breathed many times. Finally, form crawled and writhed into the blankness, and seemed to solidify beneath me as, abruptly, the blankness gave way to a dull red light. I was falling.

"I thought instantly of the forty-five thousand feet that lay between me and the solid Earth, and stiffened automatically in terror. And in the same instant I landed in a deep blanket of white snow, stained by the red light that lighted the world.

"Cold. Cold—it tore into me like the fang of a savage animal. What cold! The cold of ultimate death. It ripped through that thick, insulated suit and slashed at me viciously, as though there were no insulation there. I shivered so violently, I could scarcely turn up the alcohol valves. You know I carried alcohol tanks and catalyst grids for heating, because the only electrical fields I wanted were those of the apparatus. Even used a Diesel instead of gas engine.

"I thanked the Lord for that then. I realized that whatever had happened, I was in a spot indescribably cold and desolate. And in the same instant, realized that the sky was black. Blacker than the blackest night, and yet before me the snow field stretched to infinity, tainted by the blood-red light, and my shadow crawled in darker red at my feet.

"I turned around. As far as the eye could see in three directions the land swept off in very low, very slightly rolling hills, almost plains— red plains of snow dyed with the dripping light of sunset. I thought.

"In the fourth direction, a wall—a wall that put the Great Wall of China to shame—loomed up half a mile—a blood-red wall that had the luster of metal. It stretched across the horizon, and looked a scant hundred yards away, for the air was utterly clear. I turned up my alcohol burners a bit more and felt a little better.

"Something jerked my head around like a giant hand—a sudden thought. I stared at the Sun and gulped. It was four times—six times— the size of the Sun I knew. And it wasn't setting. It was forty-five degrees from the horizon. It was red. Blood-red. And there wasn't the slightest bit of radiant heat reaching my face from it. That Sun was cold.

"I'd just automatically assumed I was still on Earth, whatever else might have happened, but now I knew I couldn't be. It must be another planet of another sun—a frozen planet—for that snow was frozen air. I knew it absolutely. A frozen planet of a dead sun.

"And then I changed even that. I looked up at the black sky above me, and in all the vast black bowl of the heavens, not three-score stars were visible. Dim, red stars, with one single sun that stood out for its brilliance—a yellowish-red sun perhaps a tenth as bright as our Sun, but a monster here. It was another—a dead—space. For if that snow was frozen air, the only atmosphere must have been neon and helium. There wasn't any hazy air to stop the light of the stars, and that dim, red sun didn't obscure them with its light. The stars were gone.

"In that glimpse, my mind began working by itself; I was scared.

"Scared? I was so scared I was afraid I was going to be sick. Because right then I knew I was never coming back. When I felt that cold, I'd wondered when my oxygen bottles would give out, if I'd get back before they gave out. Now it was not a worry. It was simply the limiting factor on an already determined thing, the setting of the time bomb. I had just so much more time before I died right there.

"My mind was working out things, working them out all by itself, and giving answers I didn't want, didn't want to know about. For some reason it persisted in considering this was Earth, and the conviction became more and more fixed. It was right. That was Earth. And it was old Sol. Old—old Sol. It was the time axis that coil distorted—not gravity at all. My mind worked that out with a logic as cold as that planet.

"If it was time it had distorted, and this was Earth, then it had distorted time beyond imagining, to an extent as meaningless to our minds as the distance a hundred million light years is. It was simply vast—incalculable. The Sun was dead. The Earth was dead. And Earth was already, in our time, two billions of years old, and in all that geological time, the Sun had not changed measurably. Then how long was it since my time? The Sun was dead. The very stars were dead. It must have been, I thought even then, billions on billions of years. And I grossly underestimated it.

"The world was old—old—old. The very rocks and ground radiated a crushing aura of incredible age. It was old, older than—but what is there? Older than the hills? Hills? Hell, they'd been born and died and been born and worn away again, a million, a score of million times! Old as the stars? No, that wouldn't do. The stars were dead—then.

"I looked again at the metal wall, and set out for it, and the aura of age washed up at me, and dragged at me, and tried to stop this motion when all motion should have ceased. And the thin, unutterably cold wind whined in dead protest at me, and pulled at me with the ghost hands of the million million million that had been born and lived and died in the countless ages before I was born.

"I wondered as I went. I didn't think clearly; for the dead aura of the dead planet pulled at me. Age. The stars were dying, dead. They were huddled there in space, like decrepit old men, huddling for warmth. The galaxy was shrunk. So tiny, it wasn't a thousand light years across; the stars were separated by miles where there had been light years. The magnificent, proudly sprawling universe I had known, that flung itself across a million million light years, that flung radiant energy through space by the millions of millions of tons was—gone.

"It was dying—a dying miser that hoarded its last broken dregs of energy in a tiny cramped space. It was broken and shattered. A thousand billion years before, the cosmical constant had been dropped from that broken universe. The cosmical constant that flung giant galaxies whirling apart with ever greater speed had no place here. It had hurled the universe in broken fragments, till each shattered bit felt the chill of loneliness, and wrapped space about itself, to become a universe in itself while the flaming galaxies vanished.

"That had happened so long ago that the writing it had left in the fabric of space itself had worn away. Only the gravity constant remained, the hoarding constant, that drew things together, and slowly the galaxy collapsed, shrunken and old, a withered mummy.

"The very atoms were dead. The light was cold; even the red light made things look older, colder. There was no youth in the universe. I didn't belong, and the faint protesting rustle of the infinitely cold wind about me moved the snow in muted, futile protest, resenting my intrusion from a time when things were young. It whinnied at me feebly, and chilled the youth of me.

"I plodded on and on, and always the metal wall retreated, like one of those desert mirages. I was too stupefied by the age of the thing to wonder; I just walked on.

"I was getting nearer, though. The wall was real; it was fixed. As I drew slowly nearer, the polished sheen of the wall died, and the last dregs of hope died. I'd thought there might be someone still living behind that wall. Beings who could build such a thing might be able to live, even here. But I couldn't stop then; I just went on. The wall was broken and cracked. It wasn't a wall I'd seen; it was a series of broken walls, knitted by distance to a smooth front.

"There was no weather to age them, only the faintest stirring of faint, dead winds—winds of neon and helium, inert and uncorroding— as dead and inert as the universe. The city had been dead a score of billions of years. That city was dead for a time ten times longer than the age of our planet today. But nothing destroyed it. Earth was dead— too dead to suffer the racking pains of life. The air was dead, too dead to scrape away metal.

"But the universe itself was dead. There was no cosmic radiation then to level the walls by atomic disintegration. There had been a wall—a single metal wall. Something—perhaps a last wandering meteor—had chanced on it in a time incalculably remote, and broken it. I entered through the great gap. Snow covered the city—soft, white snow. The great red sun stood still just where it was. Earth's restless rotation had long since been stilled—long, long since.

"There were dead gardens above, and I wandered up to them. That was really what convinced me it was a human city, on Earth. There were frozen, huddled heaps that might once have been men. Little fellows with fear forever frozen on their faces huddled helplessly over something that must once have been a heating device. Dead, perhaps, since the last storm old Earth had known, tens of billions of years before.

"I went down. There were vastnesses in that city. It was huge. It stretched forever, it seemed, on and on, in its deadness. Machines, machines everywhere. And the machines were dead, too. I went down,

down where I thought a bit of light and heat might linger. I didn't know then how long death had been there; those corpses looked so fresh, preserved by the eternal cold.

"It grew dark down below, and only through rents and breaks did that bloody light seep in. Down and down, till I was below the level of the dead surface. The white snow persisted, and then I came to the cause of that final, sudden death. I could understand then. More and more I had puzzled, for those machines I'd seen I knew were far and beyond anything we ever conceived—machines of perfection, self-repairing, and self-energizing, self-perpetuating. They could make duplicates of themselves, and duplicate other needed machines; they were intended to be eternal, everlasting.

"But the designers couldn't cope with some things that were beyond even their majestic imaginations—the imaginations that conceived these cities that had lived beyond—a million times beyond—what they had dreamed. They must have conceived some vague future. But not a future when the Earth died, and the Sun died, and even the universe itself died.

"Cold had killed them. They had heating arrangements, devices intended to maintain forever the normal temperature despite the wildest variations of the weather. But in every electrical machine, resistances, balance resistances, and induction coils, balance condensers, and other inductances. And cold, stark, spatial cold, through ages, threw them off. Despite the heaters, cold crept in colder—cold that made their resistance balances and their induction coils super-conductors! That destroyed the city. Superconduction—like the elimination of friction, on which all things must rest. It is a drag and a thing engineers fight forever. Resistance and friction must finally be the rest and the base of all things, the force that holds the great bed-bolts firm and the brakes that stop the machines when needed.

"Electrical resistance died in the cold and the wonderful machines stopped for the replacement of defective parts. And when they were replaced, they, too, were defective. For what months must that constant stop—replacement—start—stop—replacement have gone on before, at last defeated forever, those vast machines must bow in surrender to the inevitable? Cold had defeated them by defeating and removing the greatest obstacle of the engineers that had built them—resistance.

"They must have struggled forever—as we would say—through a hundred billion years against encroaching harshness of nature, forever replacing worn, defective parts. At last, defeated forever, the great power plants, fed by dying atoms, had been forced into eternal idleness and cold. Cold conquered them at last.

"They didn't blow up. Nowhere did I see a wrecked machine; always they had stopped automatically when the defective resistances made it impossible to continue. The stored energy that was meant to re-start those machines after repairs had been made had long since leaked out. Never again could they move, I knew.

"I wondered how long they had been, how long they had gone on and on, long after the human need of them had vanished. For that vast city contained only a very few humans at the end. What untold ages of lonely functioning perfection had stretched behind those at-last-defeated mechanisms?

"I wandered out, to see perhaps more, before the necessary end came to me, too. Through the city of death. Everywhere little self-contained machines, cleaning machines that had kept that perfect city orderly and neat stood helpless and crushed by eternity and cold. They must have continued functioning for years after the great central power stations failed, for each contained its own store of energy, need-ing only occasional recharge from the central stations.

"I could see where breaks had occurred in the city, and clustered about those breaks were motionless repair machines, their mechanisms in positions of work, the debris cleared away and carefully stacked on motionless trucks. The new beams and plates were partly attached, partly fixed and left, as the last dregs of their energy was fruitlessly expended in the last, dying attempts of that great body to repair itself. The death wounds lay unmended.

"I started back up. Up to the top of the city. It was a long climb, an infinite, weary climb up half a mile of winding ramps, past deserted, dead homes; past, here and there, shops and restaurants; past motionless little automotive passenger cars.

"Up and up, to the crowning gardens that lay stiff and brittle and frozen. The breaking of the roof must have caused a sudden chill, for their leaves lay green in sheaths of white, frozen air. Brittle glass, green and perfect to the touch. Flowers blooming in wonderful perfection showed still; they didn't seem dead, but it didn't seem they could be otherwise under the blanket of cold.

"Did you ever sit up with a corpse?" Bob looked up at us—through us. "I had to once, in my little home town where they always did that. I sat with a few neighbors while the man died before my eyes. I knew he must die when I came there. He died—and I sat there all night while the neighbors filed out, one by one, and the quiet settled. The quiet of the dead.

"I had to again. I was sitting with a corpse then. The corpse of a dead world in a dead universe, and the quiet didn't have to settle there; it had settled a billion years ago, and only my coming had stirred those feeble, protesting ghosts of eon-dead hopes of that planet to softly whining protest—protest the wind tried to sob to me, the dead wind of the dead gases. I'll never be able to call them inert gases again. I know. I know they are dead gases, the dead gases of dead worlds.

"And above, through the cracked crystal of the roof, the dying suns looked down on the dead city. I couldn't stay there. I went down. Down under layer after layer of buildings, buildings of gleaming metal that reflected the dim, blood light of the Sun outside in carmine stains. I went down and down, down to the machines again. But even there hopelessness seemed more intense. Again I saw that agonizing struggle of the eternally faithful machines trying to repair themselves once more to serve the masters who were dead for countless eons. I could see it again in the frozen, exhausted postures of the repair machines, stilled forever in their hopeless endeavors, the last poor dregs of energy spilled in fruitless conflict with time.

"It mattered little. Time himself was dying now, dying with the city and the planet and the universe he had killed.

"But those machines had tried so hard to serve again—and failed. Now they could never try again. Even they—the deathless machines—were dead.

"I went out again, away from those machines, out into the illimitable corridors, on the edge of the city. I could not penetrate far before the darkness became as absolute as the cold. I passed the shops where goods untouched by time in this cold, still beckoned those strange humans, but humans for all that; beckoned the masters of the machines that were no more. I vaguely entered one to see what manner of things they used in that time.

"I nearly screamed at the motion of the thing in there, heard dimly through my suit the strangely softened sounds it made in the thin air. I watched it stagger twice—and topple. I cannot guess what manner of storage cells they had—save that they were marvelous beyond imagination. That stored energy that somehow I had released by entering was some last dreg that had remained through a time as old as our planet now. Its voice was stilled forever. But it drove me out—on.

"It had died while I watched. But somehow it made me more curious. I wondered again, less oppressed by utter death. Still, some untapped energy remained in this place, stored unimaginably. I looked more keenly, watched more closely. And when I saw a screen in one office, I wondered. It was a screen. I could see readily it was television of some type. Exploratively, I touched a stud. Sound! A humming, soft sound!

"To my mind leaped a picture of a system of these. There must be—interconnected—a vast central office somewhere with vaster accumulator cells, so huge, so tremendous in their power once, that even the little microfraction that remained was great. A storage system untouchable to the repair machines—the helpless, hopeless power machines.

"In an instant I was alive again with hope. There was a strange series of studs and dials, unknown devices. I pulled back on the stud I had pressed, and stood trembling, wondering. Was there hope?

"Then the thought died. What hope? The city was dead. Not merely that. It had been dead, dead for untold time. Then the whole planet was dead. With whom might I connect? There were none on the whole planet, so what mattered it that there was a communications system?

"I looked at the thing more blankly. Had there been—how could I interpret its multitudinous devices? There was a thing on one side that made me think of a telephone dial for some reason. A pointer over a metal sheet engraved with nine symbols in a circle under the arrow of the pointer. Now the pointer was over what was either the first or the last of these.

"Clumsily, in these gloves, I fingered one of the little symbol buttons inlaid in the metal. There was an unexpected click, a light glowed on the screen, a lighted image! It was a simple projection—but what a projection! A three-dimensional sphere floated, turning slowly before my eyes, turning majestically. And I nearly fell as understanding flooded me abruptly. The pointer was a selector! The studs beneath the pointer I understood! Nine of them. One after the other I pressed, and nine spheres—each different—swam before me.

"And right there I stopped and did some hard thinking. Nine spheres. Nine planets. Earth was shown first—a strange planet to me, but one I knew from the relative size and the position of the pointer must be Earth—then, in order, the other eight.

"Now—might there be life? Yes. In those nine worlds there might be, somewhere.

"Where? Mercury—nearest the Sun? No, the Sun was too dead, too cold, even for warmth there. And Mercury was too small. I knew, even as I thought, that I'd have one good chance, because whatever means they had for communication wouldn't work without tremendous power. If those incredible storage cells had the power for even one shot, they had no more. Somehow I guessed that this apparatus might incorporate no resistance whatever. Here would be only very high frequency alternating current, and only condensers and inductances would be used in it. Super-cooling didn't bother them any. It improved them. Not like the immense direct-current power machinery.

"But where to try? Jupiter? That was big. And then I saw what the solution must be. Cold had ruined these machines, thrown them off by making them perfect conductors. Because they weren't designed to defend themselves against spatial cold. But the machines—if there were any—on Pluto, for instance, must originally have been designed for just such conditions! There it had always been cold. There it always would be cold.

"I looked at that thing with an intensity that should have driven my bare eyesight to Pluto. It was a hope. My only hope. But—how to signal Pluto? They could not understand! If there were any 'they.'

"So I had to guess—and hope. Somehow, I knew, there must be some means of calling the intelligent attendant, that the user might get aid. There was a bank of little studs—twelve of them—with twelve symbols, each different, in the center of the panel, grouped in four rows of three. I guessed. Duodecimal system.

"Talk of the problems of interplanetary communication! Was there ever such a one? The problem of an anachronism in the city of the dead on a dead planet, seeking life somewhere, somehow.

"There were two studs, off by themselves, separate from the twelve—one green, one red. Again I guessed. Each of these had a complex series of symbols on it, so I turned the pointer on the right to Pluto, wavered, and turned it to Neptune. Pluto was farther. Neptune had been cold enough; the machines would still be working there, and it would be, perhaps, less of a strain on the dregs of energy that might remain.

"I depressed the green symbol hoping I had guessed truly, that red still meant danger, trouble and wrongness to men when that was built— that it meant release and cancellation for a wrongly depressed key. That left green to be an operative call signal.

"Nothing happened. The green key alone was not enough. I looked again, pressed the green key and that stud I had first pressed.

"The thing hummed again. But it was a deeper note now, an entirely different sound, and there was a frenzied clicking inside. Then the green stud kicked back at me. The Neptune key under the pointer glowed softly; the screen began to shimmer with a grayish light. And, abruptly, the humming groaned as though at a terrific overload; the screen turned dull; the little signal light under Neptune's key grew dim. The signal was being sent—hurled out.

"Minute after minute I stood there, staring. The screen grew very slowly, very gently duller, duller. The energy was fading. The last stored driblet was being hurled away—away into space. 'Oh,' I groaned, 'it's hopeless—hopeless to—'

"I'd realized the thing would take hours to get to that distant planet, traveling at the speed of light, even if it had been correctly aligned. But the machinery that should have done that through the years probably had long since failed for lack of power.

"But I stood there till the groaning motors ceased altogether, and the screen was as dark as I'd found it, the signal light black. I released the stud then, and backed away, dazed by the utter collapse of an insane hope. Experimentally I pressed the Neptune symbol again. So little power was left now, that only the faintest wash of murky light projected the Neptune image, little energy as that would have consumed.

"I went out. Bitter. Hopeless. Earth's last picture was long, long since painted—and mine had been the hand that spent Earth's last poor resource. To its utter exhaustion, the eternal city had striven to serve the race that created it, and I, from the dawn of time, had, at the end of time, drained its last poor atom of life. The thing was a thing done.

"Slowly I went back to the roof and the dying sun. Up the miles of winding ramp that climbed a half mile straight up. I went slowly—only life knows haste—and I was of the dead.

"I found a bench up there—a carved bench of metal in the midst of a riot of colorful, frozen flowers. I sat down, and looked out across the frozen city to the frozen world beyond, and the freezing red Sun.

"I do not know how long I sat there. And then something whispered in my mind.

" 'We sought you at the television machine.'

"I leaped from the bench and stared wildly about me.

"It was floating in the air—a shining dirigible of metal, ruby-red in that light, twenty feet long, perhaps ten in diameter, bright, warm orange light gleaming from its ports. I stared at it in amazement.

" 'It—it worked!' I gasped.

" 'The beam carried barely enough energy to energize the amplifiers when it reached Neptune, however,' replied the creature in the machine.

"I couldn't see him—I knew I wasn't hearing him, but somehow that didn't surprise me.

" 'Your oxygen has almost entirely given out, and I believe your mind is suffering from lack of oxygen. I would suggest you enter the lock; there is air in here.'

"I don't know how he knew, but the gauges confirmed his statement. The oxygen was pretty nearly gone. I had perhaps another hour's supply if I opened the valves wide—but it was a most uncomfortably near thing, even so.

"I got in. I was beaming, joyous. There was life. This universe was not so dead as I had supposed. Not on Earth, perhaps, but only because they did not choose! They had space ships! Eagerly I climbed in, a strange thrill running through my body as I crossed the threshold of the lock. The door closed behind me with a soft *shush* on its soft gaskets, locked, and a pump whined somewhere for a moment; then the inner door opened. I stepped in—and instantly turned off my alcohol burners. There was heat—heat and light and air!

"In a moment I had the outer lacings loose, and the inner zipper down. Thirty seconds later I stepped out of the suit, and took a deep breath. The air was clean and sweet and warm, invigorating, fresh-smelling, as though it had blown over miles of green sun-warmed fields. It smelled alive, and young.

"Then I looked for the man who had come for me. There was none. In the nose of the ship, by the controls, floated a four-foot globe of metal, softly glowing with a warm, golden light. The light pulsed slowly or swiftly with the rhythm of his thoughts, and I knew that this was the one who had spoken to me.

" 'You had expected a human?' he thought to me. 'There are no more. There have been none for a time I cannot express in your mind. Ah, yes, you have a mathematical means of expression, but no understanding of that time, so it is useless. But the last of humanity was allowed to end before the Sun changed from the original G-0 stage—a very, very long time ago!'

"I looked at him and wondered. Where was he from? Who—what—manner of thing? Was it an armor-encased creature or another of the perfect machines?

"I felt him watching my mind operate, pulsing softly in his golden light. And suddenly I thought to look out of the ports. The dim red suns were wheeling across those ports at an unbelievable rate. Earth was long since gone. As I looked, a dim, incredibly dim, red disk appeared, expanded—and I looked in awe at Neptune.

"The planet was scarcely visible when we were already within a dozen millions of miles. It was a jeweled world. Cities—the great, perfect cities—still glowed. They glowed in soft, golden light above, and below, the harsher brighter blue of mercury vapor lighted them.

"He was speaking again. 'We are machines—the ultimate development of man's machines. Man was almost gone when we came.

" 'With what we have learned in the uncounted dusty mega-years since, we might have been able to save him. We could not then. It was better, wiser that man end than that he sink down as low as he must, eventually. Evolution is the rise under pressure. Devolution is the gradual sinking that comes when there is no pressure—and there is no end to it. Life vanished from this system—a dusty infinity I cannot sort in my memory—my type memory, truly, for I have complete all the memories of those that went before me that I replace. But my memory cannot stretch back to that time you think of—a time when the constellations—

" 'It is useless to try. Those memories are buried under others, and those still buried under the weight of a billion centuries.

" 'We enter'—he named a city; I cannot reproduce that name—'now. You must return to Earth, though, in some seven and a quarter of your days, for the magnetic axis stretches back in collapsing field strains. I will be able to inject you into it, I believe.'

"So I entered that city, the living city of machines, that had been when time and the universe were young.

"I did not know then, that, when all this universe had dissolved away, when the last sun was black and cold, scattered dust in a fragment of a scattered universe, this planet with its machine cities would go on—a last speck of warm light in a long-dead universe. I did not know then.

" 'You still wonder that we let man die out?' asked the machine. 'It was best. In another brief million years he would have lost his high estate. It was best.

" 'Now we go on. We cannot end, as he did. It is automatic with us.'

"I felt it then, somehow. The blind, purposeless continuance of the machine cities I could understand. They had no intelligence, only functions. These machines—these living, thinking, reasoning investigators—had only one function, too. Their function was slightly different: they were designed to be eternally curious, eternally investigating. And their striving was the more purposeless of the two, for theirs could reach no end. The cities fought eternally only the blind destructiveness of nature, wear, decay, erosion.

"But their struggle had an opponent forever, so long as they existed. The intelligent—no, not quite intelligent, but something else— curious machines were without opponents. They had to be curious. They had to go on investigating. And they had been going on in just this way for such incomprehensible ages that there was no longer anything to be curious about. Whoever, whatever designed them gave them function and forgot purpose. Their only curiosity was wonder if there might, somewhere, be something to learn.

"That—and the problem they did not want to solve, but must try to solve, because of the blind functioning of their very structure.

"Those eternal cities were limited. The machines saw now that limit, and so the hope of final surcease in it. They worked on the energy of the atom. But the masses of the suns were yet tremendous. They were dead for want of energy. The masses of the planets were still enormous. But they, too, were dead for want of energy.

"The machines there on Neptune gave me food and drink—strange, synthetic foods and drinks. There had been none on all the planet. They, perforce, started a machine, unused in a billion years and more, that I might eat. Perhaps they were glad to do so. It brought the end appreciably nearer, that vast consumption of mine.

"They used so very, very little, for they were so perfectly efficient. The only possible fuel in all the universe is one—hydrogen. From hydrogen, the lightest of the elements, the heaviest can be built up, and energy released. They knew how to destroy matter utterly to energy, and could do it.

"But while the energy release of hydrogen compounding to the heavy elements is controllable, the destruction of matter to energy is a self-regenerative process. Started once, it spreads while matter lies within its direct, contiguous reach. It is wild, uncontrollable. It is impossible to utilize the full energy of matter.

"The suns had found that. They had burned their hydrogen until it was a remnant so small the action could not go on.

"On all Earth, there was not an atom of free hydrogen—nor was there on any planet, save Neptune. And there the store was not great. I used an appreciable fraction while I was there. That is their last hope. They can see the end, now.

"I stayed those few days, and the machines came and went. Always investigating, always curious. But there is in all that universe nothing to investigate save the one problem they do not want to solve—the problem they are sure they cannot solve.

"The machine took me back to Earth, set up something near me that glowed with a peculiar, steady, gray light. It would fix the magnetic axis on me, on my location, within a few hours. He could not stay near when the axis touched again. He went back to Neptune, but a few millions of miles distant, in this shrunken mummy of the solar system.

"I stood alone on the roof of the city, in the frozen garden with its deceptive look of life.

"And I thought of that night I had spent, sitting up with the dead man. I had come and watched him die. And I sat up with him in the quiet. I had wanted someone, anyone to talk to.

"I did then. Overpoweringly it came to me I was sitting up in the night of the universe, in the night and quiet of the universe, with a dead planet's body, with the dead, ashen hopes of countless nameless generations of men and women. The universe was dead, and I sat up alone—alone in the dead hush.

"Out beyond, a last flicker of life was dying on the planet Neptune—a last false flicker of aimless life, but not life. Life was dead. The world was dead.

"I knew there would never be another sound here. For all the little remainder of time. For this was the dark and the night of time and the universe. It was inevitable, the inevitable end that had been simply more distant in my day—in the long, long-gone time when the stars were mighty lighthouses of a mighty space, not the dying, flickering candles at the head of a dead planet.

"It had been inevitable then; the candles must burn out for all their brave show. But now I could see them guttering low, the last fruitless dregs of energy expiring as the machines below had spent their last dregs of energy in that hopeless, utterly faithful gesture—to attempt the repair of the city already dead.

"The universe had been dead a billion years. It had been. This, I saw, was the last radiation of the heat of life from an already-dead body—the feel of life and warmth, imitation of life by a corpse. Those suns had long and long since ceased to generate energy. They were dead, and their corpses were giving off the last, lingering life heat before they cooled.

"I ran. I think I ran—down away from the flickering, red suns in the sky. Down to the shrouding blackness of the dead city below, where neither light, nor heat, nor life, nor imitation of life bothered me.

"The utter blackness quieted me somewhat. So I turned off my oxygen valves, because I wanted to die sane, even here, and I knew I'd never come back.

"The impossible happened! I came to with that raw oxygen in my face. I don't know how I came—only that here is warmth and life.

"Somewhere, on the far side of that bismuth coil, inevitable still, is the dead planet and the flickering, guttering candles that light the death watch I must keep at the end of time."

# ELIMINATION

John Grantland looked across at his old friend's son intently and unhappily. Finally he sighed heavily and leaned back in his swivel chair. He lighted his pipe thoughtfully. Two slow puffs of smoke rose before he spoke.

"I'm a patent attorney, Dwight Edwards, and I'm at your disposal, as such, to do your bidding and help you to secure that patent you want. As you know, I'm also a civil and commercial law expert of some standing in connection with that work. I can get that patent; I know it is patentable and unpatented as yet. But before I start proceedings, I have to tell you something, Dwight.

"You have enough to live on the rest of your life, a brilliant mind to increase it, a scientific ability to keep you occupied and useful to the world. This invention is not useful to the world. If you were a poor man, I would not hesitate in making the patent applications, because some wiser men, with more money, would buy it up and destroy the thing. But you aren't poor, and you would hold out till the thing was developed and going."

"But—but, Mr. Grantland, it's a thing the world needs! We have a fast-vanishing gasoline reserve—a coal supply being drawn on endlessly and recklessly. We need a new source of power, something to make the immense waterpower supplies in inaccessible regions available. This system would do that, and conserve those vanishing resources, run automobiles, planes, even small factories and homes—"

"It would destroy our greatest resource, the financial structure of the nation. A resource is not a resource unless it is available, and only the system makes it available. The system is more valuable, more important to human happiness than any other resource, because it makes all others available.

"I know your natural desire, to develop and spread that system for canning and distributing electricity. It's a great invention. But—"

"But," the younger man said somewhat bitterly, "you feel that any

167

really great, any important invention should be destroyed. There must be, you are saying, no real improvement, only little gadgets. There must be no Faradays who discover principles, only Sam Browns who invent new can openers and better mousetraps."

Grantland laid down his pipe and leaned back in his chair silently. Bitterly, the younger man was gathering his papers.

"Dwight," said Grantland at length, "I think I'll do best if I tell you of one invention that I have in my files here. I have shown these papers to just one other man than the men who made them. Curiously, he was your father. He—"

"My father? But he was not an inventor—he was a psychiatrist, utterly uninterested—"

"He was vitally interested in this. He saw the apparatus they made, and he helped me dismantle it, secretly, and destroy the tube Hugh Kerry and Robert Darnell made. That was twenty-two years ago, and it was something of a miracle I had, at the age of thirty-six, the sense to do that.

"I'm going to tell you mighty vague things and mighty vague principles, because you're too keen. It isn't very safe to tell you this, but I believe you will keep a promise. You must swear two things before I tell you the story: First, that you will not put that surprisingly acute mind of yours to work on what I say, because I cannot tell what clues I may give. I understand too little to know how much I understood; second, of course, that you will not spread this unpleasant story."

The young man put down his papers, looked curiously at John Grantland. "I agree to that, Mr. Grantland."

Grantland stuffed his pipe thoughtfully in silence. "Hugh Kerry and Bob Darnell were one of those fortuitous miracles, where the right combination came together. Hugh Kerry was the greatest mathematician the world has seen, at thirty-two."

"I have heard of him; I've used his analytical methods. He died at thirty-three, didn't he?"

"I know," said Grantland. "The point is—so did Bob Darnell. Bob Darnell was something like Edison, on a higher level. Edison could translate theory into metal and glass and matter. Darnell could do that, but he didn't work with steel and copper and glass. He worked with atoms and electrons and radiation as familiarly as Edison worked with metal. And Darnell didn't work from theory; he worked from mathematics that no theory could be defined for.

"That was the pair the shifting probabilities of space time brought together—and separated. You've never heard of Darnell, because he did only one thing, and that one thing is on paper there, in that steel vault. In the first place, it is in a code that is burned into my memory, and not on paper. In the second place, it is safe because every equation in it is wrong, because we couldn't code equations easily, and the book that gave them right is out of print, forgotten.

"They came into my office first because they lived nearby, and I'd gone to the same school. I hadn't much of a reputation then, of course. That was when you were just about getting into the sixth grade, Dwight—a good number of years ago.

"They had the tube then. They called it the PTW tube—Probability Time Wave. They'd been trying to make a television set that would see through walls—a device that would send out its own signals and receive them back as images.

"They went wrong, something about trying for the fourth-dimensional approach and slipping into a higher dimension. They said that Einstein's curved space theory was wrong, and it was the ten-dimensional multiple theory that was right.

"But you said something about Faradays and Sam Browns. That invention I suppressed was something so enormous, Dwight, that anything that ever has or ever will be invented is picayunish squabbling beside it. It was the greatest tower looming on the road of progress. It loomed above all other things as the sun looms greater than earth. It was the greatest thing that ever was or will be, because it necessarily incorporated the discovery of everything that ever will be or can be."

"What—what could be so great? The power of the atom—"

"That was one of the lesser things it incorporated, Dwight. It would have meant that, in a year or so, and the secret of gravity, of interplanetary, interstellar flight, the conquest of age, and eternal life. Everything you can dream of, John, and all the things that any man ever will dream of.

"They knew all that when they came to me. They explained it all, and because I couldn't believe—they showed me. You cannot conceive of such a thing—anything—so inconceivably far-reaching in scope? I'm not surprised. They told me what I have told you, and but that they said it all in such quiet, assured voices, with such perfect and absolute confidence, I'd have called them liars and put it down to the vain boasting of the Sam Brown you mentioned, with his mighty new mousetrap and his miraculous can opener—the invention of the ages.

"It's simple when you know the answer, to see how true was their every claim. Their television slipped. It slipped aside, into some higher dimension, they guessed, and instead of penetrating the walls and the buildings through that fourth dimension they sought, they decided it had slipped out and beyond space and time, and looked back to review it, a mighty pageant of incredible history—the history that was to be.

"You see, in that was the incredible and infinite scope of the thing, because it showed, in the past, all that had been, the infinite sweep and march of all time from the creation to the present.

"But then the ordered ranks broke, for, from the present to the other end of infinity, no single thing or any circumstance is immutably fixed. Their PTW tube caught and displayed every possibility that was ever to exist. And somewhere in that vast sweep of probability, every possible thing existed. Somewhere, the wildest dream of the wildest optimist was, and became fact.

"On that screen tube I saw the sun born, and on it I saw the sun die a million deaths. I saw them move planets, and I saw the planets moving in birth. I saw life created, and I saw it created again in test tubes and laboratories. I saw man arise—and I saw men and women more perfect in body and mind than the dream of Praxiteles created from acetylene and ammonia. Because somewhere in the realms of possibility, remote or so near as to be probable, those dreams of every scientist came true, and with them, the unguessed dreams of unguessable intellects.

"Hugh Kerry and Bob Darnell came to me when the thing was new, and they faintly conceived of its possibilities. That was in 1950. And in five days the world would have known and been at their feet— but for two things—three, really. First, because the thing, they knew, was imperfect, and, what they didn't know, was severely limited. Second, because they had begun to trace their own life tracks, and were worried, even then. I caught some of that worry from them and held back. I never let them cast for my life tracks. Today I do not know what will come tomorrow. Third, and what was perhaps the determining reason, they were still poor, but growing rich rapidly by the information that machine brought them of the little, everyday things that were to be two days ahead.

"You could pile up an enormous fortune, Dwight, if you just knew with a probability of eighty-five on their scale of a hundred, what tomorrow and tomorrow would bring. They did, and first the number pool hated them and refused their business, then the betting rings refused their bets, and finally, even the stock market began to act unfavorably. Because they won, of course.

"But before then, they had begun to forget that, and concentrated on the life tracks the machine showed them.

"I said the machine was limited. It was limited by two factors: one was the obvious difficulty of seeing the forest and the shape of the forest when in the middle of it. They were in the middle of the parade, and there they must stay. They could not see the near future clearly, for the near forest was hidden by the trees. The far future they could see like a vast marching column that split and diverged slowly. They saw no individual figure, only the blended mass of the march to infinity.

"At a year, the parade began to blend, and the features were lost by the establishment of the trend. But, at two days, two weeks, their screen showed a figure blurred and broken by the splitting images that broke away, each following its own line of possible development.

"Look. A vision of me in the future by only ten minutes will show me in a thousand lifecourses. Primarily, there are two; I may live, or die. But even those two instantly became a thousand, for I may die now, or at any later instant. I may die by the falling of the building or the stoppage of my heart, by an assassin's bullet, by the knife of a disgruntled inventor. They are improbable, and their future images would, on Bob Darnell's screen, have been dim, and ghostly. The world might end in that ten minutes, so destroy me. That must be there, for it is possible, a very faint image, so shadowy it is scarcely visible.

"If I live, a thousand courses are open: I may sit here, smoking peacefully; the telephone may ring; a fire may break out. Probably I shall continue to sit, and smoke—so strong and solid on the screen is an image of myself sitting, smoking. But shading from it ever lighter black and gray to faintest haziness, is each of those other possibilities.

"That confused them, made exact work difficult. To get their reports of the markets, they had to determine with an absolute rigor that the next day's paper should be put on a certain stand, spread to the page they wanted, and, come hell or high water, they would yet put that paper there, and not move it so much as a hairbreadth. The image became probable, highly probable. Its ghost images faded. They read it.

"And there's one other fault. I know the reason I'd rather not give it. Just take this for one of the facts of that invention that by the very stuff of space, time shall never be overcome. The place they might determine, or the time, with absolute exactitude, but never would they ever know both for any given event.

"And the third day they cast for their future tracks. The near future was a confused haze, but I was with them when they sought in the future far enough for the haze to go. Laughing, elated, they cast a hundred years ahead, when, Bob Darnell said, 'I'll be a man with my long white beard looped through my trousers and over my shoulders for suspenders!'

"They started their machine, and set the control for probabilities in a very low range, for the chance of Bob Darnell's living to one hundred and thirty-three years of age was remote. They had a device on their machine that would automatically sweep the future, till it found a lane that was occupied, a track that was not dead, in which Bob Darnell still lived. It was limited in speed—but not greatly, for each second it looked down five hundred thousand tracks."

"Reaction speed of a photocell," said the young man slowly. "I know."

"Dwight, try not to know," pleaded Grantland. "I mean to give no such hints—but only what is needed to understand."

"If you say two times two—can you expect me to omit a mental four?" asked the young man. "Five hundred thousand a second is the reaction of a photocell. What is there in this invention that demands its suppression?"

"That is part of it. Five hundred thousand tracks a second it swept, and an hour passed, and another, and Darnell laughed at it.

" 'I guess I'm not due for a long, full life,' he said.

"And just then the machine clicked his answer. When we saw the image on the screen, we thought the range was wrong, for the Bob Darnell on the screen was a healthier, stronger, sounder man than the Bob Darnell beside me.

"He was tanned and lean and muscular; his hair was black as night, and his hands were muscular and firm-fleshed. He looked thirty, not a hundred and thirty. But his eyes were old, they were old as the hills, and keen with a burning vigor as they seemed to concentrate on us. Slowly he smiled, and firm, even teeth appeared between his lips.

"Darnell whistled softly. 'They've licked old age,' he almost whispered.

"Evidently they had. Hugh spoke. 'They probably found it in some future age with this machine,' he whispered tensely. 'You're one keen old gentleman, Bob.'

" 'But that's not a good chance for life apparently,' Darnell said. 'I wonder how I can choose the course that leads me there?'

" 'Live a clean life, drink nothing but water,' Kerry said. 'Turn on, O time, in your flight. Let's see what else we have.'

"Darnell started the machine again—and it stopped almost instantly. One of Darnell's other tracks appeared. He'd gotten there that time with no outside aid, and he was horrible. 'Ah-h-h—' said Bob distastefully. 'I like the other way better. That face—turn it along, Hugh.'

"The mean, rheumy-eyed, incredibly seamed face disappeared; the screen went blank. And it stayed blank. Those were Bob's only tracks at that age. 'Not too bad,' he said, 'though I didn't think I had a chance in the world.'

" 'Let's see what we get at ten years,' Hugh suggested. 'That's more to the point.'

" 'We'll wait all night getting through them,' objected Bob. 'But we'll take a few. Better start with about seventy probability. Ten years is long enough for me to die in, perhaps, so that ought to be fairly high.'

"They started again. And it ran for an hour—two hours. Bob Darnell had stopped laughing now, because he didn't like that blank and stubborn assurance that he had a mighty slim chance of living ten years more. Two hours and a half and it was beginning to tell on Darnell. 'Looks like I guessed too high,' was all he said.

"Then we got a track. It was Bob Darnell, all right, but his face was round and soft and flaccid, and he lay on a soft rubber floor on his back, with a little pair of trunks on, and he was grinning senselessly with a blank, stupid face at a male nurse who was feeding him some kind of gruel that he slobbered and spilled down his fat, soft cheeks. There wasn't any mind at all behind the full, round eyes.

"It took us about ten seconds to take in that scene that was something like ten years in the future. Then Bob spoke, and his voice was flat and strained. 'I'd say that was *dementia praecox,* and I'd say that damned machine was wrong, because I'm not going to be that way. I'm going to be dead first. It's the nastiest form of insanity I can think of offhand. Start that thing up, Hugh.'

"The trails got closer together there. We got another one in half an hour, and all that half hour we stood in absolute silence in the dim laboratory, while the machine clicked and hummed, and the screen writhed and flickered with blankness, because neither of us could think of anything to say to Bob, and Bob was too busy thinking to say anything.

"Then the machine stopped again. It didn't take so long to understand that scene. Hugh started it on again. It found seven trails like that in the next hour. Then it found a sane trail, more or less, but it was a Bob Darnell who had gone through insanity. He wasn't actually insane, but his nervous system was broken.

" 'Evidently you recover,' I said, trying to be hopeful.

"Bob grinned—unpleasantly. He shook his head. 'You don't recover. If you do—it wasn't *dementia praecox. Praecox* is an insanity that is simply a slow disintegration of the mind; it gets tired of worry and trouble, and decides the easiest way out is to go back to childhood, when there weren't any worries or troubles. But it goes back and discovers again the worries children have, and keeps going back and back, seeking the time when there were no troubles—and generally is stopped by pneumonia or tuberculosis or hemorrhage of the atrophied brain.

" 'But it never recovers, and it's the most ghastly form of insanity there is, because it is hopeless. It turns a strong, sound man into a helpless, mindless infant. It's not like idiocy, because an idiot never grew up. This grows up, all right—and then grows down, lower than anything normal could be.

" 'That's just one path where I had a nervous breakdown and got over it. That one—why, it might lead to the one-hundred-and-thirty-four-year-old track. But just—go on, Hugh.'

"Hugh went on—on and on, and we found three sound, sane tracks.

"I don't have to go into more detail. I think you can understand Darnell's feelings. We tried at five years, and a few more tracks showed up. At two years, that first night, we found eighteen tracks, and eleven of them were insane, and seven sane. We named the two-year tracks with the Greek alphabet.

"The track Bob wanted, the long track that took him to a hundred and thirty-four, and beyond, clear out to a point where he merged in the march of the infinite future, was his tau track. The alpha, beta, gamma, delta—all those were quite insane, and quite horrible. That meant that, by far, the greater probability led to the unpleasant tracks.

" 'Hugh, I guess, it's your turn, if you want to try,' said Bob finally. 'We'll have to check these more carefully later.'

" 'I think I do want to know,' Hugh said. 'But maybe Grantland would like to go now. He can't be here all the time.'

" 'No, thank Heaven,' I said, 'I can't, and I don't want to know my tracks. Bob, I think one of the best ways to strike that tau track is to destroy this machine now.'

"Bob stared at me, then grinned lopsidedly. 'I can't now, John. For one thing, I have no right to; it means too much to the world. For another, I've got to find what decisions will put me on that long track. I made this thing because I knew I couldn't live to see that long march we've already seen, leading on to the infinity even this can't reach. Now, by all that is to be, I've got to find how I can reach that time!'

" 'By all that is to be, Bob, I know in my bones you won't, if this machine endures.'

"Bob grinned and shook his head at me.

" 'I can't, John,' he said.

"And Hugh started the machine down his trails. He'd set it for a hundred years, like Darnell, at a slightly higher figure than had disclosed the far end of Bob's tau track. We picked up Hugh's pretty quickly, and he too looked sound and healthy. But he had no second trail—one chance to live to be a hundred and thirty-three.

" 'I'm about as good on long life as you, Bob,' he said, 'if somebody helps me, but I guess I can't make it alone.'

" 'Well, I'm not interested in going it alone myself,' Bob replied. 'It's not a hell of a lot better than some of those other things we've seen. Let's get closer to home.'

"They tried the ten-year track. And on Hugh Kerry's trails, the machine clicked and hummed for a long, long time, and Kerry began to look paler and paler in the light from that wavering screen, because he didn't even have a chance of insane life.

" 'Let's leave it for the night,' said Hugh finally. 'It's eight o'clock, and I'm hungry as a wolf. We can leave it running on the recorder, and come back after supper, maybe.'

"We came back after supper. It was ten, then. And the machine was still clicking and humming.

"We went home for the night. You see, reasonably enough, Hugh had assumed that he had a fair chance of living ten years, but he didn't, of course. The machine was examining nearly two billion chances every hour it ran—and finding them blank.

"Hugh was down at seven the next morning. I got there at ten and found Bob and Hugh sitting very quiet, trying to smoke. The machine was still humming and clicking, and there wasn't a thing at all on the recorder.

" 'Looks like I'm not slated for a long life,' Hugh greeted me unhappily, trying to grin. 'It hasn't found—thank Heaven!' The machine stopped suddenly.

"It was Hugh, quite hale and sound, his hair a bit gray, his eyes a bit sunken, his face a bit lined, but sane—and sound.

" 'That's what we called the tau track,' said Bob after a minute of examination. 'You make a hundred-year mark on the first try.'

" 'In other words,' said Kerry softly, 'I've got about as much chance of living ten years as I have of living a hundred. Yes. That's a good way to put it. A hell of a chance. What does it say at two years?'

"It took a long time, because we didn't want to start on the low probabilities, of course, and there just weren't any good ones. We didn't find anything very quickly. Eventually we knew he had three sane and one insane at ten years, and eleven altogether at two years— three insane. And they were all of them so far down in probability, they started working right away.

"But the thing that brought home the need of haste was that when we looked, just for a moment, at Bob's two-year trails—two of the sane, and five insane trails had vanished! They had been eliminated by decisions made since the previous evening. I knew, Bob and Hugh knew, what the decision was, but we didn't say anything. He had decided to look at Hugh's trails in that time, and found those few trails. They cut off at one year, we found, so they had to work on them. That, you see, reduced Bob Darnell's chances of finding the right trail—the tau trail that wasn't in tau position any more, but, thank Heaven, still existed.

" 'It's not so hard, though,' said Kerry. 'We need only look to see what developments we make tomorrow, and tomorrow's tomorrow, to find how to perfect this machine, to eliminate the near-future images. We'll get it.'

"I had my business that I was trying to build up, so I had to leave them. I couldn't see them for five days, because I had to appear out in St. Louis, and stop over in Washington.

"When I got back I went around to see them, though it was nearly eleven o'clock. They were at it.

" 'We've made some progress,' Hugh said. 'We've both mapped our trails carefully till they vanish in the near-future mists. We'll be able to hit that long trail for Bob fairly easily, but—I'm afraid I'll have to give mine up,' he said, his face twitching just a little.

" 'H-has your long trail been eliminated by a decision?' I asked.

" 'Hm-m-m—in a sense. I located one of its decision points by luck. It's only about a month away, apparently. It is less, I believe, but we can't tell. I took a snap view of the trail, and hit what is evidently a decision point on it. What you didn't know is that twenty-seven years of that long trail is hopeless paralysis in pain. I apply for euthanasia four times unsuccessfully. Since I know where that trail leads, and still apply for that—why, I think I don't want it, anyway. But the trouble is, really, that the decision point I snapped, by sheer luck, is an automobile accident.

" 'We've been trying to take instantaneous exposures of the trails, in the near future, to eliminate the blurring. We can do it by using a blurred image to get space coordinates and snapping the controls into lock position. The time register is automatically thrown out of gear, so we have only a vague idea of time. We know it's this year—but whether it's late this month, or early next, I don't know. We can't know.'

" 'But the accident—'

" 'I'd go through with it, perhaps—if I had some control. But Tom Phillips is driving. If I drive, of course, that's a different track altogether. He has my fate in his hands—and I can't bring myself to take it.'

" 'Have you told Tom?' I asked.

" 'Not yet, but I'm expecting him over. I sent a note around that he ought to get today or tomorrow, I—'

"The telephone rang, Hugh answered it. Tom Phillips was on the other end. He had the note, luckily, as he was packing then to drive up to Boston. He wanted Hugh to come over and tell him the story, or whatever it was Hugh wanted him for. Naturally, it would do no good if Tom couldn't see the machine; so, by dint of nearly fifteen minutes arguing, Hugh got him to come over.

" 'Whew—if I hadn't been so afraid of riding with Tom, I would have gone over, at that,' said Hugh, mopping his head. 'He's a stubborn cuss when he gets an idea. I hope I can—eh? What, Bob?'

"Bob Darnell, in the laboratory, had called something.

" 'What is it, Bob?' Hugh asked, going over.

"I went over, too. 'Oh, hello, John. I didn't know you were back. Patent go through all O. K.?'

" 'Fine,' I answered, 'Everything's in order. What was it you wanted to tell Hugh?'

" 'Yes—just told me. He had just finished calling Tom Phillips when you called him.'

" 'What! God! I called him—because his long track vanished while I was looking at it then! That was a decision point!'

"We looked eagerly. It was gone, all right. And suddenly Hugh stiffened. 'Bob,' he said, 'I'm afraid; I'm scared as hell—because maybe that was a decision point, because I didn't go over for Tom. I'm going to—'

"He went, too—to call up Tom Phillips. But he was too late then, and he never got him. Tom hadn't seen a gravel truck smashing down a side street, hidden from him by a stopped trolley car.

" 'I was supposed to go over for him,' was all Hugh could say. 'But how was I to know? We didn't know the time accurately. We couldn't, could we, Bob? I didn't know—I didn't know—'

"But to the day of his death, he could not shake the feeling that he had brought Tom Phillips out to be killed, almost deliberately. It meant nothing that he had called him to warn him. He had called him out to death. He had been slow in his warning.

"A week later they had mapped their future trails; they had every decision point mapped, and noted; they knew every move that they must make to take them down those trails that led to that maximum of life each was granted. Every decision, every turn and branch of the road that led to happiness, success—except those they must make in the next ten months.

"From a high peak they could see the road that led off across the broad fields of the open country to the distant city of life they sought. But the tangled, snarled traffic of the nearby city where they were, obscured the little alleys and twisting, crooked streets of the near future in an inextricable maze.

" 'We'll get it, though,' Hugh said confidently. 'We're getting it better and better now. We've found a system that will work, we think. You see, if today we can see what we will develop tomorrow, we will be a day ahead, and then if we see what comes the day after, we'll be two days. In a week we should have the thing solved. It is only that it becomes so annoying to remember—this may be the decision day, and I do not know it. And Bob is working hard to find my decisions, because I have so few lines beyond this December, apparently. He has plenty of sound lines leading on through next year.

" 'That seems to make my case the more imperative, for I do not want to die when life is so near. Yet we cannot know even this, for the paths twine and twist, and it may be that my decision point to the long trail I seek is in December. And, similarly, it may be that the decision point Bob seeks—is tomorrow. We cannot guess, we cannot know, who is in the more desperate position, the more immediately threatened state.

" 'But tomorrow we will advance faster, because we have determined as inflexibly as our determination to place that newspaper on the stand, that we shall hereafter, invariably, put on the blackboard there the discoveries of the day, and the progress made. That, we think, will clear up the images.'

" 'Will clear up the images?' I asked in some surprise. Because, you remember, Dwight, that it instantly cleared up the newspaper images.

"Hugh looked a little worried.

" 'Will,' he replied. 'You see, it didn't so very much at first, for some reason. I can't quite— But at any rate, by watching our progress that we are to make, we will make swift advance to the discovery of the secret, and long life.'

"It seemed so clear, so true, so logical. If they could steal the inventions of a million years in the future, could they not spy on their own progress of the next day and the next? So simple, so logical an advance.

"But they missed one thing. There were many, many things they could try, and though they inflexibly determined that they would write on the blackboard the progress of the day, and did, the blackboard was blurred white and gray on the screen. For each of the thousand things they might try was there, you see, and from the first day two probabilities entered: that they deciphered, and tried one of those courses, and that they did not decipher the next day's work, and had to develop it directly.

"Three times they read that blackboard. Each time the next day's blackboard read: 'Did work shown by future image yesterday.' So, when they did read it, remember, they saw only a day's work done, and the day's work was yet to be done, though they knew what it must be. If you are a repairman and know that tomorrow you must change the clutch plates and put in new transmission gears, that knowledge does not eliminate the operation.

"They thought it might spare them the blind alleys. But one of those day's work was a blind alley that they were forced to rip out the next.

"I was called over one day, the third time they read that blackboard, and they showed it to me. There were many, many images on it, and only one was legible, because it was very, very brief, and written very large.

"Hugh smiled lopsidedly at me when I came in. 'Well, John, I think we've found one of my decision points,' he said.

" 'What! Got those near futures cleared up?' I was immensely pleased. They'd advanced a lot, you know, since I first saw the instrument. Their near-future images were sometimes quite readable; their selectivity had been increased a thousandfold. But there was still a mistiness, a sort of basic mistiness.

" 'No,' Darnell interrupted. 'We read the blackboard. Come—you can see it.'

"I did. It was quite easy to read, because Hugh had always been the one to write on the board, and his writing was cramped and neat. On many of those images the writing was cramped and neat. But on many others it was a broad, looping scrawl—Darnell's hand. It said simply: 'Hugh Kerry killed today. May God have mercy on me.'

"I swallowed hard before I spoke. 'There's a lot of images there, Hugh.'

" 'Yes, but it's a decision point. Bob has sworn, and determined by all that's holy, he'll write the full facts on the case tomorrow, and not that message. The message still sticks, and none other has appeared. It's a decision point—and may God have mercy on me, too, for I don't know what that decision must be. It won't even tell me whether to stay indoors here or stay out of here.'

"Dwight, that is the thing that pressed and pressed on them. It was like the old Chinese water torture, and each day was a drop of water that fell, and they were bound to the wheel of time that cannot stop or be stopped. They had now the vision to see across that wheel to another day and another age—but they could not slow that progress through time, nor speed it by a whit.

"The days must come, and they must go, for all their knowledge of time. And the sun that day sank, as it had a thousand thousand thousand times before, and would a thousand thousand thousand times again, and it rose on a new day. No force, nor will, nor wish could stay that progress; the day must come. And Hugh could not know, because the message was so stubborn, whether his decision lay in that laboratory or out in the open.

"I could not leave them. Yet I had to, because time still went on, and the courts went on. I left, on a case I know not the faintest detail of, save that I fought it with a bitter determination to win, and somehow won it.

"It was four thirty when I got back to the laboratory. Bob Darnell met me, and his face was white and tense. 'Hugh?' I asked.

" 'He's gone over to Teckno Products for some apparatus,' said Darnell quietly. 'He wouldn't let me go. He ought to be back. Come into the laboratory. I've been watching his trails.'

"I went with him into the laboratory where the rustle and hum of the machine, and the flickering, greenish light of the screen made it seem a sorcerer's lair of necromancy. Bob looked at the screen, then he turned to me with an unpleasant grin. 'It's blank, John. Those are Hugh Kerry's trails one year from today,' he said. He walked over to the blackboard very slowly, like an automaton, and picked up a piece of chalk. Slowly he erased the words on the slate, and in a round, broad scrawl he wrote: 'Hugh Kerry killed today. May God have mercy on me.'

" 'Bob,' I said, 'Bob—that's the message you swore you wouldn't write. Erase it—wait till we know, till we know what happened to him so we can write the details. That may—'

" 'Save him?' asked Bob bitterly. 'What matter now? He's dead now. But if you like, we can find the details. But nothing will do any good at all, because he's dead now, anyway. What good will it do to change that message? He's already taken the wrong trail, and reached the end, John. But I'll find out—'

"He called up the police. He asked if they knew what had happened to Hugh Kerry, how he had been killed.

"The telephone was a noisy one, always had been, and I heard the answer where I stood. 'Hugh Kerry, eh? I have no report on anyone by that name. What makes you think he's been killed, and how?'

" 'He must be dead by this time,' said Bob. 'Ask your men, please. I—what?'

" 'The other desk man,' said the man on the telephone, 'just got a call, and he says if you're looking for a guy named Hugh Kerry, he was just killed by a girl driver at Fourteenth and Seventh. He stepped out from behind a parked car right— Say, who's calling?'

" 'Thanks, officer. Robert Darnell calling, from One Forty-three East Eighty-seventh. I'm going right over to the scene—'

"We went over in my car, got there pretty quickly, but the ambulance had already taken Hugh Kerry and the girl driver away. We heard from her later. Hugh had simply walked right into the side of her car, practically tripped over her running board. She was in the hospital with hysterics then. She kept saying he looked so surprised— as though somebody had suddenly explained something to him. Somebody had, you see—a surprisingly easy answer to a complex problem.

"Bob Darnell tried to get his car, that Hugh had driven over to Teckno Products in, but the police picked him up. I wasn't a criminal lawyer, and I had to go downtown and get Bill Poole, a classmate of mine, to come and help him out.

"It was a bad problem, too, we found out. Three weeks before, Hugh Kerry had taken out a one-year-term insurance policy for a hundred thousand dollars. And it had a double-indemnity clause in case of accidental death. The insurance company was fighting for their two hundred thousand dollars, and the police were fighting for a murder charge. Because, you remember, Bob Darnell had said over the telephone: 'He must be dead by this time.'

"The time machine was too wild. We couldn't get any clear images to show them anything to speak of. But, finally, they had to let Bob go, because it's awfully difficult to prove murder when a man is killed in an automobile accident at one end of town, and a man you're accusing is calling the police station from the other. And they never tried to involve the poor girl who was the direct instrument of death.

"I went back with Bob Darnell, when they released him. I was with him when he started up the machine, and looked at his trails. There were only five left, because Hugh Kerry's trails were gone, now, and they had crossed and intertwined with Bob Darnell's, of course. The long trail was there, and one other sane trail—that ended in three years. The other three were all insane trails.

"Bob went to work harder than ever, and because I'd gotten behind in my work while Bob was tied up, I, too, had to go to work harder than ever. It was three weeks before I could even get around to the laboratory.

"Bob Darnell greeted me at the door when I came. He had one of those slip chains on the door, and opened it only a crack when he let me in. 'Those insurance people kept bothering me,' he explained. 'They want to see what I'm doing all the time. They aren't going to, though.'

"I looked at him, and his eyes and forehead were screwed up in worry and concentration.

" 'John,' he said finally, 'you know it's too bad Hugh went after that apparatus Teckno was making. I got it and put it in, and they didn't make it right at all. I think maybe they're trying to make me order more so they can see how this works. I shouldn't have told the police about my chronoscope. But I put the apparatus in, and I think I got it in right, and, John, it makes the near-future images better, but what do you think—it cuts out some of the long-range tracks. It won't show them all now.'

"His voice seemed quite annoyed, and rather petulant, I thought.

" 'It won't?' I said, quite softly, I think. 'Let me see.'

" 'No. It won't show them right. There are five. I saw 'em myself. But this thing won't work right. It cuts out four of them, and only shows one little short one. There's something wrong with it. I figured out what once, but I can't seem to remember any more. But I don't like Teckno anymore, and I won't buy anything from 'em any more. I'm going to make 'em take this back.

" 'Help me disconnect it, John? You remember how the chronoscope works; I can't seem to find the connections since I put in the wrong stuff Teckno made. I've been so worried, John, with the insurance company bothering me, and this not working right.'

" 'It isn't working right, eh?' I asked. 'There's only one trail left? Well, you know, Bob, they change.'

" 'No. There ought to be five trails. I know, cause I saw 'em,' he said decisively.

"So I went into the laboratory with him, and I looked at the screen, and there was only one trail, as he had said. It was as I had expected since I entered the house that day. I told Bob then that I couldn't help him any more, but that I had a friend who might be able to, though I wasn't sure. So I went away and brought your father, Dwight, who was, as I told you, the only other man who ever saw the chronoscope or the drawings of it.

"He helped me take it apart and break up the parts that might have been revealing."

John Grantland paused a long minute, his head sunk forward on his chest. He raised it slowly and added, as though an after-thought: "We were glad it was a very short track. It could have been so long—"

Dwight Edwards rose slowly, dropping his papers on Grantland's desk. He sighed as he turned away. "The world doesn't need all its Faradays, does it?" And as he walked through the door, "You'll take care of those papers for me—"

# FRICTIONAL LOSSES

"But why, Hugh, do you insist on exploring always in these worst of the ruins for what you want?" asked Ban wearily. "These sharp-edged glass fragments, and the thick ashes—surely there are other parts of this junk heap that would satisfy you. I can see little difference, save that some parts are churned more than others, and this is one of the worst places."

Hugh Thompson shook his heavy, gray head slowly and straightened his aching back very slowly for he was getting old now, and the living conditions he endured were very hard for him. His back felt fragile, breakable. "No, Tom. You are only thirty-two; you do not remember. New York was divided into many districts. Perhaps you can remember that they used to dig here for the food supplies? That was because this was a food-market district, too. But right in this section once was a great number of stores devoted to radio and electrical equipment. It is not as badly churned as you think. And here is our best hope, though faint enough it is."

Ban Norman looked about doubtfully. Great mounds and heaps of semifused and disintegrated rock and metal sprawled as far as the eye could reach in one direction, to the river's edge in the other. Here and there a crumbling remnant of a tower remained, balanced by an occasional hundred-foot pock mark that, walled with glassy, fused granite, was floored now with a thin layer of muddy water and scum. The white masses of cracked stone were streaked with dark red, like the dried blood of the buildings they had been from the slowly melting iron skeletons.

"The Granthee treated this section to an exceptionally heavy lashing. Why expect anything so delicate as the radio tubes you seek, to survive?"

"Because we can do nothing else, Ban," said the old man, patiently. "I was no older than you are when this happened, and I first attempted to do what we have done for these thirty years now. Our little station has failed again, and all the people that have so faithfully sought to keep this thin thread of civilization are wondering again if the final break in the thread has come for us. Boston is gone now, has been for three months. Cincinnati is lost, we know, because Randolph Balling could get no man or woman to learn from him before he died.

"We are losing, Ban, and I hate it so. Man tried so hard, for so long—and, now, in three decades—oh, it is so wrong to give up hope."

Ban sighed, and moved toward the shade of some great tumbled blocks. "Let us eat, while we rest and talk. What was this building?"

Hugh looked about him, at the great blocks, thrown down in a moment of petulance like a scattered child's toys. He tried to determine his location by the rotting remains of the docks, the tumbled heaps behind, the Jersey shore across the river. Slowly he shook his head. "It is thirty years, Ban," he said, seating himself gingerly, and pulling the hard, blackish bread from the bag of woven reeds he carried. "I am forgetting how old New York looked. It has been so long I have seen it thus, it seems it was never otherwise. But there were few high buildings here, and this was evidently a very large one. It may have been the New York Telephone Company building."

Ban looked about the ruins and shrugged. "I see no cables, or wires."

"No. But this was an executive building, and the central offices represented little of the equipment. It would be lost in this jumble. Besides, when the clans formed they stripped every fragment of copper they could find from every building, to make pans. They could work copper more readily than any other metal, and all exposed cables were taken. There was lead, too, for the sling shots. We are fortunate, really, so much of the radio equipment was deeply buried for that would have been destroyed in those first years."

"But the buried equipment was ruined so that was no gain."

"It was not all ruined. And we can be thankful that much of the equipment had been refined to a ruggedness that resisted the strains. The metal tubes, for instance. They were but a few years old when the Granthee came. Had the old glass tubes been all we had, it would have been few, indeed, we could have salvaged."

Ban looked about sourly. "I can believe that. What was it that destroyed this section so thoroughly?"

"The atomic bombs. Some few of our own. That great crater I have shown you in the old park was one of our own, set off when the Granthee ship landed there. You cannot find even a fragment of that ship; even the metal of which it was made was ruined in that flare. The atomic bombs flared rather than exploded."

"If we had the atomic power they had, why was it that they, with their little force of a hundred ships, came so near to conquering the whole world of man?"

"We did not have atomic power. We developed, toward the end, atomic explosives, which are very different. Grant Hubert has shown you explosives, and you know how different they are from fuels. We had explosives, but before we could learn to use atomic fuels, it was too late. The men and the laboratories and the machine shops were, it seems, gone.

"The Granthee ships appeared in April, over Russia, Chicago, Brazil and Central Africa. In July the thing was a thing done. They attacked, with their fever ray—an intense radio beam—that heated men like an intense fever, till they died in seconds. They wiped out life in Africa in a few days, and they wiped out all life in Asia, nearly a billion humans, within two weeks. Japan was armed as a modern nation, and withstood the attack for a week, and destroyed seven of the Granthee ships. She might have done more, but for the Japan Deep."

"The Japan Deep—"

"Yes. Japan was an island empire, of men somewhat similar to John Lun, yellowish, small men. But they had learned the ways of the whites, and fought more stubbornly, more heroically, really, than the others. They were a fatalistic race. They conceived the idea, and used it first, of the torpedo ships. I have shown you the wrecked airplane near Newark. They had many, smaller, but far swifter—little planes that could make six hundred miles an hour.

"They took those, and put heavy metal around the engine, and many, many pounds of explosive in them, and they filled the fuel tank with a substance known as picric acid in the gasoline. Their engines could not withstand that treatment for more than ten minutes, but for those minutes they were terribly powerful.

"So those planes took off from the ground, and flew like great birds into the air, at a speed that would cover the distance from here to the clan in the Orange Mountains in less than two minutes—six hundred miles an hour.

"The Granthee ships were fast, but they were very, very large, nearly a thousand feet long. They turned their radio beams on the planes, and the engines sometimes stopped, and sometimes didn't, and the pilots always died, but not before they had lined the ship on its destination. So, several hundred ships that flew thus—great three-ton explosive shells moving as fast as the bullet of that short gun I showed you, the automatic—one might strike and penetrate and destroy the Granthee ship.

"Not all the Granthee would die then, but, of course, on the ground, without their ships, they were helpless against the many men and women, despite their poison fangs. They could run very swiftly on their six legs, but it is impossible to run far, or swiftly, when you are enveloped in men who do not in the least mind dying, if only you die, too.

"And, of course, there were guns. The Japanese had some ships, they were called battleships, made of steel, very thick and very tough, so thick and strong that the radio beam could not penetrate, so big that any beam the Granthee could throw would not seriously heat them.

"These ships carried guns, not like the automatic I showed you, but tubes two feet thick, and fifty feet long, and their shells weighed tons. Those great shells, when they succeeded in hitting a Granthee ship, caused serious damage, and sometimes brought one down. The Japanese brought down two of the seven they destroyed in this way, and, as they landed, peasants with scythes and sticks and stones attacked them.

"The Japanese were a peculiar race, but they fought as all men fought in that day, with far inferior weapons—but enormous reserves. In the taking of one ship, with its load of a thousand Granthee, which fell near Tokyo, one of their great cities, approximately one million of the Japanese died. That is what was meant by the thousand-to-one ratio. Of course, not all that million ever got a chance to attack the ship, or tried to, but that number died in Tokyo because of the Granthee ship. Perhaps seven thousand actually took part in the attack.

"But had it gone thus, it would not have been too terrible for man's civilization, because there were only one hundred thousand of the Granthee. Had we lost only one thousand for each of the Granthee we destroyed, it would have been scarcely a serious loss. One hundred millions, of humanity—and in that day we had two thousand millions. But the ratio was fifteen thousand to one."

"And even that would be endurable, were it not that, sooner or later, the second Granthee expedition will come and destroy the rest of us.

"Man fought on capital then. For a thousand years the world had been building, and for a hundred thousand man had been spreading. In three months he spent all he owned, in defeating the invasion. Japan lost everything because the vast atomic bombs of the Granthee loosened the islands, and they slipped into the Japan Deep, a hole in the ocean floor where water went down, down, for five miles, a deep that could swallow the greatest mountain of Earth, and remain unfilled.

"And Japan was gone.

"But the Granthee had flown west, too. They attacked Europe, which was a very densely settled region of high culture and civilization. But the Eurasian Granthee fleet had concentrated on Japan, and the even more populous China.

"In China, one Granthee ship fell, and six hundred million men died. India brought down two ships, because of the British defenses there, and Australia, we know, must have brought down eight, though there never was any message heard. But Australia had few cities, and vast country, so it may be that thousands roam about, unable to communicate with us. The thread of radio is so thin, so fragile.

"Europe fought and destroyed the Granthee ships, all that had come over her, and her cities vanished in the purple-red atomic flares and her people died in the fever beams. But there were many, many forts, and armored vehicles and battleships. These fought, and the fever beams could not reach the men, and the atomic bombs could not be dropped, since even to the Granthee ships, a sixteen-inch armor-piercing projectile loaded with half a ton of high explosive was no futile pebble. The Granthee shot their bombs as shells, but they could not hit the small fleet tanks, and even their might could not beat to the forts buried hundreds of feet beneath rock and soil.

"Oh, they killed the men gradually, because they turned the whole region of the forts into a lava pool, bubbling thickly like a great pot of candy cooking, so the men died. But the ships died, too. The battleships resisted them, one, even two bombs sometimes, and they were mobile and hard to hit, and even the Granthee could not boil an ocean. They hid the warships in clouds of smoke so they could not be seen, while airplanes that flew like darting midges against the sun told them where the Granthee hovered.

"So, finally, was the last Granthee ship over Europe destroyed. And nearly five million people still lived to rejoice. They started quickly, though, to work, the munitions factories starting again, the hidden, buried plants.

"The Granthee fleet over Africa came, and joined with what was left of the fleet that had destroyed Australia.

"Europe fought again. They had vast reserves in that day, because a war was forever hanging over their heads, and their armies were trained and their guns were made, and their piles of ammunition.

"They did as the Japanese did. Their men died in destroying Granthee ships with their little planes—and some new ones, rockets they called them. They were hollow metal shells packed with explosive—save for the guiding man and the fuel that drove them on wings of flame instead of metal. The Granthee could not avoid them, for even swifter and more mobile than the interstellar cruisers were these tiny things. Frequently they moved so swiftly, the screaming metal shell did not explode till it was half through the Granthee ship.

"There were not so many men, then, nor women. The Granthee ships brought down were not always totally destroyed. Some Granthee lived to fight on Earth, and because even on the ground they were deadly, trained troops advanced cautiously and destroyed them carefully. No Granthee lived long, you understand.

"And, finally, as you know, the last Granthee ships landed, only three still in navigable condition. But they landed in England, which was an island off the coast of Europe. They had battered its every weapon of destruction. Now they set out to capture its humans, and did, for there were very few and no weapons whatever. The last three ships were destroyed by humans who let themselves be captured, together with packs of high explosives, of poisonous gas bombs.

"And in America here, the cities had all been battered as have these humbled blocks. There were no more cities, nor any government, but men needed no government to fight now. The first fleet that reached the United States we destroyed, as they had destroyed the fleet in Europe. More came from South America.

"This country is very large, so large you cannot understand. There is so much land the Granthee could not cover it all with their few ships, and everywhere there were humans who hated them. A man in New York discovered one way to release the energy of the atoms, and he made a great many bombs that would do what the Granthee bombs would do. He couldn't shoot them in guns, and they required a great deal of apparatus to set them off. But four Granthee ships were destroyed by them when enslaved humans carrying food to the Granthee carried those bombs instead.

"In three months the Granthee were all destroyed, the last few who were captured were tortured horribly. The few scientists among us who still lived, after the destruction of the laboratories where they had been working, tried to question the Granthee, but the people hated the Granthee too much. The scientists heard only the defiance that the Granthee screamed at men—that the second expedition would follow.

"Man had fought, and defeated the first expedition because though his weapons were far less powerful, he had so many of them, so much material, such immense odds in his favor so far as manpower went. And such colossal hatred that suicide was nothing to him. Willingly, a thousand humans would die if only they could take a single Granthee with them.

"It actually averaged about fifteen thousand humans for each Granthee, and still all the Granthee died, and there were humans left."

"But there are only about two million humans in all the world now," said Ban. "The second expedition will find that the first has done its work. Mankind is reduced to an easily conquered remnant. So what have we gained?"

Old Hugh shook his head. "That is not the philosophy of mankind in the past. Not what have we gained—but what can we do to that second expedition to defeat them."

"Yes," said Ban bitterly, "but you accent it wrongly. What can *we* do to the second expedition?"

"The scientists who survived have been working steadily. They have the secret of the Granthee radio fever beam, and they have atomic bombs, if they can only get a suitable source of power."

"If!" said Ban. "If—and we use an old diesel automobile engine and a converted electric motor for our source of power. We burn weird fuels like the wood gas we used last spring, and we chortle our triumph of getting a staggering, weak signal into the air.

"There are no repair shops, no tools, no machines. There is nothing. We are still living on the capital mankind built up before the Granthee. We paw now in the ruins for strayed bits of that capital, helpless without the stored labor of men long dead. Only the things those dead hands reach out to give us give us this false flicker of civilization, a dying candle flame that splutters up once in extinction. We live because life is an automatic process. We have children because that is an automatic process we cannot halt. We grow food because we suffer hunger if we do not, and we fear the face of Death.

"It is false to delude ourselves we accomplish anything. What good is that triumph of the mind—that we can imitate the fever beam of the Granthee? Stolen idea from dead Granthee, made from stolen apparatus from dead cities. And even so the fever beam is useless when the enemy is behind a metal wall, and when does a Granthee come out to fight? What have we?

"Why grub in fallen ruins to communicate to people in no better state than yourself? Why try to build anything that the Granthee may tear it down? Men built a city here, a great city of steel and stone and beauty. They were far greater than we, they had a skill that is dead with them, a power that is vanished, too. And with all their weapons, with all their vast capital to expend—they are dead. We have not the skill, nor the capital nor the weapons. And the second expedition comes; they have told us that much.

"You old men who saw that civilization cannot forget it. You go on dreaming your dreams of rebuilding it. But we who have grown up since have no false hopes. We never saw it, and we know we never will.

"Man's capital is spent, his income is spent, he is pawning his last proud possessions. Man's civilization is done. He may still have pride enough and power enough in his shrunken body to destroy himself before the Granthee come to capture him. Man is the only large animal remaining on all Earth, and the Granthee must capture him. Then you know what his fate will be. Man will be the horse to labor, and his child the chicken to eat. And it is sure for many live now who have not the wit to see it, nor the will to escape it."

Old Hugh sighed. "I know, Ban, I know," he said softly. "I have felt it, and feared it, and understood that. And for two reasons I go on living and working: The first is that there are those who have not the wit nor the will; and for the sake of those who would become the horse and the chicken, we must try. There is a third reason, too, so I will say that my second is that the Granthee did not know when the second expedition would come. It was only a promise when they started—an empty promise.

"The greatest reason is that other men go on working still, with man's old courage and his old skill. You know that in Schenectady there are men who are not stealing apparatus from dead cities, but making new. And in Detroit they are making engines again—engines that burn wood and do not wear swiftly, nor easily, with bearings that are lubricated as we are lubricating ours, with oil pressed from castor oil beans we can grow here."

"Do they make guns that can blow apart Granthee ships? Do they make swift rocket ships to drive a trail of destruction through—"

"Not yet, I know, Ban, but—"

"But the second expedition will put a stop to that. Old Hugh, I love you, love you as the only father I've known; but you struggle against impossibilities. The castor beans you mentioned— You know we will have oil but a little longer, since the frost destroyed last year's crop. Then our paltry little machines will slide and grate to a stop, as frictional losses destroy their efficiency and their metal. Friction has stopped man always."

"Not friction, but inertia has stopped mankind, Ban."

"Aye, the momentum dies, and the race glides to a halt as friction slows it. But come, old Hugh, I will help you, for I know the work is dear to you. What you are attempting now I do not understand, but I know you want more tubes, more apparatus, so we will grub among the ruins, you and I."

Ban rose slowly, and picked his way over the tumbled stones and rotting wooden beams, charred and blackened by fires the atomic bombs had started and angered Nature drowned in ton on countless ton of outraged rain.

Wearily the old man picked his way along, head bent, sorrowful. He knew the truth of what Ban said. But Hugh was of a generation that had known and yielded to hope. His generation would always yield to it.

## II

The sun was sinking into long summer twilight as they made their way down to the rotting dock. They were heavy laden and old Hugh was happy, picking his way along among the tumbled blocks. Cautiously they lowered themselves to the little rowboat, looking anxiously at the sullen flow of the river, a clean, clear river now, with sunken rusty hulls visible beneath its surface.

The tide was turning soon, and the water moved slowly, gurgling very softly round the piles of the pier. Gulls swung lazily on the little choppy waves, watching the men with keen, bright eyes. Men were a source of danger to gulls; to men gulls were a source of food—a rather strong-flavored soup, but nourishing.

"Lower them, gently, Ban," said Hugh. "I'm afraid we'll have to go farther afield next time. The instruments, thank Heaven, were in working order. Here's the receiver—and that other one. It's heavy, so be careful. Look, here's something we can use that I found just as we left."

"What is it? It looks like a small motor or generator, but has no power shaft to take hold of."

"It is both, a rotary converter. They used to use these on automobiles to run radio sets; it has a 6-volt motor and a 110-volt alternator wound on one armature, so that it produced 110 A.C. from 6 volts D.C. We have lots of powerful storage batteries from old automobiles, and this is a 500-watt converter, so we have something very useful."

"Hm-m-m—it may be. I've never seen one before. Well, are we ready?"

"I'm afraid that's all. I wish I'd been able to find that roll of copper tubing the old invoice listed. He must have sold it—"

Silently they rowed across the water as the long twilight settled. Stars came out, and the moon, as they plodded along, the little child's wagon behind them. They went over the rough cobblestones of the old Meadows road till they passed the torn section, then on their bicycles to the Orange Mountains.

The moon was high when they reached the lighted buildings of the clan. Ban's wife greeted them, slightly curious, as they returned. The neighbors came in, a few at a time, to look incuriously at the treasures Hugh had collected, and to ask news of the road, for few and seldom were the trips so far from the clan. They slouched out presently, only old George staying to help them, an automobile mechanic once, venting his love of machinery on their decrepit old engine.

"They were calling you today, Hugh," he said. "I couldn't do anything, and they couldn't seem to make it with the telephone thing." He shook his head sadly. "I never could understand those buzzes and clicks. I wish they'd talk language."

"They can't always, George. Code will get through with less power, and we all have so little power. I'll send out a call and see if I can find who called me."

The little diesel pounded presently, with gnarled old George soothing its heavy knocks as best he could, and the transmitter, patched and jury-rigged, began to operate. But no answer came to their call from the silent ether—only the soft wash of static. Hugh shook his head and shut the diesel off. "No response, George. They'll call again. They always do. They always have time. I'm going to start working on that fever beam, I think."

"Fever beam," Ban said. "You might give a mouse a dangerous fever and—"

"No, you don't understand. Fevers can cure, too. I'm going to build a curative fever apparatus, one with power enough to heal, though it cannot hurt. And that metal tube you asked about is no weakling, Ban. It will handle five hundred watts, and we have six. If they are all in operable condition, as I believe they are, that is not insignificant power. It is more than we have had before, for a long time." Hugh gently reproved him.

Ban snorted again. "More than we have had for a long time—and enough to cure, but not harm anything, even a large mouse!"

"But I will learn. I will learn how to construct the beam. And you will learn. That is important, Ban; we must remember that. So help me now, while I test these tubes. Remember that they use four thousand volts, and be careful, please."

In two days they had finished the things, and set up makeshift apparatus. There had been a thyratron tube there, too, a thing that old Hugh brought along out of interest and a collector's acquisitiveness, for it was not a radio tube, capable of control, simply a type of switch capable of operating at near radio frequency in effect.

It was set up on a panel of well-dried, seasoned hardwood, for there was no more bakelite or hard rubber to be used, and slate was hard to get. And the wires were never insulated, merely spaced, because insulation had rotted and fallen off in the years since wire was made.

But they tried it, and it worked to some extent. Not as well as old Hugh had hoped, but nothing ever did, for his apparatus could never be quite the right apparatus, but the nearest equivalent to hand. By radio he held long conferences with those men in Schenectady who had not forgotten their craft, and developed ways and means to measure what he had no instrument for measuring—wave lengths and frequencies, wave forms even, after great difficulty, from an old television tube that had somehow maintained its vacuum. Television they could have no more, for television required waves so short they could be sent only with horizon distances. But the old cathode-ray television tube became an oscillograph.

Old Hugh looked at the result in dismay. "Ban, I'm afraid our apparatus is very faulty. That's not a sine wave, but a wave form for which man has never invented a name. Well, it can't be helped. We must do what we can with what we have. The men in Schenectady have sent one of their young clansmen on foot and in canoe clear out to Detroit to help the men there.

"Presently, radio equipment will be made there, too, where they have production machinery still—and vast cargoes of raw materials. Maybe then we will get new, and good equipment, tubes that always have their vacuum, and haven't gone 'soft.' They will make caterpillar tractors that burn wood gases, and use castor oil beans for lubricant. Then they can break through, and start commerce again. They are going to make big boats again, and try to ship things on the Great Lakes, and finally, even a huge diesel of hundreds of horse power to the men in Schenectady."

"Huge!" said Ban. "Hundreds of horse power! The locomotive those men at Schenectady once made stalled outside of Montclair, and it used fifty thousand horsepower, a mere fraction of the load of one substation!"

"It is huge," old Hugh maintained, hurt somewhat by the tone of Ban's voice. "We are rebuilding with a very little start. We have a great task, and that will be a huge accomplishment, Ban. Men will try very hard for that, and work with a great love and pride and honest effort that man never exceeded. It will represent the hopes and thoughts and labors of many men, an accomplishment they can be as proud of as any ever done.

"The giant machines are gone, and man labors again with the sweat of his brow and the craft of his hand. That engine will release many hands and many brows to greater, better efforts. Did I not know it useless, I would urge you again to go to Schenectady, that you may get real training and do your part in this greater labor ahead."

"The labor ahead is useless. The second expedition is ahead."

"I know, Ban; I want to show you something of interest. You remember that neon bulb I brought? Take this terminal of the new power set in one hand, and the bulb in the other. So I will turn it—no, do not loose your grip, hold tightly and remain on that insulating plate. Do not touch the ground, though that would probably harm you little, but stay there and hold the tube. So—and see."

"Eh—it lights!" Ban stared at the brilliantly glowing tube. "With but one connection—through my body. How can it be so? My body has very great resistance, you have schooled me, and for power to flow, always there must be two connections."

Old Hugh chuckled. "I shall show you something perhaps yet more remarkable. See, here is that coil I wound yesterday. I told you it was a furnace, and you looked at me askance. So. Now, will you hold this metal cylinder, and I lead the wire here, to the coil, and again to the set here. You are in the circuit, see?"

"Aye! I'm in the circuit right enough, and I like it very little. Old Hugh, are you sure of yourself?" Ban asked dubiously.

"We shall see. Now, the furnace is set on this table, and in my hand I hold a bit of asbestos, hollowed to hold a few scraps of aluminum metal. Now—I turn on the power set, and thrust my hand in the furnace—"

"By the gods of time! It's melting! Your hand—"

"As cool as you please, my son." Quickly the old man shut off the set, and tossed aside the molten metal. "The radio-frequency currents play strange tricks, for they run not through your body, but across it, like water. These extreme frequencies cannot go through any conductor, but always across its surface. It is called the skin effect. When it passes as a flow of current in a wire, or any conductor, it is only on the surface; yet when acting through an insulator, it acts all through it. In the furnace, it attacks the metal, but not my hand, for my hand is a very poor conductor, and a hard path, while the metal is a very good conductor, and an easy path.

"It is very interesting, but not useful, I am afraid," he said. "Come, we must see what we can do to correct the fever beam hook-up, to get better efficiency, and the correct wave form. I wonder if the wave form can have any peculiar effects—something unusual. I wonder perhaps—"

"What? What might it do?"

"I was thinking—thinking of the time I worked with a quartz-crystal oscillator, and built up the frequency till it exactly corresponded with the crystal's natural note and—the crystal was white dust. Maybe I could develop a wave form that would pulverize even hard steel that way—"

"Maybe. Then you could break all Joan's sewing needles, and maybe even get enough power to crack one of her knitting needles. There are many things you might do—if you had power.

"Old Hugh, I do not like to see you spend your time uselessly."

"I have nothing else to spend, Ban. Let me work. Who knows—but let me try, it costs little, and might be worth much."

"It costs a mouth to feed, and work to gather oil for the engine, and wear on the engine and tubes. It does cost us time." Ban looked at the old man sorrowfully. "The others complain. I do not; I know what you are attempting. But it is they who must work to feed you, and, as yet the communication they have maintained all these years has brought them little good. Twice only it has warned them of a killing frost, once of the great storm. Beyond that—since the bandits have all been destroyed, it has done them little good. They grow restless, Hugh."

Slowly old Hugh looked away, out through the window toward the hard-working men in the fields, women weaving again on hand looms. It had been a fad once, in the world he had known, before the Granthee. It was no fad now; it was protection against the winter, and, because the wool was never cleansed completely free of its grease, against the rains.

"I know, Ban. I told Dr. Ponting I would call him at noon today. I must call."

"And I must go," said Ban. "I will be back this evening."


III


Old Hugh sat silent, fingering slowly the crude key of his transmitter, a bit of brass spring he had cut himself, mounted with a scrap of a platinum wedding ring above and below for contact points. The platinum wedding ring had been found on a slender, bleached bone, protruding from beneath a great tumbled block of stone in the city. His lined old face grew more and more sorrowful. Finally he buried his face in his gnarled old hands, and his body rocked slowly.

"Three groups," he muttered, "three groups in all the world. So far as we know. Never have we roused Europe, never Australia. Three little groups against the vast inertia of two millions. The first expedition was destroyed, and utterly defeated—yet it has won. Ah-h-h, if only—"

Hours later he fussed with his apparatus, setting up the parabolic netting of wires he had contrived after Dr. Ponting's radioed directions that noon. He was working over it carefully to align exactly the bit of copper tubing a few inches long that was its aerial, designed to radiate these ultra-short waves. Multiplex ultra frequency they called it in Schenectady. It was ingenious, perhaps too much so for him, his wave form was so poor.

Carefully, because he had much time, and no real aim, he checked his work by the plans he had copied down from the messages over the radio. The triple generating oscillator set, the power set, the mixing oscillator, the phase indicators were all in order. But somehow they did not combine properly.

Then, quite by accident, he noticed that he had connected one of the tubes slightly more than 185 degrees out of phase, instead of slightly more than 5! And a screwed connection near it had come loose. No wonder his wave form was peculiar, his efficiency low: one tube fighting the other two!

Muttering to himself in vexation he brought a screw driver and tightened the connection down firmly, solidly. Then, just to test it really, he turned on the set. The oscilloscope began to move as heaters warmed up, then abruptly struck a weirdly shaped wave, and broke again, abruptly, into the peculiar wave he had been getting just as there sounded in the quiet little room a very sharp *ping*.

Hugh looked curiously, and shut off his set hastily. The loose connection was not merely loose now. The screw had vanished!

Vaguely worried and surprised, old Hugh replaced it, and turned on the set. This time he watched that screw. The tubes were warmer now, heated more quickly. *Ping!* Very sharp. And the screw was gone.

Old Hugh brought the soldering iron and soldered that connection in place, and wondered. Again the set started. There were five distinct *pings* this time—and a little tinny clatter of falling metal parts. The beautifully constructed little paraboloid director lay in disassembled parts on the table, quite scattered and crumpled—not harmed, merely taken apart in a hundredth of a second, with a little stinging *ping* of metal.

A man trained in research through a lifetime would have stopped there, and worked very hard with his mind, and sought some explanation, some theory, then devised a theory-testing experiment to prove or disprove that theory. Old Hugh had not done research work, real research, for thirty years. He had simply tried to make delicate mechanisms work with defective apparatus. To him, this was simply more defective apparatus. With the patience a generation of troubles had taught him, he kneeled down on the floor and hunted about the little shack till he had found five bolts, four nuts and two tiny screws.

These were precious things, these little screws, because they couldn't be made any more, and they were so hard to get—such little things— they sifted down among the debris to unattainable depths. One nut was missing and he had to replace it from his hoarded stock. Then, patiently, his stiffened fingers assembled again the little thing that had fallen apart, and bolted it firmly.

Then he started his apparatus again. But he made sure this time that the thing would not be so defective. He wired the tiny nuts in place. And now in all his circuit there were only soldered joints or bolts with nuts wired solidly in place. And he turned his projector where it would send its beam harmlessly into the mountainside half a mile away, and so started the set.

He watched his set, and it worked, so he did not look through the window where, half a mile away, a mighty mass of rock and earth and giant trees began to move in a ghastly silence down the hill. For seconds the thing moved in majestic silence, a whole section of the hill gliding downward, swifter and more swiftly. Then it broke in flying, smoking rock, crashing and roaring in monstrous shock. The shouts of men and screams of women made him rise suddenly and step hastily across the room, not even pausing to shut off his machine.

He fell with a sickening jar, heard the dull snap, felt the meteoring pain that shot up his leg to become a vast, unbearable ache. He tried to rise, and fell back whimpering softly, calling bewilderedly, mercifully numbed, as yet.

It was hours before Ban found him there, in the dark little room, with only the faint glow of the heater tubes shining in the dark. The steady pounding of the diesel had attracted him from the mystery there on the hillside that the men were looking at in awe and vague fear. They wanted old Hugh, suddenly wondering where he was, who might explain this to them.

Gently they lifted him up, unconscious now, and the old doctor showed them how to set the bone again, giving in words, the skill his hands possessed to hands that had the strength his no longer held. Then they bound the leg, and straightened it, and beside him two women watched. They fed him when he woke, feverish, mumbling.

Ban shut off the experimental set, and started the transmitter. Through space his message leaped to other sets and found them deaf. This was not communication time.

Morning came, and again Ban tried, but now the men came in. The mystery had vanished in the night. The rock slide was there, and the more distant, strangely truncated slope was visible beyond it, raw and harsh. But the strange thing had vanished.

Ban called again. Schenectady answered finally, and to them Ban poured out the message: Hugh Thompson feverish and sick with a broken leg; the mountains moving and stirring, strange rocks down which Jeff Hurley shot, slipping without resistance till brought up against a broken hull of a great boulder outside the area of damage, damaged himself beyond repair—dead; the broken mountains—

And no mention of the set. For the men of that later day, even when trained somewhat, did not so rapidly connect cause and effect. And in every mind, anyway, lurked the thought: the second expedition.

Old Hugh woke late that afternoon, and they told him of the mystery, at his insistence carried him to the little room and his key. And from that position he saw the meaning of the thing.

"Ban," he said suddenly, quite softly, "Ban, look along the axis of the paraboloid there, and tell me—"

"Eh," said Ban, "the slippage is along that line. What do you suppose made that paraboloid line up with that damage? Some magnetism—"

Old Hugh groaned softly. "Oh, Ban, can you believe nothing you see, either? Move that paraboloid one degree further toward the mountain, making sure no man is in its path—

"But no, there will be half a hundred out there now. Never mind. I must think why. But first—start the transmitter."

At the key he called, called vainly for a long time. Schenectady answered after a while, and rapidly he told them of his mistake in the connection, and the damage involved. They would try it, on a barren mountainside.

His description was too accurate. Old Hugh said, "Right through the wall."

They did not hear from Schenectady that day, or the next, as old Hugh grew more feverish, became delirious. Ban caught the weak, broken signals the third day. "—building as—gested. Something—ent wrong, for the entire building—lapsed. Transmitter ruined, as—ell—set we—ade up. No power. Will—d more later. Greatest—covery—as ever made in hist—" And no more could he catch; so he put down what he got, and turned back to old Hugh, uncomprehending.

## IV

Thirty years of harsh, rugged life lay behind old Hugh. Somehow the fever abated, the pain lessened as his sturdy old body rallied in defense. Slowly, he began to recover, and still no message came through from Schenectady, though two weeks passed. The women who cared for him had cleaned the room, and Ban told old Hugh, negligently, that the message he'd been unable to clear up had been thrown out.

Old Hugh was busy thinking. But the problem eluded him. Somehow, he was sure, he had destroyed some of the rock crystals to powder as he had hoped, yet he could not understand; it was beyond his belief that so tiny a power, a bare three horsepower, could do so much damage. Surely, it seemed, it would have taken vastly more. But, perhaps it was some really rare constituent of the rock, rare but vastly important, that held the secret, some unconsidered crystal that was the key log in the jam that made rock solid, vibrating in chance tune to his set, and vibrated to powder.

He cursed that lost nut he knew must be guilty for his fall. A little rolling nut—but the feeling as he fell had been so strange—

He didn't see his ragged, raveled clothes. When the women brought them back to him they had been carefully repaired, as all things must be where all things are worked for and made by the sweat of man's brow and the craft of his hand. Perhaps they would have given him some little hint.

But he itched to be at it again, determined now that, pointed to the skies, the thing must be safe. So he had the men bring in samples of every rock they could find at the great slide, and, when he could hobble again on his crutch with Ban's aid, he set the paraboloid on its back, and the rock specimens above it on wooden shelves, turning the power to a very low degree. Then he turned on the set that had not operated since he had fallen there by the window, and broken his leg as the mountain slid down.

Slowly the tubes warmed up. He watched with interest and care the little stones on the little platform just under the low roof of the little wooden shack.

Then the tubes were warm, and there were a great many slight *pings* of sound, and a very quiet, swift slip of the roof and the sudden heavy thrashing as the roof fell in. It was fortunate that the device was so effective, for the roof came in as separate shingles and boards.

Old Hugh groaned as they dug him out, and reached a hand to feel the device that had done this. His leg hurt, his head ached abominably, his laboratory was a ruin, evidently, but he was not seriously hurt, nor was Ban. Ban's wife was crying and dabbing at his bleeding face, questioning frantically and tongue lashing old Hugh simultaneously. She was pale, and very scared, for the shack looked as though a monstrous giant had stepped heedlessly on it.

Ban stared dazedly and bewilderedly at the wrecked laboratory. "I know," he said suddenly, looking owlishly at old Hugh. "What they said was 'building collapsed.' That was it."

Old Hugh laughed shakily. "A fine time to remember it, my boy. We can confirm their report."

"And they said it was the greatest discovery in history. I'll bet that was it. Yes. I know it was. You've got the disintegration ray, Hugh!"

Old Hugh shook his head. "It doesn't fit, Ban. It does the job, but I don't know why, nor how. That's never really safe. We must find out why."

"Why? We can work it."

"Eh? How well? How much? I'm going back in there."

Silently, other men began to clear the wreckage away, and with their efficient taciturn movements, more and more apparatus began to appear. Old Hugh interfered with them as he brought forth coils and condensers and little metal tubes, his soldering iron and the precious little alcohol soldering torch, a piece of dry, seasoned wood, a few condensers, the rotary converter. Miraculously, from the ruins, Ban brought the oscillograph.

With gnarled, skilled fingers old Hugh built up the thing on his bit of board, a foot square with one-inch tubes and a gently hammered piece of annealed copper in the form of a bowl. They brought him, silently, the things he asked for, and silently stood watching.

It formed under his fingers. At his command, Ban brought the storage battery they had built up from the sound parts of a dozen decrepit wrecks. Hugh attached his terminals, and the little converter whined. The tiny tubes grew warm and a wave form built up in the oscilloscope.

"A good research student would know just what to do, I think I know just what happened now, Ban, and the way to test it is to see if my theory will predict results. I have aimed this at the horizon. Ban, will you catch that little kid over there, and place him on that bare patch?"

Ban tried, and with the aid of three other men the struggling kid was brought and placed on the bald knoll. "He won't stay, Hugh."

"Leave him and run at right angles to the beam, Ban. You others step away now." In a moment Ban ran—and old Hugh pressed his key. The running goat bleated suddenly, tumbled and slid along the ground, his feet threshing and struggling, bleating louder now, mortally terrified. For half a minute he struggled, flashing legs flying without result—then he was up and bouncing away like a thrown rubber ball. In moments the kid was nibbling grass, tossing his head back toward them, bleating defiantly.

"Yes," said Hugh, eyes flashing, "I was right."

Open-mouthed, Ban stared at the little animal. The lean, silent men moved restlessly. "What did it, Hugh?" asked one at length. "That goat acted like he got on a cake of ice, and even then I never saw one of them sure-footed little beasts slip like that."

Old Hugh was disconnecting the battery. The rotary converter slowed from a whine to a drone, and stopped. He looked lovingly at the foot-square board and the copper bowl and the little black tubes, like dull metal acorns, less than an inch high. "Yes, that's what broke my leg that day. I know now. Old Jim Duncan, you've been wanting to tear down the old wooden house there and haven't had the time to do it right and save the nails. Well—Ban, you pack the battery, will you?"

Hugh set off down the grassy lane that was all the main street the clan had. At the end of the row was the old, rotting house, deserted, broken, preserved only so long by the original sound construction, and the fact that men who grubbed for every grain of food they ate had no time yet to tear it down carefully and pull the nails out straight and usable, keeping the boards, most of them, unbroken and sound.

They followed him silently. Talking was not a highly developed art among these people, not as it had been when old Hugh was young Hugh. Ban set down the battery at Hugh's gesture, and the old man laboriously set himself on the ground, his game leg sticking out before him. He connected the set, and the converter whined again. Old Hugh lined the copper bowl on the tumble-down house and pressed the key. A thousand, thousand sharp *pings,* a sudden settling, a clamorous rattling of boards—the building was down, and dust swirled slowly.

"Great heaven!" gasped Ban. Suddenly he was running forward, toward the house and—through the beam. In an instant he was down, skittering along the ground, threshing arms and legs. Quite unhurt, evidently, but surprised, and suddenly embarrassed.

Old Hugh cut off the key. Slowly, flushing, Ban rose to his feet, absolutely nude save for his leather belt, his leather shoes, a mass of thread and lint that reduced itself, as he moved, to individual hairs, all that remained of his clothes. A slow roll of laughter welled from the people. Then his wife was running forward, her face crimson, her eyes blazing wickedly at old Hugh as she glanced toward him in her swift passage.

"Wh-what happened?" asked the unhappy Ban Norman.

"I sort of think you better get dressed again, Ban, before you start gettin' questy," said a laconic, faintly humorous voice. "Looks like you wore out them clothes in a hell of a hurry."

Ten minutes later Ban was back, his angry wife bristling at his side. A soft murmur of chuckles ran through the folk as they straightened from their work of gathering nails and screws and useful bits of metal from the old house. Long, straight boards, mostly unharmed, were being stacked to one side.

Old Hugh looked at Ban with twinkling gray eyes. "Maybe my puttering will be some use, yet. See?"

On the ground before the humming little set a pile of lint was accumulating. The women were at work. Every old, worn-out bit of clothing in the clan had been brought and reduced to its original fibers in moments. "They can reweave them now, into new and useful material. And Ban, they are beginning to feel something else. Do you see all this little, little thing means?"

"I see something it means, you old fool!" snapped diminutive, peppery Joan Norman. "It means I have to weave Ban Norman a new suit! First you tear down the house about Ban's ears, then you tear the clothes off his very back. I had to make that, and those you're wearing too, you muddle-witted ingrate. You have less sense than two-year-old Junior and don't use what you have! You and your messy batteries and coils and wires. Every day Ban comes home with holes in his things, and now—now you're not content with just making holes in them, you tear them all to pieces, right back to lint, and make a spectacle out of my Ban. And will you—"

Gently, Ban picked up his wife and carried her back to the house. Ten minutes more and he was back grinning. "She's peeved. But Hugh, what in the name of the heavens have you got? I don't—"

"It's the skin effect, Ban. I've figured it out now. That's why so little power does so much, so very much. Look, it induces those extreme frequencies in any conductor, and almost anything is more or less of a conductor because of moisture in it, and those frequencies go, of course, to the surface. How they do it, I cannot guess. Yet, somehow, they rearrange the molecules so that they become perfectly fluid, there just on the very surface, and absolutely destroy all friction."

"Friction! But—" Ban gasped, and fell silent for a second. "But I do not understand—friction—"

"Man has always thought of friction as his worst enemy, yet he cannot do without it. Look, your clothes fell apart in a moment, because the woven strands were held together by their friction. Even the knots were held by friction. The shed fell on us, as the house fell, because the friction that held the nails in was gone, and the nails, of course, sprang out. I was vastly tempted to turn it on the diesel, and get along without oil, till I remembered—every bolt and nut would fly off as though a charge of explosive lay beneath it, for each bolt and each nut is held in place only by friction. In a hundredth of a second the diesel would have become a mass of disassembled, oil-splattered parts.

"They know it over there, I think. We have lost some of our fear now, Ban, because—"

"Then—then that little set there could tear down a small mountain! It needs no power, the weight and force of the mountain would do it all!"

"This needs no power," said old Hugh, brushing about his head at the dull hum and buzz he took to be a fly.

Only the low cries of the men over by the fallen house made him look up. Some five miles away, two or three miles up, hung two great, blackened, pointed cylinders. They buzzed like vast, angry insects, and pale, lambent flame rippled and played about their atomic exhausts.

They seemed to move slowly, so far and so high there, as they drifted across country. Then one twisted and dipped in its course. A thrilling wave of warmth seemed to reach down to them; the men by the house dropped their tools and the lumber they carried. They ran to their homes. Already women and children were coming out, joining their men and vanishing in the green depths of the wood.

Old Hugh's eyes were keen and bright as he looked up into Ban's dull, racked face. "Oh, Lord," said Ban, and turned suddenly toward the clan center, toward his home. His wife was coming out, crying for him, little Junior in her arms. Ban ran swiftly to them. The feeling of warmth and heat made him sluggish, he realized suddenly as he ran to them.

Old Hugh looked after him, and turned back, a lone little figure squatted awkwardly with his broken leg stretched out before him. From the wood came softly muffled cries. Only two words seemed to filter through—"second expedition."

Old Hugh stirred beside his softly humming little board; the old, patched battery; six little metal acorns, warm to the touch; a little copper bowl. Old Hugh's eyes were bleak and dark as he looked along the edge of the board and wondered what power he actually had in his tiny, futilely whining bit of wood and metal and insulation.

An unbearable violet flame leaped suddenly in the skies, shrieking a thousand feet in the air. A rain of black metal separated from a solid clump to spread in a long, stretching line that reached down and down in masses to the waiting earth. It settled at the base of a giant rock, finally, as a second long rain of metal reached down and down.

Somehow, miraculously, living, moving parts separated themselves and stood a moment, bewildered by sudden helplessness, perhaps, pawing at the broken wreckage, glinting peculiarly like an iridescent metal in the afternoon sun. The old man hobbled to a higher knoll, dragging the heavy battery and the little bit of wood and metal and insulation.

The great cliff stirred, moved. The afternoon quiet echoed to the vast, angry mutter of the mountain. Annoyed, it seemed to settle more comfortably over the spot where, iridescently, purple things had moved.

## V

Ban looked in at the doorway of the wrecked shed cautiously. The diesel was humming rhythmically, and the whine of the generator sounded sleepily on the quiet, late-afternoon air of the deserted little settlement. Old Hugh was propped up on three broken boards; his game leg tenderly rested on a fourth. On the bench beside him was the rough, dry board, and on the floor the old, decrepit storage battery. There were soft, quick hisses and buzzes coming from the loudspeaker on the table—a rather dented and battered loud-speaker, but functioning.

Ban listened to the familiar code. "—already," it spelled out to him. "There were eight here, thirty more came this morning. Detroit has sent three of the rocket machines, and five of the frictionless, welded tank machines have crossed the country. They left an anti-friction projector set in each clan village they passed.

"We believe those two ships you destroyed were the last of the American fleet. Our new set, though, caught a European station never before heard. We cannot get through to them, apparently, till the new transmitter is finished tomorrow, because they have no receivers as sensitive as ours. But one of the Detroit rockets is making the one-way crossing tonight, though unable to return till fuel is developed there.

"Undoubtedly, however, our strong point of resistance here will protect Europe by drawing all the Granthee fire. The tank machines ring up at a distance of thirty miles, and the rockets are waiting.

"Detroit is preparing thirty-five more now, for production has been vastly speeded since the frictionless machine tools went into operation. Have your clansmen returned?"

The speaker fell silent. Old Hugh reached out a firm hand to the key, and Ban listened to his swift keying. "One, so far, at any rate. They will drift in now, for their fear is gone. He has brought in a sample of the Granthee hand weapon, powered by atomic energy, I see. He is beside me now—Ban Norman—so, if your rocket will come for me, I can join you in three hours. Ban Norman knows the language of the key; he can teach it to others."

"You said no others would learn, and Norman was weakening," spluttered the little dented speaker.

"Others will learn now. Another has come, and is watching through the broken window. He is trying to understand now. In six months we will have fifty trained operators, and perhaps ten men who can hook up apparatus."

"That is good, Hugh Thompson. Detroit just sent word that the rocket has taken off to pick you up. We will deliver the tank machine and the medicines you asked for in three days or so, the gang plow in two weeks. Can Ban Norman take the key now?"

"Yes," said Ban Norman softly. "Going to—Schenectady—Detroit—in three hours. Old Hugh—"

"What—what does it say?" asked the keen-eyed face at the window.

"It says, young Jim Duncan," old Hugh replied slowly, as Ban Norman slipped eagerly over to the key, "that the Granthee have suffered severe frictional losses, and—that man's hesitation is over, and not his civilization."

# Forgetfulness

Ron Thule, the astronomer, stood in the lock gate and looked down across the sweep of gently rolling land. Slowly, he breathed in the strange, tangy odors of this planet. There was something of a vast triumph in his eyes, and something of sorrow. They had been here now scarcely five hours, and the sun was still low in the east, rising slowly. Out beyond, above the western horizon, a pale ghost of the strange twin world of this planet, less than a third of a million miles distant, seemed a faint, luminous cloud in the deep, serene blue of the sky.

It was triumph, for six long years of travel, at a speed close to that of light, lay behind them; three and a half light years distant was Pareeth, and the crowding people who had built and launched the mighty two-thousand-five-hundred-foot interstellar cruiser that had brought this little band of one hundred. Launched in hope and striving, seeking a new sun with new planets, new worlds to colonize. More than that, even, for this new-found planet was a stepping-stone to other infinities beyond. Ten years of unbroken travel was the maximum any ship they could build would endure. They had found a planet; in fact, nine planets. Now, the range they might explore for new worlds was extended by four light years.

And there was sorrow there, too, for there was a race here now. Ron Thule turned his eyes toward the little clustering village nestled in the swale of the hills, a village of simple, rounded domes of some opalescent, glassy material. A score of them straggled irregularly among the mighty, deep-green trees that shaded them from the morning sun, twenty-foot domes of pearl and rose and blue. The deep green of the trees and the soft green of the mosslike grass that covered all the low, rounded hills made it very beautiful; the sparkling colors of the little gardens about the domes gave it further enchantment. It was a lovely spot, a spot where space-wearied interstellar wanderers might rest in delight.

Such it was. There was a race on this planet the men of Pareeth had found after six long years of space, six years of purring, humming atomic engines and echoing gray steel fabric that carried and protected them. Harsh utility of giant girders and rubbery flooring, the snoring drone of forty quadrillion horsepower of atomic engines. It was replaced now by the soft coolness of the grassy land; the curving steel of the girders gave way to the brown of arching trees; the stern ceiling of steel plates gave way to the vast, blue arch of a planet's atmosphere. Sounds died away in infinitudes where there was no steel to echo them back; the unending drone of the mighty engines had become breezes stirring rustling leaves—an invitation to rest.

The race that lived here had long since found it such, it seemed. Ron Thule looked across the little village of domes to the largest of them, perhaps thirty feet across. Commander Shor Nun was there with his archaeologist and anthropologist, and half-a-score of the men of this planet. Rhth, they called it.

The conference was breaking up now. Shor Nun appeared, tall and powerful, his muscular figure in trim Interstellar Expedition uniform of utilitarian, silvery gray. Behind him came the other two in uniform—young, powerful men of Pareeth, selected for this expedition because of physical and mental perfection, as was every man of them.

Then came Seun, the man of Rhth. He was taller, slimmer, an almost willowy figure. His lean body was clothed in an elastic, close-fitting suit of golden stuff, while over his shoulders a glowing, magnificently shimmering cape of rich blue was thrown. Five more of these men came out, each in a golden suit, but the draped capes glowed in deep reds, and rich greens, blues and violets. They walked leisurely beside the men of Pareeth. An unconscious force made those trimly uniformed men walk in step between the great, arching trees.

They came near and Shor Nun called out, "Is the expedition ready?"

From the forward lock, Toth Mour replied, "Aye, commander. Twenty-two men. What do these people say?"

Shor Nun shook his head slightly. "That we may look as we wish. The city is deserted. I cannot understand them. What arrangements have you made?"

"The men you mentioned are coming. Each head of department, save Ron Thule. There will be no work for the astronomer."

"I will come, Shor Nun," called out the astronomer, softly. "I can sketch; I would be interested."

"Well enough, as you like. Toth Mour, call the men into formation; we will start at once. The day varies in length, but is some thirteen hours long at this season, I am told."

Ron Thule leaped down to the soft turf and walked over toward the group. Seun looked at him slowly and smiled. The man of Rhth looked taller from this distance, nearly six and a third feet in height. His face was tanned to a golden color that came near to matching the gold of his clothing. His eyes were blue and very deep. They seemed uncertain—a little puzzled, curious about these men, curious about the vast, gray bulk that had settled like a grim shadow over the low hill. Half a mile in length, four hundred feet in diameter, it loomed nearly as large as the age-old, eroded hills it had berthed on. He ran a slim-fingered hand through the glinting golden hair that curled in unruly locks above a broad, smooth brow.

"There is something for an astronomer in all this world, I think." He smiled at Ron Thule. "Are not climate and soils and atmospheres the province of astronomy, too?"

"The chemists know it better," Ron Thule replied, and wondered slightly at his replying. He knew that the man of Rhth had not spoken, simply that the thought had come to be in his mind. "Each will have his special work, save for me. I will look at the city. They will look at the buildings and girders and the carvings or mechanisms, as is their choice. I will look at the city."

Uneasily, he moved away from the group, started alone across the field. Uneasiness settled on him when he was near this Seun, this descendant of a race that had been great ten millions of years before his own first sprang from the swamps. Cheated heir to a glory five million years lost.

The low, green roll of the hill fell behind him as he climbed the grassy flank. Very slowly before his eyes, the city lifted into view. Where the swelling curve of the hill faded softly into the infinite blue of the sky, first one little point, then a score, then hundreds appeared, as he walked up the crest—the city.

Then he stood on the crest. The city towered before him, five miles away across the gently rolling green swale. Titan city of a Titan race! The towers glowed with a sun-fired opalescence in the golden light of the sun. How long, great gods of this strange world, how long had they stood thus? Three thousand feet they rose from the level of age-sifted soil at their bases, three thousand feet of mighty mass, stupendous buildings of the giants long dead.

The strange little man from a strange little world circling a dim, forgotten star looked up at them, and they did not know, or care. He walked toward them, watched them climb into the blue of the sky. He crossed the broad green of the land, and they grew in their uncaring majesty.

Sheer, colossal mass, immeasurable weights and loading they were—
and they seemed to float there on the grace of a line and a curve, half
in the deep blue of the sky, half touching the warm, bright green of
the land. They floated still on the strength of a dream dreamed by a
man dead these millions of years. A brain had dreamed in terms of
lines and curves and sweeping planes, and the brain had built in terms
of opal crystal and vast masses. The mortal mind was buried under
unknown ages, but an immortal idea had swept life into the dead
masses it molded—they lived and floated still on the memory of a
mighty glory. The glory of the race—

The race that lived in twenty-foot, rounded domes.

The astronomer turned. Hidden now by the rise of the verdant
land was one of the villages that race built today. Low, rounded things,
built, perhaps, of this same strange, gleaming crystal, a secret half-
remembered from a day that must have been—

The city flamed before him. Across ten—or was it twenty—thousand millenniums, the thought of the builders reached to this man of
another race. A builder who thought and dreamed of a mighty future,
marching on, on forever in the aisles of time. He must have looked
from some high, wind-swept balcony of the city to a star-sprinkled
sky—and seen the argosies of space: mighty treasure ships that swept
back to this remembered home, coming in from the legion worlds of
space, from far stars and unknown, clustered suns; Titan ships, burdened with strange cargoes of unguessed things.

And the city peopled itself before him; the skies stirred in a moment's
flash. It was the day of Rhth's glory then! Mile-long ships hovered in the
blue, settling, slow, slow, home from worlds they'd circled. Familiar sights,
familiar sounds, greeting their men again. Flashing darts of silver that
twisted through mazes of the upper air, the soft, vast music of the
mighty city. The builder lived, and looked out across his dream—

But, perhaps, from his height in the looming towers he could see
across the swelling ground to the low, rounded domes of his people,
his far descendants seeking the friendly shelter of the shading trees—

Ron Thule stood among the buildings of the city. He trod a pavement
of soft, green moss, and looked behind to the swell of the land. The
wind had laid this pavement. The moving air was the only force that
maintained the city's walks. A thousand thousand years it had swept
its gatherings across the plain, and deposited them as an offering at
the base of these calm towers. The land had built up slowly, age
on age, till it was five hundred feet higher than the land the builder
had seen.

But his dream was too well built for time to melt away. Slowly time was burying it, even as long since, time had buried him. The towers took no notice. They dreamed up to the blue of the skies and waited. They were patient; they had waited now a million, or was it ten million years? Some day, some year, the builders must return, dropping in their remembered argosies from the far, dim reaches of space, as they had once these ages gone. The towers waited; they were faithful to their trust. They had their memories, memories of a mighty age, when giants walked and worlds beyond the stars paid tribute to the city. Their builders would come again. Till then, naught bothered them in their silence.

But where the soft rains of a hundred thousand generations had drained from them, their infinite endurance softened to its gentle touch. Etched channels and rounded gutters, the mighty carvings dimming, rounding, their powerful features betrayed the slow effects. Perhaps—it had been so long—so long—even the city was forgetting what once it was. They had waited, these towers, for—

And the builders walked in the shade of the trees, and built rounded domes. And a new race of builders was come, a race the city did not notice in its age-long quiet. Ron Thule looked up to them and wondered if it were meant to be that his people should carry on the dream begun so long ago.

Softened by the silence, voices from the expedition reached him. "—diamond won't scratch it, Shor Nun—more elastic than beryl steel. Tough—" That was Dee Lun, the metallurgist. He would learn that secret somehow. They would all learn. And Shor Nun, commander, executive, atomic engineer, would learn the secrets that their power plants must hold. The dream—the city's life—would go on!

Ron Thule wandered on. No duty his, today; no responsibility to study carefully the form and turn of sweeping line, the hidden art that floated ten millions of tons of mass on the grace of a line. That for the archaeologist and the engineer. Nor his to study the cunning form of brace and girder, the making of the pearly walls. That for the metallurgist and the chemist.

Seun was beside him, looking slowly about the great avenues that swept away into slim canyons in the distance.

"Your people visited ours, once," said Ron Thule softly. "There are legends, the golden gods that came to Pareeth, bringing gifts of fire and the bow and the hammer. The myths have endured through two millions of our years—four and a half millions of yours. With fire and bow and hammer my people climbed to civilization. With atomic power they blasted themselves back to the swamps. Four times they climbed, discovered the secret of the atom, and blasted themselves back to the swamps. Yet all the changes could not efface the thankfulness to the golden gods, who came when Pareeth was young."

Seun nodded slowly. His unspoken thoughts formed clear and sharp in the astronomer's mind. "Yes, I know. It was the city builders. Once, your sun and ours circled in a system as a double star. A wandering star crashed through that system, breaking it, and in the breaking making planets. Your sun circled away, the new-formed planets cooling; our Sun remained, these worlds cooling till the day life appeared. We are twin races, born of the same stellar birth. The city builders knew that, and sought your worlds. They were a hundred thousand light years distant, in that time, across all the width of the galaxy, as the two suns circled in separate orbits about the mass of the galaxy.

"The city builders went to see your race but once. They had meant to return, but before the return was made they had interfered in the history of another race, helping them. For their reward the city builders were attacked by their own weapons, by their own pupils. Never again have we disturbed another race."

"Across the galaxy, though. The Great Year—how could they—so many stars—"

"The problem of multiple bodies? The city builders solved it; they traced the orbits of all the suns of all space; they knew then what sun must once have circled with ours. The mathematics of it—I have forgotten—I cannot develop it. I am afraid I cannot answer your thoughts. My people have forgotten so many things the city builders knew.

"But your people seek entrance to the buildings. I know the city, all its ways and entrances. The drifting soil has covered every doorway, save those that once were used for the great airships. They are still unblocked. I know of one at this level, I think. Perhaps—"

Ron Thule walked slowly back toward the group. Seun was speaking with Shor Nun, and now they angled off across the city. Their voices hushed; their footfalls were lost in the silence that brooded endlessly over the towers. Down timeless avenues they marched, a tiny band in the valley of the Titans. The towers marched on and on, on either side, up over low hills, beyond the horizon. Then, before them, in the side of one of the milky walls a great opening showed. Some five feet above the level of the drifted soil, it led into the vast, black maw of the building. The little party grouped at the base, then, laboriously, one of the engineers boosted and climbed his way to the threshold and dropped a rope to a companion.

Seun stood a bit apart, till Shor Nun lifted himself up to the higher level and stood on the milky floor. Then the man of Rhth seemed to glow slightly; a golden haze surrounded him and he floated effortlessly up from the ground and into the doorway.

The engineers, Shor Nun, all stood frozen, watching him. Seun stopped, turned, half-smiling. "How? It is the *lathan*, the suit I wear."

"It defies gravity?" asked Shor Nun, his dark eyes narrowing in keenest interest.

"Defies gravity? No, it does not defy, for gravity is a natural law. The city builders knew that. They made these suits shortly before they left the city. The *lathan* simply bends gravity to will. The mechanism is in the filaments of the back, servant to a wish. Its operation— I know only vague principles. I—I have forgotten so much. I will try to explain—"

Ron Thule felt the thoughts parading through his mind: Nodes and vibrations, atoms and less than atoms, a strange, invisible fabric of woven strains that were not there. His mind rebelled. Vague, inchoate stirrings of ideas that had no clarity; the thoughts were formless and indistinct, uncertain of themselves. They broke off.

"We have forgotten so much of the things the city builders knew, their arts and techniques," Seun explained. "They built things and labored that things might surround and protect them, so they thought. They labored generations that this city might be. They strove and thought and worked, and built fleets that sailed beyond the farthest star the clearest night reveals. They brought here their gains, their hard-won treasures—that they might build and make to protect these things.

"They were impermanent things, at best. How little is left of their five-million-year striving. We have no things today, nor any protecting of things. And we have forgotten the arts they developed to protect and understand these things. And with them, I am sorry, I have forgotten the thoughts that made the *lathan* understandable."

Shor Nun nodded slowly, turned to. his party. Ron Thule looked back from this slight elevation, down the long avenue. And his eyes wandered aside to this descendant of the mighty dreamers, who dreamed no more.

"Seek passages to lower levels," said Shor Nun's voice. "Their records, their main interest must have centered near the ancient ground level. The engineers—we will seek the lowest, subsurface levels, where the powers and the forces of the city must have been generated. Come."

The opalescent light that filtered through the walls of the building faded to a rose dusk as they burrowed deeper into the vast pile. Corridors branched and turned; rooms and offices dust-littered and barren opened from them. Down the great two-hundred-foot corridor by which they had entered, ships had once floated, and at the heart of the building was a cavernous place where these ships had once rested— and rested still! Great, dim shapes, half-seen in the misted light that filtered through wall on translucent wall.

The room blazed suddenly with the white light of half-a-dozen atomic torches, and the opalescent walls of the room reflected the flare across the flat, dusty sweep of the great floor. Two-score smooth shapes of flowing lines clustered on the floor, a forgotten company of travelers that had stopped here, once; when the city roared in triumphant life. A powdery, gray dust covered their crystal hulls.

Slowly, Shor Nun walked toward the nearest of them, a slim, thirty-foot-long private ship, waiting through eternity for a forgotten hand. The open lock at the side lighted suddenly at the touch of his foot, and soft lights appeared throughout the ship. Somewhere a soft, low humming began, and faded into silence in a moment. "Drus Nol— come with me. Seun, do you know the mechanism of these ships?"

The man of Rhth hesitated, then shook his head slowly. "I cannot explain it." He sighed. "They will not function now; they drew their power from the central plant of the city, and that has ceased operation. The last of the city builders shut it down as they left."

The men of Pareeth entered the ship hesitantly, and even while they walked toward the central control cabin at the nose, the white lighting dimmed through yellow, and faded out. Only their own torches remained. The stored power that had laid hidden in some cells aboard this craft was gone in a last, fitful glow. Somewhere soft, muffled thuds of relays acted, switching vainly to seek charged, emergency cells. The lights flared and died, flared and vanished. The questing relays relaxed with a tired click.

Dust-shrouded mechanism, etched in the light of flaring torches, greeted their eyes, hunched bulks, and gleaming tubes of glassy stuff that by its sparkling, fiery life must be other than any glass they knew, more nearly kin to the brilliant refraction of the diamond.

"The power plant," said Shor Nun softly, "I think we had best look at that first. These are probably decayed; there might still be some stored power in the central plant they could pick up and give us a fatal shock. The insulation here—"

But the city builders had built well. There was no sign of frayed and age-rotted insulation. Only slight gray dust lay in torn blankets, tender fabric their movements had disturbed.

Seun walked slowly toward the far end of the room, rounding the silent, lightless bulks of the ancient ships. The dust of forgotten ages stirred softly in his wake, settled behind him. The men of Pareeth gathered in his steps, followed him toward the far wall.

A doorway opened there, and they entered a small room. The archaeologist's breath whistled: the four walls were decorated with friezes of the history of the race that had built, conquered and sailed a universe—and lived in domes under sheltering trees.

Seun saw his interest, touched a panel at his side. Soundlessly, a door slid from the wall, clicked softly, and completed the frieze on that wall. The archaeologist was sketching swiftly, speaking to the chemist and the photographer as he worked. The torches flared higher for a moment, and the men moved about in the twenty-foot room, making way for the remembering eye of the little camera.

As Seun touched another stud, the door slid back into the wall. The room of the ships was gone. Hastily, the men of Pareeth turned to Seun.

"Will that elevator work safely to raise us again? You said the power was cut off—"

"There is stored power. Nearly all has leaked away, but it was designed to be sufficient to run all this city and all its ships, wherever they might be, for seven days. There is power enough. And there are foot passages if you fear the power will not be sufficient. This is the lowest level; this is the level of the machines, the heart of the city— nearly one thousand feet below the level at which we entered."

"Are the machines, the power plant, in this building?"

"There is only one building, here beneath the ground. It is the city, but it has many heads. The power plant is off here, I think. It has been a long time since I came this way. I was young then, and the city builders fascinated me. Their story is interesting and—"

"Interesting—" The thought seemed to echo in Ron Thule's mind. The story of the conquest of the universe, the story of achievement such as his race could only dream of yet. They had dreamed—and done! And that, to their descendants, that was—*interesting*. Interesting to this dark, strange labyrinth of branching corridors, and strange, hooded bulks. Production machinery, he knew, somehow, production machinery that forgotten workmen had hooded as they stepped away temporarily—for a year or two, perhaps till the waning population should increase again and make new demands on it. Then great storerooms, bundled things that might be needed, spare parts, and stored records and deeds. Libraries of dull metal under gray dust. The unneeded efforts of a thousand generations, rotting in this quiet dark that he, Ron Thule, and his companions had disturbed with the moment's rush of atomic flame.

Then the tortuous corridor branched, joined others, became suddenly a great avenue descending into the power room, the heart of the city and all that it had meant. They waited still, the mighty engines the last of the builders had shut down as he left, waited to start again the work they had dropped for the moment, taking a well-earned rest. But they must have grown tired in that rest, that waiting for the resurgence of their masters. They glowed dimly under the thin blankets of grayed dust, reflecting the clear brilliance of the prying light.

Shor Nun halted at the gate, his engineer beside him. Slowly, Seun of Rhth paced into the great chamber. "By the golden gods of Pareeth, Drus Nol, do you see that insulation—those bus-bars!"

"Five million volts, if it's no better than we build," the engineer said, "and I suppose they must be busses, though, by the stars of space, they look like columns! They're twenty-five feet through. But, man, man, the generator—for it must be a generator—it's no longer than the busses it energizes."

"When the generator operated," Seun's thoughts came, "the field it created ran through the bars, so that they, too, became nearly perfect conductors. The generator supplied the city, and its ships, wherever in all space they might be." And the further thought came into their minds, "It was the finest thing the city builders had."

Shor Nun stepped over the threshold. His eyes followed the immense busses, across in a great loop to a dimly sparkling switch panel, then across, and down to a thing in the center of the hall, a thing—

Shor Nun cried out, laughed and sobbed all at one moment. His hands clawed at his eyes; he fell to his knees, groaning. "Don't look— by the gods, don't look—" he gasped.

Drus Nol leaped forward, bent at his side. Shor Nun's feet moved in slow arcs through the dust of the floor, and his hands covered his face.

Seun of Rhth stepped over to him with a strange deliberation that yet was speed. "Shor Nun," came his thought, and the man of Pareeth straightened under it, "stand up."

Slowly, like an automaton, the commander of the expedition rose, twitching, his hands falling to his sides. His eyes were blank, white things in their sockets, and horrible to look at.

"Shor Nun, look at me, turn your eyes on me," said Seun. He stood half a head taller than the man of Pareeth, very slim and straight, and his eyes seemed to glow in the light that surrounded him.

As though pulled by a greater force, Shor Nun's eyes turned slowly, and first their brown edges, then the pupils showed again. The frozen madness in his face relaxed; he slumped softly into a more natural position—and Seun looked away.

Unsteadily, Shor Nun sat down on a great angling beam. "Don't look for the end of those busses, Dru Nol—it is not good. They knew all the universe, and the ends of it, long before they built this city. The things these men have forgotten embrace all the knowledge our race has, and a thousand thousand times more, and yet they have the ancient characteristics that made certain things possible to the city builders. I do not know what that thing may be, but my eyes had to follow it, and it went into another dimension. Seun, what is that thing?"

"The generator supplied the power for the city, and for the ships of the city, wherever they might be in space. In all the universe they could draw on the power of that generator, through that *sorgan* unit. That was the master unit; from it flowed the power of the generator, instantaneously, to any ship in all space, so long as its corresponding unit was tuned. It created a field rotating"—and the minds of his hearers refused the term—"which involves, as well, time.

"In the first revolution it made, the first day it was built, it circled to the ultimate end of time and the universe, and back to the day it was built. And in all that sweep, every *sorgan* unit tuned to it must follow. The power that drove it died when the city was deserted, but it is still making the first revolution, which it made and completed in the first hundredth-of-a-second it existed.

"Because it circled to the end of time, it passed this moment in its swing, and every other moment that ever is to be. Were you to wipe it out with your mightiest atomic blast, it would not be disturbed, for it is in the next instant, as it was when it was built. And so it is at the end of time, unchanged. Nothing in space or time can alter that, for it has already been at the end of time. That is why it rotates still, and will rotate when this world dissolves, and the stars die out and scatter as dust in space. Only when the ultimate equality is established, when no more change is, or can be, will it be at rest—for then other things will be equal to it, all space equated to it, because space, too, will be unchanged through time.

"Since, in its first swing, it turned to that time, and back to the day it was built, it radiated its power to the end of space and back. Anywhere, it might be drawn on, and was drawn on by the ships that sailed to other stars."

Ron Thule glanced very quickly toward and away from the *sorgan* unit. It rotated motionlessly, twinkling and winking in swift immobility. It was some ten feet in diameter, a round spheroid of rigidly fixed coils that slipped away and away in flashing speed. His eyes twisted and his thoughts seemed to freeze as he looked at it. Then he seemed to see beyond and through it, as though it were an infinite window, to ten thousand other immobile, swiftly spinning coils revolving in perfect harmony, and beyond them to strange stars and worlds beyond the suns—a thousand cities such as this on a thousand planets: the empire of the city builders!

And the dream faded—faded as that dream in stone and crystal and metal, everlasting reality, had faded in the softness of human tissue.

The ship hung motionless over the towers for a long moment. Sunlight, reddened as the stars sank behind the far hills, flushed their opalescent beauty with a soft tint, softened even the harsh, utilitarian gray of the great, interstellar cruiser above them into an idle, rosy dream. A dream, perhaps, such as the towers had dreamed ten thousand times ten thousand times these long aeons they had waited?

Ron Thule looked down at them, and a feeling of satisfaction and fulfillment came to him. Pareeth would send her children. A colony here on this ancient world would bring a new, stronger blood to wash up in a great tide, to carry the ideals this race had forgotten to new heights, new achievements. Over the low hills, visible from this elevation, lay the simple, rounded domes of the people of Rhth—Seun and his little clan of half-a-hundred—the dwindling representatives of a once-great race.

It would mean death to these people—these last descendants. A new world, busy with a great work of reconquering this system, then all space! They would have no time to protect and care for these forgetful ones; these people of Rhth inevitably would dwindle swiftly in a strange, busy world. They who had forgotten progress five millions of years before; they who had been untrue to the dream of the city builders.

It was for Pareeth, and the sons of Pareeth, to carry on the abandoned path again—

CONCLUSION OF THE REPORT
TO THE COMMITTEE OF PAREETH
SUBMITTED BY SHOR NUN,
COMMANDER OF THE FIRST
INTERSTELLAR EXPEDITION

—thus it seemed wise to me that we leave at the end of a single week, despite the objections of those members of the expedition personnel who had had no opportunity to see this world. It was better not to disturb the decadent inhabitants of Rhth in any further degree, and better that we return to Pareeth with these reports as soon as might be, since building operations would soon commence on the twelve new ships.

I suggest that these new ships be built of the new material *rhthite,* superior to our best previous materials. As has been shown by the incredible endurance of the buildings of the city, this material is exceedingly stable, and we have found it may be synthesized from the cheapest materials, saving many millions in the construction work to be undertaken.

It has been suggested by a certain member of the expedition, Thon Raul the anthropologist, that we may underestimate the degree of civilization actually retained by the people of Rhth, specifically that it is possible that a type of civilization exists so radically divergent from our own, that it is to us unrecognizable as civilization. His suggestion of a purely mental civilization of a high order seems untenable in the face of the fact that Seun, a man well-respected by his fellows, was unable to project his thoughts clearly at any time, nor was there any evidence that any large proportion of his thoughts were to himself of a high order of clarity. His answers were typified by "I have forgotten the development—" or "It is difficult for me to explain—" or "The exact mechanism is not understood by all of us—a few historians—"

It is, of course, impossible to disprove the assertion that such a civilization is possible, but there arises in my mind the question of advantage gained, it being a maxim of any evolutionary or advancing process that the change so made is, in some manner, beneficial to the modified organism of society. Evidently, from the statements made by Seun of Rhth, they have forgotten the knowledge once held by the mighty race that built the cities, and have receded to a state of repose without labor or progress of any kind.

Thon Raul has mentioned the effect produced on me by close observation of the *sorgan* mechanism, and further stated that Seun was able to watch this same mechanism without trouble, and able to benefit me after my unfortunate experience. I would point out that mental potentialities decline extremely slowly; it is possible that the present, decadent people have the mental potentialities, still inherent in them, that permitted the immense civilization of the city builders.

It lies there, dormant. They are lost for lack of the driving will that makes it effective. The *Pareeth,* the greatest ship our race has ever built, is powered, fueled, potentially mighty now—and inert for lack of a man's driving will, since no one is at her helm.

So it is with them. Still, the mental capacity of the race overshadows us. But the divine fire of ambition has died. They rely wholly on materials and tools given them by a long-dead people, using even these in an automatic and uncomprehending way, as they do their curious flying suits.

Finally, it is our conclusion that the twelve ships under consideration should be completed with all possible speed, and the program as at present outlined carried out in full; *i.e.,* seven thousand six hundred and thirty-eight men and women between the ages of eighteen and twenty-eight will be selected on a basis of health, previous family history, personal character and ability as determined by psychological tests. These will be transported, together with a basic list of necessities, to the new planet, leaving in the early months of the coming year.

Six years will be required for this trip. At the end of the first year on the new planet, when some degree of organization has been attained, one ship, refueled, will return to Pareeth. At the end of the second year two ships will return from Rhth with all data accumulated in that period. Thereafter, two will sail each year.

On Pareeth, new ships will be manufactured at whatever rate seems practicable, that more colonists may be sent as swiftly as they desire. It is suggested, however, that, in view of the immense scientific advancements already seen in the cities of Rhth, no new ships be made until a ship returns with the reports of the first year's studies, in order that any resultant scientific advances may be incorporated.

The present crew of the *Pareeth* have proven themselves in every way competent, courageous and cooperative. As trained and experienced interstellar operators, it is further suggested that the one hundred men be divided among the thirteen ships to sail, the *Pareeth* retaining at least fifty of her present crew and acting as guide to the remainder of the fleet. Ron Thule, it is specifically requested, shall be astronomical commander of the fleet aboard the flagship. His astronomical work in positioning and calculating the new system has been of the highest order, and his presence is vitally needed.

Signed by me, SHOR NUN,
this thirty-second day after landing.

UNANIMOUS REPORT OF THE
COMMITTEE OF PAREETH ON
THE FIRST EXPEDITION TO THE
PLANET RHTH

The Committee of Pareeth, after due consideration of the reports of Folder R127-s6-11, entitled "Interstellar Exploration Reports, Expedition I," do send to commander of said expedition, Shor Nun, greetings.

The committee finds the reports highly satisfying, both in view of the successful nature of the expedition, and in that they represent an almost unanimous opinion.

In consequence, it is ordered that the ships designated by the department of engineering plan as numbers 18834–18846 be constructed with all such speed as is possible.

It is ordered that the seven thousand six hundred and thirty-eight young people be chosen in the manner prescribed in the attached docket of details.

It is ordered that in the event of the successful termination of the new colonizing expedition, such arrangements shall be made that the present, decadent inhabitants of the planet Rhth shall be allowed free and plentiful land; that they shall be in no way molested or attacked. It is the policy of this committee of Pareeth that this race shall be wards of the newly founded Rhth State, to be protected and in all ways aided in their life.

We feel, further, a deep obligation to this race in that the archaeological and anthropological reports clearly indicate that it was the race known to them as the city builders who first brought fire, the bow and the hammer to our race in mythological times. Once their race gave ours a foothold on the climb to civilization. It is our firm policy that these last, decadent members of that great race shall be given all protection, assistance and encouragement possible to tread again the climbing path.

It is ordered that the first colony city on Rhth shall be established at the spot represented on the accompanying maps as N'yor, as called in the language of the Rhth people, near the point of landing of the first expedition. The nearby settlement of the Rhth people is not to be molested in any way, unless military action is forced upon the colonists.

It is ordered that if this condition shall arise, if the Rhth people object to the proposed settlement at the spot designated as N'yor, arbitration be attempted. Should this measure prove unsuccessful, military penalties shall be exacted, but only to the extent found necessary for effective action. The colonists shall aid in the moving of the settlement of the Rhth people, if the Rhth people do not desire to be near the city of the colonists.

In any case, it is ordered that the colonists shall, in every way within their means, aid, advance and inspire the remaining people of Rhth.

It is further ordered that Shor Nun, commander, shall be plenipotentiary representative of the committee of Pareeth, with all powers of a discretionary nature, his command to be military and of unquestioned authority until such time as the colony shall have been established for a period of two years. There shall then have been established a representative government of such nature and powers as the colonists themselves find suitable.

It is then suggested that this government, the State of Rhth, shall exchange such representatives with the committee of Pareeth as are suitable in the dealings of two sovereign powers.

Until the establishment of the State of Rhth, it is further ordered that—

The grassland rolled away very softly among the brown boles of scattered trees. It seemed unchanged. The city seemed unchanged, floating as it had a thousand thousand years halfway between the blue of the sky and the green of the planet. Only it was not alone in its opalescent beauty now; twelve great ships floated serene, motionless, above its towers, matching them in glowing color. And on the low roll of the hill, a thirteenth ship, gray and grim and scarred with eighteen years of nearly continuous space travel, rested. The locks moved; men stepped forth into the light of the low afternoon sun.

To their right, the mighty monument of the city builders; to their left, the low, rounded domes of the great race's descendants. Ron Thule stepped down from the lock to join the eight department commanders who stood looking across toward the village among the trees.

Shor Nun turned slowly to the men with him, shook his head, smiling. "I did not think to ask. I have no idea what their life span may be. Perhaps the man we knew as Seun has died. When I first landed here, I was a young man. I am middle-aged now. That time may mean old age and extinction to these people."

"There is one man coming toward us now, Shor Nun," said Ron Thule softly. "He is floating on his—what was that name?—it is a long time since I heard it."

The man came nearer leisurely; time seemed to mean little to these people. The soft, blue glow of his suit grew, and he moved a bit more rapidly, as though conscious of their importance. "I—I think that is Seun," said the archaeologist. "I have seen those pictures so many times—"

Seun stood before them again, smiling the slow, easy smile they had known twelve years before. Still he stood slim and straight, his face lined only with the easy gravings of humor and kindliness. He was as unchanged as the grassland, as the eternal city. The glow faded as he settled before them, noiselessly. "You have come back to Rhth, Shor Nun?"

"Yes, Seun. We promised you that when we left. And with some of our people as well. We hope to establish a colony here, near the ancient city; hope some day to learn again the secrets of the city builders, to roam space as they once did. Perhaps we will be able to occupy some of the long-deserted buildings of the city and bring life to it again."

"A permanent colony?" asked Seun thoughtfully.

"Yes, Seun."

"There are many other cities here, on this planet, nearly as large, equipped with all the things that made this city. To my race the quiet of the unstirred air is very dear; could you not as easily establish your colony in Shao—or Loun—any of the other places?"

Shor Nun shook his head slowly. "I am sorry, Seun. We had hoped to live near you, that we might both discover again those forgotten secrets. We must stay here, for this was the last city your people deserted; here in it are all the things they ever built, the last achievements of the city builders. We will aid you in moving your colony if you wish, to some other meadowland near the sea. All the world is the same to your people; only this city was built in this way; it was the last to be deserted."

Seun exhaled softly, looked at the ten men of Pareeth. His mind seemed groping, feeling for something. His deep blue eyes misted in thought, then cleared slowly as Ron Thule watched. Slowly, they moved from man to man of the group, pausing a moment at the anthropologist, catching Shor Nun's gaze for an instant, centering slowly on Ron Thule.

Ron Thule looked into the deep eyes for a moment, for a long eternity—deep, clear eyes, like mountain lakes. Subtly, the Rhthman's face seemed to change as he watched the eyes. The languor there changed, became a sense of timelessness, of limitlessness. The pleasant, carefree air became, somehow—different. It was the same, but as the astronomer looked into those eyes, a new interpretation came to him. A sudden, vast fear welled up in him, so that his heart contracted, and a sudden tremor came to his hands. "You have forgotten—" he mumbled unsteadily. "Yes—but you—"

Seun smiled, the firm mouth relaxing in approval. "Yes, Ron Thule. That is enough. I sought your mind. Someone must understand. Remember that only twice in the history of our race have we attempted to alter the course of another's history, for by that you will understand what I must do."

Seun's eyes turned away. Shor Nun was looking at him, and Ron Thule realized, without quite understanding his knowledge, that no time had elapsed for these others. Now he stood motionless, paralyzed with a new understanding.

"We must stay here," Seun's mind voice spoke softly. "I, too, had hoped we might live on this world together, but we are too different. We are too far apart to be so near."

"You do not wish to move?" asked Shor Nun sorrowfully.

Seun looked up. The twelve great interstellar cruisers hovered closer now, forming, almost, a roof over this conference ground. "That would be for the council to say, I know. But I think they would agree with me, Shor Nun."

Vague pictures and ideas moved through their minds, thoughts emanating from Seun's mind. Slowly, his eyes dropped from the twelve opalescent cruisers to the outstretched palm of his hand. His eyes grew bright, and the lines of his face deepened in concentration. The air seemed to stir and move; a tenseness of inaction came over the ten men of Pareeth and they moved restlessly.

Quite abruptly, a dazzling light appeared over Seun's hand, sparkling, myriad colors—and died with a tiny, crystalline clatter. Something lay in his upturned palm: a round, small thing of aquamarine crystal, shot through with veins and arteries of softly pulsing, silver light. It moved and altered as they watched, fading in color, changing the form and outline of light.

Again the tinkling, crystalline clatter came, and some rearrangement had taken place. There lay in his hand a tiny globe of ultimate night, an essence of darkness that no light could illumine, cased in a crystal surface. Stars shone in it, from the heart, from the borders, stars that moved and turned in majestic splendor in infinite smallness. Then faded.

Seun raised his eyes. The darkness faded from the crystal in his hand, and pulsing, little veins of light appeared in it. He raised it in his fingers, and nine of Pareeth's men fell back. Ron Thule looked on with frozen, wooden face.

A wave of blue haze washed out, caught and lifted the men and carried them effortlessly, intangibly back to the lock, through the lock. From the quiet of the grasslands they were suddenly in the steel of the ship that clanged and howled with alarms. Great engines bellowed suddenly to life.

Ron Thule stood at the great, clear port light of the lock. Outside, Seun, in his softly glowing suit, floated a few feet from the ground. Abruptly, the great atomic engines of the *Pareeth* shrilled a chorus of ravening hate, and from the three great projectors the annihilating beams tore out, shrieking destruction through the air—and vanished. Seun stood at the junction of death, and his crystal glowed softly. Twelve floating ships screamed to the tortured shriek of overloaded atomics, and the planet below cursed back with quarter-mile-long tongues of lightning.

Somewhere, everywhere, the universe thrummed to a vast, crystalline note, and hummed softly. In that instant, the green meadowland of Rhth vanished; the eternal city dissolved into blackness. Only blackness, starless, lightless shone outside the lock port light. The soft, clear note of the crystal hummed and beat and surged. The atomic engine's cry died full-throated. An utter, paralyzed quiet descended on the ship, so that the cry of a child somewhere echoed and reverberated noisily down the steel corridors.

The crystal in Seun's hand beat and hummed its note. The blackness beyond the port became gray. One by one, six opalescent ships shifted into view in the blackness beyond, moving with a slow deliberation, as though forced by some infinite power into a certain, predetermined configuration. Like atoms in a crystal lattice they shifted, seemed to click into place and hold steady—neatly, geometrically arranged.

Then noise came back to the ship; sounds that crept in, afraid of themselves, grew courageous and clamored; pounding feet of men, and women's screams.

"We're out of space," gasped Shor Nun. "That crystal—that thing in his hand—"

"In a space of our own," said Ron Thule. "Wait till the note of the crystal dies down. It is weakening, weakening slowly, to us, but it will be gone, and then—"

Shor Nun turned to him, his dark eyes shadowed, his face pale and drawn. "What do you know—how—"

Ron Thule stood silent. He did not know. Somewhere, a crystal echoed for a moment in rearrangement and tinkling sound; the universe echoed to it softly, as the last, faint tone died away.

"Shor Nun—Shor Nun—" a slow, wailing cry was building up in the ship. Scampering feet on metal floors became a march.

Shor Nun sobbed once. "That crystal—they had not lost the weapons of the city builders. Space of our own? No—it is like the *sorgan*: It rotates us to the end of time! This is the space we knew—when all time has died, and the stars are gone and the worlds are dust. This is the end of the nothingness. The city builders destroyed their enemies thus—by dumping them at the end of time and space. I know. They must have. And Seun had the ancient weapon. When the humming note of the crystal dies—the lingering force of translation—

"Then we shall die, too. Die in the death of death. Oh, gods—Sulon—Sulon, my dear—our son—" Shor Nun, commander, seemed to slump from his frozen rigidity. He turned abruptly away from the port light toward the inner lock door. It opened before him suddenly, and a technician stumbled down, white-faced and trembling.

"Commander—Shor Nun—the engines are stopped. The atoms will not explode; no power can be generated. The power cells are supplying emergency power, but the full strength of the drive does not move or shake the ship! What—what is this?"

Shor Nun stood silent. The ship thrummed and beat with the softening, dying note of the universe-distant crystal that held all the beginnings and the endings of time and space in a man's hand. The note was fading; very soft and sweet, it was. Through the ship the hysterical cry of voices had changed; it was softening with the thrum, softening, listening to the dying thread of infinitely sweet sound.

Shor Nun shrugged his shoulders, turned away. "It does not matter. The force is fading. Across ten million years the city builders have reached to protect their descendants."

The note was very low—very faint; a quivering hush bound the ship. Beyond the port light, the six sister ships began to move again, very stealthily away, retreating toward the positions they had held when this force first seized them. Then—

Shor Nun's choked cry was drowned in the cries of the others in the lock. Blinding white light stabbed through the port like a solid, incandescent bar. Their eyes were hot and burning.

Ron Thule, his astronomer's eyes accustomed to rapid, extreme changes of light, recovered first. His word was indistinct, a cross between a sob and a chuckle.

Shor Nun stood beside him, winking tortured eyes. The ship was waking, howling into a mad, frightened life; the children screamed in sympathetic comprehension of their elders' terror.

White, blazing sunlight on green grass and brown dirt. The weathered gray of concrete, and the angular harshness of great building cradles. A skyline of white-tipped, blue mountains, broken by nearer, less-majestic structures of steel and stone and glass, glinting in the rays of a strong, warm sun with a commonness, a familiarity that hurt. A vast nostalgia welled up in them at the sight—

And died before another wave of terror. "Darun Tara," said Shor Nun. "Darun Tara, on Pareeth. I am mad—this is mad. A crazy vision in a crazy instant as the translating force collapses. Darun Tara as it was when we left it six long years ago. Changed—that half-finished shed is still only three quarters finished. I can see Thio Rog, the port-master there, coming toward us. I am mad. I am five light years away—"

"It *is* Darun Tara, Shor Nun," Ron Thule whispered. "And the city builders could never have done this. I understand now. I—"

He stopped. The whole, great ship vibrated suddenly to thwang like the plucked bass string of a Titan's harp. Creaks and squeals, and little grunting readjustments, the fabric of the cruiser protested.

"My telescope—" cried Ron Thule. He was running toward the inner lock door, into the dark mouth of the corridor.

Again the ship thrummed to a vibrant stroke. The creaking of the girders and strakes protested bitterly; stressed rivets grunted angrily.

Men pounded on the lock door from without. Thio Rog, Ton Gareth, Hol Brawn—familiar faces staring anxiously in. Shor Nun moved dully toward the gate controls—

Shor Nun knocked gently at the closed, metal door of the ship's obser-vatory. Ron Thule's voice answered, muffled, vague, from beyond.

The commander opened the door; his breath sucked in sibilantly. "Space!" he gasped.

"Come and see, come and see," the astronomer called softly.

Shor Nun instinctively felt his way forward on tiptoe. The great observatory room was space; it was utter blackness, and the corridor lights were swallowed in it the instant the man crossed the threshold. Blackness, starred by tiny, brilliant points, scattered very sparsely, in every direction.

"Seun took the telescope, but he left me this, instead. I under-stand now; he said that only twice had they attempted to alter a race's history.

"This is space, and *that* is Troth, our own star. Watch—"

The star expanded; the whole of this imageless space exploded outward and vanished through the unseen walls of the observatory. Troth floated alone, centered in the invisible room. Seven tiny dots of light hung near it, glowing in its reflected light.

"And that is our system. Now this is the star of Rhth—"

Space contracted, shifted and exploded, leaving one shining, yel-lowish star, attended by five brightly visible worlds.

"The other planets are too small or too dimly illuminated to see. When I came there was a new system displayed. This one."

Another planetary system appeared.

"That is the system of Prother."

"Prother!" Shor Nun stared. "Five and a half light years away—and planets?"

"Planets. Uninhabited, for I can bring each planet as near as I will. But, Shor Nun"—sorrow crept into the astronomer's voice—"though I can see every detail of each planet of that system, though I can see each outline of the planets of Rhth's system—only those three stars can I see, close by."

"No other planetary systems!"

"No other planetary system that Seun will reveal to us. I understand. One we won on the right of our own minds, our own knowledge; we reached his worlds. We had won a secret from nature by our own powers; it was part of the history of our race. They do not want to molest, or in any way influence the history of a race—so they permitted us to return, if only we did not disturb them. They could not refuse us that, for it would be a breach in their feelings of justice.

"But they felt it needful to dispossess us, Shor Nun, and this Seun did. But had he done no more, our history was altered, changed vitally. So—this he gave us; he has shown us another, equally near planetary system that we may use. We have not lost vitally. That is his justice."

"His justice. Yes, I came to you, Ron Thule, because you seemed to know somewhat of the things that happened." Shor Nun's voice was low in the dark of the observatory. He looked at the floating planets of Prother. "What is—Seun? How has this happened? Do you know? You know that we were greeted by our friends—and they turned away from us.

"Six years have passed for us. They wanted to know what misfortune made us return at the end of a single year, for only one year has passed here on Pareeth. My son was born, there in space, and he has passed his fourth birthday. My daughter is two. Yet these things have not happened, for we were gone a single year. Seun has done it, but it cannot be; Seun, the decadent son of the city builders; Seun, who has forgotten the secrets of the ships that sailed beyond the stars and the building of the Titan Towers; Seun, whose people live in a tiny village sheltered from the rains and the sun by a few green trees.

"What are these people of Rhth?"

Ron Thule's voice was a whisper from the darkness. "I come from a far world, by what strange freak we will not say. I am a savage, a rising race that has not learned the secret of fire, nor bow, nor hammer. Tell me, Shor Nun, what is the nature of the two dry sticks I must rub, that fire may be born? Must they be hard, tough oak, or should one be a soft, resinous bit of pine? Tell me how I may make fire."

"Why—with matches or a heat ray— No, Ron Thule. Vague thoughts, meaningless ideas and unclear. I—I have forgotten the ten thousand generations of development. I cannot retreat to a level you, savage of an untrained world, would understand. I—I have forgotten."

"Then tell me, how I must hold the flint, and where must I press with a bit of deer horn that the chips shall fly small and even, so that the knife will be sharp and kill my prey for me? And how shall I rub and wash and treat the wood of the bow, or the skin of the slain animal that I may have a coat that will not be stiff, but soft and pliable?"

"Those, too, I have forgotten. Those are unnecessary things. I cannot help you, savage. I would greet you, and show you the relics of our deserted past in museums. I might conduct you through ancient caves, where mighty rock walls defended my ancestors against the wild things they could not control.

"Yes, Ron Thule. I have forgotten the development."

"Once"—Ron Thule's voice was tense—"the city builders made atomic generators to release the energy bound in that violent twist of space called an atom. They made the *sorgan* to distribute its power to their clumsy shells of metal and crystal—the caves that protected them from the wild things of space.

"Seun has forgotten the atom; he thinks in terms of space. The powers of space are at his direct command. He created the crystal that brought us here from the energy of space, because it made easy a task his mind alone could have done. It was no more needful than is an adding machine. His people have no ships; they are anywhere in space they will without such things. Seun is not a decadent son of the city builders. His people never forgot the dream that built the city. But it was a dream of childhood, and his people were children then. Like a child with his broomstick horse, the mind alone was not enough for thought; the city builders, just as ourselves, needed something of a solid metal and crystal, to make their dreams tangible."

"My son was born in space, and is four. Yet we were gone but a single year from Pareeth." Shor Nun sighed.

"Our fleet took six years to cross the gulf of five light years. In thirty seconds, infinitely faster than light, Seun returned us, that there might be the minimum change in our racial history. Time is a function of the velocity of light, and five light years of distance is precisely equal to five years of time multiplied by the square root of minus one. When we traversed five light years of space in no appreciable time, we dropped back, also, through five years of time.

"You and I have spent eighteen years of effort in this exploration, Shor Nun—eighteen years of our manhood. By this hurting us back Seun has forever denied us the planets we earned by those long years of effort. But now he does not deny us wholly.

"They gave us this, and by it another sun, with other planets. This Seun gave not to me, as an astronomer; it is his gift to the race. Now it is beyond us ever to make another. And this which projects this space around us will cease to be, I think, on the day we land on those other planets of that other sun, where Seun will be to watch us—as he may be here now, to see that we understand his meanings.

"I know only this—that sun I can see, and the planets circling it. The sun of Rhth I can see, and those planets, and our own. But— though these others came so near at the impulse of my thoughts, no other sun in all space can I see so near.

"That, I think, is the wish of Seun and his race."

The astronomer stiffened suddenly.

Shor Nun stood straight and tense.

"Yes," whispered Seun, very softly, in their minds.

Ron Thule sighed.

# OUT OF NIGHT

The Sarn Mother looked down at Grayth with unblinking, golden eyes. "You administer the laws under the Sarn," she clicked waspishly. "The Sarn make the laws. Men obey them. That was settled once and for all time four thousand years ago. The Sarn Mother has determined that this thing is the way of progress that is most desirable. It is clear?"

Grayth looked up at her, his slow-moving eyes following from the toe pads, up the strange, rope-flexible legs, up the rounded, golden body to the four twined arms, his lips silent. His steel-gray eyes alone conveyed his thought complete. The Sarn Mother, on her inlaid throne of State, clicked softly in annoyance.

"Aye, different races we are; the Sarn are the ruling race. The Sarn Mother will be obeyed by the slaves of her people no less than by her people. For many centuries the crazy patchwork has persisted—that the men have had freedoms that the masters have denied themselves. Henceforth men shall be ruled as the Sarn. The Sarn have been just masters; this is no more than justice. But be warned, you will see that this thing is administered at once—or the Sarn will administer it themselves."

Grayth spoke for the first time, his voice deep and powerful. "Four thousand years ago your people came to Earth and conquered our people, enslaved them, destroyed all our leaders, setting up a rabble of unintelligent slaves. Since your atomic energy, your synthetic foods, your automatic production machinery, and the enormous decrease in human population you had brought about made more of goods for each man, it worked no great hardship.

"Before ever the Sarn came to this world, your race was ruled by a matriarchy, as it is today, and must always be. To your people it is natural, for among you the females born in a generation outnumber the males five to one. You stand near seven feet tall, while the Sarn Father—as the other males of your race—is but four feet tall, but a quarter as powerful physically. Matriarchy is the inevitable heritage of your race.

"You differ from us in this fundamental of sex distribution. By pure chance our two races resemble each other superficially—two eyes, two ears, rounded heads. Your race has two, wide-separated nostrils, four arms in place of two. But internally there is no resemblance. No bone of your body is three inches long; your arms, your legs are made as a human spine, of many small bones. Your copper-bearing foods are deadly poison to us. Your *strath,* though it seems like human hair, is a sensory organ sensitive to radio waves, and a radiator of those waves. We are two races apart, fundamentally different.

"Now, like your own matriarchy, you wish to establish upon us a matriarchal government; for this reason alone, you state, the number of males to be allowed in succeeding generations is to be reduced.

"What is natural for your race is an unnatural crime upon ours. Would you insist that we should eat no better food than you eat, as we should obey no different laws? Would you legislate that we should eat your foods, as we should obey your laws? Equally, in either case you destroy us. It is to the advantage of neither race."

"Grayth, you seek to tell the Sarn Mother her mind? What is best for her good? Perhaps I have been foolish to allow such freedom to your kind, allowing this 'election' of human administrators. You, Grayth, will be replaced within this week, and not by election. The laws of the Sarn will be applied at once!"

Grayth looked at her steadily, deep-set iron-gray eyes unwavering on jewel-flecked golden ones. He sighed softly. "Your race does not know of the ancient powers of man; you are a race of people knowing and recognizing only the might of the atomic generator, the flare of the atomic-blast as power. The power of the mind is great. For ten thousand years before your coming men thought, and united in their thoughts of the unseen powers. In a hectic week your ancestors destroyed all of man's chaotic civilization, clamped on him suddenly a new world state. Before a union of thought could be attained, the thing was done, and as slow crystallization of feeling came, the poor survivors found that the conditions were not impossible. Our very difference of race protected them, to an extent, against mistreatment.

"But a crystallization has taken place during these forty centuries, a slow uniformity has built up. The mighty, chaotic thought wills of five hundred million men during three thousand generations were striving, building toward a mighty reservoir of powers, but their very disordered strivings prevented ordered formation.

"During a hundred centuries of chaotic thought, turbulent desire, those vast reservoirs of eternal, indestructible thought energies have circled space, unable to unite. During these last four millenniums those age-old forces have slowly united on a single, common thought that men destroyed by your race during the conquest have sent out.

"We of our race have felt that thing in these last years, that slowly accreting oneness of age-old will and thought, developing reality and power by the gathering of forces generated by minds released by death during ten thousand years. He is growing, a one from many, the combined thought and wisdom and power of the fifteen hundred billions of men who have lived on Earth. Aesir, he is, black as the spaces in which he formed.

"We are a different race. As you have your *strath* sensitive to radio, we have yet a more subtle sense, a sense reacting to the very essence of thought. That, too, has grown with the passing years. Over there by the wall an electrotechnician follows conduits, and his thoughts are clear to my mind, as the communications of the Sarn are to each other."

The Sarn Mother's lips twitched. "He pays no attention to us," she said very low, so that, in the huge room, only those within a few feet of her could hear. "I doubt this power you claim. Make him come here and bow down before me—and say no word."

Across the room, the human electrotechnician, clad in the stout, ungraceful clothes of his trade, the lightning emblem emblazoned on his back, looked up with a start. "Before the Sarn Mother?" his voice echoed his surprise that he, an undistinguished workman, should be called thus before the ruler of Earth. "Aye, I—" He looked about him suddenly, his face blanking in surprise as he saw no one nearer him than the gathering two hundred feet away across the black basalt floor. A red flush of confusion spread over his face, and he turned back to his task with awkward nervousness, sure that the voice from empty air, issuing an impossible summons, had been a figment of his own imagination—

The Sarn Mother looked with unwinking golden eyes at Grayth. "You may go," she said at last. "But the Law of the Sarn, that there shall be five of females and one of males, is the law of the planet."

Grayth turned slowly, his head bowed momentarily in parting salute. His body erect, and his tread firm, he walked down the lane of the gathered Sarn. Behind him, the six humans who had accompanied him fell into step. Silently, the little procession passed between the gleaming bronze of the great entrance doors and down the broad steps to the parked lawns beyond.

Bartel hastened his steps and fell in beside Grayth. "Do you think she will enforce that law? What can we do? Will she believe in this mind force, this myth from the childhood of a race?"

Grayth's eyes darkened a little. He nodded slowly. "We will go to my house. The Sarn Mother is not given to idle gestures, and she cannot lay down laws and revoke them aimlessly. But—we can talk when we reach my house." Grayth strode on thoughtfully. Sunlight lay across the lawns—sunlight and green shadows under trees. They saw the occasional darting shadow of vague huge things, high in the air, smoothlined shapes that floated wingless and soundless far above them. Then down a long avenue paved with a gray cement that would glow with soft light when night fell, they went. The broad park lands, with their jewel-like palaces of the Sarn, fell behind them, then the low wall that divided the city of the Sarn from the city of men.

The broad avenue shrank abruptly, changed from the gray, night-glowing cement to a cobbled walk. The jewel-like palaces and the sprawling parks of the Sarn gave way to neat, small houses of white-washed cement, crusted with layer on ancient layer of soft-tinted wash. For these homes nearest the Sarn City had been built after the coming of the Sarn, when the ruins of man's cities still smoldered with destruction.

The very atomic bombs that had brought that ruin to man's cities were dead now. The last traces of the cities being succumbing to the returning thrust of green, burying life. The Sarn were old on Earth and this city they had caused to be about them was old, the hard granite cobbles of the walk worn smooth and polished with the soft tread of ages.

The Sarn Mother had sat on her golden throne and watched the rains of summers smooth them, and the tread of generations of men polish them. The Sarn Mother had been old when the Sarn landed; she was unchanged now, after the passage of more than a hundred generations of men, after ten generations of the rest of her people. She was eternal.

The neat, vine-clad houses of the city of men slipped back, and the easy bustle of the square came before them, the ancient shops where a hundred and twenty generations had bought and sold and carried on their lives. He nodded absently, smiled to friends and well-wishers, noted unchanging the sullen looks of those who wore the small green-shield emblem of Drunnel's faction.

Bartel's voice spoke again at his shoulder. "Drunnel's friend, Varthil, seems less sullen today. Did you notice?" Bartel nodded faintly toward the powerful figure clad in the balance-emblemed tunic of a legal administrator. "He went so far as to smile slightly. I am undecided between two meanings."

"There is only one possible." Grayth sighed. "He has more sense than to try to make me believe he begins to regard me as a friend; therefore, he smiles not at me but to himself. You sent Thera as I suggested—"

Bartel nodded in puzzlement. "I did, Grayth, but—I cannot see the need of that. The Sarn will—"

"The Sarn Mother will do nothing. Wait till we reach the house." The square fell behind; the houses grew less ancient, subtly so, for the style of building remained unchanged, and the building had been good. There were no signs of decay in even the oldest. The lands around each house grew larger, too. There were more children in these cobbled lanes.

Grayth turned off, Bartel and three of the others with him; two, with a few words of parting, went on. Silently, they continued to the low, rambling house of faintly tinted cement that was Grayth's residence and office.

Here in this low, millennium-old building, the pyramided, loosely-knit government of the humans of Earth was concentrated. A structure based on town delegates from every human settlement of Earth, men who reported to district speakers who carried their messages to continental spokesmen and finally to the spokesman of man, and this was the spokesman's official residence. Six months ago old Tranmath, spokesman of man for twenty-two years, had died in this old building, and Grayth had been elected his successor, to "deal justly, and honorably and to the utmost of my ability so long as I may live, or until my body fails." Death or dishonesty alone could remove him from his position. Death, dishonesty, or—now—Drunnel, who for the moment represented both.

Responsible to the Sarn, responsible to the humans as well, Grayth's actual powers were limited purely to advisory capacities; he advised the Sarn, though they disregarded his suggestions as they liked. He advised the legion commanders, the police of the human towns, and they, likewise, could disregard his suggestions. The Sarn Mother knew as well as he did that he could not enforce those laws of the matriarchy, even had he desired to; the Sarn Mother did not like Grayth.

A dozen secretaries and clerks looked up as the small party entered, and looked back to their work. Enamel-and-silver disks on their headbands, the design worked into their sleeves, showed their status in society—the book and the lamp of administrators.

Grayth nodded briefly and continued across the rubberlike floor to the low door of his inner conference room. The feet of thirty generations of spokesmen had carved into that tough, rubbery stuff a channel that circled here to avoid a column, turned back to avoid a desk that had sat just so, it or its precursors, for one thousand years. Finally, it tunneled a bit under the door, and into the low-ceilinged office. It split, as the entering parties had split those thousand years, to the nine seats about the conference table, a great six-inch slab of time-stained mahogany.

Grayth seated himself at the end of the table, Bartel, the American spokesman, at his right, beside him Carron, commander of the legion of peace, Darak and Holmun, Grayth's subspokesmen. And on their heels the gray-clad electrotechnician came quietly into the room. Silently, the five men nodded greeting, while the technician placed his kit on the age-worn table. He lifted from it a shelf layer of jumbled tools, exposing tiny, banked instruments, and a thin, insulated metal rod that popped up as a spring extended it.

Skilled fingers made adjustments as tiny needles swayed delicately and came to rest. His fingers touched small controls, and the flexible metal aerial nodded and bowed and danced, bowing to every side of the room, halting suddenly as needles lifted and quivered. The technician lined it carefully, then looked along its pointing finger toward the atom-flame projector, throwing dying stars of light that settled and vanished in twinkling illumination in the air. The tiny rod glowed with bluish light as he threw a tiny stud on his instrument panel.

"That makes twelve different listeners," he grunted. "I told you the Sarn had had time to install more than one."

"And the spokesmen wondered, in years gone by, that the Sarn seemed to know their very thoughts." Grayth smiled bitterly. "We may be able to advance. I am the first spokesman in ten centuries who can hold a conference without the invisible presence of the Sarn Mother."

Carron looked angrily toward the atom-flame projector. "It's in that thing? Why don't you rip it out?"

The technician grinned. "The Sarn can hear radio waves as you hear sound. To them, that listener—a tiny radio transmitter powered probably by the atomic power of the projector—emits a clear, low hum. When we speak, the crystal modulates the radio hum with our voice frequencies. My little aerial there simply transmits a wave which, without stopping the transmitter's radio frequency carrier, strips off the modulation. If I tear out the transmitter—the hum would vanish, and the Sarn would become—curious, shall I say?"

"Furious," grunted Bartel. "Why won't they switch to another while we're in the room? They switch from one to another of those listeners irregularly."

"Ware's instrument would still work, whichever they used," Grayth explained. "He was merely curious as to which and how many they were using. There was no need to locate the listener." The technician nodded in confirmation.

Darak turned to Grayth with a sigh. "That being settled, tell me, Grayth, why does the Sarn Mother ask you to do—command you to do something she knows you have no power to accomplish?"

"Because the Sarn Mother knows I will not do it," answered the spokesman sourly, "but that Drunnel would."

"Drunnel—could he influence the Sarn Mother? I never believed she would side in human quarrels unless she was directly affected— always felt she considered them beneath her notice." Carron looked to Grayth in surprise.

Grayth settled back slowly in his great, worn chair. He lighted his pipe and began to puff, looking lazily at the gushing, soundless stars of the atom flame. "Four thousand years ago the Sarn Mother landed, and only she herself knows how many ages she had lived before that. The Sarn are long-lived—some live as long as a thousand years. But the Sarn Mother is the matriarch, immortal. Even her people have forgotten her age. The Sarn landed, and in the Battles of Conquest ninety-nine percent of mankind on Earth was destroyed. The remainder were made slaves, and they, our forefathers, were the meanest, sniveling scum of humanity."

Carron moved restlessly; his face flushed slowly and words growled in his throat. Grayth looked at him, his lean, rugged face smiling ironically. "It's true enough, Carron. Those noble forefathers of ours were no great men; the great died killing Sarn, rebelling, fighting. The unconquerable spirits died because they could not be conquered— and could die.

"Four thousand years the Sarn Mother has sat on her throne and watched mankind—listened, it would seem"—Grayth nodded toward the glowing aerial of the demodulator apparatus—"to its most secret councils. She knows man with the knowledge of one hundred and twenty generations. Unfortunately, man evolves, and being a short-lived animal, evolves more rapidly than do the Sarn. The weakness that made him submit to slavery has died out in four thousand years. For a millennium the Mother has seen man rapidly becoming man again.

"Bartel—Carron—what is that you wear on your forehead, that medallion of silver and enamel? The thing they placed on your forehead when they said you were 'called to manhood.' The Mother believes, in her mind, that it is the badge of your slavery, and your rank in her hierarchy of slavedom.

"But Ware has hollowed the solid silver of the Sarn Mother's slave badge to contain the telepath instrument. That she does not guess. She does guess, though, that man's slavery is being hollowed, a shell that may break soon. My announcement of the telepathic power troubled her more than we had guessed. We did not know, but she did. The ancients, before the Conquest, had begun to discover telepathy. Where we hoped a myth might impress her, she knew the fact already! By my telepath I followed her mind as she listened.

"That she learned from forgotten records, but this she has learned from watching one hundred and twenty generations of us. Man will fight and die for what he has not; woman will fight and die for what she has. Man will sacrifice everything he has for something he hopes for, an ideal; but while woman will fight for an ideal, she will not give up the good she has to gain it.

"The Sarn Mother knows that man is thinking again, after four thousand years, of the freedom he has not."

"The Mother, then, means to enforce the matriarchy laws on humanity!" Bartel exclaimed. "But—that will merely inflame the revolution, not stamp it out."

Grayth shook his head. "The Mother is not so direct. She has lived four thousand years; to her a century is a passing year, and three generations of misery to humanity is a bad year in her life. She knows rebellion might flare, but she plans not for a century, but for a millennium. Her will will be done—and the survivors will bless the beneficent Mother and her justness. What things must she do that the matriarchy laws may be applied to humanity?"

"Kill four out of every five men! She can't! Better she would kill the last of humanity trying that, for every woman will fight for her man—and be killed with him!" Carron snorted. "Before she accomplished any such slaughter, half her Sarn would have been throttled, and all humans, man and woman alike. To bring to effect the law of one and five, so many women would die defending their men that none would survive. And surely they would never serve the butcher."

"Drunnel," said Grayth bitterly. "Drunnel is her cat's-paw. Women will hate the butcher, true enough, so Drunnel she's groomed for the role. No hatred of Sarn, no danger to Sarn. But civil war—and Drunnel. Drunnel—and not rebellion, but rebellious energies diverted against themselves. Let men kill men, and fewer women die. Let men kill men, till the beneficent Mother steps in with her hallowed legion of Sarn and stops the slaughter—when the law of one and five is reached.

"Half the survivors will hate Drunnel for his destruction and half will love the leader of their lost men. But all will praise the Mother who stopped the bloody war. The Sarn Mother plans with the wisdom of four thousand years, and not the hot temper of forty."

Carron opened his mouth to growl something, stopped, and closed it with a snap. "I'll throttle Drunnel this afternoon," he finally vowed.

"Rendan is his lieutenant, and will take over. After Rendan is Grasun—and others follow." Bartel sighed.

"And I don't think you will throttle Drunnel this afternoon anyway," Ware said softly. "Unless he is late for his hour with the Mother, he is before her now, bargaining and discussing weapons."

"We haven't any weapons save those air guns Ware and others have made for us—and clubs," Carron groaned. "The Mother, I suppose, will give him some of the deadly weapons by which the Sarn destroyed the ancients."

Ware shook his head. "By no means; you forget her purpose. She does not want Drunnel to win. She wants him to bring about a decimating strife. If she gives him powerful weapons and easy conquest, the war is done before it is begun. No, she will give him weak weapons, and few of them, so that he will win only after long, deadly struggle. Why, she would probably supply us with weapons, if Drunnel should get too easy a victory."

Carron threw his great body back in his chair so viciously the old wood creaked in protest. The room thundered to his curses. "I'll move my blistering legion of peace this very hour, by—by Aesir! I'll throttle Drunnel with my own hands, and I'll see that every sneaking, slinking Sarn-fathered maggot of his evil crew squirms beside him!"

"We can't. Drunnel has as many men as we—and it would not be done in an hour. We must wait till Ware's work is done, and Aesir is ready to aid us," Grayth said sharply. "If we can hold off this struggle till we are ready to help ourselves, the Aesir will be strong enough to help us."

"What does Drunnel hope to gain from this?" asked Holmun. "He is spreading his organization to Europe, to Asia, as I know. Everywhere you sent me these last two months, I have found him working, promising a firmer stand against the Sarn, more freedom for humanity. Those are campaign promises, to be rejected. But if he knows this is coming—what does he hope to gain by it, knowing, as he must, that the Sarn Mother is inciting this thing to cause slaughter, not to give him power?"

Grayth's lean, tanned face hardened and the iron-gray eyes flashed. "Power, yes, but more than that; every move Drunnel has ever made, he has found me across his path. He sought the district delegateship; I won it. He had to content himself with that of city spokesman. He sought the American spokesmanship; I won it. He hated me. Six months ago we sought the spokesmanship; I won again, while Bartel here won the American spokesmanship over Rendan, his friend. That might be enough—but he wants Deya, and Deya chose me. To him it was the finishing blow. I think the man is mad. Power and the girl he wanted—and he has been blocked in every move.

"If he must, he is not averse to destroying all mankind to destroy me, and to destroy Bartel, too. If he wins, he does that—destroys us—and he believes he will then have Deya and Thera as well.

"If he wins, he destroys me, and Bartel, the men he hates. For a time at least, he will have the power he wants and the women he wants, not for themselves now, but because they refused him. He fights for those reasons. His followers—"

Grayth looked at none of them, his whole concentration turned on an inner consideration of the problem. His voice was almost a monotone, the voice of a man thinking out loud. "There will be civil war," he said softly, "because mankind is slowly growing aware of slavery and restriction. The whole race is stirring with a slow realization of confinement. But as yet, the mass of men have not realized what it is they want. The rule of the Sarn is so deep in their minds that the idea of rebellion against the Sarn Mother cannot rise to conscious levels. Mankind needs, in its restlessness demands, as never before, a leader about whom it can crystallize to express this restlessness in action. Drunnel's followers that will rebel against us are rebelling, symbolically, one might say, against the Sarn, since we represent the government the Sarn allowed.

"Drunnel has found, ready to hand, a mass of men who will act as he wants, to place him in the place of the men he hates. This is a fight between leaders, solely that. Only the leaders know why they are fighting. The people who will follow Drunnel against us will fight only because of a vague discontent that Drunnel has enlisted to aid him. Only Drunnel knows what it is he wants: power and Deya.

"Then he hopes to win the Mother to a new plan, not matriarchy, but a rule by men of a world of women. He knows the Mother's feelings, her realization of mankind's discontent, I believe. He hopes to compromise with her."

"He won't," said Ware softly. "I've spent hours near the Mother as the electrotechnician of the city of the Sarn. She has her plans, and they are as Grayth said. But she plans further. For a year or two Drunnel will have power and hatred, but she will protect him. He will have near him—his wives—the best minds of the women, and she knows them: Deya, Thera, Coson—you all know them. Then the Mother will withdraw her protection, and the hate he will have stirred will kill him. Some woman will avenge her man. Deya will be spokeswoman of man. For a day in her life, the Mother will suffer Drunnel and his annoyances, that the long-time plan may be carried out."

Carron stood up abruptly. The massive old chair crashed over backward as he strode the length of the room, trembling, his great arms knotted with angry muscles, his three hundred pounds of bone and sinew quivering with wordless anger.

Ware lingered a moment after the others had left Grayth. Slowly, he prepared to pack away his small kit of tools and apparatus. "Aesir, our black lord, seems no nearer." He sighed.

Grayth nodded silently. Then he said, "Can you give me one of those demodulators, Ware? You are the only hope of success mankind can have, you and your discovery. You must not be seen visiting the spokesman too frequently, attending the executive conferences. As an electrotechnician you are part of the gray background of the Sarn City; we want no spotlights turned on you. By the telepath you can follow every conference, and if you can teach me to operate that demodulator—"

Ware's usual slight stoop, the gray monotony of his work seemed to slip from him for a second as he stood erect, suddenly a powerful figure of a man, six feet tall, dark eyes set far under heavy brows, searching out with vibrant intelligence. The easy lines of his face straightened and deepened as he gazed steadily at Grayth for a long, silent moment. Slowly, he ran his lean-fingered hand across his head, taking the telepath band from his forehead.

"I think that we will both be busy tonight, Grayth. You with the men whom you can handle, I—I have an appointment with Aesir, whom I cannot handle." A slow smile spread across the lean, tanned cheeks. "If, in the morning, the problem is still pressing—come to my house. I will probably be behind the stone."

"There is tonight," Grayth acknowledged sadly. "Let's pray that tomorrow the problem will still be pressing. Thank—er—Aesir, you have never appeared, that even Drunnel does not see you when you walk by with that kit of tools. If things so come that we—Bartel, Carron, and I—are not here to press the problem tomorrow, I have this hope: that neither Sarn nor Drunnel realize their true source of danger.

"But do not come here again, please, Ware."

"Maybe that would be best," the electrotechnician agreed. He bent over to pack his apparatus, his tools once more.

*       *       *

Drunnel looked up to the Mother's slitted, vertical-pupiled eyes. Behind his own keen, dark eyes a swift, agile brain was weighing—guessing—planning. "But they are not so helpless; they have a weapon designed by one of their own men—a hand weapon that projects small slugs of metal. An air gun."

The Mother's expressionless eyes continued to stare at him, unwinking, the smooth, coppery skin of her face unmoving, the delicate, barely unhuman face hiding the thoughts of more than four thousand years. "I do not mix with human quarrels, save when they affect my Sarn," she said softly. "If this quarrel of yours gets out of hand, I will send my legion to stop it. But Grayth does not please me, and he has no desire to enforce my laws. I will give you those things I mentioned, no more—the crown and the glow beam. You will have one thousand of each; the rest of your forces will have to fight on terms equal with theirs.

"Sthek Tharg, take them to the hall of arms and let them have those things." The Sarn Mother's eyes closed behind opaque, coppery sheaths; she sat motionlessly as the Sarn she had called uncoiled his arms and rose slowly from his padded chair. On noiseless, padded feet he stalked off across the great hall of assembly. Behind him, Drunnel and his six companions followed.

"Call others," Sthek Tharg snapped.

"Rendan," Drunnel spoke softly, "tell Sarsun we will need seventy-five men, preferably discreet men, at the gate just after dusk. That will be in two hours now. I will send someone else to lead them when we are ready."

Rendan dropped from the group and hurried through the labyrinthine corridors to the outer park, down to the human city. Drunnel followed his silent guide through unfamiliar passages, to an elevator that dropped them one thousand feet to a dank, cold corridor that led off to unfathomed reaches of dimness, a corridor lighted only sparsely by far-scattered atom flame projectors burning at an absolute minimum.

The Sarn started off firmly toward the left. Doors opened from the corridor at long intervals—doorways opening into dim-lighted halls burned by atomic-blasts in native, sparkling granite. Something of the crystalline fury of the blasts lingered yet in their glittering, scintillating walls. Under dim lights, vague, vast structures of crystal and metal and plastic loomed in indeterminate dusk. The feeble, dying sparks of atom stars served only to make horrific outlines discernible. Vast, many-legged things of metal, built with huge ropy things that dropped dejected near them—ropy things of glinting metal ending in things strangely like Sarn hands, with their many-boned flexibility.

Other rooms were filled, cabinet above cabinet, with boxed devices—things that might, of course, be no more than searchlights. The armory of the Sarn! Unused these four thousand years.

Drunnel looked at the shrouded things with keen, dark eyes. His lean, muscular body never slowed in its step; the thin, almost ascetic face never turned. Only the dark eyes darted from dark doorway to huddled, half-glimpsed mass—the doorless doorways, without bar, or light-beam interceptor. The elevator answered to any being's control.

The Sarn turned his head, rotated it till his slitted eyes stared straight to Drunnel's, while he walked steadily forward. The line-thin gash of his mouth opened in what might have been a smile. "I will get the crown and the weapon. It is not—advisable that humans cross the threshold of these doors."

He paused a moment, and the body and head rotated in opposite directions till, alike, they faced a dark doorway. He walked toward it, and as he crossed, a spark of the atom flame in the dim room's ceiling floated down, living strangely long, to burst abruptly before him. It burned for perhaps ten seconds, dying with a shrill, clear, tinkling note during all those seconds, fading into dimness as the thin, keen note died with it.

Drunnel, twenty feet away, relaxed slowly, his knees bending under his weight, till he crouched on the floor, his powerful, six-foot body crumpled under its own weight till he was on hands and knees, his head dangling in limp agony, all his muscles quivering, jerking, dancing madly under his skin.

The thin, sweet note died. Drunnel raised his head slowly, white as chalk in the light of the corridor, streaked with sudden, clammy sweat. His dark eyes, bloodshot and wide now, stared into the slitted ruby eyes of the Sarn in the doorway. The Sarn's thin mouth twitched slightly as he moved into the room. The atom flame in the roof leaped up with his moving, and the cabinets of the rooms stood out in clear relief.

Drunnel climbed slowly to his feet, dark, bloodshot eyes snapping with an inexpressible hatred that tugged at him like a living thing. One shaky, trembling step he made toward that doorway, insane anger flooding him. Then, slowly, his mind regained control as the agony washed from him, and he stood, trembling half from weakness, half from a mad desire to crush the thin-lipped mouth of Sthek Tharg. "Drunnel"—he turned, to see Grasun, an unsteady hand stretched toward his leader, staring up into his face with tortured, worried eyes— "don't—stay here."

Drunnel snapped the hand from his sleeve. "I'll stay," he said softly. He glanced at the others: Farnos, leaning dazed against the wall, blood trickling from his nostrils; Tomus working himself to his feet with the aid of the rough wall; Blysun swaying unsteadily on his feet. The others were still helpless on the floor. "He might have told us what was coming."

"He wanted to warn us—against entering the rooms—and didn't, perhaps, realize how strongly it affected us," Farnos said.

Drunnel looked at him silently. Farnos dropped his eyes uneasily and struggled to his feet, one hand steadying him. The effects were passing swiftly. Inside the room rumbling wheels echoed softly; the Sarn was pulling a little four-wheeled truck loaded with a hundred or more small gray cases, perhaps four by twelve by three inches, and a dozen or so round cases four inches thick and a foot in diameter.

Sthek Tharg stopped, just inside the door, and eyed them. "Perhaps," he said ironically, "you would be more comfortable farther from that doorway as I pass through." He started forward. The humans scrambled away from him. They were fifty feet away when the thin, sweet note of a dying star of light thrilled through them, jerking, straining, quivering. Drunnel stood his ground, leaning slightly against the wall. The Sarn moved toward them, the low rumble of the rubber-shod wheels changing its note as the cart rolled into the corridor.

"Come here and take the crowns. They will protect you against the crystals—if you are not too close." Drunnel came toward him, took one of the round boxes, and from it the curious crown. It was a band of metal that circled his head, padded with rubber on the inner side, eight erect, outward-slanting metal rods, ending in dull-golden globes, perhaps a quarter of an inch in diameter. Nested in the center, above the curve of his skull, a tiny mechanism was inclosed in golden metal.

"It will throw a sheath of energy about you which is proof against any material thing, and deadly to any being wielding a metal object against you. It holds in near stasis the molecules of the air, so that the sound of the crystals will not reach you—if you remain at a little distance. And it is defense against the glow-beam."

Drunnel mounted the thing on his head, slipping his headband of silver and enamel into his cloak pocket. He touched a tiny stud at his brow, and a slight shock of energy lanced him momentarily. The Sarn's voice was softened, muffled by its action, and he snapped it off.

"The glow-beam"—Sthek Tharg opened one of the flat boxes to disclose an object fashioned of black plastic, dully lustrous metal, and one single crystal—"carries a charge sufficient to paralyze, for a day, five hundred men, paralyze for a moment nearly one thousand, or paralyze forever two hundred. This slide controls the action—this stud the discharge."

He raised it in flexible, many-boned fingers, his almost tentacle-like arm looping up with it. It pointed down the corridor, and as he touched the stud briefly, a clear, sweet note seemed to dart down the faintly luminous beam that shot forth, to vanish in unseen reaches of the corridor. "Its range is about a third of a mile."

Drunnel took another from its flat case, examined it, and put it quietly in his cloak. The others were fitting the curious crowns to their heads, and, a moment later, unloading the little truck.

Sthek Tharg returned to the dim room. Again the dying star shot toward him, and the atom flame leaped up. Drunnel touched the stud at his brow, and heard very dimly, as though far off, the sweet, torturing note of the crystal. It made his teeth hurt, as though an unseen drill were working in their depths. He took five cautious steps toward the doorway, till sweat started from his face and his limbs began to tremble. He snapped off the stud and walked toward his men. They, too, were snapping off the energies—

"Grasun, turn yours on." Drunnel watched; there was an instant of wavering energy, as though a sheath of heat waves had risen suddenly about the man—then nothing—nothing save the slightest of distortions that only his expectant eye could detect; that, and the slightly duller appearance of the eight metal globes on the crown's eight points. "Can you understand me readily?" Drunnel spoke in an ordinary tone.

"Perfectly," Grasun replied, nodding in confirmation.

"Good. Turn it off. We will have to move these things to the elevator, then again to the gate of the Sarn city. And—there is something I want to find out—"

The Sarn returned with the small truck. Drunnel stood alone, watching his men carrying the last of the boxed weapons to the elevator. He started in surprise at the first note of the dying crystal, snapped the little stud as he turned to watch Sthek Tharg. The Sarn stepped through expressionlessly, the little truck behind him. Drunnel walked toward him as the notes died in the air, his hands reaching toward the piled boxes—

"Stop!" snapped the Sarn. He fell back a hasty step, slitted ruby eyes blazing angrily. "You have a sheath of energy around you, fool. Turn off that crown."

Drunnel looked at him, mumbled a vague apology as he turned the stud. Rapidly, he lifted the boxes from the truck; he had learned what he sought to know. The Sarn were not immune to the sheath of the crown.

Deya opened the door at his knock, and Grayth stepped in with a backward glance at the dimly seen groups in the tree-shaded street. The last colors of sunset were fading from the sky, and the darkness slowly saturated the clear, cooling air. The spring nights were not yet hot as they would be in another two weeks. A near-full moon hung halfway up the eastern sky, its light not yet appreciably affecting the dimness of the scene.

Deya looked over his shoulder, and motioned him in. "They look more restless than ever, Grayth. Thera came this afternoon—she is fixing supper now—and told me that Bartel believed the explosion would come soon."

Grayth nodded slowly and shut the door behind his back. He looked unhappily into the clear, calm blue eyes raised to his, eyes like bits of cobalt glass in a delicately molded, determined face. Six feet two Grayth stood, but Deya was a resurgence of a four-thousand-year-forgotten blood, a clear, Norse strain. Her eyes were not three inches below his, her red-gold hair, her clean-lined body the living remembrance of a race human minds had forgotten.

Grayth sighed, took her in his arms. "The explosion will come tonight, dear girl. In three weeks—or never—we will be able to end this indeterminacy."

Deya's hands rested lightly on his shoulders as she leaned backward slightly to see him more clearly. His lean, strong face was set and serious, the etched-iron eyes worried. "The Mother has helped Drunnel as you feared?"

Grayth nodded. His finger touched the telepath disk at his brow. "Have you tried to follow any of his men's thoughts today?"

Deya smiled. "No, I tried to follow yours. I could not for some reason, only occasional snatches of ideas. You were very angry about four o'clock this afternoon."

Grayth nodded. "We had a conference. Drunnel has gotten weapons, and though I cannot follow his mind, as you know, I did follow that of Rendan. But Rendan was sent to gather men to carry away the weapons the Mother gave, and did not follow everything that happened. By Aesir, I wish I could follow Drunnel. That he should be one of those rare, complete nontelepaths!"

"What are the weapons?" Deya asked.

Grayth shrugged. "Rendan did not know—nor, I believe, did Drunnel. But you know what I have said; the Mother will not give him either a hopelessly powerful, or hopelessly numerous stock of weapons. I suspect a weak weapon of attack, and a powerful weapon of defense for a few."

"Let's go out to the kitchen." Deya moved in his arms, and started away. "Thera hopes Bartel will be able to come." For a moment the cobalt-blue eyes clouded in inner concentration, as did Grayth's. They nodded together as Bartel's thoughts reached them, weak and unclear with distance. He was coming.

For a moment more Grayth caught the strong, lithe body in his arms, then they moved on to the kitchen. Thera had placed a table on the stone-flagged terrace behind the kitchen, under the trellis-work of dark-leaved climbing roses. A few first buds were opening in the cool night air. The last washing colors of sunset had faded from the sky and the shadows now were those cast by the moon, and by the silently flaring atom flame projector.

The table was set and the food being brought when Bartel knocked. Thera went to admit him, and as she passed Grayth he suggested softly that she bolt the door when Bartel had entered.

A moment later the two returned. "They are standing around in groups," Bartel said, seating himself wearily. "I got a number of hate thoughts, and a number of friendly thoughts as I passed them. The groups seem about equally distributed as to sympathy, and I think that is one reason why I was not bothered at all on my way here. Perhaps we had best eat quickly. We may be—called out later."

Three-quarters of an hour later, Grayth and Bartel sat in the moon dusk, puffing slowly at their pipes. Deya and Thera moved quietly, stacking and washing utensils. Grayth pulled a small, flat jar from his cloak and put it on the table, looking questioningly toward Bartel. "Perhaps we might apply a little now."

Bartel grunted. "Moon cream. Does it work as well as Ware thought it might?"

Grayth smiled. "Better. I see you are wearing your official crimson and blue. Mine are about the same. With this—" Grayth rubbed the paste over his hands and arms to the elbows, then over his face and neck. It vanished on his skin, colorless and invisible, in the light of the atomic flame. He rose and walked the length of the terrace, down into the garden, where only the pale moonlight reached him. As he stepped into the shadow of a gnarled, spreading apple tree—he vanished, a black shadow in blackness. As he stepped out into the moonlight again, crimson cloak, dark-blue jacket and trousers, face and hands alike were jet black. Slowly, he rejoined Bartel.

"It works," agreed Bartel, smearing the colorless stuff into his skin. "I hope it's harmless."

"It is. A harmless substance that will not reflect polarized light. You know the moonlight will not show colors—though the eye and the brain are tricked by it. Tonight it will serve both to make us invisible in shadow, and as a badge; Drunnel does not have it. All our men do."

"Carron was gathering the men and distributing these things when I left him." Bartel looked out over the moonlighted town. "He was still busy. Listen!"

A voice cried out somewhere in the direction of the square, the center of the human town—a dim, unrecognizable voice, crying out a blurred word time and again. Other voices joined. It grew and washed across the city, a many-times-repeated chant that grew with its moving, washing toward them in unrecognizable syllables, till a half-dozen voices two hundred feet away took it up with a gleeful howl: "Drunnel— Drunnel!" Feet pounded with a muffled beat across lawns, hardening momentarily as they traversed stone-flagged walks, dying in the distance.

"He was busy, but the human town is annular, with the huge area of the Sarn city in the middle. Many men from the far sections had not been able to reach him yet. We were not able to use the vision instruments to spread our messages—Drunnel, since he has the Mother's help, did," Bartel finished hurriedly.

"He has another swift method of communication," Grayth pointed out. "It has rolled around the city in less than a minute and a half. They will be pouring into the square."

Somewhere outside a man shouted, screamed a curse as a muffled *thonk* cut it off abruptly. A bedlam was loosed, a score of cursing voices, a great bull-roaring voice giving orders, scurrying feet and the clang of metal on metal—and on flesh. It stopped with a long-drawn, thin scream that died away in gurgling bubbles of sound. The door of the cottage trembled to heavy blows.

Grayth was halfway through the house before the second blow sounded, moving in slow-seeming strides that propelled him as though half-floating through kitchen and hallway. In his hand a bluely lustrous bit of metal gleamed. "Who's there?" he demanded.

"Carron, you fool. Let me in. There's more coming down the street, and there's no need for arguing with them."

Carron burst in, an immense figure in torn greenish cloak of the legion of peace, a dozen men at his heels. In his immense hand a three-inch-thick table leg, nicked deeply in three places, and smeared with blood, seemed a thin wand. The door bellowed like a sail in the wind, as his huge hand cuffed it shut. "Bars," he grunted. Two of his men slammed over the heavy metal, locking bolts.

"They've started, Grayth, and my men are gathering. They put their messages out faster, since they could use the vision—and we couldn't. Damn the Sarn! But we'll be evenly matched in the square, if the Mother didn't give Drunnel half her armory."

"She didn't," Grayth answered positively. "I told you she wants us matched—with Drunnel having a bit of an edge."

"Why couldn't we use the vision?" asked Thera, looking into the crowded room.

"Perhaps you had best lower those shutters," said Deya softly, "or turn out the lights. You are conspicuous and crowded in that window."

Carron smiled broadly at her, ducking his head to pass under the door beam six and a half feet from the floor. "I should have thought of that." He reached for the control rope, and the thin metal vanes of the shutters slipped almost noiselessly into place over the windows.

"The vision central offices are in the Sarn city," Deya explained to Thera. "The Sarn watch them; they offer no chance to send through messages we would want and the Sarn did not. Coded messages might work, if every man knew the code, but if every man knew, the Sarn would also know soon enough."

"The rest of the speakers are coming here later," Grayth said to Carron. "We must get them here safely—"

"I sent three strong detachments to gather them in," Carron grunted. "And I came here myself. I'm going to get the whole lot of you in here and throw one good guard ring about the place. That'll save me men and allow a better guard. I've got men in every house about here; not a man of Drunnel's could weave his way through without alarm being sent in. The moonlight is tricky, a crawling man seems a bit of a shrub, but these men are in their own houses. By Aesir, they know what shrubs they have—and Drunnel's men have no face-blackening moon cream."

"They have lamp black," said Deya. "They may use that."

"If they think of it. It makes them conspicuous then when they are in the light." Carron nodded. "What plans have you made, Grayth?"

"No detailed plans, for we are not ready. Had we had another month—even a week, perhaps—we might have learned then to summon Aesir to our aid, and we had plans for that. But now—we must do as we can. Look; first the leaders, the speakers, must be concentrated and guarded here. Then, to stop this battle, we must somehow destroy three men: Drunnel, Rendan and Grasun. Beyond that succession the power of the leadership is not determined among them, and they'd fight among themselves. If that could be done this night, the month we need would be gained. The Mother would see that one of the others took up the fight, but not immediately; time would elapse. Drunnel, Rendan, and Grasun."

"Right." Carron nodded. "But they'll be at the square, in the center of their men. They'll be hard men to catch, and quick-footed men."

Grayth touched his headband fleetingly, his eyes intent on Carron. "We may be able to outguess them." Carron's eyes lighted with understanding.

"Aye—we might. We can try."

"The speakers with their escorts are almost here," Deya said, her eyes clearing from an effort of concentration. "Perhaps the door—"

A man sprang to draw the bolts as a knock sounded outside. A moment later ten men in the crimson cloaks of the speakers entered, crowding about in the tiny room. Fifty men in the dark green of the legion of peace, and a score in civilian motley, waited outside. Carron stepped to the door. "A line of you—about the cottage and move outward till you surround the block. Make sure there's no man of Drunnel's within your line."

The men faded into nothingness under, the shadowed trees, vanishing in silence and darkness under the deceptive moonlight, seeming so bright, yet actually colorless and dim. Carron closed and barred the door behind him.

"We'll take those men and join at the square. I haven't heard a sound since the call of Drunnel's men," Grayth said. "I'll go with you, Carron, and we'll start at once. Somehow we must get Drunnel, Rendan, and Grasun."

"They won't agree with us," said Bartel sourly. "They no doubt have similar plans on you. It seems to me that you would be much better off staying here and letting us do that, for just as surely as Drunnel's forces collapse with his disappearance, ours collapse if you are taken. The battle would be over, right enough—with Drunnel in power."

Grayth shook his head. "The speakers are here; they will be goal for many of Drunnel's men, but Drunnel will not want them," he said softly. "Drunnel wants me, and you. Therefore, we will go where he cannot find us. If we stay, he can lay plans to attack us. If we are somewhere in the city, our group can lay plans of defense, knowing where we are, while Drunnel, not knowing, cannot plan attack. And— we have work."

Bartel stepped through the door after him. As the three faded into the shadows, the dry grating of the bolts rattled the door behind them. In a moment their eyes became accustomed to the moonlight, the dimness seemed to roll back, and the silvery light grew stronger. Presently it seemed that it was illumination as effective, as strong as daylight. Then, abruptly, a shadowy being emerged from the darkness under a tree, appearing as though from thin air. "There's no one between the cottage here and the ring of watchers," he murmured.

Carron nodded. "Gather the men near Phalun's cottage. We'll make for the square." Carron hefted the table leg in his hand, and slipped into the shadow with the others. Grayth halted him, took the heavy weapon from him.

"Whatever the Mother has given them, it will more than likely be electric in nature," he said after a moment. "Discard metal and take wooden weapons. Warn your men against metal things."

At the corner of a tree-shadowed cottage they met the troop of men, and Carron passed the warning along. The soft clink and thud of metal followed slowly, reluctantly. The force dispersed quietly, groups of two and three wandering off to return moments later, silent, drifting shadows in the moonlight, carrying faintly lustrous table legs and chair legs of nonconducting, plastic material, one with a five-foot, pointed plastic rod ripped from an atom flame projector. And at the hip of each swung the blued-metal air guns.

Silent, drifting ghosts, they passed down the streets, scattered under clumps of moon shadow, following the lawns and dust-muffled roads. Slow accretions joined the party as the stragglers from outlying districts appeared. Three times there were brief scufflings and cries that were silenced under dull, muffled blows. White faces in the moonlight looked up sightlessly as they passed on—white faces, the badge of Drunnel's men.

There were lights in the square ahead, far down the street. Early arrivals stood about in tense idleness, awaiting the coming of reinforcements for both sides. Grayth turned down a side street, crossing at right angles toward the sound of a compact body of men advancing on a parallel street. A moment later they saw them, dark figures with white faces, marching toward the square, a group of half a dozen in the lead, wearing curious gemmed crowns and carrying foot-long instruments in their hands.

The drifting shadows in the deeper shadow of trees dispersed, vanished save for little wraiths of blackness moving behind cottages, in absolute silence. The troop of Drunnel's men moved on alertly, eyes darting about, clubs and knives ready. A dense mass of three great trees darkened the road ahead, and they marched into it.

A dozen were down before they fully realized the assault. Carron's great voice boomed out in exaltation as he recognized the leader.

"Grasun, by Aesir, Grasun!" A roar went up from the compact group of Grasun's companions.

And through it came the sweet, thrilling, killing note of the glow-beam Grasun carried in his hand. Its faint light shot out straight for the black shadow of a charging man bearing the mace of a bulky table leg in his upraised hands. The beam touched him, sang through him, and roared in sweet, chilling vibrations as though his twisting, tortured body were a sounding board. The men near him writhed and fell, twisting, helpless, their weapons dropping from numbed, paralyzed hands. Drunnel's men charged forward with a cry of triumph as the beam of the glow-tube swerved. Again the thin, shrill note stabbed out toward a darkened figure. For a moment he glowed, writhing, falling, his joints cracking suddenly as maddened muscles distorted him impossibly, his dying body a sounding resonator that paralyzed those near him.

Another glow-beam came into action as Carron's great figure lunged forward, the table leg upraised in huge arms. Leaping Drunnelians tumbled from the mighty, charging body; for a fraction of a second he loomed over Grasun.

Grasun stared up, his white face lifted to the moonlight, a smile of pure joy in it as he turned his weapon slowly toward the colossus towering six inches above him, three hundred pounds of bone and sinew. The table leg crashed down toward what Grasun knew was an impenetrable, invisible, shielding force. He pressed the stud of his gun as the mace contacted his shield, with all the force and momentum Carron's shoulders could give it.

Grasun fell to the ground, while the pale beam of his ray shrieked its way through the treetops. Carron dropped his splintered club from numbed fingers. The sheer momentum of the blow, unable to crack the shield though it may have been, served to stun the man inside by the vicious jerking it imparted to him. Carron saw the strange, glowing rod wavering toward him again, felt the stunning impact of another attacker's club on his shoulder, and spun with a roar of rage. His immense hands closed on the attacker, the giant arms lifted him like a squalling child above Carron's shoulders, to crash him on the force shield of the fallen man. A high, thin wail of terror escaped him as the arcing energies of the field crashed through him. He fell, a smoldering, quivering thing, at the feet of Grasun.

"Rocks!" roared Carron, leaping from the scene of battle. "Rocks for those with the crowns! Bombard 'em!"

Others of Grayth's men had not leaped so hastily to close contact. The soft coughing air guns were bringing down many of the Drunnelians, groaning as heavy slugs broke bones, silent when they struck an instantly vital spot. The bullets fell away from those who wore the crowns, who stood unscathed, their whining weapons of the Sarn Mother stabbing at vague shadows retreated now into the greater shadows of the trees.

A cobble of granite the size of a man's head hurtled out of the darkness toward Grasun as he staggered uncertainly to his feet—a cobble hurled by an unseen giant. The shield deflected it, stopped it, but the meshed forces transmitted shattering momentum to the man who wore the crown. Grasun huddled on his knees, shaking his head, his weapon fallen to the ground beside him.

"Rocks!" Carron roared. "Rocks—big rocks, you blasted, withering idiots! Not pebbles, you howling fools, rocks! They have a shield— a shield of force. But it shakes 'em when the rocks hit 'em—"

"Throw at Grasun." Grayth's voice snapped out of the night, low and tensely clear. "A dozen of you—heavy stuff."

A rain of granite cobbles, unearthed from a forgotten pile, stormed out of the night. Half a dozen struck the fallen man's shield with a blasting force. From barely within the protective shadow of the tree, Carron's huge arms heaved a boulder of eighty pounds weight. The deadly thing crashed down on the straining shield with a snapping of energies, held for a moment as though bouncing on unseen rubber, and fell to one side. Grasun rolled end over end under the impact, struggling dazedly to rise. His voice called out in muffled syllables to the milling men around him, but they dared not help him; the shield was death to touch.

"Carron—Carron—think!" Grayth's clear, sharp voice penetrated the roar of fighting men. Carron stopped bewildered for a moment, then strong in the telepath came his orders. Immediately his great hands swept a dozen others of his men into formation about him, each with a boulder in his hands. They burst from the shadows, and heavy rocks flew. The crowned men fell, staggered aside at the heavy burst of ammunition. The giant charged in at the head of his men, two great table legs flailing in his hands. The disorganized mob of Drunnelians parted as he charged toward the groggy Grasun. But before he came too near the invisible death of the shield, he bent and picked up the glow-beam projector Grasun had dropped. Carron fled again to the protective trees.

Boulders were effective on crowned and unshielded alike. The steady rain of deadly ammunition was disrupting the aim of the glow-beam wielders. The apologetic little cough of the air guns in the hands of practiced men was making the Drunnelians fall like blighted grain.

The last of Drunnel's unshielded men were down, or gone. Half a dozen wearers of the crowns stood in a tight circle firing their strange death into the shadows. Grayth joined Carron beneath a great tree, and took from him the slim, warm tube of the weapon taken from the fallen Grasun. "A man you can trust," he snapped. "Send it to Ware; we must get others. Don't let those men escape; we must get Grasun."

"Tarnor—take this. You know the house of Ware. Take it to him. Run." The man was a crawling figure, sprinting across a lawn, then gone from sight. "Now"—Carron turned to Grayth—"we can keep their fire ineffective so long as the rocks hold out, but how can we crush those shields? It is death to touch them, it seems. I saw eight of their own men die when they stumbled into them."

A man materialized out of shadow beside Carron, a great wooden bucket in his hands, his invisible face split by a toothy grin. Carron took the thing in huge hands, and stepped forward; his huge arms creaked to the strain as it leaped into the air, to fall in a silver rain over the shielded men, running, trickling, wetting the ground at their feet. From another side another bucket leaped into the air, to drop over them, some few drops resting for a moment on the invisible sheath in darting, arcing energies. Another and another—

Grasun howled—a shrill scream of terror and agony. Water had short-circuited the thing on his head; it was smoking; as he tore it from him it grew red-hot—white; it exploded with a roar of sound, a burst of incandescent energy that limned attackers and attacked alike in glaring light. Grasun fell to the ground twitching, rolling—and suddenly stilled as he touched the hem of another's shield. A roar of triumph went up from every tree, every cottage corner.

The pistoled legion of peace had been driven into the buildings surrounding the square. In the center of the square, surrounded by two score figures, Drunnel and Rendan directed the battle.

Grayth waited in the darkness just beyond, while Carron closed up his communications. Darting runners brought messages. Eyes dulled with an inner concentration, Grayth sat motionless, gathering information by telepath from a hundred hidden points, from men in the cottage they had left, from Deya, from Ware in his underground workshop. The secret of the glow-beam—

"The shields muffled voices," Grayth said to Carron. "They also stop the glow-beam then, for Ware says it projects a beam that carries an ultrasonic vibration that is death to man—and probably harmless to Sarn."

Carron grunted. "The men in the buildings had already found the danger of metal, but they hadn't learned the trick of the rocks. I—"

Somewhere in a building, lightless and darkened, a sudden, terrific glare appeared. The windows were solid squares of thrusting radiance, spotlight beams that shot their brilliant knives through weak moonlight to limn for an instant the crouching figures in the center of the square. Drunnel stood up, badly outlined against a fierce beam of light, his face surprised, startled.

"Water." Grayth smiled. "I got the message through to Paultur. One of Drunnel's shielded men was trying to drive them out of the building. I wonder—" His eyes closed for a moment. "No, the weapon was destroyed, too."

Another virulent flash burned through the windows of a nearby house; in the first a duller, redder light was growing. Men were darting out of the place, smoke trailing behind them. The exploding crown had set fire to the age-dried woodwork.

Men were filtering out of the shadows, dim clots of a more solid black in the blackness under the tree. A fitful redness was growing in the moon-drenched square as the ancient woodwork of the ignited house yielded to the growing flame. The dimly seen messengers came near to Carron, speaking in low voices, Carron's deep bass growling in reply, till they vanished again on some mission of communication.

"Grayth," the giant's voice rumbled in its softest tones, "the men in the buildings can't get near enough to Drunnel's group to throw the heavy rocks. The glow-beams make it impossible, and until they get near they can't disturb the aim. Is there any way we can shield our men against the beams?"

Grayth was silent, but in his telepath Carron could feel the tenuous thread of mind energies reaching out to Ware, to others of their group. And dimly, he could feel Ware's answering thought. Screening—each man wrapped in sheet metal carefully grounded, worn over a thick padding of cotton, or quilting.

Carron muttered disgustedly. Grayth looked up at him, nodding. "Impossible, I know."

Shielded men were leaking away from the group in the center of the square, darting down narrow side streets before the rocks buried from nearby buildings could knock them from their feet. Other shielded men were coming toward the square from every direction, men from more distant sections of the annular city. They were waiting in the back streets outside the square, moving in restless circles.

Carron touched Grayth's sleeve. "We can't do it in this try, Grayth," he growled. "The shielded ones with their weapons are surrounding the square. We'll be caught helplessly if we don't retreat. I've sent word to those others that—"

"If we don't reach Drunnel tonight, we'll never be able to," Grayth groaned. "The Sarn Mother will give him better weapons, and waverers who had joined us will transfer to him when they see us in retreat."

"We must retreat at once," insisted Carron unhappily. "If we only had some means of swift communication—if we had only been able to map out a plan, and put it across to all our scattered people. We didn't have time; we didn't know what weapons Drunnel would have until too late. I know now what we should have done. Perhaps it is not too late, if we can once join our forces. Because all meetings have always been held in the square, all our men are rushing toward it. I'll call the men out of those buildings at—"

A wild rush of feet sounded down the great, radial artery. A hundred men with the darkened faces of Grayth's supporters swept down the street, half-a-dozen glow-tubes in their hands, and many empty water pails among them. The hidden men in the buildings of the square cheered them on, and a fusillade of air-gun pellets rattled on the stone flags. The mass of men broke up, scattering before they came in range of the pale beams of death. Long before Carron's messenger reached them their compact formation was gone; they were filtering through back streets into every building of the square.

But Carron's runner brought back a new interpretation of this re-enforcement; they were not running to the charge, but falling back before more than fifty armed, shielded Drunnelians. Another band of Grayth's men rushed in from another artery, vanishing like smoke in shadows and shadowed buildings. The torch lighted by an exploding crown was growing; the red flare of a burning building was rapidly making the moonlight unimportant, the moon cream useless. The fire was spreading.

Two score of Drunnel's fighters appeared down the street that had recently brought Carron's green-cloaked legionnaires. Carron settled back under the tree in helpless rage. "We won't retreat, Grayth. We can't now, for Drunnel has driven half our men into this square, between his central, unassailable group and the ring of other men, and the buildings sheltering them are burning. I haven't seen a score of Drunnel's unshielded fighters; they're probably in the outskirts, keeping the rest of our men from relieving those inside the ring."

Grayth looked at the spreading flames consuming the buildings. Stone for the most part, they were roofed with metal or slate, but the floors, walls and supporting beams were of wood. These were burning furiously. A burning house collapsed as he watched, the fierce heat of the internal furnace crumbling age-hardened mortar, loosening the aged stone.

Drunnel stood in the light of the fire, watching his circling fighters on the outskirts. His arms moved, giving orders, pointing out directions of movement. A messenger ran toward a broad artery, down which a score of weaponed men were moving. A rain of half-a-hundred great stones crushed him to the ground and a stream of water drowned his screen into exploding fire as he passed too near a house. Another messenger started after him, dodging, running in irregular movements. A well-thrown rock knocked him from his feet, and a steady rain of them held him helpless till water drowned his screen in turn. A roar of angry triumph went up.

Drunnel's arm stayed another man who started toward a broader road. Drunnel shook his head, shrugged his shoulders as the man motioned violently, attempted to pull away.

"They can't enter the buildings," Carron growled. "The water and rocks stop that. But they don't have to. The fire is already there." He nodded toward a group of men working on a roof top with a garden hose, their dark-green cloaks flapping in the faint wind. A glow-beam reached up from somewhere beyond the square, and a man crumpled in death. Three near him stiffened and jerked, one to slide from his position into the growing furnace.

A messenger panted up from the shadows, the glow of the flames giving color to his cloak, washing the blackness of the moonlight from his face. In his hand he held three of the crowns. His face split in a grin. "They don't have them turned on all the time."

Grayth stepped forward eagerly. "Three of them. How did you get them intact?"

"A dozen of us—we saw them coming down the road, and hid in the shadows. They did not have their shields turned on, and three fell in the first volley of the air guns. The others we washed out with water, but these we saved."

"Well," Carron pointed out bitterly, "that improves the odds. We now have three effective men who can stand up against their near thousand—maybe. Your technician friend may be able to duplicate them, though—in a month."

"Tarnsun," Grayth called softly to the figure half visible in the light of the flames, "take this to Ware. You can penetrate the lines Drunnel is drawing about us by wearing this, turned on full. If— Never mind, just go back and wait." Grayth had caught the weary denial Ware had sent. Grayth's thought had reached Ware at once, reached a tired, immensely busy technician, struggling with things of more immediate consequence.

Grayth turned the things in his hand, gave one to Carron. The giant spoke suddenly, pointing toward the square. One of the shielded men had stepped from the group, carrying a blazing ball of cotton on the end of a bit of wire. It sailed out from his arm to land on the roof of the building near the artery down which their messengers had attempted to go. It blazed feebly for a moment and went out. But a dozen more followed it, blazing, oil-soaked cotton wrapped around a stone. Light things that could be hurled a distance the heavy rocks Carron's men had used could not cover. Three crashed through windows. The feeble blazes grew stronger. Water hissed viciously; for a moment the flame wavered, then grew swiftly brilliant.

Dark figures dropped from windows to dart toward nearby buildings. Four stopped halfway, never to reach their goal, as glow-beams found them. The red flower of the flames spread slowly at first; then windows burst in the heat and they grew swiftly. The house on the opposite corner was burning now.

A messenger walked down the alley between the flames to a group of shielded men beyond. They moved away in planned unison when he reached them, the band splitting in two, marching in opposite directions about the square.

Carron stiffened suddenly; his eyes darted sideward toward Grayth's shadowed figure. Grayth, too, was stiffened, tense. A soft, unreal voice whispered in their minds, a voice and more than a voice, for with it whispered sights and sounds and odors: soft odors of a garden under moonlight, the sounds of men crashing through ruined flower beds, and the thrilling, keening wail of the glow-beams. A garden in black and white, scattered with darting figures hurling water pails and rocks at an advancing troop of thirty shielded figures. Deya was watching through a window, with a score of the divisional speakers about her. The troop of Carron's legionnaires were falling back before the concerted assault of a mass of shielded, armed Drunnelians.

"They can't stop them," Grayth muttered.

Carron's voice rumbled unintelligibly. "We didn't."

"Another month—even a week, perhaps—and we might have learned to summon Aesir to aid us. Do you think the Mother knew— that she did this just early enough to prevent us—"

"What can we do now?" Carron demanded. "We might try a mass attack—all of the men swarming at once down on Drunnel and Rendan there—"

"Rendan isn't there." Grayth sighed. "It was he who went to the outer ring to order them. A mass attack would only lead to a thousand deaths for everyone we have had tonight. There are nearly five thousand of our friends in those buildings. Somehow they must be released."

Slowly, Grayth got to his feet. Deya's thought pictures came so clear to his mind that it seemed almost that he must avoid the old oak which stood by the flagged terrace where he had eaten dinner, and the charging Drunnelians behind their shields. The last of Carron's green-cloaked legionnaires was down. They would not use their glow-beams on the speakers; Grayth knew with a terrible certainty that they would not use them on Deya and Thera.

Grayth reached to his forehead and touched the little stud of the crown he had donned. Carron watched him in surprise, started after him as he walked out of the shadow of the tree into the full light of the flames. "Stay there, Carron," Grayth called. Then he was striding across the last of the lawn onto the flagged pavement of the square. He stood still for a moment, as a half-dozen glowing beams lanced toward him, to die soundlessly against the invisible sheath of his crown. The beams stopped. Drunnel stepped toward him, till he stood in the forefront of his little force.

"What terms, Drunnel?" Grayth called. The sheath seemed to drink in his voice, but somehow Drunnel had heard.

Drunnel laughed softly. "And may I ask, why terms? Why should I want terms from you?"

"Because you have no real desire to destroy these men in the buildings." Grayth nodded to the silent watchers in the windows facing the square. "Because you only want to make sure that I do not escape—and because you cannot hold me. We have captured a score or so of these crowns the Mother gave you. With them I, a score or so of my men, Deya, Thera—and a few others—can leave you. We will have time and opportunity then to do something more, perhaps. But certainly I can find my way to safety on this world you cannot ever hope to search, though the Sarn Mother herself should aid you."

Grayth looked at Drunnel steadily, wondering if Drunnel had, of course, any way of knowing how many crowns had been captured intact. One, at least, he knew. And he had no way of knowing that Deya and Thera were even then arguing with a group of shielded men led by Barthun.

"What do you want?" Drunnel spoke after a moment's silence, broken only by the crackling lap of the flames, the restless creak of ancient houses crowded now with men.

"The men that fought for me go free, every man or woman or child you have surrounded, captured or blockaded. I will surrender to you."

"I do not like your terms." Drunnel laughed. "You cannot escape from this point now; the outer ring of my men would stop you."

Grayth shook his head. "You know better than that. What offer will you make?"

"I will release these men and women of no importance; but I will demand your surrender, and that of Bartel, Carron, and the spokesmen of the districts." Drunnel stood out before his men, his dark eyes flashing, a smile of sweeping satisfaction on his face. "And that is concession enough for what I hold in my hand this night. What fight have you, Grayth? Your men are bottled between my inner center here, and my outer ring. And the fire spreads in between.

"A clever trick your water was, and clever enough that hurling of rocks, but it gains you nothing. I have more sense of realities than you, Grayth. I don't lay humanity open to the anger of the Sarn Mother, and she is just. She appreciates and aids those who aid her.

"Your futile air guns have merely tempted your men into a closing trap. You, who have never seen a book on military strategy, never practiced warfare, hoping to defeat one tutored by the generals of the Sarn! You may be wise enough in working the minds of cattle such as these in my burning pens—but for practical matters your knowledge is nothing.

"Well, what do you say, Grayth? I'll release these men, these stupid followers of a stupid leader—but the leaders must face the Mother."

Grayth shook his head. "We are not caught. We are quicksilver under your fingers, escaping as you try to hold us. Bartel you want for personal reasons, personal hatred, as you want me. I will surrender to you if you will swear by the name of the Mother, by Kathal Sargthan herself, that my people, including all others save only myself and Bartel, shall be free and undisturbed. Bartel, I except with his consent—and catch him if you may! You claim your ring tight—"

Drunnel stared at the tall figure of his enemy. Quicksilver under his fingers, to slip through the teeth of his closing trap. Bartel—

"Let Bartel join you, then," he called carelessly. "The sheep will fall apart in squabbles when the goats are gone."

"You swear by the name of the Mother, by Kathal Sargthan, that those who have fought for me shall be free and unmolested, on equal grounds with those who have fought with you and with those who have not fought?"

"By Kathal Sargthan, I swear that." Drunnel nodded.

"By Kathal Sargthan you swear that we shall have trial before the Mother, as the law of the Sarn demands?"

Drunnel laughed, eyes flashing in the light of the flames. "Aye—if you want that so badly, Grayth, you and Bartel shall surrender to me, and together you shall appear before the Mother. And by the Mother's name, I'll have you there at the morning audience, too!"

Bartel's figure emerged from the dark entranceway of a building, striding forward to join Grayth. Grayth snapped off the tiny stud of his crown as Drunnel came forward, took it from his head and restored the silver-and-enamel disk of the Mother's slaves. Drunnel took it from his hands, eyes bright, white teeth flashing in an almost friendly smile of triumph. The game was played out; Grayth and Bartel were no longer obstacles in his path to power.

The Sarn stood in solidly massed ranks leading up to the high, golden throne of the Sarn Mother. The great hall of audience was quiet, a hush so deep the faint rustle of the atom-flame projectors far above in the lofty dome trickled down to them like the rustle of autumn's falling leaves.

Grayth and Bartel stood side by side before the Mother, their official crimson cloaks stripped from them, draped instead over the tall forms of Drunnel and Rendan standing close behind. A long, slanting ray of morning sunlight stabbed through a window to wash on the crimson cloth, rebounding in reddening glare.

For long minutes the motionless, slitted eyes of the Mother looked into Grayth's calm face. Her line-thin mouth seemed scarcely to move as she spoke. "You told us that the law of the Sarn could not be enforced, and that you were unable to enforce it. Therefore, Grayth, it was my desire that you be removed.

"By the law of the Sarn, the inefficient administrator is worthy of removal, and the rebellious administrator is worthy of death.

"By the common law of the humans, the inefficient are removed, and the treasonous are worthy of death.

"By the law of the Sarn and the law of man, you have earned no appeal to me. Why then do you protest your ancient privilege of appeal to the Mother of laws and justice?"

"By the law of Sarn and humans, the inefficient should be removed and the rebellious or treasonous destroyed," Grayth acknowledged. His voice was low and clear, its tones dying slowly in the vast hall. "If these things are proved against me, I am guilty. But no man has accused me of inefficiency, for I am not inefficient in failing to do that which the law forbids me to do. The law of the Sarn forbids that the spokesman of man be also the commander of the legion, or that he raise a police power for his office. The law of the humans forbids the spokesman of man doing other than offer advice. I have given the

Mother advice, as the laws require; the laws of the Sarn cannot be forced onto humanity without destruction. You ordered that I enforce them, yet the law of Sarn and of man forbids my raising the power I must have to do this. Had I done so, I would have rebelled against the law of the Sarn and been traitorous to human law. I did not do so; therein I am not traitorous, nor am I inefficient."

"The word of the Mother is the law of the Sarn." The Sarn Mother's masking, translucent lids slid across her eyes for a moment. "There is no law above it. The decisions of the Mother are the law of the Earth; there is no law above them. You have acted inefficiently, or rebelliously. I find your actions rebellious. The law defines the manner of your death.

"So, also, I find Bartel rebellious. The law defines the manner of your death." The unwinking eyes swung slowly to Bartel and held him for a moment. Then, suddenly, they moved from his face, to look down the long hall of audiences to the great entranceway. The expressionless face remained unchanged, the line-thin slit of her lips did not move. But in the silence the breath whistled softly into her nostrils. Grayth turned slowly to follow the unmoving stare of the Sarn Mother.

In the bright radiance of the atom flames, across lancing beams of early sunlight, a vague, amorphous thing moved, a thing of utter blackness. Shifting suggestions of blocky, heavy legs moved it forward. Slowly, in the sunlight and the radiance of the projectors, it seemed to solidify, condensing upon itself. A gigantic, manlike figure looming twelve feet—a figure not *in* black, but of blackness, a sheer absence of all vision, a solid shadow of utter night.

As it moved closer in ponderous, soundless strides, the condensation and solidification went on, more clearly the arms, the great legs became visible. A great, featureless head of jet surmounted the heroic figure, a face of eyeless, mouthless, noseless blackness, swirling, moving unsteadily.

And behind it on the great floor, where the formless feet touched, white sprang out, white flowers of frost. Slowly, the figure moved forward, an aura of cold, a faint, whispering wind from unguessed, icy spaces drawing about it, behind it. A stabbing beam of brilliant sunlight struck down from a high window, lanced into it like a great shaft—and vanished. It did not illuminate nor reflect from that figure of blackness.

"Aesir—" Grayth gasped the name, falling back a step.

Thirty feet from the Mother the figure halted, the mighty arms at rest by its sides. The paralyzed Sarn began to stir, a voice broke out in hissing syllables—and quieted. The blackness spoke, spoke not in words, but in thoughts, thoughts that danced and lanced through every mind, human and Sarn alike.

"There is neither justice nor right in your ruling, daughter of the Sarn. Your race and the race of my people are different. You must change that ruling, in the name of the justice you invoke."

The Sarn Mother's hand moved like a flashing serpent's tongue to a tiny stud set in her throne. A pencil of ravening, intolerable fury burst from the carven mouth of the crouching metal beast at her side, a pencil of inconceivable energies that reft the air in its path in screaming, shattered atoms—and died soundless, lightless on the breast of the lord of blackness. From her massed guards a thousand tongues of death shrieked out, ravening rods of annihilation—that died unseen in his blackness. From the plaque above the throne of the Sarn Mother a roaring column of the atomic-blast, a force designed to wash down mountains, vomited forth, drowning in colossal thunders the pricking bubbles of the lesser rays. No spark of light, no faintest sight of illumination appeared on the motionless giant.

The shouting voice of the rays died out, stopped, and their echoes wandered lonely in the vast silence of the hall. The blackness spoke again, in a soundless voice that seemed to echo like a vast organ's song, yet lacked all quality of sound.

"I am not matter, nor of forces such as your beams, your rays can touch, daughter of the Sarn. Your wisdom, the ancient powers of your race are useless. You are still but one; I am all of mankind that has ever been, the fifteen hundred billions who have died since the first man. I am the billions you slaughtered at the Conquest. Ten thousand generations of mankind have willed, dreamed, and struggled for success and freedom. I am the crystallization of those wills, those dreams. I am mankind, an incarnate ideal half-formed. No force, no ray, no thing of matter can influence my being.

"All space was saturated with the deathless energies of forgotten strivers, the eternal wills of all man's myriads since the lost beginning of time. In glacial epoch I died under rending tiger's claws, yet lived in the child protected by that sacrifice. I died while the world was young—and I died last night under the rays you gave these men, and with the leaden shot of the air guns in me.

"I am the wills of mankind, raised into substance by your own acts, daughter of the Sarn. Three billions died at the Conquest, and their wills released to eternal space carried one single thought: to save Earth from your slavery. They were the crystallizing point, on that heart and nucleus the space-ranging wills of unremembered generations have united into me. Four thousand years have passed, and slowly

I have grown, till my powers made contact with Earth's space and time last night, when once again wills and minds went from Earth in striving for freedom.

"I am Aesir, the pantheon of mankind, and mankind itself. All that ever died, under blazing desert sun or in freezing arctic waste, when the first dim stirrings of mind arose and struggled with a tool, and through all time to the will that became of me while I spoke here— the will of one wounded last night and dying this morning.

"For whatever cause they strove and died, they are of me, daughter of the Sarn. Mankind must have justice, for each of those who died sought in his own way for what his mind believed was truth. Grayth and Bartel have striven that justice might be, and they shall go on with their works.

"Drunnel and Rendan have sought to sell mankind for their own ends. They, too, shall have justice."

The vast blackness of his arm reached out and a formless finger of jet touched once on Drunnel's forehead for a fraction of a second, before it passed to Rendan's terror-frozen countenance. Slowly, Drunnel swayed, his legs loosened, and he fell to the floor as a soft, white blanket spread over his face. His head clicked like brittle metal on the black basalt of the floor. Like dropped ice it shivered in a dozen fragments. Kindly, swift-spreading, white frost crystals softened and concealed it, and the broken skull of Rendan.

Aesir turned. Before him a lane opened as the Sarn stumbled back, making a way that led him straight to the vast gold-flecked wall of the hall of audiences, polished slabs of jade-green stone. Silently, Aesir stepped into it; the solid matter misted and vanished at his touch, opening to the empty corridor beyond. For a moment it remained so, the vast, black figure striding soundless down the deserted corridor beyond the wall—then the wall closed in behind him. But it was black, black with the blackness of Aesir himself.

A guard turned on it a stabbing beam that crushed the atoms of a rising column into sparkling dust. But the blackness of the wall remained, untouched, unlighted. The beam died, and very slowly, before their eyes, the blackness faded from the wall, evaporating in little curling wisps of jet fog. For a moment, a distorted profile remained, a vast, black shadow of a man thrown on green stone.

Then only green polished stone glowed in the warm light of the rising sun.

The Mother's expressionless eyes looked into Grayth's for long, silent seconds. The Sarn shifted restlessly, little whisperings of a rising sound. "You shall both go, Grayth and Bartel, and see that order is restored in the human city." The Sarn Mother's voice halted for a moment, then continued. "At the hour of sunset of this day all the weapons and crowns I allowed to leave my arsenal will be returned to me.

"The law of the one and the five shall not apply to humans."

The Mother's eyes closed. Grayth and Bartel turned and walked silently down the long aisle between ranks of silent Sarn. Behind them followed the six, silent men who had come that morning with Drunnel and Rendan. Outside the great entranceway, the six went hastily away across the green lawn. For a moment Grayth and Bartel stood alone.

An electrotechnician, a man so commonly seen working about the Sarn city that few noticed him, joined them there. In one hand he carried a large, snap-locked bag, a somewhat large kit, containing, no doubt, the tools, the instruments and delicate bits of apparatus of his trade. In the other hand he carried a pair of stiltlike things of light metal tubing, things that ended with a curious webbing that resembled broad, splayed feet.

"I had the luck of the gods," said Ware softly. "It was perfectly impossible to complete the thing in the time that—"

"Yes," said Grayth with a chuckle that was half a sigh, "we had the luck of the gods, too."

# CLOAK OF AESIR

The Sarn Mother's tiny, almost-human face was lined with the fatigue of forty hours of continued strain. Now, she feared greatly, a new and greater tension was ahead. For the eight City Mothers, taking their places about the Conference Hall of the Sarn, were not going to be sympathetic to the Mother's story.

To them, the ancient Sarn Mother well knew, the humans of Earth were slaves. Slaves bred for work, of little mentality and no importance. Earth was the planet of the Sarn, the planet the Sarn had taken, some four thousand years before, from the race of small-bodied, small-minded weaklings called Man that had originally inhabited it.

And that idea was going to be extremely hard to change. Particularly, it would be hard for the Sarn Mother to change that idea, for she was somewhat—not of them. The Sarn Mother was the Immortal. She was, therefore, disliked.

These eight, these Mothers of Cities, were the matriarchic governors of Earth under the Sarn. Each had risen to overlordship of a continent, or near-continental area, by competitive brilliance among all their people. They had won their places, merited them, they felt.

But the Sarn Mother? The ultimate ruler of all Earth, all Sarn and humans alike? She had not *inherited* her position exactly—she had simply been there forever. Her winning of it was forgotten in the mists of antiquity. The Sarn were a long-lived people—some lived a thousand years—but the Sarn Mother was immortal; she had lived in the mythical days of the Forgotten Planet, before the home world of the Sarn had disrupted in cosmic catastrophe, forcing the race to seek new worlds.

The Sarn Mother had won this world for them, but that—and all others who had fought mankind in that four-thousand-years-gone time—was forgotten. The Sarn Mother was simply a hang-over from an era that should have died. So felt the Mothers of Cities, ambitious Sarn who saw a place above them that—because of the Mother's cursed immortality—they could never hope to reach.

269

The old Sarn Mother knew that, and knew, too, that only her own possession of secret science those millenniums of her life had given her, made her place safe. The City Mothers feared two things: that well-held secret science, and the jealousy of their sisters.

The old Sarn was tired with mental struggle, and she knew, as soundly as she knew the City Mothers hated her, that she was facing another struggle. The humans of Earth were rising in a slow, half-understood revolt. She and these eight City Mothers knew that.

But the City Mothers did not, and would not, admit that those humans were capable of revolt. For all their lives humans had been slaves, pets, a sort of domesticated animal. That they or the similarly domesticated cows might attempt to set up a civilization—

For the Sarn Mother alone had been alive the four thousand years that had passed since Mankind's defense of Earth all but succeeded in defeating the invading Sarn. The City Mothers could not understand. Subconsciously they had no intention of understanding anything so unpleasant.

The Sarn Mother's pointed, elfin face smiled weary greeting. Her fluting, many-toned speech betrayed her fatigue as she spoke to them. "I call you together, daughters, because something of grave importance has arisen. You have heard, perhaps, of the judging of Grayth and Bartel?"

"Rumors," said the Mother of Targlan, the city perched high in the crystal clarity of the mighty Himalaya Mountains. "You reversed your judgment, I heard." Her voice was silky smooth—and bitter.

The Sarn Mother's small, pointed face did not change. The trouble, definitely, was beginning. "I told you at the last Council that the human stock was rebuilding, that the submerged intelligence and will that built, before our invasion of this planet, a high civilization, were mounting again. It is, I believe, equal in power to that before the Conquest. And, under our rule, it has been purified in some respects. There is less violence, and more determination.

"It is somewhat hard for you to appreciate that, for you do not remember human beings as other than slaves.

"I recognize a certain growing restlessness at restraint. The majority of those humans do not yet know—understand—the reason for a vague restlessness that they feel. Their leaders do. They are restless of government and restraint, and I hoped to use that vagueness of feeling to destroy the tendency toward rebellion. I thought the rebellion might be turned against their own, proxy government. Therefore, I caused the humans to revolt against their government under us, instead of against the Sarn.

"Even I had underestimated them. Grayth and Bartel, the leaders of Mankind, appeared before me accompanied by Drunnel, the rival leader. I will not detail their quarrel, save to say that Drunnel was my tool. I sentenced Grayth and Bartel.

"Then—Aesir, he called himself—appeared. He was a blackness— a three-dimensional shadow. He stood some four feet taller than I, nearly twelve feet tall, twice the height of humans. But he was shaped like a human in bulk, though the vague blackness made any feature impossible. He claimed that he was not made of any form of matter, but was the crystallization of the wills of all humans who have died in any age, while seeking freedom.

"Aesir spoke by telepathy. Mind to mind. We know the humans had been near that before the Conquest, and that our own minds are not so adapted to that as are the humans'. Aesir used that method.

"He stood before me, and made these statements that were clear to the minds of all humans and Sarn in the Hall of Judgment. His hand of blackness reached out and touched Drunnel, and the man fell to the floor and broke apart like a fragile vase. The corpse was frozen glass-hard in an instant of time.

"Therefore, I released Grayth and Bartel. But I turned on Aesir's blackness the forces of certain protective devices I have built. There is an atomic blast of one-sixteenth aperture. It is, at maximum, capable of disintegrating half a cubic mile of matter per minute. There was also a focused atomic flame of two-inch aperture, sufficient to fuse about twenty-two tons of steel per second.

"These were my first tests. At maximum aperture the blackness absorbed both without sound or static discharge, or any lightening of that three-dimensional shadow."

The Sarn Mother's mouth moved in a faint, ironic smile. "There are," she went on softly, "certain other weapons there. The Death of the Mother, which I employed once on a rebellious City Mother, some thirteen hundred years gone. Tathan Shoal, she was, of Bish-Waln." The Sarn Mother's slitted eyes lit amusedly on the present Mother of Bish-Waln, capital city of the continent of Africa.

"Tathan Shoal had the mistaken idea that she might gain by attacking me. She came with many devices, including a screen capable of turning all the weapons she knew. It cost me the South Wall of the Hall of Judgment and an effective and efficient administrator to convince her. For she had been effective and efficient.

"Daughter of Targlan, it is best for the Race that we share knowledge. Tell your sister of Bish-Waln the remarkable progress your physicist has made with the field she knows as R-439-K."

The Mother of Targlan's face remained unchanged, save for a faint golden flush that spread over it, and the sudden angry fire of her eyes. Field R-439-K—her most treasured secret—

"It is a field," she said in a pleasant, friendly tone, "which causes the collapse of atoms within it, bringing about a spreading disruption that continues so long as the generator is activated. It is necessarily spherical in shape, destroying the generator very quickly, however. It would be excellent as a sort of bomb." She added that last as a sort of afterthought, a hazy, bitter dream in her voice.

The Sarn Mother smiled and nodded toward the Mother of Bish-Waln. That City Ruler's eyes were angry as had been her predecessor's as she responded to the unspoken command. But her voice betrayed no emotion.

"No, Sister, it can be projected to some extent. The generator need not be destroyed, though the projector is, if you employ a field of ellipsoidal form."

The Mother of Uhrnol smiled, but her smile was only half amusement. "The projector can be saved, too. It is too bad I could not have known of your efforts. I could have saved you considerable work."

The three smiled at each other in seeming friendliness. Each felt slightly relieved; she stood alone neither in her chastisement nor in the loss of treasured secrets.

"The point of interest," the Sarn Mother pointed out softly, "is that none of you can stop that field. There is no protection. Some twenty-two centuries ago I discovered that interesting modification of the atomic-blast field, and within a century I had projected it. Ten centuries ago I had it tamed to the extent of a cylindrical tube of force of controllable dimensions. If Tathan Shoal had waited another five centuries before attacking me, she would not have cost me the South Wall. It still does not match perfectly the other three. But I cannot screen that force."

"Nor I," admitted the three City Mothers, in turn. There was a hint of bitter defeat in their tones, for each had hoped that field that could not be screened might make them safe in disposing of the old harridan, the Immortal Sarn Mother, who ruled them from a forgotten generation. She was a bitter, anachronistic hang-over from a forgotten time, from even the Forgotten Planet, and should have been forgotten with it.

"Aesir," said the Sarn Mother softly, "took the Death of the Mother into his blackness, and seemingly drew strength from it. At any rate, both the apparatus and the atomic generator which fed it were blown out from sudden overload.

"It might be wise to cooperate more closely than in the past. Once, remember, our race had a very bitter struggle with this race. What do you Mothers of Cities believe this Aesir to be?"

The Mother of Targlan stirred angrily. "There are clowns among the humans of my district who amuse their fellows by trickery. Humans have stiff legs, bending only in certain, few joints. That lack of flexibility gives them amusing powers. They can, for instance, advance the stiffness by the use of poles of light metal, representing longer, artificial bones. I have seen such clowns walk on legs that made them not twelve, but seventeen feet high."

"Yes," said the Sarn Mother sweetly, "the clowns of my North America are of a very inferior brand. They can appear but twelve feet tall. But—"

"Many," said the Mother of Bish-Waln, "of my humans have shown they can talk mind to mind among themselves. If it is new among your people here, it is—"

"Yes," said the Sarn Mother sweetly, "the humans of my North America are of an inferior brand, evidently. But—I am curious of these clowns and mind-talkers. Do they, perhaps, absorb atomic-blast beams for nourishment, and warm themselves at a focused flame? Do they so overload your atomic-collapse field generators as to burn them in molten rubbish?

"Or do they, perhaps, unlike yourselves, remember that the Sarn Mother has watched humans, and the minds and tricks of humans, for some eight times your not-inconsequential five hundred years?

"There were, in the Hall, humans, Sarn, and myself. By telepathy, Aesir spoke to us all, telling a myth of his origin among immaterial wills. He was, in his way, quite noisy, and quite conspicuous. Also, he was an excellent psychologist. Had I been warned—had I known beforehand and had time to think—I would not have turned the blast, the focused flame, nor, certainly, the Death of the Mother against him.

"Now do any of you, who see so clearly through the trickery of my poor little, twelve-foot clown, and the trickery of my slow-developing telepathist—do any of you see through to the message Aesir meant for my intellect, and not my mind? A message he did not speak, but acted?" The Sarn Mother's elfin face looked down the Council table, and there was nothing of laughter in it.

The City Mothers moved uneasily under the lash of biting scorn. The Sarn Mother's voice dropped, softer still, till the tinklings of the atom flame above muffled her words.

"Mummery for fools, my Daughters. I am interested that you are so attracted by the mummery as to forget the purpose, and so pleased with your cleverness that saw the human behind it.

"But I am—irritated that you underestimate, not merely the mind of a human of deadly, blazingly brilliant intellect, but, even more, my own mind.

"Humans are a smaller people, better adapted to this somewhat heavier planet than we are. But we are no longer on the Forgotten World. The humans have learned to respect height; the ruling Race is tall.

"Is Aesir a fool, then, to make himself yet taller, and to fill out his slenderness with vague blackness?

"We have no hair on our skulls, as have humans, but the more useful *sterthan* which seems, to humans, practical telepathy, since we can talk among ourselves by what they know only through microwave radio sets.

"Is Aesir a fool, then, to use telepathy himself, talking truly mind to mind? Men know the limitations of microwave radio, that it ends at the horizon. But they do not know what vague limits telepathy may or may not have, and it is very wonderful, therefore.

"That mummery, my Daughters, was intended only for humans, that mass of restless humans who do not know what they want. That was not meant for me—save that he wanted me to know what others heard.

"I am proud of my humans, Daughters. But I am afraid, for you. You have not shown the intelligence that that Man expected. That mind telepathy he used was not the message he meant for me. To me he said: 'Mother, a new balance must be reached. You are the ruler of Earth—but for me. I challenge you to try your weapons—which I know, as does everyone on Earth, you have in your throne—and see if you can destroy me.' And when I, not thinking, but reacting spontaneously to the evident menace of his blackness, did just this, he said more. He touched Drunnel, and Drunnel fell dead. 'I have an impregnable shield,' his actions spoke, 'and it is more; a weapon. You cannot destroy me, Mother of the Sarn—but I can destroy you.

" 'Therefore, we seek a new balance. You could destroy all my people—but not destroy me. And I could destroy you, or any of your people.

" 'Release these two, Grayth and Bartel, and we will think again. This is not the time for hasty action.'

"Aesir, Daughters, is no fool. He is no trickster—save for his own sound purposes—but a mind of astounding brilliance. He has discovered a principle, a weapon, unknown to us and of immense power.

"And, my Daughters, I respect him. I released Grayth and Bartel, since they are, evidently, pawns in this game. Or, at least, they are two of the few humans on Earth I know are not—Aesir.

"And I have more liking"—the Sarn Mother's voice was bitter and ironic—"for one who expects my mind to see beyond mummery to a deep and important sincerity, than for those who explain trickery and point out the inferiority of my humans."

"You are reading words that are not written," said the Mother of Targlan flatly.

For an instant the eyes of the Sarn Mother burned with a white anger, a blazing intolerance of such sheer stupidity. Then it faded to a look of deep concern.

The Sarn Mother was unhuman, unhuman in the same way her elfin face was. It was very wrong, taken as a human face, with its pointed chin and tiny mouth, the slit-pupiled, golden eyes, and peaked hairline that was not hair. But there was the fundamental parallelism of two eyes, a mouth, a high, rounded forehead. Her body was grotesquely unhuman, but again there was a parallelism of articulated arms carried high on a strong torso and legs, though her arms were like four powerful snakes.

And—she was un-Sarn. The Mother was immortal, an unchanging intellect in a world that waxed and waned and changed about her. She had living memories of a world crushed in cosmic dust. She had memories of great Sarn who had dared and won a world, of a human civilization of magnitude near equal to this present Sarn world.

And the process that had made her immortal, had made her unable to have descendants. There was no direct link from her to this newer generation. Her only link was through a planet wiped from the face of Time.

Four thousand years she had ruled this planet. Two thousand more she'd lived on the Forgotten World before the desperate colonization attempt had been conceived. These creatures—these Sarn—were ephemeral things about her, for all their five hundred years.

Sixty centuries are long, for any intellect. All things exhaust themselves in that long time, save one—the curiosity of the mind, the play and counterplay of intellect. The Mother was the perfect seeker after knowledge, for no other thoughts could ponderably intrude. Those others she had met long ago.

She was un-Sarn by her immortality, by her separation of six thousand years from all direct contact with her equals.

She was unhuman only by a difference in body. And the body is wearied and forgotten in that time. Only the intellect, the mind, remains of interest, expanding and changing forever.

The intellect behind Aesir's cloak of blackness was the keenest, the finest, this planet had ever seen. And—that human appreciated that she, the Sarn Mother, was a keen intelligence.

The City Mothers did not.

The Sarn Mother turned her eyes slowly from the Mother of Targlan. "The words that spell the secret of that blackness are not written." she said mildly. *These were the daughters of her race. These were the descendants of Sarn she had known and worked with and liked during six thousand years. These were—*

"I must see more of that cloak, and investigate it more adequately." She sighed. "And you, my Daughters, must not underestimate an enemy. And the humans are, I fear—or will be soon.

"They have been slaves for many generations—very short generations—and they have evolved. They evolve more swiftly than we, because of that short life span. And, remember this: at least one of them is sufficiently brilliant, of sufficient mental caliber, to develop a screen weapon superior to anything we know of. That alone makes him, potentially, extremely dangerous."

The City Mothers sat silent for long seconds. The thought was, as the Mother had known, extremely upsetting. Their matriarchic minds rebelled at the thought that there was a human—and a *male* human, at that—who was capable of developing something scientifically superior to anything in their possession.

"If," said the Mother of Targlan, "he has this remarkable weapon—proof against all ours, and deadly to us—I am extremely thankful that he has shown such kindliness toward our race." Her fluting voice was sugary. "He has not equipped any of his compatriots nor attacked us in any way."

The seven other City Mothers twitched slightly straighter in their chairs and looked with pleased smiles at the Sarn Mother's fine, small face.

The Mother smiled bitterly. "Undoubtedly that would be your own reaction were you possessed of such a weapon," she admitted. The Mother of Targlan stolidly continued to look into the Mother's half-angry, half-annoyed eyes.

"But you," the Mother explained, "have never done more than to say 'a thousand pounds of tungsten' when you had need of it. Or order fifty No. 27-R-29 oscillator tubes, when you hoped to make a satisfactory lie detector. Incidentally, Daughter, I have an effective invisibility generator. And your lie detector will not operate. You'd do far better to use common sense and simplicity instead of outrageously expensive mummery that doesn't work. That spy you sent to—one of the other cities—last week had a very slipshod invisibility. I watched her a whole afternoon from here. She set off seven different alarms, and finally was caught in a delightful booby trap. Your sister believes in simplicity instead of gadgets."

The Mother of Targlan sat silent and stony. Her slitted eyes contracted slowly in flaming hatred.

The old harridan was becoming cattish. The old harridan was tired. She was wearied to death of the bickerings and annoyances of these City Mothers with too little to do to occupy their time. Furthermore, she hadn't slept in forty hours, and knew it. And the Mother of Targlan was being unbearably stupid.

The Mother of Bish-Waln was interested. So—that was the source of that spy. And the old Mother, for all her foolishness about these humans, had some sense. The secret of success is simplicity. Though that Targlan spy *had* had a fearful and wonderful array of apparatus strapped about her, it also had made her—even when dead—remarkably hard to see. She'd sounded like a collapse in a glass factory when she fell, though.

"To get back to my remarks," said the Sarn Mother abruptly, "you have never had to want something without getting it. Except," she added with a flash of tiny, pointed, green-white teeth, "understanding. If you want materials, they are brought.

"If a human wants materials, he steals them. And I will say this for you—you have all been remarkable organizers. The anti-theft measures you have developed are outstanding. But I should think that the fact that humans still succeed in thieving would convince you they are clever."

"So," snapped the Mother of Targlan, "are rats. But they aren't intelligent."

"Quite true," admitted the Mother. The Mother of Targlan was becoming annoyed, which vaguely pleased the old Sarn Mother, who was very annoyed. "But humans are both. It took me twelve years to find exactly how it was approximately thirty ounces of platinum disappeared each month, despite my electrostatic balance detectors. Now I make all workers clip their fingernails and hair. It was truly startling how much dust they could carry that way.

"To acquire materials, humans must steal them. And they must find it extremely difficult to gather such things as metallic caesium, gaseous fluorine, and rare gases like helium and neon. Unfortunately, I believe a considerable quantity of material is obtained from ingeniously acquired atom flame lamps." The Mother nodded toward the softly rustling lamps overhead.

"So your workers secrete complete atom flame lamps under their nails?" said the Mother of Targlan. "Your theft measures are indeed remarkable. The atom destructor of one atom lamp would power a dangerous weapon. They will stand a load of nearly ten thousand horsepower."

The Sarn Mother smiled. "How many atom flame lamps have you lost through theft, Daughter?"

"None. Not one!" snapped the Mother of Targlan.

"And what," asked the Mother kindly, "of lamps destroyed in burning human homes?"

"Perhaps ten a year."

"I'd say five a year, then, are acquired by humans. I've proven two homes were burned to the ground to secure the atom lamps the occupants wanted."

"We," said the City Mother loftily, "require that the wreckage be produced."

"Excellent," sighed the Mother. "An excellent provision. Do you have a chemist analyze the molten waste? The humans generally find it very difficult to obtain scandium, and the analyses usually skimp badly on that. But the other elements you'll find. They smelt up a careful mixture of all the proper elements, with the exception of gallium. But they can always claim that boiled away."

The Mother of Targlan looked startled. The Sarn Mother's eyes twinkled slightly in satisfaction. She had discovered *that* trick only four days before, herself.

"As I said, the humans find it hard to get materials and apparatus. But they are really ingenious, and I rather respect them for it. If you wish to assure yourselves of your cities," she added, looking about the table, "I'd advise you to acknowledge the power of your opponents.

"That is the reason this human, Aesir, has not done more. He has a weapon and a protection—for one. So long as he cannot obtain material, he cannot do more.

"But he will obtain materials." The Mother's annoyed air was dropped now. This, she knew, meant the safety of the Sarn race. "If he obtains sufficient materials before we learn the secret of that cloak, *the Sarn will not rule this planet.*"

The Mother of Bish-Waln looked at the Immortal steadily. Suddenly she spoke. "I have always considered the humans stupid. That they had the cleverness of other lower animals, in greater degree, I realized. But we, Mother, have no memories of their civilization before we came. How far advanced was it, actually?"

The Sarn Mother looked at the City Mother keenly for a moment.

It was anomalous; this City Mother, less than one twentieth the Immortal's age, looked far older. Her face, pointed in the manner typical of her race, was graven with fine lines. There was a power and strength of purpose in its deeply tanned, leathery molding. Ruler of a tropical continent, her city centered in the warmth and cloudless air of the Sahara, she was one of the most active of the City Mothers.

The old Sarn Mother smiled slightly and nodded. "I can tell you very little now. But call in your archeologist. She is a brilliant and learned Sarn. Briefly, when we landed, the humans had had civilization for some fifteen thousand years. It was, by their calendar, 1977. They had recently developed atomic power of the first order, involving vapor turbines heated by atomic combustion, driving electromagnetic generators. They mined the world, their transportation systems were heavily interlinked and efficient.

"And—of our fifty-two ships, we lost thirty-nine during the Conquest. They were intelligent, efficient, and deadly fighters. We captured and enslaved only the scum of the race; the best of humankind died fighting with a grim tenacity that appalled us. They were a fighting breed, slightly given to attack, but utterly and insanely given to defense.

"It is worth noting in this case. If they once attack us, then we will, of course, attack, in reply. Whereupon their inherited defensiveness will come into play. If it does, I seriously assure you that, whether they have weapons or not, even if they fight with their bare hands, you will find the human race a perfectly deadly thing to tangle with. They have no conception of when to stop. It is good military tactics to stop, if any reasonably equitable settlement can be reached, after losing ten percent of your forces. The human race does not know that, and never will. They stop when, and only when, they are convinced they have won their point. They simply do not show good sense.

"But they are extremely deadly.

"That is true of the mass of humanity. They have leaders now, and Aesir is the principal leader. We can, and must, control them through him. He knows, instinctively, the attitude of his people, and will try, therefore, to prevent suicidal war.

"Wherefore, if we obtain the secret of his cloak of blackness, we can proceed."

"I will ask my archeologist, Mother," said the Mother of Bish-Waln.

"Whatever you may say of the dreadful, deadly, human race," said the Mother of Targlan ironically, "it would be interesting to know the mechanism of that shield. But—maybe he will not explain. And it would be extremely difficult to force him to, if what you say of it is true."

"We shall have to analyze it, of course," said the Mother wearily. There were many more hours of work and sleeplessness ahead. "Some hours ago I instructed my physicists to set up all the instruments they thought might be useful in the House of the Rocks."

The Mother of Targlan stared blankly; then, acidly, commented: "Of all places in the Sarn City here, I should say that that would show the absolute minimum of probability for an appearance of Aesir."

"And," continued the Mother, wearied of interruptions, "they will be ready for him in about an hour and a half. It is evident that Aesir will come to the aid of Grayth, if we capture him. To make assurance doubly sure—since Grayth is not, actually, absolutely necessary to them—we will take also Deya, Spokeswoman of Human Women. Grayth plans to marry her, and I am sure that Aesir will aid in releasing her."

The Mother of Bish-Waln frowned slightly. "Is it not bad policy, Mother, to arrest, and then release this man again? And—again at the insistence of Aesir."

"Therefore, the House of the Rocks. No human can approach. No human will know of the actual escape—save those humans already closely associated with Grayth, and, therefore, Aesir. Those humans already know what powers Aesir has, even better than we, and they will recognize this maneuver not as an arrest that failed, but as a test that did not fail. Our policy will be good, not bad, to those who know. The mass of humans simply will not know."

"They will not, I suppose," said the Mother of Drulon, at the far, stormy tip of South America, "notice that Grayth, their Spokesman, is being taken in Sarn custody—and returns?"

"They will not," smiled the Mother. With an uncoiled finger, she pressed a tiny button.

At the far end of the long Council room, a silver door opened in the jet black of the wall. The heavy metal portal swung aside, and a Guard snapped to attention in its opening, a giant Sarn standing over eight feet tall. Her powerful, supple arms were corded with the smooth-flowing muscles of a boa constrictor. Vaguely, her trappings indicated the rank of a Decalon—a commander of a Ten. Her cloak, though, was a deep, rich maroon, and in the center the gold, silver, and bright-purple metal threads wove a pattern that was the Mother's personal symbol.

And her face—to one who knew Sarn physiognomy—was not that of a mere Decalon. The slitted eyes were deepset and widely separated. Her mouth was firm, and the face, small and pointed to human experience, was square and powerful in a Sarn. The golden skin had been tanned to a leathery, weather-beaten brown, crossed by a myriad of fine lines of character. This was no mere commander over ten guards.

"Decalon," said the Mother softly, "bring the Cloaks of the Mother, and your command. There is an errand."

The Decalon turned sharply, noiselessly, closing the metal door.

"Once," explained the Mother, "Darath Toplar was Commander-in-chief of the Guard of the Sarn City. She is now a Decalon. That is because there are but ten in my personal Guard.

"Now this is a time of emergency. I have revealed to each of you something of the things each thought a secret, and some of the things that I held secret. I am showing you the Cloaks of the Mother. That they existed, rumors have stated. They do. They have the properties the rumors suggest. Because it is necessary, they will be used."

The Decalon was back, behind her ten guards dressed in the same type of maroon uniform. Ten powerful, eight-foot Sarn warriors. On the face of each was stamped a keen, loyal intelligence. In the arms of the Decalon was a case of dark hardwood, inlaid with heavy, silvery metal straps. She put it down at the end of the great Council table, and the Mother's hand flicked out as her supple arm uncoiled to shoot a scrap of carefully cut metal the length of the polished table. The Decalon fitted it into a concealed lock with a motion of familiar dexterity.

The case, opened, revealed a space two by three by one-half foot. In it, racked neatly along one side, were twenty little battery cases, with coiled, flexible cables attached, and twenty headsets, bearing curiously complex goggles. The case was practically empty.

The Decalon reached in, and with practiced movements passed to her command the goggles and battery cases. Then she reached more carefully into the body of the case. The reaching hand vanished. Presently, queerly section by section, the Decalon was wiped out, till only a pair of feet remained, dwindling off into space. These vanished as some unseen boots were pulled over them.

In a moment, only the City Mothers and the Mother of the Sarn remained in the room—seemingly. The City Mothers stirred uneasily. The eyes of the Mother of Targlan were golden fires of anger and chagrin. These—these picked eleven of the Mother's personal guard and spy force—knew every secret of her laboratories.

And the old immortal harridan knew them, too. Her crackling laughter must have been spurred a thousand times by the futile attempts and doomed plans the Mother of Targlan had made and thought over. The Mother of Targlan felt a rising pressure of helpless anger well up, an anger that was suppressed by its very helplessness. Even the satisfaction that the Mother was old, a cackling hag, was denied. For— salt on her wounded pride—the Mother had done, seemingly centuries ago, what the Mother of Targlan struggled with vainly! The Mother was a far better scientist.

It was a very different Council room, this chamber where the Spokesmen of Man had met—an inner office of the elected representative of Mankind, the spokesman of man. It was a warm room, mellowed by a thousand years of time; ancient woods, waxed and cared for for ten centuries and more, had taken on a fine, soft patina. Long, slanting fingers of afternoon sunlight did not glare on cold jet stone here; it was softened by the richness of the panels. Each was of a different wood; one from each of the continents, and one for each Continental Spokesman.

The great table in the center was worn in soft hummocks and swales by the arms of forty generations of Spokesmen, the thick rubberlike floor carven by their feet.

But as in the great Council room of the Hall of the Sarn in nearby Sarn City, here, too, atom flame lamps rustled softly with dying atoms, whitening the light of the setting sun. Four men only were at this Council table, four who sat motioning, gesturing with a curious alertness, their faces intent. Yet—utterly silent.

Grayth, tall, lean, keen-faced Spokesman of Man, an elected representative who had won his honor by a keen understanding of the practical psychology of the men he represented before the Sarn Mother, political leader of Mankind. Bartel, shorter, more solidly built Spokesman of North America, close friend of Grayth, who had stood beside him before the Sarn Mother, when—Aesir—had come.

And Carron, the gigantic Commander of the Legion of Peace, the only semblance of an army allowed humans. A police force armed with tiny gas throwers capable of a single, stupefying shot, and rubber truncheons.

Also, one more. Darak, Grayth's Sub-Spokesman. He sat silent now, making occasional pothooks on a pad of paper, his round, uninteresting face bored and boring. Darak's office was appointive, given him at Grayth's order, for the blankly unimpressive face and uninteresting character of the man made him few friends—as he had found by many years of careful study of the subject. Few friends, and few who paid him any attention whatever.

Darak had no need of the Cloak of the Mother; his own, based not on laws of physics but of psychology, was nearly as effective. People did not see Darak. He wasn't worth seeing.

Four humans at the ancient Council table, four men as free as possible in this day of the Sarn, each wearing on his cloak the symbol of his rank in human society. Each wearing on a band round his forehead the medallion given every human at the age of eighteen. The band of Manhood or Womanhood, the Sarn informed them. The mark of Mankind's submission to the Sarn.

Or was, till Ware made certain slight alterations, alterations that hollowed out the solid three-inch disk of silver to contain a minute thing of spider-web coils and microscopic crystal oscillators. The first of the telepaths that rendered this soundless Council meaningful.

And rendered quite useless the listening devices that had followed every Council of Mankind for a thousand years. Grayth smiled upward to the swell of the atom flame lamp. In the mechanism of that device, in a dozen other places in the room, the Sarn had long ago hidden radio transmitters. For a millennium, every Council of Mankind had been directly open to the strange radio-sense of the Mother and her advisers. For the hairlike growth on the Sarn skulls were the sense organ of a type Man did not have, directly sensitive to radio.

"Four men in here," Grayth thought to his companions, "four men rustling papers. But the Sarn must be very curious as to the silence."

Carron's broad, tanned face broke into a wide grin. "After a thousand years, a bit of silence from this room is due. The Mother knows well enough we aren't minding her business. But I don't think she'll be anxious to investigate after—Aesir."

"The Sarn Mother," the thought whispered in their minds from a more distant telepath, "is busy holding a conference of her own. I've been trying for weeks to get the pattern of Sarn thoughts. I get annoying flashes, but no more. The Mother is tired, and the City Mothers are being stubborn, I gather. But the thought patterns are just enough different from human thought to make the telepaths ineffective at more than about one hundred feet. And the most assiduous electrotechnician can't spend *all* his time tracing conduits in the Sarn Palace."

"I'd suggest you do absolutely nothing that an ordinary electrotechnician wouldn't do, Ware," Grayth hurriedly advised. "And for Aesir's sake, stay home when you're supposed to have off hours."

"Have you reached any conclusions? I've been sleeping, and woke only a few minutes ago." Ware's mental voice seemed to yawn. "I've been trying to think of some way to get more metal. Ye gods, if I could just get into one of the Sarn electrical plants for a day, I'd have a dozen things I need fixed up. The math was none too simple, but I've gotten it, I think." He chuckled. "Thanks, in fact, to a very wise old Sarn.

"Just below conscious level, a thought came to him, a bothersome equation. While a certain electrotechnician fussed with conduits fifty feet away, he fussed with the equation. The Sarn have some mathematical methods our ancestors never developed, and that I haven't had a chance to learn. Carron, if you ever feel urged to crack the skull of old Rath Largun, spare him for that."

"Can you use him again?" asked Carron amusedly.

"Oh, I have. He's old. and his mind wanders. Nearly a thousand years old, I think, which is exceptionally old for even a Sarn male. Since he is a male, he gets less credit among his people than he deserves, but he's the most brilliant mathematician the Sarn have. Because his mind wanders—he believes he thinks up the equations."

"Might they give him a clue later?" asked Grayth sharply.

"T . . . P . . ." said Ware easily. "What word am I spelling? When you have correctly answered that, the Sarn may get that clue."

"Good." Grayth nodded silently. "Ware, Carron has seven technicians in his Legion of Peace who will procure some of those things you need. They have volunteered."

"I have not said what I wanted, nor will I," Ware answered instantly. "Every technician caught stealing metal now will be destroyed by the Sarn instantly. No man is going to lose his life on something I wouldn't attempt myself. Further, we need two classes of men now more vitally than ever before: technicians and fighters. Humans haven't fought and are not fighters. Carron's Legionnaires are the only trained, experienced fighters—with the will and emotion needed for fighting—that we have. And when they are also technicians, we can't spare them.

"Have you told Darak what's to be done, and given him the disks?" Ware changed the subject abruptly, with an air of "that's that." It was because Carron didn't know what metals Ware wanted; had he, he would have gotten them somehow, anyway.

Darak replied softly. "I have been told, and I have the disks. Twenty-five telepaths, each equipped with destroying apparatus reacting to one key thought. I know how the destroying mechanism is to be disconnected if successful delivery is made. Grayth has supplied me with sufficient official dispatches for both Durban City and Targlan. I am starting in twenty-two minutes."

"Then—good luck, Darak."

"Thank you. The wish is, perhaps, the luck of the gods?"

"Yes. The luck of Aesir—very appropriate." Ware chuckled. "You will lose contact with me, except when I use the large telepath here in the laboratory. You know the schedule hours for that?"

"Yes, thanks."

"We will be going, too, I think." Carron rose ponderously. His huge form dwarfed even the great Council table. And, since he spoke for the first time, his heavy voice seemed to explode in the room. "I'll see you to the Sarn City gates, Darak."

He glanced down at the Sub-Spokesman's busy fingers. They were chubby, soft-looking fingers, rather thick and clumsy. An ink bottle flickered and wavered in and out of existence under the flicking, incredibly deft fingers. Then it flickered, without seeming to move under his caressing, chubby hand, from a round, red ink bottle to a square black one. "Thank you, Carron. The dispatches, Grayth?" Darak's voice was rather high for a man, quite undistinguished. Darak was, next to Ware, the cleverest human on Earth in that era. But his mentality was as utterly different as was Grayth's. Grayth was a practical psychologist, the only living man capable of unifying and moving the masses of mankind. Ware was the scientist, the epitomization of centuries of the Sarn efforts to develop capable human technicians. And Darak?

Darak had the curiosity of the scientist in Ware, the psychological sense of Grayth, and the love of action that made giant Carron what he was.

Grayth tossed a mass of papers toward the Sub-Spokesman, a mass that bulged and crinkled. Darak leafed them swiftly into a brief case that he carried. "One thing I will have to remedy," he telepathed silently. "The metal gleams." Twenty-five silvery disks flickered momentarily among the rapidly leafed papers, and vanished as his thick fingers passed them. "All here," he said aloud. "Goodbye. I should be back in about four days."

His feet made no noticeable noise on the floor—an accomplishment far more difficult than a soundless tread. An unnoticeable step involves exactly sufficient sound to satisfy the ear, without enough to attract it. A soundless tread is very startling, particularly in a rather stout, heavily built man.

He walked through the outer office, past a battery of secretaries and clerks working over statistics from all the human world, correlating and arranging them for Grayth and the Human Government. Two looked up as he passed, but neither saw him. They missed him as completely as they missed the passing of eleven eight-foot Sarn Guards walking past in the opposite direction on the soundless toe pads nature had given them. For neither party wished to be seen, and each had its own unseen cloak wrapping it.

The door stood open a moment as giant Carron and Grayth spoke a few last words. Bartel stepped out, and then Carron, holding the door wide for his own exit, lingered a moment longer. Soundless feet carried the three Sarn, larger even than Carron's six feet six, through the door.

The door closed behind the Commander of the Legion of Peace, and Grayth stood alone, silent. "Aesir—Aesir—Aesir—" his telepath was sending out.

"Yes?" snapped Ware.

"Three Sarn are standing in the room, invisible to me. Eight more are in the outer office. Both Carron and Bartel are trying to call you— they stood in the door delaying the entrance of the invisible three. All are invisible. Their thoughts I can detect, but not decipher."

"I know. I've learned to 'hear' their thoughts. It takes a little adjusting, due to the different patterns. I'm trying to get them now. Too distant. I don't like it."

"Grayth, Spokesman of Man." The Decalon spoke from the air in the curious accents of the Sarn, speaking the tongue common to humans and Sarn.

Grayth started, looked about him, shook his head violently, and reached for a call button with a look of unhappy doubt.

"Stop," snapped the Sarn. Grayth's hand halted in midair. "The Sarn Mother sent us for you. Stand up."

"Wh-where are you? Are you—"

Grayth stopped abruptly. A Sarn's powerful, muscle-corded arms gripped him suddenly, and simultaneously an intense blackness fell over him. A blackness more utterly complete than could have been produced by any substance thin enough and flexible enough to give the clothlike sensations that accompanied it. A very faint, rubbery rustling sound came to his ears, and simultaneously the jerking and pulling of the Sarn Guard adjusting the cloak.

"We wear the Cloak of the Mother," the Guard fluted sharply. "You will be quiet. You will make no sound, say no word. It is understood?"

"Yes," sighed Grayth. Then silently: "You've caught my impressions, Ware?"

"Yes." It whispered in his mind, the reassuring solidity of another human in close contact. The blackness, the utter blackness, baffled and brought a welling of panic. The huge, corded arms of the Sarn, the secrecy of this invisible arrest, all brought a feeling of irrepressible panic.

Then Ware's calm mind obtruded powerfully, silently. "The blackness is not related to mine. It is caused, I suspect, by the complete refraction of light about your body. To be invisible, you must be rendered blind to visible light, since any organ capable of seeing must, by its nature, intercept light. Struggle slightly. Strike the face of one of the Guard."

Grayth shuddered. A Guard was working swiftly at his feet. A tremor passed through him, and for a moment he fought off the powerful arms, surprising their grip by a sudden thrust and a gasp as of panic. His arm flailed out gropingly. Then with a second gasp, half-sob, he quieted at the soft, tensely sharp command of the Decalon.

"Goggles," said Ware softly. "Transformers, probably, operating on ultravisible light, thus making vision possible with invisibility."

Tensely, in Grayth's mind came the impression of half a hundred other human minds attending this exchange, half a hundred humans throughout this central city, the Sarn City, capital alike of human and Sarn affairs.

"You must stop them," Grayth felt a mind whisper urgently. "Ware—you must release him. Secret capture—they hope to loose him where Aesir cannot find him to release him." Deya's mind, turbulent and fearful, now. Leader of Human Women, determined and ready to defy the age-long, mind-burdening hold of the Sarn, this sudden, half-magic descent of the invisible guards terrified her for the sake of the man she loved.

"Stay where you are, Ware," Grayth rapped out mentally. "They're moving me now—leading—no, carrying me out through my office. In thirty seconds, I'll be lost utterly; the darkness is totally blinding and bewildering." Grayth felt solid ground under his feet suddenly, then he was standing, and spinning in the four cable arms of the giant Sarn. The darkness spun madly about him for a moment, then he stood waveringly on his feet, without the faintest idea of position as powerful arms urged him forward. "Stay where you are. I don't know where I am, anyway, and I'm convinced this is intended as a trap to bring you where the Mother's prepared weapons can destroy you and all hope of the revolution. She wants me only as bait for you. Stay!"

Softly in Grayth's mind came Ware's easy chuckle. "If I knew where you were, my friend, I would come. I will know soon enough. In good time, the Mother will see that you—and hence I—know. She realizes you have telepathic communication with me. Never, to my knowledge, has she revealed these invisible cloaks—"

"There have been other unexplained disappearances; this is the first time a telepath has been available to carry word," Deya snapped out.

"No matter. In good time, for no force, no power, no weapon or ray, no bomb or any other thing can serve to disrupt the—Cloak of Aesir. No energy, however great, can break down that shield. That is not the Mother's hope, for this morning in the Hall of Judgment she tested that cloak to all her powers—and one or two, Grayth, no other Sarn of all Earth knows, save the Mother alone. It did not fail then, nor can it. She makes no further trial of it, but wants an analysis of its forces." Ware's easy jubilance rode through to Grayth, lessening the tension.

"She will not learn one iota of that, Grayth. No, she wants a demonstration, a demonstration on her own terms, at her own time, in her chosen place. By Aesir and all the gods of Earth, Grayth, we'll give her the demonstration she seeks. By every god from Mithra to Thor, we'll give her one. I'll chill her prized palace there on the Sarn Hill till her old bones ache. No Sarn yet ever had rheumatism, but, by Earth and Man, we'll find out this night whether a Sarn's thousand bones can't breed a mighty case!"

"You'll stay where you are, you braggart fool," Grayth howled through his telepath. "You are the revolution, not I. Bartel's an abler man, if he does lack a bit in fine words and simple phrases. The Sarn Mother's lived five centuries to your year; she has studied space and time and all of energy with tools and instruments you never guessed, or will guess. You are a child, a prattling fool of a child, to her, Ware. Stay where you are! You may not know of any way to analyze or defeat that shield of yours, but what do you know of the Sarn's ten-thousand-year-old science?"

Ware's bubbling laughter echoed queerly in telepathy. "All Sarn science, Grayth, that has been published. The telepath, my friend, is not without its powers as an educator, tuned inward to catch, amplify and reflect each thought to a solid impression. And all human science, Grayth. Under my house—when I was trying to make a lab the Sarn wouldn't find—I found an ancient subway and a buried lab some striving humans had contrived in the last days before explosives and gas killed them. Books and periodicals, tons of them, heaped clumsily. A forgotten legacy."

Grayth groaned. The skin of his back seemed suddenly oppressed in the queer manner a telepath contrives when absolute rapport is established between two powerful minds. A heavy pack strapped on Ware's back. The screaming hiss of an atom flame lamp unit readjusted, rebuilt to carry a million times the load it had been designed for, a scream that vanished in inaudible shrillness. Sketchily, waveringly, the rock-walled, hidden laboratory of Ware's contriving stood

out before Grayth's eyes, lighted against the utter blackness that
shrouded him. Then that, too, became a blackness, a stranger, straining blackness and chill as Ware pressed a contact at his belt.

"Ware," pleaded Grayth, "I don't know where I am. If you don't
promise now to stop this expedition at least until I give further intelligent information, I'll grind the Mother's medallion under my heel,
and by the gods, you'll never know."

"I'll wait,"sighed Ware.

"But—you'll go later, Ware—you'll go?" demanded Deya.

"I'll promise that, too, Deya." Ware's mind smiled to her.

"Grayth, I shall continue." Darak's thoughts, faint with distance,
came in.

"Right," replied Grayth. "Bartel!"

"Yes."

"And Carron and Oburn, Tharnot, Barlmew, Todd—all of you,
continue your duties, without any change or shift. Do not hint you
know of my disappearance till the appropriate time. Todd, you take
charge of that outer office; you did a good job, apparently, when you
knew I was being carried by, invisible, ten feet from you. You are in
charge there. Keep the girls out of my inner office, for any reason,
until I can give some idea of what is to take place. Got it?"

"Right."

"Deya," said Ware, "has stopped sending. Further, she does not
answer; she's blanked her mind."

"We've been walking—stopped now!" Grayth's mind raced.
"Deya—Deya, answer me!"

There was a tense silence of mind; only the low, multitudinous
mutter of a thousand human minds in normal thought about him.

"Oburn, where are you?" snapped Ware.

"At home."

"Stroll out in front; you live within three doors of Deya. Grayth,
stumble in the dust—do you feel dust under your feet?"

"Yes." Grayth stumbled awkwardly against a giant Sarn Guard,
dragging his foot sharply across a dusty walk, unseen.

"Dust rose," said Oburn softly. "Deya, will you answer me?"

"Yes." Her telepath thoughts were half angry, half miserable.

"We're moving again, though, so—they spun me. I don't know
which way."

"You will stop dragging your foot." A Sarn voice low and tense in
Grayth's ear warned him.

"Ware, I—I don't like this." Grayth's thought was tense and very
worried.

Deya's was bitter. "It was well enough when you were the one; now you are not so anxious Ware stay back, I take it. Ware, you stay right where you are, because if that was wise for Grayth, the only one of us who can really move the men of his following, it is a hundred times wiser so far as I am concerned."

"I think," said Ware, annoyed, "that I had better start designing a telepath locating-device. It should be relatively simple, and if this continues, we'll need one. I'll join you as soon as I know where you are. In the meantime, I have a little work to do preparing. Please stop ordering and counter-ordering. We need you both; the Mother wants to study this apparatus, and she won't stop taking people until she gets the chance. It won't do her any good whatever, so she'll get that chance."

"I fear you're right," Grayth agreed. "It should be getting dark now."

"It is. The moon rises at one forty-five, so we have plenty of time. I think . . . I think it is going to be heavily overcast," predicted Ware suddenly. A chaos of thoughts raced suddenly through his mind, thoughts too lightly touched for others to follow.

Utter jet, and the sound of people moving, voices and low laughter. Hasty side-steps to avoid unseen passers that brushed by, feet sounding softly on the dusty walks or grassy lanes. Then rough cobbles under their feet, rounded by the tread of more than a hundred generations of Mankind, and behind them, the low murmur of the Square fading away.

The rough cobbles gave way, suddenly, to the smooth, glassy pavement of the roads of the Sarn City. They had passed the low, ancient wall that marked the boundaries where men might walk unchallenged. Only low, sleepy cheeps of birds in nearby parklike gardens now, and the shrill notes of crickets and night insects tuning up.

The pace of the Sarn Guards accelerated, their long legs, and the curious manner in which they retracted them with each step, making a pace swift for the humans to match. Grayth heard Deya's soft breathing accelerate as they moved at a near trot up the slow rise that led to the Sarn Palace.

Then steps under his feet, strong Sarn arms guiding him upward, steadying stumbling feet. The echo of corridors answered to his tread, and for an instant he knew where he was; this was no unfamiliar walk to him now, and he was mentally readjusted. To the right, then, and a half-dozen turns, and he was beyond any area of the vast, sprawling Sarn Palace that he knew.

An arm detained him; he stood motionless in utter darkness, while, beyond, something hummed for an instant, then a soft shuffling of a sliding door, two steps forward, and the soft clang of the door's return. The sensation of a sudden drop in a swift elevator was nerve-tearing in this darkness, this total unknowingness of place, time, or intent of captors. Grayth stiffened, heard Deya's soft gasps as the floor seemed cut from beneath her. Then the steadiness of the floor returned, and only the soft humming of the gravity controls told of their movement downward. Time became confused, there was no clue to their speed, yet Grayth was certain that they dropped many thousands of feet. The air pressure mounted till swallowing had relieved it so many times he lost track of that crude barometric method. More than five thousand feet, though—

More than a mile! No human had ever guessed at the depths of the Sarn Palace. Only once had humans ever been permitted to see those depths, and then it was the upper caverns only, when Drunnel and his men had been given a few feeble weapons by the Mother's orders. Weapons to overcome Grayth and Ware.

"More than a mile—we're slowing, Ware. The air is thick; it must be nearly two miles down. The air itself seems denser and richer in my lungs. Unless we are brought upward again—"

"I'll come down to you," Ware's calm mind replied. "Can you receive there clearly?"

"Perfectly," Grayth acknowledged.

"Two facts I wanted; antigravity units of the cars do not disturb the reception. Two miles of solid rock do not disturb it. Thought waves are a level below all known radiations, a force unto themselves. The Cloak of Aesir stops all other things."

"We are walking down a corridor, wide, rock-floored and walled, low-ceilinged. There are columns," said Deya. "Ahead, I hear Sarn."

They halted, and the echoes of their feet died away slowly, the curious *zing-zing-zing* of sound reflected from rows of columns disappeared in unknown, unseeing distances.

"Mother of Sarn! Decalon Toplar reports with her Ten, and the two humans for whom she was sent," the Decalon's fluting voice called out.

"Remove the Cloak of the Mother, Decalon. Place all of the Cloaks in this case, and with them the visors."

A giant Sarn tugged at Grayth, the curious rustle of the cloak rose about him, then abruptly he was blinded by a flood of intolerably brilliant light. Gradually his eyes adjusted themselves; it was 'no more than normal illumination from a score of giant atom flame lamps set high above in the arched and groined stone of the ceiling. Black, glittering, granitic rock, studded with two huge plaques on opposite sides. A twenty-foot disk of gold mapping Earth, a twenty-foot golden disk mapping the Forgotten Planet. From a concealed atom flame lamp in the lofty dome, two projectors shot stabbing rays against the golden disks. On Earth's, a ray of brilliant yellow-white; on the other, a ray of dim, chill blue.

The Mother sat on a Chair of State, about her the eight Mothers of the Cities and a score of giant Sarn Guards. From air, eleven more were emerging, as Deya emerged piecemeal, while goggled Sarn packed into the silver-and-hardwood case on the long table something unseen and tenderly treated. The Decalon stood by the case, tucking unseen folds carefully into its corners, taking goggles and batteries from the Guards to place on tiny pins.

"It is the Given Law that no being, human or Sarn, shall twice be accused of a single thing," said Grayth. "Yesterday in the Hall of Judgment I was tried and acquitted. It is the Given Law that no being, human or Sarn, shall be brought for judging without an opportunity of defense, save he waive that right.

"Neither I nor this woman, Deya, has committed any offense against any being, human or Sarn. As is our right, we ask our accuser to appear and explain before us and the Mother the reason for this arrest."

The Mother's slitted eyes closed slowly and opened sleepily. Her powerful body remained as motionless as the stone of the Hall; the Mothers of the Cities neither moved nor seemed so much as to breathe.

The Mother spoke in the fluting tongue of the Sarn. "The Given Law is the Law of the Mother; by it I have promised to abide, save in time of emergency. This, Grayth, is such a time. You, this woman, and perhaps certain others have sought to plot against the Sarn and the Sarn Mother. That is the accusation; I am the accuser. What answer do you make?"

"If one be brought before the Mother, and faced with his accuser, he has then twenty-four hours to consider his reply. The accusation must have evidence enough to make it seem just in the Mother's eyes that an answer be made, and complete enough that the accused know why this thing is charged.

"The Mother is the accuser, but I may ask—by the Given Law—what reasoned facts bring forth this accusation?"

The Mother's eyes sparkled. Almost, a smile touched her tiny lips as she looked at Grayth's keen, gray eyes. The Sarn were proud that never in the millenniums of Man's enslavement had cruelty been applied, nor intentional injustice. Where the Law of the Sarn could apply logically to humans, both races worked under the same law;

where—as in the nature of two races such things must be—the laws could not apply identically, justice had been applied.

The Sarn were just; no human could say otherwise. The Sarn Mother's age covered six-score generations of Mankind, and to some extent her immortality removed her alike from human and Sarn. Wherefore, it was easier for her, who had known Man's greatness, to appreciate the keenness and strength that lay in Grayth's stubborn face. And, knowing Mankind, to appreciate the steadfastness with which he would fight by every law or trick of law to win freedom back for Deya.

And—she appreciated the searching quickness with which Grayth had forced her once again on the defensive. Her case was true and solid—but made of ten thousand thousand little things, of things that had not happened as well as of things that had. Of subtle, reasoned psychology—and not half-a-dozen solid facts. Of those few, three were ruled out of this consideration, because they had been dealt with in that earlier trial, when Grayth was released.

She had no time to argue now with a mind that she knew was fully as keen as that of her own City Mothers. There were other, more important things afoot, as that gray-eyed man well knew. And he knew as well as she that her case was not a thing to be stated in a dozen sentences. And also that it was a perfectly just, though unprovable, accusation.

"This is a time of emergency, Grayth," said the Mother softly. "I will give you the twenty-four hours you demand, however. And your companion, Deya.

"Decalon, let these two be taken to the fifteenth cell in the House of the Rocks."

The Decalon and her squad of ten moved forward. Grayth turned to Deya, a slight smile on his lips, as the Ten surrounded them. Back toward the great pillared corridor leading off into unseen distances, lighted by dwindling atom flames, the Guards led them.

"The House of the Rocks. This, then, is the rumored prison of the Sarn. Ware—Ware—" Grayth called mentally.

"I am coming, Grayth. I will join you in an hour. You need not call continuously as I have made rapport with you and can follow your normal thoughts. The sky, as I suggested, is becoming overcast. It will be a very dark night."

"We could not leave unaided," sighed Deya.

"I do not believe it would be probable." Grayth laughed uneasily.

Grayth moved about the cell restlessly. The Decalon and her squad-ron were gone, down that tube that had brought them. The single huge old Sarn that served as warden, turnkey, and guard had set the tumblers on the steel door, and left with soft, shuffling toe pads.

Grayth stopped in the center of the room, his head high and tense, furrows of concentration on his forehead. Deya, in her chair, sat motionless, her deep-blue eyes clouded in sudden thought. She rose slowly, a magnificent throwback to a race five thousand years forgotten, a viking's daughter, bearing a golden tan of the more southern sun of this region, but golden-haired and blue-eyed, tall and powerful.

Slowly her eyes cleared, and a slight frown of understanding met Grayth's eyes. "There are Sarn close by. At least a dozen. And if those Sarn are prisoners here, then all the Mother's laboratories have been stripped of talent," she said softly.

"Echoes," thought Grayth sharply. "Do not use voice."

Deya smiled. "They do, and yet no intelligible word is audible. The echoes do not carry words; they carry sounds, confusing, blended, intermingled sound. And concentration on telepaths might make impressions on instruments, where normal thought did not. Perhaps speech is better."

Grayth nodded. "There are a dozen Sarn, at least, all scientists. They are in the cell above, the cell below, the cells on each side. And the only clear things of their thoughts that I can make is—Aesir—and instruments."

"I've found that shaft," came Ware's thoughts. "I haven't traced every circuit of the palace for nothing, and as the palace electrotechnician, I've found many that were not on my charts. The sky is becoming heavily overcast. It will be very dark indeed. I will join you shortly."

The Mother pointed silently. Across the room, a section of rock had swung aside, and a broad signal board was revealed. A green light blinked irregularly, then went out. A blue bulb winked for a moment, and died in turn, as a yellow bulb glowed steadily. "By the shaft, then. The air is not open to him."

The Mothers of the Cities stirred restlessly. A second yellow light flashed. "If he goes below the sixth level—" suggested the Mother of Durban.

"The cage will remain down there, but probably he will not. He walked through a solid wall once; he may walk through solid rock." A third and fourth bulb flashed. The Mother watched quietly; the Mothers of Cities tensed as the fifth lighted. Abruptly it was out, and in sudden succession the blue and green bulbs winked.

"He knew," said the Mother, almost approvingly. "The car did not fall. Go."

A section of rock wall swung open. Silently the Mothers of Cities vanished behind it, and with them went the tall figures of the Guards. The rock swung to. The Mother, alone on her tall throne, saw a darkening of the farther lights of the long corridor.

Aesir stood again before the Mother, a blackness, a thing that was not black, but was blackness incarnate. A thing some seven feet in height, vaguely manlike in form.

The Mother's thin lips smiled. "You have shrunk, Aesir. Have some of those billions of wills you mentioned left you, then?"

A voice stirred in her mind, a respecting, yet laughing voice. "Perhaps that may be it; a few wills more of cold metal than warm human flesh. But for the good of my race, two wills you hold captive must be freed. For this I have come again. And—perhaps that you and those who wait in five adjoining cells may know me somewhat better.

"I am the crystallization of a billion, and more than a billion wills, Mother of the Sarn."

"There are no humans here; the Sarn need no such tales." The Mother moved annoyedly.

"It is no tale; it is pure fact. This blackness is their product, not as, perhaps, I might explain to humans, but still their product." The voice that stirred soundless in the Mother's mind smiled.

The Mother nodded slowly in comprehension. "Wills and knowledge. That may be. We seek a new balance, you and I."

"We seek a new balance, your race and mine," corrected that blackness. "You and I might reach a balance in this minute, if it were we two alone. The balance would be—that your plan went down to a depth that none, neither Sarn nor human, knows, while I remained."

"Yes," acknowledged the Mother. "I might be wiped out, and you remain. But your race would go, and mine remain, save that you alone continued."

"There is no need to exchange these thoughts; each knows the other to that extent. Man has one great advantage over Sarn; that, as a race, Man is more nearly developed to universal telepathy. A few of my people can already talk among themselves; I have learned the different pattern that is Sarn telepathy. I can speak with you as Grayth cannot."

"Though he appears aware of Sarn thoughts when near us," sighed the Mother. "I had not thought of that."

"We make an exchange now," Aesir's thoughts laughed. "You wanted observations of my—my body stuff. I will give you that, and in exchange—"

Aesir stepped forward, and swept from the long table the silver case that contained the Cloaks of the Mother and the goggles. Simultaneously, the Mother's finger moved, and a carven bit of her high throne sank under it. From unseen projectors, a shrieking hell of flame screamed out, intolerable—blasting— The rocky floor of the great chamber screamed and puffed out in incandescent fury. The great table boomed dully in the corridors, a sudden, expanding blot of livid gas. The mad shrieking screamed and thundered down the corridors, the floor of the vast cavern slumped in annihilation that speared down through a hundred feet of rock in a single second of cosmic fury—

And died in silence. The Mother dropped three curled arms before her face, blinking tear-blurred eyes. Aesir stood, blackness against fiery incandescence of the cooling rocks, unsupported in the air. His form was altered, a clumsy thing with a strange, angular belly. An almost rectangular protuberance. But the thing was not rectangular; one corner was twisted and bitten away.

"I never knew," said Aesir softly, "but I am certain now; the world of the Sarn was not so heavy as Earth. You move slowly, Mother."

Silently the blackness glided down the corridor, dwindling from the Mother's sight. Furious golden eyes glittered after the hunched, disfigured mass. Slowly the glitter faded from her eyes, and a concentration of thought appeared, perhaps even a mischievous twinkle of approbation.

The Mother's finger touched another button, and instantly a score of tense-faced Guards leaped through the door, clumsy-seeming, funnel-mouthed hand weapons ready. They stopped at the door, staring at the fiery incandescence in the floor.

The Mothers of Cities crowded through their ranks, a slow, dawning smile of satisfaction on their thin lips as they looked into the glow. The Mother of Targlan took her seat slowly. "Then the revolution is ended," she said with soft satisfaction.

The Mother turned angry eyes on her. "Daughter," she asked bitterly, "do you think I mount here weapons of the power I have in the Hall of Judgment? I did not turn that weapon on him—but on the Cloaks. No more than a corner of them did I get; he moved too swiftly. My thoughts have been disturbed in this emergency, and I have not rested in fifty hours, or I would never have left that case where he might reach it.

"Aesir must win on this exchange, for he *will* know what makes the Cloak of the Mother, while I *may* know what makes the Cloak of Aesir."

The Mother looked calmly down the long corridor, where a figure of hunched blackness turned into a narrow cleft in the great wall of the rocky tunnel.

The old Sarn Warder of the House of Rocks had been instructed. The Sarn Mother had no desire to lose Sarn lives—and she wanted Aesir in that grim citadel. The Warder, as Aesir appeared, turned away and left the passages open to him. The invisible Guards at the narrow cleft that led into the impregnable citadel remained inactive, wrapped in invisibility.

Up the stairways carved in the glinting rock the Blackness strode. Down the corridor to the gray steel door behind which Grayth's and Deya's minds acted as directive calls.

And—between ranks and files of recording instruments set in every wall, in every doorway he passed. Tiny atom flames finer than the slimmest wire reached out to touch and feel at the black texture of his cloak. Unseen force fields caressed delicately at the fringes of blackness. Bolometers and thermometers felt and sampled the chill that poured from the blackness. Frigid air, like chilled puddles, flowed from that blackness and trickled across the stone floor behind him. White of frost coated the corridor pavement as he, in his dead blackness, passed.

"Grayth—Deya—stand back from the door. The door will fade to a vague transparency. Step through it instantly." Through the impenetrable blackness, the subtle mystery of thought reached out to contact and explain to the imprisoned humans.

The formless blackness of Aesir's hand waved stubbily over the gray metal of the door. As though that hand were a wet cloth, the door a chalked picture on slate, it vanished. Where the hand had passed in quick circles, the grim metal roiled and twisted—and vanished.

Deya's hand reached out uncertainly, touched the space where the door had been to feel a vague opposition, as though a thick and incredibly viscous gassy stuff remained. It was utterly without temperature sensation. She lunged through it sharply, overcome by an instant's strangling suffocation, then stood beside Aesir in the corridor. Grayth joined them silently.

"The Cloaks?" he asked.

"They are useless save for information. The Mother's rays cut through the corner of the case, and cut strange patterns in them, no doubt. You could not use them. We'll have to go out as we are. Now come, and stay close behind me. We must put walls behind us, and that won't be easy."

"Can we go into the rock—or would that be impossible?" Deya asked.

Aesir's misshapen hand pointed. Behind them, the door of the cell was blackness similar to Aesir's own, a blackness rapidly congealing about two bent shadows overlapping on the surface. Two shadows where Deya and Grayth had passed through. A deadly chill was radiating from the door, a growing chill that sucked the light of the atom flame lamps in the ceiling, and ice from the air.

"You felt that momentary suffocation. You can't breathe inside that steel, or inside rock. And that condition of interpenetrability is both temporary and frightfully treacherous. We'll have to go."

Ware went ahead, and now, as he passed the hair-fine atom flames that had probed for his cloak, a finger pointed and sharp cracklings of lightning snapped where the jet beam of blackness struck the probing beams. Harmless to Aesir's blackness, they were hairlines of death to unshielded humans.

The flames ahead on their course abruptly sputtered and went out. The Sarn saw no reason to lose good instruments.

Down the stair, and out into the glare of the great atom flames lighting the House of the Rocks. "There are invisible Guards," said Aesir. "The Mother, I take it, warned them to let me pass in unhindered. They may seek to stop you—"

It was against the Mother's orders. But those Sarn Guards, in their eight-foot power, in their contempt for humans, in the pride they held that never had any being imprisoned in the House of the Rocks escaped, raised unseen weapons toward Grayth and Deya.

A long, stretching finger of jet shot out from Aesir's stubby hand. Something crackled in the air, darting lightnings and a wild, many-toned shriek of agony chopped off abruptly. A Sarn figure black as Aesir's jet stumbled from nothingness and faded behind a swiftly formed white curtain of frost crystals. The black finger swept around, and the Sarn Guards died in blue lightnings and blackness.

"Run," commanded Ware. The three started down the straight narrow cleft that led to the outer corridor. Aesir turned right, then right again, into a low-roofed tunnel. Another elevator bank, the cars undamaged. The heavy, locked metal door faded under his hand to disclose a black shaft leading down and up in emptiness to unseen depths and heights. Another door—and another—

Then a car was found, and the three hastened through. Behind them in the main corridor a heavy pounding of running feet and clanking accouterments sounded. The blunt, dull-glossed nose of a war-blast swerved clumsily round the corridor with half-a-dozen giant Sarn tugging at it. Degravitized, it floated free, but its tons of mass were clumsy and hard to manage there in narrow rock corridors. Shouting, musical commands twisted it into place, settled it, and it thudded to the floor as the degravitizer was cut. Two Sarn swung the trajectory controls, and a third held the lanyard ready.

Aesir reached for the controls of the elevator cab as the blast roared in throaty fury at dissolving, flaming walls. The rock walls to the left and right flared into deadly flame of dying atoms. And the view was lost as the translucency of the metal door snapped instantly into blackness, a blackness that licked up the furious energy greedily and pulled with freezing fingers at the heat of the two human bodies within.

"That button, Grayth. Quickly. I cannot touch it through this cloak," Ware snapped.

Grayth pushed the thing, one among a bank of hundreds. The floor of the cab pushed against them momentarily, then a sense of weightless falling gripped them as Ware's black finger pointed at something in the control mechanism. Blackness and frightful cold drained every trace of warmth from a resistor in the controls, and the full current drove through the degravitator control. The car shot madly upward.

"The Mother has many of these cars wired with power cut-offs. If this is one—as it probably is—and she learns in time which car we took, she may cut out our circuit. If so—we still have one chance, though I have never dared try it."

"Better cut that resistance back in," said Grayth quietly. "Listen to the howl of the air above."

The shriek was mounting. Far above in the closed tube, compressed by the upward plunge of the tube-fitting car, the air was howling through some vent. It was a vast organ pipe that changed its tune upward, upward—more and more swiftly as the tube length shortened and the pressure mounted—

"I can't." Ware's hidden head shook. "The air pressure must stop us. But not until we reach the top of the building and the automatic safeguards go into action. They'll cut the current in the car and apply brakes as we pass the topmost floor. If the Mother hasn't already—"

The shriek mounted. Abruptly the drive of the car vanished. Grayth, already firmly gripping the carved cage walls, flung a protecting arm about Deya and gripped more tightly. Aesir tumbled upward toward the roof of the cab, inverted himself somehow in mid-flight, and hung poised.

"Don't touch me," snapped Ware's thoughts in their minds. "It would be death—"

A new sibilant hiss cut through the roar of the air in the tube above, and Ware sighed in relief. "The Mother was too late. She cut the power—but not before we had come so high, and so fast that the automatic safeguards tripped. The emergency brakes have gone on."

The deceleration died, and Ware floated back to the floor. The car was stopped, was sinking slowly. It clicked again, and a ratchet locked somewhere beneath their feet. The door of the car opened with a rumble, and an outer door slipped aside. The three stepped out into a corridor, a corridor lighted by the atom flame lamps of the Sarn, lamps carved in alabaster and golden amber stone. They were in the uppermost floor of the Palace of the Sarn.

Far below, the Sarn Mother looked thoughtfully at the little lighted column of signal lamps. The City Mothers followed her gaze, furious as they saw the double red bulbs of the safety guard signals go on. "I am curious," said the Sarn Mother softly. "He froze the resistor in the degravitizer circuit with his blackness, surely, to get any such mad climb rate. But I have a thought that Aesir does nothing that he does not know some remedy for, nor attempt anything that he does not have some second, saving escape. What would he have done had I been able to cut his power before he could reach the safety trips?"

The City Mothers were not curious. They waited impatiently as the Mother let seconds slip away without flinging a rank of Guards about that upper floor.

The Mother made no move. She saw no gain in throwing her Guards against the blackness, that, so far as she could see, had no weakness. She saw, rather, that her best policy was to wait the report of her scientists. Knowledge was the power she needed now. That, and the power she already had; control over all sources of the materials whose lack rendered Aesir harmless—so far as revolution went.

Aesir stood in the entranceway of the Hall of Judgment. Behind, through the ever-open doors, the Gardens of the Sarn were visible. Aesir—Ware—smiled. "I said it might be an overcast night," his thought whispered softly.

Grayth and Deya shivered. The gardens knelt before a wind that howled in maniac fury. In the reflected light that shone against the low-pressed sky, a wrack of storm boiled overhead. And it was cold. The wind that shrieked across the Gardens was a breath of savage winter cutting through this summer night.

"I think," said Ware, "that it will rain."

As he spoke the sky burst into flame. Vast tongues of lightning ripped across the sky, stabbing down to Earth in a mighty network of electric fire. The air exploded with a blast of thunder that rattled the mighty fabric of the Sarn Palace to its bones. Instantly the floodgates opened. The clouds split up and tumbled down in liquid streams. The shouting wind lashed the water droplets before it in a horizontal spray that was half falling water, half water slashed from the ground that was suddenly a pond. The twinkling lights of the Human City beyond the Sarn City walls were suddenly gone.

"Perhaps," said Ware pleasedly, "I used too much."

"You?" gasped Grayth. "*You* did this?"

"The Sarn hate cold, and they hate the wet more than any cat ever did. You'll find no Sarn loose in the Gardens tonight. Our way should be clear to the gates."

Deya shuddered and looked at Aesir's blackness. "That wind is cold; that rain must be near sleet. And I am dressed for June—not a February night."

"I used too much power." Ware shrugged. "I never did this thing before. Put it down to inexperience."

"Experimental error." Grayth sighed. "Gods, man, you've washed the city away. Come, let's start before we have to swim."

"Not yet," said Ware. "I've something else to do. The Mother wanted to study this blackness of mine. Well, by all the gods there are, I'll give her all she wants. I'll make her think again before she summons Aesir for her pleasure!"

He turned about and faced into the great Hall of Judgment. It was magnificent beneath the dim light of a few big lamps. It was jet stone and chrome, gold and sparkling, inlaid crystal. Aesir's arm became a funnel of blackness that pointed in slow circles around the room. Where that arm passed, the sparkle of polished stone and shining metal or gem vanished. It became a dead blackness. The walls ceased to have the appearance of walls, but became empty spaces that stretched off to some eternity of night.

The glint and whisper of the atom flames died away; their strong light dulled to something somber and depressing.

And cold—cold welled out of the place in a tangible flood. The humans shivered violently and fled from the doorway that dripped, suddenly, with frozen mist. Puddled air, chilled near its freezing point, it seemed, flowed down the walls and out the door. A breeze sprang up, a throaty gurgle of air rushing into the room at the top of the great door to rush out at the bottom in a freezing, unseen torrent.

Grayth and Deya hurried aside, shivering in unbearable chill. The torrent of air poured out, across the vestibule to the entranceway of the Palace. It flowed down the steps, and as they watched, the howling rain turned to snow and froze as sleet on the stone.

"Yes," said Ware in satisfaction, "the Sarn hate cold. It will be a month before that room is habitable again. Now come."

He walked through the flood, and down the steps toward the windlashed Gardens. The wind howled by him, swirled around his cloak of blackness, and the figure was outlined in white that swirled and glinted in the faint light radiated from the building. Behind him, Grayth and Deya made their way, white figures against the blackness. In a moment they were lost behind driving, glistening curtains of rain.

They were soaked and freezing in an instant. In his arms Grayth felt Deya shivering violently. "Ware," he called abruptly. "Ware—go on; we will meet you. We can follow that blackness only by the snow that forms around you, and on a night like this, may I be cursed if I follow a walking snowstorm. I'm freezing now, and Deya, too."

"Frozen," the girl chattered.

"I can't cut off this shield," Ware answered. "The instruments aren't insulated well enough. If water touches them—there'll be neither Sarn nor Human City to squabble over. Meet me at my house. You can find your way?"

"I think so," nodded Grayth, shivering.

"Strike for the road. It will glow tonight, as usual. And there will be no Sarn upon it, with this liquid blizzard howling."

"Good." Grayth and Deya set out, half-running. Black wind and water thundered through the Gardens. The sky exploded once more in blinding light, the waves of sound rocking the ground beneath their feet so that even half frozen as they were, they felt its shaking.

In the ruck of that wild night, no eyes saw Grayth and Deya reach their goal. Rain in solid, blinding sheets hid them as they slipped between wind-bowed trees to Ware's small stone cottage, into its unlighted doorway. Ware's hand found Grayth's, and led the shivering, dripping pair through the tiny room, abruptly brilliant in the explosion of another lightning flash. At the far wall, Ware fumbled at a stone that grated and moved. Silently he led them down to a yet smaller room lined with rough granite. The stone above them swung back, and a light sprang up. But again Ware was fumbling, and again he led them down, down to a musty cavernous place, walled with age-rusted steel, supported by rusted columns of steel hidden at the heart of thicker columns—stalagmites and stalactites formed about and buttressing the corroded metal.

"The old subway," Ware explained. "It goes for a quarter of a mile in that direction and nearly a mile in the other before cave-ins block it. All, you see, beneath the Human City—and most at a depth of more than one hundred and twenty feet. My lab's over here." It was set up on the concrete platform of a forgotten station.

"But here—strip off those wet things and stand before these heaters." Ware turned to a crude control panel, and a network of iron bars grew warm, hot, then faintly red as a welcome heat poured out.

"Do we hide," asked Deya softly, "or frankly return?"

"If," said Ware sadly, "I knew how much longer this queer status of half-revealed-half-concealed revolt was going to continue before I could get somewhere, we might be in a better position to know what to do."

"Which makes me wonder, Ware. Half-concealed-half-revealed, I mean. The Mother's Cloaks have the goggles to make vision possible. I don't know what that blackness of yours is—beyond that it is infernally cold; I'm still congealed—but if no ray can pierce it, pray tell me how you see where you are going."

Ware looked up, laughing. "I don't. Yet I found my way across that swamp called the Garden of the Sarn more easily than you, tonight. The telepath is the answer—I see through others' eyes. The Mother told me where her Cloaks were hidden." He nodded toward the truncated case. "Without her eyes—I'd never have seen to reach them."

"Perhaps," said Deya, "if we knew better what you have, and what you lack, we could help more efficiently."

"Perhaps," suggested Grayth grimly, "you can wash the blasted Sarn out of their city. Another such 'overcast night' and you may do it."

"The Sarn City's higher than we are." Ware smiled. "But our people do stand cold and wet better than theirs."

"But," said Deya, "it isn't practical—nor fast enough. What have you there? My slowly thawing bones give me a very personal interest in that cloak of yours."

Ware sighed gustily. "It's hard to explain. About ninety percent of it isn't in words, or explainable in words. It's a mathematical concept that has reality.

"Wherefore I will now give you a typical pre-Sarn analogy, because neither you nor Grayth can get pictures from mathematics. It's a language, you know—as much a language as the one we normally speak, or the Sarn language. Some terms you can translate, and some can't be. For instance $x^2 + y^2 = c^2$ is mathematics language for 'circle.' I will give you analogies which I guarantee are not sound, and neatly conceal the truth. But I can't do any better.

"Dirac, a physicist of the pre-Sarn days, explained the positron as a hole in a continuum of electrons in negative energy states. Space, he said, was completely filled with electrons possessed of negative energies. It was full to the brim, and overflowed into the electrons we can detect—ordinary matter electrons.

"Shortly before the Sarn came, men were developing hints that there might be more to that. There was. Electrons in positive energy states, when vibrated, gave off radiation—light, heat, and so on. If you use energy concentrated enough, you can vibrate electrons in negative states. You might say they give off negative energy radiation. They produce photons of energy in negative energy states.

"As I said, it's an analogy that I can't honestly describe, but the effect is radiated negative energy. Radiant cold or radiant darkness or radiant lack-of-X-rays—whatever you want.

"Energy being conserved, of course, the result is that the source of that radiation, instead of consuming energy, gives it off. My pack does not radiate negative energy; it sets up a condition in the air about me that makes the air atoms radiate negative energy.

"The atomic flame the Mother turned on me satisfied, to some extent, the ravening demand for energy that negative energy setup caused. The force that makes the air atoms radiate in that way makes them unstable—sort of splits them into two parts, two half-formed atoms of matter. In that state, neither half is real, but each has a terrible demand for sufficient mass—in the form of energy—to raise it to reality. In that median state, matter is interpenetrable. We walk through steel doors and stone floors, for instance. It will hang on that unstable point of half-and-half momentarily, before re-forming to matter. It's as dependable as a rattlesnake or a 'tame' tiger. While we're interpenetrating, it may fall off that delicate balance and consume our mass-energy in re-forming. When Sarn Guards send atomic flames after us, the unstable matter greedily drinks in the energy, and starts definitely toward re-forming with the air of that energy. If left alone, one-half of the semiatoms absorbs the other half, and it's normal again. In the meantime, it's black. And cold—like the Mother's Hall of Judgment right now.

"When the Mother's beams were tearing at me, the energy was actively making extra atoms of air. It didn't make any difference what kind of beam she used—the energy was consumed. Her atomic flame had lots of power—and made a lot of air. Her curious atom-disruption beam didn't carry much energy, but the particular form of the beam was most deadly. The form passed through my shield quite unchanged, theoretically. But the energy had been removed from it.

"Naturally, the Mother's physicists are badly puzzled now by a completely unanimous report of 'nothing' on the part of their instruments.

None of them, of course, read below absolute zero. That shield has a temperature of minus fifty-five thousand Absolute—or thereabouts.

"I could wipe out the Sarn very readily. But"—Ware shrugged his shoulders—"they'd wipe out all humans while I was at it."

"What do you need?"

"An hour," Ware sighed. "One hour—in the Sarn workshops. A few pounds of molybdenum, some wire-drawing apparatus, a few ounces of scandium, and special glass-blowing machinery. Then I'd have a duplicate of this toy of mine that would protect this whole city for fifty miles about."

"In other words," said Grayth, smiling slightly, "if you could drive the Sarn out, you could drive them away."

"Precisely," acknowledged Ware. "Which is comforting, if useless."

Deya rubbed her left arm with her right hand thoughtfully, and turned sideways to the heater. "How far," she asked thoughtfully, "will your present apparatus reach?"

"That, too, is helpful." Ware grinned. "Just about far enough to blanket completely the Sarn City. I could protect that against any attack. But not, not by any means, the Human City."

"That might help, though." Deya nodded. "I have something in mind. My dress is dry, if somewhat crumpled. Could you get us something to eat, Ware? My chill has left me hungry."

"What's your thought?" asked Ware eagerly, half annoyedly. The telepaths did not carry thoughts the wearer wished to conceal.

"I—I'd rather talk with Grayth first." Deya shook her head slowly. "I may be wrong."

Resignedly, Ware went up the crude stairway, up to the kitchen of his cottage one hundred and fifty feet above. Deya looked at Grayth as each in turn pulled off the telepath.

Deya pulled on her dress, smoothing the still slightly damp crinkles down. "How is Simons, Grayth?"

Grayth looked at her in slight puzzlement, his shirt half on. "Hopeless, as you know—but why do you ask now? He could not help us, anyway."

Deya's lips set in a slight, tight smile, her eyes bright and thoughtful. "I'm not so sure, Grayth. Not—so—sure. Ware has said that anything that he can run through an amplifier can be recorded, hasn't he? And if it can be recorded, it could be rebroadcast on a different wavelength, perhaps—"

Grayth started, went rigid. "By Aesir and all the gods of Earth! Deya! What fantastic idea have you now? That man is mad, horribly, loathsomely mad—"

"Negative energy," said Deya shortly, deft fingers arranging her hair. "If we could make the Sarn give up without fighting—in despair and hopelessness— And there are energies other than those purely physical ones that the Sarn are so thoroughly equipped to resist."

Grayth stood silent for a moment, his swift-working mind forgetting for the moment the task of driving his tired body. "You've talked with Doctor Wesson?" he asked intently.

Deya nodded slowly, "Yes—just this morning," then thought a moment before going on. "Or rather yesterday. It will be dawn in about three hours, if the storm has stopped. We should bring him here before then. You see what I have in mind?"

"Yes! I'll have Carron—"

Ware came down the steps slowly, bearing two trays with bread and cheese and cold meat, some cups, cream, and coffee. "If you will use those beakers for the water, the laboratory hot plates for a stove, Deya, I'd prefer your coffee to mine."

"Ware," asked Grayth tensely, "can you record a thought—a telepath thought?"

Ware stopped, brows suddenly furrowed. "Record it? Why? I've never tried—it's easier to think it again."

"Could it be done?"

"Hm-m-m—yes. I think so."

"How long to make the apparatus?" Grayth asked anxiously.

Ware hesitated. Shrugged. "A few hours. I can make that. Telepath apparatus, because of its very nature, has to be tiny. A few grains of the hard-to-get elements go a long way when the whole apparatus is less than a cubic millimeter in volume. But it takes time. A recorder and reproducer—say, two days, once I get the design. I think—yes, I know I can do it."

Grayth swept the telepath back to his head. Rapidly his thoughts drove out. "Carron—Carron—"

"Yes?" Sleepily Carron responded to the call.

"It's three hours to dawn. Carron—this must be done before the first people stir. Get Ohrman, the instrument maker, to Ware's at once. There are telepaths to be made. Get Doctor Wesson and tell him to call at Ware's. Then rouse one of the other men to receive and transmit my orders and get some sleep yourself.

"Now, Ware, draw out the plans for the parts you'll need for that apparatus, so Ohrman can start while you get some sleep. Oh—you can, I assume, make some translator arrangement that will twist human thought to Sarn telepath levels?"

"Eh? Human to Sarn levels—I don't know about that. I've been working on that problem on and off for weeks."

"Good—it'll be on, and not off, now. If you can do that, Ware, we win Earth again!"

The thing was incredibly tiny. It lay in Ware's palm, two small, enclosed reels connected by a bridge of bulging metal, the size, perhaps, of a half-peanut, between two slices of inch-thick steel rod. But the workmanship was wonderfully fine.

"This is only the reproducer." Ware sighed. His eyes were red and weary. "The recorder is there. You said that needn't be portable. And it records, as you wanted, in Sarn-type bands from the human thoughts, on a silver ribbon. The ribbon is endless, and repeats as long as this little spring is wound.

"Now, may I ask what you want of it? I've concentrated so on this that no question could enter my mind, I think. How is recorded thought to dislodge the Sarn? By repeating, 'Go away—go away,' endlessly? Telepathic commands have no more force than words, you know."

"Not if they are resisted," Deya acknowledged. "But they can enter below conscious strength level. Do you want to see who—why—"

The stone above moved. Grayth and Deya and Ware looked up. Only the heavily sleeping, exhausted Ohrman remained unconscious of the intruder.

"Down, Simons," said Dr. Wesson's voice. There was a gentle urgency in it, a pitying yet firm tenderness. A pair of feet appeared, slowly, wearily, with an air of terrible, unending exhaustion—tired beyond all rest, misery and hopelessness subtly expressed in the dull, shambling descent of those heavy feet.

Loosely, miserably they came down the long flight, their mechanical, rhythmic drumming a muffled beat of defeat. The man came into view. His figure was lax, powerfully muscled arms and shoulders bent under a soul-deadening weight of overwhelming despair. Down—down—

"Down, Simons." The doctor's voice was weary with a queer despair caught somehow from that doom-weighted figure.

Ware turned slowly to look at Deya, at Grayth. "Who is he—Simons?"

They did not answer, and he turned back to look at the figure that stood unmoving now beneath the powerful lights of this buried laboratory. His face was pale and lined, powerful with the strength drained from it, set in a dead mask of uncaring despair. His eyes were black,

black pits that looked without hope, or hope of hope, into the keen gray eyes of Aesir.

Ware felt something within him chill under the gaze of those eyes that no longer cared or hoped. The soul beyond them was not dead and longed for death. The lights of the bright room seemed cold and drear. Fatigue and hopelessness of the endless struggle against the overwhelming Sarn surged up in Ware, hopelessness and despair so deep he did not mind that the cause was lost before—

He tore his eyes away. "Deya—in the name of the gods, what—who—what is this thing!" he gasped.

"That is negative energy, Ware. That is the negative energy of the mind, the blackness of Aesir applied to all hope, all ambition. He is mad; he is a manic depressive. He has no hope, no thought of escape from that negative hell of despair that is beyond despair. He is mad, for no sane mind could conceive that awful blackness, the hopelessness that is a positive, devouring force that infests his being.

"If ever his mind should start to mend, he will become a suicidal maniac, driven to kill himself in any way he can, at any horrible expense. He cannot think of that escape now. That is struggle, that is in itself a hope—and he has none. To conceive of death as an escape is to hope, to believe that something better can be.

"That is beyond him now, for hope—struggle—effort to escape—all involve a will that mind has lost.

"He is mad, Ware, because no mind can hold the terrible despair his thoughts now know and remain sane.

"Record his thoughts. Record them there on that silver ribbon. Record that hopelessness that knows no resistance, no will to struggle. Record it, and broadcast that through the Sarn City!"

The Sarn Mother sat motionless at the high window of her tower, dull eyes looking out over the Gardens of the Sarn. Rich cloaks and heavy blankets wrapped her—useless things. The cold seeped through to her bones and drank her warmth. The great chamber, windowed on every side, was darkened by a heavy gloom, chilled by a cold that had grown slowly through the hours and the days she had sat here, almost unmoving. The bleak, cold stone of the walls was damp with a cold sweat of moisture. Great heaters in the walls ran at red heat and the dark air drank their warmth. Magnificent atom flame lamps rustled softly in the high ceiling; their faint, silken whisper mumbled meaningless in her ears, and their strong light had lost its sparkle. Some subtle change in the air made it seem gray and very cold.

The sun did not shine here. A cold, steady rain beat down on the

Gardens below, ran endlessly over the clear windowpanes, stirring under vague, listless winds. The sun did not shine here. Through the fog of slowly dripping rain, beyond the limits of her Gardens, the sun shone. It was brilliant there, she knew, a bright, hot sun sparkling in the bright clean air. It was June out there. The year was dead here, dead in a creeping, growing chill that burdened the land. The creeping, growing chill of—

That hellish thing of blackness. Almost, she felt angered at it, squatting there, dejected, black, unutterably woeful in the center of her Gardens. Or what had been her Gardens. It was a ravaged place now, plowed and harrowed by howling beams of atomic death, a shrieking incandescent effort to move that crouched thing of blackness. It had meant only the destruction of one slight spot of beauty in a dreary, cold world.

But that meant little, for there was no beauty now, or ever would be again. Only the chill that stole the heat from the air, the walls, her tired old body and the subtle darkness that cut through the brilliance of the atom flames and left light without sparkle, colors that all tinged gray.

A finger stirred listlessly and pressed a control. No, it was over. Full heat. She had known that; what sense to try again what she had tried a thousand times before during these endless, sleepless days that changed only from one shade of gray to a deeper black.

Dull eyes looked at the sweating walls. Cold, stone walls. When had it ever been that she had ordered stone? Warm marbles of rose and green. Warm? The rose of dying day before night's chill. The green of endless arctic ice. It mocked her and drove its chill to her age-old body.

Age-old. Unending years that had wheeled and rolled while she waited, useless. Waited for the coming of her people, or when she might again seek in space. Useless years of fruitless attempts to learn that one, lost secret of speed bettering light's swift flight. Lost—lost with the ten trained Sarn that died those four thousand years gone in the blasting of this city once called New York. Too much else she'd had to do then to learn that secret.

Time she had now; four thousand wheeling years. But now she could not learn; it eluded her dulled mind, and the weakened minds of the decadent race.

As Aesir eluded her, and squatted miserable in the midst of misery his works had brought.

She stirred. The cold worked through. Hot food, hot drinks—they warmed a moment, then added dead, cold mass to the chill within her. A deadness that, she knew now, had been within her before this glooming chill had made her more aware. Her Sarn were weak; the soft product of an easy world, too sanely organized to require of them sharp, sharpening competition in endeavor.

And she was old. Immortality she had, and everlasting youth of tissue. But the mind grew old and dull, the courses of its thoughts narrowed and chilled with years and millenniums that passed. She was never to recall that exact age—but what matter? A stupid thing. What mattered that she thought of it or not; the years had passed, they'd graved their mark and narrowing on her. And on her race.

They had weakened. Humankind had strengthened, grown with the years that sapped the Sarn. Now, in her Gardens, that hunched figure of dejection squatted, chilling all her city, defying the minds of all the Sarn. It had been a matter of time, inevitable as the fated motion of the planets. And the time had come. The humans were the stronger.

The door behind her opened slowly, but her brooding eyes remained fixed on the far wall till the intruder moved before her gaze. Barken Thil. Once, the Mother had thought her brilliant, hoped this physicist might find the forgotten secret of the speed drive. Now her eight-foot figure was shrunken, dimmed by the fog and gloom that curdled the air about them. "Yes?" The Mother spoke wearily.

"Nothing." The physicist shook her head. "It's useless, Mother of the Sarn. The blackness is there. No screen, no substance shuts it off. It registers no more than the cold we feel on our instruments; they tell us only what we know, that the air transmits less light, less heat. It is absorbed somehow, and yet does not warm thereby. A vacuum transmits energy as before—but we cannot live in vacua.

"Thard Nilo has gone mad. She sits on her stool and stares at the wall, saying: 'The sun is warm—the sun is bright. The sun is warm—the sun is bright!' She will not move save when we lead her. She does not resist—but she does not act."

"The sun—is warm," the Mother said softly. "The sun—is bright. The sun—never shines here now. But the sun is bright and hot and the air is clean and dry in Bish-Waln."

The tired eyes looked up slowly toward the lax figure of the physicist. "I—I think I will visit. Bish-Waln. Where the sun is hot and bright and the air—

"I have never been there; never in all the time since Earth became ours, four thousand years ago, have I left Sarn City. I have never seen Targlan of the ever-blue skies and the ever-white mountains. I have never seen Bish-Waln in the golden sands—the hot sands.

"I think that now, before humanity rises finally, I should like to see it. I think—yes, perhaps I will go."

Two hours later, she roused herself to give orders, vaguely, and hours later to enter her ship. The chill leaked out of metal and crystal as from the cold, green stone. She stared blankly through the rain-washed windows as the gloom-crowned Gardens and the Sarn City dropped behind. One more ship rose slowly, listlessly behind her. Vaguely, she wondered that so few Sarn had been still there that these two ships could carry all.

For the first time in four thousand years she was leaving her city. For the first time in four thousand years no Sarn remained in Sarn City.

The clouds and gloom were suddenly below, a dull grayness that heaved and writhed like a living dome over Sarn City. June sunlight angled from the setting redness in the west across the Human City stirring vaguely there below. A warmth she had not known in six unending days shot through her ancient body, and a blissfulness of sleep lapped her as the ship accelerated strongly, confidently, toward the sparkling waters beyond, toward Bish-Waln, bright and hot in the Golden Sahara.

Her eyes closed, and she did not see through the dissolving clouds to the black figure that slowly rose erect, nor to the ordered division of the Legion of Peace that marched toward the blank, silent windows of the Sarn Palace. Behind them came a loose group of work-clad men to disperse among the dead, lightless shops of this, the city that had marked the landing of the Sarn.

# DEAD KNOWLEDGE

The sun was a red ball sinking at the end of the broad, paved avenue that ran straight to the east. Its long rays slanted down across the city, across the towers, gilding their clean-lined hulks with a parting gold. An absolute silence wrapped the whole majestic city, a silence that had settled on and into the three men standing immobile on the short, green grass of the circle that was the city's center. In a dozen directions great arteries radiated through vast chasms between artificial cliffs that lifted a hundred stories, a thousand feet into the dark blue of the sky.

A restless breeze, stirred by the approaching chill of twilight, soughed softly down the street, around the immense bulks of towering buildings leaping upward, sweep on sweep of fine-drawn graceful line. Bar Young stirred restlessly, obliquely eyed his companions with an uneasy intensity. "That—that's why nobody noticed us."

"There were lights in this city last night," Hall said in a voice lowered unconsciously by the pressing weight of silence. "It can't—can't be deserted."

"I thought for a while that the people might be a race of day-sleepers—an owl people—but even at 4 a.m. no Earth-city could be this quiet, so motionless. And however alien these people of a strange solar system may be, they must be in many ways similar to man. Those buildings—this park—all their works might be those of some city of Earth. It's a ghost-city, deserted place like the abandoned mining camps." Ross looked about with a vast unease.

"We could try one of the other cities—" suggested Young. "We have to find them—the people—somehow. Twenty-seven light years—three years of traveling—to reach this system, to find five dead worlds, and only this one habitable. And inhabited; such cities as this cannot be simply—abandoned. There was no place for the people to go, no other planet they might have migrated to. And no signs of space-travel or space-ports that might accommodate spaceships, even such small ones as ours." Over his shoulder he glanced back toward the 300-foot bubble of steel and quartz that had brought them across vast gulfs of emptiness.

The swift-sinking sun shrank below the eastern horizon, its beams lifting from the level of the park, climbing slowly up the sides of the towers, painting green and blue and pale-yellow stone to red. Polished metal reflected its brilliance in flashing gleams from the curving, rising buildings that towered about them, a ring of 1000-foot giants dwarfing the low trees of the park, and the 100-foot sapphire needle of crystalline light at the center of the circle. Slowly, the lifting light left the feet of the buildings, the deep blue of the sky overhead darkened with a fast-running twilight.

Still darkness crept in to replace the silent daylight, welling up from the pavements into the shadows. The thin, clear air of the planet, utterly quiet and dustless, held no light within it; the shadows became black and sharp. The deserted city of daylight began to people itself with unseen things that moved soundless in the silence, pressing the lengthening shadows toward the three men with a soundless, eager menace.

Ross shook his head slowly. "We've got to find out what happened here—why this city was deserted. There is something—wrong. A ghost town is something understandable—a town, built by a lode of mineral, that ceases to be when the mineral is gone. But a city—a magnificent city of 1000-foot towers and ten million homes stretched over fifty miles of meadowland cannot be deserted. It's impossible. Even—and I thought of this for a moment—even a plague could not drive out every man, every woman and child. There would be watchmen, caretakers, there would be sanitation corps men to work and rehabilitate the city. It is too much, too much of labor and thought and effort to be neglected utterly, however fearful the plague might be.

"There is something wrong." He watched the uneasy shadows creep across the pavements toward them, engulfing them as the light of the city faded, the last faint sun-rays touched the tips of the highest towers for a lingering instant—and vanished. The night-wind grew, murmurous and mumbling behind the buildings, freighted with the communications of the unknown rising on the flowing tide of dark.

He turned abruptly; a soft, blue light was growing on the building walls—something behind them— At his start the others turned, nervous hands grappling suddenly to heat-guns. The sapphire needle behind them was a crystal of living fire that wavered, grew in a rising rush, and retreated for a moment to gather strength for another upward rush in the dusk. Waves of shadows forced back by it seemed to gather denser in the buildings' outskirts, spreading invaders hurled back by the light.

With a rush the light mounted suddenly to a needle beam that stabbed into the dark sky, to winking, unfamiliar stars, in strange constellations. Simultaneously with the jetting light beam, a low, sweet hum built up, up to a ringing music that floated out across the silent, darkening bulks about the park. It rose and fell and rose again in sweet cadences, to fade away in plaintive notes. As it faded, light, a million lights on a thousand streets grew, a vast lighting system coming to life to drive back again the shadows crouching angrily at the feet of the towers.

Swift darkness fell with the sun's disappearance, a darkness that made the unlighted buildings vanish in black needles against the black, star-flecked sky. Only their lowermost levels were clear in the soft rays of the street lights, fading into rising dimness of black, lightless eyes—polished glass that gleamed dimly without being illuminated, unexpected winkings of light from ranges far above the effective limits of the lamps.

Bar Young's breath sucked softly. "Automatic—automatic lights controlled by the coming of night. No light—no window shows a trace of illumination within. Only the city's mechanical watchman functioning to turn on the lights of a deserted waste. That was the light we saw last night from space, as we came in. Those were the lights we saw in the western cities already in night when we were landing.

"They are gone—gone, it must be, forever, and gone not hurriedly, but calmly, putting away all cars, all traces of their occupancy in neat order. But why, *why* have they left this place?"

Hall moved forward into the light of the crystal and out of the lean shadow of their cruiser. "I don't like this city—particularly at night. There is something wrong with it, the same thing that made the people leave. It was the city, I feel somehow, not the people that made this desertion necessary."

Ross moved his head in a vague gesture, half agreement, half negation. "The city—well—I have the feeling you do, the oppression of the silence and the dusk. Those buildings stand there, crouching in the darkness, half-seen things that have a suggestion, in this city of deserted mystery, of some menacing thing. But isn't it more our own vague feelings—strangers from an alien world and solar system, who have stumbled on this cosmic mystery as the quick dusk of this planet set in—that are to blame?"

Young looked at him under frowning brows, a wry grimace twisting his mouth. "The original builders deserted it. Something, human or inhuman, forced them to a course unbelievably extreme. Yet—there is no sign of wreckage, of invasion, of trouble. The city is clean, so clean that even the normal litter of a great city does not appear. We have to investigate, but—I don't like this city of night. We can go to one of the daylight cities."

"This is one deserted city," said Ross abruptly stubborn. "I feel I'm fooling myself with man's instinctive, age-old fear of darkness, and unknown things. The others probably aren't deserted, and this is our opportunity to study the race unhampered. Their language, perhaps, from books and pictures. I say we should investigate, visit some of the homes we saw on the outskirts. Our ship is slim enough to move down that main artery without striking anything, and in a few moments we can get some indication of what the people who deserted this place were. Therein may lie the whole answer, a vagrant, migratory people descended, perhaps, from birds, who move en masse from city to city as the seasons—"

Young looked at him keenly, and his voice trailed off apologetically. "You know as well as I that no civilization of 1000-foot towers would rise from a race of migratory habits. No, the people who labored for this city intended to remain, generation after generation, and they built with lofty permanence in mind. Hall, what about that language? I think—but you're probably the expert."

"You saw what I did—you're probably right. As a guess—the signs, that posted notice on the tree, looked to me like an ideographic writing."

"Ideograph—" Ross repeated vaguely.

"Picture writing, like Chinese or ancient Egyptian. It is a sort of completely conventionalized rebus writing. In a civilization such as this, it must be highly idiomatic, impossible to decipher without a hundred years of study."

Ross shook his head stubbornly. "Then we'll have to investigate. We can go down that main avenue, out toward the suburban districts, and stop at some apartment house." He pointed down the great avenue that stretched out straight toward the east. A faint lingering of lighter sky gave substance to the vast, hunched shadows that waited down the long passage. The night pressed down on the thin line of lights, crushing their illumination to the ground, obscuring the unseen things that went on in the higher, darker silence. The silence of the city brooded again, unbroken. The dusk-wind died away as night gained full sway. A moonless sky—sprinkled with the myriad bright, blind eyes of the stars—looked down sightlessly.

The silence held them in its grasp, froze them for long seconds before Ross moved, half-angrily. "Let's go down there." He spoke in a voice that echoed in startled protest against the blind, high walls. "This silence gets you." His voice was suddenly softened. He turned and walked to the open lock of the ship, his rubber-soled feet seeming noisy in the ringing corridor.

A silent ghost, the ship lifted on her antigravity field and drifted down the broad avenue, the space-fields meshing in the soundless structure of space to pull it forward, as noiseless as the city itself. Only the soft purr of the atomics, the familiar whine of the circulators, changed the soundless menace of the city to a world of reality, of living things moving in the light.

The hot, white beams of the forward landing light swept brilliance down the avenue ahead as the silent, waiting towers moved by in stately procession—broad, brown-paved streets, gray concrete side-walks, a thousand shops, their broad windows sparkling in the light of the ship. Goods of strange pattern and unguessed purposes lay still behind the windows of the locked, dark stores. "They did not take their possessions," Young said softly.

Ross's fingers flickered over the controls, his iron-gray eyes level and intent on the avenue before him, his powerful, stocky body hunched over the controls in self-determined blindness to the dark mystery beyond the windows. Hall's lean face looked strained and tense; to him the presence of the goods seemed no surprise, nor would their absence have changed his opinion one iota. His dark, keen eyes followed the moving windows silently, watching them slip behind.

The towers shortened, pulled down from the skies to become squatter, smaller buildings as they left the city's heart. Swift miles fled behind the cruiser's sleek, bright-metal form. Ten times the speed of light lay within the powers of her fields; she idled now, and the wind of her passage chuckled meaningful laughter in her wake. The shops gave way to blank-walled business houses, then again as five-story apartment houses, set back from the avenue, spaced by green, tree-dotted lawns, appeared.

The cruiser slowed, halted in the street. The burbling of the wind died away and the silence of the city wrapped it again. No cheep of insect or ruffled piping of birds disturbed the utter quiet as the purr of the atomics died away. Ross rose, his feet scraping noisily. "Bring your camera, Hall, and let's see what we can get. There must be some indication in there—some reason for this desertion." His voice echoed pleasantly in the ship, breaking the pressing silence in rolling sounds that continued, gave life to his voice. The vastness of the city's ways drank in the sound, made voices flat and as unnatural as the city.

There was no door, but a grilled gateway that led into a courtyard open to the still night sky. A dozen doors opened from that; a fountain pool lay with unruffled waters, reflecting the starlight save where the smooth surface was broken by the spider-web fronds of some water plant showing minute red flowers in the light of their atom flares. The three floors of the building were terraced back from the courtyard, so that each story had a small, railed terrace running entirely round the court. Onto these the doors of the apartments opened. Pale-blue wash of some sort laid over a plaster-like material reflected the light of their flares, limning each detail of the patio clearly—the winding stairs that led up from terrace to terrace, the bright blue and white tiles of the fountain pool—

"They knew how to live," said Young softly. "Three years in that metal bubble and this place, even in the silence, looks attractive. Why—why—*why* should any being, who loved life and beauty as the creators of this must have, leave this building, neat and ordered, a perfect home?"

"Try that first door, Hall," said Ross steadily. "I'll try the one on this side. Young, you want to take the second one?" Ross reached his goal first, studied the knob of the portal of golden metal for a moment, pulled at it gently. The door opened toward him, and his call brought the others.

Curiously familiar the furnishings seemed, chairs of gracefully curved, glowing metal—an aluminum bronze with a matte, golden glow—upholstered in bright blue and white, a studio couch in similar materials, a desk in a dully glowing, dark-red wood. The silence of the city seemed to leak into the place with the opening of the door, making these ultimately human things more deserted, more poignantly alone, than had been the vast masses of the City, towering into the black hush of the night skies.

The room was lived in, the desk untidied by a torn bit of paper, scattered sheets of faintly yellowish parchment-like material, a few scattered instruments evidently—humanly—pens. Hall moved toward the desk soundlessly, on rubber-soled feet over a carpet of bright, dark blue. A dozen lines of characters ran smoothly across the exposed sheet, from right to left, many-dotted, rounded characters, curiously like Arabic script; unfamiliarly dissimilar to Hall, who read half Earth's polyglot tongues with ease.

Ross turned his head slowly, seeing the lattice-fronted cabinet faced with meters and three small knobs, the well stocked bookcase, scattered pictures on walls, small tables. Discarded a moment before, it seemed, a newspaper in the strangely curved, many-dotted characters slashed a message across all its front page. The entire page seemed devoted to that one item—the secret?

Hall looked up at Ross's low word and followed his pointing finger. Slowly he shrugged and shook his head. "It's ideographic, I'm sure. The secret lies there, all right, open to be read. In full detail, no doubt, the story of the silence—the dark city under dark skies.

"We'll never know. These people, when they left, did not prepare for visitors. Why should they? They alone on the only habitable planet of their system, alone in a gulf of space we never would have guessed could be crossed by living intelligence, but for Hargreave's Accident and its consequence, the speed-drive.

"They left no primers for those to come, in their ordered—ordered? Why this paper dropped so carelessly, as though suddenly?"

"There is a door there," pointed out Young, quietly.

Ross strode forward, his square, blocky body determined in its movements. Slowly he opened the door, letting the strong white light of his atomic flare reach in. Abruptly he stiffened, his breath sucked in sharply, then slowly he relaxed. His head lifted slightly, and he seemed to look without seeing at the ceiling of the room beyond, his body curiously half-tense, half-loosened. "They were very human," he said softly. "But for that bright blue hair, she would seem a girl of Earth.

"Hall—Young, they did not leave. Here, here everywhere in their homes throughout the city they wait in silence. They are here, forever—everywhere, all about us, the ten millions of them who loved life and beauty."

Silently, slowly, as though reluctant minds dragged on by bodies captured by an alien will, the two moved toward him. Over his shoulder they saw the little room, the low, broad bed, two figures seeming asleep only now that dusk had fallen, wrapping the city in its silent cloak. A girl—twenty, she might have been if of Earth—slim and young, her smooth, warm face still now, with a look of tired unhappiness half smoothed away. From beneath the white, closed lids, tears had trickled and dried long, long since. The arms of the man who had held her close were stiffened forever, yet so quiet, so easy had been their passing that no sign of death save their soft, gray blankets indicated more than a nighttime's sleep. Soft, gray fabric of dust lay deep over them, as it lay over all the furniture in this place.

Something gleamed with a brilliant ruby light on the bed beside the girl, dropped from her relaxed hand. Softly, on tiptoe as though to save disturbing this sleeping pair, Ross plucked it from its place, and brushed the dust from its surface—deep-cut sparkling red glass, formed in a graceful bottle, labeled in bright green characters on whitish background on an inlet smooth surface of the bottle. Enigmatic, rounded characters, made plain by the blurred thing below—a rounded, evident skull, framed by a pair of fleshless hands.

Softly the three left the room., went out to the courtyard of pale, pleasant blue under the sparkling night sky. Far off, the mighty tower of a building rose a dark finger against the pattern of the stars. Silently, Young lifted a pointing finger toward a strange constellation, a leering devil's head, with crooked, twisted mouth, and one winked eye. A bright star, and a lesser one for eyes; blind eyes, of which Sol, the ruler of a certain planetary system 27 light-years distant, was the lesser.

"Three years," said Ross dully. "Let's try these other doors."

Hall moved slowly toward another golden panel and opened it. The glare of the atomic flares lanced in. As the others came up behind his motionless figure, their eyes, too, saw into this room—this once lived-in room.

A child—a boy ten years old?—slept in a chair, sprawled carelessly. Slowly Ross led the way in. Not till they rounded him did they see the dark hole in his temple. The door of the room beyond stood open. And as their lights moved, beams reached into the space beyond. Another child, a girl perhaps two, lay in the lap of a hunched woman's figure. Each was marked with the dark hole of a bullet wound; Hall saw the other marks first, small pricks in blanched, whitened areas—one in the child's thigh, one in the mother's throat. Only when they entered the room did they see the twisted, contorted body of the man, his lips drawn back in a toothy, hideous grin, his arm swollen, enpurpled still, clasped in the death-loosened grip of the other hand.

"Preservative," said Young softly. "Effective, a poison that killed in agony. He shot the others and protected them; himself he could only protect. That other couple—that poison must have had the same effect.

"Need we see more apartments—more of the tens of millions who built and labored and loved this city—and left, to go beyond the stars in the only way they knew?"

"No," said Ross softly. Then his voice became sharply agonized. "But why—why? No sign of danger, no sign of damage. What struck at them, forced them to this? A foreign state of this world? But what could war, or attack of any sort, offer that made this preferable? And this is the greatest city, by far, on this planet. It would have a greater backing of man power and machines than any other, if there are those silly artificial boundaries no visitor from space could see.

"No unproven threat could do this; no *threat* of death can make ten million people seek death.

"I know—we do not *know* that they have all killed themselves, but—" He stopped, and the silence of the city poured in, drinking the little sounds they made and washing them away.

"There could be no invasion from the other worlds of this system. We know them—and they're dead rocks. Two blistered in unbearable heat, one an airless boulder too small for atmosphere, and two frozen utterly. No alien race could menace them from their own system.

"Is there some other ranging race in space, some stock of slavers perhaps, working on a cosmic scale? No race that fought its way from mud to magnificence as these people did would kill themselves without fight. And fight of the magnitude that must result—they have atomic power, I'm pretty sure, for the city power is still functioning and gray dust gathering half-inch coats over the people—that fight would leave scars we couldn't miss.

"Why? What deadly thing could drive them to this, a century or ten centuries ago?"

"That long?" asked Hall softly.

Ross gestured, and again the silence welled in. "No sounds, no action. This is a cloudless, almost rainless world, the temperature so constant, the air so clear, only a few light showers can have fallen. There are no seasons, and no winds or living animals to damage buildings. The grass grows on, the trees we saw seem long-lived. I don't know.

"But we must—we must—" He looked about him jerkily, his face whitened by three years of sunless spaces, whiter still in the flame of the atom-flares. "The menace cannot be from this system. It must have come from outer space, a power that wanders from star to star—a power that could wander to Earth.

"That may *have* wandered to Earth—" He stopped aghast, looking at the other two. "Three years—and it will be six years before we get a word of news from Earth."

Earth—a planet of silent cities, its wandering ships stilled once, forever, the soughing wind alone whispering through crumbling cities—

"No." Young spoke sharply. His voice bombarded back from the shocked, protesting silence. "Let's go out—go to the ship," he muttered, turning sharply. The room fell dark behind them, a quiet, dark hush that was accustomed here stealing back as the flares passed out.

"We can try other cities. Somehow, crazily, I had not thought of nationalism. I had more the idea of a world state, such as Earth has now. But ours is only half a century old—long to us, but not to history. Other cities here may have different languages, as different nations on Earth did have. Those other languages might be such that we could translate them in time, and a lot shorter time. Primers not, perhaps, for people of other worlds, but for people new to this world, learning the story of its development from as little background as we have. Children come with no more language than we."

"No," Hall shook his head. "That isn't true altogether. For a phonetic language a child's primer might serve, but not for an ideograph. An ideograph is a rebus, a symbolized, conventionalized puzzle, from which all trace of origin has fallen away, tacked onto a highly modern idiom. That is not for unlearned children, but for those who know already the spoken language from which the thing takes start.

"We can try those other cities, there might be a living people— incredible—but if there is another language, a phonetic one, we have some hope of gaining essentials in a city where books for children might exist." The silent ship gained life and sound as the lock took them in. A circulator whined into soft sound near them and the silence of the city rested, knitting up its briefly tattered fabric as the shining metal bubble leapt away in startled, frantic flight. For an instant, the delicate fernlike fronds of the trees waved in the vacuum of its passage. Then the stillness and dark crept in and regained a long-held sway. Vague things stirred busily in the shadows that reached out again with the vanishment of the white, clear atom-flames.

The silent world fled beneath the slanted rise of the ship, darkness giving way to a swift-returning twilight as the rise and movement brought the sun again above the horizon. Wordlessly, the three watched mist-shrouded hills rise from the plains, climb, and fall behind in diminishing foothills. A vast river-valley opened out, shadowed at one edge 100 miles beneath, sunlit at the far side.

The ship angled down again toward the soundless planet. The patchwork of farmed land mottled the green-brown of the ancient river-system's valley. Where two tributaries joined the stream a many-colored blot of steel and stone shadowed the land. The ship slanted down and the city below gained reality and a third dimension as their altitude diminished from miles to feet.

Slow as a settling dust-grain, the interstellar cruiser drifted down on her antigravity fields, down toward a parkland in the city's heart. Dense, dark-green trees around a small lake, fed by a tiny meandering stream. Flowers had run riot, spreading in the unattended years back from the stream, around the borders of the lake.

No sun-tipped 1000-foot towers ringed this park; the buildings were broad and low, colonnaded structures of white and green and pale-blue stone. Glinting walls of glass brick poured the rays of the setting sun into the buildings to escape again through other glass walls as a mockery of internal illumination shining out into the evening sky.

Slowly the ship settled while Ross's gray eyes tightened. This park was not deserted. On smooth lawns, under clear waters of the pond, at ease in a hundred places, sleeping figures lay. Tiny, graceful cockle-shell boats lay upturned beneath the waters, beside their spilled occupants. On the lawns couples, trios, lay in an eternal sleep. The warm strong rays of the sun, heat, the soft rains had bleached away the bright colors of the clothes they wore. Slow oxidation and time had embrittled them and the stirring breezes had torn the fabric to broken tatters.

Young moved toward the lock, out onto the soft turf, yielding under his feet. A group of four lay beneath a grotesquely gnarled, gracefully twisted tree. Two elderly people, man and wife, and a younger couple, the girl's bright blue silkens faded now to a color as soft as the wall of the building that rose two hundred feet away, beyond the brown-paved highway. Long rays of the setting sun reached down to illuminate her body, bent forward over the head of the man in her lap. Nestling beside it lay a ruby crystal green-labeled flask.

Hall walked past them and automatically Young and Ross fell into step behind him. "That building," said Hall slowly, "must have been an office building, or a public building. There must be written material there, and we can find in five minutes whether there is any need to stay in this city. These people took their poison—the same one apparently—in the parks, in many places. Look—parked cars. Their psychology was, in that degree, different. Their language may have been."

"If it is—the menace was not national, but planetary," Ross added.

Broad doors stood open, a layer of sifting dust laid down in the farther passages where the other breezes had not stirred it. On one white-stoned wall, between a series of small bronze doors, an inset panel of dark stuff behind glass covering showed the curved, many-dotted characters of the strange, yet familiar language. Hall sighed. "The language is the same. We could try once more, say half around this world."

Silently, the three walked back, the smooth carpet of dust tearing beneath their feet. The quick dusk was setting in once more, the sun's last rays lighting the sky, but lifted already above the city's streets. Moments later the spherical ship lifted once more into the light, and rose beyond the atmosphere's dim carpet to race around the world.

Shallow inland seas, their smooth waters darkened under night skies, fell behind; the glowing patches of great cities operating long after their creators had given way to death and some unknown that hovered still about this dark world. Great cities, like mouldering patches of phosphorescent decay on the dark trunk of a fallen tree, and lesser towns that sparkled only faintly.

"This is a temperate zone," Ross suddenly. "I'll head for the tropics. If there were two races on this planet, the difference in climate would be the most probably dividing factor, and this is our best opportunity to find a second language and a clue."

The sun rose again with the fleeting ship's motion, rose and held as they cruised a thousand miles around the bulge of the planet, to slant down once more as the dark green of temperate foliage gave way to the brilliant colors of a tropical jungle. The ship slowed over a broken patch in the spreading jungle growth, a city whose buildings lay in broken ruins beneath the thrust of climbing plant-life. Shattered stone and glass half-hid, half-revealed the crushed bodies of the people who had built and died here. Broken rubbery pavements twisted and writhed over thrusting roots of giant trees towering half a thousand feet above the low white buildings. There was sound here, the faint rustle of a billion leaves in the slow-stirring morning air, and sharp tinkle and crack of masonry disturbed by a life that thrust out blindly, voraciously for more, and yet more room.

Hall pointed silently to a broken, tumbled wall of glass bricks, fallen to jagged splinters in the sunlight, half obscuring the metal shelving it had protected. A crumbled, sodden mass of books bleached under the hot sun—the color and printed symbols lost under soft tropic rains and harsh, white sunlight. "The same language," said Hall briefly. "It was the universal language of this planet. We will find no comparative tongues to give clues and hints. There can be no Rosetta Stone in three languages. Everywhere there must lie a thousand, written complete accounts—a million notes of explanation, a thousand printed accounts complete and exact, written by dead scientists.

"The answer of a million eye witnesses from the views of every type and class of man or woman. Why it was that parents murdered children, and then themselves."

"Why it was," added Ross thoughtfully, "they all, each one took such precautions their bodies should not decay. There is that which puzzles me. They went out of their way—the one we saw who shot those he'd tend to protect and injected some preservative, but poisoned himself—unpleasantly."

Hall shook his head uncertainly. "I don't know; a lot of races made a fetish of preserving the body, for rehabilitation in another time, a reincarnation in that flesh." Hall looked about him. A thousand bodies, some crushed, but none, never, a skeleton. "The red-flask poison must have been rare and hard to obtain, the injected stuff a common substance any one could get."

Ross shook his head with an air of ending the subject. "There is more to it than that. These people died, a world of them, by their own hands. Why, in a world without war, without threat of damage? And why in a world of scientific achievement should this fetish of body preservation have survived, and it alone, in the face of acts that denied every other custom, even the law of self-preservation?"

Hall shrugged wearily. "Let's go out to space. We are tired now, and in the atmosphere of this world our thoughts are mixed. Perhaps after rest, we'll understand it better—perhaps not. But we'll have to make a thousand photographs and ten thousand reports. There must be samples of soil and air, water and minerals.

"We aren't through. We'll have to study this morgue world for three months at least. Come on."

The ship floated up as silent as the world it left, the antigravity field increasing, and the slow throw of the planet's spin sending it again into space. The drive-fields gripped, and the cool and dark of space received it. The spinning world shrank away in distance, the vastness of its puzzle contracting in their minds as the planetary ship with its cargo of death, stilled happiness, and unguessed mystery shrank in size.

Young and Hall sat beside Ross, watching with unseeing concentration the skilled manipulations of his fingers, lulled by the soft purr of the atomics aft. Slowly Hall rose to his feet and turned down the corridor toward his room.

Young shook himself, the dark horror in his eyes fading suddenly, his tense mouth relaxing in a startled, half-sheepish grin. "Ye gods, that world gets you! I'll start the galley; *they* may be dead, but *we're* still living."

Ross nodded wearily, then nodded again abruptly as his eyes, too, cleared. "Gets you, is right!" he exploded. "Yes—go ahead. I suppose I do have an appetite, but—" He shook his head with the jerkiness of a boxer trying to clear away the fog of a blow. He looked up with dazed eyes, a new intentness and questioning in them.

"Back there, it's a dream. It's been three years since we saw a living soul, Bar, and something of the wear we've had on each other in this damned tin bubble eats down your resistance and appreciation of reality. Already that whole thing back there is beginning to seem a dream, another of those damnable nightmares you get from sleeping while the speed-drive is on. A world—cities, their millions dead by suicide, without a sign, an indication of the slightest trouble that might have affected them to make them do it. And—Lord, the silence! That silence is as unnatural as those almost-living corpses. Weren't there ever any birds to sing, no insects at all?

"That great dead city was too unreal to make the thing comprehensible; it seemed more like a posed question visualized with a ghastly accuracy."

"That was no vision, or if it was, we have to live and labor in it for three months or more. And think it over for three years going back." Young stared down from the port toward the slowly turning, mottled world, not 50,000 miles away. The faint blue haze of its atmosphere drew a blurring veil over its features, disclosing the gross outlines of land-locked seas and mountain ranges. The great river valleys showed as wide depressions, while the mantling, faint haze of blue reflected from the atmosphere veiled the thin silver threads of rivers that had caused them.

Young turned sharply and strode back to the galley. Presently he heard the strains of one of their stock of records grow in the ship as one of the others—probably Ross, he thought—started the amplifier. The lifting, quick-paced song caught him for a moment, and speeded his movements. The mystery floating there in space contracted into unreality; the strong, deep channels of familiarity and accustomed work diverted his conscious mind. Somewhere deep beneath the surface a vast weight of impending trouble stirred, and rose to bother him into uneasiness and haste as the record stopped and another started—a faint-toned plaintive song of the Martian colonists composed of the thin whine of Martian dust-winds and the sough of compressors. Surely, the composer had woven into it the same sphinx-mystery of the Martian sands, the scattered, cut blocks that never could have been assembled to form anything, but were shaped and cut on a world that never, in all its history, could have supported intelligent life—

His mind stirred uneasily. "Hey, pilot! Hall! Come and feed."

The song died jerkily as the needle-light died and the record-reel rewound automatically. Ross's heavy feet came down the corridor, and his stocky body swung round the corner. With half-unconscious eagerness, Young found himself watching him vaguely; he sighed gustily, familiarly, as he seated himself and Young turned away, vaguely satisfied. Three years of familiarity in the cramped "tin bubble"—that unimportant thing, the invariable sigh as he seated himself. Always,

Young caught himself watching for it; always it came. His eyes swung to watch for Hall. He would pause in the doorway, lift his head just— so and sniff. As unconscious as Ross's sigh. Then he would enter.

"Hey, Hall—come on," Ross called. Leisurely Young slid the metal plates across the table, pans of food. In a momentary pause, the ship was suddenly silent, the air mechanism off, the atomics cut down to soundless idle.

"Hall—" Young stepped into the corridor doorway. The vague unease welled up in him as the silence of the ship stirred strong memories that had seemed to fade into the limbo of nightmares and things of unreality. "Hall—" He walked with spaced, hesitant steps toward the closed door of Hall's cabin, threw it open and grunted in disgust. "He's asleep," he threw over his shoulder to Ross, peering round the corridor. "I don't see—how he could have—

"Ross," Young's voice was very low and still in the corridor, "he's got—"

Ross's bulk edged by him somehow, darting into the little room. For an instant his great, thick-fingered hand clutched the green-la-beled ruby bit of glass, then dropped it to crashing fragments on the metal floor-plates. Roughly he turned Hall's quiet figure to the light. It moved with a curious solidity, as though in one stiff, solid piece— legs, arms and head in the same rigid position. Ross jerked back, rub-bing his finger stiffly on the tough fabric of his trousers, darkened eyes tense on the face before him.

They of the planet had died, always, with closed eyes. Yet Hall lay with eyes wide-opened. Jerkily, Young snatched a carelessly dropped shirt, and threw it over the white, staring face, over the black misery of horror in the eyes.

"It got him," Ross gurgled unpleasantly. "Hall—it got Hall. Hall's a man—"

"Notes—" Young clawed frantically at the little desk let into the metal wall. "This thing's locked—get his keys. Notes—"

"No." Ross shook his head groggily. "No notes—if he wrote a note it'd be out—open for us."

"If it got him he must have known why—why they died, why he was dying," Young pleaded. "He must have. Lord, Ross, he didn't lie down and drink that to see what it was."

"Maybe he did!" Ross straightened slightly, then slumped again. "No. He's the chemist. He knew. He knew what it was and why— why they died, why—we—will—die."

"He couldn't have! No, we won't die. We have to find out."

"So did he. He didn't even tell us. Didn't tell us to warn us. Why?

That's another why." Ross looked at the still frozen figure. A queer hatred was growing in his eyes, bitterness and horror, hatred and a bit of madness. Suddenly all the weight of oppression that had ridden them in the city rose again and crushed him. The comforting, shock-proof feeling of unreality was rent and cast aside. Hall did that; Hall laid his mind open to that deadly pressure of realization and reality. His lip lifted slowly, lifted and snapped down.

"Will you stop that," snapped Young. "Stop grinning, you crack-headed ape."

Ross glowered at him. "It's damned unfair of Hall. If he knew—he must have known. Why didn't he tell us? Why did he make another 'why' to bother us? Why—why—"

Young shook himself, and looked down at the figure under the shirt. It looked contorted, agonized now, because it was rigid and stiff. It should be lying on its other side, so he grasped it abruptly and heaved it back.

Ross stalked out of the doorway. Suddenly the amplifier began to roar out a recorded storm of music, blaring forth an echoing shock of sound that shattered silence.

Young joined him in the control room. "What do we do?"

For answer, Ross's fingers flew over the controls. Behind them the slumberous atomics woke to a straining throb that drowned the roar of the speaker for a moment, then died away as vast potentials built up. A dark mantle, a trickery of unseen lenses had acted. The sphere of space about them rushed in suddenly and contracted close to them. From the port, in one single direction, Young saw the planet that had been below them, the sun that had been ahead, and all the field of stars that had been on every side. Yet they did not overlap. From every other port, he knew, he would see the same. Abruptly, the planet puffed, and vanished. The nearby sun puffed and snapped down to dwindle at crazy speed.

Tense eyes in white face, Ross labored over his controls. The calcu-lators hummed and clicked softly under the protecting screen that kept out the clawing silence that struggled to reach them, gnawing at the walls of the ship, pressing savagely—

"We're headed back," said Ross. Slowly he straightened, then slumped forward to look at his work. Minutes passed; the record ran out, stuttered, and a new one fed itself in. White-faced, Ross looked up again, a saner terror in his eyes. Slowly that submerged as reason and courage came back. "I guess that's best, at that," he said quietly.

Young nodded vaguely. "We need help. I wouldn't stay there. That planet is *wrong*—and Hall knew why."

A light of bitterness blazed in Ross's eyes, his face set angrily. "No matter what the thing might be, he should have told."

"I wonder if it could have been a thing—that isn't tellable. An explanation that does not exist, without the lack of explanation."

Ross glared up at him. "Talk sense; stop words and make sentences."

"I mean—an hysteria. It nearly caught us. Hall was a more sensitive man than you and I; we know that. We lived with him—damn near inside his skin—in this bubble for three years. It might have been an hysteria that, mounting and growing, swept round that world and destroyed them all. Made it a morgue world without reason or sense."

Ross muttered vaguely. "It isn't sensible. Some few in any race are too utterly selfish to permit the thought of possessing all the world to be overcome by an hysteria of death. No. The misers and the antisocial would be dancing in joy. No, it doesn't explain. Hall knew. Hall knew the secret, the answer to all those 'why's,' damn him. He died as all those millions did—sealing the secret forever." Ross swung abruptly, a sudden fierce flame in his face. "And listen, if you get it—get a hint of it—and don't tell me before attempting suicide— If I find you still alive, I'll roast you slowly. I'll tear each separate nerve out of your carcass one by one. I'll—"

"Hell. You tell me. That's all."

Stubbornly, Ross turned back to his controls and pecked at them as a small blue light gleamed. The light winked out. A green one lit, faded, and finally a white one lit and burned steady on the board. "We still have to eat."

Only the tinyness of the star they had left indicated the motion at ten times light's speed, hours later. The stars from every port appeared the same; there was no shifting of position, no changing in constellations of the vastly distant suns. The ship plunged on, a silent, darkened metal bubble in a silent immensity of space. The atomics were silent now, the speed-fields built to saturation. Ross stood at the portlight motionless, his eyes unseeingly staring into the strange, twisted maze of stars compressed in unnatural clarity to any line of sight.

"It must have been hysteria. It must have been. Hall would have spoken. He'd have told us, sure, if he knew and realized what struck him." Ross blurted out the words, swinging to Young.

Young looked up from his lab bench, fragments of ruby glass and a dozen drops of liquid beside his microscope. "Nothing I recognize." He shrugged morosely. "I'm no chemist, just an inept physicist out of his field. I wouldn't know anything more complex than a few muscarine derivatives—and this is complex and new to man, I suspect. Surely we know of no such precipitation. One fragment of a drop of it solidified an egg white like lightning.

"And—it may have been hysteria. Hall was 50,000 miles in space when it got him. How many millions—" He stopped and looked at Ross with a twisted grin. "One of us will fail to reach Earth, in all probability. Stop to think of that?"

Ross looked at him in sudden suspicion. "Listen, if you get some idea of what this is all about—"

"No, damn it. But why were there three of us sent in the first place?"

"The energy concentrations needed by a larger ship couldn't be built up by known means. The atomics couldn't handle the potentials. They couldn't carry food, air, supplies for more than three men."

"Why not two men?" suggested Young smoothly.

"Why, two men—" said Ross blankly and stopped. "Because," he went on in suddenly tense, hard voice, "two men for three years, in a tin can, makes one man. Nerve friction, as they call it."

"Two men in a sealed tube for three years. Two men, one corpse, and one—vast—mystery. The mystery of a dead planet and a dead man. The cargo of this ship won't stay that way." Young rose and went abruptly to his room. The air recirculator cut off with a soft pop as though to emphasize his words.

For a long time Ross sat silent, listening to the creak of Young's feet on the floorplates. He began to move restlessly, his fingers twitching slightly; then his arm. A vague uneasiness seemed to stir him. Then the unseeing lethargy seemed to drain from his eyes, a sharpening, widening horror flooding in—

He rose to his feet, and on soundless toes moved past the laboratory bench, toward the corridor leading to the rooms.

Hours later, Young looked down into his face with a look of frozen bitterness. Ross stared back at him, his face relaxed in a gentle smile of complete satisfaction. "You damned, sneaking rat. You rotten louse. One man to operate this ship for three years—and you *knew*, you unutterable skunk, you knew. You, *you* shouting about knowing and telling, and then ducking like that—"

The cold smile on Ross's lips remained unchanged; growing wildness in Young's eyes matched the tic that formed in his cheek, jerking the muscles in little, rhythmic twitches.

He straightened slowly from the cooling corpse, and slunk down the echoing corridor of the ship, a dull hatred and hopelessness in his mind. Nightmares—nightmares of a horror planet riding in a death ship with the speed-fields up. He wouldn't dare to lower them for three full years, until they cut off of themselves. Ross and Hall were the pilots, the ones who knew the manipulations of the speed-field finders. They had escaped, had escaped with the infinite velocity of death.

And Ross had known. Somehow, he'd guessed the secret of the planet and its dead millions, guessed it as Hall had. But what clue, what unremembered thing, had given them the path that led to understanding? And what was that understanding that drove these men, sound and safe, already trillions of miles from that world, to follow the builders of the ghost cities?

Young started at the tinkling of a falling water drop, and jabbed at the tap angrily. A sudden tinkling stream of water bubbled down and stopped. They had known—and said nothing.

And more than that—knowing, realizing that some menace hung there still, a menace they escaped by death, and death alone—Ross had taken the last few drops of that sudden poison of the death world, leaving none if he—

A cold fury settled on Young, a seething anger that cleared his mind and filled him with a determination to bring this ship, bring it back to Earth, and know the full story of the planet before he did. If, somewhere, both Hall and Ross had picked up the clue that gave them understanding, then he, too—by the gods—he, too, would find that clue!

Some understanding of possibilities came to him slowly. He moved with a swift surety to his room and gathered a few things he needed. Then, to the pilot's bench and the ship's log. Swiftly he wrote into it the account of what had passed since Ross's last entry after Hall had died. Then laboriously, he calculated many things—the exact specific heat of the ship as a whole, the energy content of the ship at 700° absolute, and studied all the ship to determine what might and might not happen.

He was a physicist and atomic engineer. Piloting this ship from the closed space of the speed-drive was beyond him; a practical knowledge he didn't have. But not the designing and building of the controls he wanted or the construction of the cylinder he would need—if things happened.

He made his connections, pressed a small switch. A tiny synchronous motor turned slowly to the low, smooth hum of a tuning fork; a slow creep of the rotary switch assured him. In twelve hours that must be reversed to halt its action.

Then he went again to the pilot room and stared unseeing at the queerly clustered stars. Slowly, every item that they had seen, had touched, went through his mind. The cold hatred for the two blankly unspeaking, yet informative corpses he suppressed; they told him only this—that it could be known. It could be, knowing the why of those dead millions, the reason for that suicide, the nature of the cosmic menace that had overcome them so utterly that they, the supreme fighting type of their world, had gone down unresisting. And that, somehow, that knowledge impelled a bond of final secrecy.

It came to him with sudden surprise, the numbness of his hand. The faint ticking of his finger nails in the startled silence of the ship brought a slow fading of that intense concentration. Idly at first he rubbed the numbed hand to restore circulation—and paused.

A tremor shook him, and a shocked horror flooded his mind. A million voices shouted and commanded deep within him, a growing clamor that was, somehow, united and fiercely determined. A conscious force growing discoverable abruptly, noticed for the first time—

It seemed, then, to take long minutes of slow growth, yet in the confusion he knew simultaneously that it was like the time-rate of a dream, started by the slam of a door, ending with the slam of the door as the closing sequence of the dream. A flash of mental action of incredible rapidity vouchsafed him in the infinitesimal instant of time between his awareness of attack, and his defeat.

In that atom of time, he saw through other minds, a million billion other minds, and yet thought with his own. He lived in another universe, a universe of infinitesimals, thinking, conscious, intelligent molecules. Single molecules of a vast complexity driving forward to a racial goal through the medium of countless billions of keen-thinking units—units that were single, conscious molecules. What body cells were to Young, single atoms were to them. Their thought was a swift shifting of atomic strains within their molecule-bodies; their senses not sight, nor sound, nor any thing humans might know, but finer, subtler things of electric, magnetic, gravitic strains. A fineness that made chemical action a stupendous, gross thing.

Light came to them as great blundering, fuzzy balls of energy which they absorbed as food, Their thought processes, flashing with the speed of electric stress, outstripped man's clumsy mechanism a million times. Yet one great thing they lacked; they could have no control of gross matter, their very minuteness made that thing to them unthinkable. A hundred million atoms composed each molecule-body. A vastly swollen intelligent molecule—yet withal so minute that a hundred millions of them were undetectable to man.

Intelligence, swift, keen intelligence—unable to control their own environment by the handicap of size. Yet, eating the hurtling quanta of light and radiant heat as food, they could ride the streaming light-currents of space from world to world. For temperature was unknown to them, light, food enough. Only the extreme battering of high-temperature molecules could destroy them. Beyond that one thing, their conscious control of their own molecular forces made them immune, eternal.

But the delicate, immensely organized chemistry of intelligent beings like man were susceptible to the race control of billions of them. Immense organizations of them, working in planned unison, could affect the delicate chemistry of nerves and brain to give orders, relayed by the grosser, greater organism into action that could control that physical environment beyond their own control.

And, like many high protein molecules, they had this other attribute; they were, chemically, enzymatic. They could force lesser unconscious proteins that to them appeared as lesser animals, to shape and form themselves into replicas of the Intelligences. Man would serve them both as breeding ground, and relay control, subjected utterly to the unseen will of beings whose smallness put them beyond the greatest microscope.

An understanding that swept up and through Young's mind in that last instant of consciousness, before his mind fell before their final comprehension of the intricate network of nerve cells that long study, since first they entered his body on the dead world, had brought.

And Young understood, too, the suicides, the preservation that Ross had puzzled at. The red-flask poison the Intelligences knew, and hated. A lesser, swifter enzyme protein that shook down the proteins of man, or any proteinous material, to its own form. One that destroyed equally the protein molecule that had gained intelligence. The injected stuff, a simple chemical poison, that, like formaldehyde, precipitated and hardened any protein, rendering the dead flesh forever useless to the Intelligences.

His body surged up from its chair as a last fierce urge whipped through him before the rising tide of molecules destroyed his last conscious will. The familiar control room, the lab bench, reeled and faded behind red mist in the same instant that he rose. His mind had fallen to the planned attack of a billion unseen enemies, seeking through him to gain control of all space, for all time—

The dark mist faded very slowly from his eyes. Before he could see, even, he knew where he would find himself. His eyes opened on the metal walls of his own cabin, familiar things seen through a slow growing haze. A warm lethargy that had crept into legs and arms, was creeping inward to this last core that was himself. Fading memory and knowledge gained from the attackers made it clear; their greater, more complex molecules fell easier prey to the enzyme poison of the Planet of Death. For this last, brief second of time before it finally overcame him, too, in its warm lethargy, he understood.

Already the warm paralysis had reached, and stopped, his motor nerves; he could not speak, or write, or signal now, just as before him Hall and then Ross had been helpless to warn, or explain.

The last brief flash of action though, had gone unstayed, for the yet more complex paths of his subconscious mind had not so easily been traced. Unhampered, it had carried out his last strong will. The last drop of poison Ross had taken, but the egg— Dimly he saw it, half eaten beyond the growing haze of warm gray before his closing eyes.

And memory satisfied him of other things. The log, with a scrawled warning "Intelligent molecules—" that he had thrust in self-hypnosis in the prepared, heat-proof cylinder. The synchronous motor turning slow before the drive of a humming tuning fork that molecules could not halt.

The circuit would close, the automatic controls would bring the ship to Earth's system, and halt it as the speed-fields collapsed. And slowly, because of that closed circuit, the atomics would labor and build up a temperature of 700° absolute, where metal glowed dull and warning red—

And destroyed any molecule save only the very simplest, even those that might be partly sheltered in the asbestos cylinder, where even paper would be somewhat scorched—

# WHO GOES THERE?

The place stank. A queer, mingled stench that only the ice-buried cabins of an Antarctic camp know, compounded of reeking human sweat, and the heavy, fish-oil stench of melted seal blubber. An overtone of liniment combated the musty smell of sweat-and-snow-drenched furs. The acrid odor of burnt cooking fat, and the animal, not-unpleasant smell of dogs, diluted by time, hung in the air.

Lingering odors of machine oil contrasted sharply with the taint of harness dressing and leather. Yet, somehow, through all that reek of human beings and their associates—dogs, machines, and cooking—came another taint. It was a queer, neck-ruffling thing, a faintest suggestion of an odor alien among the smells of industry and life. And it was a life-smell. But it came from the thing that lay bound with cord and tarpaulin on the table, dripping slowly, methodically onto the heavy planks, dank and gaunt under the unshielded glare of the electric light.

Blair, the little bald-pated biologist of the expedition, twitched nervously at the wrappings, exposing clear, dark ice beneath and then pulling the tarpaulin back into place restlessly. His little birdlike motions of suppressed eagerness danced his shadow across the fringe of dingy gray underwear hanging from the low ceiling, the equatorial fringe of stiff, graying hair around his naked skull a comical halo about the shadow's head.

Commander Garry brushed aside the lax legs of a suit of underwear, and stepped toward the table. Slowly his eyes traced around the rings of men sardined into the Administration Building. His tall, stiff body straightened finally, and he nodded. "Thirty-seven. All here." His voice was low, yet carried the clear authority of the commander by nature, as well as by title.

"You know the outline of the story back of that find of the Secondary Pole Expedition. I have been conferring with Second-in-Command McReady, and Norris, as well as Blair and Doctor Copper. There is a difference of opinion, and because it involves the entire group, it is only just that the entire Expedition personnel act on it.

"I am going to ask McReady to give you the details of the story, because each of you has been too busy with his own work to follow closely the endeavors of the others. McReady?"

Moving from the smoke-blued background, McReady was a figure from some forgotten myth, a looming, bronze statue that held life, and walked. Six feet four inches he stood as he halted beside the table, and with a characteristic glance upward to assure himself of room under the low ceiling beams, straightened. His rough, clashingly orange windproof jacket he still had on, yet on his huge frame it did not seem misplaced. Even here, four feet beneath the drift-wind that droned across the Antarctic waste above the ceiling, the cold of the frozen continent leaked in, and gave meaning to the harshness of the man. And he was bronze—his great red-bronze beard, the heavy hair that matched it. The gnarled, corded hands gripping, relaxing, gripping and relaxing on the table planks were bronze. Even the deep-sunken eyes beneath heavy brows were bronzed.

Age-resisting endurance of the metal spoke in the cragged heavy outlines of his face, and the mellow tones of the heavy voice. "Norris and Blair agree on one thing; that animal we found was not—terrestrial in origin. Norris fears there may be danger in that; Blair says there is none.

"But I'll go back to how and why we found it. From all that was known before we came here, it appeared that this point was exactly over the South Magnetic Pole of Earth. The compass does point straight down here, as you all know. The more delicate instruments of the physicists, instruments especially designed for this expedition and its study of the magnetic pole, detected a secondary effect, a secondary, less powerful magnetic influence about eighty miles southwest of here.

"The Secondary Magnetic Expedition went out to investigate it. There is no need for details. We found it, but it was not the huge meteorite or magnetic mountain Norris had expected to find. Iron ore is magnetic, of course; iron more so—and certain special steels even more magnetic. From the surface indications, the secondary pole we found was small, so small that the magnetic effect it had was preposterous. No magnetic material conceivable could have that effect. Soundings through the ice indicated it was within one hundred feet of the glacier surface.

"I think you should know the structure of the place. There is a broad plateau, a level sweep that runs more than one hundred and fifty miles due south from the Secondary Station, Van Wall says. He didn't have time or fuel to fly farther, but it was running smoothly due south then. Right there, where that buried thing was, there is an ice-drowned mountain ridge, a granite wall of unshakable strength that has dammed back the ice creeping from the south.

"And four hundred miles due south is the South Polar Plateau. You have asked me at various times why it gets warmer here when the wind rises, and most of you know. As a meteorologist I'd have staked my word that no wind could blow at minus seventy degrees; that no more than a five-mile wind could blow at minus fifty; without causing warming due to friction with ground, snow and ice, and the air itself.

"We camped there on the lip of that ice-drowned mountain range for twelve days. We dug our camp into the blue ice that formed the surface, and escaped most of it. But for twelve consecutive days the wind blew at forty-five miles an hour. It went as high as forty-eight, and fell to forty-one at times. The temperature was  minus sixty-three degrees. It rose to minus sixty and fell to minus sixty-eight. It was meteorologically impossible, and it went on uninterruptedly for twelve days and twelve nights.

"Somewhere to the south, the frozen air of the South Polar Plateau slides down from that eighteen-thousand-foot bowl, down a mountain pass, over a glacier, and starts north. There must be a funneling mountain chain that directs it, and sweeps it away for four hundred miles to hit that bald plateau where we found the secondary pole, and three hundred and fifty miles farther north reaches the Antarctic Ocean.

"It's been frozen there since Antarctica froze twenty million years ago. There never has been a thaw there.

"Twenty million years ago Antarctica was beginning to freeze. We've investigated, though, and built speculations. What we believe happened was about like this.

"Something came down out of space, a ship. We saw it there in the blue ice, a thing like a submarine without a conning tower or directive vanes, two hundred and eighty feet long and forty-five feet in diameter at its thickest.

"Eh, Van Wall? Space? Yes, but I'll explain that better later." McReady's steady voice went on.

"It came down from space, driven and lifted by forces men haven't discovered yet, and somehow—perhaps something went wrong then—it tangled with Earth's magnetic field. It came south here, out of control probably, circling the magnetic pole. That's a savage country there; but when Antarctica was still freezing, it must have been a thousand times more savage. There must have been blizzard snow, as well as drift, new snow falling as the continent glaciated. The swirl there must have been particularly bad, the wind hurling a solid blanket of white over the lip of that now-buried mountain.

"The ship struck solid granite head-on, and cracked up. Not every one of the passengers in it was killed, but the ship must have been ruined, her driving mechanism locked. It tangled with Earth's field, Norris believes. No thing made by intelligent beings can tangle with the dead immensity of a planet's natural forces and survive.

"One of its passengers stepped out. The wind we saw there never fell below forty-one, and the temperature never rose above minus sixty. Then—the wind must have been stronger. And there was drift falling in a solid sheet. The *thing* was lost completely in ten paces." He paused for a moment, the deep, steady voice giving way to the drone of wind overhead and the uneasy, malicious gurgling in the pipe of the galley stove.

Drift—a drift-wind was sweeping by overhead. Right now the snow picked up by the mumbling wind fled in level, blinding lines across the face of the buried camp. If a man stepped out of the tunnels that connected each of the camp buildings beneath the surface, he'd be lost in ten paces. Out there, the slim, black finger of the radio mast lifted three hundred feet into the air, and at its peak was the clear night sky. A sky of thin, whining wind rushing steadily from beyond to another beyond under the licking, curling mantle of the aurora. And off north, the horizon flamed with queer, angry colors of the midnight twilight. That was spring three hundred feet above Antarctica.

At the surface—it was white death. Death of a needle-fingered cold driven before the wind, sucking heat from any warm thing. Cold—and white mist of endless, everlasting drift, the fine, fine particles of licking snow that obscured all things.

Kinner, the little scar-faced cook, winced. Five days ago he had stepped out to the surface to reach a cache of frozen beef. He had reached it, started back—and the drift-wind leaped out of the south. Cold, white death that streamed across the ground blinded him in twenty seconds. He stumbled on wildly in circles. It was half an hour before rope-guided men from below found him in the impenetrable murk.

It was easy for man—or *thing*—to get lost in ten paces.

"And the drift-wind then was probably more impenetrable than we know." McReady's voice snapped Kinner's mind back. Back to the welcome, dank warmth of the Ad Building. "The passenger of the ship wasn't prepared either, it appears. It froze within ten feet of the ship.

"We dug down to find the ship, and our tunnel happened to find the frozen—animal. Barclay's ice-ax struck its skull.

"When we saw what it was, Barclay went back to the tractor, started the fire up, and when the steam pressure built, sent a call for Blair and Doctor Copper. Barclay himself was sick then. Stayed sick for three days, as a matter of fact.

"When Blair and Copper came, we cut out the animal in a block of ice, as you see, wrapped it and loaded it on the tractor for return here. We wanted to get into that ship.

"We reached the side and found the metal was something we didn't know. Our beryllium-bronze, non-magnetic tools wouldn't touch it. Barclay had some tool steel on the tractor, and that wouldn't scratch it, either. We made reasonable tests—even tried some acid from the batteries with no results.

"They must have had a passivating process to make magnesium metal resist acid that way, and the alloy must have been at least ninety-five percent magnesium. But we had no way of guessing that, so when we spotted the barely opened lock door, we cut around it. There was clear, hard ice inside the lock, where we couldn't reach it. Through the little crack we could look in and see that only metal and tools were in there, so we decided to loosen the ice with a bomb.

"We had decanite bombs and thermite. Thermite is the ice-softener; decanite might have shattered valuable things, where the thermite's heat would just loosen the ice. Doctor Copper, Norris and I placed a twenty-five-pound thermite bomb, wired it, and took the connector up the tunnel to the surface, where Blair had the steam tractor waiting. A hundred yards the other side of that granite wall we set off the thermite bomb.

"The magnesium metal of the ship caught, of course. The glow of the bomb flared and died, then it began to flare again. We ran back to the tractor, and gradually the glare built up. From where we were we could see the whole ice field illuminated from beneath with an unbearable light; the ship's shadow was a great, dark cone reaching off toward the north, where the twilight was just about gone. For a moment it lasted, and we counted three other shadow-things that might have been other—passengers—frozen there. Then the ice was crashing down and against the ship.

"That's why I told you about that place. The wind sweeping down from the Pole was at our backs. Steam and hydrogen flame were torn away in white ice-fog; the flaming heat under the ice there was yanked away toward the Antarctic Ocean before it touched us. Otherwise we wouldn't have come back, even with the shelter of that granite ridge that stopped the light.

"Somehow in the blinding inferno we could see great hunched

things—black bulks. They shed even the furious incandescence of the magnesium for a time. Those must have been the engines, we knew. Secrets going in blazing glory—secrets that might have given Man the planets. Mysterious things that could lift and hurl that ship—and had soaked in the force of the Earth's magnetic field. I saw Norris's mouth move, and ducked. I couldn't hear him.

"Insulation—something—gave way. All Earth's field they'd soaked up twenty million years before broke loose. The aurora in the sky above licked down, and the whole plateau there was bathed in cold fire that blanketed vision. The ice-ax in my hand got red hot, and hissed on the ice. Metal buttons on my clothes burned into me. And a flash of electric blue seared upward from beyond the granite wall.

"Then the walls of ice crashed down on it. For an instant it squealed the way dry ice does when it's pressed between metal.

"We were blind and groping in the dark for hours while our eyes recovered. We found every coil within a mile was fused rubbish, the dynamo and every radio set, the earphones and speakers. If we hadn't had the steam tractor, we wouldn't have gotten over to the Secondary Camp.

"Van Wall flew in from Big Magnet at sunup, as you know. We came home as soon as possible. That is the history of—that." McReady's great bronze beard gestured toward the thing on the table.

## II

Blair stirred uneasily, his little, bony fingers wriggling under the harsh light. Little brown freckles on his knuckles slid back and forth as the tendons under the skin twitched. He pulled aside a bit of the tarpaulin and looked impatiently at the dark ice-bound thing inside.

McReady's big body straightened somewhat. He'd ridden the rocking, jarring steam tractor forty miles that day, pushing on to Big Magnet here. Even his calm will had been pressed by the anxiety to mix again with humans. It was lone and quiet out there in Secondary Camp, where a wolf-wind howled down from the Pole. Wolf-wind howling in his sleep—winds droning and the evil, unspeakable face of that monster leering up as he'd first seen it through clear, blue ice, with a bronze ice-ax buried in its skull.

The giant meteorologist spoke again. "The problem is this. Blair wants to examine the thing. Thaw it out and make micro slides of its tissues and so forth. Norris doesn't believe that is safe, and Blair does. Doctor Copper agrees pretty much with Blair. Norris is a physicist, of course, not a biologist. But he makes a point I think we should all hear. Blair has described the microscopic life-forms biologists find living, even in this cold and inhospitable place. They freeze every winter, and thaw every summer—for three months—and live.

"The point Norris makes is—they thaw and live again. There must have been microscopic life associated with this creature. There is with every living thing we know. And Norris is afraid that we may release a plague—some germ disease unknown to Earth—if we thaw those microscopic things that have been frozen there for twenty million years.

"Blair admits that such micro-life might retain the power of living. Such unorganized things as individual cells can retain life for unknown periods, when solidly frozen. The beast itself is as dead as those frozen mammoths they find in Siberia. Organized, highly developed life forms can't stand that treatment.

"But micro-life could. Norris suggests that we may release some disease-form that man, never having met it before, will be utterly defenseless against.

"Blair's answer is that there may be such still-living germs, but that Norris has the case reversed. They are utterly non-immune to man. Our life-chemistry probably—"

"Probably!" The little biologist's head lifted in a quick, birdlike motion. The halo of gray hair about his bald head ruffled as though angry. "Heh, one look—"

"I know," McReady acknowledged. "The thing is not Earthly. It does not seem likely it can have a life chemistry sufficiently like ours to make cross infection remotely possible. I would say that there is no danger."

McReady looked toward Doctor Copper. The physician shook his head slowly. "None whatever," he asserted confidently. "Man cannot infect or be infected by germs that live in such comparatively close relatives as the snakes. And they are, I assure you," his clean-shaven face grimaced uneasily, "*much* nearer to us than—*that.*"

Vance Norris moved angrily. He was comparatively short in this gathering of big men, some five-feet-eight, and his stocky, powerful build tended to make him seem shorter. His black hair was crisp and hard, like short, steel wires, and his eyes were the gray of fractured steel. If McReady was a man of bronze, Norris was all steel. His movements, his thoughts, his whole bearing had the quick, hard impulse of a steel spring. His nerves were steel—hard, quick-acting—swift corroding.

He was decided on his point now, and he lashed out in its defense with a characteristic quick, clipped flow of words. "Different chemistry be damned. That thing may be dead—or, by God, it may not—but I don't like it. Damn it, Blair, let them see the monstrosity you are petting over there. Let them see the foul thing and decide for themselves whether they want that thing thawed out in this camp.

"Thawed out, by the way. That's got to be thawed out in one of the shacks tonight, if it is thawed out. Somebody—who's watchman tonight? Magnetics—oh, Connant. Cosmic rays tonight. Well, you get to sit up with that twenty-million-year-old mummy of his. Unwrap it, Blair. How the hell can they tell what they are buying, if they can't see it? It may have a different chemistry. I don't care what else it has, but I know it has something I don't want. If you can judge by the look on its face—it isn't human so maybe you can't—it was annoyed when it froze. Annoyed, in fact, is just about as close an approximation of the way it felt, as crazy, mad, insane hatred. Neither one touches the subject.

"How the hell can these birds tell what they are voting on? They haven't seen those three red eyes and that blue hair like crawling worms. Crawling—damn, it's crawling there in the ice right now!

"Nothing Earth ever spawned had the unutterable sublimation of devastating wrath that thing let loose in its face when it looked around its frozen desolation twenty million years ago. Mad? It was mad clear through—searing, blistering mad!

"Hell, I've had bad dreams ever since I looked at those three red eyes. Nightmares. Dreaming the thing thawed out and came to life—that it wasn't dead, or even wholly unconscious all those twenty million years, but just slowed, waiting—waiting. You'll dream, too, while that damned thing that Earth wouldn't own is dripping, dripping in the Cosmos House tonight.

"And, Connant," Norris whipped toward the cosmic ray specialist, "won't you have fun sitting up all night in the quiet. Wind whining above—and that thing dripping—" He stopped for a moment, and looked around.

"I know. That's not science. But this is, it's psychology. You'll have nightmares for a year to come. Every night since I looked at that thing I've had 'em. That's why I hate it—sure I do—and don't want it around. Put it back where it came from and let it freeze for another twenty million years. I had some swell nightmares—that it wasn't made like we are—which is obvious—but of a different kind of flesh that it can really control. That it can change its shape, and look like a man—and wait to kill and eat—

"That's not a logical argument. I know it isn't. The thing isn't Earth-logic anyway.

"Maybe it has an alien body chemistry, and maybe its bugs do have a different body chemistry. A germ might not stand that, but, Blair and Copper, how about a virus? That's just an enzyme molecule, you've said. That wouldn't need anything but a protein molecule of any body to work on.

"And how are you so sure that, of the million varieties of microscopic life it may have, *none* of them are dangerous. How about diseases like hydrophobia—rabies—that attack any warm-blooded creature, whatever its body chemistry may be? And parrot fever? Have you a body like a parrot, Blair? And plain rot—gangrene—necrosis if you want? *That* isn't choosy about body chemistry!"

Blair looked up from his puttering long enough to meet Norris's angry, gray eyes for an instant. "So far the only thing you have said this thing gave off that was catching was dreams. I'll go so far as to admit that." An impish, slightly malignant grin crossed the little man's seamed face. "I had some, too. So. It's dream-infectious. No doubt an exceedingly dangerous malady.

"So far as your other things go, you have a badly mistaken idea about viruses. In the first place, nobody has shown that the enzyme-molecule theory, and that alone, explains them. And in the second place, when you catch tobacco mosaic or wheat rust, let me know. A wheat plant is a lot nearer your body chemistry than this other-world creature is.

"And your rabies is limited, strictly limited. You can't get it from, nor give it to, a wheat plant or a fish—which is a collateral descendant of a common ancestor of yours. Which this, Norris, is not." Blair nodded pleasantly toward the tarpaulined bulk on the table.

"Well, thaw the damned thing in a tub of Formalin if you must. I've suggested that—"

"And I've said there would be no sense in it. You can't compromise. Why did you and Commander Garry come down here to study magnetism? Why weren't you content to stay at home? There's magnetic force enough in New York. I could no more study the life this thing once had from a Formalin-pickled sample than you could get the information you wanted back in New York. And—if this one is so treated, *never in all time to come can there be a duplicate!* The race it came from must have passed away in the twenty million years it lay frozen, so that even if it came from Mars then, we'd never find its like. And—the ship is gone.

"There's only one way to do this—and that's the best possible way. It must be thawed slowly, carefully, and not in Formalin."

Commander Garry stood forward again, and Norris stepped back muttering angrily. "I think Blair is right, gentlemen. What do you say?"

Connant grunted. "It sounds right to us, I think—only perhaps he ought to stand watch over it while it's thawing." He grinned ruefully, brushing a stray lock of ripe-cherry hair back from his forehead. "Swell idea, in fact—if he sits up with his jolly little corpse."

Garry smiled slightly. A general chuckle of agreement rippled over the group. "I should think any ghost it may have had would have starved to death if it hung around here that long, Connant," Garry suggested. "And you look capable of taking care of it. 'Ironman' Connant ought to be able to take out any opposing players still."

Connant shook himself uneasily. "I'm not worrying about ghosts. Let's see that thing. I—"

Eagerly Blair was stripping back the ropes. A single throw of the tarpaulin revealed the thing. The ice had melted somewhat in the heat of the room, and it was clear and blue as thick, good glass. It shone wet and sleek under the harsh light of the unshielded globe above.

The room stiffened abruptly. It was face up there on the plain, greasy planks of the table. The broken haft of the bronze ice-ax was still buried in the queer skull. Three mad, hate-filled eyes blazed up with a living fire, bright as fresh-spilled blood, from a face ringed with a writhing, loathsome nest of worms, blue, mobile worms that crawled where hair should grow—

Van Wall, six feet and two hundred pounds of ice-nerved pilot, gave a queer, strangled gasp, and butted, stumbled his way out to the corridor. Half the company broke for the doors. The others stumbled away from the table.

McReady stood at the end of the table watching them, his great body planted solid on his powerful legs. Norris from the opposite end glowered at the thing with smoldering hate. Outside the door, Garry was talking with half a dozen of the men at once.

Blair had a tack hammer. The ice that cased the thing *schluffed* crisply under its steel claw as it peeled from the thing it had cased for twenty thousand thousand years—

### III

"I know you don't like the thing, Connant, but it just has to be thawed out right. You say leave it as it is till we get back to civilization. All right, I'll admit your argument that we could do a better and more complete job there is sound. But—how are we going to get this across the Line? We have to take this through one temperate zone, the equatorial zone, and halfway through the other temperate zone before we get it to New York. You don't want to sit with it one night, but you suggest, then, that I hang its corpse in the freezer with the beef?" Blair looked up from his cautious chipping, his bald freckled skull nodding triumphantly.

Kinner, the stocky, scar-faced cook, saved Connant the trouble of answering. "Hey, you listen, mister. You put that thing in the box with the meat, and by all the gods there ever were, I'll put you in to keep it company. You birds have brought everything movable in this camp in onto my mess tables here already, and I had to stand for that. But you go putting things like that in my meat box, or even my meat cache here, and you cook your own damn grub."

"But, Kinner, this is the only table in Big Magnet that's big enough to work on," Blair objected. "Everybody's explained that."

"Yeah, and everybody's brought everything in here. Clark brings his dogs every time there's a fight and sews them up on that table. Ralsen brings in his sledges. Hell, the only thing you haven't had on that table is the Boeing. And you'd 'a' had that in if you coulda figured a way to get it through the tunnels."

Commander Garry chuckled and grinned at Van Wall, the huge Chief Pilot. Van Wall's great blond beard twitched suspiciously as he nodded gravely to Kinner. "You're right, Kinner. The aviation department is the only one that treats you right."

"It does get crowded, Kinner," Garry acknowledged. "But I'm afraid we all find it that way at times. Not much privacy in an Antarctic camp."

"Privacy? What the hell's that? You know, the thing that really made me weep, was when I saw Barclay marchin' through here chantin' 'The last lumber in the camp! The last lumber in the camp!' and carryin' it out to build that house on his tractor. Damn it, I missed that moon cut in the door he carried out more'n I missed the sun when it set. That wasn't just the last lumber Barclay was walkin' off with. He was carryin' off the last bit of privacy in this blasted place."

A grin rode even on Connant's heavy face as Kinner's perennial, good-natured grouch came up again. But it died away quickly as his dark, deepset eyes turned again to the red-eyed thing Blair was chipping from its cocoon of ice. A big hand ruffed his shoulder-length hair, and tugged at a twisted lock that fell behind his ear, in a familiar gesture. "I know that cosmic ray shack's going to be too crowded if I have to sit up with that thing," he growled. "Why can't you go on chipping the ice away from around it—you can do that without anybody butting in, I assure you—and then hang the thing up over the power-plant boiler? That's warm enough. It'll thaw out a chicken, even a whole side of beef, in a few hours."

"I know," Blair protested, dropping the tack hammer to gesture more effectively with his bony, freckled fingers, his small body tense with eagerness, "but this is too important to take any chances. There never was a find like this; there never can be again. It's the only chance men will ever have, and it has to be done exactly right.

"Look, you know how the fish we caught down near the Ross Sea would freeze almost as soon as we got them on deck, and come to life again if we thawed them gently? Low forms of life aren't killed by quick freezing and slow thawing. We have—"

"Hey, for the love of Heaven—you mean that damned thing will come to life!" Connant yelled. "You get the damned thing— Let me at it! That's going to be in so many pieces—"

"No! No, you fool—" Blair jumped in front of Connant to protect his precious find. "No. Just low forms of life. For Pete's sake let me finish. You can't thaw higher forms of life and have them come to. Wait a moment now—hold it! A fish can come to after freezing because it's so low a form of life that the individual cells of its body can revive, and that alone is enough to reestablish life. Any higher forms thawed out that way are dead. Though the individual cells revive, they die because there must be organization and cooperative effort to live. That cooperation cannot be reestablished. There is a sort of potential life in any uninjured, quick-frozen animal. But it can't—can't under any circumstances—become active life in higher animals. The higher animals are too complex, too delicate. This is an intelligent creature as high in its evolution as we are in ours. Perhaps higher. It is as dead as a frozen man would be."

"How do you know?" demanded Connant, hefting the ice-ax he had seized a moment before.

Commander Garry laid a restraining hand on his heavy shoulder. "Wait a minute, Connant. I want to get this straight. I agree that there is going to be no thawing of this thing if there is the remotest chance of its revival. I quite agree it is much too unpleasant to have alive, but I had no idea there was the remotest possibility."

Doctor Copper pulled his pipe from between his teeth and heaved his stocky, dark body from the bunk he had been sitting in. "Blair's being technical. That's dead. As dead as the mammoths they find frozen in Siberia. We have all sorts of proof that things don't live after being frozen—not even fish, generally speaking—and no proof that higher animal life can under any circumstances. What's the point, Blair?"

The little biologist shook himself. The little ruff of hair standing out around his bald pate waved in righteous anger. "The point is," he said in an injured tone, "that the individual cells might show the characteristics they had in life if it is properly thawed. A man's muscle cells live many hours after he has died. Just because they live, and a few things like hair and fingernail cells still live, you wouldn't accuse a corpse of being a zombie, or something.

"Now if I thaw this right, I may have a chance to determine what sort of world it's native to. We don't and can't know by any other means, whether it came from Earth or Mars or Venus or from beyond the stars.

"And just because it looks unlike men, you don't have to accuse it of being evil or vicious or something. Maybe that expression on its face is its equivalent to a resignation to fate. White is the color of mourning to the Chinese. If men can have different customs, why can't a so-different race have different understandings of facial expressions?"

Connant laughed softly, mirthlessly. "Peaceful resignation! If that is the best it could do in the way of resignation, I should exceedingly dislike seeing it when it was looking mad. That face was never designed to express peace. It just didn't have any philosophical thoughts like peace in its make-up.

"I know it's your pet—but be sane about it. That thing grew up on evil, adolesced slowly roasting alive the local equivalent of kittens, and amused itself through maturity on new and ingenious torture."

"You haven't the slightest right to say that," snapped Blair. "How do you know the first thing about the meaning of a facial expression inherently inhuman? It may well have no human equivalent whatever. That is just a different development of Nature, another example of Nature's wonderful adaptability. Growing on another, perhaps harsher world, it has different form and features. But it is just as much a legitimate child of Nature as you are. You are displaying that childish human weakness of hating the different. On its own world it would probably class you as a fish-belly, white monstrosity with an insufficient number of eyes and a fungoid body pale and bloated with gas.

"Just because its nature is different, you haven't any right to say it's necessarily evil."

Norris burst out a single, explosive, "Haw!" He looked down at the thing. "May be that things from other worlds don't *have* to be evil just because they're different. But that thing *was!* Child of Nature, eh? Well, it was a hell of an evil Nature."

"Aw, will you mugs cut crabbing at each other and get the damned thing off my table?" Kinner growled. "And put a canvas over it. It looks indecent."

"Kinner's gone modest," jeered Connant.

Kinner slanted his eyes up to the big physicist. The scarred cheek twisted to join the line of his tight lips in a twisted grin. "All right, big boy, and what were you grousing about a minute ago? We can set the thing in a chair next to you tonight, if you want."

"I'm not afraid of its face," Connant snapped. "I don't like keeping a wake over its corpse particularly, but I'm going to do it."

Kinner's grin spread. "Uh-huh." He went off to the galley stove and shook down ashes vigorously, drowning the brittle chipping of the ice as Blair fell to work again.

## IV

*"Cluck,"* reported the cosmic-ray counter, *"cluck-burrrp-cluck."*

Connant started and dropped his pencil.

"Damnation." The physicist looked toward the far corner, back at the Geiger counter on the table near that corner. And crawled under the desk at which he had been working to retrieve the pencil. He sat down at his work again, trying to make his writing more even. It tended to have jerks and quavers in it, in time with the abrupt proud-hen noises of the Geiger counter. The muted whoosh of the pressure lamp he was using for illumination, the mingled gargles and bugle calls of a dozen men sleeping down the corridor in Paradise House formed the background sounds for the irregular, clucking noises of the counter, the occasional rustle of falling coal in the copper-bellied stove. And a soft, steady *drip-drip-drip* from the thing in the corner.

Connant jerked a pack of cigarettes from his pocket, snapped it so that a cigarette protruded, and jabbed the cylinder into his mouth. The lighter failed to function, and he pawed angrily through the pile of papers in search of a match. He scratched the wheel of the lighter several times, dropped it with a curse, and got up to pluck a hot coal from the stove with the coal tongs.

The lighter functioned instantly when he tried it on returning to the desk. The counter ripped out a series of chuckling guffaws as a burst of cosmic rays struck through to it. Connant turned to glower at it, and tried to concentrate on the interpretation of data collected during the past week. The weekly summary—

He gave up and yielded to curiosity, or nervousness. He lifted the pressure lamp from the desk and carried it over to the table in the corner. Then he returned to the stove and picked up the coal tongs. The beast had been thawing for nearly eighteen hours now. He poked at it with an unconscious caution; the flesh was no longer hard as armor plate, but had assumed a rubbery texture. It looked like wet, blue rubber glistening under droplets of water like little round jewels in the glare of the gasoline pressure lantern. Connant felt an unreasoning desire to pour the contents of the lamp's reservoir over the thing in its box and drop the cigarette into it. The three red eyes glared up at him sightlessly, the ruby eyeballs reflecting murky, smoky rays of light.

He realized vaguely that he had been looking at them for a very long time, even vaguely understood that they were no longer sightless. But it did not seem of importance, of no more importance than the labored, slow motion of the tentacular things that sprouted from the base of the scrawny, slowly pulsing neck.

Connant picked up the pressure lamp and returned to his chair. He sat down, staring at the pages of mathematics before him. The clucking of the counter was strangely less disturbing, the rustle of the coals in the stove no longer distracting.

The creak of the floor boards behind him didn't interrupt his thoughts as he went about his weekly report in an automatic manner, filling in columns of data and making brief, summarizing notes.

The creak of the floor boards sounded nearer.

## V

Blair came up from the nightmare-haunted depths of sleep abruptly. Connant's face floated vaguely above him; for a moment it seemed a continuance of the wild horror of the dream. But Connant's face was angry, and a little frightened. "Blair—Blair, you damned log, wake up."

"Uh-eh?" the little biologist rubbed his eyes, his bony freckled finger crooked to a mutilated child-fist. From surrounding bunks other faces lifted to stare down at them.

Connant straightened up. "Get up—and get a lift on. Your damned animal's escaped."

"Escaped—what!" Chief Pilot Van Wall's bull voice roared out with a volume that shook the walls. Down the communication tunnels other voices yelled suddenly. The dozen inhabitants of Paradise House tumbled in abruptly, Barclay, stocky and bulbous in long woolen underwear, carrying a fire extinguisher.

"What the hell's the matter?" Barclay demanded.

"Your damned beast got loose. I fell asleep about twenty minutes ago, and when I woke up, the thing was gone. Hey, Doc, the hell you say those things can't come to life. Blair's blasted potential life developed a hell of a lot of potential and walked out on us."

Copper stared blankly. "It wasn't—earthly," he sighed suddenly. "I—I guess earthly laws don't apply."

"Well, it applied for leave of absence and took it. We've got to find it and capture it somehow." Connant swore bitterly, his deepset black eyes sullen and angry. "It's a wonder the hellish creature didn't eat me in my sleep."

Blair stared back, his pale eyes suddenly fear-struck. "Maybe it di—er—uh—we'll have to find it."

"You find it. It's your pet. I've had all I want to do with it, sitting there for seven hours with the counter clucking every few seconds, and you birds in here singing night music. It's a wonder I got to sleep. I'm going through to the Ad Building."

Commander Garry ducked through the doorway, pulling his belt tight. "You won't have to. Van's roar sounded like the Boeing taking off downwind. So it wasn't dead?"

"I didn't carry it off in my arms, I assure you," Connant snapped. "The last I saw, the split skull was oozing green goo, like a squashed caterpillar. Doc just said our laws don't work—it's unearthly. Well, it's an unearthly monster, with an unearthly disposition, judging by the face, wandering around with a split skull and brains oozing out."

Norris and McReady appeared in the doorway, a doorway filling with other shivering men. "Has anybody seen it coming over here?" Norris asked innocently. "About four feet tall—three red eyes—brains oozing out— Hey, has anybody checked to make sure this isn't a cracked idea of humor? If it is, I think we'll unite in tying Blair's pet around Connant's neck like the Ancient Mariner's albatross."

"It's no humor." Connant shivered. "Lord, I wish it were. I'd rather wear—" He stopped. A wild, weird howl shrieked through the corridors. The men stiffened abruptly, and half turned.

"I think it's been located," Connant finished. His dark eyes shifted with a queer unease. He darted back to his bunk in Paradise House, to return almost immediately with a heavy .45 revolver and an ice-ax. He hefted both gently as he started for the corridor toward Dogtown.

"It blundered down the wrong corridor—and landed among the huskies. Listen—the dogs have broken their chains—"

The half-terrorized howl of the dog pack had changed to a wild hunting melee. The voices of the dogs thundered in the narrow corridors, and through them came a low rippling snarl of distilled hate. A shrill of pain, a dozen snarling yelps.

Connant broke for the door. Close behind him, McReady, then Barclay and Commander Garry came. Other men broke for the Ad Building, and weapons—the sledge house. Pomroy, in charge of Big

Magnet's five cows, started down the corridor in the opposite direction—he had a six-foot-handled, long-tined pitchfork in mind.

Barclay slid to a halt, as McReady's giant bulk turned abruptly away from the tunnel leading to Dogtown and vanished off at an angle. Uncertainly, the mechanician wavered a moment, the fire extinguisher in his hands, hesitating from one side to the other. Then he was racing after Connant's broad back. Whatever McReady had in mind, he could be trusted to make it work.

Connant stopped at the bend in the corridor. His breath hissed suddenly through his throat. "Great God—" The revolver exploded thunderously; three numbing, palpable waves of sound crashed through the confined corridors. Two more. The revolver dropped to the hard-packed snow of the trail, and Barclay saw the ice-ax shift into defensive position. Connant's powerful body blocked his vision, but beyond he heard something mewing, and, insanely, chuckling. The dogs were quieter; there was a deadly seriousness in their low snarls. Taloned feet scratched at hard-packed snow, broken chains were clinking and tangling.

Connant shifted abruptly, and Barclay could see what lay beyond. For a second he stood frozen, then his breath went out in a gusty curse. The thing launched itself at Connant, and the powerful arms of the man swung the ice-ax flat-side first at what might have been a head. It scrunched horribly, and the tattered flesh, ripped by a half-dozen savage huskies, leapt to its feet again. The red eyes blazed with an unearthly hatred, an unearthly unkillable vitality.

Barclay turned the fire extinguisher on it; the blinding, blistering stream of chemical spray confused it, baffled it, together with the savage attacks of the huskies, not for long afraid of anything that did, or could live, and held it at bay.

McReady wedged men out of his way and drove down the narrow corridor packed with men unable to reach the scene. There was a sure foreplanned drive to McReady's attack. One of the giant blowtorches used in warming the plane's engines was in his bronzed hands. It roared gustily as he turned the corner and opened the valve. The mad mewing hissed louder. The dogs scrambled back from the three-foot lance of blue-hot flame.

"Bar, get a power cable, run it in somehow. And a handle. We can electrocute this—monster, if I don't incinerate it." McReady spoke with an authority of planned action. Barclay turned down the long corridor to the power plant, but already before him Norris and Van Wall were racing down.

Barclay found the cable in the electrical cache in the tunnel wall.

In a half minute he was hacking at it, walking back. Van Wall's voice rang out in warning shout of "Power!" as the emergency gasoline-powered dynamo thudded into action. Half a dozen other men were down there now; the coal, kindling were going into the firebox of the steam power plant. Norris, cursing in a low, deadly monotone, was working with quick, sure fingers on the other end of Barclay's cable, splicing a contacter into one of the power leads.

The dogs had fallen back when Barclay reached the corridor bend, fallen back before a furious monstrosity that glared from baleful red eyes, mewing in trapped hatred. The dogs were a semicircle of red-dipped muzzles with a fringe of glistening white teeth, whining with a vicious eagerness that near matched the fury of the red eyes. McReady stood confidently alert at the corridor bend, the gustily muttering torch held loose and ready for action in his hands. He stepped aside without moving his eyes from the beast as Barclay came up. There was a slight, tight smile on his lean, bronzed face.

Norris's voice called down the corridor, and Barclay stepped forward. The cable was taped to the long handle of a snow shovel, the two conductors split and held eighteen inches apart by a scrap of lumber lashed at right angles across the far end of the handle. Bare copper conductors, charged with 220 volts, glinted in the light of pressure lamps. The thing mewed and hated and dodged. McReady advanced to Barclay's side. The dogs beyond sensed the plan with the almost telepathic intelligence of trained huskies. Their whining grew shriller, softer, their mincing steps carried them nearer. Abruptly a huge night-black Alaskan leapt onto the trapped thing. It turned squalling, saber-clawed feet slashing.

Barclay leaped forward and jabbed. A weird, shrill scream rose and choked out. The smell of burnt flesh in the corridor intensified; greasy smoke curled up. The echoing pound of the gas-electric dynamo down the corridor became a slogging thud.

The red eyes clouded over in a stiffening, jerking travesty of a face. Armlike, leglike members quivered and jerked. The dogs leaped forward, and Barclay yanked back his shovel-handled weapon. The thing on the snow did not move as gleaming teeth ripped it open.

## VI

Garry looked about the crowded room. Thirty-two men, some tensed nervously standing against the wall, some uneasily relaxed, some sitting, most perforce standing as intimate as sardines. Thirty-two, plus the five engaged in sewing up wounded dogs, made thirty-seven, the total personnel.

Garry started speaking. "All right, I guess we're here. Some of you—three or four at most—saw what happened. All of you have seen that thing on the table, and can get a general idea. Anyone hasn't, I'll lift—" His hand strayed to the tarpaulin bulking over the thing on the table. There was an acrid odor of singed flesh seeping out of it. The men stirred restlessly; there were hasty denials.

"It looks rather as though Charnauk isn't going to lead any more teams," Garry went on. "Blair wants to get at this thing, and make some more detailed examination. We want to know what happened, and make sure right now that this is permanently, totally dead. Right?"

Connant grinned. "Anybody that doesn't can sit up with it to-night."

"All right then, Blair, what can you say about it? What was it?" Garry turned to the little biologist.

"I wonder if we ever saw its natural form." Blair looked at the covered mass. "It may have been imitating the beings that built that ship—but I don't think it was. I think that was its true form. Those of us who were up near the bend saw the thing in action; the thing on the table is the result. When it got loose, apparently, it started looking around. Antarctica still frozen as it was ages ago when the creature first saw it—and froze. From my observations while it was thawing out, and the bits of tissue I cut and hardened then, I think it was native to a hotter planet than Earth. It couldn't, in its natural form, stand the temperature. There is no life form on Earth that can live in Antarctica during the winter, but the best compromise is the dog. It found the dogs, and somehow got near enough to Charnauk to get him. The others smelled it—heard it—I don't know—anyway they went wild and broke chains and attacked it before it was finished. The thing we found was part Charnauk, queerly only half-dead, part Charnauk half-digested by the jellylike protoplasm of that creature, and part the remains of the thing we originally found, sort of melted down to the basic protoplasm.

"When the dogs attacked it, it turned into the best fighting thing it could think of. Some other-world beast apparently."

"Turned," snapped Garry. "How?"

"Every living thing is made up of jelly—protoplasm and minute, submicroscopic things called nuclei, which control the bulk, the protoplasm. This thing was just a modification of that same world-wide plan of Nature; cells made up of protoplasm, controlled by infinitely tinier nuclei. You physicists might compare it—an individual cell of any living thing—with an atom; the bulk of the atom, the space-filling part, is made up of the electron orbits, but the character of the thing is determined by the atomic nucleus.

"This isn't wildly beyond what we already know. It's just a modification we haven't seen before. It's as natural, as logical, as any other manifestation of life. It obeys exactly the same laws. The cells are made of protoplasm, their character determined by the nucleus.

"Only, in this creature, the cell nuclei can control those cells *at will*. It digested Charnauk, and as it digested, studied every cell of his tissue, and shaped its own cells to imitate them exactly. Parts of it—parts that had time to finish changing—are dog-cells. But they don't have dog-cell nuclei." Blair lifted a fraction of the tarpaulin. A torn dog's leg, with stiff gray fur, protruded. "That, for instance, isn't a dog at all; it's imitation. Some parts I'm uncertain about; the nucleus was hiding itself, covering up with dog-cell imitation nucleus. In time, not even a microscope would have shown the difference."

"Suppose," asked Norris bitterly, "it had had lots of time?"

"Then it would have been a dog. The other dogs would have accepted it. We would have accepted it. I don't think anything would have distinguished it, not microscope, nor X-ray, nor any other means. This is a member of a supremely intelligent race, a race that has learned the deepest secrets of biology, and turned them to its use."

"What was it planning to do?" Barclay looked at the humped tarpaulin.

Blair grinned unpleasantly. The wavering halo of thin hair round his bald pate wavered in a stir of air. "Take over the world, I imagine."

"Take over the world! Just it, all by itself?" Connant gasped. "Set itself up as a lone dictator?"

"No," Blair shook his head. The scalpel he had been fumbling in his bony fingers dropped; he bent to pick it up, so that his face was hidden as he spoke. "It would become the population of the world."

"Become—populate the world? Does it reproduce asexually?"

Blair shook his head and gulped. "It's—it doesn't have to. It weighed eighty-five pounds. Charnauk weighed about ninety. It would have become Charnauk, and had eighty-five pounds left, to become—oh, Jack, for instance, or Chinook. It can imitate anything—that is, become anything. If it had reached the Antarctic Sea, it would have become a seal, maybe two seals. They might have attacked a killer whale, and become either killers, or a herd of seals. Or maybe it would have caught an albatross, or a skua gull, and flown to South America."

Norris cursed softly. "And every time it digested something, and imitated it—"

"It would have had its original bulk left, to start again," Blair finished. "Nothing would kill it. It has no natural enemies, because it becomes whatever it wants to. If a killer whale attacked it, it would become a killer whale. If it was an albatross, and an eagle attacked it, it would become an eagle. Lord, it might become a female eagle. Go back—build a nest and lay eggs!"

"Are you sure that thing from hell is dead?" Doctor Copper asked softly.

"Yes, thank Heaven," the little biologist gasped. "After they drove the dogs off, I stood there poking Bar's electrocution thing into it for five minutes. It's dead and—cooked."

"Then we can only give thanks that this is Antarctica, where there is not one, single, solitary, living thing for it to imitate, except these animals in camp."

"Us," Blair giggled. "It can imitate us. Dogs can't make four hundred miles to the sea; there's no food. There aren't any skua gulls to imitate at this season. There aren't any penguins this far inland. There's nothing that can reach the sea from this point—except us. We've got brains. We can do it. Don't you see—*it's got to imitate us—it's got to be one of us—that's the only way it can fly an airplane—fly a plane for two hours, and rule—be—all Earth's inhabitants. A world for the taking—if it imitates us!*

"It didn't know yet. It hadn't had a chance to learn. It was rushed—hurried—took the thing nearest its own size. Look—I'm Pandora! I opened the box! And the only hope that can come out is—that nothing can come out. You didn't see me. I did it. I fixed it. I smashed every magneto. Not a plane can fly. Nothing can fly." Blair giggled and lay down on the floor crying.

Chief Pilot Van Wall made for the door. His feet were fading echoes in the corridors as Doctor Copper bent unhurriedly over the little man on the floor. From his office at the end of the room he brought something and injected a solution into Blair's arm. "He might come out of it when he wakes up," he sighed, rising. McReady helped him lift the biologist onto a nearby bunk. "It all depends on whether we can convince him that thing is dead."

Van Wall ducked into the shack, brushing his heavy blond beard absently. "I didn't think a biologist would do a thing like that up thoroughly. He missed the spares in the second cache. It's all right. I smashed them."

Commander Garry nodded. "I was wondering about the radio."

Doctor Copper snorted. "You don't think it can leak out on a radio wave, do you? You'd have five rescue attempts in the next three months if you stop the broadcasts. The thing to do is talk loud and not make a sound. Now I wonder—"

McReady looked speculatively at the doctor. "It might be like an infectious disease. Everything that drank any of its blood—"

Copper shook his head. "Blair missed something. Imitate it may, but it has, to a certain extent, its own body chemistry, its own metabolism. If it didn't, it would become a dog—and be a dog and nothing more. It has to be an imitation dog. Therefore you can detect it by serum tests. And its chemistry, since it comes from another world, must be so wholly, radically different that a few cells, such as gained by drops of blood, would be treated as disease germs by the dog, or human body."

"Blood—would one of those imitations bleed?" Norris demanded.

"Surely. Nothing mystic about blood. Muscle is about ninety-percent water; blood differs only in having a couple percent more water, and less connective tissue. They'd bleed all right," Copper assured him.

Blair sat up in his bunk suddenly. "Connant—where's Connant?"

The physicist moved over toward the little biologist. "Here I am. What do you want?"

"Are you?" giggled Blair. He lapsed back into the bunk contorted with silent laughter.

Connant looked at him blankly. "Huh? Am I what?"

"*Are* you there?" Blair burst into gales of laughter. "*Are* you Connant? The beast wanted to be a *man*—not a dog—"

## VII

Doctor Copper rose wearily from the bunk, and washed the hypodermic carefully. The little tinkles it made seemed loud in the packed room, now that Blair's gurgling laughter had finally quieted. Copper looked toward Garry and shook his head slowly. "Hopeless, I'm afraid. I don't think we can ever convince him the thing is dead now."

Norris laughed uncertainly. "I'm not sure you can convince me. Oh, damn you, McReady."

"McReady?" Commander Garry turned to look from Norris to McReady curiously.

"The nightmares," Norris explained. "He had a theory about the nightmares we had at the Secondary Station after finding that thing."

"And that was?" Garry looked at McReady levelly.

Norris answered for him, jerkily, uneasily. "That the creature wasn't dead, had a sort of enormously slowed existence, an existence that permitted it, nonetheless, to be vaguely aware of the passing of time, of our coming, after endless years. I had a dream it could imitate things."

"Well," Copper grunted, "it can."

"Don't be an ass," Norris snapped. "That's not what's bothering me. In the dream it could read minds, read thoughts and ideas and mannerisms."

"What's so bad about that? It seems to be worrying you more than the thought of the joy we're going to have with a madman in an Antarctic camp." Copper nodded toward Blair's sleeping form.

McReady shook his great head slowly. "You know that Connant is Connant, because he not merely looks like Connant—which we're beginning to believe that beast might be able to do—but he thinks like Connant, moves himself around as Connant does. That takes more than merely a body that looks like him; that takes Connant's own mind, and thoughts and mannerisms. Therefore, though you know that the thing might make itself *look* like Connant, you aren't much bothered, because you know it has a mind from another world, a totally unhuman mind, that couldn't possibly react and think and talk like a man we know, and do it so well as to fool us for a moment. The idea of the creature imitating one of us is fascinating, but unreal, because it is too completely unhuman to deceive us. It doesn't have a human mind."

"As I said before," Norris repeated, looking steadily at McReady, "you can say the damnedest things at the damnedest times. Will you be so good as to finish that thought—one way or the other?"

Kinner, the scar-faced expedition cook, had been standing near Connant. Suddenly he moved down the length of the crowded room toward his familiar galley. He shook the ashes from the galley stove noisily.

"It would do it no good," said Doctor Copper, softly as though thinking out loud, "to merely look like something it was trying to imitate; it would have to understand its feelings, its reactions. It *is* unhuman; it has powers of imitation beyond any conception of man. A good actor, by training himself, can imitate another man, another man's mannerisms, well enough to fool most people. Of course no actor could imitate so perfectly as to deceive men who had been living with the imitated one in the complete lack of privacy of an Antarctic camp. That would take a superhuman skill."

"Oh, you've got the bug, too?" Norris cursed softly.

Connant, standing alone at one end of the room, looked about himself wildly, his face white. A gentle eddying of the men had crowded them slowly down toward the other end of the room, so that he stood quite alone. "My God, will you two Jeremiahs shut up?" Connant's voice shook. "What am I? Some kind of a microscopic specimen you're dissecting? Some unpleasant worm you're discussing in the third person?"

McReady looked up at him; his slowly twisting hands stopped for a moment. "Having a lovely time. Wish you were here. Signed: Everybody.

"Connant, if you think you're having a hell of a time, just move over on the other end for a while. You've got one thing we haven't; you know what the answer is. I'll tell you this, right now you're the most feared and respected man in Big Magnet."

"Lord, I wish you could see your eyes," Connant gasped. "Stop staring, will you! What the hell are you going to do?"

"Have you any suggestions, Doctor Copper?" Commander Garry asked steadily. "The present situation is impossible."

"Oh, is it?" Connant snapped. "Come over here and look at that crowd. By Heaven, they look exactly like that gang of huskies around the corridor bend. Benning, will you stop hefting that damned ice-ax?"

The coppery blade rang on the floor as the aviation mechanic nervously dropped it. He bent over and picked it up instantly, hefting it slowly, turning it in his hands, his brown eyes moving jerkily about the room.

Copper sat down on the bunk beside Blair. The wood creaked noisily in the room. Far down a corridor, a dog yelped in pain, and the dog drivers' tense voices floated softly back. "Microscopic examination," said the doctor thoughtfully, "would be useless, as Blair pointed out. Considerable time has passed. However, serum tests would be definitive."

"Serum tests? What do you mean exactly?" Commander Garry asked.

"If I had a rabbit that had been injected with human blood—a poison to rabbits, of course, as is the blood of any animal save that of another rabbit—and the injections continued in increasing doses for some time, the rabbit would be human-immune. If a small quantity of its blood were drawn off, allowed to separate in a test tube, and to the clear serum, a bit of human blood were added, there would be a visible reaction, proving the blood was human. If cow or dog blood were added—or any protein material other than that one thing, human blood—no reaction would take place. That would prove definitely."

"Can you suggest where I might catch a rabbit for you, Doc?"

Norris asked. "That is, nearer than Australia; we don't want to waste time going that far."

"I know there aren't any rabbits in Antarctica," Copper nodded, "but that is simply the usual animal. Any animal except man will do. A dog, for instance. But it will take several days, and due to the greater size of the animal, considerable blood. Two of us will have to contribute."

"Would I do?" Garry asked.

"That will make two," Copper nodded. "I'll get to work on it right away."

"What about Connant in the meantime?" Kinner demanded. "I'm going out that door and head off for the Ross Sea before I cook for him."

"He may be human—" Copper started.

Connant burst out in a flood of curses. "Human! *May* be human, you damned sawbones! What in hell do you think I am?"

"A monster," Copper snapped sharply. "Now shut up and listen." Connant's face drained of color and he sat down heavily as the indictment was put in words. "Until we know—you know as well as we do that we have reason to question the fact, and only you know how that question is to be answered—we may reasonably be expected to lock you up. If you are—unhuman—you're a lot more dangerous than poor Blair there, and I'm going to see that he's locked up thoroughly. I expect that his next stage will be a violent desire to kill you, all the dogs, and probably all of us. When he wakes, he will be convinced we're all unhuman, and nothing on the planet will ever change his conviction. It would be kinder to let him die, but we can't do that, of course. He's going in one shack, and you can stay in Cosmos House with your cosmic-ray apparatus. Which is about what you'd do anyway. I've got to fix up a couple of dogs."

Connant nodded bitterly. "I'm human. Hurry that test. Your eyes— Lord, I wish you could see your eyes staring—"

Commander Garry watched anxiously as Clark, the dog handler, held the big brown Alaskan husky, while Copper began the injection treatment. The dog was not anxious to cooperate; the needle was painful, and already he'd experienced considerable needle work that morning. Five stitches held closed a slash that ran from his shoulder, across the ribs, halfway down his body. One long fang was broken off short; the missing part was to be found half buried in the shoulder bone of the monstrous thing on the table in the Ad Building.

"How long will that take?" Garry asked, pressing his arm gently. It was sore from the prick of the needle Doctor Copper had used to withdraw blood.

Copper shrugged. "I don't know, to be frank. I know the general method. I've used it on rabbits. But I haven't experimented with dogs. They're big, clumsy animals to work with; naturally rabbits are preferable, and serve ordinarily. In civilized places you can buy a stock of human-immune rabbits from suppliers, and not many investigators take the trouble to prepare their own."

"What do they want with them back there?" Clark asked.

"Criminology is one large field. A says he didn't murder B, but that the blood on his shirt came from killing a chicken. The State makes a test, then it's up to A to explain how it is the blood reacts on human-immune rabbits, but not on chicken-immunes."

"What are we going to do with Blair in the meantime?" Garry asked wearily. "It's all right to let him sleep where he is for a while, but when he wakes up—"

"Barclay and Benning are fitting some bolts on the door of Cosmos House," Copper replied grimly. "Connant's acting like a gentleman. I think perhaps the way the other men look at him makes him rather want privacy. Lord knows, heretofore we've all of us individually prayed for a little privacy."

Clark laughed brittlely. "Not any more, thank you. The more the merrier."

"Blair," Copper went on, "will also have to have privacy—and locks. He's going to have a pretty definite plan in mind when he wakes up. Ever hear the old story of how to stop hoof-and-mouth disease in cattle?"

Clark and Garry shook their heads silently.

"If there isn't any hoof-and-mouth disease, there won't be any hoof-and-mouth disease," Copper explained. "You get rid of it by killing every animal that exhibits it, and every animal that's been near the diseased animal. Blair's a biologist, and knows that story. He's afraid of this thing we loosed. The answer is probably pretty clear in his mind now. Kill everybody and everything in this camp before a skua gull or a wandering albatross coming in with the spring chances out this way and—catches the disease."

Clark's lips curled in a twisted grin. "Sounds logical to me. If things get too bad—maybe we'd better let Blair get loose. It would save us committing suicide. We might also make something of a vow that if things get bad, we see that that does happen."

Copper laughed softly. "The last man alive in Big Magnet— wouldn't be a man," he pointed out. "Somebody's got to kill those— creatures that don't desire to kill themselves, you know. We don't have enough thermite to do it all at once, and the decanite explosive wouldn't help much. I have an idea that even small pieces of one of those beings would be self-sufficient."

"If," said Garry thoughtfully, "they can modify their protoplasm at will, won't they simply modify themselves to birds and fly away? They can read all about birds, and imitate their structure without even meeting them. Or imitate, perhaps, birds of their home planet."

Copper shook his head, and helped Clark to free the dog. "Man studied birds for centuries, trying to learn how to make a machine to fly like them. He never did do the trick; his final success came when he broke away entirely and tried new methods. Knowing the general idea, and knowing the detailed structure of wing and bone and nerve tissue is something far, far different. And as for other-world birds, perhaps, in fact very probably, the atmospheric conditions here are so vastly different that their birds couldn't fly. Perhaps, even, the being came from a planet like Mars with such a thin atmosphere that there were no birds."

Barclay came into the building, trailing a length of airplane control cable. "It's finished, Doc. Cosmos House can't be opened from the inside. Now where do we put Blair?"

Copper looked toward Garry. "There wasn't any biology building. I don't know where we can isolate him."

"How about East Cache?" Garry said after a moment's thought. "Will Blair be able to look after himself—or need attention?"

"He'll be capable enough. We'll be the ones to watch out," Copper assured him grimly. "Take a stove, a couple of bags of coal, necessary supplies, and a few tools to fix it up. Nobody's been out there since last fall, have they?"

Garry shook his head. "If he gets noisy—I thought that might be a good idea."

Barclay hefted the tools he was carrying and looked up at Garry. "If the muttering he's doing now is any sign, he's going to sing away the night hours. And we won't like his song."

"What's he saying?" Copper asked.

Barclay shook his head. "I didn't care to listen much. You can if you want to. But I gathered that the blasted idiot had all the dreams McReady had, and a few more. He slept beside the thing when we stopped on the trail coming in from Secondary Magnetic, remember. He dreamed the thing was alive, and dreamed more details. And— damn his soul—knew it wasn't all dream, or had reason to. He knew it had telepathic powers that were stirring vaguely, and that it could not only read minds, but project thoughts. They weren't dreams, you see.

They were stray thoughts that thing was broadcasting, the way Blair's broadcasting his thoughts now—a sort of telepathic muttering in its sleep. That's why he knew so much about its powers. I guess you and I, Doc, weren't so sensitive—if you want to believe in telepathy."

"I have to," Copper sighed. "Doctor Rhine of Duke University has shown that it exists, shown that some are much more sensitive than others."

"Well, if you want to learn a lot of details, go listen in on Blair's broadcast. He's driven most of the boys out of the Ad Building; Kinner's rattling pans like coal going down a chute. When he can't rattle a pan, he shakes ashes."

"By the way, Commander, what are we going to do this spring, now the planes are out of it?"

Garry sighed. "I'm afraid our expedition is going to be a loss. We cannot divide our strength now."

"It won't be a loss—if we continue to live, and come out of this," Copper promised him. "The find we've made, if we can get it under control, is important enough. The cosmic-ray data, magnetic work, and atmospheric work won't be greatly hindered."

Garry laughed mirthlessly. "I was just thinking of the radio broadcasts. Telling half the world about the wonderful results of our exploration flights, trying to fool men like Byrd and Ellsworth back home there that we're doing something."

Copper nodded gravely. "They'll know something's wrong. But men like that have judgment enough to know we wouldn't do tricks without some sort of reason, and will wait for our return to judge us. I think it comes to this: men who know enough to recognize our deception will wait for our return. Men who haven't discretion and faith enough to wait will not have the experience to detect any fraud. We know enough of the conditions here to put through a good bluff."

"Just so they don't send 'rescue' expeditions," Garry prayed. "When—if—we're ever ready to come out, we'll have to send word to Captain Forsythe to bring a stock of magnetos with him when he comes down. But—never mind that."

"You mean if we don't come out?" asked Barclay. "I was wondering if a nice running account of an eruption or an earthquake via radio—with a swell wind up by using a stick of decanite under the microphone—would help. Nothing, of course, will entirely keep people out. One of those swell, melodramatic 'last-man-alive scenes' might make 'em go easy, though."

Garry smiled with genuine humor. "Is everybody in camp trying to figure that out, too?"

Copper laughed. "What do you think, Garry? We're confident we can win out. But not too easy about it, I guess."

Clark grinned up from the dog he was petting into calmness. "Confident, did you say, Doc?"

## VIII

Blair moved restlessly around the small shack. His eyes jerked and quivered in vague, fleeting glances at the four men with him: Barclay, six feet tall and weighing over 190 pounds; McReady, a bronze giant of a man; Doctor Copper, short, squatly powerful; and Benning, five-feet-ten of wiry strength.

Blair was huddled up against the far wall of the East Cache cabin, his gear piled in the middle of the floor beside the heating-stove, forming an island between him and the four men. His bony hands clenched and fluttered, terrified. His pale eyes wavered uneasily as his bald, freckled head darted about in birdlike motion.

"I don't want anybody coming here. I'll cook my own food," he snapped nervously. "Kinner may be human now, but I don't believe it. I'm going to get out of here, but I'm not going to eat any food you send me. I want cans. Sealed cans."

"Okay, Blair, we'll bring 'em tonight," Barclay promised. "You've got coal, and the fire's started. I'll make a last—" Barclay started forward.

Blair instantly scurried to the farthest corner. "Get out! Keep away from me, you monster!" the little biologist shrieked, and tried to claw his way through the wall of the shack. "Keep away from me—keep away—I won't be absorbed—I won't be—"

Barclay relaxed and moved back. Doctor Copper shook his head. "Leave him alone, Bar. It's easier for him to fix the thing himself. We'll have to fix the door, I think—"

The four men let themselves out. Efficiently, Benning and Barclay fell to work. There were no locks in Antarctica; there wasn't enough privacy to make them needed. But powerful screws had been driven in each side of the door frame, and the spare aviation control cable, immensely strong woven steel wire, was rapidly caught between them and drawn taut. Barclay went to work with a drill and a keyhole saw. Presently he had a trap cut in the door through which goods could be passed without unlashing the entrance. Three powerful hinges from a stock crate, two hasps and a pair of three-inch cotter-pins made it proof against opening from the other side.

Blair moved about restlessly inside. He was dragging something over to the door with panting gasps, and muttering frantic curses.

Barclay opened the hatch and glanced in, Doctor Copper peering over his shoulder. Blair had moved the heavy bunk against the door. It could not be opened without his cooperation now.

"Don't know but what the poor man's right at that," McReady sighed. "If he gets loose, it is his avowed intention to kill each and all of us as quickly as possible, which is something we don't agree with. But we've something on our side of that door that is worse than a homicidal maniac. If one or the other has to get loose, I think I'll come up and undo these lashings here."

Barclay grinned. "You let me know, and I'll show you how to get these off fast. Let's go back."

The sun was painting the northern horizon in multi-colored rainbows still, though it was two hours below the horizon. The field of drift swept off to the north, sparkling under its flaming colors in a million reflected glories. Low mounds of rounded white on the northern horizon showed the Magnet Range was barely awash above the sweeping drift. Little eddies of wind-lifted snow swirled away from their skis as they set out toward the main encampment two miles away. The spidery finger of the broadcast radiator lifted a gaunt black needle against the white of the Antarctic continent. The snow under their skis was like fine sand, hard and gritty.

"Spring," said Benning bitterly, "is come. Ain't we got fun! And I've been looking forward to getting away from this blasted hole in the ice."

"I wouldn't try it now, if I were you." Barclay grunted. "Guys that set out from here in the next few days are going to be marvelously unpopular."

"How is your dog getting along, Doctor Copper?" McReady asked. "Any results yet?"

"In thirty hours? I wish there were. I gave him an injection of my blood today. But I imagine another five days will be needed. I don't know certainly enough to stop sooner."

"I've been wondering—if Connant were—changed, would he have warned us so soon after the animal escaped? Wouldn't he have waited long enough for it to have a real chance to fix itself? Until we woke up naturally?" McReady asked slowly.

"The thing is selfish. You didn't think it looked as though it were possessed of a store of the higher justices, did you?" Doctor Copper pointed out. "Every part of it is all of it, every part of it is all for itself, I imagine. If Connant were changed, to save his skin, he'd have to— but Connant's feelings aren't changed; they're imitated perfectly, or they're his own. Naturally, the imitation, imitating perfectly Connant's feelings, would do exactly what Connant would do."

"Say, couldn't Norris or Vane give Connant some kind of a test? If the thing is brighter than men, it might know more physics than Connant should, and they'd catch it out," Barclay suggested.

Copper shook his head wearily. "Not if it reads minds. You can't plan a trap for it. Vane suggested that last night. He hoped it would answer some of the questions of physics he'd like to know answers to."

"This expedition-of-four idea is going to make life happy." Benning looked at his companions. "Each of us with an eye on the other to make sure he doesn't do something—peculiar. Man, aren't we going to be a trusting bunch! Each man eyeing his neighbors with the grandest exhibition of faith and trust—I'm beginning to know what Connant meant by 'I wish you could see your eyes.' Every now and then we all have it, I guess. One of you looks around with a sort of I-wonder-if-the-other-*three*-are look.' Incidentally, I'm not excepting myself."

"So far as we know, the animal is dead, with a slight question as to Connant. No other is suspected," McReady stated slowly. "The always-four order is merely a precautionary measure."

"I'm waiting for Garry to make it four-in-a-bunk," Barclay sighed. "I thought I didn't have any privacy before, but since that order—"

## IX

None watched more tensely than Connant. A little sterile glass test tube, half filled with straw-colored fluid. One—two—three—four—five drops of the clear solution Doctor Copper had prepared from the drops of blood from Connant's arm. The tube was shaken carefully, then set in a beaker of clear, warm water. The thermometer read blood heat, a little thermostat clicked noisily, and the electric hotplate began to glow as the lights flickered slightly. Then—little white flecks of precipitation were forming, snowing down in the clear straw-colored fluid. "Lord," said Connant. He dropped heavily into a bunk, crying like a baby. "Six days—" Connant sobbed, "six days in there—wondering if that damned test would lie—"

Garry moved over silently, and slipped his arm across the physicist's back.

"It couldn't lie," Doctor Copper said. "The dog was human-immune—and the serum reacted."

"He's—all right?" Norris gasped. "Then—the animal is dead—dead forever?"

"He is human," Copper spoke definitely, "and the animal is dead."

Kinner burst out laughing, laughing hysterically. McReady turned toward him and slapped his face with a methodical one-two, one-two action. The cook laughed, gulped, cried a moment, and sat up rubbing his cheeks, mumbling his thanks vaguely. "I was scared. Lord, I was scared—"

Norris laughed brittlely. "You think we weren't, you ape? You think maybe Connant wasn't?"

The Ad Building stirred with a sudden rejuvenation. Voices laughed, the men clustering around Connant spoke with unnecessarily loud voices, jittery, nervous voices relievedly friendly again. Somebody called out a suggestion, and a dozen started for their skis. Blair, Blair might recover— Doctor Copper fussed with his test tubes in nervous relief, trying solutions. The party of relief for Blair's shack started out the door, skis clapping noisily. Down the corridor, the dogs set up a quick yelping howl as the air of excited relief reached them.

Doctor Copper fussed with his tubes. McReady noticed him first, sitting on the edge of the bunk, with two precipitin-whitened test tubes of straw-colored fluid, his face whiter than the stuff in the tubes, silent tears slipping down from horror-widened eyes.

McReady felt a cold knife of fear pierce through his heart and freeze in his breast. Doctor Copper looked up. "Garry," he called hoarsely. "Garry, for God's sake, come here."

Commander Garry walked toward him sharply. Silence clapped down on the Ad Building. Connant looked up, rose stiffly from his seat.

"Garry—tissue from the monster—precipitates, too. It proves nothing. Nothing but—but the dog was monster-immune too. That *one of the two contributing blood—one of us two,* you and I, Garry—*one of us is a monster.*"

## X

"Bar, call back those men before they tell Blair," McReady said quietly. Barclay went to the door; faintly his shouts came back to the tensely silent men in the room. Then he was back.

"They're coming," he said. "I didn't tell them why. Just that Doctor Copper said not to go."

"McReady," Garry sighed, "you're in command now. May God help you. I cannot."

The bronzed giant nodded slowly, his deep eyes on Commander Garry.

"I may be the one," Garry added. "I know I'm not, but I cannot prove it to you in any way. Doctor Copper's test has broken down. The fact that he showed it was useless, when it was to the advantage of the monster to have that uselessness not known, would seem to prove he was human."

Copper rocked back and forth slowly on the bunk. "I know I'm human. I can't prove it either. One of us two is a liar, for that test cannot lie, and it says one of us is. I gave proof that the test was wrong, which seems to prove I'm human, and now Garry has given that argument which proves me human—which he, as the monster, should not do. Round and round and round and round and—"

Doctor Copper's head, then his neck and shoulders began circling slowly in time to the words. Suddenly he was lying back on the bunk, roaring with laughter. "It doesn't have to prove *one* of us is a monster! It doesn't have to prove that at all! Ho-ho. If we're *all* monsters it works the same—we're all monsters—all of us—Connant and Garry and I—and all of you."

"McReady," Van Wall, the blond-bearded Chief Pilot, called softly, "you were on the way to an M.D. when you took up meteorology, weren't you? Can you make some kind of test?"

McReady went over to Copper slowly, took the hypodermic from his hand, and washed it carefully in ninety-five percent alcohol. Garry sat on the bunk edge with wooden face, watching Copper and McReady expressionlessly. "What Copper said is possible." McReady sighed. "Van, will you help here? Thanks." The filled needle jabbed into Copper's thigh. The man's laughter did not stop, but slowly faded into sobs, then sound sleep as the morphia took hold.

McReady turned again. The men who had started for Blair stood at the far end of the room, skis dripping snow, their faces as white as their skis. Connant had a lighted cigarette in each hand; one he was puffing absently, and staring at the floor. The heat of the one in his left hand attracted him and he stared at it and the one in the other hand stupidly for a moment. He dropped one and crushed it under his heel slowly.

"Doctor Copper," McReady repeated, "could be right. I know I'm human—but, of course, can't prove it. I'll repeat the test for my own information. Any of you others who wish to may do the same."

Two minutes later, McReady held a test tube with white precipitin settling slowly from straw-colored serum. "It reacts to human blood too, so they aren't both monsters."

"I didn't think they were," Van Wall sighed. "That wouldn't suit the monster, either; we could have destroyed them if we knew. Why hasn't the monster destroyed us, do you suppose? It seems to be loose."

McReady snorted. Then laughed softly. "Elementary, my dear Watson. The monster wants to have life forms available. It cannot animate a dead body, apparently. It is just waiting—waiting until the best opportunities come. We who remain human, it is holding in reserve."

Kinner shuddered violently. "Hey. Hey, Mac. Mac, would I know if I was a monster? Would I know if the monster had already got me? Oh, Lord, I may be a monster already."

"You'd know," McReady answered.

"But we wouldn't." Norris laughed shortly, half hysterically.

McReady looked at the vial of serum remaining. "There's one thing this damned stuff is good for, at that," he said thoughtfully. "Clark, will you and Van help me? The rest of the gang better stick together here. Keep an eye on each other," he said bitterly. "See that you don't get into mischief, shall we say?"

McReady started down the tunnel toward Dog Town, with Clark and Van Wall behind him. "You need more serum?" Clark asked.

McReady shook his head. "Tests. There's four cows and a bull, and nearly seventy dogs down there. This stuff reacts only to human blood and—monsters."

XI

McReady came back to the Ad Building and went silently to the washstand. Clark and Van Wall joined him a moment later. Clark's lips had developed a tic, jerking into sudden, unexpected sneers.

"What did you do?" Connant exploded suddenly. "More immunizing?"

Clark snickered, and stopped with a hiccup. "Immunizing. Haw! Immune all right."

"That monster," said Van Wall steadily, "is quite logical. Our immune dog was quite all right, and we drew a little more serum for the tests. But we won't make any more."

"Can't—can't you use one man's blood on another dog?" Norris began.

"There aren't," said McReady softly, "any more dogs. Nor cattle, I might add."

"No more dogs?" Benning sat down slowly.

"They're very nasty when they start changing," Van Wall said precisely. "But slow. That electrocution iron you made up, Barclay, is very fast. There is only one dog left—our immune. The monster left that for us, so we could play with our little test. The rest—" He shrugged and dried his hands.

"The cattle—" gulped Kinner.

"Also. Reacted very nicely. They look funny as hell when they start melting. The beast hasn't any quick escape, when it's tied in dog chains, or halters, and it had to be to imitate."

Kinner stood up slowly. His eyes darted around the room, and came to rest horribly quivering on a tin bucket in the galley. Slowly, step by step he retreated toward the door, his mouth opening and closing silently, like a fish out of water.

"The milk—" he gasped. "I milked 'em an hour ago—" His voice broke into a scream as he dived through the door. He was out on the ice cap without windproof or heavy clothing.

Van Wall looked after him for a moment thoughtfully. "He's probably hopelessly mad," he said at length, "but he might be a monster escaping. He hasn't skis. Take a blowtorch—in case."

The physical motion of the chase helped them; something that needed doing. Three of the other men were quietly being sick. Norris was lying flat on his back, his face greenish, looking steadily at the bottom of the bunk above him.

"Mac, how long have the—cows been not-cows—"

McReady shrugged his shoulders hopelessly. He went over to the milk bucket and with his little tube of serum went to work on it. The milk clouded it, making certainty difficult. Finally he dropped the test tube into the stand, and shook his head. "It tests negatively. Which means either they were cows then, or that, being perfect imitations, they gave perfectly good milk."

Copper stirred restlessly in his sleep and gave a gurgling cross between a snore and a laugh. Silent eyes fastened on him. "Would morphia—a monster—" somebody started to ask.

"Lord knows," McReady shrugged. "It affects every earthly animal I know of."

Connant suddenly raised his head. "Mac! The dogs must have swallowed pieces of the monster, and the pieces destroyed them! The dogs were where the monster resided. I was locked up. Doesn't that prove—"

Van Wall shook his head. "Sorry. Proves nothing about what you are, only proves what you didn't do."

"It doesn't do that," McReady sighed. "We are helpless because we don't know enough, and so jittery we don't think straight. Locked up! Ever watch a white corpuscle of the blood go through the wall of a blood vessel? No? It sticks out a pseudopod. And there it is—on the far side of the wall."

"Oh," said Van Wall unhappily. "The cattle tried to melt down, didn't they? They could have melted down—become just a thread of

stuff and leaked under a door to re-collect on the other side. Ropes—
no—no, that wouldn't do it. They couldn't live in a sealed tank or—"

"If," said McReady, "you shoot it through the heart, and it doesn't
die, it's a monster. That's the best test I can think of, offhand."

"No dogs," said Garry quietly, "and no cattle. It has to imitate
men now. And locking up doesn't do any good. Your test might work,
Mac, but I'm afraid it would be hard on the men."

XII

Clark looked up from the galley stove as Van Wall, Barclay, McReady,
and Benning came in, brushing the drift from their clothes. The other
men jammed into the Ad Building continued studiously to do as they
were doing, playing chess, poker, reading. Ralsen was fixing a sledge
on the table; Vane and Norris had their heads together over magnetic
data, while Harvey read tables in a low voice.

Doctor Copper snored softly on the bunk. Garry was working with
Dutton over a sheaf of radio messages on the corner of Dutton's bunk
and a small fraction of the radio table. Connant was using most of the
table for cosmic-ray sheets.

Quite plainly through the corridor, despite two closed doors, they
could hear Kinner's voice. Clark banged a kettle onto the galley stove
and beckoned McReady silently. The meteorologist went over to him.

"I don't mind the cooking so damn much," Clark said nervously,
"but isn't there some way to stop that bird? We all agreed that it
would be safe to move him into Cosmos House."

"Kinner?" McReady nodded toward the door. "I'm afraid not. I
can dope him, I suppose, but we don't have an unlimited supply of
morphia, and he's not in danger of losing his mind. Just hysterical."

"Well, we're in danger of losing ours. You've been out for an hour
and a half. That's been going on steadily ever since, and it was going
for two hours before. There's a limit, you know."

Garry wandered over slowly, apologetically. For an instant,
McReady caught the feral spark of fear—horror—in Clark's eyes, and
knew at the same instant it was in his own. Garry—Garry or Copper—was certainly a monster.

"If you could stop that, I think it would be a sound policy, Mac,"
Garry spoke quietly. "There are—tensions enough in this room. We
agreed that it would be safe for Kinner in there, because everyone else
in camp is under constant eyeing." Garry shivered slightly. "And try,
try in God's name, to find some test that will work."

McReady sighed. "Watched or unwatched, everyone's tense. Blair's jammed the trap so it won't open now. Says he's got food enough, and keeps screaming, 'Go away, go away—you're monsters. I won't be absorbed. I won't. I'll tell men when they come. Go away.' So—we went away."

"There's no other test?" Garry pleaded.

McReady shrugged his shoulders. "Copper was perfectly right. The serum test could be absolutely definitive if it hadn't been—contaminated. But that's the only dog left, and he's fixed now."

"Chemicals? Chemical tests?"

McReady shook his head. "Our chemistry isn't that good. I tried the microscope, you know."

Garry nodded. "Monster-dog and real dog were identical. But—you've got to go on. What are we going to do after dinner?"

Van Wall had joined them quietly. "Rotation sleeping. Half the crowd sleep; half stay awake. I wonder how many of us are monsters? All the dogs were. We thought we were safe, but somehow it got Copper—or you." Van Wall's eyes flashed uneasily. "It may have gotten every one of you—all of you but myself may be wondering, looking. No, that's not possible. You'd just spring then, I'd be helpless. We humans must somehow have the greater numbers now. But—" he stopped.

McReady laughed shortly. "You're doing what Norris complained of in me. Leaving it hanging. 'But if one more is changed—that may shift the balance of power.' It doesn't fight. I don't think it ever fights. It must be a peaceable thing, in its own—inimitable—way. It never had to, because it always gained its end otherwise."

Van Wall's mouth twisted in a sickly grin. "You're suggesting, then, that perhaps it already *has* the greater numbers, but is just waiting—waiting, all of them—all of you, for all I know—waiting till I, the last human, drop my wariness in sleep. Mac, did you notice their eyes, all looking at us?"

Garry sighed. "You haven't been sitting here for four straight hours, while all their eyes silently weighed the information that one of us two, Copper or I, is a monster certainly—perhaps both of us."

Clark repeated his request. "Will you stop that bird's noise? He's driving me nuts. Make him tone down, anyway."

"Still praying?" McReady asked.

"Still praying," Clark groaned. "He hasn't stopped for a second. I don't mind his praying if it relieves him, but he yells, he sings psalms and hymns and shouts prayers. He thinks God can't hear well way down here."

"Maybe He can't," Barclay grunted. "Or He'd have done something about this thing loosed from hell."

"Somebody's going to try that test you mentioned, if you don't stop him," Clark stated grimly. "I think a cleaver in the head would be as positive a test as a bullet in the heart."

"Go ahead with the food. I'll see what I can do. There may be something in the cabinets." McReady moved wearily toward the corner Copper had used as his dispensary. Three tall cabinets of rough boards, two locked, were the repositories of the camp's medical supplies. Twelve years ago, McReady had graduated, started for an internship, and been diverted to meteorology. Copper was a picked man, a man who knew his profession thoroughly and modernly. More than half the drugs available were totally unfamiliar to McReady; many of the others he had forgotten. There was no huge medical library here, no series of journals available to learn the things he had forgotten, the elementary, simple things to Copper, things that did not merit inclusion in the small library he had been forced to content himself with. Books are heavy, and every ounce of supplies had been freighted in by air.

McReady picked a barbiturate hopefully. Barclay and Van Wall went with him. One man never went anywhere alone in Big Magnet.

Ralsen had his sledge put away, and the physicists had moved off the table, the poker game broken up when they got back. Clark was putting out the food. The click of spoons and the muffled sounds of eating were the only sign of life in the room. There were no words spoken as the three returned; simply all eyes focused on them questioningly while the jaws moved methodically.

McReady stiffened suddenly. Kinner was screeching out a hymn in a hoarse, cracked voice. He looked wearily at Van Wall with a twisted grin and shook his head. "Uh-uh."

Van Wall cursed bitterly and sat down at the table. "We'll just plumb have to take that till his voice wears out. He can't yell like that forever."

"He's got a brass throat and a cast-iron larynx," Norris declared savagely. "Then we could be hopeful, and suggest he's one of our friends. In that case he could go on renewing his throat till doomsday."

Silence clamped down. For twenty minutes they ate without a word. Then Connant jumped up with an angry violence. "You sit as still as a bunch of graven images. You don't say a word, but oh, Lord, what expressive eyes you've got. They roll around like a bunch of glass marbles spilling down a table. They wink and blink and stare—and whisper things. Can you guys look somewhere else for a change, please?"

"Listen, Mac, you're in charge here. Let's run movies for the rest of the night. We've been saving those reels to make 'em last. Last for what? Who is it's going to see those last reels, eh? Let's see 'em while we can, and look at something other than each other."

"Sound idea, Connant. I, for one, am quite willing to change this in any way I can."

"Turn the sound up loud, Dutton. Maybe you can drown out the hymns," Clark suggested.

"But don't," Norris said softly, "don't turn off the lights altogether."

"The lights will be out." McReady shook his head. "We'll show all the cartoon movies we have. You won't mind seeing the old cartoons, will you?"

"Goody, goody—a moom-pitcher show. I'm just in the mood." McReady turned to look at the speaker, a lean, lanky New Englander, by the name of Caldwell. Caldwell was stuffing his pipe slowly, a sour eye cocked up to McReady.

The bronze giant was forced to laugh. "Okay, Bart, you win. Maybe we aren't quite in the mood for Popeye and trick ducks, but it's something."

"Let's play Classifications," Caldwell suggested slowly. "Or maybe you call it Guggenheim. You draw lines on a piece of paper, and put down classes of things—like animals, you know. One for 'H' and one for 'U' and so on. Like 'Human' and 'Unknown' for instance. I think that would be a hell of a lot better game. Classifications, I sort of figure, is what we need right now a lot more than movies. Maybe somebody's got a pencil that he can draw lines with, draw lines between the 'U' animals and the 'H' animals for instance."

"McReady's trying to find that kind of a pencil," Van Wall answered quietly, "but we've got three kinds of animals here, you know. One that begins with 'M.' We don't want any more."

"Mad ones, you mean. Uh-huh. Clark, I'll help you with those pots so we can get our little peep show going." Caldwell got up slowly.

Dutton and Barclay and Benning, in charge of the projector and sound mechanism arrangements, went about their job silently, while the Ad Building was cleared and the dishes and pans disposed of. McReady drifted over toward Van Wall slowly, and leaned back in the bunk beside him. "I've been wondering, Van," he said with a wry grin, "whether or not to report my ideas in advance. I forgot the 'U animal' as Caldwell named it, could read minds. I've a vague idea of something that might work. It's too vague to bother with, though. Go ahead with your show, while I try to figure out the logic of the thing. I'll take this bunk."

Van Wall glanced up and nodded. The movie screen would be practically on a line with this bunk, hence making the pictures least distracting here, because least intelligible. "Perhaps you should tell us what you have in mind. As it is, only the unknowns know what you plan. You might be—unknown before you got it into operation."

"Won't take long, if I get it figured out right. But I don't want any more all-but-the-test-dog-monsters things. We better move Copper into this bunk directly above me. He won't be watching the screen, either." McReady nodded toward Copper's gently snoring bulk. Garry helped them lift and move the doctor.

McReady leaned back against the bunk and sank into a trance, almost, of concentration, trying to calculate chances, operations, methods. He was scarcely aware as the others distributed themselves silently, and the screen lit up. Vaguely Kinner's hectic, shouted prayers and his rasping hymn-singing annoyed him till the sound accompaniment started. The lights were turned out, but the large, light-colored areas of the screen reflected enough light for ready visibility. It made men's eyes sparkle as they moved restlessly. Kinner was still praying, shouting, his voice a raucous accompaniment to the mechanical sound. Dutton stepped up the amplification.

So long had the voice been going on that only vaguely at first was McReady aware that something seemed missing. Lying as he was, just across the narrow room from the corridor leading to Cosmos House, Kinner's voice had reached him fairly clearly, despite the sound accompaniment of the pictures. It struck him abruptly that it had stopped.

"Dutton, cut that sound," McReady called as he sat up abruptly. The pictures flickered a moment, soundless and strangely futile in the sudden, deep silence. The rising wind on the surface above bubbled melancholy tears of sound down the stove pipes. "Kinner's stopped," McReady said softly.

"For God's sake start that sound, then; he may have stopped to listen," Norris snapped.

McReady rose and went down the corridor. Barclay and Van Wall left their places at the far end of the room to follow him. The flickers bulged and twisted on the back of Barclay's gray underwear as he crossed the still-functioning beam of the projector. Dutton snapped on the lights, and the pictures vanished.

Norris stood at the door as McReady had asked. Garry sat down quietly in the bunk nearest the door, forcing Clark to make room for him. Most of the others had stayed exactly where they were. Only Connant walked slowly up and down the room, in steady, unvarying rhythm.

"If you're going to do that, Connant," Clark spat, "we can get along without you altogether, whether you're human or not. Will you stop that damned rhythm?"

"Sorry." The physicist sat down in a bunk and watched his toes thoughtfully. It was almost five minutes, five ages, while the wind made the only sound, before McReady appeared at the door.

"We," he announced, "haven't got enough grief here already. Somebody's tried to help us out. Kinner has a knife in his throat, which was why he stopped singing, probably. We've got monsters, madmen and murderers. Any more 'M's' you can think of, Caldwell? If there are, we'll probably have 'em before long."

### XIII

"Is Blair loose?" someone asked.

"Blair is not loose. Or he flew in. If there's any doubt about where our gentle helper came from—this may clear it up." Van Wall held a foot-long, thin-bladed knife in a cloth. The wooden handle was half burned, charred with the peculiar pattern of the top of the galley stove.

Clark stared at it. "I did that this afternoon. I forgot the damn thing and left it on the stove."

Van Wall nodded. "I smelled it, if you remember. I knew the knife came from the galley."

"I wonder," said Benning looking around at the party warily, "how many more monsters have we? If somebody could slip out of his place, go back of the screen to the galley and then down to the Cosmos House and back—he did come back, didn't he? Yes—everybody's here. Well, if one of the gang could do all that—"

"Maybe a monster did it," Garry suggested quietly. "There's that possibility."

"The monster, as you pointed out today, has only men left to imitate. Would he decrease his—supply, shall we say?" Van Wall pointed out. "No, we just have a plain, ordinary louse, a murderer to deal with. Ordinarily we'd call him an 'inhuman murderer,' I suppose, but we have to distinguish now. We have inhuman murderers, and now we have human murderers. Or one, at least."

"There's one less human," Norris said softly. "Maybe the monsters have the balance of power now."

"Never mind that." McReady sighed and turned to Barclay. "Bar, will you get your electric gadget? I'm going to make certain—"

Barclay turned down the corridor to get the pronged electrocuter, while McReady and Van Wall went back toward Cosmos House. Barclay followed them in some thirty seconds.

The corridor to Cosmos House twisted, as did nearly all corridors in Big Magnet, and Norris stood at the entrance again. But they heard, rather muffled, McReady's sudden shout. There was a savage flurry of blows, dull *ch-thunk, shluff* sounds. "Bar—Bar—" And a curious, savage mewing scream, silenced before even quick-moving Norris had reached the bend.

Kinner—or what had been Kinner—lay on the floor, cut half in two by the great knife McReady had had. The meteorologist stood against the wall, the knife dripping red in his hand. Van Wall was stirring vaguely on the floor, moaning, his hand half-consciously rubbing at his jaw. Barclay, an unutterably savage gleam in his eyes, was methodically leaning on the pronged weapon in his hand, jabbing—jabbing, jabbing.

Kinner's arms had developed a queer, scaly fur, and the flesh had twisted. The fingers had shortened, the hand rounded, the fingernails become three-inch-long things of dull red horn, keened to steel-hard, razor-sharp talons.

McReady raised his head, looked at the knife in his hand, and dropped it. "Well, whoever did it can speak up now. He was an inhuman murderer at that—in that he murdered an inhuman. I swear by all that's holy, Kinner was a lifeless corpse on the floor here when we arrived. But when It found we were going to jab It with the power—It changed."

Norris stared unsteadily. "Oh, Lord, those things can act. Ye gods—sitting in here for hours, mouthing prayers to a God it hated! Shouting hymns in a cracked voice—hymns about a Church it never knew. Driving us mad with its ceaseless howling—"

"Well. Speak up, whoever did it. You didn't know it, but you did the camp a favor. And I want to know how in blazes you got out of the room without anyone seeing you. It might help in guarding ourselves."

"His screaming—his singing. Even the sound projector couldn't drown it." Clark shivered. "It was a monster."

"Oh," said Van Wall in sudden comprehension. "You were sitting right next to the door, weren't you? And almost behind the projection screen already."

Clark nodded dumbly. "He—it's quiet now. It's a dead— Mac, your test's no damn good. It was dead anyway, monster or man, it was dead."

McReady chuckled softly. "Boys, meet Clark, the only one we know is human! Meet Clark, the one who proves he's human by trying to commit murder—and failing. Will the rest of you please refrain from trying to prove you're human for a while? I think we may have another test."

"A test!" Connant snapped joyfully, then his face sagged in disappointment. "I suppose it's another either-way-you-want-it."

"No," said McReady steadily. "Look sharp and be careful. Come into the Ad Building. Barclay, bring your electrocuter. And somebody—Dutton—stand with Barclay to make sure he does it. Watch every neighbor, for by the hell these monsters came from, I've got something, and they know it. They're going to get dangerous!"

The group tensed abruptly. An air of crushing menace entered into every man's body, sharply they looked at each other. More keenly than ever before—*is that man next to me an inhuman monster?*

"What is it?" Garry asked, as they stood again in the main room. "How long will it take?"

"I don't know, exactly," said McReady, his voice brittle with angry determination. "But I *know* it will work, and no two ways about it. It depends on a basic quality of the *monsters,* not on us. 'Kinner' just convinced me." He stood heavy and solid in bronzed immobility, completely sure of himself again at last.

"This," said Barclay, hefting the wooden-handled weapon tipped with its two sharp-pointed, charged conductors,' "is going to be rather necessary, I take it. Is the power plant assured?"

Dutton nodded sharply. "The automatic stoker bin is full. The gas power plant is on standby. Van Wall and I set it for the movie operation—and we've checked it over rather carefully several times, you know. Anything those wires touch, dies," he assured them grimly. "*I* know that."

Doctor Copper stirred vaguely in his bunk, rubbed his eyes with fumbling hand. He sat up slowly, blinked his eyes blurred with sleep and drugs, widened with an unutterable horror of drug-ridden nightmares. "Garry," he mumbled, "Garry—listen. Selfish—from hell they came, and hellish shellfish—I mean self— Do I? What do I mean?" He sank back in his bunk and snored softly.

McReady looked at him thoughtfully. "We'll know presently." He nodded slowly. "But selfish is what you mean, all right. You may have thought of that, half sleeping, dreaming there. I didn't stop to think what dreams you might be having. But that's all right. Selfish is the word. They must be, you see." He turned to the men in the cabin, tense, silent men staring with wolfish eyes each at his neighbor. "Selfish, and as Doctor Copper said—*every part is a whole.* Every piece is self-sufficient, an animal in itself.

"That, and one other thing, tell the story. There's nothing mysterious about blood; it's just as normal a body tissue as a piece of muscle, or a piece of liver. But it hasn't so much connective tissue, though it has millions, billions of life cells."

McReady's great bronze beard ruffled in a grim smile. "This is satisfying, in a way. I'm pretty sure we humans still outnumber you—others. Others standing here. And we have what you, your other-world race, evidently doesn't. Not an imitated, but a bred-in-the-bone instinct, a driving, unquenchable fire that's genuine. We'll fight, fight with a ferocity you may attempt to imitate, but you'll never equal! We're human. We're real. You're imitations, false to the core of your every cell."

"All right. It's a showdown now. *You* know. You, with your mind reading. You've lifted the idea from my brain. You can't do a thing about it.

"Standing here—

"Let it pass. Blood is tissue. They have to bleed; if they don't bleed when cut, then by Heaven, they're phony from hell! If they bleed—then that blood, separated from them, is an individual—*a newly formed individual in its own right, just as they—split, all of them, from one original—are individuals!*

"Get it, Van? See the answer, Bar?"

Van Wall laughed very softly. "The blood—the blood will not obey. It's a new individual, with all the desire to protect its own life that the original—the main mass from which it was split—has. The *blood* will live—and try to crawl away from a hot needle, say!"

McReady picked up the scalpel from the table. From the cabinet he took a rack of test tubes, a tiny alcohol lamp, and a length of platinum wire set in a little glass rod. A smile of grim satisfaction rode his lips. For a moment he glanced up at those around him. Barclay and Dutton moved toward him slowly, the wooden-handled electric instrument alert.

"Dutton," said McReady, "suppose you stand over by the splice there where you've connected that in. Just make sure no—thing pulls it loose."

Dutton moved away. "Now, Van, suppose you be first on this."

White-faced, Van Wall stepped forward. With a delicate precision, McReady cut a vein in the base of his thumb. Van Wall winced slightly, then held steady as a half inch of bright blood collected in the tube. McReady put the tube in the rack, gave Van Wall a bit of alum, and indicated the iodine bottle.

Van Wall stood motionlessly watching. McReady heated the platinum wire in the alcohol lamp flame, then dipped it into the tube. It hissed softly. Five times he repeated the test. "Human, I'd say." McReady sighed, and straightened. "As yet, my theory hasn't been actually proven—but I have hopes. I have hopes."

"Don't, by the way, get too interested in this. We have with us some unwelcome ones, no doubt. Van, will you relieve Barclay at the switch? Thanks. OK, Barclay, and may I say I hope you stay with us? You're a damned good guy."

Barclay grinned uncertainly; winced under the keen edge of the scalpel. Presently, smiling widely, he retrieved his long-handled weapon.

"Mr. Samuel Dutt—*Bar!*"

The tensity was released in that second. Whatever of hell the monsters may have had within them, the men in that instant matched it. Barclay had no chance to move his weapon, as a score of men poured down on the thing that had seemed Dutton. It mewed and spat and tried to grow fangs—and was a hundred broken, torn pieces. Without knives, or any weapon save the brute-given strength of a staff of picked men, the thing was crushed, rent.

Slowly they picked themselves up, their eyes smoldering, very quiet in their motions. A curious wrinkling of their lips betrayed a species of nervousness.

Barclay went over with the electric weapon. Things smoldered and stank. The caustic acid Van Wall dropped on each spilled drop of blood gave off tickling, cough-provoking fumes.

McReady grinned, his deep-set eyes alight and dancing. "Maybe," he said softly, "I underrated man's abilities when I said nothing human could have the ferocity in the eyes of that thing we found. I wish we could have the opportunity to treat in a more befitting manner these things. Something with boiling oil, or melted lead in it, or maybe slow roasting in the power boiler. When I think what a man Dutton was—

"Never mind. My theory is confirmed by—by one who knew? Well, Van Wall and Barclay are proven. I think, then, that I'll try to show you what I already know. That I, too, am human." McReady swished the scalpel in absolute alcohol, burned it off the metal blade, and cut the base of his thumb expertly.

Twenty seconds later he looked up from the desk at the waiting men. There were more grins out there now, friendly grins, yet withal, something else in the eyes.

"Connant," McReady laughed softly, "was right. The huskies watching that thing in the corridor bend had nothing on you. Wonder why we think only the wolf blood has the right to ferocity? Maybe on spontaneous viciousness a wolf takes tops, but after these seven days—abandon all hope, ye wolves who enter here!

"Maybe we can save time. Connant, would you step for—"

Again Barclay was too slow. There were more grins, less tensity still, when Barclay and Van Wall finished their work.

Garry spoke in a low, bitter voice. "Connant was one of the finest men we had here—and five minutes ago I'd have sworn he was a man. Those damnable things are more than imitation." Garry shuddered and sat back in his bunk.

And thirty seconds later, Garry's blood shrank from the hot platinum wire, and struggled to escape the tube, struggled as frantically as a suddenly feral, red-eyed, dissolving imitation of Garry struggled to dodge the snake-tongue weapon Barclay advanced at him, white-faced and sweating. The Thing in the test tube screamed with a tiny, tinny voice as McReady dropped it into the glowing coal of the galley stove.

XIV

"The last of it?" Doctor Copper looked down from his bunk with bloodshot, saddened eyes. "Fourteen of them—"

McReady nodded shortly. "In some ways—if only we could have permanently prevented their spreading—I'd like to have even the imitations back. Commander Garry—Connant—Dutton—Clark—"

"Where are they taking those things?" Copper nodded to the stretcher Barclay and Norris were carrying out.

"Outside. Outside on the ice, where they've got fifteen smashed crates, half a ton of coal, and presently will add ten gallons of kerosene. We've dumped acid on every spilled drop, every torn fragment. We're going to incinerate those."

"Sounds like a good plan." Copper nodded wearily. "I wonder, you haven't said whether Blair—"

McReady started. "We forgot him? We had so much else! I wonder—do you suppose we can cure him now?"

"If—" began Doctor Copper, and stopped meaningfully.

McReady started a second time. "Even a madman. It imitated Kinner and his praying hysteria—" McReady turned toward Van Wall at the long table. "Van, we've got to make an expedition to Blair's shack."

Van looked up sharply, the frown of worry faded for an instant in surprised remembrance. Then he rose, nodded. "Barclay better go along. He applied the lashings, and may figure how to get in without frightening Blair too much."

Three quarters of an hour, through minus thrity-seven degrees cold, while the aurora curtain bellied overhead. The twilight was nearly twelve hours long, flaming in the north on snow like white, crystalline sand under their skis. A five-mile wind piled it in drift-lines pointing off to the northwest. Three quarters of an hour to reach the snow-buried shack. No smoke came from the little shack, and the men hastened.

"Blair!" Barclay roared into the wind when he was still a hundred yards away. "Blair!"

"Shut up," said McReady softly. "And hurry. He may be trying a lone hike. If we have to go after him—no planes, the tractors disabled—"

"Would a monster have the stamina a man has?"

"A broken leg wouldn't stop it for more than a minute," McReady pointed out.

Barclay gasped suddenly and pointed aloft. Dim in the twilit sky, a winged thing circled in curves of indescribable grace and ease. Great white wings tipped gently, and the bird swept over them in silent curiosity.

"Albatross—" Barclay said softly. "First of the season, and wandering way inland for some reason. If a monster's loose—"

Norris bent down on the ice, and tore hurriedly at his heavy, windproof clothing. He straightened, his coat flapping open, a grim blue-metaled weapon in his hand. It roared a challenge to the white silence of Antarctica.

The thing in the air screamed hoarsely. Its great wings worked frantically as a dozen feathers floated down from its tail. Norris fired again. The bird was moving swiftly now, but in an almost straight line of retreat. It screamed again, more feathers dropped, and with beating wings it soared behind a ridge of pressure ice, to vanish.

Norris hurried after the others. "It won't come back," he panted.

Barclay cautioned him to silence, pointing. A curious, fiercely blue light beat out from the cracks of the shack's door. A very low, soft humming sounded inside, a low, soft humming and a clink and click of tools, the very sounds somehow bearing a message of frantic haste.

McReady's face paled. "Lord help us if that thing has—" He grabbed Barclay's shoulder and made snipping motions with his fingers, pointing toward the lacing of control cables that held the door.

Barclay drew the wire cutters from his pocket, and knelt soundlessly at the door. The snap and twang of cut wires made an unbearable racket in the utter quiet of the Antarctic hush. There was only that strange, sweetly soft hum from within the shack, and the queer, hectically clipped clicking and rattling of tools to drown their noises.

McReady peered through a crack in the door. His breath sucked in huskily and his great fingers clamped cruelly on Barclay's shoulder. The meteorologist backed down. "It isn't," he explained very softly, "Blair. It's kneeling on something on the bunk—something that keeps lifting. Whatever it's working on is a thing like a knapsack—and it lifts."

"All at once," Barclay said grimly. "No. Norris, hang back, and get that iron of yours out. It may have—weapons."

Together, Barclay's powerful body and McReady's giant strength struck the door. Inside, the bunk jammed against the door screeched madly and crackled into kindling. The door flung down from broken hinges, the patched lumber of the doorpost dropping inward.

Like a blue rubber ball, a thing bounced up. One of its four tentacle-like arms looped out like a striking snake. In a seven-tentacled hand a six-inch pencil of winking, shining metal glinted and swung upward to face them. Its line-thin lips twitched back from snake fangs in a grin of hate, red eyes blazing.

Norris's revolver thundered in the confined space. The hate-washed face twitched in agony, the looping tentacle snatched back. The silvery thing in its hand a smashed ruin of metal, the seven-tentacled hand became a mass of mangled flesh oozing greenish-yellow ichor. The revolver thundered three times more. Dark holes drilled each of the three eyes before Norris hurled the empty weapon against its face.

The thing screamed in feral hate, a lashing tentacle wiping at blinded eyes. For a moment it crawled on the floor, savage tentacles lashing out, the body twitching. Then it staggered up again, blinded eyes working, boiling hideously, the crushed flesh sloughing away in sodden gobbets.

Barclay lurched to his feet and dove forward with an ice-ax. The flat of the weighty thing crushed against the side of the head. Again the unkillable monster went down. The tentacles lashed out, and suddenly Barclay fell to his feet in the grip of a living, livid rope. The thing dissolved as he held it, a white-hot band that ate into the flesh of his hands like living fire. Frantically he tore the stuff from him, held his hands where they could not be reached. The blind thing felt and ripped at the tough, heavy, windproof cloth, seeking flesh—flesh it could convert—

The huge blowtorch McReady had brought coughed solemnly. Abruptly it rumbled disapproval throatily. Then it laughed gurglingly, and thrust out a blue-white, three-foot tongue. The thing on the floor shrieked, flailed out blindly with tentacles that writhed and withered in the bubbling wrath of the blowtorch. It crawled and turned on the floor, it shrieked and hobbled madly, but always McReady held the blowtorch on the face, the dead eyes burning and bubbling uselessly. Frantically the thing crawled and howled.

A tentacle sprouted a savage talon—and crisped in the flame. Steadily McReady moved with a planned, grim campaign. Helpless, maddened, the thing retreated from the grunting torch, the caressing, licking tongue. For a moment it rebelled, squalling in inhuman hatred at the touch of the icy snow. Then it fell back before the charring breath of the torch, the stench of its flesh bathing it. Hopelessly it retreated— on and on across the Antarctic snow. The bitter wind swept over it, twisting the torch-tongue; vainly it flopped, a trail of oily, stinking smoke bubbling away from it—

McReady walked back toward the shack silently. Barclay met him at the door. "No more?" the giant meteorologist asked grimly.

Barclay shook his head. "No more. It didn't split?"

"It had other things to think about," McReady assured him. "When I left it, it was a glowing coal. What was it doing?"

Norris laughed shortly. "Wise boys, we are. Smash magnetos, so planes won't work. Rip the boiler tubing out of the tractors. And leave that thing alone for a week in this shack. Alone and undisturbed."

McReady looked in at the shack more carefully. The air, despite the ripped door, was hot and humid. On a table at the far end of the room rested a thing of coiled wires and small magnets, glass tubing, and radio tubes. At the center a block of rough stone rested. From the center of the block came the light that flooded the place, the fiercely blue light, bluer than the glare of an electric arc, and from it came the sweetly soft hum. Off to one side was another mechanism of crystal glass, blown with an incredible neatness and delicacy, metal plates and a queer, shimmery sphere of insubstantiality.

"What is that?" McReady moved nearer.

Norris grunted. "Leave it for investigation. But I can guess pretty well. That's atomic power. That stuff to the left—that's a neat little thing for doing what men have been trying to do with one-hundred-ton cyclotrons and so forth. It separates neutrons from heavy water, which he was getting from the surrounding ice."

"Where did he get all—oh. Of course. A monster couldn't be locked in—or out. He's been through the apparatus caches." McReady stared at the apparatus. "Lord, what minds that race must have—"

"The shimmery sphere—I think it's a sphere of pure force. Neutrons can pass through any matter, and he wanted a supply reservoir of neutrons. Just project neutrons against silica—calcium—beryllium—almost anything, and the atomic energy is released. That thing is the atomic generator."

McReady plucked a thermometer from his coat. "It's one hundred and twenty degrees in here, despite the open door. Our clothes have kept the heat out to an extent, but I'm sweating now."

Norris nodded. "The light's cold. I found that. But it gives off heat to warm the place through that coil. He had all the power in the world. He could keep it warm and pleasant, as his race thought of warmth and pleasantness. Did you notice the light, the color of it?"

McReady nodded. "Beyond the stars is the answer. From beyond the stars. From a hotter planet that circled a brighter, bluer sun they came."

McReady glanced out the door toward the blasted, smoke-stained trail that flopped and wandered blindly off across the drift. "There won't be any more coming. I guess. Sheer accident it landed here, and that was twenty million years ago. What did it do all that for?" He nodded toward the apparatus.

Barclay laughed softly. "Did you notice what it was working on when we came? Look." He pointed toward the ceiling of the shack.

Like a knapsack made of flattened coffee tins, with dangling cloth straps and leather belts, the mechanism clung to the ceiling. A tiny, glaring heart of supernal flame burned in it, yet burned through the ceiling's wood without scorching it. Barclay walked over to it, grasped two of the dangling straps in his hands, and pulled it down with an effort. He strapped it about his body. A slight jump carried him in a weirdly slow arc across the room.

"Antigravity," said McReady softly.

"Antigravity," Norris nodded. "Yes, we had 'em stopped, with no planes, and no birds. The birds hadn't come—but it had coffee tins and radio parts, and glass and the machine shop at night. And a week— a whole week—all to itself. America in a single jump—with antigravity powered by the atomic energy of matter.

"We had 'em stopped. Another half hour—it was just tightening these straps on the device so it could wear it—and we'd have stayed in Antarctica, and shot down any moving thing that came from the rest of the world."

"The albatross—" McReady said softly. "Do you suppose—"

"With this thing almost finished? With that death weapon it held in its hand?

"No, by the grace of God, who evidently does hear very well, even down here, and the margin of half an hour, we keep our world, and the planets of the system, too. Antigravity, you know, and atomic power. Because They came from another sun, a star beyond the stars. *They* came from a world with a bluer sun."

# The Elder Gods

[WITH ARTHUR J. BURKS]

Lord Nazun, chief of the Elder Gods, looked down at the city of Tordu, and sighed softly. Beside him, Talun snorted angrily, a pleasant dilute odor of drying kelp and salt sea eddying about him in the soft breeze. Lady Tammar chuckled and spoke softly, "It oppresses you more than usual tonight, Talun?"

"It's sure we'll gain nothing in this way. Nazun, tell me, what was in the minds of men when we appeared first?"

Nazun stirred uneasily, a vague, lean bulk against the midnight blue of the sky. "I know, my friend—but there was a certain fear, too, that we would not change with the changing times. Perhaps that is our flaw."

"And the greater flaw," the sea lord growled, "is standing by in idleness and watching the destruction of our people. The Invisible Ones are death—death not of the body, but of the spirit and mind. Where are my sea rovers gone? Dead and decayed. Fishermen—good, stout workmen though they be—lack the spark that makes the sea rover."

"We cannot attack the Invisible Ones by attacking, by taking over the minds of our people; that is the First Law," Nazun pointed out.

"No—and ye need a solid right arm to attack the Invisible Ones, which none of us possesses. But, all the same, we possess neither a solid thing that keeps us subject to material weapons such as a solid right arm may wield!"

"You'll turn no man of Tordu against the Invisible Ones. The pattern and movement of every Azuni is so set and known to the Invisible Ones, as to us, that he would be dead at the hands of the priests of the Invisible Ones before he moved half across Tordu," Lord Martal pointed out. "There are chances in the lives of men—but not when the Invisible Ones have time to plot out those chances first!"

"No stranger has reached these islands in five centuries," Nazun sighed. "Your sea rovers, Talun, rove as close by the shore as a chick by the old hen's feet. While they rove the shorelines of the continents, they'll never find Azun . . . and without wider knowledge of the pointing needle, no seaman ventures far. It will be a century yet before men wander the oceans freely once more."

Talun's sea-squinted eyes narrowed farther. "They wander," he said explosively, "where the will of the winds drives them, my friend. Now if ye want a stranger here on these islands, we'll see what the winds and my seas can do!"

Nazun stood silent, squinting thoughtfully at the sea beyond, and the town below. "One stranger, Talun—only one. One stranger, without background known to us or the Invisible Ones, is beyond calculation and the prophecy of the gods; half a dozen strangers, and there would be more factors on which to base foreknowledge—and defeat!"

"One then," growled Talun. "One good sea rover, with a spark and flame within him that these damned Invisible Ones can't read or quench!"

Lord Nazun looked down at the wilted form on the pebbled beach with a wry, dry smile on his lips, and a twinkle of amusement in his narrowed gray eyes. "A sorry specimen you've fished up for us, Talun. And did you need to cause so violent a storm as the recent one to capture this bit of drift?"

Talun's dark face knotted in a grimace of anger, then smoothed in resignation. His roaring voice cut through the dying whine of winds and the *broom* of surf on the beach below. "I never know, Nazun, whether you mean your words. The scholars that fathered you forgot me, and forgot to give me wisdom—a sad lack in this day. That washed-up thing may be a bit bedewed, a bit softened by immersion in good brine, but he'll dry out again. And he's a man, a real man! There's more than mush in his back, and more than jelly in his heart. These Azuni men that sail by the bark of a dog and the twitter of a bird will be the vanishment of me!

"By the sea, I'd say such a storm as that last was needed to net that man! There was courage in him to build his ship on the edge of the brine, and sail straight out from land! A man who uses land as a guide only to show him how to get farthest from it quickest has my liking, and my protection."

Talun's heavy brows pulled down belligerently as he looked Nazun in the eye defiantly. Then his gaze shifted back to the man uneasily. Nazun's deep-set, narrow gray eyes were friendly, twinkling with pleasant good humor, but there was in them a depth beyond depths that left Talun, for all his own powers, ill at ease and unsettled.

Lady Tammar laughed softly. "And while you argue, he dries out. Now, good Nazun, you have netted your fish, or Talun has netted him for you and brought him to this beach. What plans have you for him next?"

"He's been well stripped," Lord Martal grunted. He waved a muscle-knotted, stout-fingered hand at the man who was beginning to stir again on the lumpy mattress of hard quartz. "He has neither gold, nor sword to carve it out with, nor any other thing. I'd say he was fitted to take advice for his next move. He could have used a sword for defense, Talun. You might have left him that. By the cut of his figure. I'd say he would sooner fight than ask for help, weapon or no."

Talun scratched his bearded chin uneasily and snorted. The dying wind permitted the faint aroma of fish to cling about the bulky figure once again in a not unpleasant intensity. More a signature or card of identity than an offense. "Your favorite irons don't float," he said, half annoyed. "The man showed sense when he parted with that when his cockleshell went down. Now leave my works alone, and let me worry about my sea. I've done my task—a man, such as you asked, at your feet, stripped as you asked, but sound. You can find him swords and breastplates enough in the junk shops of Tordu, where your ex-friends have left them, Martal. My fishermen are still with me."

Lord Martal laughed. "Good enough, friend, and right enough. We'll equip him once again. There's a house, a small temple where men worship chance and probabilities, where I may find a way to help our new-found friend. Ah, he's getting up."

Weakly, Daron pushed his elbows under him, sneezed vigorously, and gasped. He looked about him at the empty beach. The pebbles that had left a faithful imprint on every aching muscle of his back and shoulders gave way to broken rock a hundred feet away, and that in turn became a rocky cliff. Daron turned his head wearily, heaved himself erect, and dragged himself over to the nearest good-sized boulder. He held his head firmly in place till the dizziness left, then looked about. The wind was dying away but the surf still made hungry, disappointed noises on the beach as it tried to reach him.

He looked at it resentfully. "You took my ship, and you took my crew, which seems enough. Also you took from me all sense of where I am, which was more than enough to rob me of. May the gods give that there are men somewhere near—though it seems unlikely. No men of sense would inhabit so unpleasant a coast."

He looked up the beach, which curved away somewhere beyond

the rain mists into a gray, formless blank. Down the beach, the high rocky cliff dwindled away just before it, too, was swallowed by the gray, wind-driven mists. Overhead, the dull gray was darkened to night, and the dull gray of his spirits darkened with it.

He followed the line of the cliff speculatively, and looked at the smug, uplifted brow of it near him. There was no sense struggling up here if it fell away to an easy slope half a mile down the beach. He heaved himself up from the boulder and started, annoyed that he had not the faintest idea whether he was moving south, east, north or west. To his sea rover's mind it was a feeling of nakedness equal to the undressed feeling the lack of his sword gave him.

Half a mile and the cliff did give way to a cragged set of natural steps. Above, he found his dizziness returned by the effort of climbing, and the beginnings of a mist-obscured meadow of some wiry grass that thrived on salt-spray. He set off across it doggedly as the gray of the skies gave way to almost total blackness. The wiry grass clutched at his toes, and he felt too weary to lift his feet above it.

Resignedly, he lay down to wait for daylight. Half an hour later, the chilling, dying wind induced him to change his mind. He stood up again and started on. The wind had swept away the last of the rain mist, and presently he made out a gleam of light that came and went erratically. He stood still, squinting his eyes, and watched.

"It may be like the pools I saw in the Dryland, a dream of something I want, but again, it may merely be that trees are blowing in front of the light. In any case, it's something other than gray mist to walk toward."

He stopped a hundred yards from the little building and watched more carefully. Strangers were not welcome in most of the world he'd known, but a rough gauge of the way an unknown people received a stranger lay in their buildings. Sticks and wattles—the stranger was apt to be the dinner. Good timber and thatch—the stranger was welcomed to dinner, usually roast sheep or lamb. Crude stone—the stranger was allowed to enter, if he could pay for his dinner. Finished stone—the stranger was shown the way to the public house.

It augured ill. The house was built of fieldstone, well mortared. But still—they'd be less likely to make dinner of him, even though they might not make dinner for him.

He knocked, noting, for all his weariness, that the door was singularly ill-kept. It opened, and Daron paused in measurement of the man who faced him. Six feet and more, Daron stood, but the man before him was four inches more, built long and supple, with an ease and grace of movement that spoke of well-ordered muscles.

But the face eased the sea rover's mind. It was high and narrow but broad above the eyes—strange eyes—gray and deep, almost black as they looked out from the warm firelight of the room beyond. The rugged strongly hewn features were keen with intelligence; the eyes and the tiny wrinkles around them deep with a queerly eternal wisdom.

"Your coast, yonder," said Daron, his mouth twisted in a grim smile, "offers poor bedding for a man whose ship is gone, and the grass of your meadows seems wiry for human gullets. I've naught but my gratitude left to buy me a meal and a night away from the wind, but if that be good value in your land—"

The face of the native wrinkled in good-humored acquiescence as he opened the door more fully. "It is a depreciated currency, much debased with counterfeit, a strange trouble of our land. But come in, we'll try the worth of yours."

Daron stepped in, and passed his host. Rather quickly he sought a chair made of X members supporting leather bands. It creaked under his weight as he looked up at his host. "My knees have yet to learn their manners, friend, and they seemed unwilling to wait your invitation."

"Sit then. How long have you been without food?"

"Some twenty hours—since the storm came up. It's not the lack of food, I think, but the too-free drinking of the last five of those hours. Wine has made my knees as unsteady, but I liked the process better."

"I have little here to offer you—a shepherd's fare. Tordu is some two days' journey away, beyond the Chinur Mountains."

"Hm-m-m . . . then this is some expansive land I've reached. Friend . . . but stay, if I may eat, the questions and the answers both will boil more freely. If you have the bread and cheese of the shepherds I know, they'll serve most excellently to sop this water I've imbibed."

"Sit here and rest, or warm yourself nearer the fire. The wind is dying, but turning colder, too." The tall man moved away, through a doorway at the far side of the stonewalled room, and Daron's eyes roved over the furnishings.

There were simple things, chairs—stools of leather straps and wooden X's, some simple, wooden slabs—a table of darkened, well-worn oak. Some sense of unease haunted Daron's mind, a feeling of decay about the smoke-grimed stone of the walls not matched by the simple furnishings.

Then his host was back with a stone jug, an oval loaf of bread, and a crumbling mass of well-ripened cheese on an earthenware plate. He set them on the table, as Daron moved over, for the first time observing closely the dress of his host. His clothes were of some blue-green stuff, loosely draped to fall nearly to his leather-sandaled feet, bunched behind his head in a hooded cowl thrown back between the shoulders now.

Daron's quick eyes studied the fingers that set out the food even as he reached toward it. They were long, slim, supple fingers, and the forearm that stretched from the loose sleeve of the blue-green cloak was muscled magnificently with the ropey, slim, deceptive cords of the swift-actioned man's strength.

Daron's eyes rose to the face of his host. The level, gray eyes looked down into his for a long moment, and Daron shrugged easily and turned back to his food. The eyes had regarded him with honesty of good intent—and the green-robed man was his host. If he chose to call himself a shepherd within his own house, to a stranger he befriended, that, then, was his business.

"I am called Nazun," his host said presently. His voice was deep and resonant, friendly, yet holding within it an air of certainty and power that the sea rover had heard in few men before. One had been his friend, and had carved out an empire. None of them had been shepherds—for long.

"I am Daron, of Kyprost—which I think you may not know. I am afflicted with a strange curse—like quicksilver, I cannot long remain in any place, yet in all my wanderings I've never heard of land that lay halfway from Western world to Eastern. And—unless I swam back in five hours over the course my vessel spent twelve days laying—this is a land I never knew existed."

"This is the island Ator, of the Azun islands. Some few of our people have sailed eastward to the borders of the great continent from which you came, but not in many generations have the Azuni been the sea rovers they once were. They wandered here from the lands you know, long ago, but now they see no joy in roving. Azun is very pleasant; they forget the old ways and the old gods, and worship new ideas and new gods."

Daron grinned. "Pleasant, is it? It was a hard, gray place I found. But for your light, it seemed I might find no more of it, for that the wind was cooling, I found for myself before I found your door."

Daron looked up again into Nazun's eyes, his blue eyes drawn to the gray. For an instant the firelight fell strong and clear on the sun-tanned face of the giant before him. The deep-sunk gray eyes looked into his levelly, from a face set for an instant in thought, a face of undeterminable age, as such strongly hewn faces of men may be. There was kindliness about it, but in that instant kindliness was hidden by overwhelming power. Daron's careless smile dropped away so that his own strongly chiseled face was serious and intent.

The gray eyes, he suddenly saw, were old. They were very, very old, and something of the chill of the dying wind outside leaked into Daron from those eyes.

The sea rover dropped his eyes to his food, broke a bit of bread and some cheese, ate it, and washed it down with the full-bodied wine from the stone jug.

The room was quiet, strangely quiet, with only the rustle of the fire to move the drapes of silence. Daron did not look up as he spoke, slowly, thoughtfully. His easy, laughing voice was deeper, more serious. "I am a stranger to this section of the world—friend. I . . . I think I would do better if you would give me some advice as to how I might repay you for this meal, which, at this time, is life."

Nazun's voice was soft against the silence, and Daron listened without looking up. "Yes, it is a strange corner of the world, Daron. Many generations ago the Azuni came, sea rovers such as you, and settled here. They found rich land, good temperatures, a good life. For a long time they roved the sea, but Azun was home. They built a peaceful country—there were no other sea rovers then to menace them—and prospered here.

"It was a peaceful home—they stayed by it more and more. Why wander in harsher lands? The Azuni have not wandered now in many generations. There is no need. And with peace, comes wisdom. They grew too wise to worship the old gods, and found new gods—you'll learn of them, the Invisible Ones, in Tordu, the capital of Azun—in new ways.

"But you will learn of this. Primarily, for safety and for pleasure here, remember this: the Azuni know more of minds and the works of the power of mind than any people of the Earth. This power may make things uncertain for you . . . but only some of the Azuni have the full knowledge now.

"For good reasons, friend, I cannot have you here the night. Go from the door straight out. There is a broken wall of stone some two hundred paces out, which you will see by the light of the moon—the clouds are broken to a scudding wrack, now—and beyond it is a cart road. Turn right on this, and follow it along. You'll find a public house along the road within the hour. And—if someone offers you a game, accept and you may have luck. Take this—it's a small coin, but planted well, it may grow a large crop."

Daron rose from the table. Turning as he rose so that his eyes sought the glowing fire. He slipped the small silver coin into his palm, tapped his hand, and the coin spun neatly in the air to slip, edge on, between his fingers and be caught. "Aye, friend. To the right. And—I will learn later, I think, how I may return this favor. Tordu would seem to be the goal of a sound man on this island of yours."

"To the right," Nazun nodded.

Daron stepped to the door, opened it, and stepped out into the night. The moon shone through rents in the shattered cloud veil. He went on steadily to the broken wall, crossed over, and turned right. He flipped the silver coin in his fingers and noticed to himself that the bright fire in the stone house no longer shone through the windows. For that matter, the moonlight shone through the ruined roof to make a patch of light in the room beyond the shattered, unhinged door.

Daron shrugged uneasily, and remembered the friendly creases about the deep-set gray eyes and tossed the coin into a pocket with an expert flip. He swung easily down the rutted cart road.

"Nazun," he said, and cocked an eye at the scudding cloud wrack. "Now the local people might know that name—and there are other ways than asking questions to learn an answer."

## II

The wiry grass gave way to scrub, and the stunted brush to patches of trees. The stone inn house nestled in a group of the trees, half hidden by them, but a signpost hung out over the road to rectify that flaw; the traveler would not miss it. Daron fingered his single coin and squinted at the signboard as the moonlight flickered across it like the glow of a draft-stirred candle.

"That," said Daron softly, "means 'The Dolphin,' which would be a right goodly name for such a place, so near the sea; but that lettering is like to none I've seen before!" He let it go at that, and went on toward the door, with a clearer idea in mind as to the meaning of the name of Nazun. He had, seemingly, acquired a new fund of wisdom, a new language!

The voices of men and the laughter of a girl came through the heavy oaken panels of the door as he raised the knocker; and he heard the heavy, rolling tread of the host as he dropped it down again. The man who faced the sea rover now was no giant, but a short, round-bellied little man with a face all creases, sprouting seedling whiskers of a red beard as the only clue to what his vanished hair might once have been.

"Aye, and come in, for though the night is bettering, it's foul enough yet, my friend."

Daron smiled in answer to the infectious good humor of the inn-

keeper. "And who knows better than I? Pray your drinks are better
than brine, for I've had my fill of that, and your beds are better than
the quartz the waves laid me out on. I've lost a ship, a crew, a sword,
and all but one silver coin." Daron looped it upward so it glinted in
the light of a hanging lamp and the glow of the fire.

The innkeeper's smile-creased mouth pursed worriedly. "Your luck
seems bad, and . . . and your coin small," he said doubtfully.

"Ah, but you think too quickly, friend," laughed Daron. "Look,
out of a crew of a dozen stout lads, I lived. You say my luck is bad?
Out of all that I possessed, this bit of silver stayed with me like a true
friend and you think it will leave me now?

"Now let us test this thing. Look; I want a bit of meat, a bit of
bread, and perhaps some wine. You want my coin. Fair enough, but
you say my luck is bad, which is a curse on any seaman. Let's see,
then; we'll try this coin. If it falls against me, it is yours, and I seek
another place for food. If it is the friend I say—"

The innkeeper shrugged. "I am no worshiper of Lord Martal, and
I've no faith in the luck he rules. Go back through yonder door, and
you'll find his truest worshipers in all Ator, I swear. They gamble away
two fortunes in an evening, and gamble it back between 'em. But they
gamble away my wine, and pay for that, wherefore they're welcome.
Perhaps I should thank Lord Martal at that."

Daron chuckled. "By all means, man! He smiles on you, and the
old gods are good protectors, I feel." The seaman swung across the
little entrance room toward the curtained entrance to the main dining
hall beyond. The smoke-stained oaken beams hung low enough to
make him stoop his head as he pushed the curtain aside and looked
beyond. A dozen men, some in well-worn, stout clothing bearing the
faintly sour, wholly pleasant odor of the sea, some with the heavier
smells of earth and horses, clustered about a table where five men in
finer clothes were seated. Three girls, in tight-bodiced, wide-skirted
costumes, watched and moved about to fill the orders of the men.

None saw him at first, as they watched the play of the dice that
leaped and danced on the dark wood of the table top. Daron moved
over, and some of the outer fringe looked up at him, their boisterous
voices quieting for an instant, then resuming at his easy grin and nod.
The ring of farming people and fishermen made way a bit, uncertain
by his dress, for, sea-stained and flavored, it showed fine-woven cloth
of good linen, worked in an unfamiliar pattern with bits of gold and
silver wire.

The seated men looked up at him, and back at the dice, and rolled
again. Daron leaned forward, putting his widespread hands on the

table. "My friends," he said seriously, "I have an unpleasant mission here. My ship is lost, my crew is gone, and all possessions left me save this coin." The single silver bit clinked down. "Our good host has said my luck is foul; I feel that it is good. Wherein does this concern you? It is this; if I would sleep softer than the stones outside, and eat fare tenderer than twigs, I must plant this seedling coin and reap a harvest. I fear it is from your pockets, then, the harvest must come."

The nearest of the players laughed, spun Daron's coin, and nodded. "One stake, friend, and we'll finish the work the seas began! A man with such a thing is hard put—it would buy a bit of food, or a bed, but not both, and the decision would be hard. We shall relieve you!"

"Now, by Nazun, you won't, I feel!" Daron laughed—and watched their eyes.

The player shook his head and laughed. "Now by the Invisible Ones, I know we shall. If you still put your faith in outworn gods, it is small surprise they stripped you thus."

Daron relaxed, and nodded to himself. "We shall see."

"And," said the holder of the dice, passing them to Daron, "this is no field for Nazun, for there's no wisdom in these bits of bone. If the old gods appeal to you, why then Martal, I'd say, would be the one you'd swear by here."

"No wisdom in the dice—no, that may be. But wisdom may reside in fingers, thus?" Daron spun out the three polished cubes, and saw them turn a five, a five and a six. "What would you have me throw?"

"I'll take your stake," said the hawk-nosed player to Daron's right. "Better this." His fingers caressed the dice, spun them, and shot them forth. They settled for a total of twelve.

"With two dice, I'd match it, with three—" Daron's roll produced fourteen. "But even so," as he picked up two silver coins, "we need some further crops. A bed and board I have, but Tordu is farther than a seaman walks. A horse, I think— Will some one match me more?"

A sword filled the scabbard at his thigh, and a good dirk was thrust in his belt, a horse was his, and money for a day or two when he sought his bed that night. He whistled a bit of a tune as he laid aside his things, dropped the thick oak bar across the door, and settled for sleep. "I'll say this for this land," he muttered, "very practical gods they have. Unique in my experience. They do a man very material good turns. Wisdom, it is, eh? I thought as much—"

The sun was bright, the air warm, but not uncomfortable, and the horse better even than the lamp's weak light had suggested in the night, when Daron started off. The cart road had broadened to a highway, and this to one well-traveled within a pair of hours. The scrub bush and sheep-dotted meadows gave way to farmlands bordered with fences growing neatly from the ground, well-barbed fences of some cactus bush for which the sheep showed sound respect.

There was little timber here, but under the clear sun, the meadowlands and farms stretched off into pleasantly blue-hazed distance, where the banking of the haze seemed to indicate a mountain range stretching off from east to west. The road led south, but like most farmland roads, seemed unconcerned with haste and directness. It visited from door to door and rolled aside when some small swale of land suggested climbing hills. The horse was sound and strong, seeming to have a nature as blithe as Daron's own, with little mind to bother a fair day about a change in masters.

Toward noon, the rising ground began to show some signs of timber, and the stone-walled farm cottages began to trail attendants in wooden walls, and sheep appeared again more frequently. The haze rolled up by the rising sun still banked to the south, but the shining gleam above it indicated that the haze had retreated to solid mountain fastnesses, with a snow-crowned peak above.

The sun was warmer now, and where a small stream trickled through a woodpatch, Daron dismounted, tethered his mount to a bush near the stream, and spread his food. He ate, and leaned back in easy contemplation and thought. The wandering breeze brought some faint hint to him of a visitor, and his swift thoughts placed his line of action before the odor was more than identifiable to him. He looked up with a smile as the footsteps of the newcomer crunched on the twigs nearby.

He saw a wind-blown, sun-tanned man, rather stocky and heavily muscled, with eyes squinting permanently from the glare of the sun on water. A sailor's cap perched solidly on his round, dark-haired head. A black stubble of beard showed on his heavy jowls and on his thick, muscular arms, and an impudent tuft thrust out from each ear.

"My friend," said Daron, "you're a way from the sea, which, by your gait, would be more homelike to you."

The stocky one seated himself with a grunt. "Aye, and the same to you. Those linens were never stained in a brook, and, unless you ride yon horse lying on your back, it's not the sweat of your beast.

"Bound for Tordu?"

"One I met last night named such a city. I am not familiar with this country—a remarkable land I find it—and it seemed the part of wisdom to seek the center of the place. And, by the bye, men call me Daron."

"Talun," granted the stocky one, seemingly annoyed. "Tordu's a foul place for an honest seaman, though seamen of that ilk seem fewer with every season. The whole race of Azuni have grown soft and stupid, and the stupidest have gathered in Tordu to admire their overweening stupidity. They have no sense or judgment, and they shun the sea like the plague. Time was when the Bay of Tor was a harbor."

Talun snorted disgustedly. "They've got it cluttered so with fancy barges now no merchant ship can enter, and they've set a temple to those precious Invisible Ones of theirs across the mouth of the bay—they call it Temple Isle now; it used to be the finest shipyard in Azun—and their slinking Invisible Ones hang over the bay mouth till the good clean sea stays out in disgust."

"Invisible Ones? Hm-m-m. I'm somewhat unacquainted here, though I've heard a dozen times of these Invisible Ones—not including several references to them, both prayerful and annoyed last night, from certain gentlemen of the countryside I gamed with—but little explanation of them. Gods, are they?"

"Gods?" Talun snorted angrily. "They pray to them as to gods, and say they are not gods. The people of Tordu are fools and crazed ones at that. 'No gods,' they say. They scorn the old gods of their fathers, for, say they, the old gods are foolishness—made in the image of men, and hence no more than projected men and the power of men's minds. The true god-being, these wise thinkers say, is certainly no man, a thing of force in form mere mortal mind cannot conceive. So they build themselves these Invisible Ones, and give them power, and curse the old gods.

"They're fools, and have no wisdom, and admire each other's mighty thoughts."

"The wise thinkers, eh?" mused Daron. "We have such thinkers in my land, and we have certain other thinkers who have one certain trait that sets them off—a remarkable thing. They think long, study much, and confess to those who ask that they learn steadily that they know little. Some think that a crabwise way to knowledge—but I am prejudiced; I learned from such a man."

Talun stirred uneasily, and his squinted eyes turned upward to the clear blue bowl of the sky. The blistering sun was burning down from it to his face, but as he stared upward a fleecy cloud formed, rolled, expanded and hid the sun. Talun settled back comfortably.

"Learning never appealed much to me. One of my friends—but not to me. The wisdom of the fools appeals not so strongly to the countrymen, nor to the sailors, and on that alone these Invisible Ones would gain no strength, for these thinkers are few, if noisy with their thoughts.

"But another thing has influenced them," continued Talun. "The gods, these deep thinkers say, should know the future—else what's the use of consulting gods? Now the old gods did not know—or did not explain, at least."

Daron sat more upright, looked harder at this stocky, hairy figure, the very image of a sailor or fisherman, from whom the shifting breezes brought a gentle tang of salt and fish and drying kelp. "Your gods, in this land, are most unique to me," said Daron softly. "Perhaps men have a certain reservation in their thoughts of gods in other lands—a thought that a god is some vague thing, whose statue man may carve, and to whom offerings may be made, but a remote being who does strangely little manifest for his worshipers . . . Now the gods of this country, I find, are most substantial beings—and most helpful. The Lord of Chance, of Contests, let us say: he wished me well last night, I think." Daron nodded toward the browsing horse. "Now if a people blessed by gods who have such usefulness complain, it would seem they set hard standards indeed."

Talun grumbled and rolled over. Daron cast an eye upward; alone in the blue vault of the sky the single white fleece of cloud remained motionless between them and the sun, casting a pleasant tempering shade. "Men want more than they have—and that, my friends tell me, is good, and the reason seems enough," answered Talun. "If a man be satisfied with what he has, why surely, he will get no more. If a man catch a dozen fish, which is enough to feed his wife and a child, and fish no more, I'd think little of his courage, or his sense.

"But now this knowing the future. It is not always good. These wise thinkers of Tordu, they put it that the gods should know, and the gods should tell men—and their Invisible Ones do. But the priests of the Lord of Wisdom, the wisest of the old gods, say gods should know—but should not explain all things."

"Why not?" asked Daron.

"If a god should tell you that this night you would wager your horse against a slave girl, and lose both girl and horse on a toss of the dice, what would you do?"

"Why, sure I'd be a fool indeed to wager then!"

"Whereby, if you do not, you make a liar of the god," said Talun with a snort. "The god's prophecy of the future was not accurate, for you did not. Now such a prophecy the old gods made. 'If,' might the priest report, 'you cast your nets at Seven-Fathom Bank, you'll snare a swordfish and spend three days mending nets.' Now the fishermen would not, but would lose a good day's fishing, and rumble that the prophecies were vague.

"But these Invisible Ones; they have no vagueness. They tell a man, 'As you walk home this night a horse shall kick and break your skull. Farewell, worshiper!' And, that night the man is dead. He swears no horse shall come near him—they did at first—but the prophecy is right, of course. If the Invisible Ones read future right, then that must be his fate. If he has wit to escape that end, why then he's made a liar of the gods." Talun dropped one heavy lid, and his dark-blue eye speared Daron sharply. "And, young friend, old gods or new, no mortal man makes a liar of the gods!"

"That calls for thought," sighed Daron. "I see no joy in knowing my end if I have no hope of changing it."

Talun grunted and stretched himself up. "Nor did the country folk or fishermen at first. But try a human with that thought for long, and not even the gods will make him stand firm. Live a year beside a temple of these Invisible Ones, knowing every day that there you can find sure and absolute the day and manner of your death—No. Men are mortal, and they fear old Barak, the dread god of their mortality, but the sharp, itching bite of curiosity will drive them on. You've seen the countryman twist the ox's tail to drive it in the pen in which the ox can smell death? So curiosity sends men into that temple which they know means loss of hope."

Talun shrugged. "Once there—what man has courage and will to walk away? They sink like wine sots, drunk with future knowledge, giving up all strength and drive of spirit, for the Invisible Ones tell them what is coming—and they know it will come, try how they may, so you may be sure they do not try.

"Go your way, friend. I have business at times in Tordu, too, so I may see you again." Talun wandered off through the woodpatch and vanished behind a tree.

Daron lay back to stare at the cloud. It hung still precisely between the sun and the spot where Talun had sat. But it was evaporating rapidly now, and presently the blue vault of sky was clear. Daron chuckled as he untethered his horse and swung onto his back. Convenient, that trick.

His horse trotted on easily across the plain, passing a farm wagon here, neighing to a browsing horse along the way, and Daron sat straight and thought. A notion formed at the back of his mind that Talun had not altogether been a friend. That storm that took his ship and crew—

Well, it was evident he had a mission here, and surely no higher adventure had he sought than this! With gods like those this land boasted—they did not seem a stingy lot!

The day passed, and he stopped that night in another inn, the

Sheath and Scythe, it was, and the men who drank the lank, cadaverous host's wine had no smell of sea or fish about them. The heavy, earthy smell that permeated the inn was thick to Daron's sea-trained nostrils.

Experimentally, he tossed the dice again this night. He lost three throws, won two, and knew his answer. What he needed, seemingly was his—but these gods did not take the spice of gambling from him by constant winning. He settled down then, and what Martal's help did not bring him a certain deftness of fingering did. The night grew fatter then, when he found that, somehow, this land had never learned the mighty magic of the three snail shells and the pebble.

Content, and more than warmed by good wine—his shells had betrayed him with clumsiness, else he'd have stayed longer—he went to sleep.

III

With a sailor's instinct, for all his hoofed carrier, Daron found his way to the docks of Tordu straightway—and snorted as he saw them. No smell of good fish and bad, no circling, wide-winged argosies of gulls. The broad, V-shaped Bay of Tor spread out, its mouth plugged by the Temple Isle, its waves showering familiar gold and diamond back to the blue skies and the sun. But the clean, salt-and-fish smell of any coastal sea was gone, buried, drowned away in a scent that reeked in the sea rover's nostrils. Incense! The bay was dotted with hoggish, bloat-belly barges, with white canvas mocked in pretty silks, good yellow cordage tinseled with golden threads.

The final insult to the sea was the crews. Girls! Golden-tanned pink skins, and dainty figures playing seamen! Slave girls with beribboned chains of gold pulling at the oars that drifted the silly barges out.

Daron groaned. The sailor's eye roved around the harbor, and his sea rover's soul writhed in anguish. High, granite-glinting cliffs, impregnable to any storm, formed a solid wall broken in two deep, sharp clefts, the twin mouths of the bay. Set like a grim, squat fort across it was the island, a grim, stanch island of black, pinnacled basalt bedecked with carved and spidery-lined temples, beflowered with beds of plants in artificial soil.

Here was a harbor the gods had made impregnable! They'd set across its mouth such harsh defenses as no sea could smash, nor any force of men invade, for but a few score of good catapults could make those deep-cloven channels—wide enough for peaceful shipping— invulnerable to all assault.

Yet the great walls of granite fell away in rapid slopes so that the city of Tordu, at the head of the bay, straddling the Tor River, was on a level beach-front.

And barges—pretty barges mocking galleys with their silly, slim slave girls—monopolized this port!

Daron clunked his heels disgustedly against the stout ribs of his horse, and turned his back on the place. The horse *plop-plopped* away in an easy trot, while Daron's ire mounted within him. The horse, not Daron, avoided the rumbling carriages of gaily decked men and women, skirted the shoreside area of marble-fronted shops selling things for temple decorations and offerings.

Even the sound of this section of the city was unlike any Daron had known before. It rang with the voices of men and women, as any good town must, and the creak and *plop* of harness and horses' hoofs. But the ringing jingle of good steel swords, the strong, hard ring of vital, active voices was gone. The calls were vague, unimportant, even to themselves; the faces of the men were interested, but more from seeking interest than because they found interest in each small thing of life.

Daron drove westward across the city, away from the bay. The level of the ground swelled upward gently, and the street was bordered by high, plastered walls, tinted white and pale blues and greens and pinks, as pale as the life force of this silly city.

Then the ground dropped down again; and as it fell, the view of the bay was lost behind, and the large estates that hid behind those plastered walls shrank quickly. The broad street split, and narrowed—and Daron began to look about more keenly. The pale color of the walls gave way, the pale, soft voices changed, the timbre of the city's sounds changed, and the smoky, spicy scent of incense gave way with it. From the east a breeze was sweeping the smell of a true city, the odor of foods and men and the green of growing things.

A good two miles back from the bay he found the sector he sought. The men were taller, heavier; two women leaned from nearby windows listening with hand-cupped ears to the angry voices floating from a neighboring house. The sweetly sour smell of wine floated out of a whitewashed inn, and the smell of hay turned the horse's nose to the stable yard as easily as the other turned his master's course.

Daron dropped the reins into the hand of the boy that roused himself from whistling lethargy to split his freckled face in a friendly grin. "You've seen a man become a fool with the aid of wine?" said Daron gruffly.

The boy's eyes rounded. "My . . . my father runs the inn—"

"A horse may do the same with food and water. Feed the beast, but mind he's no more sense than you, so feed him light, and water him gently." Daron grinned, and a coin flashed suddenly in the air and winked into nothingness as the boy's hand moved.

Daron swung from the courtyard to the street, and filled his lungs with a grunt of satisfaction. The air had not the tang of clean sea sweeps but the insult of the incense was out of his nostrils. He blinked his eyes and entered the inn.

A half dozen townsmen, in loose armless cotton shirts that slipped on over their heads, and woolen breeches falling loose to their knees, contracting sharply to mold the shins, looked at his different garb. The shirts were blue or green or yellow, but all the breeches were brown.

Daron grinned. "You've a good eye for color, lads, but tell me this; is it good brown earth or dye that makes your breeches match?"

One of the townsmen looked casually round the room and chewed on something slowly before replying. "And where would you be from, stranger? It's clear you never heard of the Elder Vows."

"That might be, and that might be an answer. What is this Elder Vow? And is it the custom here, too, that the host so hides himself a guest goes thirsty?"

"No guest goes thirsty, but the host wears no more badge than does the guest." The man rose slowly, unfolding from behind his table like an endless python pouring from his hole. Lank as a ship's mainmast, he towered over Daron, his long arms dangling downward like wet rags hung out to dry.

Daron stepped back and eyed him up and down. "By Talun, now, you'd serve as jury-rig in any tall-sparred ship! If your drinks be as long as you, then there's good value for the money here! Give me something cool and wet that has less of the vinegar than the wine I've had since I landed on this shore."

The innkeeper grinned, leaned slightly, and plucked a cobwebbed bottle from a little door that sprung open at his touch, put it on the table and gestured broadly. "You've learned the trouble of the wines here quick enough.

"Now as to the color of our breeches; it seems small account of yours, but a long morning makes for easy talk, so sit. The answer's short enough, but there's little joy in short answers."

Daron smacked his lips and sighed contentedly. "Hm-m-m . . . a drink at last that wouldn't eat its way through marble stones! Let's hear this answer then, be it long or short. I'll leave when my business presses."

"I'm a fool," said the innkeeper sadly. "My friends"—he waved his queerly flexible long arm—"are fools. My foolishness—our foolishness—lies in this; we like to think that what we strive for we get, and what we get we get by striving for."

"A sound-seeming thought. Wherein lies the foolishness?"

The lanky one waved his arm again. "The street is full of those who will tell you. The temples on the isle are full of Invisible Ones and priests who will prove it for you.

"We go to the Older Gods. We wear these breeches to save us headaches."

Daron cocked his head. "A curious custom. In the Dryland, where once I was, there was a race of men who wrapped a white cloth about their heads to keep it cool and save them headaches, but this trick of wrapping the nether end seems somewhat strange. Still, one cannot tell. It seemed insane enough—that wrapping up the head to keep it cool—until I tried it, after twice finding that the sun was no puny light for man's convenience there. So I suppose you have some logic in your acts."

The man on the innkeeper's left blinked his eyes slowly, combed a full, spade-shaped beard of curly hairs, and patted a pate as bald as an empty seascape. "We tried wrapping our ears. The worshipers of the Invisible Ones still argued. So we wore the brown breeches and simply knocked down those who argued with us. A year or so—and they stopped arguing."

"By Nazun, that's wisdom!" Daron laughed. "But still I seek the explanation of the foolishness of striving for your wants."

"I," said the innkeeper, "am Shorhun." He stopped and chewed thoughtfully, looking at his sandaled foot.

"Daron, I'm called."

"If I go to the Temple Isle, the Invisible Ones will tell me whether or not the landlord of this place—who believes that I am a fool because I do not go—is going to throw me forth into the street. Incidentally, I'd be a fool in truth to seek an answer from the Invisible Ones on that; I know he is. But they might also tell me where I next will go, and whether I will prosper. Say that they say I will. The Invisible Ones prophesy always what *will* happen. Wherefore, if they say I will prosper, it will mean little to me what I do. It seems no prize of my good effort. If, through carelessness, I crack my pate on yonder doorframe, even that I prefer to think of as my own, my personally blundering act. If the Invisible Ones prophesy it—why, I have yet to crack my pate, and lack the satisfaction of cursing myself for a blind and imbecilic nitwit in the doing of it.

"Wherefore it is foolishness. I should go and learn my fate and then sit back to live it, like a twice-told tale, mumbling in my teeth as my pre-known date of death draws near.

"No, I prefer old Nazun. He deals in warning of things he well knows will not happen, I suppose—things I am warned against and, by avoiding, avoid trouble. Things—so the Invisible Ones say—I was not fated to meet in any case." Shorhun shrugged, a mighty thing that started like a tidal wave running up a narrow bay to crash in final jerkings at his head.

"I had thought," said Daron slowly, "to see the temples of the Old Gods. I saw none near the bay front."

Shorhun barked, a laugh that seemed half cadaverous cough. "Talun's Temple moved first. It fell to pieces one night with a mighty roaring and cursing, a sound that satisfied my feelings in its depth and originality, if it did disturb me next day in seeing his retreat."

"Eh? Talun was driven from his temple?"

"Aye. The old sea lord brought down a storm that ripped up every tree and all the neatly planted gardens of the Temple Isle, but that stubborn basalt was a bit too much for him. The isle stood."

"But what drove him out?" Daron asked intently.

Shorhun barked—or coughed—again. "Incense," he said lugubriously. "Before Tan Lormus, High Priest of the Invisible Ones, invented that, old Talun came near to driving out the pretty barges of the rich devotees of the Invisible Ones. Talun, like the true Old God he is, was using only natural things—though the number of fish that died on the beach that year was natural only by a wide stretch of allowance."

Daron burst into a roar of laughter till the tears rolled down his leathery cheeks. "Praised be Talun! Now that was an idea well worthy of the sea rover's god, and may this Tan Lormus live again in a fish's body for his rupture of so fine a plan!"

"But Talun moved," sighed Shorhun. "And the others moved after him, one by one, till last of all sweet Lady Tammar moved. She lacked not for worshipers, even with the Invisible Ones, for, Invisible Ones or not, men and women yet must have love, and no fine thoughts or wise prophecy can satisfy in place of that."

"But—she moved? The bay, foul as it may be for a sailor's eye, might still, with a good round moon, be a goodly place in a lover's eye," said Daron.

"It was—it was. But Lady Tammar is strangest of the gods in many ways. Lady of Love, she is all loves, all things to all men. She is the strong adventurer's companion mate, as strong as he, and as faithful.

She is the young man's first love, very young, and never wise. She is the mature man's wife—his ideal of her, understanding, wise, ever ready to aid him in his troubles. But—she is, too, the fop's simpering coquette, for she is the ideal of every man, however weak that ideal may be.

"So she moved back, back from the bay and its lack of common men in honest need. Lady Tammar had no joy in appearing thus to any man."

Daron sipped quietly at his wine. "I think," he said softly, "that I must see the new temple of Tammar."

Shorhun shook his great head slowly, and a little smile touched his face, changing it from the harsh look of weather-slit granite. "You can go—but Lady Tammar is wise. She does not appear to every man—for every man cannot find his perfect ideal, save in Tammar herself. And she is for no man. Once each month I go to her temple; three times she has appeared to me, and I go always in hopes. My wife is dead, and Tammar—"

"But you can go."

"Are all the temples of the Old Gods near together?" asked Daron.

"Near together, yes. But some six miles beyond Tordu, six miles up the slopes of Mt. Kalun, looking out across the city to the sea."

"I think that I shall go there, then. There are inns nearby?"

Shorhun shook his head slowly. "None nearer than Tordu. The Old Ones ruled it thus. Only the priests and priestesses and the temple people live on Mt. Kalun."

"Then this shall be my home. And—you have a tailor who could produce such fine brown breeches for me, perhaps?"

## IV

Daron sniffed, and his head nodded approval to the easy motion of the horse. There was incense here, on this road up Mt. Kalun, to the temples of the Old Gods—but incense he liked. The smell of spicy pine tar, baked from the tall, straight trees in the hot sun. The high air here was clear and crisp as a sea breeze, cleared by the luminous green masses of the trees.

The horse stopped abruptly, blew through his nostrils vigorously, and looked back at his rider. Daron laughed and patted the arching, sweaty neck. "Enough, my friend? A bit of climb it is. Good, then, it's near high noon, for all we started early. Tammar's temple has stood these good few years, and will, I think, wait while we rest. And Tammar . . . well, Lady Tammar has lasted longer still. We'll stop—and there's a nicely sheltered place." Daron slid off his mount, threw the reins over the animal's head, and led him off the trail. A hundred yards to the right, the pine-needle carpet of soft brown gave way to a little clearing, green with grass.

From the saddlebags, Daron lifted a flask of wine, wrapped in a dozen layers of crushed green leaves, wilted now and somewhat dried. But the wine within was pleasantly cooled. A loaf of bread and a cut of meat was food enough, and Daron settled comfortably. The horse was browsing at the grass, and blowing annoyedly. He was a lowland horse, it seemed, and the effects of some seven thousand feet of altitude were puzzling to him.

Hidden beyond the stand of straight-trunked pines, the road that led up to the temples carried a sprinkling of other visitors—hardy countrymen and tough-muscled seamen, the common men who had the will and muscle, too, to climb that narrow track.

No carriage road—those who came this way did not so from indolence and lack of other occupation, but because their minds and spirits drove them on. Daron, himself unseen, watched the steady, strong-backed walk of a man browned with the sun, hands dark with rich brown soil, bearing an offering of ripe, round melons slung in twin sacks across his shoulders.

"Now there," said Daron, his eyes closed down to slits of concentration, "goes a man who knows his mind. No fine-tongued orator would quickly move him to war—but, I would be loath to meet his kind as an enemy."

A pair of sailors, the breeze bringing even here the good, round talisman of their calling and proof of the god they'd worship, went noisily up the trail, blowing, laughing, rolling slightly in their walk, spurring each the other with insults of his weakness. Blowing like a hard north gale on this small slope? The wine had washed away his strength!

"Gods," said Daron to himself, "have little need of help in working miracles—but these gods of Azun be strange gods. Why might a god call on a man for help? Why, to lead and work with other men. A god is no doubt a mighty leader—but men and gods are different things. I'd fight for a god in whom I found just cause—but not behind such a one. There would seem to me a certain delicacy in the question. A man who leads against the enemy is credited not perhaps with skill, but in any case with more than jelly up his spine.

"But a god? An immortal god? Is courage needed for one who cannot die to face a deadly foe? And would such anomalous courage hearten those strong, if odorous, fishers? Why, the god might be courage itself—but still lack proof, where he cannot die or feel steel cutting!

"So—perhaps this is a certain question of leading men against those foppish ones that rule Tordu. Foppish—but from the nice-kept stable yards I saw, well mounted. And your mounted cavalry is a savage thing for simple farming men to face, no matter how ill-trained the mounted man may be."

Daron looked out and down. Two giant old pines, their trunks scaled like yellow-brown bodies of gigantic, uprearing serpents, had throttled out lesser competition to the northeast. Between their mighty boles, Tordu was visible, a sprawl of white and green and pastel blues against the green-brown farming land. The sparkling blue of the bay, with the white-crowned Temple Isle across its mouth, mocked up at him with tiny, bright-ribboned barges plying slowly back and forth on languid oars, like water beetles crawling across a puddle.

Daron fingered a single coin tucked well down in one pocket, and looked out across the town. "Tammar I'll see—I think—for this bit of silver should be more than coin, keeping in mind its source. And gods do not favor mortals for naught, and if this Nazun, chief of Azun's gods, sees fit to speak to me, why Tammar—"

He paused, his slit-narrow, night-blue eyes widening and easing away the straight furrows of concentration. Mixed visions swam before his mind—oval faces framed in spun-golden hair, with wide-opened eyes like sapphires staring out in seeming wonder, and black-haired heads, round and olive-skinned, with black-jet eyes. Tall bodies willowy slim, and lithe as temple dancers, figures strong and tall and fine, free-swinging, life-loving—

He shook his head and laughed. "No one—but part of all, perhaps. But Lady Tammar will know—and be, if Shorhun tells me right." He leaned back, eyes rising to the vaulted roof of interlacing, dark-green boughs.

A footstep near brought his eyes down, and his hand shifted half an inch to reach in one flashing drive, if need should be, the long, well-balanced weapon at his side. His hand fell away, his eyes narrowed, then widened slowly as a smile overspread his tanned face.

"You are too late, good friend. My wine is gone, my meat and bread consumed—and I cannot repay a meal of some few evenings gone. But my accommodations here are good in many ways. The seats are soft, the needles pad them well, and keep away the ground's damp chill. Would you be seated?"

Nazun's gray eyes smiled, and his head nodded easily. His lean, muscular body folded gracefully, till he was seated at the base of a mighty pine, facing Daron's curious eyes. Nazun's eyes flickered swiftly over horse, silver-mounted saddle, Daron's good and well-stitched clothing, and the jewel-hilted sword he carried. "A single coin has seeded well, since last we met."

Daron laughed easily. "One crop it raised—but the next night I found a planted pebble—planted beneath the shelter of three small snail shells—grew better still in the good soil of Azun."

Nazun's eyes laughed, and he nodded gravely. "Strange plants flourish well where the ground has not been sowed before. Yet the thing is very old."

"Perhaps," said Daron, "you could tell me its age?" He looked at Nazun's grave, unchanging face through narrowed eyes.

Nazun shook his head. "I've seen this earth somewhat longer than you, Daron, but this is older still. What legends of antiquity do your people know, Daron?"

Daron's gaze swung up to watch the bowing, swaying, stately dance of dark green boughs against a clear blue sky. His long, powerfully muscled figure looked relaxed and easy, his dark-green jacket blending here, and his gray-blue woolen breeches loose and floppy about well-corded legs. His face looked blankly easy—save for the eyes, where fine networks of tiny creases gathered about the night-blue eyes peering upward at the moon-blue heavens.

"Legends? Legends—and this Nazun is no mortal man, but Lord of Wisdom. Now legends are for children's ears, it seemed to me, but—but I am not Lord of Wisdom." Daron's thoughts flashed swiftly over years and nations—and legends. A pattern formed abruptly in his mind, a pattern he'd never seen before, and with his understanding, he started so he moved and looked deep in Nazun's eyes.

"Now by the gods!" said Daron, soft-voiced. "I've seen a hundred nations, and heard a hundred tales, and spent long nights around the fires to the music of the ballads and the thrill of long-drawn legends. I've heard how Bummeur of the Tutz nations defeated Lacoor of the Parrys from the Tutz balladeers. And, two nights later, heard how, in that self-same battle, Lacoor of the Parrys drew Bummeur of the Tutz to follow his retreat, and trapped him—from a balladeer in Par.

"But in the Tutz ballads, and in those of the Parrys, in those of every nation I have met, there is one common basis of ancient, ancient legend, stories older than the histories of nations. Once men were gods—and flew in air. And men were gods, to ride on fire, beyond the air, and spoke with the voices of gods, heard across all Earth, from nation to nation, and they had thunderbolts of gods.

"But men were men—not gods. They flew on their wings, and loosed their thunderbolts at one another, till each had stripped all godhood from the other. And—men were men, and grubbed in ground again, and rode the air no more, but plodded earth on old Shank's mare.

"Now a man may lie, and having taken council aforehand, a dozen men may lie, and lie alike. But when a hundred men, in a hundred nations, men who have never met, lie the same fine tale—there's more than lying there!"

Nazun's gray eyes twinkled, deep beneath their shadowing brows, and his head nodded lazily. "I've heard such legends among the peoples of Azun—and one legend heard only here. That, when man stripped man of god-like powers, and the world rocked and heaved in torture to their thrusts, lands sank and new lands rose from the sea-beds. The island group that is Azun rose from the seas then, and some hundred peaceful men, who had certain wisdom of those things that made for godhood, took council. Now tell me, friend, if the nations tore like mad dogs at each other's throats and every nation was embroiled, and new lands rose from the sea—"

"I," said Daron, "would found a new nation on that untainted land."

Nazun nodded slowly, settled back against the tree and looked up to where a scarlet-breasted bird cocked wary eyes downward before he drew back his head to rap a resounding tattoo on the great trunk. "Now," said Nazun, looking upward, "let us think what wise men might do—in days when the world was mad with bloodlust and mighty powers. Say you were such a refugee that settled here on Ator, largest of this Azun group."

His eyes wandered down again to rest on a hopping bird fighting with a stubborn worm. "That bird there walks, but he can fly, thanks to a certain mechanism—a sort of machine that he was gifted with. Pity we have not that machine."

Daron cocked a squinted eye, and watched the triumphant bird gobble quickly, ruffle his feathers, crouch and leap into the air. "I've tried a thousand times to do the same," the sea rover sighed. "I've seen coasts no ship could reach, and no walking man could find. And the bird flew where I could not." He shrugged. "I could not make such mechanism."

"But once—men were, the legends say, near godlike—men might have had the wit for that, perhaps," suggested Nazun.

"Ah," said Daron softly, and watched the bowing, dancing, swirling limbs above his head. Thoughts flashed through his mind such as he'd never contemplated. Gods, or godlike, the legends said. But—if their godhood had rested in mechanisms, in cleverness of tool and trickery—that was a sort of godhood one could well strip away, as one force took the catapults of another, to leave them helpless, wandering in rout.

"They'd need," said Nazun's soft, almost dreaming voice, "most wonderful tools for that, no doubt. Better, finer tools than we. Springs, perhaps, of a steel better than we know, and mighty forges to make the steel."

The picture roiled and cleared in Daron's mind. That was the source of legend, then! They had been godlike, those men of old! But their godhood had rested in machines—and the tools to make the machines. Once smash those tools—and machines wore out, with no more tools to replace them—

"They," said Daron slowly, "had wit, perhaps, but, it seems, more trickery than godhood. Wit, knowledge—but no judgment, and wisdom is also judgment."

"Men's minds are strange, are they not, my friend? And little known. Had such ones, as these ancient legends speak of, known more of themselves, perhaps their godlike knowledge of the things they bent to toys might have made them gods indeed."

Daron looked closely at the pine-needle-strewn ground on which he sat, and thought. There was a story here—a further story. Gods did not speak to men to while away the time. There would be reward, perhaps, but also—when the affairs of gods were concerned, and mortal men were brought to enter—danger, adventure! "Had I escaped," said Daron softly, "from a world, and founded on an island, unmolested, a new city, a new nation, having some remnant of that godlike knowledge—I think I would forget it. I think, perhaps, more knowledge of myself would make life worthier to myself. How does man think—and how go mad? Some say a demon enters the spirit of the mad, and some say only that his mind is sick, like the belly with a colic. And some are only queer, and growing somewhat queerer, we say are mad.

"I know the thousand riggings of a hundred nations' ships—and know not how that knowledge lodges in my skull. I think, were I to build a new nation on the wreckage of that old, I'd learn myself a bit, before I tried the rebuilding of such powers as once destroyed men."

"And wait, before you learned again those things, till every man in all the race had judgment enough to carry burning brands through the granary of man without setting fire? Wait, as the ages passed, till there was not, and never would be again, a madman to loose the spark? Yes," said Nazun softly, "that would be—safe, at least."

Daron laughed, and nodded slowly. "Safe," he chuckled, "and stupid, as the turtle in his shell. We need— Oh!" said Daron suddenly, and looked at Nazun with a sudden, overwhelming understanding. "Man needs a *god, or godlike guide who acts, who interferes to direct man upward as he longs, and halt the downward settling of his urge!*"

Nazun moved easily, his long, blue-green-clad body rippling blithely to whipcord muscles under tanned and healthy skin. "Man needs his ideals personified, made real and given power. Given power enough, indeed, to stop the individual man who errs, but judgment enough to spare the man who sees ahead. One who is not man—for man is jealous of man, and unyielding to man's suggestions."

Daron sat very still, and concentrated on the soft brown mass of needles at his feet. "A mighty plan," he sighed. "And if man, through centuries, learned once to rule the rest of the world with godlike powers, perhaps through other centuries he might learn to rule himself. But how, I wonder, might it be?"

"The compass needle points to north, drawn by a thread of force unseen, unfelt by men. The brain of man is made of many tiny parts, working one against the other, millions on millions of them, by threads of force like the force that moves the compass needle, perhaps. A somewhat different force, more akin to the sparks that come from combing hair on cold, dry nights, it might be. If these small parts—these cells—act thus against each other, and it is their interaction, not the cells themselves, that is thought, then it is the force the cells generate, *and not the cells themselves,* which is thought."

"Yes," said Daron, his eyes narrowed and alert on those bottomless gray wells of Nazun's eyes. "And—the force that is the interaction is not material, as invisible as the fine thread of pull that turns the compass needle."

Nazun relaxed, and his eyes wandered from Daron's, as though the important story were told. "If these things were true, men might then learn to make those interactions that are thought self-existent, apart from the materials of the cells. A group of many men, wise and learned, might cause a concentration of such forces to take an independent existence, a self-thinking, immaterial thought. It would be—almost godlike.

"It would be the essence of man—his ideas, without his needs, his heights, without his weakness.

"And the minds of many men might mold and build it better, nearer to human kind, while yet it had the power to reject the wrong in men.

"With such—man might go onward safely, for such a guardian of man could guide and aid men."

"Why"—Daron halted, licked his lips with tip of tongue, and rephrased his thought. If Nazun wished indirection, there might be reason, must be reason here—"if such a thing should be attained, say—five centuries ago—"

"Perhaps seven and a half," suggested Nazun.

"—or so long as seven and a half centuries ago, then men so protected might advance that knowledge of material things once more in safety. It seems to me, they would."

"But if," said Nazun, "some twelve long centuries had passed since Azun first was settled, and twelve long centuries of valifying those studies had established strong tradition— And does the young man choose the stony hillside, though it have rich and virgin soil beneath the rocks, when the proven, fertile soil of the valley is there?

"Daron, where would you start the search for facts that lead to knowledge that might make men fly again?"

"Why . . . with birds."

"There is a tradition, I have heard, handed down from the days of legends. It is very strong, and probably true. The way to flight is not the way of birds. The wings men fly upon must not move."

"I'd like," said Daron dryly, "to study this science of the mind."

"So many did. But that is gone—since the Invisible Ones came."

"These thought-force things might be invisible, might they not?"

"But, being thought," Nazun said, lazily turning to shade from the shifting sun, "might make themselves have form in man's mind."

"But any form!" said Daron softly, thinking suddenly of Lady Tammar, who was, so Shorhun said, every man's ideal, but not for any man.

"But why should they? These gods—men are men; they are limited as men, and cannot truly conceive of a god, can they? It is not logic. To imbue a god with human qualities is basic contradiction. They are more than human, and hence, by definition, not human. A human, then, could not conceive them. A god should see the future, and be possessed of absolute logic."

"The logic is sound," Daron nodded, eyes narrowed, "but the logic of a wise man of Tharsun, in the Tutz nation, was sound, too. It was logic that a heavy rock should drop much faster than a light one. It doesn't, incidentally. I had him show me, by test, the soundness of his proof.

"A god such as you describe might be a god! I could not know. But he'd be a poor neighbor, with his absolutes. The laws of nature are absolute, and logical. But I've seen a small child thrust its hand into the pretty glow of molten brass—and be punished with the absolutes of nature's laws."

Nazun shrugged. "I repeat the logic of the priests of the Invisible Ones. They have no root in human brain—though they draw their powers from the tiny generators of the force of thought that make up human brains. They live by the energies of the thoughts their worshipers give. But their root and existence lies within a . . . crystal ball, a thing some three feet through."

Daron stiffened where he lay. "That is material?"

"It is material, and may be crushed by a blow."

Daron knew, that instant, what his task must be. "Where might this crystal be?"

"On the Temple Isle—but no one knows. The Invisible Ones guard that knowledge—with certain reason. But it is not readily seen, nor wisely seen. The priests of the Invisible Ones, the Invisible Ones themselves—and the sphere itself. Three defenses makes it safe."

Daron nodded, and shivered slightly.

"I . . . I saw a thing of similar nature. And thereby came near to being no more! A certain wizard of the Tahly folk showed me it, and, but for a friend, I'd be standing paralyzed before him yet! He learned, though, and taught me certain things. Hypnotism, where the mind is slaved!"

Nazun nodded. "Its strong defense, a final barrier. It was not meant so originally, but meant only as the basis of the Invisible Ones, its weaving lights their patterned thoughts, and, being mechanism, they are uninfluenced by anything but logic."

Daron snorted softly. "Cold comfort in such gods as that!"

"No comfort—but knowledge."

"Useless knowledge, if what I hear be truth."

"Useless—but satisfying, at times. To know the result of tomorrow's deeds. The Invisible Ones are there, that knowledge can be had. No good it can do, for, being truth, it can't be changed. But—a young man's wife is suffering in labor—and he can know the true result, two lives—or none! Or a child is sick, and the father sleepless with prodding fear, which might—and the Invisible Ones know—be needless.

"A day, you'll stay away, not caring greatly for that ultimate knowledge what day and hour Lord Barak has closed your book—but a month, a year, a dozen years. The knowledge is there—"

Daron nodded. "No man has will to fight such steady pull forever. And once indulged—the man's mind and will is trapped. Aye—that is logic, but lacks ideals. But—I wonder if the Invisible Ones"—Daron looked at Nazun's rugged face through narrowed lids—"could tell me when I shall die? Or—when they shall die?"

"They cannot. The course of a man is straight through time, from past to future, basing actions of the present on the memories and knowledge gained in the past. But a god acts on his knowledge of the past and future! That is chaos—and cannot be predicted. And those of men who associate themselves with gods—cannot be predicted."

Daron's eyes looked upward again. The lowering sun was casting longer rays, and the zenith sky was dark, deep blue, with the clarity of high mountain air. The darkening branches wove across the spot of sky, and whispered soft accompaniment to eager, anxious birds. A three-foot crystal ball with moving, weaving, hypnotic lights. A material thing that a blow could smash—but which, because it was material, no immaterial thing could harm!

Daron's eyes swept down—and widened sharply. The tree across the way swayed gently to the breeze, but Nazun was gone. There was a helmet where he had sat, a thing of woven wires of silver and gold, wires fine and soft as young lamb's wool, and five strange jewels. A blue-green, queerly luminous bit of stuff lodged at the front, a bit of stone that matched in color Nazun's garb. A bit of stone like agate, red-streaked and white, above the right ear, a bit of rose quartz above the left, and a sea-green crystal at the rear.

At the peak, a blob of utter night made solid was fixed in the fabric of the weave. "Barak, Lord of Fate and Death," said Daron softly. "And the others—Talun's sea-green, my Lady Tammar's rose, and Martal's streaked stone, Lord Martal's Stone of Chance."

Abruptly, as he settled it upon his head, it occurred to him that immaterial forces such as thought did not ordinarily move weighty gold and silver.

Slowly he caught up the reins of his browsing horse and mounted. Lost in thought, he nodded gently to the motion of the animal, and wondered further how it might be that clouds should form, and a howling storm move up at the behest of a wholly immaterial Talun. And puzzled at how much of a full, round truth Nazun had seen fit to gift him with.

A good hour later he roused, and looked about—and cursed himself for a fool. The horse, in natural course, had found the going easier down the mountainside. The temples, and Lady Tammar, were far above, and for this day, he must wait.

## V

The sun was set, and the moon well up, a round, pale lantern of lies, pretending to light the city of Tordu, when Daron turned down the cobbled street toward Shorhun's inn. The moon's light was a snare and a deception, as Daron well knew; it lied about the colors of the walls, saying that dirt-streaked muddy yard wall there was touched with silver paint, and that yonder wall was built of glinting gold. Daron well knew it was blue-tinged plaster, and the black tiled roof was bright green by day.

And the shadows, where only low voices and soft laughter originated, were people—though the moon would not reveal it. Deceptive. The glow of light on walls and streets, smelling with the faint and blended odors over which prevailed the queer, wet scent of water poured on hot stone cobbles and lawns at sunset. The little trees and sunken entrances casting shadows sharp and black, the narrow, canyon alleyways black gouges through the twisting buildings of the section.

Daron was deep in thought—but Daron had visited more nations than one, and in most, he'd found an eye that didn't sleep of more than slight aid for long and healthy life. The black shadow of an entrance arch, cut through a high plastered garden wall, spouted figures, two clumps of shadow that ran, topped with white blobs of faces, and lightening with moon-glimmer on steel.

The horse reared and screamed and twisted round in panic as Daron's sharp spurs raked his sides in a way he'd not known since this new master mounted him. He lurched and pawed forward—and the two shadows ducked aside from the sharp shod hoofs. Daron was off on the far side of the horse. The animal snorted once, and felt his rider gone. Startled, hurt, he clattered away. Daron was on his feet, balancing lightly in the shadow of the wall, while the two shadows turned to face him. Full moonlight struck at them now, while the wall's high shadow engulfed and blotted out clear sight of Daron's figure.

"Right!" said a low voice, and one of the pair leaped to Daron's right, the other to his left. They wore cloaks of some dark stuff, and cowls that snugged about their heads. The cloaks hung close about them, no hindrance now as they came on mincing, dancing feet, and lunged, a trained chorus that attacked from two sides at once.

Daron blotted out in shadow, and was behind the one as he spun on his heel. His cloak swirled loose at the hem, and the moon-glimmer of his sword reached up—and fouled in it. Moonlight silvered on his face, a lean, bony face with hollow, blackened eyes and line-thin lips that writhed in blazing anger. Daron's sword licked out, twisted neatly round the fouled weapon, and sent it flying, a glinting fragment of light, across the garden wall. Somewhere beyond, it landed with a ringing clang.

"Hold!" said Daron sharply. "I have no enemies here."

The second man danced forward, his face lifting in a smile of keenest pleasure as his blade darted under Daron's momentarily lifted sword. Daron's body shifted slightly at the final instant—and the blade bent double as it scraped on the thin steel plate beneath the sea rover's jacket at the breast.

The cowled man danced back as Daron's blade came down, a soft-voiced vicious snarl on his lips. The second man was circling, his cloak stripped off in an instant's time and wrapped about his left arm, the glint of a dirk in his right hand.

"So be it, then!" Daron snapped. "I *had* no enemies here!"

"And," the sword bearer whispered, "you will have none—for the dead have neither friend nor foe!"

Daron slipped aside, backed toward the wall as he caught the other's sword on his own, the swift wrist play making the steel *thrum* and sing, and the close, keen following of blade on blade making scarce a click of contact. Daron danced and moved and wove, and watched the moon-whitened faces of his attackers. They were twins, twin meal-white faces with twin sooted, shadowed eyes. But one stood forth in lighter clothing, loose trousers gathered at the calf to tight stocking breeches, loose jacket hanging below the waist. But each arm carried an armlet of jewel-glinted metal, and across the breast was woven a pattern of spheres and many jewels.

Daron danced back and back, feeling out the swordsman, and knowing in the spring and slash of the blade he faced that this was one who'd handled weapons before and handled them well. He moved and danced and backed away, and the dirkman, short of reach with his small blade, circled helplessly.

Daron moved forward in a deceptive glide that scarcely seemed motion, and twisted as he moved. The long, thin blade lunged out, flicked once, and laid open his opponent's arm from wrist to elbow. A soft, thick inhalation of pain, and whispered curse; the cloaked one held his blade in his left hand, and charged in for revenge. Daron backed, circled left to avoid the lunge of the dirk. His twisting, glimmering blade lunged out once more and buried in the swordsman's throat. An instant's scream was throttled in a rush of blood, and the sword dropped down to ring on cobbled pavement.

Simultaneously, as Daron freed his blade, the dirk rang on the street, and the second man had swept up the fallen sword. Daron leaped forward, and in the engagement wrapped his blade about the base of the other's, and sent it flying. His own straightened out, and hovered near the jewel-sprinkled breast.

"Now how is this, my jeweled dandy, that you seek strangers for your murdering? Would not wisdom suggest you know your victim and his capabilities before you practice up on assassination? I have no knowledge of your laws here, but there is one of mine I think good. Who attacks me is an enemy—or gives good account of why he sought me out. Speak, and speak truth!"

The moon-whitened face was motionless, the thin, straight lips held shut. He faced the moon now, and the shadowed eyes were lighted, gleaming fish-belly white against the face. They shifted minutely—and Daron leaped aside and whirled.

The sword he had just thrown with his blade licked past his shoulder like metal lightning. The man whose throat Daron had spitted whirled, and leveled the blade for a second attack as the other swooped to retrieve the dirk, glowing like molten silver on the cobbles.

Daron cursed softly, and engaged the dead man's blade. It swept and swung and danced to meet every move. It glinted like a sweep of sunlit rain, a thousand lines of steel in place of one. Daron danced back, drew back his arm as the dead man lurched forward clumsily, blood bubbling through slow-formed words. "Stand still, fool; you die!"

Daron's arm swept downward, and his sword flew hilt-foremost toward the dead, white face. The dead man's sword swept up too slow, and the heavy hilt crashed true across his eyes, with all the strength of Daron's arm behind it.

The second attacker lunged in, grasped Daron's sword before it fell, and reached out for Daron's dancing form. The dead thing squalled, raked at blinded eyes, and twisted vainly. Barely, Daron retrieved the blind thing's sword and danced away with skin still whole.

"Men," said Daron tensely, "I'll fight fair—but when the fairly killed come back again—why, there's an end to fairness!"

"You'll die," the rustling, laughing whisper of the other assured him. His cloaked arm reached, and suddenly, as the two blades engaged, grasped Daron's sword. Daron released the blade, dropped his hand to his dirk before the other, expecting a frantic pull, recovered balance. The dagger flashed, spun through the air, and buried in the bejeweled man's face. He screamed and stumbled forward, dropping the two blades he held to claw at the dagger.

Daron whipped up his own blade from the street, and slashed coldly at the fallen man's throat. The watchful sword rang against it, and sent it dancing down the street.

The thing stood up and stared at him with blank, dead eyes. "You die," it said. "You must—for I cannot!" The words were whistling, nasal, but half formed. The slashed throat whistled and moaned as air sucked in and out.

"You cannot die," Daron agreed with cold, live things squirming in his belly, "but blind, you cannot see!" The sword he held danced out again, swept, parried, darted in—and in a second time. Daron stepped back, his blade lowered, to watch the blinded thing—and almost died on the lunging blade!

Desperately, the sea rover met the blade that danced and lunged and parried at his own, a dead, blind thing seeking out his every move and driving him back—back—with tireless speed, while lead flowed down Daron's veins and settled in his wrist. "Nazun—Lord Nazun," Daron whispered softly, "I ask no help in things I know, I ask no help in doing—but give me knowledge to stop this *thing!*"

The swords sang and danced and winked, and soft leather sandals scraped on cobblestones—and Daron felt the blade come nearer. Air whistled in the dead throat, and in his own dry throat, and he glanced sharply at the corpse that lay outstretched beside the dirk—and wondered when it would again rise!

Daron's breath sucked in in sudden understanding. For an instant, the leaden load of tiring muscles lightened with glimpse of relief. His defense grew bolder, then an attack that wrapped the dead thing's blade gave him the chance he sought. His own blade lunged forward again as he twisted—and laid open the dead thing's arm from wrist to elbow. The severed tendons dropped the blade, and as the other arm swept down, a slashing exit at the left wrist left it with useless fingers.

"You may not die, you may not blind," Daron panted hoarsely, "but those hands will grip no more!"

The dead man dropped like an emptied sack, lay limp an instant in the street and, as Daron watched, the limbs stiffened in rigor.

Cold gnawed at the sea rover's brain as he walked silently down the street, rubbing the tired muscles of his forearm. This section of the city was quiet as those men had at last become, the silvering of the moon alone remaining. The low voices and the laughter had vanished. Only far away across the still rustle of trees in the night wind came sounds of a city's movement, the restless, rustling tone that rises and falls and never dies while a city lives. The smell of flower gardens and fresh salt air swept from the bay on the wings of the inshore breeze. But no sound nearby.

Then, a block away, he heard the hesitating *clop-clop* of a shod horse's hoofs, the irregular rhythm of an unridden horse, uncertain of its way, feeling the weight of loneliness, lacking human guidance. Daron started toward the sound, loping silently, his mind skipping agilely, yet numbed withal, and bewildered mightily. His enemy was clear—for none but a god could make those dead things dance to their strings. But his friends—

Or had he thought that solution for himself? Had his own mind seen clear the ripped arm of the abandoned corpse, and the reason for its desertion? It was no more than he had done before—save that that dead, blind face opposing him with inhuman skill had frozen and numbed his thoughts beyond any experience he had ever known.

He thrust the thing to the back of his mind, and turned down a narrow street. His gray stallion tossed its head uneasily, and faced him, whickering uncertainly. "So, boy, it's easy now. I raked you then to save you from being spitted. Come, now—it hurt, I know, but a foot man does not fight a mounted man, but first his horse. Come—ah!" Daron swung up, and soothed the uncertain animal to an easy walk, and guided him once more toward the inn. But the sea rover's eyes kept sharper watch than ever they had at a good ship's bow.

## VI

The hanging lamp was dark, with charred and smoking wick, and Shorhun's lanky figure draped uneasily in the fireside chair, asleep and snoring gently. His long, lean arms, like knotted ropes, hung loose beside the chair, his fingers half opened to the glow of the dying fire. Across the room, the boy was curled upon a bench, head pillowed on an elbow, and one long arm, a small duplicate of Shorhun's knotted cables, reached down to grip in lax fingers a dog's collar.

The dog looked up abruptly, with wide-opened eyes as Daron's horse *clopped* softly in the courtyard, and the creak and grunt of leather harness attested to the stabling of the animal. His quick eyes watched Daron enter the room. He snorted softly, and lowered his massive head upon his paws, eyes watchfully awake.

Daron rubbed his arm and smiled. Softly he stepped over to Shorhun and laid a friendly hand upon his arm. The lanky innkeeper moved and raised his head.

"Daron?" he said, his voice mechanical and toneless with broken sleep.

"Aye, Daron—and with a throat as dry as Fraka's plains. And— But get me wine, my friend."

Shorhun heaved up, and ambled toward his supply, to return with a bottle and a glass on a small tray. He set the lot before Daron, and slumped into his chair, resting his head within his palms.

"Ho, am I to drink alone? Come, Shorhun, another glass, and join me in it. And tell me, is it customary for this town that men should seek to murder strangers on sight?"

Shorhun raised himself, and fetched another glass. "No," he said tonelessly, pouring wine into the two.

Daron looked up into the lank, tired man's eyes. He was quiet for a moment as he watched the eyes, and watched Shorhun pick up the glass. Then his strong, brown fingers gripped Shorhun's wrist and stayed the hand. "Wait, friend. I think—I think your lamp needs oil, and I need light, I know. I would not drink until I see the color of my wine."

Shorhun moved wordlessly to the task, pulling down the counter-weighted lamp, filling the reservoir, trimming the wick and lighting it so that the room was warm with yellow light.

Daron's fingers were busy then with an aimless spinning of a bit of polished metal on a cord, a polished metal mirror that spun first one way, then the other. "Sit here," said Daron, as the innkeeper finished, "and listen, friend. I have a tale to tell."

Wearily, Shorhun sat down across the table and Daron began. His voice was low and soft, and he described his start that morning, following Shorhun's directions, and Shorhun's sleepy eyes were watching the dancing, spinning mirror on the cord, and the swirling reflections of the lamp that danced with it.

"Once before," said Daron softly, in a sleepy voice, "I traveled such a hill-climbing road, to the dwelling of a wizard of the Ind people. I was tired as you are tired, and wanted sleep—as you want sleep—the rest and ease of sleep—sleep—sleep—"

Daron's voice was toneless, sleepy—but his eyes were bright and hard, and the mirror in the lamplight spun and spun, and hesitated to spin the other way at the end of its cord. "Sleep you need—sleep—" Shorhun's sleepy eyes sank lower, then abruptly tried to rise, his body seemed to struggle to rise, his head to turn from the mirror. "You hear only my voice, as you sleep—sleep—and forget all other things, but see the mirror that tires your eyes and makes you sleep. Shorhun, you hear only your friend, Daron, Daron who, like you, seeks only the Old Gods. You hear no voice but mine, and obey me in all things. You obey me, and only me, Shorhun!"

The tonelessness was gone, and there was the whip of sharp command in Daron's tone—and the mirror spun. "You will and must answer any question I ask. That is true!"

"Y-yes," said Shorhun.

"I am your friend, and friend to your friends."

"Yes," said Shorhun promptly.

Daron's eyes were tense and dark. Very softly to himself, he whistled a little tune, and thought. "Now this is clear; someone has been here

and worked upon this man, and thanks be to old white-headed
Barhamu for what he taught me in the hills of Ind! But what is
the purpose? No god did this, for the look of his eyes in good close
view was clumsy revelation. But a man—if Barhamu knew enough to
match at all these god-making wizards of Azun—cannot make another do what that other would object to—such as murdering his
friends!"

Daron thought deeply, then: "Shorhun," he snapped, "is this wine
good?"

"Y-yes," said Shorhun, and stirred uneasily, his forehead careworn
and weather-browned, wrinkling in a frown of childish puzzlement.

"Shorhun, there was a stranger here who laid commands on you?"

Shorhun's face worked, his mouth moved and knotted and fell still.
Daron nodded grimly. "But that stranger, while no god, knew this
mind art well. Now how to break that spell—"

A thought came to him, and he rose. "Shorhun," he snapped, "sit
there, and do not move until I return." Then, thinking of certain
things that lay upon a cobbled street—"Or," he added—"until the
sun rises and the day is here."

Daron strode out the door, and sought down the road. It was half
an hour before he returned, swearing softly, with a mewing cat in his
arms. His clothes were torn somewhat, and stained with varicolored
plaster dust from climbing many walls.

He set the cat upon the table stroking it. "Shorhun," he said softly,
"I know. You can tell me, because I know these things already. The
stranger came and talked with you, and laid command on you to
forget. But you were to give me this wine, and do whatever was needed
that I might drink it."

"Yes," said Shorhun, uneasily. "It is good wine. The flavor is better
than my own."

"Watch," commanded Daron. He spilled a bit of wine, and forced
some down the cat's unwilling throat. The cat mewed and spit and
scratched, and, relaxed, sat down and cleaned its fur. Daron waited
patiently. Abruptly the cat jumped, doubled up, screeched in agony—
then straightened down with ruffled fur to lick itself clean. Two minutes later it doubled up again, screeched louder, and writhed unhappily. The spasm stopped, to resume again within a minute more.

Within five minutes the cat was dead, in one last spasm wherein
its cries were choked in a muscle-knotted throat, and its muscles con-
vulsed so violently the broad abdominal muscles ripped themselves
across in frightful spasm, and every muscle tore, so that the carcass
was a loose bag of death wrapped up in skin.

Softly Daron spoke. "That is the wine you would have fed your friend, Shorhun. That is the wine you would have drunk with me! That is murder in its foulest form!"

Shorhun shuddered, his face worked in knotted muscles, and his staring eyes twitched and danced. Abruptly he shook himself, and stumbled erect, "Eh? Daron! You here? Eh—it's night!"

Daron nodded, smiling. "Aye, it's night, my friend, and you may thank a man you never knew, one Barhamu, that you and I live now, and are not—that!"

Shorhun looked at the body of the cat, then picked it up and dropped it sharply in disgust, rubbing his hands as though they were contaminated by the contact. "What . . . what is this? And where is that dandied priest of the Invisible Ones that visited me here?"

"Ah, now the tale appears! I thought it might. Now listen to me, friend, and in the future look not so keenly at spinning mirrors, glittering jewels, or other tricks of wizards. I'll tell you something of a tale to straighten up that knotted hair of yours, but first bring me some wine—some wine of your own, and no more of this hell's brew. In the meantime, I sense a bit of trickery in your son's sleep."

An hour later, Daron was dreaming. Now even one with the easygoing conscience and the tough stomach that Daron had, dreams now and then, but no such dream as this. He dreamed, and, moreover, knew he was dreaming.

For that last hour before he went to bed, the helmet of woven gold-and-silver wire beside him, he had been thinking as he talked with lanky, grimly boiling Shorhun. With half his mind he'd told his tale, and explained many things to Shorhun that he had learned in a high, dry old building far up the slopes of the shattered mountains of the Ind. And with the other, deeper half of his mind, he had been thinking, stewing about one problem; the problem of the sphere.

The menace of iron and flesh and blood that was the priests of the Invisible Ones, he set aside. *That* sort of menace he had known before, and would know again—with luck! But the Invisible Ones themselves? That, it seemed, was in the immaterial, potent province of the Lord Nazun. But the sphere—

A single strong blow could smash it—but to see it was to be paralyzed. His keen, smoothly working mind was baffled, brought solid and firm against a thing that, he knew, was the one thing in all the world against which it could not fight effectively: itself. Too long and well had old Barhamu taught him for self-deception here. The trick of the Spinning Mirror and the Trick of the Winking Light were, alike, tricks that no mind could well resist—for they were tricks that turned that mind upon itself.

And then the dream had come, as he sought sleep. He stood before an altar of blue-green beryl, a mighty, perfect gem four feet high, by three feet square, his head bowed down in prayer. Behind the altar stood Nazun, his gray eyes deep as night, with unplumbed depths so vast that the lack of bottom made them black. The eyes drew up his bowed head, till his own blue eyes looked into them, and through them, swallowed by them—and saw with the eyes of Nazun!

His sight hurled out across the night, driving through walls of blue-green stone, through the dark, whispering forests of the mountain, across the city, where Tordu lay dark beneath the setting moon, with only here and there some late light gleaming. The world was a painted map, luminous with moon-glow, and the Bay of Tordu was a lake of quicksilver, marred by the black gash of the Temple Isle. For half an instant the world held in suspense; then, as though his point of sight had plunged like a falling meteor, the Temple Isle exploded upward, turned black and silver as buildings appeared, exploded outward, and his sight penetrated through. For an instant of time he was deep, deep within the heart of one, deep in a room whose black walls, carved from the living basalt of the isle's foundations, were lighted with a glow that seemed pure white.

A circle of warrior guards stood round the sphere, the three-foot sphere of crystal, like a fragile bubble floating in a three-clawed rest of gold. Uncounted myriads of pin-point lights circled in darting, swooping, patterned orbits, a mathematically precise involvement of inextricable cycles and epicycles, progressions and ordered, intricate orbits. The row of warrior guards stood firm about the sphere—but every back was toward it, and every guard stood with hand on sword and metal shield.

In a fraction of a second—then the vision was gone, chopped off with a hollow sensation of frightful fall that gripped and wrenched at Daron's mind and soul.

His mind retched and quivered in terror—then quieted as some vast thing of calm touched it, soothing, stilling. And Daron stood again before the blue-green altar gem of beryl. Lord Nazun stood behind it, and his gray eyes were tensed and tired; his strong-muscled hands leaned on the altar top, gripping it, it seemed, for support. The tanned, rough-hewn face of the Lord of Wisdom was white with strain and very tired.

Lord Nazun's voice was vastly weary as it whispered in the dream. "The Invisible Ones are wary; they cut off the vision soon. No further sight of that can I afford, for the cost is more than human mind could understand. But you have seen. Now—sleep again, and think!"

## VII

Daron sipped fragrant feya, and with drowsy eyes watched the sun shadows play in the courtyard. The sounds of Tordu City were waking round him; the cries of women, the shrill voice of a small boy carrying on conversation with some friend two blocks away, the heavy creak of a laden ox-cart plodding toward the market, bearing round, green melons and green-wrapped ears of corn.

Behind the drowsing eyes, the vision of the sphere danced and spun and moved, the myriad lights flashed in their orbit there, and, despite the strong protection of Nazun's mighty will, half hypnotized him still. Slowly to Daron's inward gaze, one fact was forming from the vision. Those myriad points of light moved not aimlessly, but with an order more precise than the swinging, ticking pendulum of the clock upon the wall. They looped and moved and danced—in ordered, plotted curves.

And abruptly Daron started. The drowsing eyes became alive, and the immobile face moved in a sudden, grim smile. He laughed softly, and swung to his feet. Shorhun, sitting silent at his table, looked up, and opened sleepy eyes.

"Ten minutes more, my friend," the lanky innkeeper sighed, "and for all your concentration I'd have broken in. I have a question of some small moment I would ask."

Daron laughed, and swung his sword belt round to a position of greater comfort. "Then ask away, Shorhun, for one cactus-spined and triply damned question that's festered in my mind is solved. Perhaps I can solve yours."

The innkeeper unfolded upward and shrugged. "It was merely this. I live today, because your eyes do more than see, and your brain holds more than most. But—I know not your plans, of course, but if they do not include your death within some three hours. I'd advise you seek some other seat."

"Hm-m-m. My plans did not include quite that," Daron nodded. He cocked a half-closed eye at Shorhun's ugly, solemn face. "But why should this seat—a very comfortable one seeming—be so sadly dangerous?"

"The priests of the Invisible Ones know it's here. If half your tale of last evening be true, then you murdered one priest. If it be wholly true, then you did murder enough to bring down the wrath of all the Invisible Ones on a dozen men."

Daron grunted softly. "They are slow to anger, then. I'd act without thinking over the problem a whole night through."

Shorhun nodded. "They would. But King Elmanus wouldn't. And it's King Elmanus' word that's needed. He wakes at eight, has breakfast at eight and a half, and holds no audience before nine and a half. It's nine and a quarter now."

Daron looked up at Shorhun with interest. "Now if this King Elmanus has these haughty priests of the Invisible Ones trained so well to leave his sleep alone, he holds my strong respect. He is unique among the monarchs of the world I've seen; he can make a high priest wait as high priests should, until he's had his breakfast. What potent secret does he hold for this?"

Shorhun sighed. "Old Elmanus is near eighty years old now, and he's reigned for fifty-five. For fifty-five long years, the Old God's priests have howled in his left ear, and for fifty-five long years the priests of the Invisible Ones have shrieked into his right.

"It's reached a sorry state, where now he can hear very little in either ear, and not at all when he is sleeping. But he has curiously sensitive hearing to the wail of countrymen and seamen both. His nobles he hears continuously, wherefore he need not listen hard to them."

"I'd think," said Daron shrewdly, "the priests would have found another king."

Shorhun chuckled. "Old Elmanus has not the slightest fear of death. He's lived too long, and during that life the two sets of gods have grown apart and hatred grown between. Now each fears a new king more than they loathe the old."

"Has neither worked on the will of Elmanus' successor?"

"Elmanus has no son, and his daughter is a priestess of Lady Tammar—but no woman may hold the throne. His successor must be elected."

"He'd be a noble, and the nobles—so you say—are all besotted with the future knowledge of the Invisible Ones."

"He'd be no noble," said Shorhun sourly. "The nobles all know well that several hundred exceedingly tough seamen loathe their blood and bones and several thousand countrymen obey old Elmanus blindly because he's just."

"Hm-m-m. . . . it would make a throne as hot as the sun's own fires! But—perhaps I'd best be on my way. Where would you suggest?"

"It depends upon your plans," said Shorhun, shrugging like a beaching wave. "If you intend permanent escape from Elmanus' guard I'd say your own land would be a sound place to seek. If for a day—start west, and I'll say north. They'll find you, though."

Daron rose, stretched mightily, and started through the door. "Call up that imp you name your son, and have him fix my horse. I saw a watchmaker's place two blocks away, and I have business there."

"I'll call my son, but his memory is short. He may remember long enough to bring the horse to Granner's place." Shorhun vanished through the kitchen door.

The sun was warm and the breeze that slid joyously down the mountainside was fresh with pine-laden scent, and the smell of many breakfasts pleasant to the nostrils. The cobbles, round beneath the feet, were easy walking, and Daron's eyes alert as he swung down the street. Two blocks away he came upon the little doorway that he sought, signed without by a huge wooden cog bearing the symbols "WATCH-MAKING."

The place was dark, and still cool with last night's air, and the watchmaker who looked up at him a half-seen figure in the gloom. His head was bald and polished as the faces of his products, but fringed around with a halo of white hair so fine it floated in the air. His face was a wizened, dried up apple, split by a smiling mouth, and sharp blue eyes as old as the skies, and laughing with them.

"And what is time and a timepiece to one as young as ye?" he snapped as Daron entered.

"Father, I am touched by a strange malady. The malady is never fatal, I am told, but long enduring," Daron said solemnly. "The malady some call inventor's itch."

The bright-blue eyes speared up at him. "Huy-hu, now. Unless this thing you have invented is the size and crudeness of an ox cart, those fingers of yours will never make it."

"Alas, father, they won't," Daron sighed. "Yours will, though, I suspect."

"I've work enough with things I know, and things that work, without befuddling my old head with foolishness. What have you in mind?"

"A thing about the size of a pocket watch, but of special and strange making. Now look you here, for all my handling of ships' cordage, still my fingers have certain skill at drawing things, and this is what I'd need. I'll pay you for it with twice its weight in gold, and add another weight if it is done by the third hour of the afternoon."

Rapidly Daron sketched, and the old watchmaker's keen eyes followed him. A dozen sketches, and many special strictures and explanations were demanded, but at last the old man snorted understanding.

"That malady you call inventor's itch, we call more often madness.

The thing is mad, and has no use, but I shall make it as you say. You'll have it by the second hour after noon."

"Good," said Daron. "Now here is proof of my madness, for I'll give you now the gold." Four round, hard coins he laid on the old man's desk and stepped outside, where Shorhun's freckled son lounged by his horse.

"My father says," the boy whispered softly, giving him the reins, "that guards are popping out of ash receivers, and springing up among the flowers. I'm going to the house of my grandmother for a week or so. Good-bye."

Daron stood an instant in thought, then stepped around the corner of the building where the lad had vanished to take him on his way. Two legs scrambling over a roof top disappeared as Daron turned the corner, and the lad was lost.

Shrugging, Daron set off across the town, his mind busy with his plans. Deeper and deeper into the city he went, stopping once at an inn where he was not known. Two hours later—the loungers there had learned a certain respect for three snail shells and a pebble that made longer stay imprudent—Daron sought out a small tailor's shop, and took off his hands some misfit clothes that reeked in Daron's nostrils of earthy sweat. But, at least, they did not betray the seaman's origin.

For three long hours more he visited in armorer's shops, obscure secondhand places, seeking a shield. It was well afternoon before he found the place he sought, a tiny cubbyhole left when two haughty buildings had not quite met, a mere alleyway between them roofed over by some sad-faced individual with the salesmanship of Jeremiah.

"A shield," he sighed, and sat firm on the broken chair before his door. "I don't think I have many. What kind?"

Daron looked at him sourly. His beard was of the sort that prolonged and persistent laziness, not art, produces, and his hands stained not with the grime of toil but, it seemed to the sea rover, the dust that settles on anything long motionless. "A round shield," said Daron carefully. "A round, flat shield of good steel or of silver-plated bronze."

"Silver-plated bronze? I had one such—I think it's gone—but they are not practical, I'm told," he added hastily. "A shield of hard-tanned hide will turn an arrow, or stop a blade, and is far lighter. Tharmun's shop, two blocks from here, specializes in them."

"Aye, so?" said Daron patiently. "That's what I learned some five minutes past. Now look you, friend, your aura is that of a wild goat, increased in strength by your advanced age and greater size. The spiders have spun their webs between your feet, and how one so immobile has escaped a load of flowing fat surprises me. Or can it be that your colossal lethargy forbids you rising to seek food?

"Be that as it may, I'll see your shields, my friend, if I must prick your dusted hide to make you seek them in defense. Now move!" Daron's sword left its scabbard of its own volition, seemingly, and pricked the cadaverous, sad-faced one.

With a howl of anguish he bounced within his shop, with Daron at his heels.

The sea rover halted. The place was dark as the maw of some deep cave, and rank with lack of cleaning. Very slowly Daron's eyes made out its contents, while the whine of the proprietor sought to convince him he wanted none of the merchandise.

"Be quiet, or by Martal, I'll let that noise out through your throat," snapped Daron. "Now bring me that bronze shield you have. Is it not clear to you that I am mad, and not to be reasoned with?"

The shield was brought. It was bronze, a well-made shield that some craftsman had labored over, and in seeing it, Daron knew that chance had favored him. Unlike any shield he'd seen before, its face was absolutely flat and plain, without decoration save a very chaste and simple geometric pattern that inscribed a circle round the edge. The face was bronze, very thin, for lightness, but by its ring a hard, true melt. The back was crossed with a patterned grid of bars that made it strong enough to turn a broadax swing.

"Now by Martal, chance is behind me this day indeed," said Daron with satisfaction. "What price do you want, Goaty One?"

"Ten *thords* I paid for it and less than twenty I cannot take and stay in business," the merchant whined.

"Ten thords it is then," said Daron, dropping two golden coins, "and good day."

"No, no! Twenty, I said!"

Daron swung on his horse, and started down the street. Behind him he heard a long, sad sigh, and the heavy creak of the broken chair. The shield, he saw, was bronze, plated well with silver, and the price was fair. The silver was black as night with lack of care, and a dark, old bronze patina had coated over the gridwork at the back.

Daron rode directly to the watchmaker's shop, and entered. The old man looked up from his work and nodded. "Ten minutes more, son, and your madness will spin as gaily as you like. You are early."

"No," said Daron wearily. "I'm late. I needs must polish my shield."

The old man's sharp eyes turned on the metal shield and narrowed down. "Now, by Nazun, I know your wits have left you, or you've more strength than even those none-too-puny arms suggest. That thing

may make a fine display—old Elmanus' guards once carried those, I think—
but as protection, they're as light and dainty as a good stone wall."

Daron laughed. "I'm vain as the peacock of Ind, and must make a
flashing display, father. Give me polish, then, and a bit of cloth, that
I may dazzle those who look at me."

The old man bent, and drew out soft rags, and a cake of black-
streaked rouge, and some white, moist paste. "Damp the rag at the
pump yonder, rub on the rouge and mix the white paste with it. If
there's any silver left, that thing should shine."

For half an hour more, Daron rubbed till his back and shoulders
ached, and his new-old garments were stained with a dozen shades of
red and black and green from the bronze. But when he finished, the
old shield's face shone like the sun, with scarce a dozen bad scratches.

"So it's old Elmanus I've to thank for finding this shield, eh? I
knew it was mad to hope to find so useless a thing, but this thing was
what I needed, none the less."

"King Elmanus it was. He had a special guard of twenty men, who
used those things. Elmanus found that a good spot of sunlight cast
back by twenty mirror shields would stop men quicker, and with less
stain of blood, than twenty swords. With those twenty shields, the
guard could blind a man for half a week.

"Wherefore all Elmanus' enemies came at him after dusk, and found,
of course, his twenty guards as well protected by those heavy shields
as though they each were weighted down with chains. Elmanus lost
three full complements of guards before he gave up those shields.

"You being only one, I'd think you had poor chance to learn wisdom—but that, my son, is your own task. It is your skin that shield is
supposed to defend."

"Ah, yes, and so it is. Now tell me, is that thing finished?" Daron
asked.

"Done. And here it is. I owe you also a coin, for, having an affec-
tion for those who are mad, I made it very light. Undoubtedly, it
shows I am a kindred spirit, and mad as you."

"Mm-m-m," said Daron, holding the tiny thing, "it seems good
enough indeed. I know good workmanship, and that is here. Keep the
extra coin. Good day, father."

"Good day, and if you now seek Nazun's temple, he will cure your
madness."

"I have no time. I have another appointment. Elmanus' guards are
seeking me for certain questions involving the death of two priests,
and I must find them."

Whistling, Daron went out, and the old man looked after him

with shrewd, hard eyes. With sudden decision, brought on by over-powering itch of curiosity, the old man swung heavy shutters across his tiny window, barred them, barred the door, and hobbled off across the town. On his weak legs, it would take him some time to reach Elmanus' court.

## VIII

On the highest crest of the rolling land that fronted on the bay, the palace of Elmanus set, overlooking the estates of the nobles. The avenue here was broad, and paved with bricks of well-baked, hard, red clay. Daron's horse trotted along easily and turned into the broad way that led up to the gate. A half dozen uniformed guards, in bright blue-and-white foppish cut, barred his way with neat precision. Daron stopped at their hail and demand of identity, and looked them up and down.

"Now, lads, for all that foppish rig, you've bone and muscle underneath, I do swear! Now let me— Officer, I should say by your stance, and the broadness of your palm, you've walked behind a plow and seen a furrow turn. And a good half of you knows the smell of drying kelp."

"Enough of that!" snapped the officer. "I ask no guesses as to whence we come, but whence you come. In the name of the king, answer, or you'll find time to answer in the keep."

"Now that, my friend, is no threat at all, for there be few places safer in this land. Further, your good king would favor seeing me. I understand certain of your brother guards have marched hot streets the whole day through seeking me. Men call me Daron, and my origin is something even I am not too certain of."

"Daron! Ho, forward, *round!*" The guardsmen moved with perfect military precision, and with a smoothness Daron admired. He was instantly the center of a small circle hedged with good steel lance points.

"Daron, dismount, in the name of King Elmanus."

"Now softly, friend. What other purpose, think you, brings me here? Take down that hedge, and ease your nervousness. Good. Now, you of the infant mustache, take the horse, and feed him well. I'll want him back. Take sound advice, too. When your friends tell you that is not a mustache, but merely evidence of laziness, believe them. Either shave it off, or dye it dark. On your tanned face, the blond hair seems somewhat weakened, and like drought-burned grain."

The mustached guardsman's face turned red, and his eyes dropped, but he took the horse's reins, his young face sullen. The officers eyes were lighting with a suppressed amusement and liking.

"Enough, Daron; I give the orders here. But take his horse, Kahlmur—and, by Nazun, his advice! Now forward. Elmanus has ordered your arrest."

"Your statement, officer—very incourteous officer, too, it seems. I know not your name, though you know mine—is exact. He has ordered my arrest; he does not want to see me."

"Pordan Holum, Daron. Holum, Pordan of the Outer Guards. Maybe his majesty does not desire to see you, but you may rest assured the priests of the Invisible Ones do."

The Inner Guards they passed, and to the doors of King Elmanus' Hall of Justice they were passed. Abruptly, there was an eruption of activity about Daron, and shouting officers. Priests began to appear from a dozen ways, priests in the flaming orange-scarlet of the Invisible Ones, and in the blue-green of Nazun, the deep, sea-green of Talun's temple, and the red-streaked white of Martal's retinue.

A tall, gray-eyed priest of Nazun first approached Daron, where he waited easily among the group of Holum's men. The priest was as tall as Daron, lean and thoughtful of mien, but there seemed some lack of fire in his eyes and face, a worried, tired and strained appearance round his mouth, and a crease between his brows.

"In the name of my lord, Nazun, I appear for you, Daron. The adepts of the Invisible Ones accuse you of murdering two of their neophytes within the streets of Tordu." There was a hasty, uneasy pressure to his words, and a curiously worried, uncertain tone in his voice. And, withal, a look of deep respect with which he regarded Daron. Very softly, so that only Daron himself could hear, he added: "Lord Nazun himself has ordered this appearance—but I fear their case is strong!"

Daron laughed. "I have no knowledge of the laws and rulings of this land, wherein your kindly aid is much to be desired, but none save Nazun himself and, perhaps, the Invisible Ones, knows more of this case than I. I think we may manage, and—if Nazun has given you some charge regarding me, perhaps he gave a charge to follow somewhat as I lead in my argument."

"Aye," said the priest uneasily. "He—Lord Nazun—takes interest in few men."

A priest in scarlet-orange, bedecked with gold and flaming jewels, hurried up, a fat, round man waddling busily, with sweat-bedewed pate glistening in the light. "Pordan," he howled, "this man is armed. What manner of arrest is this! Take that shield, that sword and dirk

from him. The man is a murderer; would you have an armed killer
brought before our king!"

Daron turned to him, and bent a steady, hard-eyed gaze upon his
fat, sweaty face. "Now by Nazun, my fat friend, you'll need no murdering. Have not your Formless Ones told you you'll die of bursted
veins? And would you make a liar out of them by dying before your
time?"

The fat-faced priest paled, and panted heavily. "You have no knowledge of that!" he gasped.

"So, I have not. I know nothing of what they say? But yet I do, it
seems. Now, be that as it may, remember this. This is the house of
King Elmanus, and your orders here are wanted no more than mine;
in fact, I think, some several degrees less. I came to this place seeking
justice, and of my own free will. Wherefore, my friend, Pordan Holum
shows more courtesy than you.

"Now, Pordan Holum," said Daron, turning to the officer, "I give
my sword and dirk and shield into your keeping, as an officer of the
sea to an officer of the king's guard, to hold and protect with honor,
till I may call for them."

"I take them as an officer, to hold and protect," replied Pordan
Holum formally—with a gleam of satisfaction directed at the fat priest.

The great oaken doors, bound with mighty hinges of black wrought
iron, before which they stood, swung slowly open, and a herald spoke.
"In the name of King Elmanus, in the name of Ator, and the people of
Azun, the Hall of Justice opens. Bring in those who seek justice before
the king."

The crowd surged forward, and it was a growing crowd. A half
score of priests in scarlet-orange, and a score in the assorted colors of
the Old Gods, flanked the little group of Holum's guards that marched
with Daron toward the throne.

The room was vast and cool after the heat of outside, the light
softened and dimmed. Great slabs of translucent milky quartz made
the roof, pouring in the sun's light diluted and cooled. The walls were
made of cool, green stone, and the floor was black basalt, soft and
soothing to the eye. Great pillars of sea-green stone reached up, carved
in intricate and graceful geometric designs.

At the far end of the long, high room sat King Elmanus, on a
throne that narrowed Daron's eyes. There was a dais of red granite,
and a backdrop of night-blue velvet behind. A ring of guards in that
same night-blue velvet faded into it almost unseen, save for the flicker
of their unsheathed swords, and their faces. Those faces were tanned
and strong, and the men were big, broad-shouldered men with taper-

ing build of speed and stamina. These were no city breed, but strong countrymen and seamen, every one.

But the throne itself! It was a chair of good blue leather, and deeply padded, without hint of gold or jewel, or any frippery. It was a broad, deep seat, with broad, comfortable arms, and the man that sat in it was broad and comfortable.

Daron's narrowed eyes slanted in a smile. Now here was a king who knew his dignity was beyond reproach, and sought the comfort aging bones enjoyed! Two slim and pretty girls stood beside and slightly behind the throne, and Daron's respect increased. They were dressed in simple, easy-falling robes of some light linen stuff, and in the very simplicity of their garments Daron saw more the character of their master.

With neat precision the guards drew up and halted before Elmanus' throne, and behind them stood the fat priest of the Invisible Ones, and the lean and worried priest of Nazun. Directly before Elmanus, Daron halted.

Elmanus was old, his head crowned with a wealth of white hair that gleamed and shone against the backing of the night-blue velvet drape. He wore a simple jacket of white silk, on which was embroidered in golden threads and scarlet, a crest and coat of arms. And, beneath it, in the oldest language known to man, a brief motto. His breeches were night-blue linen, with gold thread tracery, and in his hand he carried a staff of pure gold, chased with a deep-cut formal design. At the peak of the staff there gleamed a single, monster sapphire, as deep as skies, and large as a man's two fists.

Elmanus' face was tired, the dark eyes sunken in old and leathery skin, his mouth creased about with the graven lines of many years of struggle, but over all lay lines of easy humor, and his eyes twinkled with good humor as they looked back into Daron's steady gaze.

"And this is the man you bring me, Tor Lamon, as double murderer? I say with satisfaction, you are a liar or mistaken." Elmanus snorted gently, and nodded to himself. "What is your case?"

The fat priest quivered angrily. "The Invisible Ones, your majesty, have stated that this is the man."

"Well, what say you for yourself . . . er . . . Daron, isn't it?"

Daron shrugged, and smiled. "It is a matter of temperament. These two annoyed me. I was forced to remove them."

Elmanus' jetting brows of white, stiff hairs drew down. "Annoyed you, eh? Are you given to these mad tempers, then?"

"Aye, in case of such annoyance. One sought to spit me on his blade, and the other tried hard with dirk and cloak."

Elmanus snorted and leaned back. "Annoyance enough. What said the Invisible Ones of that, priest?"

"If this man's words be true, then why is it that, not content with killing them, he coldly mutilated their corpses so? One, Rehsal, a neophyte of two years' practice, was run through the throat, and blinded too. Now if the man be blinded, what need to run him through, and if he be run through, why blind a corpse, save out of coldly murderous temperament?

"And the other was yet more fiendishly mutilated! Shulthas was with us on the Temple Isle seven years, and was a man of good and even temper, yet his body we found run through the throat, blinded, and with the hands cut off.

"This Daron, I say, is a madman, a fiendish maniac. Give him to us, before this voyager from other, barbaric lands destroys more. He must be done away with."

Elmanus looked at Daron with lowered brows. "Your temper seems extreme, for even such provocation. What brought this thing about?"

"The power of the Invisible Ones, your majesty. These things I did; I ran the one attacker through the throat and he died as any good man should. I turned to face his companion—and the dead man rose and attacked me with a dirk. I blinded him—and he fought me with a skill he had not shown alive! Now such things I do not like, and it seemed the best thing was to make those hands incapable of grasping blade, and only then did that dead thing lie down as a dead man should!"

"Eh?" Elmanus gasped. "The dead fought!"

"The man lies to save his skin! The dead cannot move!" Tor Lamon roared.

Daron turned to the priest, and regarded him through narrowed eyes. "Now tell me this, priest, your gods can predict the future, can they not?"

"As every Azuni knows."

"And you can tell me the exact and final end to each and every power these gods of yours possess?"

"No, for they are gods, and no true god can be envisaged by a man," the priest replied haughtily, looking pointedly at the lean and worried priest of Nazun. "Their powers are unknown, and unknowable."

"Then," said Daron with finality, "they can raise their dead neophytes to fight again. That may be unknown and unknowable to you; I saw them, you did not."

Elmanus leaned back, his old eyes brightening.

Tor Lamon sputtered. "The dead cannot rise!" he snapped. "It is preposterous, insane! No—"

"Man," said Daron firmly, "can envisage the powers of a god. So. I saw your Invisible Ones bring the dead to life. Go back to your temples now, and learn more about your gods."

"I think," said Elmanus, with a chuckle in his voice, "his point is very sound. Now on his testimony alone, I would not ordinarily have ruled that he was attacked, but since his arguments are so sound and his logic good enough to meet that of Tor Lamon, who seems sane enough, he must be sane. And if he is sane, he would not make an insane defense. The defense he has presented is insane, or true. If not insane, then it is true. We have shown him sane—sane at least as Tor Lamon—and therefore we must accept his statement and defense as true."

Elmanus leaned back with satisfaction in his sparkling old eyes, and watched the empurpling countenance of Tor Lamon. "I dismiss the charge. Daron is free."

"Your majesty," said Tor Lamon with difficulty, "there is a further vital point. I must accept your ruling that this outlander can mur-der—"

Elmanus' heavy brows shot down, and his finger shot out to stab at the fat priest violently. "I said the charge was dismissed!" he roared, in a voice that blasted at the great room's roof, and set Tor Lamon back in shock. "You deny my ruling by that statement."

"I—I retract my words. I . . . I spoke without due thought. But, your majesty, there is a further trouble this outlander brings."

"Speak then," snapped the old king, his deep eyes sparkling.

"The predictions of the future that our whole country depends upon today—"

"And more fools they," said Daron softly. Elmanus' lips twitched.

"—are upset by this outlander. These predictions are based on a knowledge of all things that enter into life upon this empire you rule. Now this outlander has appeared, and injected a new and disturbing element, an element not in the orbits of the peoples of Azun, and upsets the prediction of the longer range."

"Your gods are strong," said Daron softly. "They are mighty, beyond the understanding of man. One man upsets their powers, which is, indeed, beyond the understanding of man, as far beyond his understanding as that a heavy ox cart be upset by a single grain of dust. Strange are the ways of the Invisible Ones."

Tor Lamon purpled with rage. "As much," he ground out, "as the power to predict the future is beyond your comprehension."

"The man's point," said Elmanus mildly, "is well made. It does seem strange." Elmanus relaxed back into his chair with a deep satisfaction. This was, beyond doubt, one of the most excellent examples of priest-baiting he had seen in fifty-five years of weary tending to dry and wordy cases. This Daron was a man to have around!

Tor Lamon's cheeks paled from their fat-bleached dusky red to a cold, white rage. "If a man have two children, and each of these children have but two, and these in turn have no more than two, there will be sixteen then, in the course of one man's lifetime. Now if the man—and his children like him—be an active man, given to killing neighbors who annoy him, at the rate of two in four days, such a family may have profound effect. In fact, it would appear, but some four generations of such men and we would have no more Azuni left in our empire!"

"That sounds somewhat improbable, but still seems a point possible of argument," said Elmanus weightily. "Surely you have asked the Invisible Ones when this man shall die?"

Tor Lamon writhed, and Daron, who had studied more than one useful art, spoke softly. "The Invisible Ones could not give him that answer, for their powers are strangely limited, but they could, and did, tell him this: Tor Lamon dies here, this day!"

The paleness of Tor Lamon's face became ghastly, his lips and eyelids became blued and purpled slowly as he stood, and stark fear shone in his eyes, all rage dying out. "You . . . you cannot know!" he gasped— and screamed as he said it, doubling up and clutching at his heart. He rolled, and fell at Elmanus' feet, dead.

A dozen lesser priests sprang forward, and knelt by the fallen Tor Lamon's side. Slowly they straightened. "Tor Lamon knew that he would die here," they acknowledged.

"How," asked Elmanus uneasily, "did you know this? Are you some newer god still, another god to plague my people here with death?"

Daron shook his head slowly. "There is a vein in the neck, even so fat a neck, and a swelling at the base of his neck, even beyond his fat, and many other small signs that the skilled may learn. I learned those signs. If the man's brain be exposed, there may be found a small but fatal leakage of blood. It may be, though, that the bursting of the great vein of the heart did this. The man was doomed, and being given to anger, doomed him doubly."

"Your majesty," a scarlet-orange robed priest said, "we ask one thing. This man should die; his very presence has, now, three times taken Azuni lives."

"Through defense against attack, twice, and only by the over-

weening anger of Tor Lamon, the third time. The man lives," said
Elmanus decisively.

"Then, in the name of the Invisible Ones, let this man be taken for
study to the Temple Isle, that he may be fitted into the pattern, that
the knowledge of the future may not be disrupted."

"With the proviso," said Elmanus, "that he be returned to me,
healthy, whole, and sane as he is now, that seems a fair request." Elmanus
looked at Daron.

"With that proviso," said Daron distastefully, "and the additional
one that I be given time to see the sun and breathe the air, I suppose
I must agree."

"So be it then," Elmanus nodded. "Take him and all his possessions with him, save his horse, to be returned to him when, one month
hence, he returns here before me."

Daron looked slowly at the silent priest of Nazun. The man looked
worried, tired, and wearied by his worry. He looked baffled, too, as he
looked into Daron's eyes and saw therein a deep total satisfaction!

IX

Daron stood motionless, weaponless, helmetless, before the scarlet-
orange robed high priest of the Invisible Ones. This temple room was
small, its walls pure white marble, their decorations, a bas-relief of
symbolic scenes in the creation of the Invisible Ones. Behind the high
priest stood a block of basalt as black as the pit, streaked and grained
with flaming scarlet-orange veins in lighting darts of brilliant color.

There was no other thing in the room, and light that entered came
through plates of pure white marble shaved thin as heavy paper, dif-
fused and softened, shadowless. But above that altar there remained a
feel of vast and angry tension, a straining, malignant drive that sought
to reach and tear at the mind of the sea rover standing between four
heavy-thewed and brawny priest guards.

Priests those four might be, but by the ripple of their scarlet-orange cloaks across their broad and heavy shoulders, their training had
come in larger degree from the hilt of a sword and the grip of a shield
than from the pages of a book. They gripped their silvery needle swords
now with an easy sureness that spoke conclusively of confidence in
handling them.

But confidence was gone now from the face of the high priest; his
brows were contracted in a frown of futile anger, his eyes blazing with
rage, and his lips strangely tense with fear and lack of surety.

"Who are you, outlander? Was that aged fool, Elmanus, right in naming you some new and potent god, a god both material and of force, too? The Invisible Ones shy off from you, cannot reach and touch your brain. Speak, what are you—man or god?"

A slow, easy smile of complete and easy satisfaction touched Daron's lips. "Now that, friend priest, it seems to me, is the purpose of my being here; you seek to find that answer. Sure it seems, Elmanus gave you thirty days to learn, and me no orders to inform you.

"This I will say; you'll know before the thirty days are gone—but not from my lips." Daron's smile changed to a solemn frown of thought. "But hold. You and your priests have maintained that no true god can appear as a man. A god, you say, by very definition is non-human, beyond conception of a human mind. Now that is a point I would not agree upon, but your own definition shows you, it would seem, that I must be a man, and no god."

"Why do you dispute that definition?" snapped the priest. "It is clear that a man-thing is no god, for, by very definition, a god is superhuman."

Daron laughed. "True enough, and sound logic that may be. But you have lost, here, it seems, the principles of logic. Have you heard, perhaps, of the 'undistributed middle'? Look you, a fish swims in the sea."

"Aye."

"I swim in the sea. Therefore I am a fish."

"And of what importance is your false and silly sophistry?"

"A god is more than man," said Daron pointedly.

"By definition, that is so."

"And more than man's conception can hold. Wherefore you limit his powers stringently in one thing; whatever he may be, it must be unfamiliar, he cannot appear a man. So—and, swimming in the sea, I am a fish."

The high priest cursed softly to himself, and glared at Daron's mocking eyes, and cursed again at old—but potent!—King Elmanus.

"Your mind is a maze of silly, tricking traps and nonsense thoughts. The Invisible Ones appear in any form they choose; watch now the altar top, watch closely, see the darkening there—the slow darkening and condensation— see it grow, grow darker, more solid, a vague cloud at first—solidifying, strengthening—forming to no normal man but a winged being of luminosity—a glowing, slowly forming thing—"

Daron smiled and nodded to himself, and stole a sideward glance at the four priest guards who stood beside him. Awe and fear were growing on their faces; and in Daron's mind a dry old voice repeated an old refrain in the liquid, fluent syllables of the Ind: "No mind but yours can rule your thoughts, no mind but yours can control your inner self. But your mind will, if you permit it, follow after any other mind, and see and feel and be as that other mind desires—if you will let it! I can make you see the flower or the tiger, smell the perfume or the acrid breath, but it is your mind, not mine, that does that thing."

And Daron looked at the empty altar and smiled at the futile mouthings of the fat and sweating priest. His hands moved and waved in futile gropings, and Daron let his mind laugh at the futility and pay no heed at all to all the high priest's exhortations.

"Your men," said Daron softly, "see wondrous things. I see an empty altar. Cease your foolish mouthings, and get on with what you seek to do."

The high priest's eyes blazed in exasperation, and he collapsed from mighty dignity like a pricked bladder of air. "Wake!" he snapped fretfully. "You see no more."

Four priest guards started, their eyes blinked rapidly, and their mouths gaped foolishly at empty air. With the white calm of incandescent fury, the high priest spoke again. "Take this accursed outlander to the South Wing of cells, and keep him there. I'll search him later."

Angrily the high priest turned away, and vanished through a door that seemed a part of the marble wall. Daron turned to the awed guards, and looked at them through lowered lids, a broad grin splitting his face. "Remarkable! These Invisible Ones are invisible indeed. You seemed to see something there?"

"Quiet!" snapped the leader of the four. "March, and step along."

Daron followed easily, his mind busy with his thoughts. For one thing old Barhamu had said was true; no mind but his could touch his inner self. And one thing he had said was not true of these Azuni— they could trick the minds of many men, a mass of worshipers!

Down from the upper levels of the temple they went, and through corridors hollowed out in black basalt that formed the foundations of the isle, then across half the width of the isle it seemed, to rise again into a building of gray, hard granite, and huge oaken, iron-bound doors. A guard in dull-blue cloak and well-worn leather turned a huge iron lock and passed them through, accompanying them, to use his key again upon another door.

The passageway before them now—walked and floored and ceiled with hard gray stone—was lined with heavy doors, iron bound and locked. It was a narrow passageway, so that but two men could walk abreast, and at the far end an open door opened into a guard room where four blue-caped and well-weaponed guards lounged at their ease, to straighten into interest as the men came up the hall.

"In the name of the high priest, Shor Lang, we bring this prisoner. By King Elmanus' given order, one month he stays, to be guarded, fed and kept in health. And these are the orders of Shor Lang," said the scarlet-orange garbed leader of the priest guards formally.

One of the blue-caped prison guards, his head covered by a good steel helmet, worn at a jaunty, carefree angle, nodded, grunted, and tossed a heavy iron key to the priest guard. "Number three, down the way. If he's the howling menace to peace of mind that stinking fisherman we just threw out of there has been, you can have him back and welcome."

Daron's swift eyes took in the room. Two benches, two chairs, all hard and made of slabbed wood. One table, with a good and comfortable chair. A paneled case on one wall filled with bound volumes with a thousand titles—all religious. The table was littered with a dozen stacks of a dozen different forms, ink and pens, and odds and ends. As Daron turned away, the captain of the guards was filling in one of the forms.

"Where's his equipment, or does he walk the streets as naked of blade as he is now?" he asked.

"His materials will be brought to you for storing in the locker room. Elmanus ordered all returned to him one month hence. A shield—and it's one of those mirror things old Elmanus finally got sense to dispense with—a sword, a dirk, and a helmet of gold and silver wire and phony jewels."

"Wire?" The captain of the guards looked up, and then looked toward Daron's retreating back. "A fool. If he had gold and silver, he could get good steel and leather. I'll hold this form till the things arrive. Here's receipt for your man. Hm-m-m, he rolls like a seaman but his garb stinks of earth."

Daron stepped through the oaken door to his cell. The walls were gray granite, too tough it seemed for even prisoners' patient scratching of names and decorations. One cot, one chair of hard oak slabs, and little other furnishing. The door closed behind him with a *thunk* of very sound and solid oak, and the lock turned with an oily grate of heavy steel.

Daron paced the room with eyes keen in observation. The door was no flimsy thing, but it was pierced by a spy-hole with a little sliding plate that let the guards look in whenever they might think of it, but left the prisoner blind as to passings in the corridor.

A window, high on the other side of the tiny cell, was barred with inch-thick wrought iron, blackened by weather, but resistant to rust. They were let into a granite block of size and strength that echoed clearly: "No—not this way, my friend."

Daron lay down to pass the time and think a bit. A month he had to plan his way—which should be time enough. An hour after he came, a guard came down on feet so soft they made no noise through thick oak panels. Only the sudden *clank* of the sliding spy-hole plate, and the gleam of a weirdly unsupported eye, apprised Daron of his coming. Daron grunted. With that sudden sort of inspection, there'd be no safe working out of tools within this room.

Restlessly, he went over to the spy-hole again. Six close-spaced bars of metal stopped it from the inner side. Bronze, though, and Daron eyed them speculatively. Daron carried a dirk-blade without handle beneath his clothes, a handy thing, he'd found.

The light died out of the high window, and the cell was dark. Daron slept.

With morning, the door was opened by two guardsmen, accompanying a single small and worried man in a greasy apron. The small and worried man edged nervously into Daron's room, and offered him a tray of wood, bearing two bowls of food.

The sea rover laughed. "My friend, I eat men only when most direly hungry. Keep me well fed, and your bones are safe enough."

The little, gray-haired man's lips pulled aside in a mechanical and nervous smile. "Yes. Yes, yes, oh yes. Food. Yes, sir. I—"

Daron looked at the grinning guards. "Has some one been frowning at him?"

"There's a fisherman with hair and strength enough to be old Talun himself down the way, and this goat-eared thing that calls itself a cook has been underfeeding him. Drathun, our fishing friend, swears he'll eat him yet," said one of the guards.

"Why, if I know seamen and their ways, there'd be peace and safety for him if he'd feed him," Daron commented.

"Eat up yourself, and get ready," said the guard as the little man danced nervously through the closing door. "Old Elmanus, so they tell me, ordered exercise and air. And Shor Lang says the gardens. So . . . so you'll learn some gardening in an hour more."

An hour later, the little man was back to pick up the empty bowls. The food was bad enough, but fairly plentiful, so Daron felt easy as he strolled out to the passageway. Six guards were there now, and the captain of them was going down the hall, opening the great cell doors one at a time, with a huge brass key. A dozen assorted prisoners came out, some seamen, browned and smelling of dried kelp and fish scales, some farming men, with brown-stained hands, and shambling, easy walk, and one man with the mold of lumbering.

Daron watched the process keenly. The corridor was lined up all one side with cells, and heavy doors that opened outward into the passage. Two cells opened from the other wall. At one end of the passage—the end but two doors from his own cell—there was a heavy oaken door that let out to the main building. At the opposite end were the guardroom's ever-watchful doors.

As Daron stepped into the corridor the men from the cells nearest the outer door were already waiting. One, a massive, squat chunk of a man with bearlike arms and legs, and bearlike forward-slanting neck, looked up at him from deep sunken eyes beneath enormous bushy eyebrows, black as charcoal marks. His body, through torn and salt-stained jacket and breeches, was as hairy as an animal's.

But the little, far-sunk eyes were twinkling with good humor, and the mouth was wide and strong, the creases round its corners slanting upward.

"So," he said, in a gentle rumble, like a starting avalanche, "this be the outlander then? I'm Drathun, fisherman because no other of the scum of Nozos have the guts to sail beyond a dog's bark or a birdie's peep. What are these other lands? As big as Azun, then?"

"Nozos?" said Daron. "Hm-m-m, that's on the Isle of Eran, is it not? Ah yes. As to the outer world. There's more sea than land, man, but there's far more land than ever you've seen. What brings you here?"

"Catching fishes in the isle's shadow!" he boomed in laughter. "They feared their pretty barges would smell of good, clean food."

"So they teach you now the beauty of the little pansy and the delicacy of the rose's sweet perfume? A new trade for you then?"

"Gardening!" Drathun snorted. "And two more months of that. Solmun, my helper—aye, the lad with midget mustache on his lips—goes free in another week."

"Quiet," roared the guard captain. "Now, *march!*"

He led them to the door, worked at the lock with his great key, and the little troop was led outside, down an angling corridor to stop before another oaken door. Three guards remained with them, and three stepped through the doorway as the captain unlocked it with his key. Racked tools occupied one wall, and on the other, Daron's sharpening eyes saw a miscellany of possessions. Nets and clubs and hats and—a silver-plated bronze shield, a long, strong sword, a jewel-hilted dirk, and a familiar helmet of gold and silver wires and curious jewels.

A heavy mattock in his hands, Daron followed quietly to the gardens outside. A tangled mass of weeds and tough-rooted creepers sprang from an uneven plot of newly imported soil that lay upon the barren basalt rock. Two lanky farming lads, Daron, and Drathun, the chunky fisherman, were set to work, watched by one crossbow-armed guard.

The sun was hot, the air was still, and the roots were tough. The position of work was one Daron was not accustomed to, and his muscles ached before the day was done. He slept that night with the heavy, solid sleep of exhaustion. And—of contentment. He had a month.

X

Daron sat down with his back to a tree, and the heavy odor of new turned, sun-baked earth in his nostrils. Only faintly the salt, clear scent of the sea swept in, and he looked with sour eyes at the glint of sun on wind-ruffled waters.

"Drathun, my friend," he sighed at last, "that, and not this stubborn land, is the place for men. Now a plant belongs in soil, rooted and fixed, unchanging itself in a never-changing stuff. But for a man to grow—and growth is change—he needs must live where change is constant on the sea."

"Aye—and a month, a week, and two more days before I get back to it." Drathun's deep-buried, twinkling eyes looked saddened.

"I think," said Daron softly, looking up through the tracery of an ornamental tree, "that we might leave these people here without their full consent. If you don't roar it out like a captain calling the bow-watch in a storm."

"Eh?" said Drathun sharply, in a much reduced bellow. His powerful, blocky body tensed.

"Do you," asked Daron, "like our aid and helper there, Tarmun, the farmer?"

"He's a solid ox, but good enough."

"Tarmun!" called Daron, turning toward the farmer lolling under a hedge, a floppy hat of straw across his face.

The gangling farmer raised his head, and the hat fell away. His face was long and sad and brown, and the man himself was long and sad and brown—and only Daron had the strength of arm to equal that of the slow-moving farmer.

"This shade is cooler here—and our brief hour of rest draws to a close. Come nearer, friend. I want to know that triply distilled essence of vegetable evil the next time I pull its root. That—what is its name?"

"Snake-bite root." The farmer roused himself gradually, stretched, and ambled over. "You can tell it," he sighed lugubriously, "by the purple veining of the root, and"—his voice fell as he sat near them, and farther from the guard still munching on his lunch in the shade of another tree—"you're a liar, my friend. You know it well after one bite, being above the wit of a hog, which learns likewise, in one good sting. What do you seamen want of me?"

"You like it here, perhaps, in the Temple of the Invisible Ones, my friend?"

"I loathe their rotten ways as heartily as you men of Talun do, as you well know."

"Then, my strong-armed friend," said Daron easily, staring up through the tree to the free blue sky, "do me the favor of tying this lumpy one in a goodly running bowline as the guard puts us in the cell this night. You know perhaps an insult or two to sting a seaman's hide?"

"Oh, the seaman's good enough in his place, but the place has too much smell. That stinking merchandise that Drathun would have us think is food, makes right good nourishment for plants, when well rotted at their roots."

Drathun's deep-sunk eyes grew somewhat brighter, and his wide, friendly mouth grew harder. "My oxlike friend, you learn your wit and knowledge from the horses you nurse about your farm. I'll knot those hawser-things that you call arms with greatest joy tonight."

"Aye, so?" said Tarmun sadly. "But then, Daron perhaps knows better why and when and where this thing should find its working out."

"In the passage before our cells, when all but we have been locked away. Drathun, your cell is nearest to the door, on that same side on which my cell is placed. Tarmun, your cell is across from my own. The cell on your side nearest to the outer way is unoccupied. We three will be last to be put away. If you would fight—"

"Aye," said Drathun. "We will, but, friend—" His brows drew down in puzzled wonder, and his tiny, deep-set eyes looked up at Daron from under paint-brush brows.

A guard stood up, stretched leisurely, and roared a call to work. The three beneath the tree moved apart reluctantly, Daron's voice rising slowly in "—know the accursed rope next time I spot it, and I'll fry it slow and happily."

Tarmun yawned. "Do that, seaman, and you'll learn that plants have better protection than your brainless fish. Fry it, and the vapors will give you such an itch on all your body as you've never known, nor ever will forget. Drop that—it's mine. It's lighter."

"Yours, you mud-footed farmer, that tool is mine!" roared Drathun, grabbing at the mattock angrily, well knowing it was his, and Tarmun knew it, too.

"Let loose, fish-skin. You'll never swing a mattock like a man, and that will bring more aches than results, with your soft-muscled flesh."

"Why, you horse-faced flounder of the land! Let go that hold, before I try the mattock blade in that dried clay you call a head! I'll—"

"You," said a bored guard, "will drop that thing, seaman. If your friend, the ox, wants to play with it, let him. Sure it fits his hand better than yours, but I'll try a rope's end on your back if you prefer to argue."

Growling, Drathun picked up another mattock, and swung to his work, his brow-hidden eyes darting at the shambling, long-armed farmer.

From a dozen ornamental trees about the gardens, Daron collected bits of exuding gum, and chewed them placidly, to moisten his work-dried mouth. The guards sat comfortably in the shade, and joked at the laboring men, and kept the water bottles handy.

Twice through the long, hot afternoon the stubby, bearlike seaman and the horse-faced farmer came near blows, and twice the bored guard captain stopped their angry voices. With sunset, the dozen men were gathered together, and marched back to their cells, placed before their doors, and one by one locked in.

The captain locked away the fourth from last, and turned to Daron. In a slow, drawling voice the lanky farmer spoke. "Was it," he asked of Drathun gently, "your mother or your father that was the bear? For surely you cannot be full human with such a pelt as that. You should use a currycomb more frequently, and comb the stink of fish from it."

From the gray granite floor, Drathun swung a calloused fist toward the farmer's heavy jaw. With the slightest, slowest movement possible, Tarmun moved aside. His long arm reached out, grabbed Drathun's fist, and in an instant the two were rolling, struggling on the floor.

The captain of the guard looked down with exasperated boredom. Daron roared in laughter. "Ho guard, give me that key! They've been wanting to fight this out all day; we'll let 'em try it for a night."

Grinning, the captain released the key, and Daron, with a mighty heave of his foot, sent both the struggling pair into the vacant cell, and locked the door on them, to toss the key to the captain. He stared through the peephole slot, till the guard captain shoved him aside.

"Now, my fine buckoes, you two can fight the whole night through," said the captain sourly, "if such be your mind, or you can learn the part of men and stand up here. Your supper will be in your cell, but by the Invisible Ones, there'll be no scrap of food in that place you've got now."

Sullenly, the two men rose, eyeing each other angrily. Equally sullenly, they came out, to be locked in their separate cells, as Daron stepped into his. In Daron's closed palm, however, was an impression on the gums he'd gathered of that master key that turned all locks in this whole wing!

And in Daron's mind—lest the Invisible Ones be seeking to read his thoughts and plans—was a turmoil that defied their every effort. And that, too, was thanks to the old wizard of the Ind. Daron was trying to remember places, people, and happenings he had forgotten, and since most forgetting is caused by a subconscious barrier to remembrance, both conscious and subconscious minds were in a fine fog.

Under the tree, the next noon hour, Daron and Drathun sat, and at long and patient calling, Tarmun at last came over, mollified. He sank down beside Daron, well away from Drathun, the half-amused, half-bored guard captain watching Daron's laughing eyes as he smoothed their anger down.

"And now, since Drathun plays with closed fists, I have an eye two shades darker than the other," sighed Tarmun, "and no good reason for it. I like the man—and he's as slippery as one of his own eels. What was the reason for this?"

"An impression in a bit of gum. I've a design of that magic bit of metal called a key our guard captain conjures our doors open with. Within another pair of nights, I could carve out a key to do the same—but for that thrice-accursed peephole in my door. But—I've a mind to block it up."

"The guard," said Tarmun sourly, "will approve of that."

"He will," laughed Daron, "when he sees my block! Now Drathun; you say your assistant was held less blameworthy, less punished for the crime of fishing in the bay?"

"Aye. The Invisible Ones are touchy on the score since old Talun sent droves of dying fish to pollute the bay, and drive the noble pretties on their way."

"He goes in two days, I think?"

"Aye."

"Now if I were a fisherman released from this place, I'd go to Talun's good temple on Mt. Kalun, and give thanks to him. And, if I were released at such a time as this, I'd tell the priests of Talun that the fishing fleets might well be here—following a heavy run, perhaps—when next the moon is dark. Say five days hence."

"Aye, would you now? Daron, you seem to me a man of sense; I'll tell the boy your good advice." Drathun's deep eyes looked uneasily at Daron's immobile, placid face. "A run of fish, the whole fleet would follow willingly—if Talun would grant such things at any man's request."

"And were I released, a seaman, now, after seeing Talun's temple, I'd seek the fishing fleet, and tell them of my strong dislike for this prettied isle, and this misused harbor that has beribbon-decked girls for sailors. I'd even try to urge them to sail in here in force."

"Their reluctance would not be overwhelming—if they saw a reason there," remarked Drathun.

"Now," said Daron, "if such things had been suggested to you, as a fisherman, and it had been mentioned that, if Talun approved, a run of fish would come—would you follow such a run, and enter the harbor?"

"And every man of Nozos, and every other fishing port as well!" Drathun answered.

"And," said Tarmun lazily, "you might mention that idea to a farmer here and there. Who be ye, Daron? Man or god?"

"None," agreed Drathun, stretching mightily, and standing up. He wandered off to settle heavily beside his young assistant, a hundred yards away.

Daron was wandering about picking up some bits of wood and twigs. Presently the guard called them to work again.

The captain of the guard walked down the row of cell doors on soft feet, mechanically slipping open the peepholes of the doors to glance at the men within. He came to No. 3, leaned toward the peephole and slipped the plate aside—and jumped back with a howl of dismay—

Abruptly from within came a roar of echoing laughter, and the captain of the guard looked again, heard the running feet of the guardsmen down the corridor, and cursed luridly.

"By the Invisible Ones!" he roared, "that triply-damned slot nipped out a piece of my thumb as neatly as you please. Go on back, ye fools. I'll fix the thing."

Angrily he unlocked the door and swung it open as his men turned back. He stepped inside the door, and pulled it halfway shut behind him. On the cot, doubled up in the light of his lamp, Daron was laughing soundlessly now.

He wiped his eyes, and looked up at the furious face of the captain of the guard. "By the gods, captain, do me this small turn; leave up the thing, and let your men bite as hard as you! So it nipped your thumb, eh?"

The captain glared at him. "Nipped my thumb? Blazes, no, as you well know, fish-skinner! It stuck its leering face out into mine when I slid that peephole cover aside, and I liked to jump out of my sandals with the startlement!"

Daron laughed silently, and through his laughter managed: "My respects, captain! Ye've a mind that works fast."

The captain snorted softly and turned toward the door and its peephole. "And have my men make me a laughing stock for crying 'Guard! Guard!' for fright at a silly jack-in-the-box—though, by the gods, a more obscene face my eyes have never laid on before! What is the cursed thing?"

One of the light bronze bars had been twisted from the peephole grate to make room for the contraption of paper, twigs and strings. A knotty root supplied an evil, tiny face with hideous, wormy beard, held on a springy twig that had been compressed behind the peephole plate to thrust the startling obscenity of the twisted root in the captain's face when the plate was moved. A bit of luridly red paper supplied a body of snakelike form, a wholly startling thing.

"A root!" the captain grated in disgust.

"A root!" said Daron, shaken with laughter. "Let not this art be sacrificed with but one showing, friend!"

In silent anger at his own stupidity, the captain closed the door, and slipped the peephole shutter back. He could hear the scratchings as Daron fitted up his contraption again.

He walked on his rounds, and so did not hear the further scratchings as Daron carved, from the removed bronze rod, a duplicate of the captain's key that had been hidden against his belly when the captain opened the door.

An hour later, there was another howl of terror, a moment's silence, and a lurid cursing of a nipping slide. Daron, in silent laughter, stared out the hole into the red and foolish face of the guard. In determined silence the guard replaced the trap, and Daron returned to his carving. Slow work, for even good hard steel does not make fast progress on well-tempered bronze. But the key was shaping.

## XI

"Mayan's a fool—he never brought in more than a thousand pounds of fish at once in his life—but he's agreed to do it tonight. And Tarmun will be ready," Drathun whispered as he passed Daron. The guard snapped something at him, and he turned into the cell.

Thirty seconds later, Daron was locked in his cell, and within an hour, the last meal of the day was gone, and the little timid man had collected the bowls of their food.

Then: "Guard! Ho, guard!" Tarmun was roaring.

The guardsman walked down the corridor lazily. "Aye, what is it?"

"The captain gave me permission to wash the earth from my jacket this evening. Let me down to the washroom."

"Captain, Tarmun, the farmer, wants to wash his jacket down the passage."

"Let him go," called the captain boredly, "but keep an eye on him."

Daron heard the click and scrape of the heavy key in Tarmun's lock, then the heavy tread of the farmer, passing by his door.

"Hey, guard!"

"Aye, what now?"

"I be going mad of sitting here in one small room. In the name of the gods, will you let me get something to read. at least?"

"Captain! Mayan, the fisherman, wants something to read. Shall I send him down?"

"Now by the Invisible Ones! I didn't think the fool had brains enough! Aye, send him down the hall, and if he must read, he'll read of the true gods."

Again the great bronze key scraped in a lock, and the heavy hinges creaked as the door was forced open. Mayan's rolling steps echoed down the stone-walled hall.

Mayan's cell was but one door beyond Daron's and on Daron's side of the corridor. Tarmun's cell was directly across the corridor. With the two men out of their cells, one walking by the guard down to the washroom, the other bound down the long hall to the guardroom—

With a single flowing motion, Daron was up and at his door. The five remaining bronze bars behind the peephole clinked in Daron's hand, and noiselessly, the peephole plate slid back. Through the hole, Daron saw what he had prayed for. With both men out of their cells, their great oak doors stood open—open into the narrow passageway from opposite sides, completely cutting off the view from the guardroom! And the guard was watching Tarmun wash his jacket.

Daron's long arm snaked out through the peephole, reached down, and thrust the key he'd carved into the lock of the door. It scraped, stuck a bit, turned—and the door opened. Instantly, Daron's arm was back, the five bronze bars were refixed in the peephole, and the contraption of roots and paper blocked the hole again.

Daron swung through the door, and as the door closed soundlessly behind him, he stiffened in horror.

"Ho!" came the roar of Tarmun's great voice down the passageway. Daron had the door half open again, and was darting through as the voice roared on.

"—on a fair spring day,
"When the snow's away,
"We'll plant the seed and pull the weed,
"And wait the harvest's sway—ay—"

Daron cursed weakly, and stepped out the door again. The lock clicked to behind him, and the key was in his hand again. Two steps, two motions, and Drathun's door swung open, and the squat, powerful seaman moved soundlessly out. Two steps more, the door was shut and locked behind him, and the outer door swung open. Instantly Drathun was through, then Daron, and that door, too, was locked tight behind.

"Left," whispered Daron, and the two were off on soundless, shoeless feet—each, at Daron's strict order, thinking furiously of things they could not remember! Left, and down, and across a deserted corridor, and the key slipped in another iron-bound oaken door. The unoiled hinge creaked softly, and Daron cursed beneath his breath, then they were in.

From beneath his jacket, Drathun pulled a stub of candle, lit it, and the door was closed behind them. In the light of the candle's glow, the locker room was ghostly with hunched things, unnameable and unrecognizable. Two tense-nerved men danced lightly on their feet as each made his way to his own things.

Ten seconds later, Daron was out, and Drathun close behind. On Daron's head sat now the gold-and-silver wired cap of Nazun, and in his hand he carried his own good sword. Drathun, behind him, had a helmet of good round steel he'd looted from some temple guard, and bore a sword like a good ship's spar for length and mass.

Daron's mind went blank for just an instant's time, as he sent a frantic prayer to Nazun for guidance—then something smashed into his mind, and exploded in his brain. In the instant it came, it died—but left its trace on Daron's mind.

"Remember forgotten things," Daron whispered to Drathun, and the squat seaman nodded, his deep-set eyes blank with thought. Daron took his arm, and jerked him to motion down a side corridor.

In that instant's flash of understanding, a map of the entire Temple Isle had been engraved upon his mind—and the room of the sphere he knew! On fleeing, soundless feet he set out, with Drathun's shorter legs rolling fast and noiseless behind. Down long gray corridors of granite he went, then down a stair that led to black basalt corridors.

The candle flickered in the lightless gloom, and shadows writhed behind them and before. There was an odor of musty dark, and the faintly sour smell of sea-washed rock about them. Through long, long tunnels they fled, till they were far beneath the main temple of marble.

"There's something pricking at my mind," Drathun whispered.

As he spoke, Daron felt the first strange tingling of the cap he wore, and a soft, dim glow of bluish lights like the lights of the winter sky in the far north, played round his head. Simultaneously, Daron was turning off, and down, along a horizontal corridor of black basaltic rock, then down a stair. Another corridor branched off, turned, and descended once more. But now the black basalt of the isle was not fine enough. This run was lined with white marble blocks.

The candle was out, and far ahead Daron heard the stir of men, and excited voices. A light sprang into being ahead, and the two dropped aside in a branching corridor to wait.

A pair of scarlet-orange cloaked priestly guards ran by, their voices tense and angry, bearing a crystal lamp. Behind them another pair appeared. Then the lights were all upon the way the seamen had come. They started on, had made a hundred yards, when from a black tunnel mouth two guards sprang out with roaring cries that mouthed and mumbled down the bore, and lost all semblance of voices to become vague animal cries.

"Their hands!" snapped Daron. "Take off their hands or these things will not die!"

Drathun snorted, and his broad mouth opened in a grin. The great sword he bore he twirled like a staff of wheat, his great thick wrists untiring in its lightning glimmer. It struck the priest guard's lighter weapon, twisted, flung the thing aside to clatter on the floor—and drank at the man's heart. The figure in scarlet-orange slumped, fell forward, and measured its length on the floor. Drathun turned to find Daron engaged with a left-handed opponent now—and gasped as the man he'd killed stabbed up at him from the floor, dead eyes white and ghastly in the light of the lamp the priests had carried.

"They can't die!" the fisherman gasped, his blade slowed by his very fear of this unholy thing.

"No, fool—their hands, take off the hands, and dead or alive, they can't grip blades!"

Two minutes lost, two handless corpses behind, they pressed down the corridor. The men they dodged were ranging back now, their shouts

and cries an echoing confusion down the corridors. Daron ran on,
eyes grim and determined. Drathun beside him sweating cold with
horror. This thing was new to him, and none too old to Daron.

"Two turns more, Drathun, and we reach the room. Look not
within, or you fall paralyzed. Believe me there, as you did not believe
what I said of those undead guards. I'll go within; you guard my back,
and look not in the room until I call. Hear?"

"Aye. I'll wait outside."

They turned a corner—turned another, and met a dozen guards,
looking this way and that to locate the source of echoing calls that
resounded endlessly in the halls. The two were in their midst and
through them to the doorway before they well knew they'd come.

And at that doorway, a sheet of livid lightning struck, struck—and
held! Blue curling flame, that writhed and danced and shrieked! A
scarlet-orange guard backed away in leaping panic of the thing at his
back, and Daron tripped him with a flying foot. The man stumbled,
twisted, shrieked as he touched the wall of flame.

Then he fell through, but was not consumed. Instead, he wavered
slowly to his feet, as guards and attackers stopped alike in fascination.
The man stood up, and his face was blank, his lips lax, his arms helpless, flabby things that swung at his sides. He laughed and chuckled,
and the chilling sound rattled loosely in the corridor. He laughed,
and the laughter grew in Gargantuan reboundings, thrusting fingers
of madness in their brains.

Then the soldier-priest was dancing, dancing, skipping down the
hall, and the men drew back and let him pass.

Daron stiffened, and his face went white and tense. "Nazun!" he
called—and leaped toward that sheet of waving flame.

He touched it, and the helmet of his head grew warm while icy
pricklings tore at his scalp. A shrieking hell of warring forces danced
and sang and shattered in crystalline trumpetings about him, his body
ran in crimson flame, blue laced, and wrapped in the blue lightnings
of the Invisible Ones, a sheath of flickerings that blinded.

Warring things struggled there, with low mumblings of sound and
silent fury that underran the root of their blasting. Then slowly, from
the very peak, where the dead, black stone of Barak, Lord of Fate,
reposed, a veil of black welled out, a heavy, clinging smoke of night
that rippled, spread out, and overran, tumbling down about the figure that stood paralyzed, a helpless point on which two unseen forces
concentrated.

The black lapped out, and drank the blue curtain of flame, drank
and pulled and grew, and the howling hell of lightning died down,

weakened, till only the mad, maddening mutterings remained, and even they grew weak. The icy pricklings left his scalp; the crimson cocoon of fire withdrew—

Abruptly he was through the doorway, and in the same instant that the cloaking cloud of blackness vanished, Daron pulled from a hidden pocket the little mechanism the watchmaker had made for him, and clamped it in his eye, a monocle of mechanism. He touched a button, and it whirred, softly, swiftly. Behind him he heard the roar of fear-struck guards coming again to life and action, and the clang of Drathun's mighty sword. Before him, in the same instant, he saw the circle of guards.

A dozen picked fighting men, men in cloaks of pure white wool, with harness of creamy leather, studded heavily with silver fittings, leaping toward him who faced at last the three-foot globe that was the root and being of the Invisible Ones!

There was fear and stark amazement on the faces of the guards, a fear and unknowingness that hampered their minds, and slowed their movement. This huge and bearded warrior who stood before them, with one blue eye closed and a monocle of whirring mechanism mounted in his other eye, this—man or god—who passed the veil of madness!

Daron's silver shield swept up, and every warrior of them looked to it, as any trained and instant-reaction warrior must—

And every man of them slowed, stiffened—and became a rigid, useless thing, eyes fixed and glazed, staring at the image of the thing of mystery that they had never seen! In the polished perfect mirror of the shield, they stared into the mystery of the whirling, circling, patterned lights, the lights that boiled and raved and twisted now, as though some maddening thing was driving, hurrying, forcing them on.

Daron moved forward, two slow steps. His heavy blade came up— and fell.

A high, clear and piercing note sang out, a sweet, cloying sound of exquisite tone, as from a mighty, perfect bell. Again the heavy blade came up, and fell. Louder rang the note—but perfect still.

The silver shield moved, streaked forward, and clanged in brazen wrath—and the silver sphere exploded in a mighty blast of light, a shrieking, howling tornado of more-than-sound, a light that seared and darkened eyes.

The sphere was gone.

Daron snatched the whirring mechanism from his eye, opened his closed eye—and had by that one eye the advantage of every other. The twelve white-cloaked guards were down, down in limp and broken postures that told the warrior's eye a tale of ultimate defeat.

*These men were corpses—and had been!*

The power that animated them—the Invisible Ones—was gone!

Daron turned. Drathun was standing, half leaning against the doorway, holding a streaming wound in his left arm. "They fled when that bubble burst—and all shrieking furies of the world fled by me, too! By Talun and Martal, man, what deadly stuff is this we battered into?"

"That was the death-howl of the Invisible Ones, my friend," said Daron grimly. "Now we've a rendezvous above, I think."

"The fishermen's ships!" Drathun gasped. "The Invisible Ones are gone!"

"Come up—they'll need guidance, they'll need to know!"

Along the winding passages they ran, passages that seemed like veins of some dead animal now, drawn of all life, dead things that had been living. The guards had fled; they saw no men, but far away they heard the howling, shouting clamor of men in terror and in pursuit.

They vomited from a sloping ramp, and stood in a garden torn and trampled now, a score of corpses, dead and useless things—with no mark to show their death! Fallen, Daron knew, in the instant that the crystal shell that was the root and basis of the Invisible Ones was shattered.

Daron charged across the gardens toward the main entrance to the vast, snowy temple of the Invisible Ones. A line of blue-cloaked guards was fighting, holding back a horde of howling, rough-clad seamen. And at their very head, roaring in a voice of thunder, stood a rough and hairy figure, a very squat giant of a man—

"Talun!" roared Daron, and charged forward. "By Talun and the Old Gods all, they're gone, ye seamen, they're gone! The Invisible Ones are fallen! Their power is broken for all time to come! Take back your harbor, seamen! Take back your island, too!"

"Ah, Daron!" the mighty, squat, old figure roared. "Come on, lad— fight, don't waste good breath in idle talk! Drive out these scum! We'll bring the good, clean sea back to Tordu, and drive that stink of incense out forever!"

## XII

Daron looked up and ahead, where, in the early sunlight, the topmost parts of Nazun's blue-green temple loomed above the trees. He halted momentarily, and breathed deep of the clear, crisp mountain air.

Drathun, panting, looked up at him. "Ye be a determined man, Daron. This air is thin. Now while you rest and get a bit of breath, give me one more bit of fact. You drive me mad, friend! What was that whirring thing ye wore in your eye last night as you broke the sphere?"

Daron laughed, and pulled the little thing from his pocket. "Here, Drathun, look at it. Look through it, and press this button here."

The seaman did. A hole drilled through front and back, covered by smooth glass surfaces, was darkened suddenly as a plate of metal began to revolve, passing in front of it, then circling back. Swiftly it gained, till the moving metal was but a blur, a haze that slightly dimmed the clear sight through the pierced hole.

The seaman grunted and passed it back. "A hole, with a bit of metal revolving past so fast it is not seen. A blur—no more. Now what is the magic of this thing?"

"In the lowlands of Looz Yan, in the land of the West, I saw a similar thing. They have there great windmills, and this thing they call a *strobe*. Now the magic of the thing is this: if you peer through this at a whirling thing, that thing seems to stand still! When I looked through this at the ordered whirling of the lights of the sphere—the lights moved slow, and lost all order, and made no sense. The magic of their power was broken, just as my view of them was broken by that metal plate. Yet, because they did not whirl in ordered circles, I could see them move in normal lines."

"Hm-m-m, there's more magic in simple things than I thought. Now, one more thing—"

"We climb the mountain now," laughed Daron. "And while you go to Talun's temple, I pay respects to good Nazun—and visit Lady Tammar. Up, my friend."

Drathun grunted. "Aye, up. My bones grow wearied, for I've had no sleep this night, and action enough for a dozen nights. I'm no young man such as you, or those who seem to be following us."

Daron looked back for the first time. Below them, a rushing crowd of men and women struggled up the path, panting, calling, beckoning. Daron smiled.

"I think the Old Gods have gained in popularity, with the death of the new."

"So the wine-sot turns to water his affliction is withdrawn," Drathun growled. "Half those who worshiped at the Temple Isle could not stay away, though they willed it. Well—we have given them sound cure for that! A hundred tons of fish were offered there to Talun this night, on the red-orange altar of the Invisible Ones!"

Daron walked on, steady and slow, as the mountain man must,

who would gain his goal in health. The high hills of the Ind had taught him that, as well as other things. "The fools will kill themselves in running up that mountain."

A voice, a shade more piercing than the rest, reached up to them. "Daron—Daron—wait there!"

"Eh?" Daron turned. "Someone called my name."

Drathun laughed, a deep roar of amusement. "Are you fool enough to think that name unknown after this night! All Tordu calls your name now!"

Daron shrugged. Again the call came up, clearer now, and the speaker, a long-legged youth, blowing like a spent horse, shouted out again. "Wait there for us, Daron! We've need of you!"

Daron turned and looked up at the tops of the temples above, clustering in the long-slanting rays of the risen sun. He looked back at the crowd, and the youth, and said to Drathun: "I'll wait, or the young fool will run his heart out."

"Elmanus"—called the youth. He slowed now, gulping deep breaths of air, and stumbled nearer, to throw himself on the pathside grass. "Elmanus is dead!"

"Eh?" snapped Drathun. "Old Elmanus gone?"

"Aye—he died this night."

A half dozen other men were struggling up, blowing hard. Long-legged farm men, and a seaman with rolling gait. The seaman laughed and panted all at once, and stuttered out the tale.

"Aye, the good old king is gone—may the gods protect his name—and gone happy, at that."

"What struck him down?" Daron asked. The king had been old, but seemed strong and well for all that.

"Joy," panted a horse-faced farmer. "And foolishness."

"He had a wine bottle in one hand," the youth panted.

"And a slave-maiden of his on the other," the seaman managed, between a laugh and a gasp for air.

"And the old fool danced a jig! At his age! He was howling in glee, and dancing round, and the girl had more sense than he!"

"She tried to stop him," the seaman nodded. "But he was howling praises on your name, and curses on the vanished Invisible Ones, and shrieking—"

"—that," the farmer interrupted gleefully, "he didn't give a damn what gods were gone, so one set or the other was destroyed."

"Ah," said Daron, a half-smile tugging at his lips. "Too much release from pressure—and he exploded."

"Aye, he tried to dance, and tripped and fell. His leg bent under him, and broke his hip. He was old and drunk with wine, and the shock killed him two hours gone."

"But," the seaman panted, "as he died, he was conscious again, and he said to his ministers, 'Bring me that Daron! Bring him here! He's the only one in all this land with force enough to be a king!' "

The crowd was growing, surging, panting all around them now, and shouting out to Daron. Suddenly they parted, and an officer in old Elmanus' livery came up, panting hard, his face red and sweating. "I near killed my horse, I fear, Daron, and these seamen and farmers beat me even so. King Elmanus is gone—gone from joy, and gone demanding that you take his place."

"I—" said Daron, and looked about the crowd. Every hot and sweating face looked up at him eagerly. Abruptly, he spotted one face that was cool, and slightly smiling, a round, rough-hewn face, with dark and heavy brows, and leathery, tanned skin.

Old Talun shut one eye slowly and nodded to him. Beyond, behind him, even, Daron saw a tall, lean man in blue-green robes.

"Now this land," said Daron with a sudden laugh, "is a broad, and right good land, and one thing I like about it. It has good gods, gods who act and do, and fight for what is theirs! And, better, these gods pay those who help them in their own way, and show no stinginess!

"So be it then; not for King Elmanus alone, but if ye people—fishermen and farmers both—want me there—why there I'll go!"

There was a roar of cheers that washed up about him like a pounding surf, and a hundred hands laid hold of him. Before he well knew what had happened, he was riding down the mountainside on the shoulders of a howling, cheering crowd.

His roars and protests went unheard, and, at last, he grinned and accepted it. But, back across his shoulder, he looked toward Tammar's temple, glowing rose-quartz vanishing behind, gleaming in the sun.

He'd reach that temple yet!

# STRANGE WORLDS

We're bound and blinded here by the same thing that gives us life; we trust our flesh too much, perhaps. I've seen a world with other eyes, a world where the sky's black pall presses down on strange trees, bent and twisted things with gray boles and cotton-white leaves. A river of ink flowed between salt-white banks into an inky sea. Strange manlike shapes that glowed with shifting luminosity walked across a field spotted with animals that burned with ghostly light, and only snakes and crawling things were black. A silver mirror did not reveal my face, and the inky pools of the river showed me no reflection.

For I saw with the infrared eyes of a camera.

A homing pigeon turns bewildered, baffled and uncertain, when the thing we know only by a radio receiver floods its strange directive sense. Somehow the radio broadcast makes it lose all its strange power of direction. It has some other sense than those we know; more than that we cannot understand.

Our senses loop in a deceiving circle, seeing infrared, at the deepest red of the spectrum, as black—and showing the farthest, most brilliant, violets as black. And at the farthest red and highest violet they close the circle—and call them both red-violet. The eyes close our sight beyond those ranges, circling back to trick us with the false concept that they see all colors, all there is, without a break.

Our ears fail below the level of many insect notes. There is a world of life and sound beyond our knowing.

And Man accepts as all there is those things his senses choose to show him!

Strange worlds, whole universes, exist beyond those smugly closed boundaries, beyond the circling fence our own deceiving eyes weave around us. "It cannot be—I've never seen it!" And the closed circle of our vision shuts it out!

Faintly, dimly, men perceive things in some other way, a sense so delicate, so weak it cannot serve us forcefully and with assurance, cannot even make us know how we have perceived it. Telepathy and clairvoyance—the reading of minds, and the perceiving of things without the intervention of the eye. Science hardly recognize that these powers exist; tends uneasily to deny them till some logic makes them mechanical and predictable.

The ghostly image on a camera plate led to the finding of radium, the atom that shattered, and, shattering itself, shattered a whole structure of theories of the universe. Science missed it, lacked an essential bit of knowledge that went to the shaping of the universe.

It lacks an explanation of telepathy, of clairvoyance, that makes these things understandable in terms of other things we know. But had men "not believed in" radium until it fitted in with the things then known, it would be still a myth!

There was a time when men did "not believe in" hypnotism. It was something from the discarded pages of the stupid books of black magic, books where goblins, unicorns, griffins, witches and demons stalked. Obviously, because it rubbed shoulders with such rubbish, it was fantasy. Those who tried to use it found, perhaps, that they could not, and reported, "It can't be done—I can't do it."

Now, all that is, to each of us, is that our minds perceive. But the brain is a blind, gray thing, shut away forever from the outer world, itself so helpless, so senseless, it cannot feel pain. Any reality the world can have to us must be brought in and made apparent to this gray stuff that barely seems to live. But each man is a world to himself, each brain and mind shut off behind its wall of flesh and gray bone— and each mind is, itself, all the world it knows, each a strange, lone world that must conceive for itself some picture of that outer universe. And all its senses lie.

Yet men have studied those inner worlds far less than they have the outer universe; men know far less of how that strange gray mass works and knows and understands—what powers it may have—than they know of the stars.

The brain is blind and gray and senseless, shut off forever from the world, and its every avenue of sense a liar.

Is it so strange a thing that this unknown mass should have some unguessed power by which to feel and see beyond, directly, meeting mind to mind in telepathy, sensing direct the truth of things by clairvoyance? Is it all untruth that we sense, somehow, that, beyond the false accounts of eyes and ears and touch, there lie unknown worlds that only mind can reach?

# WOULDST WRITE, WEE ONE?

How much of writing is an art—that is, a more or less unplanned, unthought-out result of a sort of instinct—and how much of it is a development of the science of plotting, I can't know. It seems that all of the part that makes the story effective, the actual wording and expression, is as completely unscientific and unanalyzable as walking. Walking robots walk scientifically, based on accurate and detailed analyses of the mechanics of walking, and stalk with the stiff gracelessness of a forced story.

The story "Forgetfulness," which seems to have been one of the best-liked stories I've done, was rejected the first time I submitted it to Mr. Tremaine. I had labored on that work. I wrote it out, then rewrote it, section by section, building up the characters necessary in precisely the way I felt they must go to explain my story. Some parts were rewritten five and six times before I submitted it.

When it came back, I stuck it on the shelf for nearly a year. Then, having had better than ten months to forget the self-pleasing phrases and the pleasure they had evoked, I was a little better able to read it from "outside" the story.

It was all there—everything of plot and idea that appeared in the final version. It wasn't bad, because the plot and idea were fairly sound. But it was, too, not good. It walked with the precision, the scientifically exact placement of words and phrases and incident that five or six carefully studied rewritings had built into it, word by word.

A story is a vehicle for expressing an idea. That one was, but the mechanism of the vehicle was there for any who looked to see. I rewrote it, from beginning to end, without reference to the original copy. That time, knowing what I was going to tell, it told itself smoothly.

For every story there must be mechanism, motivation, and plotting, consistency of action and incident. And for every mechanism containing these things, there is not, by any means, a story. Short story courses and books can teach only mechanism; but the mecha-

459

nism of a story means so little that these courses, books—and the present analysis, of course—mean nothing as far as learning to write, or writing itself, goes.

One of the greatest of the science fiction authors, Murray Leinster, has told me that he did one series of stories with the aid of a book on short story writing, getting all his inspiration from the "do's" and "don'ts" in that book. One by one he took their rules and consciously, intentionally violated them flagrantly. A really capable writer can, by his writing alone, commit any sin against mechanism and thrive by it.

L. Ron Hubbard sold a series of stories to one magazine, each story based on an idea given him by one of the editorial taboos the magazine listed for the benefit of would-be authors. The magazine—a detective book—listed as one requirement that their stories must have action—movement—somebody doing something in every paragraph. Hubbard wrote a story in which every character was afflicted with spring fever; the desk-sergeant snored at his desk in the next room throughout the story; and the detective hero sat down with his feet on his desk, and waited for a watch to run down for 6000 words. The magazine bought it.

Mechanism and idea cannot carry a story; mechanism intentionally made wrong cannot stop a story if the author is a true writer.

But, naturally, mechanism carefully and properly constructed is an enormous help to the ordinary writer. It helps him to order his story logically and devote his attention to the telling of his tale. In the working out of that mechanism, the short story courses can help. Where they can't help is in giving that unteachable, innate thing that a writer has to be born with, just as some people are born with red hair or six fingers per hand. It isn't that they're intellectually superior in conceiving the idea of red hair or six fingers or in having word-sense; they just happened that way.

What is word-sense? It's like Life; we can't define it, or make it, but it's evident when it's there in degree that's useful. L. Ron Hubbard and E. E. Smith and Murray Leinster and L. Sprague de Camp—all the really widely-liked authors have it. They use just the word that is precisely right in the exact connection they need. They don't think about it; it just pops up form their minds when they need it. It's as subtle, but as necessary for strong writing, as flavor in food. And it evaporates as swiftly under attempts to force it. You can't can the pleasant tang of orange juice; the canned product has the same sweetness, the same acid flavor, every chemical constituent is there in precisely the right proportion. The mechanism is there—but the style is flown. The subtle and indefinable necessity cannot be pinnhed down.

Similarly, de Camp, Hubbard, any of them, tend to find their material wooden when they press to hard.

And, strangely, that does not mean too fast. Hubbard's work is at its best when it flows from his electric typewriter—the ordinary kind is too slow for his thoughts—at 10 or 12 pages an hour, for then the story is covering itself in words smoothly and naturally, without pressure to distort it.

A good story flows that way, swiftly, easily, as it should read swiftly and easily. When rewrite must be done, it is done similarly: smoothly and swiftly, not paragraph by paragraph, but in five and ten page sections so that the natural fluidity of the story has a chance to establish itself.

But the greatest of crimes against science fiction that the amateur tends to commit, it seems to me, is that desire to paint on a broad canvas with broad strokes. The desire to have a great idea, briefly and broadly used. Not in that, but in the littlest of ideas, minutely pigeonholed in its own proper place, working into the story easily and naturally, is the real strength of the best science fiction. The small, practical difficulties that never appeared in the old science fiction make the realities of life and science fiction alike. Vic Phillips's "Maiden Voyage" or Gold's "A Matter of Form" or John Berryman's "Special Flight" were alike in that. Vic Phillips made a strong story on the idea of a commercial man misinterpreting the value of a military device, because the action of the story was not warped to that idea but laid on the natural theme of ordinary difficulties of a machine under that future world's conditions. Berryman tied his story into reality by a dozen deft touches that must have been but half noticed, yet reacted to still. The atomic rockets in difficulties because the injectors hadn't been lapped. The idea was stolen, lifted bodily, from the diesel engine field, where the ignition problems of the gas engine are countered by the injector troubles of the diesel. The calculator that corrected their path to avoid meteors was made by International Business Machines. Right! Of course it would be!

They weren't vague troubles with rockets, or vague calculators labeled "super"; by detail touches they had body and reality.

And another thing that hides behind the surface in many science fiction stories, apparent only to those who seek it, is the exact scientific background theory behind some weapon or machine in such detail stories. When a machine or weapon is to be used, modern science fiction does not go into detailed explanation, giving theory, logic, and development; but gives only the weapon and its possibilities, or the machine and its functions. But, properly handled, those functions and possibilities must be consistent. Therein many fail in a detail that means reality or annoyance to fiction.

Each author has his tricks to prevent this; my own is the detective story method, you might say. The detective story writer avoids inconsistencies readily; the author knows the answer beforehand. Figure out your machine, weapon, or whatever it may be beforehand, with science theory and logic. But don't put that in the smooth flow of a story to annoy the reader by yanking him abruptly from a tense situation on Mars in 3783 back to Earth, 1940. Use the weapon, knowing its action is always consistent with the theory.

Too few build civilizations before they build stories. But a story is only an incident, and an incident takes place against and because of the civilization—and a civilization is a mass of a billion details, each interacting with the others. Histories tell of kings and emperors and dictators; to get a picture of the civilizations they ruled, archeologists seek broken pots and beds and plowshares, the details of life that give the forgotten times realities. Not kings but broken pots paint life's realities.

Not Presidents and Admirals of Space Navies, but the broken pots of another age, is the need of science fiction.

## Editor's Note

This article appeared in the February 1940 issue of Scienti-Snaps, a fanzine edited by Walter E. Marconette and J. Chapman Miske. The editors had the following to say about the essay:

> Mr. Stuart, better known to fantasy enthusiasts as John W. Campbell, Jr., editor of *Astounding* and *Unknown*, has advised us that this is his first and last appearance in fan magazines. His contract with Street & Smith forbids that his fiction, and even his ideas for stories, appear outside of S & S publications; and, in his own words, "writing science fiction fan articles is too hard work." While we regret that Mr. Stuart will not be available in the future, we are proud that his only appearance has been in the pages of this magazine.

This book was set in Adobe Garamond using PageMaker 6.5 on an IBM Thinkpad running Windows 98 SE. The dust jacket was created on a Macintosh G3 using PageMaker and PhotoShop. The book was printed and bound by the Maple-Vail Company of Binghamton, NY.

# The New England Science Fiction Association (NESFA) and NESFA Press

## Books from NESFA Press:

## The New England Science Fiction Association:

NESFA is an all-volunteer, non-profit organization of science fiction and fantasy fans. Besides publishing, our activities include running Boskone (New England's oldest SF convention) in February each year, producing a semi-monthly newsletter, holding discussion groups relating to the field, and hosting a variety of social events. If you are interested in learning more about us, we'd like to hear from you. Write to our address above!